MAN, MAE, AND THE MOTHS

A NOVEL

MAN, MAE, AND THE MOTHS

A NOVEL

LILLIAN ROSE

Man, Mae, and the Moths
Copyright © 2019 by Lillian Rose
All rights reserved. No part of this book may be used or reproduced in any manner whatsoever including Internet usage, without written permission of the author.

This is a work of fiction. The names, characters, places, or events used in this book are the product of the author's imagination or used fictitiously. Any resemblance to actual people, alive or deceased, events or locales is completely coincidental.

ISBN: 978-1709201257

Dedicated to Davey's Pond

Wade in the Water, Children, Wade.
God's A-Gonna Trouble the Water.
— AFRICAN-AMERICAN SPIRITUAL, ARR. MOSES HOGAN

1

Vaughn perched forward on the rolling nubs of his elbows over his infant son in the dark, lightless nursery. The tips of his hips in his stomach laid flat into the floor like the legs of a tilted tripod. The baby was unswaddled beneath him and practiced catching his chubby feet and toes in his tiny human hands, careful not to swipe his bean-sized digits against his father's chest. Not that he could make that decision consciously, his brain only the size of a shriveled avocado, but Vaughn liked to pretend his baby was considerate in that way.

Careful not to kick dad.

Vaughn's ten-year-old daughter sat downstairs at the kitchen nook, hunched less pleasantly over her homework—her light hair jostled loosely back into an almost acceptable French braid. Vaughn had crafted the girl's hairstyle himself after school with his callused, worker man's fingers that somehow forgot how to weave conditioned soft hair into a three-strand design. If he'd ever known how to in the first place, that is. He knew she would have preferred her mother to do such work, drawing this conclusion from her *"ouch dad"*'s and *"mom should teach you."*'s

Vaughn smiled down at his bubble blowing, six-month-old son.

Yeah.

Huh.

It had been obvious once he looked at it from all angles. Specifically, the angle that looked down at the top of his daughter's head while he yanked and worked the hair into spots he wasn't sure was right, his daughter's head pulling back to reveal her unhappy, scrunched eyebrows.

Vaughn would have loved to have his wife's help—even let her take the wheel while he only watched her delicate fingers lace under and over their daughter's hair while the girl spoke circles around the kind of day she had. *"Lindsey did this, Mrs. Hall did that. Did you know that Kyle's mom is a lawyer, she came and talked to the class today —"* And Vaughn would nod, dimples pressed into the corners of his mouth as he listened to his daughter.

Vaughn, however, didn't have such an option since he hadn't had the best of luck keeping tabs on his wife lately. Her car was always gone and her phone always off. Every chance she got, it seemed like, she'd disappear off the grid, from him, from their two kids, from the world.

He tried to not feel bitter about his wife's choices as his face slacked down into a frown and he mentally traced his thumb over his boy's pudgy new baby scented cheek—wishing he could have the pleasure of stroking it for real. The baby puckered his lips and tried to latch onto the air. Hungry for the breast.

"I love you," he whispered to the infant with latex lips nested beneath a heavy layer of graying facial hair.

The bald baby boy stared at his father with his round, undecided color, eyes. His tiny lines of eyebrows flexing as if deep in baby thought as his tongue rolled out over his lips, like a pink fish.

Vaughn couldn't blame his wife. A father who didn't touch his son wasn't a father worth being married to at all. She'd run off with someone who coddled the boy in their arms and kissed his tiny lips soon—the whisker faced father understood that.

Vaughn wished he could touch his boy, but he couldn't. Incapable to explain or even fathom why himself—let alone explain it to Sherie—a wife unwilling to hear the God awful excuse for his *lack of interest* in their child. Because, to her, that's what it was. But it wasn't. His boy, meant to be loved and held, could only be handled in his father's grasp for mere seconds, no matter how hard he tried to make it work. The nurse had handed his son to him in the hospital and Vaughn had stumbled into her, handing the crying baby back instantly.

The father pressed his nose into the infant's to test *it*. Check. Try me. Trial period to see if *it* was still there. The world swept up from under him and Vaughn made a plugged recoil away from his son who choked a wide-lipped cry and kicked his bean toed feet like he was in pain. Vaughn's vision played catch up, still rolling back and forth like he'd hit his head.

It was still there.

He'd experienced the phenomenon before the boy was born too. Soon after conceiving, Vaughn could hardly even snuggle into his wife. Her growing stomach an orb of dizzy spirals every time he neared it. Vaughn sighed an unintentional breath against his baby who had stopped crying and now worked his lips against the air displeased, still hungry for a breast. He supposed that had been what pushed Sherie to start falling out of love with him, what is a husband if a husband cannot love on his pregnant wife. It occurred to him then, as it had more often than not, that his wife more than likely feared she'd married a psychopath.

And, as if to help the situation, he himself began to think that maybe he was.

2

The door to the nursery swung open behind the man, expanding the small line of hallway light out over his back and the baby boy's face like an unfolding Chinese fan before silently retracting back to its pencil-thin beam, the door once again shut.

Vaughn could hear bare feet bounce on the balls carefully behind him on the rolled out blue, woven carpet, the aging hardwood floors creaking beneath the eighty-pounds of girl. He sat up in response, to his knees, keeping his brown, tired eyes on his son. "Hey, Marilyn Mae." He called windlessly to his approaching daughter, "did you get that homework done?" Division. Tricky stuff for a ten-year-old with a botched braid.

His daughter pressed up behind him with no response.

He made a good-natured '*hm?*' Sound with the back of his throat, meaning: *answer my question, sweetie?* He pushed his curled fists into the tops of his bent thighs to crack his knuckles absentmindedly, waiting for his daughter's response.

The young girl poked her finger into the bottom rung of his spine in a single jab that sent a puzzled expression of minute pain to the father's face, his eyebrows arching and mouth parting. Her knife-like finger then traveled up the length of his back and stopped cold between his pointed shoulder blades. It left a pinched, dull sting as it rolled over each vertebra like a heavy weighted pinwheel. Vaughn's back jerked into an arch and the pained expression on his face expanded, "Ow, Marilyn!" He scolded. Although, hushed, careful not to startle his son.

She retreated, her warmth removing from his backside in a sweeping motion.

He turned his head over a shoulder to ask her what was wrong, why she had felt the need to do such a thing—but Marilyn Mae wasn't there to ask.

The darkened nursery empty.

Almost.

Vaughn's stomach tightened into one mammoth knot and he blindly reached out for his infant son, his head still turned over his tense shoulder and his eyes trying to wean through the darkness like search lamps.

Someone, not his daughter, had entered the room and now sat watching from a corner like a neglected guard dog, snarling its canine teeth.

Vaughn's fingers brushed, then grabbed, the fat around his boy's infant bicep—the room instantly swirling into a vertigo sway from the connection between son and father. Vaughn snapped his head back to his boy while baring teeth and seized him up off the floor with a fluid, dizzying, yank. The baby let out a yelped cry as he crashed into a tight hold against his father's chest.

That something in the corner was coming closer to the man now, its heat coming back up behind him like sweltering black smoke.

Vaughn stacked his shins under his knees and stood with compressed eyesight. The room did a full loop around him and he crashed drunkenly into the baby's white crib. A hand-me-down from when the child's sister was a small infant. The crib squealed on rusted, locked wheels an inch or two as his son began to scream. Vaughn rounded the crib and continued to stumble forward like he was in a tumbler tunnel at a fairground towards the back of the nursery, away from the creeping being behind him. He spun reluctantly and lowered his back into the cool room wall to try to gain a sense of stability, the world in front of him thrashing violently through a straw of consciousness. This moment the longest he'd held his son, and the hardest his head had been knocked around by a spell of disequilibrium.

His shoulders softened into the wall and his neck hardened with strung veins like it was trying to stay above agitated water.

Through the thin straw line of sight, Vaughn could see it. The being in the corner.

Vaughn buckled his knees and planted his socked feet flatter into the floor, the bridge between toes and heel straightened into the hardwood as the dark shape in the corner peered at him, emaciated and hunched over. The world lurched up once, then twice, and the man contracted his eyelids over his watering brown eyes in a tight scrunch, thinking about his daughter who must've still been on the bottom floor, and how he was going to get to her.

The world swept upside down three times.

The shape, which was not human, leaned closer to the center of the room, the slice of hallway light illuminating one beady eye squished deep into its hollowed features. The baby roared out a mangled cry as the room vibrated in an internal earthquake between the man and his son.

The creature was colorless and raw. its bottom jowl basketed out like the unhinged jaw of a snake brushing in counterclockwise swipes against its stretched flesh.

A stench stabbed out across the room and Vaughn's face tightened, his nose flaring and eyelashes fighting away wetting tear ducts. *A dream* he told himself but knew it wasn't true, the odor intoxicating and his world collapsing around him.

The creature reached an elongated taloned limb out to the scooted crib and pulled it back into its rightful place, the reverse scrap of its wheels locking metal bolts into the joints in Vaughn's jaw and tightening his teeth together.

Its head swiveled, its breath switching directions across the man's body.

He crammed his fear back and squeezed his son into him tighter, despite the vomit-inducing sensation, thinking of his daughter once more.

3

His daughter, Marilyn, had been the one to find her father that night, in the nursery.

She had hopped up the tall, silent stairwell of the old Victorian home like any other night, one step to the next, her hand sliding crookedly over the painted wood railing, her mind sliding smoothly over the thoughts of her division homework. (Finished and stacked on the kitchen table under her dulling, pink pencil.) A borrowed gift from a girl at school. She reached the top and tip-toed over unpolished floorboards and an old vent towards the nursery, pushing through the glass knobbed door, like any other night.

She had noticed her brother first—neatly swaddled into his crib, fast asleep next to a row of decorative baby pillows her mother had bought.

She noticed her father second.

He would've gone unnoticed if her dopey eyes hadn't seen his grey tipped, white cotton socked feet–dangling–at eye level.

She followed them up with a stopped heart and paused at his face, swollen and sealed off from the rest of his swinging body by his own black work belt being used against him as a leather noose. It carried her lifeless father on the room's ceiling fan like a skinned deer, his pants sagging where the waistband lacked support.

All at once, Marilyn threw her hands to her face to cover her vibrating eyes from the sight. Her fingers pulsed into curled claws and began to stream down her cheeks and eyes as a sharp shriek fled from her throat like a burning siren.

Her baby brother awoke and begun to sob along with the cry she hated most, and she collapsed into a jittering pile against the ground. Her hands found her scalp and began to rip chunks of her hair out, strands of her father's version of a braid clumping out beneath her fingertips as the unforgettable wreak of death shrink wrapped around her.

4

The policeman with the tight beer belly said it had been suicide.

Marilyn's mother had said she knew there was something mentally wrong with her husband, she had already been planning to divorce.

MAN, MAE, AND THE MOTHS

LILLIAN ROSE

Part One: Bear Kingsley

1

He stood still.

The showers hot torrent weakened into a tepid stream that curved and creased into the warmest centers of his body but Brent Kingsley kept still. His temples ached with early morning disorientation and lingering soap suds crackled chaotically under the dark brunette laps of his hair. A crisp September beam of the sun made an incision through a slit in the plastic shower curtain from the tiny, vented window that hung parallel to the shower. It welcomed Monday morning in an opaque glare and Brent shut his sleep crusted eyes away from it.

He dropped his head under the shower nozzle and scrunched the shampoo from his hair with spindly fingers. The bubbly water rushed down his forearms and shot off his elbows like a fountain at a busy park in the summer. The ones where parents sat around and filmed their little ones crash through the groundwater jets.

The water rocketed in streams off his elbows and splashed havoc into the pooling water around his ankles. The drain had been clogged and showers turned into baths if he let them run long. The man supposed he could always *clean* the drain with a pair of store bought tweezers, but that meant knowing what type of hair the tenant before him had gotten stuck in the bath pipe, and he wasn't confident he could handle that. Warm liquid collecting into a quarter sized lump inside his throat at the thought.

Brent nudged the still water with his foot to create a gentle ripple.

He had thought of giving up and just taking a bath altogether. Forget the shower and just lay in his, and the past tenant's, swirly filth. However, the thought of a bath made his stomach ache like it was full of river rocks that compressed his organs and weighed him down, planting his feet heavily into the wet porcelain glass.

He kicked his foot again and the wading blue tinted liquid seemed to grip at his ankle and calf as it splashed.

He closed his eyes against the thumping water on the back of his soggy skull and thought of his childhood. The one spent in foster care—a long term family, Onslow's, jutting out in his memory like a broken tree branch.

They had been Baptist, Christian, the kind that wore dresses and ironed suit pants to church, only. The mother a down-in-the-dirt, ranch life, woman of dignity and the father a mole faced, jelly body, plumber. Mom and Dad Onslow, even though they weren't the real Mom and Dad. Not to him, at least. Dad, the real one, was a man he never knew, and Mom, the real one, left him to foster care, too young to know any better, he supposed.

The Onslow's had other children, real ones to them, all much older than the cowardly boy they all cared for. The oldest, Greg, used young Brent as a chick magnet—the man realized as he got older. Greg would take the boy to church and school events, kissing the boy's cheek lovingly the second a fluttering female eyelid was batted in their direction. Then, swatting the plump foster child's cheek away when no longer being admired by those flirty, mascara eyes.

The other boy was Christopher, just a year younger than his prodigy of a brother, Greg. They looked similar and both attended the same high school, trading Brent off to one another at basketball games to spread the luck of maybe finding a girl to take to Sunday class with them that weekend. A victim to their creepy, Christian game.

The timeless apartment water pipes shuddered out the last of the warm water onto Brent's skin and a heatless tide fell in its wake. He turned the silver handle under the plastic shower head and the water receded—like an ocean tide. Goosebumps kissed up his body and the skin on his face tightened, steamed out pours now swallowing to the cold. A diving hand plummeted through the slit in the plastic where the sun came through and grappled for a purple, damp towel hung over a plastic hook. Once clutched in his pruney fingers and palm, he pulled it back through and wrapped it around his shivering, long frame. The copper drain sucked and wheezed and he watched as the water around the bottom of his legs struggled to evacuate itself. It hung onto uncurled leg hairs for safety. Brent found himself amused at tug on his furry shin for a moment before his leg lifted and he stepped from the shallow tub.

There had been another, the youngest Onslow, fourteen and a woman. Amanda. She was technically an eighth grader, but Brent had never seen her attend the middle school in town. Instead, she watched over him, the buzzed head foster child, while both her parents worked. At night was when she would ignore him, leaned wearily over thick, tattered school books and write out papers under her mother's instruction—*homeschool.* A term Brent hadn't understood as a child. It meant free *day care* to the Onslow's with the young foster *responsibility.*

He had loved Amanda during this beginning period with the Onslow's. She had a single dimple and blonde hair that was always pulled loosely behind her round head in one of her mother's scrunchies, revealing her round and heated tipped ears. He'd always imagined her as his real mother. A warm young woman who raised her hands high in the church. Yes, that's what he had liked.

When the weather was good she'd take young Brent for a long walk, usually ending at a brightly colored park, where they'd play tag or hide and seek. When the weather was bad, which was more often than not, she'd draw Brent a bath. Early in the afternoon to be clear it wasn't for body cleaning, but for playing.

Even now, at age thirty-one, Brent smiled at what would become a rotten memory, his mental cap hung on the innocence of it in the beginning, for just a moment.

He dropped the purple towel to the floor after swiping drying streaks across his body and began to dress. Black briefs, black socks. khakis, a white undershirt—that clung to his *not completely* dry skin, a tucked blue button-up, and a brown belt. He brushed his teeth with a near empty tube of *Glacier Mint* and fixed his floppy hair with gel lubed fingers in a neatly clean, speckless mirror.

Amanda had brought him a new toy for bath time one morning, her allowance spent on it the night before while out running errands with Dad Onslow. A toy boat with a dark green bottom and a plastic grey deck. Little windows were cut in circles at the side and if he looked close enough he could see small crew members partying through the portholes like plastic sculptures. She had explained to him, as he examined the boat, shivering naked in front of her, that it was a *cruise ship*. She went on to say through light smiles at his bewildered expression that adults and children would go on them for *fun* out at sea. He'd smiled back at her, in like with the idea, and had told her that maybe one day, when he was big and strong, *they* could go on a *cruise ship* together.

"Maybe we can!" She had agreed over the loud roar of water as she prepared that specific day's bubble bath. *Not for body cleaning, but for playing.*

He had grinned, naked, at her and clenched his tiny four-year-old butt cheeks as his eyes fell back to the boat. His baby carrot fingers tracing the boat's detail.

Thirty-one-year-old Brent stared at his reflection in the early autumn light and listened to the gurgling of his bathtub drain, now almost complete with its slurp of dirty liquid from the porcelain tub. He chewed the inside of his scruffy cheek and watched it cave against his slender face before he cracked the medicine cabinet door open and sent his reflection sideways. His long hand searching out for a face razor tucked away on the middle shelf.

He recalled that Amanda had left the room to read after he settled into the steamed bath lined with her apple-scented, white foam, and all had been normal —seeing as she usually read on the couch in the shag carpet living room, her legs tucked under her and a blanket pulled while he splashed about freely.

His new toy boat floated fine and he pushed it around large mounds of bubbles with the insides of his fingers. "It's getting foggy out here," he murmured like he was a little, plastic carved crew member in the party. The *cruise ship* nose dove through a large mound of soapy fizz. *Foggy*. It was a term Mom Onslow had taught him once as they came into the valley of the town and the roads began to look *foggy*. He had stopped the boat with his index finger and it teetered in place like it was being held down by an anchor, plunged deep below, into the floor of the bathtime sea bed. Young Brent had begun to then push on it. He had pushed downward so the portholes filled with the sud water and watched as the boat resisted. It contended to stay above the water but eventually gave in and caved below the child's persistent pressure. The cabin was weighed down with gargled water and it had sunk with ease.

Brent had propelled it to the bottom of the tub then lifted his hand from the plastic toy. He'd watched with fascination as it slowly worked its way to the top of the bathwater again where it poured the warm liquid from its openings and began to bob back along the water line properly.

He'd forced it under a second time, then a third, amused with the way it animated the gurgling water from its toy body. After time, and time again, of doing the fine motor skill, Amanda re-entered the bathroom, dry towel in her hand. "Hey, Brenty Boy," She had said melodramatically, "let's get out and dry off."

Brent had remembered now that the bath had been *so* warm that particular day and the bubbles had yet to be popped, some hardly even popping on their own yet. It had been unfair to the four-year-old. He wanted more time to play, so he had propelled his toddler backside into the furthest lip of the tub and glared at her with a pout in his lip.

"Brent," she had insisted then as she knelt to the edge of the tub and reached for him.

He wasn't getting out. He had been having fun with his new *cruise ship* that she had bought *special* for him and he was going to *play* with it. Young Brent kicked the water. He hadn't thought about it and only threw his leg out in a hyperextended-knee apathetic tantrum. But the bridge of his foot had caught water, rather than wind, and had paddled it out into Amanda's face. Her blonde hair had stuck to the sides of her round appearance like men's sideburns under the sudsy fluid. She looked like her father that way.

Brent had giggled youthfully. He hadn't meant to splash her and he expected she'd splash him back. Call him a '*twirp*' jokingly like Greg always did. It'd be fine, and funny, and he'd then get out.

She didn't splash him back, on that specific day, with the bubble bath and the green bellied boat he'd subconsciously named Boat Kingsley. After himself, of course.

The adult man lumbered through the memory and his dark apartment simultaneously with long feet that trailed to the small kitchen. His floorboards hissed, then snapped like a smoldering campfire, under his tall weight. A pot of coffee brewed as he shuffled to his pantry and threw the thin door open to pluck a shelved box of cereal from its lonely spot. The cereal stung the glass bowl he had removed from the neighboring cupboard as he poured the crunchy, sugar flakes. The milk from his fridge filled the empty gaps as the cereal shifted to welcome its cold partner. He walked the bowl to his wooden dining table and set it down with a muffled glass *'clunch'* before going back to his kitchen to retrieve his coffee and a silver spoon.

Amanda's beautiful smile had broken into a foreign, inflamed, coral frown and she lunged herself out to grab his shoulder. Her squeeze clamped his skin and nerves into the dull edges of his bones and he yelped like a stepped-on pet.

"*Get out you little BASTARD!*" Her voice had been thin and stabbed at his ears.

He'd driven back against her bruising hold, terrified and confused. His four-year-old brain at work to try and comprehend the sudden anger—anger he'd never experienced in one single human, not even on the TV, in his young —starting life. *BASTARD.* He'd known that word. Dad Onslow had used it before. A *bastard* was the President on the T.V., a bastard was the car when it didn't work, a bastard was the bad thing that you were *mad at.* He was *not* a bastard. And she was not *mad* at him, was she? It had punched at him and the tears had hurt as they welled up in his eyes.

Adult Brent sat at his dining table and took a long sip from the dark caffeine that swallowed down his esophagus like lava from a canister. The memory spindled the outer corners of his brain like a funnel web and he paid no mind to the mountain view across from him at the table, through his apartment glass window. His head kept down and eyes glared as he thought distastefully about his temporary sister and munched on his breakfast.

She had released her abrasive grip on him and sat back on her heels. Inspecting his dastardly demeanor. Her fingertip imprints were dug into his shoulder socket, red and sore.

"You don't want to get out yet?" She had asked, her voice suddenly breathy, like normal.

Brent had rubbed his shoulder and felt the splinters run wildly through it, tears spilling from his small lidded eyes, "No," he squeaked with a tight throat.

Her apologetic, soft grin faltered like a bad video connection, "okay." The way she spoke plain and robotic.

Okay, Brent had thought and ignorantly reached his little arm out for his boat with a naive faith in his sister's new-to-him temper.

He had been ambushed by Amanda's weight then—abruptly being conjured on top of him in a burst of fitted rage. She shoved against both his shoulders from above like a bag of cement. His fragile spin compressed into an involuntary slouch as she pressed him into the tub—his small ass jutted against the grainy, marbled beige floor and skipped out from under him. Like the boat, Brent was forcibly held to the bathtub bottom. He had felt like a balloon against the pressure of her hands pinning him down at the shoulders. He tried to fight the briny water, but it filled his nose and poured down his windpipe.

He hadn't meant to make her mad.

He hadn't meant to—

The man chugged the lingering milk in his now cereal-less bowl before getting up to move back to the kitchen. A zombie footed puppet to the memory.

Young Brent convulsed his insufficient body against her unbudging hold. The water filled and pumped through his lungs with bright, burning electricity as he stayed submerged. He had tried to wedge his elbows under his back to give himself some leverage, but his little chicken wings kept slipping and slamming his elbows into the edge of the tub with a drowned *whack!* Sour and distant in his water-absorbing ears. He had been blanketed by the thick layer of bath around him. He eventually stretched his hands out of the water and felt chilled, feathery air breeze past and through them. His body then began to numb and his sense of what part of him was out of the water, and what part was in, fuzzed together in one singular sensation. His lungs ached to breathe air, but his groping lips were helpless. At age four he had thought of death.

Amanda had let her grip up then—just as he had begun to accept the idea—and Brent had projected himself up out of the water like his toy boat, the air stinging his nose and eyes. He had draped his body over the lip of the tub and ejected the water from all openings in his feverish face. His chest shuddered and jerked as he tried to hold down a gulp of air. The sensation of suffocation intensified as he gagged and gaped in the steamy bathroom. Bile crept its course up through his gasps and he vomited out his nose.

Amanda clasped the back of his neck as he wheezed and sobbed and pinned his chin to the outside of the glass cylinder, "next time I ask you to do something, you will do it."

It took concentration to work his exhausted muscled into a contracted nod against her hold—but he had managed.

She had fumed a thank you before standing and turning out of the bathroom.

Her sudden flipped switched personality had confused the young boy then.

And confused the adult man now, still haunting him with each wading watered shower.

He released his bowl into the metal kitchen sink and worked his hands into it to scrub it clean. Its clear exterior scraped against the surface of the sink as he scrubbed and his skin shuttered. He deadpanned a stare into the silver appliance as the chill pasted.

Brent dried his scrubbing hands off on a kitchen rag, killed the pouring faucet, then threw the old memory into a mental black garbage bag and poured a second cup of coffee. He left his apartment to lock it, revolve, and descend down the cement flight of apartment stairs that echoed a musically slapped beat into the stairwell of the surrounding homes.

The stairs led him to the parking lot where his black 2015 4Runner sat waiting for him like an obedient dog. He walked towards it while he held his coffee tight between two hands. The wind curled off an Oregon-meets-Washington mountain line and turned through the valley with a bitter cold the September sun couldn't touch through the thick smoke from a set of surrounding forest fires.

The frozen morning atoms crept through Brent's thin blue button-up and delivered an iced frown to his lips. *Tomorrow his outfit would include a jacket.*

He slid into the SUV and set his coffee mug carefully into the cupholder closest to the dashboard and automatic gear shift. He stuck the key into the ignition with a slick jab and a slight tremble in his jaw. His hand turned and the vehicle came alive with a rumbled purr that sent air blasting from its vents like the blow dryers at the end of car washes. Brent sat and shivered against the grey cloth seat as he waited for the car to warm before he buckled and backed out of his parking spot. He pulled onto a side street and head towards the back, forgotten about, side of town.

2

A one-story, rectangular-shaped grade school stood on the south side of town. The *forgotten* side, populated by low income-folks and folks smart enough to save their money by *living* in the low-income folks' territory. Brent turned into the building's nearly vacant parking lot and killed the now warm vents and engine of his SUV. The school was constructed of aging bricks and flat, metal beams—painted a chipping turquoise blue. Angled, tall windows pointed upward in a peak above the main entrance and gave the building the effect that it was much larger on the inside. It compensated for the school's seven-foot hallways that met the pointed main entrance. Brent shut the headlights off, their beam dropping down to only an automated glow at the front of the black Toyota. He took a long sip from his coffee mug with anticipation for the long burn down the back of his throat and he grimaced a little as it passed.

The school buses hadn't shown up yet with their morning loads of children and the parent drop off lane was unoccupied. Empty, eerie, elementary.

Brent abandoned his vehicle and headed into his place of work.

A burst of motion, fluid like a small explosion from behind the main office windows, caught his peripheral vision as he entered the pencil and Playdoh scented structure—so he glanced. Debra, Grant Elementary School's head receptionist was perched in her rolling, mesh, office chair like a hawk. She waved an extended hand persistently at the entering man, her underarm flab wobbled side to side like a featherless wing.

Brent gave a scuff and jokingly rolled his eyes at the middle-aged Hispanic woman before making a small pivot to the office doors, "happiest Monday to you, Deb." He greeted as the office door seal broke and he pressed through the entrance.

Featherless hawk catches mouse.

She gave an addressing beam up at her young coworker as she settled back into her rolling seat, "Good morning, handsome." She gestured her once flapping arm and hand to his coffee mug with a thirsty nod, her dark curls bouncing over her rounded, dress strapped shoulders, "need me some of that this morning." She laughed.

Brent wiggled his eyebrows at her as he took a final deep swig to empty the cup, "you're telling me." He breathed out the steam of the hot drink and checked the knotted black garbage bag of bad memories in his brain to make sure that memory of Amanda wouldn't come back out to visit.

"Mondays." She rested her head in the palm of her hand and reflected on her measly office woman life.

Brent plodded to the mail cubbies built against the wall that shared right side of the woman's desk, "gonna be a good one," he insured in a buggy sing-song tone. Debra winced at his song. He reached a hand into the cubby labeled with his name and retrieved a new manila folder left just for him. Brent tilted his head to read a name scribbled on its tab, rather than angling the folder itself. *Matthews, David.*

"That's actually what I needed you to come in here for." Debra gave reason to the girthy folder now flopped over in his hand.

Brent moved back to the front of her desk with a smug smirk, "it wasn't because you wanted to say hi to me?" He acted hurt but then winked to excuse it in verbal sugar.

She blushed under a layer of makeup in a way that flicked anxiety against the back of his neck, "He's a new student." She pointed to the folder and Brent glanced back down at the etched blue pen name—*Matthews, David*—no longer joking with her, "I need you to read his file before meeting him."

The lick of nerves behind him vanished then and a tight eyebrow raised, *I need you to,* "Debra," her name came out of his mouth in a belittling way that he hadn't meant, "did you read it?"

Her blush grew deeper but her eyes narrowed.

"That's my job." He made clear, as he had done a thousand times before, it had felt. Her mouth opened but he continued, "you aren't the counselor," he poked the corner of the folder into his chest like it was his own finger, "I am." His voice smirked but his lips did not.

Debra held her hand with the flabby wing back out to save the lecture, "Ei! I know." She shook her head like it mattered, "but Brent—"

"Will you bring him to my office once he gets dropped off?" Brent questioned sensitively.

Debra frowned and paired it with a sharp, jabbing look from over the top of her rounded green glasses, "yeah," her voice was peeled in a thin line.

"Great!" Brent let her offended expression go unnoticed, "I'll show him around and get to know him then." He tilted half a caffeinated grin at her, "get to know him first, rather than the file first." He felt the need to explain this to her, though he had, *a thousand times before*. "Reading a report someone else made of a kid is worse than reading a book by its cover, Deb." He winked again, trying to lasso their conversation back into friendly banter, "Reading a file first is something caseworkers do." She hadn't the slightest bit of knowledge of what that meant to him. His past of caseworkers and foster care kept neatly hidden in that mental garbage bag of his.

"Yes." She nodded because *yes*. She had heard his righteous speech *a thousand damned times before*. "But this time, I think it's important." There was a sudden, cold sternness to Debra—the head receptionist—that Brent submissively nodded too.

"Fine." he lied, "what grade is he?" *Lassoing the conversation back.*

"Third.–enrolled into Engels' class."

Brent smiled at the name as he turned and threw a *"perfect"* over his shoulder. He exited the office without a goodbye, folder and empty coffee cup balanced in hand.

He patted the file against his side as he sauntered down the muted hallways, chewing on the inside of his cheek. Soon the seven-foot-tall corridors would be filled with disruptive schoolyard talk, squeaky sneakers, and backpack zippers. Soon he would be meeting *Matthews, David.*

The long sided hall of the rectangular building led to an office catty-corner to the fifth-grade classrooms. Brent used his elbow to flip on the light before he entered.

The counseling room was cold and clean, as he had left it. He placed the empty coffee cup at the bottom of his keyboard and tossed the folder gently to the edge of his desk. His thoughts already spiraling down a rabbit hole checklist of things he had to get done before Monday was over. A progressive headache joined as he dropped into his office seat.

3

The drop off lane became lively with the traffic of parents and their headlights in the overcast forest fire *fog* morning. Some were sharply dressed and bopped useless buttons on their phones as they coasted through the curbed lane. The '*yes, yes honey—mommy has to go to work*' kind of parents. Other parents put their cars into park regardless of the posted exhaust pollution signs that asked them to keep their cars slowly puttering through the drop off. The '*okay, I love you so much. Do you have your lunch? Your homework? Did you brush your teeth? Have the office ladies call me if you need me*' kind.

All the children wrapped tightly in warm jackets that they'd shed later in the mid-afternoon, September heat, eventually left their parent and joined their friends on the covered playground in the back of the old school. Staff members for Grant Elementary with neon caution vests and first aid fanny packs policed through the playground like extremely boring security guards in knitted old lady sweaters.

Some children, not all, made *ninja missions* out of the morning duty teachers. "Don't let them see you!" they'd yell and dive into the gaping mouth of a closed spiral slide as their friends fell back and hid behind the slanted side of the rock wall.

Girls met at the swing sets and practiced their swing *tricks*. One girl with auburn curls performed her newly learned *backflip* off the swings for her friends to admire. Boys at the monkey bars mocked her.

On the dried grass end of the playground a group of second graders collected acorns in their hands and pockets from a neighboring tree that hung its branches over the silver fence lining of the schoolyard. One boy with shaggy hair and pink skin pulled the bottom of his shirt up to make a bowl at his front—collecting double the amount of acorns than his friends. The children then walked about the bark chip field and placed acorns sporadically throughout the entire gated play structure. The goal was to plant a *jungle*.

The playground was full and only unknowingly missed one more child, *Matthews, David*. Newbie's didn't get to play backflips, or acorn burial.

The bell rang and the vested teachers began to wrangle the kids into nearly neat lines sorted by grade. The doors hoisted open and herded single file lines were introduced to empty, eerie, elementary. The halls filled with their noise that bounced across the short walls. The lines orderly fashioned enough to laced like needle and thread through the school. The lines of children that shuffled like tiny soldiers past Brent's office door while he clicked through unopened emails.

"Hi."

Brent lifted his hands off his desk and turned his chair around to his room entrance, "Hi, Nancy," he smiled at the first grader leaning into his office. Nancy had plastic brown cheetah print glasses that stayed secure around her head with black rubber straps. Her eyes magnified beneath them like an adorable cartoon character. Baby Betty Boop with dusty blonde hair instead of animated black.

"Hi." She repeated as she spun for the exit and scampered down the hallway back towards her friends. She flapped the sleeve of her oversized jacket against her sides as she ran.

A laugh tickled the counselor as he turned back to his emails, his hands laid back down onto his desk. *Cuter than a bug's ear.* He thought. His headache began to drop off softly and he rubbed at his temple to help it move along, still smiling after the girl.

Time passed and after the hallways fell silent, the school kids' hype tucked away in their individual classrooms, Brent found himself staring attentively at the folder on the corner of his faux wood desk. *'This time, I think it's important.'* Debra's voice lectured within his head. He began to reach out for it with a glacier hand. When hadn't new news been important to her? Debra was like *TMZ* but for children.

"Mr. Kingsley?"

4

A hardly freckled boy with caramel brown hair stood sheepishly between the lumber frame of Brent's office door. His cheeks were flushed and his brown, wide eyes wandered like a lighthouse over a smooth ocean top. Debra stood behind the boy with one hand firmly against his tiny shoulder. A hand the counselor tisked a mental finger at—the garbage bag in his mind wiggling and wanting to come undone. "David," she addressed the child, "this is Mr. Kingsley."

    Brent stood from his chair and the boy's drifting eyes skated across his tall figure long enough for acknowledgment before they bounced tirelessly off into another direction. The boy noticed the texture of the stranger's office walls—bumpy and painted over with burgundy. Different than the walls in the elongated hallways because those were beige and smooth. He noticed a round table in the back of the room, for mini conferences, with mini people. He noticed the spot beside it, which shared a corner with the adult, paper blessed desk, was a wooden bookshelf. Stacked with *Goodwill* games and toys the boy only skimmed his attention across.

    A poster of a green lanky frog with a dapper gentleman grin was tacked to the left wall behind the desk and chair and the boy's eyes went to that, instead. The frog leaned against a vertical wheel, like the ones' the boy had seen in old game shows like *Wheel of Fortune*. Brent observed as the boy's stare traced over the mustard yellow bubble lettering at the top of the poster that spelled out *Kelso's Wheel.* The child's small fists clenched and unclenched at the seams of his jean pockets.

Debra shot Brent a troubled look that he dismissed to pass a glare at her hand on the boy's shoulder. A hand she then removed.

Grant Elementary's counselor hiked his khakis up at the knee and squatted in front of the new student. The joints between his bones trapped air and cracked on the way down to support his new position. The snap brought the boy's attention to him and his anxious fists relaxed against his thighs.

Brent smiled at him with closed lips and developing crow feet wrinkles, "hello," he said.

The boy's eyes fell to his shoes. They were cheap, white sneakers with dark blue rubber. The boy was sure he'd once saw an old man with the same pair. One lace was in a bow the other in a jumbled knot caked in dirt. The lace had frayed ends where old dried mud replaced the aglets. Distracted by the knot the boy knelt to make a matching bow and his left knee made a mimicking crack.

A smirk pushed up on his blotchy red cheeks as he worked at the tangled yarn, "my knees pop too," the boy confessed.

Brent's eyebrows raised the length of his forehead at the boy's raspy mumble.

Debra became bored and sent herself away to her coil-cord phone where there may be new, newer news to feed her sanity. She slumped her way down the hallway with heavy *heal-toe-heal-toe* clicks of her booties.

The boy became more relaxed with the woman gone and the attentive counselor's own shoulders untensed and rolled forward empathetically as he observed the child.

"It's kind of a funny thing, isn't it, David?" Brent asked in reference to their popping joints.

The swell in the boy's cheeks exhausted and he sucked his bottom lip into his mouth, "Davey," the boy sighed as he stood. His eyes stayed to his shoes in admiration of his matching rabbit-ear, loopy-loop, bows—an easy excuse to avoid the adult's evaluating eyes. It was an awful habit—*sucking on his lip*. His sister had asked him politely to stop once or twice before because of that red rash that would always start rimming the base of his mouth. And he had stopped —*sorta*.

It had come back when they moved. His sister said she understood. *Falling off the wagon* she had called it. The boy hadn't quite understood the phrase but had always imagined the red razor wagon that had been at his old home. The one with the broken handle their mother had thrown out. *That would hurt to fall off of,* he always thought.

"You like to go by Davey?"

The boy's lip dropped from his mouth and he pulled it along with a wipe from the cuff of his hand me down, green jacket. His eyes failed to meet Brent's directly, still. "Some people like to call me David, but I like Davey better."

Brent grinned genuinely with his teeth this time, "I love that name."

Brown diverging eyes latched onto Brent's older, more tired eyes.

"Do you like being called Mr. Kingsley?" Davey asked a fair question with a shy squeak of a voice.

Brent tipped his head back and hummed at it. His Adam's apple bobbed slowly under the thin layer of shaved prickles on his neck, "Yes, I do." He pressed his lips together and thought some more before they smacked apart, "but not by everyone."

Davey dipped his head in understanding even if reasons weren't particularly clear to him. "What's your real, real name?" His eyes blinked rapidly, just for a moment, as he asked and a hand came up to press at his bottom lip. He was thinking about pulling it back in.

The man's inclined head tipped back down to be level, "Brent," he answered then stood, his pant legs falling back down to cup around his black tube socks.

"Brent," the boy intoned back to himself then smiled with two front adult teeth like it was an afterthought. He had never heard the name before, though believed it was a real one. Even if it did roll out of his mouth like a funny accent.

Brent looked into the hallway with a familiar routine, "would it be alright if I showed you around?" He watched the boy from above as he spoke.

Davey rolled his head over his shoulders indecisively, *nod yes, or nod no? That is the question.* Then, rather than giving a nod or verbal answer, he shuffled into the hallway. Eyes low and feet scooting. Brent understood and followed.

They walked down the long corridor of the rectangular building side by side. Brent cutting his lengthy strides in half to stay with the young child. Davey dressed warmly in old clothes and had a plain black backpack strapped loosely to his shoulders. It was too big and meant for a teenager, and had fuzz matted into the glue spot where a logo once was. The man took his eyes off of it and put them in the hallway walls, careful not to develop assumptions.

Child art stapled itself down blue billboards that stretched the full length of the hallway and Davey stopped a moment to adore one drawing of a dog's face. A springer spaniel with wide eyes and a dropped tongue, neatly crafted in three shades of blue pencil. It was more unique than the adolescent Crayola art of the other students, "who did this one?" He asked Brent who had also stopped to look.

The man squinted at the art like he needed glasses. The name written lightly in plain graphite pencil in the right corner, "Alexis Adams," he answered, "She's a fifth-grader here." Brent then tossed a hand in the air and waved it around flamboyantly, "one of the most astounding artists of this time." He used his best high held, nasally, museum tour guide voices hoping Davey would understand his joke.

The boy turned his head over his green jacket shoulder and watched the act with a gentle giggle to say he did. Brent lowered his hand then and smirked, "she's a good kid." He said, fitted back in his normal voice, and meant it.

Davey responded politely after a long pause for calculated thought. "Do you know everybody here?" He meant in the school.

Brent took a step forward, back down the hallway, and the boy followed, "I think so," he recalled, "at least I try." He thought for a moment longer, "I'm pretty new here too, you know?"

"You are?" The boy's muscles in his face and body relaxed by a notch and a half at the possibility of not being so alone on his new journey.

"Sure," Brent kept his hands behind his back as he stepped, "this is only year three, for me."

A snort left the boy's body and was chased immediately by a lowered head in a recoiling attempt to apologize for the laugh.

Brent thought: *don't be sorry.*

"That's not really being new," Davey justified his snotty sound.

This time it was Brent that chuckled, "Sure I am. There are a lot of students in this place, it takes a really long time to get to know them all." Davey's face contorted, "okay," Brent admitted with a slight shake of his head, "Maybe I'm not so new anymore." They reached the end of the hall and had to make a left turn towards the library, now on the short stroke of the rectangle. "But I do remember what it was like to be new. Even as a kid, I was new a lot when I was around your age."

"You're like me?"

Brent looked away from the kid for a brief second, "sure!" He spoke kindly as the garbage bag in his head stretching open a little as he looked back at Davey.

They sauntered quietly until they reached the main hall, to their left was the library and to their right was the front doors with the angled windows and the main office. Brent peeked through the office window at Debra—she didn't notice—and he was thankful. He knew too well that her meeting eyes would have asked, '*did you read the folder?*' And the answer was no.

"Would you like to see our library area?"

Two flags stood on either side of the doorway, one for America and the other for Oregon. Both hung limp with a golden beaver for one and red, white stripes for the other.

Davey considered the double doors that lead to the child athenaeum, "sure," he shrugged.

It reminded Davey of a courtroom.

5

The library had smelled of uncoated paper and fermented rose perfume. Sweet, bitter and all-at-once too strong for Davey's nose. A woman sat and scanned the barcode of books at a computer at the far end of the room. Davey's face scrunched at that tart rose sting coming from her. Burnt brown hair fuzzed around her aging features and a red sweater draped off her shoulders in an unflattering manner. "Who is that?" He queried Brent.

Brent let out a held sigh through flexed nostrils, "Mrs. Roland." He kept his head low as he answered, careful not to poke the book scanning beast.

Davey caught his whisper and carried it on under the rasp of his low voice, "She wears—"

"Too much perfume?" Brent finished the sentence without hesitation, then watched amusedly as the boy swung his head up at him with shock and smiled. He gestured without touch for the boy to walk forward, guiding him in the opposite direction of the librarian, "yeah," he continued, "I know." He led Davey to a group of tables lined up in the center of the dim-lit library, "we all know." Including parents who'd complained their child was getting ill from the woman's chemical sprayed scent. Brent never did doubt it.

"Alright," The man stopped at a table and pulled out a chair, "time to get to know each other a little more." And as he lowered himself into the chair he asked the child, "is that alright with you?"

Davey's bottom lip twitched as he fought an urge to suck it under his front teeth.

"Don't worry," the counselor smiled, "it'll be easy."

Davey rocked back on his heal and waited anxiously. There was a hesitation that Brent Kingsley dragged out, pausing long enough to watch Davey rock back forward to his toes and pull his eyes away from the man.

"Can you find me your most favorite book?" Brent's head twitched at another incline and he noticed the boy's lip now folding into his mouth for the second time since meeting him. He mentally noted it as a nervous tick, "take your time," he added to his gifted task and watched the lip come out, wet with slobber the boy swept away again with a green sleeve.

Davey glanced around the carpeted library and felt it's depth intimidate his small frame like kicks to the shin. Each wall-hung-shelf colored with dark wood that stretched far beyond his reach. He rocked again, but sideways this time, switching the weight to his right foot, then his left, then back again to his right. His hands started to tingle as he twisted them against each other at the front of his body as if he were washing them under a sink's faucet. He glanced at the soft spoken counselor, seated back in a royal blue, metal chair and suddenly wanted to press into him. The same way his lip always wanted to press into his mouth. He studied the man's lap and thought about the risk of climbing into it and saying *"no thank you, I'd like if I just stayed next to you because you feel —"*. Davey looked away from the counselor and back at the walls hidden by books and their shelves and let the thought carry itself to a complete sentence: *"safe."* What a strange emotion. One Davey only ever felt around his sister, *safe*. And now the stranger felt *safe* and he wanted to fold into that, and not let it go away.

Brent tilted back on two legs of the chair, then dropped back forward, "You don't have to find a book, Davey."

Davey looked back at him and suddenly really wanted to.

He let a final rock to his left foot follow through to his full weight and stepped his right foot over it. His body turned to the biggest shelves and he continued to walk to them, his legs like prosthetics screwed loosely into his hips. His hands, again, twirling back over each other like he was a fly.

He stopped at the wall-hung-shelves with the dark wood and stared up at them. He skimmed over the books at eye level, scanning them like the perfume wearing librarian on the other side of the room did with the red laser and their barcode. They were all thick and far too advanced. *Fifth grade (and sixth grade for the smart readers) level.* He didn't think he had read any of them or even heard of them from his older sister, so he moved to the next shelf. He waddled like his legs really were prosthetic—or strapped to stilts. On this shelf the books were thin, and their spines were glossy. Yet, still, the titles seemed rare and unheard of. The boy took a stilted step back and bent his head up to read the sign taped to the top of the shelf.

Non-Fiction.

He made a face, privately, at it. *No wonder,* he thought. *Non -Fiction* meant *Not - fake.* Or *Not* his *favorite.*

Across the library, where a circular carpet and reading chair sat in the focal point under a bright, bulb lamp, was a sign for *'Fiction and Fun Reads'.* It was a sign painted into the wall, like a scribe, over a mural of two small children curled up and reading with a green tree python. The python wore glasses and gleamed a human smile that made Davey feel strange.

He glanced at Brent, worried that he was wasting the man's time and thinking again about curling against him, the word *safe* bouncing through his head like a tennis ball. The man's head was down as he scratched up old calluses on his hand and seemed to be in no rush. So, Davey crossed the room to the *'Fiction and Fun Reads'* section with his head low to avoid any mistaken eye contact with the snake on the wall. His backpack whooshed against his back as he walked with legs that were starting to feel more like his own.

He studied three different white, half his height, shelves before he stood still and studied a rotating, clear one. He turned it to watch the titles sweep past, and smiled absently. It reminded him of the rotating racks of sunglasses at drug stores. He stopped the clockwise rotation with two fingers, then began to push it in the opposite direction, counter-clockwise. He turned it slower and actually read the titles as they swiveled by. These ones were all paperback, and well loved, he noticed as he stretched a hand out and let it brush over their ripped spines. He trailed his fingers over the long line of books, the swinging shelf stopped completely now and paused at one. His forefinger pressed into its tattered backbone and his eyes glistened as he mouthed the title to himself. A sense of nostalgia washed bearably through him and he plucked the book from its place to hold it to his chest. *This one was his most favorite book.*

He scampered back to Brent with a hop in his normal legged step and stopped a few feet in front of him. The man was leaned fully forward in his chair now and was studying his shoes. Davey noticed they were nicer than his and wondered if the counselor had noticed the same thing. He'd hoped not.

Brent looked up from the floor then and met the boy with a calm smirk, "find one?" He asked.

Davey nodded and handed the used book to the man.

"*Matilda?!*" It was a delightful, and quite surprising choice–the man thought–as he turned it over in his hold. Feeling the weight of its thinning papers and studying its bent front cover. A picture of Mara Wilson, from the movie adaptation, smiled up at him. Her hair swept back with a red ribbon bow. He thought of *Itty Bitty Pretty One* by Thurston Harris.

"My sister read it to me when I was in the first grade," Davey explained in a shy whisper with eyes that trailed up as he thought back, she'd read him a lot of books before they moved.

"I love it! Great choice, kiddo!" Brent watched Davey's lower lip as he spoke. Curious to see if affirmation caused the anxious twitch. It did. The lip went into his mouth. That was okay, Brent was new to the child and nerves were expected.

He opened the book to the middle and skimmed the lines. The garbage bag in his mind tore as he remembered stealing *Matilda* from Amanda's hoard of books under her bed. He ran his thumb over the browning pages and flicked it against a folded corner as he thought of Amanda's room. Her bed on a box spring and a metal headboard that would screech like a wind instrument every time she got into it. Below its surface and behind the yellow bed skirt was the land of her keepsake books. Before Amanda's bedroom was scary to him, and her bed was something he was forced into, beneath it was somewhere he'd hide with the books like it was his own reading nook. Even if he couldn't read them yet, he'd just grab and flip through them, to smell them, usually. *Matilda* was one of those books.

"What's yours?" Davey spoke while he pulled a chair from the table and took a seat next to the man.

Brent looked at him with a despondent glaze that hung like window blinds over his iris'.

Davey elaborated, "Favorite book?" Unsure of himself now as the counselor looked up at him.

Brent closed the book and removed himself from the memory of Amanda's bedroom as he leaned back in his chair with his normal delight that made the boy relax, "easy." He said without a second thought, "*Double Fudge.*" He expected Davey to give a look of confusion or cower away at the unfamiliar title, but instead, his posture straightened and his low features on his face brightened.

"By Judy Blume?" He asked, his voice pitched up, breaking through the low rasp he had been speaking with.

Brent slid *Matilda* into the center of the table and clapped his hands together, "How'd you know that?" The boy was beaming at him now.

"My sister!" He exclaimed proudly.

Brent was impressed, "your sister sounds wonderful!"

Davey's lip did not go into his mouth this time.

Brent felt Mrs. Roland's eyes lift up and shoot a pointed glare at him like they were arrows. He lowered his hands back down into his lap and his voice back into his chest in response to her cranky stare.

"Thank you," Davey rebuked back to the comment on his sister.

Brent blinked his eyes once over a laced up smile, "you're welcome."

They left the library with the book back where Davey had found it and ambled again down a long sided hall, a different one than the last, the other side of the rectangle. Davey jarred his head from left to right to take in all the new details. This hall was also painted beige but the art on the billboards was from different children. Younger grades, *K* through second. Some drawings were mere scribbles in led, some were stick figures. Davey didn't mind them, but also didn't stare for long.

His eyes fell forward onto the long hallway linoleum ground that was only a shade lighter than the walls with a marble swept finish. He thought as they stepped with his voice stuck in his throat. It wasn't until he felt the man's glance fall to him while wondering why the kid had stopped looking at the art on the walls and found the floor was more interesting, that Davey blurted, "Can I call you Brent?" His voice cracked under the blunt pressure and his face reddened.

Brent grinned sympathetically and pulled his eyes back up to look over the hallway, "sure," he said with a voice that shrugged with his word, "but don't call me Brent in front of your peers."

Davey thought of ocean piers and cocked his head with a bit of puzzlement.

Brent turned his eyes back down to the boy, "kids your age," he clarified, "they all have to call me Mr. Kingsley."

Davey nodded, "because you like to be called Mr. Kingsley, but not by everyone?"

"Right." Brent nodded across their deal, "And because students have to call their teachers by their last name." They made eye contact, his head tilted down, Davey's tilted up, and Brent winked.

Davey understood, he was *special.*

The man and boy fell into a silent stride, Brent's nice shoes making small *thud* noises against the tan, glossy ground. Davey noticed his long arm and how it swung gently against his tall frame and thought again about how Grant Elementary's counselor was *safe*. He stared at the man's hand, unable to remember the last time someone other than his sister showed interest in him. *Real* interest–like Brent, *but Mr. Kingsley to the peers,* had. Davey lifted his own hand. It cuffed into Brent's swinging one and held on, the warmth of the man's palm and fingers spreading down into Davey's toes. *Safe.*

Brent had nearly jumped at the boy's touch as if it were a loud noise and his hand clamped around Davey's in a startled jerk as a wave of affection crashed through his tall figure. It was a stark, bold move that he hadn't expected from the boy. He looked down, anticipating eye contact, but was denied; Davey's face turned the opposite direction as he stared again at more art. His arm at a loose sway below Brent's grip.

6

They took the last turn in the rectangular building and stopped at the front of a heavy wooden door. Davey made a quick glance at the art on the walls in the other short hallway and surmised the art was similar to his own.

Brent swung the boy's dangled arm at an easy tempo to grab his attention, "this is your stop," he said and watched as the kid's lip retracted into his mouth. "It's okay," Brent used his fingers to tightly embrace the small hand in his palm, "this classroom is amazing–I'm *so* glad you were enrolled into class with these children." He smiled and spoke with his body, his knees dipping as he said '*so* glad'. He hoped the boy believed him and squeezed his small hand for good measure.

Davey squeezed back.

Brent slowed and studied the red in the boy's face as it resurfaced and masked what little freckles he had. "It's okay." He repeated and stepped towards the door solemnly. Davey tugged back, unsure. Brent gave him a wink over a shoulder to remind him it was alright before he broke the door's seal and popped his head through the thin opening to the classroom. Davey shrunk behind the man and the half opened door with his hand still clutched against the counselor's.

Small heads turned away from their lesson and towards Brent.

A crash bang of cheering "*Mr. Kingsley!*"'s slammed through the open door, past the counselor, and surrounded Davey. The mangle of voices flapped around him like bat wings from his hiding place behind the man and he pulled Brent's hand instinctively. He was given another squeeze in response, one that held him in place and told him he'd be fine. He teetered his weight and bit down on the lip in his mouth, suddenly provoked with a cattle prod of jealousy. So many voices were excited to see the man that their whoop of his name morphed together in an ugly, inaudible sound monster trudging forward to bust down the door jam and swallow Davey whole. So many voices already liked the man as much as Davey did and that made his stomach burn.

He wanted something *special* all to himself.

He rolled the skin on his lip around in his mouth and thought of ocean piers came back to him. The jealousy seemed to leap off the piers in his mind then as he remembered they all had to call him *Mr. Kingsley* but he could call him *Brent*. The jealousy swam below the dock and knocked at his feet and he stomped at the boardwalk vibrations.

Brent, who had smiled at the roar of his name, now made a hushed noise with his lips to the children, "hi, everyone." He spoke evenly towards the chorus of children. He made eye contact with the woman at the front of the room who stood patiently waiting with a ruler slacked in her hand. "*Sorry*," he mouthed to her and she gave a forgiving nod. A crinkle in her lips hinted into a grin. She tucked her ruler under her arm and her hands came together in a patterned clap, loud and metallic. The golden jewelry that decorated her fingers and wrists clunk together in a vibrating sting, like a bell.

Slow, slow. Quick, quick, quick.

The children brought their attention around, back to her, and clapped an echo of the pattern in a silly, unified response.

Slow, slow. Quick, quick, quick.

The classroom fell into a silent murmur then as they waited for further instruction from the woman at the front of the room. Some children still turned in their seats towards Brent and mouthing "*hellos*".

"Do you need me, Mr. Kingsley?" The young teacher asked with her smooth, apricot voice.

"Yes, please." He insisted with a final squeeze back to Davey's hand.

She sat her ruler down gently onto the classroom projector table and raised her arms into a petite shrug—her fingers spread out and her lips tight to one side, "looks like free time is starting early today, friends!" The room erupted into another thrilled roar that drowned out her giggle at their wild faces.

Brent backed out of the room then and turned a reassuring smile to Davey. The boy half gestured his unsure lips back as the rest of him noticed the fire red shades in Brent's cheeks. His head lined up curiously with the embrued burn beneath the man's eyes as he wondered if he were alright.

The teacher caught the slow closing door and as she came through and Brent also reached and pulled his side of the door in a gentlemen kind of way. She gave a thank you to him as she joined the impromptu stand-up meeting. The classroom door shut behind her to mask the children's noise and her thick eyebrows snaked up the length of her forehead, "Oh, hello." She sighed at Davey and ran two hands down the bottom tail of her shirt to straighten it out.

She had natural black hair that hung just below the collarbone of her olive shoulders and river green eyes, surrounded by brown pencil eyeliner and a smooth swipe of mascara. Her lips were full and wrinkled when she smiled. She was, Davey could see, a genuinely stunning lady.

He looked back at his counselor's blushing cheeks and his loose smile kited at the corners—because Davey Matthews' understood the primal urges between adults—even if he couldn't feel it himself.

"Mrs. Engles," Brent spoke on queue to the sudden silence, "meet Davey Matthews, your newest trooper." He stepped aside to showcase the bashful child who'd been shielding himself behind Brent's leg as he evaluated the adults' relationship.

"Hi," She repeated.

Davey dropped his eyes and leaned into the back of the counselor, *Mrs?* Davey knew what that meant, and he felt sorry for the man.

She scanned Brent under her thick black eyebrows and he gave her a vowed nod, "Davey," he said with his safe voice. Davey looked at him. "Mrs. Engles is a great friend of mine—I promise you will like her."

Davey looked at her.

She smiled.

Davey looked away.

Mrs. Engles wasn't offended by this, instead, she mixed a smile somewhere into her features and placed her ring decorated fingers over her rounded hip bones. "Would you like to choose your spot in the classroom?" She asked with a fruity voice that was supposed to make the idea sound like a treat. "Anywhere you'd like to sit." She added.

Davey inspected Brent's face as if the correct answer was going to pop up on a sign over his forehead. Brent shrugged at the boy, "I don't know kiddo, it's your choice, not mine."

Davey's head tossed back to her and he raised his shoulders into a mirrored shrug.

Mrs. Engels shrugged also then, being funny—but not being mean. Reciprocating all in good faith. "That's okay if you don't know," she chimed just as fruity, "I think I may have a great spot already planned for you." She looked into the top corners of her eyes as a gesture of thought, "however, Davey, if you don't like it, please let me know."

Davey nodded as his bottom lip sunk deeper into his quicksand mouth.

"Great," Brent and Mrs. Engles sighed in a soft unison. Then made eye contact.

Mrs. Engles stretched her wedding band hand out for Davey to take, in place of his counselor's safe, warm one. He stared at it in consideration and as he eyed the diamond a pit started to stir in his stomach. He slipped his hand from Brent's light grip and dropped it to his pocket.

"That's okay," she smirked. Then turned to pull open the door.

The noise and classroom clutter rushed back to the hollow hallway walls and plastered against the teacher, counselor, and new student.

7

The adult's hadn't brought Davey to the front of the classroom and he was grateful for it. Brent had taken Davey's teenager sized backpack from him after he'd received a glance of approval from the socially overstimulated child with quivery knees. He walked it over and hung it in a small cubby amongst the other students' bags while Mrs. Engels took him to his seat—a desk in the back next to her long, cluttered one.

His was a hollow desk with lots of room to store crayons, paper and books from the library. Maybe *Matilda*. He could get it on library day, Mrs. Ronald scanning it out just for him, and he could read it for himself. Absorb the words without his sister, now that he was older. Maybe *Super Fudge* too.

"Class," Mrs. Engles addressed her students once Davey was seated as if their eyes weren't already on him and their mouths weren't already whispering, "This is Davey Matthews', our new friend. Please say hello." A cheer of "*hellos*" and beams fled the boy's way promptly.

Davey stifled a smile. Then looked for Brent.

He stood in the back by the heavy door entrance—watching Davey. They caught each other's stare and Brent flashed a thumbs up to the kid, like a coach during a tough play, before he backed out into the hallway. His hung-on-a-lanyard employee badge bounced off his abdomen and smiled white at Davey as the man turned and the door shut behind him. It felt as if someone had ripped a warm blanket off of him as he watched Brent exit. His stomach tightened and he looked to the front of the strange classroom, fighting the sting in his nose and water in his eyes.

His teeth bit down on his lip.

In the burgundy counseling office, Brent resumed his inquisitive glare on the manila folder labeled *Matthews, David.* He thought of crossing *David* out and writing *Davey* as he rubbed a light circle into his palm where the boys' hand had sat.

"What does Deb know, that I don't?" The man pondered the idea. A knot tangling towards the front of his spin, just behind his gnawing stomach. *What's the big deal?*

Probably nothing but he grabbed the folder anyway. Its weight pressed firm into his skin. His thumb trailed the edge of its thick manila stock, the contact was dull and dry, and it scraped in Brent's ears. The sound forced his molars to tighten down, an instruction from his bothered eardrums.

He pushed the card stock flap open.

He starred with sudden fatigue at the fine print enrollment papers and forgot about any type of urgency Debra had shown. His eyes drifted to his white and black traditional clock on the wall and avoided the long read in front of him.

9:13

Brent let out a long, compressed, groan.

He closed the folder and dropped it on the top of his keyboard where it made a weak *thwap* in its landing. Paper slid out of its front and showed only their edge like a woman attempting to tease by slipping a lacy sleeve down over the shiny skin on her shoulder. Brent wasn't interested. He quickly shuffled the papers back in to the card stock as he stood from his chair. He collected a notepad, pen from a dusty mug under his monitor, and an 'Evaluation Sheet' from his desk drawer. He slid it back in with the creased sting of plastic rolling over metal and led his chair gently beneath his desk. He's late.

The counselor hustled to the first-grade hallway, just past the library, like a high school student avoiding the hall monitor. He nudged through the door of Ms. Gus' classroom and snuck to the back. The room was lit with high beam, white fluorescent lights and decorated with grey tables, all round and low to the Aegean carpeted ground. Brent went to a vacant table and dragged a yellow, metal chair out from under it. He squatted into the seat, his knees to his chest, the notepad and paper laid out on his lap.

The class of first graders hardly noticed his presence, their focal point on printed out coloring pages, various sized color pencils hugged tight in their small fists. They scribbled and giggled amongst each other. Brent thought of Davey admiring all the art in the hallways and tucked a blossomed smile into his cheeks.

Ms. Gus was sat bowlegged at her snot green desk and peered at the children over her rhinestone reading spectacles like she had a pinpoint migraine. They were secure to her neck with a purple, beaded spectacle cord. Her aged eyes met Brent's and they made a featureless bow of their heads to one another. Brent's lips tightened like they wanted to greet her with a smile but failed to get there. She had fluffed white haircut so short to her head you could see the pink of her oblong scalp, the elder poodle pooch of the school. Brent dropped focus back to his papers and scribbled the time at the top of the Evaluation Sheet, under a name, *Jamie Carpenter*.

Ms. Gus had demanded that he come down to her classroom at nine to evaluate the *'melancholy'* child. Brent glanced at the clock again, fifteen minutes late, but she hadn't seemed to notice. Which came as a relief to the grade school counselor.

Brent began to observe the child reluctantly with his pen out and ready to jot down important notes, wild epiphanies and behavioral dilemmas. The boy named Jamie Carpenter colored thoughtfully with a red pinky length pencil. Brent twisted in his chair uncomfortably at her incoherent concern but watched anyway.

Jamie Carpenter's head was dipped sideways, his eyebrows furrowed, and his tongue was jutting from the corner of his mouth like it controlled the strokes of red—a rotary engine to his hand. His table group chatted as they colored similar art. He'd hardly lift his head in response to their ramble but would invite a kind smirk to his face every time a joke was made or a child laughed loud enough for his busy mind to hear it.

Brent leaned back in the yellow classroom chair and stretched his size thirteen feet farther forward on the carpet with a released breath.

Ms. Gus was anal-retentive—and crazy?

He scribbled on the evaluation sheet beneath Jamie's name and the time.

Jamie Carpenter

9:15am.

9:21am. Evaluation complete.

8

Davey, who hadn't been sat with a group like Ms. Gus' first graders, but rather at the end of the furthest row, now examined a foam apple at the edge of Mrs. Engels' desk. It was plump and wrinkled from being squeezed and toyed with. Its red body in a sea of clutter made up of papers, erasers, and big black clips with the folding, silver tabs. *An apple a day keeps the doctor away. (But what does a foam apple do?)* Davey imagined Mrs. Engels' nibbling the wet foam and bit a smile into his lower lip.

What a silly idea.

A girl with blonde pigtails sat in front of him, hair bands with pink marbles held up the thin locks. She occasionally whirled her body around to study the new student but then change her mind and whip back to face the front, unsatisfied with Davey's inattentiveness to her curious eye. The plastic marble hair bands would clack every time she spun like she was a music machine of impatient swirls.

Davey didn't just ignore the pigtail girl but his new teacher too as she practiced cursive "L"'s for the class to see under the projector screen. He scanned the new class like they had scanned him. A boy three rows down and four seats up (*hit, you sunk my ship*) dug his finger through the inside of his nose. He pulled out after scrapping the inner walls with his twisting tiny limb and placed it at the tip of his lips to use his teeth and scrape the dry mucus from under his overgrown fingernail.

Davey watched with a prickle of sweat sickly inside his chest.

You can pick your friends. You can pick your nose. But you can't pick your friend's nose. He remembered once reading the saying off a poster in the store to his mother. He had thought it was good humor, she had not, making it clear that he had disturbed her with his slow, sounded out reading voice, then wild giggle. His sister had laughed with him, instead, to make him feel better. They were lashed out on, together.

He eventually turned his attention back to Mrs. Engels.

She was writing an 'M' now, with inked curls at the tips. "M," she hinted to the kids who couldn't tell. Which was probably nobody, Davey assumed, but his eyes did take a second to trip back over to nose picker. "Like Mrs." She continued and penned out her name below the cursive letter. '*Mrs. Engels*'.

Davey's tighten jowls slackened into a frown at that darned honorific. *Poor Brent.*

Class motored through two more lessons before the lunch bell rang. An old-timey bowl and hammer screwed to the wall in the long corridors. Davey wanted to shut it off or plug his ears to it as his hands twitched. One hand came up to create a tight band around the other wrist like a human handcuff. Mrs. Engels stood the same way as him, one hand cuffed over the other's wrist, but not anxiously like he was. Instead, she stood in a woman's power stance and waited patiently for the class to quiet down. All children prattled with rumbling tummies and excited speech.

The chaotic cackle of the morphed children voices that turned into an inaudible sound monster began to grow so Mrs. Engels did her special clap.

Slow, slow. Quick, quick, quick.

Heads turned to attention and the children echoed the pattern back. Davey joined as if his motor skills couldn't help it. Like a test dog responding to a bell. Pavlov's children.

Slow, slow. Quick, quick, quick.

"Everybody, line up." The woman requested then popped her lips apart to add, "calmly." The request a far cry from the response as children began to rush to their spots. One boy pushed another to claim first and through the rebirthed inaudible sound monster, there was a pitched whine of protest. "Children!" Mrs. Engels' raised voice made her appear less beautiful, the fruity now replaced with veggies. Davey shrunk away from it. The teacher's black, soft angled, eyebrows lowered like the volume bar on a TV as her class began to quiet. She looked at the shrunken boy, "Davey, hon, would you like to be our line leader?" She gestured to the tight space between the children and the barricading door as if it was meant to look fun to him. *Not* oppressing. The boy at the front of the line who had just shoved to get there had a chest that billowed out like he was the son of a lumberjack.

Davey opened his mouth to answer with a polite, *'no, thank you,'* but could only manage a dry shake of the head. The saliva replenishing his mouth as he swallowed. He could feel the classes' eyes on him again, scanning, and he fell back into the end of the line.

Mrs. Engels gave a neighborly shrug like when she had mimicked the two males in the hallway, "that's okay." She also sounded the same way she had when Davey declined to hold her hand—a replay button of two hours earlier. "Isabel, how about you lead the line today?"

The tallest girl in class threw her hands up in a victorious cheer like a contestant chosen for *The Price Is Right*, "Yes!" She hissed in a way Davey envied. He wouldn't be brave enough to show that much enjoyment in front of this many people, he burrowed further away from the front of the children, backing himself into Mrs. Engels' desk, glancing at the foam apple. Isabel skipped to the front of the line like it was a routined dance and pressed open the wooden door. The wooden door that, in no way, would protect them from a shooter. Davey scratched at the tops of his wrists anxiously.

The class followed Isabel into the hallway in the best orderly fashion a third grade could able. Some children weebled from the line to drag their fingers against the beige walls, adding their own prints to layers of pencil led finger smudges. They paraded past other classes of children stretched out in snaked lines that all headed to the cafeteria like them.

The cafeteria was an expansion to the original rectangular building and was to the left of Mrs. Engels' room, just past Brent's office, which had darkened windows and a closed door—Davey checked. As he walked with the class he began to notice the scent of warmed food and milk and his stomach churned. Mrs. Engels had stayed back in her classroom, Davey wished he could have done the same. Alternatively, he was stuck following a new class.

The girl with pigtails fell out of line and stood still until the back, where Davey walked, reached her. Then she cha-cha'd in and began to troop behind him.

The boy kept his eyes forward. He yearned for the quiet walk with his counselor then, to silently enjoy the art again, rather than stack his feet along with the other booger picking soldiers in front of him. *And now, also behind him.* "I'm Daisy." She spoke as if her mouth was stuffed with three sticks of pink bubble gum, "Daisy and Davey," she continued to smack despite Davey's vacant responses. "Don't you think that's special?" Her question was accompanied by an obnoxious giggle.

Davey chewed the dry skin from his bottom lip.

A boy in front of him with a small face spun around with a mischievous glare more interested in the name similarities than Davey ever would be, "Daisy and Davey sitting in a tree, K.I.S.S.—"

"Stop," Davey spoke with quiet assertion, pressing his nails into sharp crescent shapes on the palm of his hands. He'd heard the rhyme many times before and never had appreciated it, even if it wasn't directed towards him.

The boy with the shrunken face scrunched his piglet nose and snickered through a gap in his front teeth, "you like her, huh?" His voice as annoying as a rusted can opener.

Davey's nails dug deeper and his eyes stretched past the boy, "no." He thought of his sister and how powerful she was. Nobody would tease him if he was powerful like her.

The boy's conniving laugh repeated, "yes, you do," it was thick with mockery—Davey thought it made him seem stupid.

"No," Daisy said this time with a snarky, upturned lip. "Leave us alone, tiny face." The boy laughed at her, but then turned around all the same, and lifted a hand to his face as he overplayed the insult through his third-grade brain. Davey dropped his head a little. She was powerful, like his sister. A woman who stood up for the little guy, women were good for that.

Mrs. Engels' class reached the kitchen and began to file through the claustrophobic lunch line. Davey strained his arm out over the rutted metal counter to grab an orange speckled tray but Daisy's hand was already on it. She removed it from the pile and held it out to him as a peace offering for the teasing she unpurposefully brought on.

Davey gave a glance to his left to ensure little face boy wouldn't see as he accepted the plastic tray from the girl in nineties fashioned pigtails—without any gratitude, too overstimulated to express it.

They slid their trays along, Daisy's occasionally bumped into Davey's, and grabbed from the covered hot plates. Davey grabbed a grilled cheese secure in a canary yellow wrapper that dripped with steamy condensation from the inside, the bread soaking up the moisture and becoming soggy. The wrapper had a cartoon sandwich at the corner. He had a gentleman's grin and stared at Davey with wide, iris-less, eyes. A cartoon hand reaching from his breaded side and waving. Davey dropped the wrapper and sandwich to his tray.

They reached the cold food section, laid out on *cold* plates, and he collected a paper cup full of thawed fruit that came fresh—*straight from a plastic bag in the back of the freezer*. A blue carton of milk was next, and he fit it nicely into the square shape of his tray. As he lifted his tray from the lipped bar he noticed the carton of milk was printed with a winking cow on the side. He wondered why there was a fascination with humanized food in a brief, fleeting, thought before the line spit him out into the open cafeteria.

Davey stopped with his old man sneakers and stood paralyzed as he watched the disarray of hungry youth. There were shouts under the bright white lights and clatters of trays against wood painted plastic tables that set his teeth on edge and he was forced to suck his lower lip in to cushion them.

Almost on queue, the pigtailed blonde named Daisy was close to him, peering over the cafeteria, but not with fear like the buckled boy next to her. She was an old veteran to the madness, "do you want to sit with me, Davey?"

Davey turned his body to her with his tray clenched in white-knuckled fists. He noticed she had blue eyes then.

Daisy and Davey sitting in a tree.

"No." he railed.

Her untamed eyebrows knitted a tight yellow line as she cross-examined him, "you're better when you're quiet." She said matter-of-factly and Davey wasn't sure he could disagree. His face beamed red as she turned and strutted away in jeans and a lime green t-shirt. One from the Goodwill, with a smiling monkey on the front, covered in sparkles.

He was alone.

Sweat prickled his hairline and he peeked at the cafeteria exit.

Lillian Rose

9

Brent left the days *third evaluation* with a growl in his stomach like a knocking engine. Amanda had once pinned him to the floor and tried to drive one of her mother's sewing needles through his earlobe, despite the shrill pleas he was vibrating with. Her forced knees held him to the crusty wood floors by the bend in his elbows. His bones rolled and pinched his skin from the inside each time Amanda shifted her weight to get a better shot at his ear.

Evaluations gave Brent the same feeling Amanda had that day. *Sure,* and earring would've been stellar but only for her, not for the kid. He grimaced at the memory and scratched the scar on his soft earlobe. He traced the destroyed garbage bag of bad thoughts over in his mind as he chewed the side of his cheek. There was a perk for foster kids and their garbage bags—they always got two, the man remembered that well. He mentally collected the spilled memories into a second black bag and double knotted it this time. He tossed it further back into his abyss of brain matter.

Brent managed his way through the front office doors, past the mail cubbies, and into the teachers' lounge without a bump into Debra. He could feel the lashing, *'No! I haven't looked at the kid's file yet!'* Ready to leap out if she happened to round the corner at the last minute. She hadn't. Debra was probably off sight to grab her lunch at her famous favorite Hawaiian grill.

It looked as though most of the staff with the 11:30 lunch break had the same idea as the Hispanic office woman seeing that the teacher lounge was empty, other than Mr. Patterson, the bald fifth-grade teacher that hid his lips under a greying mustache. He lifted his almond nostrils nose from a book to take note of his entering coworker. Brent gave him a passing smile but the older man didn't pay mind to it as he lowered his head back down and traced each line of the pages in front of him with a trembling finger.

Brent hauled the door open on the employee fridge. The condiment bottles all danced and clinked against each other as the swung door stopped abruptly in his hold. He half knelt and peered in past Tupperware and to-go boxes. A saran wrap, half-eaten, mess of a turkey sandwich sat snug behind the other covered food. He widened his bent stance and swooped a relaxed arm into the cool depths of the box and twirled his fingers around his old lunch.

He removed it to examine the sandwich that had been in there over the weekend and no doubt had soggy bread. He kneaded a thumb into the saran wrap and watched the bread beneath it wet slightly. He decided he didn't mind.

His stomach rumbled.

Definitely didn't mind.

The man balanced his sandwich on his notepad and papers while he chewed on the tip of his pin and ventured back down the hallway to his darkened office. He rounded the corner and dropped the pen from his mouth to his hand, surprised to find a body sat up against his closed office door, working on a bite of grilled cheese.

"Davey?" He paced up to the boy.

Davey tilted his head up and gave a nervous stare to the man, his mouth packed with chewed, orange cheese.

Brent looked down at him and asked, "Did someone excuse you from the cafeteria?"

Davey paused his slow chew momentarily then declined the idea. There had been a few staff members that had been stepping slowly around the perimeter of the cafeteria and he supposed they had been there to enforce the children to stay in the lunchroom until recess was introduced, but he hadn't seen the harm in sneaking past them.

A light chuckle absorbed into Brent's chest and out his lips as he shook his head, "I like you, kid." He reached for the doorknob above the boy and twisted it. The door creaked open and cool air rushed against Davey's back.

The kid shivered then shuffled to his feet, lunch tray in hand, and allowed Brent to enter the office first, before him.

Brent flipped on a light and immediately reached for the manila folder on his keyboard, *Matthews, David.* He rolled open his top desk drawer with the urgency of a teenager hiding illegal substances from an adult and tossed it in. He then jammed the drawer shut before the boy's always wandering eyes could see.

He talked over his shoulder to Davey who stood in the entrance of the burgundy room, "you can take a seat at the table, I'm just going to let Mrs. Engels know you're safe with me." He picked up the black coiled wall phone and Davey stepped to the round table in the back. *For mini-conferences, with mini people.* He set his tray down but continued to stand.

Deeper in the office Davey could see more than he had before. Like how Brent didn't have pictures on his desk of loved ones. He pondered an idea of Brent not having anyone he loved then immediately thought of Mrs. Engels' with an internal frown. No loved ones seemed strange.

He observed as Brent nodded on the phone, "yes," he spoke, "I have Davey in my office," he paused to laugh at something Mrs. Engels said then continued, "I'll bring him back to you at the bell."

Davey's chest tightened in a hug of anxiousness. He didn't want to go back.

"Mhm, okay, yes. Good—" hesitate, "Goodbye." Brent hung up the phone and rotated to the boy, "want to sit down?" He gestured an open hand to the chair without concern, his face kind, and lightly shaded with wrinkles.

Davey looked at the table, then his lunch, then the plastic school chair against the wall next to the table and found Brent's offer compelling him. It was silly to be standing next to a perfectly good chair. So he sat. Brent took a seat for himself and untangled his soggy turkey sandwich from its saran wrapping.

Davey made a face at the sandwich and Brent tweaked his shoulders dismissively as he took a gracious bite out of the corner then licked the mayonnaise from the top of his lip. Davey let his face simmer as he watched, then too took a bite of his cheesy sandwich.

They chewed together in silence.

After a deep swallow of moist cafeteria bread, Davey's short arm hiked up and an outstretched forefinger pointed to Brent's desk. Brent's eyes followed. "Where are your pictures?" Davey questioned.

Brent stared at his work table with a cocked eyebrow and chewed meditatively at the mushed turkey smushed between his cheek and teeth.

"Of your loved ones?" Davey finished the thought casually.

Brent turned his lips down in consideration and swallowed, "good question, bud." He looked down at his wet sandwich, "I guess I don't have very many."

Davey thumbed a thawed grape into his mouth and crushed it under his molars, its juice shooting out over his tongue with a sweet flavor, "yeah. Me either." He popped another grape in and chewed.

Brent gave him a curious glance but didn't press, just crossed his legs and gave the boy the impression that he understood. Davey liked that about the man. *Safe.*

"I've got a sister I love." Davey sucked a grape skin from his front tooth then folded it against the roof of his mouth before he flicked it down the back of his throat, "she's really the best." He wasn't talking to Brent anymore, but to the table, as he thought about his sister who was at home with their roommate.

Brent hoisted a smile onto his lips, "sisters can be pretty cool," the bag in his head rattled Amanda's name and he concealed a shutter, tucking his free hand between his legs to keep composure. "What's her name?" He asked about the kid's sister, but Davey was distracted, his brown eyes tracing something on the tall game shelf next to Brent's desk.

He mumbled a response the counselor didn't catch then slid slowly from his chair, his belly rolled into his ribs and his toes stretched out for the floor absentmindedly.

Brent watched.

Davey ambled to the shelf and stood on the tips of his sneakers to reach the top. The bookshelf teetered and Brent reached out a safety hand in case it tried to topple over on the expanded boy. A nineteen-sixties *Winnie the Pooh* bear was the boy's interest, a toy he hadn't noticed in his brisk brush by earlier in the day. He grappled at it, its fur like a sponge between his fingers, and started to pull it from the shelf. He removed it like a doctor would remove a tumor, careful not to spill over the other things sharing the same top-shelf. He snaked it around the objects and let out a tiny breath of relief as it came out into the open air and he dropped back onto the flats of his feet, winning a round of *Operation*.

Brent removed his cautioned hand from the shelf and tucked it low between his legs again, "Bear Kingsley." His dusty voice startled the child who then whipped his head around to the counselor who gestured his head to the stuffed animal in his hand. "I named it when I was really young, kind of goofy, huh?" He scrunched his nose as he spoke and Davey wondered if he was going to sneeze.

The boy studied the plush toy in his hand. Despite the common style of the bear, it didn't have a red shirt or a pudgy face, instead, its face was slim and had black glass eyes, and its honey yellow fur was more of an olive green. He ran his fingers over its mushy and matted fur belly. It was soft. "No." he answered, "it's clever." He folded the bear into a loose hug.

Brent's chest tightened and something in the mental garbage bag shifted and stretched the thin plastic material.

Davey moved back to his seat with the bear in his arms. He placed it on top of his lap and faced outward like a mother with a small toddler as he sat back down and scooted his chair into the table.

They fell back into silent eating.

Brent finished his sandwich and stood to toss out the balled-up saran wrap from his hand to the trash bin under his desk. As he turned back to the table he side stepped to the bookshelf and scanned a low shelf full of board games from a thrift store. He grabbed one from the top of the stack and brought it up over the table to shake at Davey.

Davey stopped chewing and watched the box. He understood the gesture. Brent was asking if he wanted to play. He shook his head no at the counselor, his hair wisping forward onto his forehead.

Brent lowered the box to Bear Kingsley's glass eye level and shook it again, the contents inside the cardboard folds rattling about one another.

Davey began to giggle, *plush toys cannot play games.* He grabbed Bear by the back base if his head and slid his index and thumb together—left then right as he puppeted Brent's bear to shake its head no.

Brent frowned and gave a tiny shrug, "suit yourself, Lil' Kingsley."

It made Davey laugh and Brent echoed the laughter. He used a long limb to place the box back to its shelf and took a seat once more, with a grunt this time.

"Brent?" Davey tossed his name off his tongue with a tilted upright voice. Brent raised his eyebrows and the corners of his closed mouth at the boy. "Are you like Miss Honey?"

Brent thought of the teacher from *Matilda*. The one with an affectionate heart and a haunted past. He considered with a pushed up chin, "I don't know," his chin dropped into a grin thoughtfully.

The boy studied him with imaginative eyes and Brent studied back. "I think you are like her." The child concluded after a warm pause.

Brent gave a considerable nod and opened his mouth to respond but Davey interrupted.

"I think you're Miss Honey—and I think I'm Matilda." He squeezed the bear in his lap.

The man had felt the way he had when Davey grabbed his hand in the hallway. Like he could love the boy. His chest tightened and he had to clear his throat before he spoke, "you're Matilda, huh?" Matilda Wormwood—neglected child. This made him frown so he replaced the thought with '*Matilda Wormwood—the child with telekinesis.*' And it made him feel better.

Davey gave him a surefire grin and nodded as his fingers ran circles around Bear's old ear.

Brent sat forward and placed his head in his palm.

The hammering school bell rang then. High and sharp like a blade through the silence. Both males jumped in their seats and Davey blinked at the noise. His hands shot up to cover his ears but instead only scratched at them because he was embarrassed. He bit down onto his lip.

Brent gripped the top of his peck to let the insecure child know he wasn't alone, "That scared me!" He panted his words out with a laugh.

Davey hesitated, then smiled on top of his bottom lip before popping it back out, "Yeah, me too." He admitted. He pulled the bear up to his mouth and dabbed the slobber from his lip. It looked like he was kissing the bear.

Brent's chest soothed as he watched the boy with the bear. Then he chuckled, "ready?"

The child instantly wilted into the back of his chair and pushed the fuzzy back of Bear's head into his cheek, *ready for what?*

"You have to go to class now, pal," Brent spoke as if he read Davey's inner thoughts.

"I have too?" The bear was tugged back down to his lap.

The man's face softened and the inside corner of his brows lifted in compassion, "I'm afraid so." Relaxation released through the man's muscles as he looked over to the child in the chair in front of him. He rubbed the center of the hand Davey had held and eyed the bear in the boy's grasp, his stomach turning over once—"But, hey—" twice. He pointed to Bear Kingsley and paused with a chilled face and parted lips. *Bear Kingsley.* In his garbage bag, the real one he had as a child, Bear Kingsley had always lived. Always jammed in, always the first priority, always the first to be unpacked. The fake garbage bag, the one in his head, tore a tiny hole and reminded him that Amanda would take Bear away from him when she didn't get what she wanted from him. His breath caught—"Why don't you take him." He wagged his finger at the toy.

Davey's eyes stretched and bogged down to the animal in his hand, "*Really?!*" He held it out to Brent with uncertainty. As if it was a final offer for Brent to take his words back—and the bear.

Brent waved the plush object away, as if he didn't, at that moment, want to yank the bear from the child and hold it in his own lap. Say, *'nevermind, I'll keep him to myself. I don't want to lose him.'* "Sure, kid." He smiled when he spoke but his voice came out like cold clay. He rubbed his hands together as if to warm his voice up in them then verbalized the last part of his thought, "but I don't want to lose him." He pointed absently at the words as they came out because they had come out sounding young and he hadn't meant that.

The shy child cracked through a layer of shell as he practically leaped into the air to Brent and wrapped a green hoodie grip around Brent's tall legs and torso. "You won't!" Brent placed a hand between Davey's shoulder blades in a giant's attempt to hug back and knew then that he could believe the child. "Thank you!" Davey whined into his shirt, "thanks!" Then he backed up and stared up at Brent like the man had just saved Christmas.

"You're welcome." He tapped his nose in thought, "Whenever I felt shy Bear helped me out." And that was true. Bear Kingsley had helped him out with a lot of things. His stomach flipped for the third time and left his spin tingly.

Davey held the bear up to his eye level and stared into its glass gaze, "Okay," he said to the bear with an overgrown, black smile. Then he turned his head back up to Brent, "you're my best friend."

Brent folded his arms and leaned back into his desk to eye the child, "thank you, Davey." He spoke with a crinkle in his dry throat. He blinked away from the kid and glanced up at the ceiling. He then looked back, "Are you going to be able to make it the whole rest of the day with Mrs. Engles now?" He chuckled at the child's suddenly dropped chin and gestured to the bear, "Since you have a new friend to help you conquer the scary shyness?" He made claws with his hands and creased a single eyebrow to look like the *Scary Shyness Monster.*

Davey giggled and tucked the bear into the crease of his arm, "I guess so!"

"Right on." Brent winked and pointed to the open doorway, "Go get 'em, Matthews. I'll see you and Lil' Kingsley tomorrow."

The boy left then, and as he left Brent focused his eyes on his Kelso's Wheel poster. He anticipated a fourth stomach turn like a quitting engine but it never delivered.

You're my best friend.

10

A scant hand pawed up the outer side of Marilyn's leg.

The portly, pale skin stretched over the man's bones was encrypted with calluses that tugged at the stubble on her thigh. Her hairs stood erect over goosebumps against his stroking touch. She didn't turn to confront him. Instead, she leaned back into the body as she danced, if you could call swaying hips to a heavy beat that; *dancing.*

His penis was hard through his dirty jeans and he played it over her lower back. It conjured an eye roll that she shot across her young adult features in the dark club lights, but still, she continued to sway with vanilla, stout, mystery man.

She thought of a grocery list she needed to make while she danced along with the hard penis, then thought of the dirty laundry in her bedroom she needed to wash, then thought of her brother. Her stomach nagged as she hoped he'd gotten on the bus, then home, okay. The Hispanic woman in the front office had promised he would, and she'd make sure of it. She had paired her reassuring comment with a pitiful look that Marilyn hadn't cared for and had dismissed. *Whatever,* she had thought as she handed her little brother over to the woman, *as long as he gets home alright.* She frowned and considered getting the little guy a phone, so he could call her when he got in the house okay, and she wouldn't have to wonder. Another hand skimmed her bare thigh and she contemplated having enough money to purchase something like that for him. Then frowned again.

The club song changed to something much softer, queue for people to stop grooving and fuel up on more alcohol, but she and the man continued to sway into each other. "Where are you going after this?" The man's whiskey-soaked breath flanked against Marilyn's hot ears as he spoke. His voice low and silky like hot car oil. *Dipstick.*

He had startled the girl but she masked it with a bitten lip hum, "Wherever you're going." She answered and *yes,* it was supposed to invite the idea of the man's bedroom into his head if it wasn't already nesting there.

"Yeah?"

Marilyn echoed, "yeah," back and pivoted on her stiletto heels to meet him face-to-face and wrap her arms around his neck. She locked her wrists behind his head and stared deep at his features. He wasn't handsome. This came to no surprise to the girl. The ugliest were always the boldest when given a bit of liquor. She thought: *damnit.* Then: *just once could it be a perv with a chiseled jaw and expensive cologne?* But knew it was like asking for rain in the desert.

The man's grey-haired jowls hung and his eyebrows furrowed as he looked over her face, his body sways becoming hesitant, "let's keep dancing." She encouraged it, turning her chin to the side and gave him a dared sideways glance, her lips parted in a way that men normally were distracted by.

The man's wrinkled head tilted back, "are you sure you're daddy didn't give you a curfew, you look—"

Marilyn's lip slid out in a pout, "young?" He smiled with uncertainty and revealed his yellow teeth and the girl giggled, "it's a curse." The look she gave him under her brow agitated the hard spot in his pants and she continued with a grin, "how young do I look?"

The muscles in the man's chin stretched as he puckered his dry lips and thought. He then dropped them back into their sag and gave a reasonable, "seventeen." As he said the age his hands slide down her flat back, like the idea of a minor rubbing on him was enough to get off on.

She lifted an arched eyebrow and let out a flirty giggle, "Twenty-two." She lied and laid in closer to keep grinding. *Eighteen.* She was eighteen. Her fake ID rubbed against her thigh in her front skirt pocket and made the top of her leg feel warm.

He believed her bluff and slid his hands down to cup her ass.

She thought longingly of the chiseled jaw and expensive cologne again.

She could smell the brand of whiskey that coated his tongue and walls of his cheeks now and her stomach churned against it, her heart sputtering a little heavier like a car filled with diesel, rather than regular. *Fill it up, diesel!* She could feel a hint of warm, acidic, bile in the pit of her chest as it yanked its way up to her throat.

Marilyn used her hands to massage against his jelly pecs and guide him. He followed her hands and began to purr backward with shuffled steps past the not-yet-drunk-enough people watching them either curiously or with a bit of disgust. The underaged girl didn't mind. They moved together through the small crowd to the darkest corner of the floor, near a thick wooden post, one she knew well. Marilyn turned and lightly pressed her back against it.

This intrigued the man. She could feel the pressure of his drunk eyes roll up the length of her exposed legs, hips, breasts, then stop at her bitten raw lips. Marilyn gave him an evil smile that made his nose flare. She was a baited hook. She thought: *Take the apple, Adam.*

He did.

The man closed her into the space between the post and his body and locked his loose lips against the hinge in her neck. Or to her: the kink. The not-yet-drunk-enough people now glared, some laughed, one pulled out a phone. Marilyn arched her back in fake arousal then bucked back against the pole. *Get closer.* She laced her tingling hands around his waist and kneaded at his hips.

He came closer. Enticed. She grinned into the dark as adrenaline pricked through her veins.

Her hands inched down his back and to his wide, cargo pants, ass. The man gave a whiskey gurgle against her hot, sweaty flesh. Marilyn took a deep breath to compress her growing nausea. She could feel his erection on the inside of her open leg. "Hey," he muttered as Marilyn crawled her fingers down the back of his pants, towards the back pockets of the clothing, "Want to get out of here?" She dropped her hands into his dirty pockets. *Leave? Already? You're so, so forward, dude.* Her right hand fingered a thick cloth wallet and she released a rib pulled sigh. *A-fucking-men.*

"Sure," she complied with a creamy voice. His head came up to watch her as she held her face close enough for him to feel her sweet breath rolling past her pink lips, "wait here for me, I have to use the ladies room." Her free hand gave a tight squeeze to his ass cheek while the other retracted the cloth fold from his worn pocket. He hadn't noticed, like she intended, and took a step back to let her pass. A stupid smirk crafted to his face like a bad joke.

She stuffed the wallet against her stomach and turned her back to him. He watched her strut away towards the bathroom without an idea the hand against her abdomen also pinned his cash and cards.

As she neared the bathroom she flicked her head over her shoulder to see if he was still watching her. He was. His greasy head bobbed to the beat of the club music which was now something by Rihanna. The bass so heavy it distorted the pop stars vocals and palpitated each person's' heart in an unnaturally beat rhythm. She gave him a wink before she ducked into the ladies room.

Once in the vacant, shit and febreeze stench bathroom Marilyn let her hand fall slack to her side as her thumb traced against the woven cloth. She stopped at the counter and took a look into her reflection.

Jesus H. Christ.

Her ponytail of dyed almond hair had been loosened as she danced and now spit out baby hairs that frizzed out around her ears like chick wings. She combed her fingers over her grown-out bangs that had been straightened and frowned at the way her hair bounced back from her fingertips in curls, the straightening gone. Forget looking a questionable seventeen. *I look like a fifteen-year-old transvestite.*

It had been a long day.

Her brown suede skirt from a Portland thrift shop was bunched up from the man's rubby, grubby hands. She placed the wallet between her chin and chest and held onto it like her neck was a clamp while she used both hands to stretch the sides of the skirt fabric into its rightful place on her legs. She glanced up at her mirrored image again and almost thought hot mess. But settled just for mess.

Marilyn turned to a bathroom stall and dropped the wallet from her chin and chest back into her palm before she shouldered through the cold metal door and locked it with its oddly sticky twist lock.

Vanilla, stout, mystery man had a name, Jeremy Walsh. Marilyn stared at his ID as she sat man spread over the toilet bowl. He was forty-six, at least the license said so. "Kind of a pedo, Jerr-bear." She snorted and peeled open the cloth money pocket of the wallet. Her stomach began to burn as she took in what was inside.

The girth of Jeremy's fold had been a jumbled strip of tin foil and plastic packaged condoms. (a wrapper, for your wrapper) One five-dollar-bill wadded between the rubbers. Her head lowered then tilted back to stretch the tense muscles in her neck, "fuck," she muttered to the water damaged ceiling panels. The night was over. She was going home with a soggy five and twelve dollars in tips that she stole from dining tables earlier.

Her head throbbed as she plucked the five from the man's wallet and stood. The thick woven cloth now felt sad in her hands—just condoms. *They weren't even the good kind.* Condoms that'd feel like a cotton swab being smeared and thrust into a vagina and dosing the room in a thick, burnt rubber scent. Like wheels on an old car ran bald on the skankiest asphalt.

She left the small stall and tossed the fold on the wet bathroom counter while a hand pocketed the five. "Someone will return it to you, Jerr-Bear." She spoke against the empty room as her hair swayed and her head bobbed towards the wallet.

Marilyn turned for the door irritably then paused with her hand tilted on the handle. Her heart began to hammer as she hesitated. If good ol' *Jerr-Bear* saw her she was screwed. She glared at the door and used her tongue to wet her lips.

Pull.

Without more thought, her arm contracted back and the door swung wide as the bump of the bass wafted back around her like a cocoon. She was exposed as her eyes searched for the man.

He was there, exactly where she had left him against the post, but his attention was not on her, his eyes shaping up the next young ass he saw. *Perfect.* Marilyn's thought purred as she dodged to the side and walked down the back bar hallway. A fearful sensation nipped at the bottom of her spine as the image of an angry, drunk man chasing after flashed across her mind. Her feet wanted to respond and pick up pace like someone might when walking up a dark stairwell after shutting off the basement lights but she didn't let them. She fought the sensation and kept her steps steady and eyes on the door.

Door. She fought it, and *knew* he wasn't following her, he hadn't even noticed she left the bathroom. Unless he noticed the light from the room expand out into the club then vanish back with a drowned thud of the swinging door...

Door! Maybe he'd seen the tail end of her skirt after she had already turned around and headed for the back entrance. Maybe he was already against a race up behind her to beat her to the door.

DOOR!

Her hands clasped around its push-bar handle and shoved it open. She fell out into the autumn air and gulped a quick breath of relief before she strolled through the graffitied, Portland parking lot to her green, 1998 Saturn S-series. She glanced back at the exit once her car keys were fiddled into the jacked handle of her driver's side. He hadn't seen her, he hadn't followed her. *She knew that.* She glared at her reflection in the car's window and dropped her head to mutter it again, "fuck."

11

Warm air misted from the green Saturn's vents and onto Marilyn's bare arms. A cigarette sat balanced between her lips as she drove the divider of Highway 217, the Portland tavern behind her now. Jeremy Walsh's five-dollar bill sat jumbled with the waitresses' tips in her front pocket. She sucked at the raisin scented cigarette and exhaled the glassy grey smoke from flared nostrils. It danced over her vision to create a hazy mask between her and the windshield and she thought about wrecking. It was a brief thought, one that lasted only as long as the vision-impairing cigarette puff that the air vents blew away.

Grant, where Marilyn's home sat on a cracked platform, was only twenty-one miles from the tavern in Portland where she stole Jerr-Bear's wallet. She took exit 6A to blow through a yellow light in the right lane that spit her out onto Pacific Highway. She followed the road until a light in front of her went yellow, then red, at an intersection adjacent to a turn off labeled *Beef Bend*. She slowed the car to a stop and glared at the green *Beef Bend* road sign. *What a name.* She then rolled her window down. It was a crank window and she had to drop her shoulder to maneuver the handle—her cigarette teetered in her mouth as she twisted the grey knob.

The cooling end of summer air plundered through the car and held her face to soothe her hot cheeks. She laid her head out of the window until the light was bright green. As the pad of her foot lifted from the break and the car coasted forward she sat back up and snaked the long, lightly smoked cigarette from her lips to drop it to the black asphalt. She watched the flicking embers bounce over the flopping white stick through her dirty side mirror as she drove across the intersection. She glanced up from the orange sparks at the now blurry, passing the green sign and thought: *See ya next time Beef Bend.*

Marilyn drove until Pacific Highway blended into 99W–South.

Stoplight, stoplight, stoplight, hillside. She drove down the elongated hillside swallowed by Oregon trees that dropped down into Grant. Once in town, she changed lanes to take a left turn into a familiar burger joint with a flipped up blinker. Her car jumped and jittered over the cracked drive-in ramp of the heavily trafficked parking lot and she made a hard turn into the closest empty spot. Her green Saturn came in sideways between the parallel lines with a front tire over into the other parking spot. She threw it into park, too lazy to correct her sloppy parking job, and killed the engine. The car came to a puttering halt and the dull inside cabin light flipped on.

"I got my parking from Mom," she admitted aloud and imagined her father laughing from a deep corner in her mind. His laugh changed three separate times like a bad radio signal that faded in and out. It was her fault—she couldn't quite remember how the laugh sounded. She frowned and the thought of her father dripped off the corners of her lips and left her only thinking about food now. Her stomach rumbled and the busy restaurant stared at her.

The wind was bitter when she stepped from the car into it. Its tentacled gusts frilled her skirt and dusted her shoulders with the frizzing curls of her loose hair as she paced to the building's entrance. It had warm-toned interior that made it seem fancier than the grease stain it really was. A woman in a buttoned sweater came out the front doors, a small child tethered by it's holding fingers to the belt loop of her expensive jeans. She gave a polite smile to Marilyn and kept the door open for her. Marilyn returned the smile with a courteous jog to the entrance and slipped into the warm restaurant. "Thank you," She said as the woman released the door and began to walk away. The woman flashed a smile over her shoulder before the front door swung shut completely, *no problem,* the smile said.

A line of strangers shuffled in front of the ordering counter where a short, strawberry blonde stood, tapping a screen as the demand came at her. Marilyn took her place in the back of the line and waited.

It inched along as the front of the line fell to the pick-up side of the counter after their order went through. She watched the cashier closely as she moved forward with the slow, steady line. The cashier was a female with obese cheeks stretched in oil and acne scars. Her customer service grin never wavered or fell into a neutral expression. Her voice was loud, loud enough for Marilyn to pick out the bubbly undertones and southern drawl over the conversations around her. She bit at the dry skin around her thumbnail as she listened to the burger girl ramble. Southern didn't match their forest range and Marilyn immediately assumed the drawl was a part of a tactic— come off sweeter—make more tips. Sweeter like *Sweet Tea.* The eighteen-year-old with the twenty-two-year-old ID skimmed the greasy ordering counter for a tip box that didn't seem to exist. Against store policies? She glanced back up at order taking burger girl and thought maybe the accent *was* real.

The line shuffled up one more step as another customer fell out of it and took a place on the pick-up side. Marilyn could see now that bubbly burger girl was younger than her, at least sixteen. Marilyn smiled to herself and hoped the girl was as gullible as she needed her to be because unlike her, Marilyn *did* have a tactic.

The line continued to bustle forward and eventually ended with Marilyn at the front, staring at the menus while chubby burger girl stared up at her.

"How may I help you today, ma'am?" The girl chirped with sparkles in her voice. Marilyn wanted to flinch away from her bird squawk but managed to keep it at a subtle cringe.

She gave the girl a glance then bounced her eyes back up to the menu while a stiletto heel rolled below her foot and she hummed at the menu. Busty burger girl waited. "May I please get two value meals?" She asked after a moment's pause. Two burgers, two small fries.

"Suuuuure!!!" The girl pounded a sausage finger against the smudged cashier screen as her voice slid through Marilyn's chest like a sword, "anything else for you, ma'am?" She blinked at Marilyn with unfaltering focus.

Marilyn gave a soft smile to smother out her irritation and prematurely reached her hand into her skirt pocket for money, "No, that'll be it."

The girl dropped her eyes to the screen, "six, ninety-eight is your total tonight, ma'am."

Say ma'am one more goddamn time, I swear to Jesus—the thought went through Marilyn's mind but she continued a delicate smile to hide it, "sure." She nodded with her word, *suuuuuure!*, And carefully removed two bills from her pocket with mentally crossed fingers that neither was the five-dollar bill from Jerr-bear.

Two dollar bills. The two of the twelve dollars a waitress got. *Could I be any –fucking–luckier?*

She leaned forward with one hip and relaxed her chin in a dramatic display of defeat, "oh my goodness," Marilyn whined to herself, but loudly enough for the burger girl to hear. *Again,* she had a tactic. The eighteen-year-old had to bite her lip and tipped her head back.

Oh my goodness, oh my goodness, oh my goodness.

Marilyn worked with her performance for the oily burger girl and began to pout out her lip, "I'm so sorry." The burger girl lifted an eyebrow and Marilyn sighed, "This is so embarrassing. I thought I had more money than this." Her voice pitched up with raw emotion.

Strawberry blonde burger girl bit the side of her cheek, "oh dear," she re-checked the screen.

Yes, so sad. Be so sad for me. Marilyn shifted her weight and the pout of her lip. *Give me my meal for free.*

Acne scarred burger girl didn't take the bait, "I'm sorry ma'am." She said with no give that she actually felt sorry.

Bitch, Marilyn thought as she opened her mouth to cancel her order begrudgingly. Couldn't pay full price now, not after she claimed to only have two soggy fucking dollar bills.

She was interrupted by a thin, warm hand that placed itself against her shoulder.

What an unexpected turn of events. She was trying to play the bitch burger girl but the middle-aged soccer mom in the line behind her showed more gullibility. Marilyn imagined her face stretched and smiled like the *Grinch*. Curled lips, ear-to-ear.

"I'll get it, dear." The woman spoke heartily.

"Oh," a gust of wind escaped Marilyn's lunges in a pitiful sight, "you don't have to do that." She turned her attention back to bubble-blowing burger girl, "What can I get for two dollars?" She waved the limp bills at the cashier because letting someone pay for you without denying it at least once just makes you an outright *dick.* Southern burger girl turned to look at the menu above her head, *I don't know, what can you get for two dollars here...?* Marilyn wanted to roll her eyes at the young employee.

She could feel the soccer mom's heart grow from her own chest into Marilyn's fucking back in an *'I'm a good citizen—it's my chance prove it'* kind of way as she rubbed a light circle against the con-artists shoulder blade. "No, no, honey. I got it. It's okay." The woman turned to the cashier who was now staring at the both of them with wide eyes and parted lips.

Marilyn knew she was probably thinking. *'Y'all ma'ams need to speed it up now, ya hear?'*

"Sweetie, please keep the two happy meals—but make the fries a medium size and —" The woman looked at Marilyn, "a milkshake?"

Marilyn tucked the arm with her two dollars under the other and pinched at the skin behind her elbow as she dipped her head down and gave a shy nod. *Oh so shy and so sad. Poor, poor me.*

The soccer mom grinned at the cashier, "yes, a milkshake."

Colossal burger girl's wide smile was back, "yoooooou got it! Anything else, ladies?"

Ma'am retired from her vocabulary. Now it was *ladies*. Marilyn wanted to gag.

"No," the woman answered with pride.

"Can I get a name for that order?" both innocent females looked to the deceiving, kinky-haired female.

Marilyn passed a stare between both of them, "Marilyn," she croaked towards busty-burger girl.

"Okaaay! For here or to go, Marilyn?" Annoying-as-shit burger girl asked.

"Um," she twisted her heal bashfully, "to go please." She was a woeful sight.

Umpa-lumpa burger girl nodded and finalized the order, "it'll be right up."

"Thank you," Marilyn smiled timidly as her brother would then looked at the woman, "thank you so much."

The woman gave a wide smile that showed she felt like a *fucking* hero, "no problem, dear." She stepped closer to the register to pay as Marilyn meandered to the pick-up side. She leaned against the wall awkwardly to show how *unsocial and sad* she was. She shoved the two dollars back into her pocket with the other fifteen buck-a-roos and grinned to herself. Everyone loves a victim.

Another skill she stole from her mother.

"I like your shoes." Marilyn looked up from her Goodwill stilettos, the soccer mom stood directly in front of her and the young adult now noticed that the woman smelled nice.

"Oh, thank you," She squeaked back and let her face turn red, "I'm still trying to learn to walk in them." *A lie.*

The woman laughed like she understood, "yeah, heels can be tricky."

Marilyn nodded.

"Have a good night, sweetheart."

Marilyn smiled, a genuine one, "I will, thank you."

The woman gave a wave to the pathetically bashful actor and stepped away to leave Marilyn back to her thoughts.

Her mother was the best at the victim game. It's probably what killed her father.

An image of her father, pristine and dangled from her brother's ceiling fan dashed against her forehead like a blistering fever and her stomach lurched, as it always did when she let herself *think*. She pressed a soothing hand against it.

"Order for Marilyn?" Someone called from the counter but Marilyn didn't move. "Marilyn?" They called again and Marilyn glanced up to see nosy burger girl staring directly at her.

Marilyn walked forward and grabbed the greasy brown bag and a medium vanilla milkshake. *I prefer chocolate,* she thought as she moved to her door and back out to the cold.

12

Brent jogged up the musical stairwell to his apartment in a reverse beat of the morning's jog down. He stopped at his front door with keys in hand and eye's locked against a pink sticky note. It was taped just under his golden peephole.

It asked, "How was work?" in heavy cursive ink.

A smile on his lips, he turned back to the stairs to leap up one more flight while pocketing his keys. He stopped at the door directly above his own with the numbers *337* screwed to its wood siding. He bounced his knuckles off the door softly and waited. His eyes drifted and he brushed his finger under the chin of a wilted flower beside the apartment's mailbox.

There was a slippered shuffle behind the thin wood before the lock latches started to click open and the door swung inward. An eighty-six-year-old, chestnut skinned, woman stood in the space of the doorway with an overweight Maine Coon tilted in her gaunt arms. She grinned with white dentures at her tall, handsome neighbor. Her slippers were neatly woven red and had begun to fray at the rubber edge. They matched her loose pink nightgown fit for a child. "Would you like me to water your flowers, Winnie?" He asked and pointed to the sad flower's pot and covered cobwebs.

The African woman cocked an eyebrow, "I can take care of myself."

Brent crossed his arms and leaned against the jam of her door, "Like you walked down those stairs by yourself to put the note on my door?" He had a quarter smile as he eyed down the woman.

Her bluing cataract eyes jerked up into her skull and she tilted slightly on a hip, being careful not to throw it out, "No, I didn't." She shook her head with her words then hoisted her fat cat up a little further against her body, "I had Tulsa with me." Tulsa made a low moan against her owner and flicked the tip of her tail.

"Tulsa's not going to save you if you fall, Winn."

Winnifred Williams' facial expression dropped into an unamused stare, "Fine. Forget the note. I hope you had a shit time at work." She snorted when Brent's jaw unlocked and dropped forward, "come in asshole." She shuffled to the side.

Brent smirked at her and stepped through the doorway. The apartment smelled of humidifiers and a musty mask of shedding black cat too. He turned his head and gave a glare at Tulsa who stared back from wrinkled, brown arms. Her eyes were yellow and her ears twitched in their own askew rhythm.

Winnifred closed the apartment door and slid the top chain lock, that was screwed in at four feet so she could reach it easily, closed. Tulsa bucked her back legs and tumbled her weight to the ground with an upset meow. The old woman kicked a frayed slipper foot at her cat, "cunt." She grumbled and scratched a green-veined hand through her thinning grey Afro, a single clipper size away from a buzz cut.

Her living room was gently lit with lamps and their blue lamp shades painted with budding roses. Brent shook his head and shielded a smirk at his foul-mouthed neighbor, like a parent who doesn't want to encourage inappropriate behavior from their child. He moved forward through her doily living room and dropped to her cracked leather couch. A towel matted with fur was draped over the cushions and he scrunched it away from himself with a made-up face of disinterest.

The walls of Winnifred's apartment were white, like his, but were decorated with various frames of quilt patterns, cut straight from *Country Living* and *Joann Fabric* magazines. No frames with family, children...grandchildren.

Where are your pictures? Of loved ones? Davey's voice leaked through his parietal lobe and he looked to his neighbor who stumbled forward with an arched back to her recliner, diagonal to his resting spot on the couch. She lowered herself with a grunt.

"Hey," Brent slowly spoke, "Winnie." He smiled as the woman deadpanned his direction and popped a top denture out just to then suck it back in. "Can I take a picture with you?" The question came out awkward and strangled and he laughed at it. Then laughed at the way her face contorted and the top denture slid back out.

"Wha duh—" she pushed the denture back in, "fuck?" She glared at his wide laugh, "Why?"

He waved a hand at her to dismiss her bad language, "I want to frame a picture of us for my office." He shrugged and turned his eyes to her quilt cut out walls, "Maybe we could frame two, one can go on your wall."

The sour look didn't leave her face but an intrigued white eyebrow joined the party, "Will you be shirtless in the photo?"

Brent glared, "no."

"Then no."

Brent rolled his eyes at the woman and dumped his head back onto her couch cushion. He could see Davey's finger pointed out at his desk, "Winn. You don't have any loved ones on your walls." He brought his head back up to her and flashed her a cheeky grin, "I'm a loved one."

"You ain't." She frowned at him, "I don't got no loved ones."

Brent pointed at his own face.

"You're cocky Brent Taylor Kingsley."

He dropped his head back to her cushion realizing for a millionth time that he should have never told her his middle name that one Christmas Eve while they were taking shots of eggnog. She *abused* it.

"I ain't got nooo oneee." She sang with a single minor note. When he lifted his head back up to scowl at her he noticed she'd pulled her top denture out again and was running a tongue across her empty gums. She smiled toothless at him and held an end of her dentures in her fist to point the other end at him like some sort of curved handgun. He waved a dismissing hand at that too.

"Please?" He was being serious this time, "can we take a picture together."

Denture went back in, "Will you be sh–"

"Winnifred!" He scolded her in an adolescent whine like he was her son. Maybe, *grandson.*

She smiled at him, "fine."

"Thank you!" Brent sat up and rifled a finger into his back pocket to get ahold of a phone he hardly used. The screen illuminated as it flipped out into his hand and he clicked a few screen icons that made the sound of popped bubbles to get to his photo collection. It was a sad sight. Six generic background pictures that came with the phone, a snap of a bumblebee on a flower from summer, and a picture of the back of a cereal box. Although now, as he stared at the calorie intake of *Life* cereal, he couldn't remember why he'd taken that photo.

"Well?"

Brent clicked the live photo button and lifted the phone up to snap a picture of Winnifred's scowl.

Winnifred gave him the bird.

He took a picture of her with her trembling middle finger tilted up to her ceiling, "Beautiful, Winn." He joked.

She gave him a jeered look to go with the hand signal and he took a picture of that too.

"Are we going to take the fucking picture together, or what?" She sucked at her false teeth, "I want to take my dentures out." The old woman began to wiggle to the edge of her seat anxiously. A hand-stitched pillow she had been leaned against fell forward and she reached an arthritic arm behind her to ungainly push it back up.

Brent reversed the camera to face him and stood to cross the room to his neighbor. His neighbor who was just as lonely as him. Their Halloweens, Thanksgivings, and Christmas' only filled with one another. He squatted down next to her soft recliner and pressed his cheek against hers. She was posed with a grin before he even had his, hardly used, phone up from his side. The phone made a bubbly click and Brent sat back on his heels, away from the woman.

Her eyes lit up and she shoved herself further to the edge of the seat, the pillow falling again, "wait!" She demanded as she wobbled upward out of the chair. Her slippers scuffed against the dark wood and she hobbled forward to Tulsa who sat away from them, near a leg of the woman's fold-out dining table as she cleaned between the pads of her paws. Brent watched with amusement as Winnifred heaved her cat into the air by her front armpits. Tulsa growled through her small chest as her tail flicked under her stretched body. "The whole family!" The woman cried as she dragged the cat back to her chair.

Their Halloweens, Thanksgivings, and Christmas' only filled with one another, and Tulsa.

They posed, Brent clicked the bubble button, and Tulsa kicked from the woman's grasp. Winnifred grumbled and Brent kissed her fragile temple in thanks. His desk would now have a loved one on it. He watched Tulsa cower against the side of the couch and begin to clean between her paw once more. *Two loved ones* he thought. Davey would be impressed.

Brent had gotten up and retrieved her dental saline in a glass cup so she could take out her sore dentures. As he returned he watched her pop them into her hand and drop them to the arm of her chair, surrounded by Tulsa's fur. He scurried forward with the saline and scolded his friend before dropping the fur and saliva dentures into her glass cup. A fantom hairball tickled the back of his throat at the sight of them. She smiled at him with saggy lips and browning gums.

He'd then gone back to the kitchen for a glass of faucet water and watered her flowers, despite her protest from her spot on the chair in toothless mumbles. He had glared at her as a glass of water was tipped into the flower pot and she had flipped him the bird once more for the day. He opened his mouth to say something but the woman had grabbed the remote, stuck in the crease of her cushion, and flipped on the TV before he could. Two men in pinstripe suits argued through split screens. American flags hung in their backdrop.

Brent put her cup back with a smile and slumped back to the couch.

13

Marilyn sat beside her brother on a cement platform step in front of their new-to-them duplex.

He had seen her car pull up from the smeared living room window and ran out to greet her with a howl of her name, "Marilyn!!"

She had wiggled from her low car and done the same to him, "Davey!" And he had grabbed her in a hug around the stomach in pajamas. Pajamas she now envied as they sat in the chilled weather against the step while he coddled a teddy bear she hadn't seen before.

She looked at it now, tucked in Davey's tiny lap while he munched on french fries.

Davey noticed her stare and smiled down at his plush friend, "his name is Bear Kingsley–" he chewed a mouthful of fries as he spoke. Marilyn cocked her head at the unusual name, "I decided to call him Beary for short."

Beary and Davey sitting in a tree. P.L.A.Y.I.N.G.

Davey kept a grin to himself–he liked that rhyme much better.

Marilyn sucked at their shared vanilla milkshake despite the shivered goosebumps over her exposed, and thinly clothed, skin, "Where'd you find him?" She asked innocently and wondered if her brother had picked up on her knack for stealing.

Davey shook his head, "I didn't find." He tousled the fuzzy patches on top of the bear's head, "my friend gave it to me."

Friend. Marilyn's chest tightened at the sound of the word until it almost became physically painful for her to breath. She had to bite against her tongue to keep from gasping '*FRIEND?!*' from her tightened throat that seemed to be strangled in a good ol' scarf of complete disbelief. After a moment she gave a solid nod, "you made a friend today?" Her voice was pinched and eighty-percent of her was convinced he was just joshing. Yanking her chain. Pulling her leg. She thought of her mother for a second time that night—how she always swore there was something wrong with Davey—*that brat won't make friends. He's a psychopath. Like your father.*

Marilyn grimaced.

Davey shrugged cooly, "yeah," he said without thought, "I think we're best friends."

Best friends.

Marilyn blinked at her brother and coaxed another suck from the straw. The milkshake gave her mouth something to do while she thought of her brother with a friend as the cold ground seeped through her thin clothing. Their little faces' bright as they grinned at one another and a little boy offered the bear to Davey. As the iced drink settled in her stomach she thought of how her mother would've twisted this into something sickly like, *'The Columbine boys were best friends.'* Marilyn sat the milkshake down with a *whack* to clear the ugly thought and dropped herself back onto the cool cement platform to stare up at the sky.

Davey began to rub his eyes and, unaware he'd absolutely boggled his sister's mind, he easily changed the subject, his conversation bounced naturally to something more important. Davey, the tangent man. "You know how sometimes an eyelash will get in your eyes?" Marilyn smiled at the sky and nodded. "Sometimes they don't come out, they disappear." He looked at his sister then.

She looked back at him with a double chin as her head angled against the cement to see him clearer and she nodded again. Slower this time. Her brother looked like an old professor as he stared at her, sternly in thought. Her smile widened.

"Do you think those hairs roll behind your eyes and there's just a big nest sitting back there?"

"Jesus, Dave!" Marilyn's smile dropped off and she jammed fists into her sockets at the unnerving image of pointed, coarse hairs jumbled behind the round slugs in her head. Their black lines tickling and poking.

Davey shrugged and slurped another fry into his mouth, "dunno," he chewed, "just a thought."

The front door opened and Marilyn removed her hands from her face just to have her vision constructed by the upside-down view of her roommate. He stood over her with his hands dug into his malnourished sides and a cigarette between his thin lips like some eighties film. Marilyn sat up like the cold cement had suddenly been set on fire and her head pulsed with the forced momentum. "Money?" His migrained voice was gruff and thick with an added layer of tobacco.

Shit.

Nick was an aspiring musician. A career on Soundcloud kind of guy that shot up heroin in groups, drank *Pabst* rather than water and sniffed coke, rather than drank it.

Marilyn hadn't known that when she moved in.

He'd been a friend of hers from the sixth grade that she'd stayed in touch with over jolly fucking *Facebook*. He—the aspiring musician—seemed like a good spot to nestle down with her brother until she found her adult pair of feet to land on. Cheap rent and a stringy-haired guy to play them guitar from the coke (the drink this time) stained (cream, but should be white) couch in his den living room.

She'd moved in, her little brother in toe, and what she thought she understood had been demolished.

An almost month of drunken slaps to her face and a buzzed-outta-my-mind penis being forced into her and this was where they were at.

She stayed because wanna be Marshall Mathers didn't seem all that awful to her after years at her mother's. The catch was the money. *Owe me everything and I'll keep a roof over Davey's head.* Though he'd never said as much as that it was what was implied. A renter's agreement between the two.

Marilyn groaned and stood to meet him face-to-face. She could feel Davey's eyes follow her up and she suddenly wished he wasn't there. "Can we talk inside?" Nick's jaw clenched in a bullshit attempt to come off as *frightening* and *stubborn*. Bullshit, bullshit, bullshit! "Please," She spoke beneath the awning of her set glare.

He took a drag from the cigarette in his mouth, the orange embers alive, then offered it to her. She crossed her arms and ignored it. The ash had begun to build up at the end of the stick as he held it out with two fingers. He locked his intoxicated eyes on Marilyn and flicked the filter with his grim coated thumb. The ash danced down towards Davey purposefully.

Davey tucked his head away from the embers and they swirled to the ground. Davey stomped on them with his loosely tied, old man shoes. He thought *Nick the Dick*—then felt a bit guilty for thinking of the dirty curse word.

Marilyn balled her fists that were crossed over her chest, "inside." She demanded, unafraid of her happy-slappy roommate.

Nick stepped aside with a gesture of a bruised, discolored arm to the open duplex door, "you first." He muttered. Marilyn stomped past him into the house and he followed to slam the door shut behind them.

The nearly empty duplex smelled like dirty underpants and old pizza boxes piled on top of the flip lid trash can. A smell Marilyn would never get used to— or want to get used to—if that mattered at all. It made her stomach turn as she tried to convince herself that Nick was still better than living with her mother.

We're better off. She turned to face Nick again, *Davey made a friend.* The thought settled like ice against a hot plate in her stomach.

Nick stepped close to her and dragged the one-worded question from his lungs again like a limp dog on a leash, "money?"

The single word pricked the base of Marilyn's spine the same way the thought of Jerr-bear chasing her as she left the Portland club had. Her hand sank into the front pocket of her skirt and the crumpled seventeen dollars shook her hand weakly. She pulled the green from her pocket and offered it to him with a raised eyebrow and puckered lips in her own bullshit window display of dominance. Bullshit, bullshit, bullshit.

He took the dollars from her stiff fingers and turned it over in his filthy hands. Inspecting them.

Marilyn shifted her baring weight to one heel, "it's all I could do tonight. A wallet and some waiting tips—" She spoke the excuse with a dry mouth and flat expression. Nick threw the money back at her like it was some sort of fancy card trick he was trying to preform. She pinched her lips together and followed the fluttering cash to the floor.

"Money!?" His thick saliva caked between his teeth was filled with vinegar as he grumbled the same word like a broken fucking record.

"Yeah—" Marilyn spoke sharply with a hot face. Anger napped behind her ears as she spoke, "I paid you." She waved furiously at the bills that dusted the ground. "Seventeen *fucki—*"

Nick stepped closer to her, his breath dancing circles over her snub nose, "How'd you buy the food?"

She glanced at the closed door with Davey on the other side munching fries, "I got it for free." She admitted. "I stole it." Davey would say *'stoled.'*

Nick squeezed with a thumb and forefinger against her cheeks, puffing her lips out like one of those spiky fish that blow up like a balloon when frightened, and he closed the space between them, "Now you're lying?" Marilyn swatted his hand away and her face slacked back down against the insides of her mouth that burned from being rolled against her molars. Nick was the ugliest of all the men she dealt with, she thought that now as their bodies were pushed together and a scent of stale marijuana wafted up from his stiff shirt. Thick disgust began to pump up from her stomach and into the back of her throat. It made the saliva in her mouth froth and her nose flare. He opened his mouth to accuse her again but before he could she shoved him. It was a hard shove but Nick only stumbled a step back from it.

"I'm not lying," she growled with the froth.

The back of his hand smacked across her mouth, not harder than usual, and she stepped forward to shove him again like they were in a high school girl fight. Her hands came up short and shoved weakly through the air as he tipped back to miss it then swung another wide hand at her. This one came across the side of her head and pulled hair from the ponytail in tired curls. Marilyn reeled back from it, stunned. Her skull rattled unevenly against the top vertebra of her neck and her stomach felt queasy. *That* was harder than he'd ever done before.

"That food belongs to me." A shaky tobacco finger was held up in her face like the barrel of a gun and she had a strange urge to bite it off, "Mine." He spun to the doorway that led to the boy on the stairs and pocketed his accusing finger.

A steel bar of panic jammed into Marilyn's back and she lunged forward at him, "Let him eat!" She cuffed both Nick's deteriorating biceps and yanked backward like she were working a cement-filled wheelbarrow towards her. Heaving like a busty construction worker with wide eyes. Nick pivoted back to her with a swung elbow. It caught her eye and a burst of bright light fled through her vision and a bold red back light-filled a watering eye socket. It pinched at her twisted nerves as hot fluids rushed into the pockets of her flesh. She wavered a moment and pressed a clammy hand into her throbbing eye to relieve the ache.

But that wasn't enough for Nick, not tonight. He was fed up, angry and underpaid.

He ripped her hand away from her cradled eye and she let out a scream of frustration before a rounded, solid punch was thrown into the sore eye. Another burst of light shattered through her head but this time it was charged with an electrical current that turned her scream into silence and her standing legs into jelly. It was a punch you'd throw at a man harassing a woman. A punch that Jeff Gillooly probably would've thrown at Tonya Harding. His knuckles tore at her eyelid and as she fell back against the crumb covered kitchen counter she felt the warmth of blood, or imagined it, as heat trickled out into her eyelashes. There was a moment where it was dark, like a sticky blink, and then Marilyn was cradling her cheek and forehead in her palms again and thinking: *fuck*.

The front door was flung open and its gold knob slammed into the wall where a crater had begun to form in the wood paneling.

Davey had been pretending to feed Bear Kingsley the long salty fries and thinking about his burger when Nick barged out of the house. He was fuming. His hand shot down towards Davey and the boy recoiled back out of instinct. Nick slipped the greasy fast food bag into his hand and separated it from Davey's grip. It tore a small hole and some fries fell to the ground like jumbo sprinkles. The man stomped on them like Davey had stomped on the ashes of his cigarette and turned back to the open home.

Marilyn stood in the doorway as she glared Nick down with one clear eye, "Give him his food." Her command was weak and her eye leaked tears she couldn't control.

Davey sprung from his spot, "No!" He grabbed Nick's arm gently. "It's okay," He looked up at the roommate and patted his arm, "It's okay." The boy brought his head back down and watched the swell in his sister's eye pulse. Marilyn's good eye swiveled and held his stare.

"Smart," Nick sighed. He used his shoulder as a bard to shove Marilyn to the side. She obliged and moved. He went into the underpants and pizza scented building.

Marilyn looked at her brother a moment longer then turned in after him. Embarrassed.

Davey sucked his bottom lip in. It was okay, really. He shrugged it off, then shrugged again at himself, despite the low rumble of hunger in his gut. The thought of the burger bobbed through his head.

The grilled cheese and grapes for lunch were good enough.

He looked at his bear, "I hope you weren't hungry."

Marilyn had fallen asleep with a lump in her throat that night as Davey stirred beside her in their shared bed, his rumbling stomach rattled her awake like a bad snore until she was too exhausted to worry. Then it just became a white noise that rocked her into a purple socket lull.

14

Cold smokey air snuggled against Davey as he balanced on the edge of the yellow-painted curb. The last of the Oregon forest fires dwindled off to the Washington side and the smoke smelled distant as he waited at the curb for the big yellow school bus. His body wobbled back and forth against the edge as he balanced and he hummed to himself to keep his mind off the biting valley wind.

Marilyn had still been asleep when he left and he had crossed to her side of the bed and kissed her cheek, being extra careful not to disturb the ugly wound over her soft eyelid. It was black/purple today. Davey's stomach made a tight rumble and he frowned. He would have grabbed something for breakfast but he had seen Nick slumped over the dining table in the kitchen and he didn't want to bother the man. Davey was sorry for the night before. He knew it was because of his hungry tummy that Marilyn was hurt. He got her in trouble. It was his fault.

His frown deepened.

He thought of the salty fries and the still wrapped burger.

His stomach gnawed louder, like an empty lawnmower.

The yellow bus he waited for veered widely around a dense tree corner four blocks down from where he stood. It stopped and the red sign swung out like an industrial kitchen door. He watched as stranger kids trickled into the yellow tube as they talked and laughed with each other. Their heads' tipped back and their mouths cawed the *Ha Ha Ha!'s*

Davey glanced over his shoulder to take inventory on how many kids waited at his stop. Zero. It was him. No one else. No *bullies*.

Daisy and Davey sitting in a tree.

He shook his head and felt the weight of Bear Kingsley jiggle from the big pouch of his adult backpack. He thought of Brent and his stomach knotted. '*Go get 'em, Matthews. I'll see you and Lil' Kingsley tomorrow.*' The red sign on the bus clunked back against the vehicle's side and the motorcoach began to roll forward towards Davey. One intersection. Two intersections. He watched it and the knot thickened in his belly.

He thought of his sister's bruised eye again. The way he had to kiss around it.

That's when he imagined Bear Kingsley kicking his plush foot against his backpack material in an attempt to escape, (*Com'on Davey!*) Another footed kick that shook his backpack against his back, (*We have to protect your sister!*)

Davey bit at his lip and considered it. Then considered Nick being mad he was home.

Bear Kingsley rattled in his imagination and his bag, (*He won't see us! We'll be spies!*)

A mischievous schoolboy grin crept onto Davey's mouth and his lip popped back into the air. He liked that idea. His feet rocked back and he stepped off the curb into the sidewalk's square of grass. "I'm really sorry, Brent." He spoke aloud to the air and turned to face the neighborhood of tilted houses. He could hear the bus as it puttered through the third intersection and he began to sprint. Bear Kingsley was right. They had to protect her from *Nick the Dick*. "I'll see you tomorrow!" He yelped to the approaching yellow school bus and its laughing children, and to Brent.

15

Brent Kingsley's morning had started the same as before, slowly and with an early pound at his brain. Today, however, the wading water didn't bring rotten memories of his sister, Amanda. He thanked his second mental garbage bag tied tightly for that.

Brent had been sure to grab his neglected phone when he left that morning and tucked it into his jacket pocket.

He played with it now as he walked through the hollow school hallways to his small office. *Hollow-ways.* He flipped the phone between his fingers underneath the fabric of his jacket and chewed the inside of his cheek. He'd get the pictures developed in the afternoon, after he was off work, at the local *We-Have-Everything-Here* store. He thought back to Winnifred as her frail arms worked to squeeze her less-than-thrilled Maine Coon between them for the photo and tucked a grin into his cheeks as he slipped into his dark office.

The office was frigid and the cold air slammed into him like a slip on ice. Brent tugged his wool jacket tight around himself and nudged the door closed with his hip. He faced the seat of the chair to himself and the room and plopped into it with a sigh. He used his legs to swivel it back towards his work table then crab-walked it in to wake his computer. The monitor flashed on with a faint click and the computer gave a drowned buzz—deep and full of low, grandpa static.

He clicked through his emails once the old PC hummed alive. He stopped at one with the header *James Carpenter* and glared. His finger jabbed at the left side of his wireless mouse at the email. He hadn't been cranky, on his way to work, or in the *hollow-way* but he considered being cranky now as the email from Ms. Gus expanded across his single monitor for him to read.

It was typed out in comic sans, blue font, and a few typing sizes too big. He began to read through it dully, his chin rested in his left palm. She requested later evaluating dates her and the counselor could schedule out on their calendars. Brent looked to his forehead and remembered he hadn't finished his coffee, he'd left it in the 4Runner, the drink probably icy by now. *Great.* He hovered his mouse over the reply tab before selecting it with mild hesitation.

"*Wendy,*" (as in Wendy Gus)

Brent started.

"*I will no longer be evaluating Jamie unless a more concerning behavior is brought to my attention. If this occurs then I will determine what actions need to be taken per your request.*"

Indent.

"*There is nothing to be worried about.*"

He indented again and added, "*We can chat in person about it, if you'd prefer, please let me know.*"

Then signed his name, "*Brent Kingsley.*" Perhaps Wendy Gus would read the email, call it good, and not bug him about it again but that was only hopeful thinking. He clicked send and the draft made a *whoosh* sound as it finalized and shrunk to the top corner of his computer.

A roll of knocks shook his door and startled his chin from its resting spot in his palm. "Come in!" he announced and spun himself towards the closed entryway.

The door opened and Debra stepped into his room. Her eyebrow was pointed up and she peered over her glasses at him like a scolding parent. The kind that say, '*I'm not mad. Just disappointed.*'

He glanced behind himself at the closed desk drawer where he'd stuffed the folder the day before. Where he'd forgotten it.

"Have you looked at it?" Debra's voice was angled and poked at him like the edge of broken glass.

Brent let his shoulders roll forward, "I'm sorry Deb, I spaced it." He was being honest. She shut his office door and the urge to flinch away from a slap passed through him. The out of place sensation disturbed him and he sat up taller against it.

Debra shook her head and her hot iron curls brushed around the wide build of her jaw. She looked like she might be sick, something the counselor subconsciously pegged as melodramatic. "Ei, Brent." She leaned back against his burgundy wall, "honey, you need to look at it."

Her voice sounded patient and certain which was a different pace than the frantic it had been yesterday and it unsettled him even more. He cleared his throat and turned back to his desk against the slow swivel of his chair, "sure." He said. Debra stepped away from the wall and stood close so she could peer over his shoulder as he removed the folder from the skinny desk drawer, "you really shouldn't be viewing this with me." He reminded her, "It's against my policies." His neck prickled against her body heat hovered over him and micromanaging.

Debra smacked her lips, "I've already seen it, handsome."

Brent bit the inside of his cheek. He dropped the folder to his desk and swung open the stock card top. The inside papers, bleach white, grinned up at him like white teeth. Or snarled. He hadn't decided yet as Debra continued to breathe over him. He exhaled pressure in his chest and lifted the first paper that slacked away from his hold, he shook it and it snapped erect and upward. He scanned its black lines.

Debra leaned over his shoulder and waved a hand at the paper which then fell back into a slack, "no," she instructed, "that's not important."

The man arched his head back to give her a sideways stare that she didn't notice, her face solid and stuck to the papers on his desk while she continued to persist for him to leaf through them. He looked back at the pages and put the first one from the side.

"It's in the back," Debra snapped, "it's a drawing."

Brent felt warm at the thought of artwork done by Davey, the boy who appreciated and studied each drawing in the lengthy hallways just the day before. "Okay." He began to rifle the top pages to the side.

Purple Crayola strokes caught his attention and he lifted the page up from the pile to study. Debra responded to the hoisted art with a high whine from somewhere in her chest, like a burp and Brent's heart gave an extra thump, a little heavier than normal, against his strung ribcage. Neatly drawn on this page were a boy and girl stick figure. The girl was taller and held the boy's stick figure hand.

Both cried. Large teardrop lines sprinkling from their circle faces.

Brent sat further back into his chair with a low exhale from his lips as his eyes drifted along with the paper. In the corner, behind the boy and girl was another stick figure, this one *dangled*. Hanged by a purple line that stretched to the top of the page. A purple noose. The stick figure's arms and legs drawn to dangle, and his eyes were a set of heavy X's. Under the hanged man was a name, "*Dad.*" Brent ran his finger over the wax indents of *dad.*

Debra's internal burp whine came out of her mouth in a sad squawk that jolted Brent upright with cold electricity in his spine. He sat the paper down gently on top of the others and angled his head back to her, this time they made eye contact and she was flossing a strand of her nail through her teeth. "Debra," he addressed her with a faulty voice, "can you leave?" He blinked to wet his dry eyes, "please."

The woman dropped the tip of her finger from her mouth and rolled the nail end over on her tongue, swallowed it, and glared. "Fine." She answered, "you see why I was worried? That kid has seen something dark. He–". Brent turned back to the papers, no longer listening. She cleared her throat, "'right then." she mumbled and left the room. The door made a deep thud as it shut and Brent could hear her heels clop down the *hollow-way* unhappily.

He set the artwork aside and began to file through the other papers. Past Davey's director information, *David Niles Matthews* it said, past a second-grade and first-grade report card, and a personal sheet with birth date. He shook his head and continued to leaf. Why was that picture kept in the records? Why had Davey drawn it?

A wave of sudden sadness lapped at his feet, rose high tide over his legs, and eventually swallowed him as he began to run out of papers. He licked his thumb and forefinger to keep a steady, sticky grasp at the sheets and furrowed his eyebrows. '*Dark,*' Debra had said. The word fired through him like a misused bullet and struck each neuron as it passed. His head in a blaze as the last sheet was leafed out and there was still no answer. "How–" His voice bounced off his desk and rattled back at him, "does a school transfer a child's drawing of a hanged dad and not explain?" He went back and studied the drawing itself. He searched it for a jotted note from an adult giving at least a mention to what the picture meant; *nothing.*

The bell had rung and children chatter with squeaky sneakers began to stomp past his office. His door clicked with a twist of the handle and swung open. A sweet, "hi." passed through his room, unmuffled by the grown noise from the hallway.

Brent stretched a hand to shield the drawing of the dead father and tilted his head in the direction of the voice, "Hi, Nancy." He said with a nod for acknowledgment.

The girl behind him with thick spectacles smiled, "hi." she repeated then turned and darted for her friends, her large jacket flapped against her sides as she ran, just as every morning.

Something heavy and uneasy began to settle in the man's stomach as he tapped his foot anxiously and stared at the name, *dad*. He heard a child say, "Good Morning Mrs. A—" then the call was shut out by the solid *womp* of the classroom door as it fell shut. The hallways were silent, once again. *Hollow-ways*. He stood from his seat and the office chair bounced back and the wheels squeaked over his rugged floor.

Mrs. Engels was tucked behind her desk in a deep blue raincoat when Brent had slipped into the classroom, unannounced. She questioned him with a stare but he acted as if he hadn't seen it. The children were still getting settled into their seats, their fuzzy morning heads separated hesitantly from chatting groups and to their individual desks and he hardly paid mind to them either.

Daisy, who had her blonde hair styled into a fishtail braid today, noticed Brent's stare as it unwavered from Davey's empty desk. She turned and studied the table and child's chair herself, then turned her head back to her counselor with a simple shrug, "he's not here today, Mr. Kingsley." she informed, over the chatter, her voice almost getting lost on the way to him.

That something heavy and uneasy hit the bottom of Brent's gut and he stepped forward from its imagined force. As he stepped, the garbage bag in his head rustled and for a moment he thought of a childhood word: *abandoned*. It had vanished as soon as it had come and he was left feeling a little cold and looking at the young female teacher for an answer. She looked back at him, uncertain, with her chin dipped closer to her chest. The man could feel the small eyes of the third-grade classroom begin to watch him too as they quieted and became aware of his presence. His face reddened.

The boy with the small face from the lunch line the day before decided to speak up from his seat in the classroom, "he's probably sick, Mr. Kingsley."

Then the boy snickered and continued with, "sick with cooties, from kissing her." He pointed a finger at Daisy and some other children began to giggle with him. Others gasped dramatically.

"Shut up! I don't even like him!" Daisy cried as she spun forward in her seat to snarl at the boy.

Mrs. Engels raised from her desk, "okay!" She used her scary voice as she unzipped her blue rain jacket, "we are not starting our Tuesday off this way!"

The small faced boy opened his smart mouth, ready for a rigor response, but was cut off by Brent who snapped his fingers at him. The snap was crisp and catastrophic to the chatter in the room—all eyes certainly on Brent now as he waved the snap at the boy, "do I need to see you in my office, Zachary?" He threatened.

Zachary rolled his eyes but kept quiet.

Brent frowned distastefully at the boy and passed his stare back to Mrs. Engels and his face softened, "Emily," he sighed it, like he had given up on something and her eyes widened at the use of her first name in front of her students, like it was a taboo, "can you please send Davey to my office when he shows up?" Because he would show up. *Just late.* Brent thought, *probably missed the bus.* That made the pressure ease up a little.

Emily Engles gave a weary smile at the man's sudden distant stare, "Of course, Mr. Kingsley."

He turned and headed back to his office.

He sat in front of the purple artwork with his hands laced together and limp in his lap. It wasn't a big deal. *No.* Kids have crazy imaginations and this was probably just something Davey had seen on TV. *Yes.* The thought hadn't seemed to help the man and his laced hands laced tighter.

Brent pressed back into his oval cushioned office chair for a second time that morning, realizing how much better he'd feel if he could just talk to the kid. "*Why isn't he here?*" He thought aloud as his pulse thickened and that word from his childhood bounced back: *abandoned.* He glared at the papers and cursed the ridiculous word. Davey didn't abandon him, it was impossible for him too because Davey wasn't Brent's mother or countless foster parents after that–he was only a student at Grant Elementary so he couldn't *abandon* the adult. Brent began to shuffle back through the other papers laid out in a spread on his desk.

A list of guardians caught his eye, except it wasn't much of a list at all, but one single name. *Marilyn M. Matthews,* it said. Maybe the boy's mother. The drawing had a hung father, but not a hung mother... Brent glanced at the girl stick figure on Davey's artwork then turned back to the Guardian's name and empty emergency contact slots with a sigh. The sheet lacked a phone number. The sigh turned into an irritated hum.

He grabbed for his phone reluctantly with the tightly coiled cord and jabbed in Debra's receptionist extension.

The phone rang a deep call against his ear and then clicked, "This is Debra."

"Deb," Brent answered immediately to her voice, which sounded metallic through the phone line, "Do you have a phone number to call home for Davey?"

The woman's voice breathed against her end of the phone, "why?" She asked butting-ly, "what'd you find out?"

Brent shook his head as if she could see it, "he's not here, do you have a number?"

"He's not here?" Her voice was high and tight.

Brent's head dropped, "no—"

"Nobody has called to excuse him."

Brent pinched the bridge of his nose and asked for the number again.

Debra scrolled her computer and sighed into her phone, "found it." She confirmed after a long pause that twisted Brent's internal organs.

"Great," Brent said as he stretched a long arm out and grabbed a black *Z Mulsion* pen from a red plastic cup located under his monitor.

Debra read it out to him and he scribbled the line of numbers at the corner of the *Guardians* sheet that should really be called, *'Guardian sheet.'* Singular. One. "Thanks," he mumbled into the receiver and put the phone into its holder to end the call, the line dropped off dead and buzzed.

Brent hoisted the phone back up to his ear and squeezed it between his face and shoulder, he listened to the soft fizzle a moment before he dialed the number.

It rang three times against his squished ear then a man with a sleepy voice answered, "who the fuck is calling me in the middle of the night?"

Brent's eyebrows raised and his face beat a little red, surprised by both being cussed at and by the man's disorientation. *Middle of the night?* He glanced at the clock behind him, "Sir, it's eight, forty-three in the morning."

A loud scuff shot through the phone and into his ear like a bullet from a hand pistol–he winced. "Who the fu–" The man was going to repeat himself and Brent had to cut him off before he could.

"Brent Kingsley at Grant Elementary school," he tapped the black pen against his desk, "I'd appreciate if you didn't cuss at me, sir."

"Oh my god –" the man growled into the phone with an annoyance so potent that it trickled into Brent's own bloodstream, "What the *fudge* do you want?" The man thought he was funny, Brent did not, Brent thought he was a bit infuriating and *stupid*.

He looked over the drawing Davey made and contemplated the man on the phone *being* the boy's father. Enough hate for the man and Davey could possibly *want* him hanged. Brent's eyes went to the stick figure tears flowing to the bottom of the page and felt his theory wilt beneath them. Besides, the man on the other end sounded young, ignorant, *stupid.* That word went through his head another time and Brent decided he didn't like it—it was too distasteful and negative for him. He straightened his posture and cleared his throat as he stopped tapping his pen and tapped his foot against the ground instead. "Who am I speaking to?" He asked and was happy to find his voice still sounded silky, and calm.

A laugh, wet and delirious now absorbed into the phone line, "Nick." The man's voice was clogged.

"Hi Nick," his foot stopped tapping, "Is Davey Matthews' home?" He waved his pen in the air absently as he talked, "your number is listed under his home address so I was hoping you could help me with this. I haven't seen him today and I really was looking forward to chatting wi—"

"Fuck bro... " The young man's voice broke through the line and cut Brent's spiel, "why are you bugging me with this shit." Brent could hear Nick rub a heavy hand over his face and imagined it combing up through his greasy hair.

"Is Davey home," Brent repeated. His foot tapped again, quicker this time.

"Sure," was Nick's reply.

Brent's tapping foot slammed into the ground in a final stomp and his eyebrows knitted together, which created a headache behind his eyes, "is he... or is he not?" He asked, his voice pinched and the silky-calm wavered.

"I'm sure the little asshole is," Nick chatted casually now, "His sister is shit at keeping track of him."

Jolts ripped through Brent's *trying-to-stay-calm* posture and his jaw tightened, "please call the school and excuse him from class." The counselor dropped the phone down into its hook like it was hot before he could hear another sigh or moan from the man on the other end. Unwanted rage rippled through him as his back molars locked together. Insanely, he thought of driving to find Davey and that man, *Nick,* as he searched back over the helpless guardian's sheet. He knew he couldn't do that, and besides, there wasn't an address, just a name. *Marilyn M. Matthews.* He stared at it and thought of what Nick said: *"his sister is shit at keeping track of him."* Not mom, not dad, sister.

His eyes went back to the drawing and he put his finger on the woman stick figure, "That's your sister." *She reads Davey books like Matilda and Double Fudge.* The something unsettling in him bottomed again.

16

Davey jogged along the edge of the house on his tiptoes. *Like a spy,* he thought as his backpack thumped against his back, Bear Kingsley silent and along for the ride. He stopped and knelt at the latched back yard gate of their duplex with a caught breath. He slipped an arm from his backpack strap and slung the black bag over the front of his body, cautious not to make a noise as he began to work the curved crease of the backpack's zipper. Each zipper claw popped open slowly, and nearly silently. Bear Kingsley had fallen over and now laid on his side at the bottom of the bag, one stuffed arm twisted behind him uncomfortably. Davey's own shoulder ached empathetically as he rescued his new plush friend from the back and cradled him in his arms. He apologized, as he rocked the bear, for having to keep him crammed in the old sack that smelled a little like rotten lunch from its years of use from his sister. He wondered what kind of lunch she'd let simmer and soak into the material of his hand-me-down school bag years ago. If he asked she'd shrug and probably say, *"nothing good."* with a scrunched up nose.

Davey stood and secured the school bag back in its rightful spot, both straps loose and frayed around his little shoulders. He eyed the height of the wooden fence created from old planks that splintered off in all directions. Designed, unpurposefully, like a thick thorn bush.

Davey lifted his bear up and whispered into his ear like it was the speaker of a walkie talkie, "this will be the trickiest part, Beary." He imagined Bear

Kingsley trembled with fear and he patted his fuzzy butt like you would do for an upset baby. He then walked his feet up to the fence and lined his toes up to the bottom of the gate door. His knees bent and his ankles stretched into his shins as his butt pushed out, then he leaped. It was a big leap that tousled Beary around in his grasp like a man in a car accident as the boy hooked his arm over the top of the gate door. His body slammed against the splintered planks of the door and the fence shook unstably. The latch rattled from the blow and Davey held his lip in his mouth until it settled. *(Quiet!)* the plush toy scolded inside of Davey's head while he worked to get his fingers around the vibrating latch. Davey nodded. He would be more careful next time.

The latch was made of thin aluminum and had a switch at the top like the tab of a pop can. Davey flicked the switch up with his middle finger. The latch unhinged and he had to rock his body back, then forward, to maneuver the gate open with swung momentum. It squeaked and brushed its bottom over the back yard grass as both boy and bear dangled on it.

Davey dropped solidly into the ground and swung around to catch the planked backyard door before it slammed shut. It bounced into his hand and he guided it slowly to the latch that fell forward on it like a mousetrap. *See Beary,* he thought as he hardly made a noise, *I'm being more careful already.* The little bear was impressed by this.

His hand began to ache, so hot that it burned, and he hoisted it into the light to study it. Embedded beneath the ball of skin and fat at the bottom of his thumb was a light brown slice of wood. Davey pulled his lip in and tucked Bear Kingsley into the crease of his armpit. "Don't look," he instructed the bear aloud, "this could be nasty." He felt lightheaded for a moment and he bit his lip like a hand would grasp something sturdy to stay upright as the spell passed. He used his index and thumb to delicately pluck the sliver from his tender flesh and flicked it into the breeze. Davey released a breath he hadn't known he was holding and the knot in his stomach dissipated.

Both bear and boy began to creep through the overgrown, wet lawn of the backyard to the duplex's sliding glass door, saturated with smudges and speckles of dead bugs. Davey peered in and held the bear forward so he could get a glance to. The boy froze as all the color left his face, his lips parted and his eyes widened to show all of the surrounding whites. Nick was awake and stood just on the other side of the glass. His back was to the deer-in-headlights boy and he had the landline phone pressed deep against his ear. His hands swung as he talked and occasionally swiped at his groggy face and disheveled hair. Nick sure liked to use his hands a lot. Davey blinked his eyes rapidly and tried to pretend that he didn't feel sick inside.

(If he turns around...)

"He'll see us." Davey murmured the rest of the bear's imagined thought. "We can't go into the house yet." He added with a reluctant shiver. Bear Kingsley agreed. Together they skimmed the yard for an escape as Davey stepped them back, away from the glass door. Bear pointed to the rained on glass table at the opposite end of the small yard with the help of Davey's hand guiding his arm. Davey nodded, he understood. The table and single plastic chair were out of sight from the glass doors, they could hide there until Nick stumbled back to sleep, as he often did.

He took the bear by the ear and whispered into it like it was a walkie-talkie again, "we're going to have to make a run for it." He braced his back toe against the smushed grass and crouched forward like an Olympic runner. *Ready.* He took a deep breath in and let his eyes slide to the glass door, angled in front of him. *Set.* He watched as the reflection of Nick walked away from the glass door and back to the kitchen to put the phone on the hook. *Go!*

It was a lunge into the dead center view from the glass door, then a wet, dewy sprint forward through the rest of the back lawn to the table. His sneakers slid and Bear Kingsley swung furiously in his hold. The single, rain caught, chair at the glass table faced him like an open mouth and he leaped into it, crashing his knees into the water. The chair tipped and Davey had to lean back to balance it on all four while he soothed, "*Woah Boy, woahh.*" Like the white plastic seat was the back of a spooked horse. He pivoted against his knee and slouched criss-cross into the seat. He huffed. *Phase one. Mission one—complete.*

Davey placed the bear upright on the lip of the table and smiled at him. "What do you think of my house, Beary?" He asked genuinely and imagined his small friend shrugged his soft shoulders. Davey understood. It was *alright.*

"Yeah," he nodded slowly, "I sometimes like it." He licked his bottom lip in a quick flash of pink, "but Nick–"

(The dick.) Bear Kingsley's fictional voice interrupted to finish the boy's sentence.

"Right." Davey kicked his feet under the spiderwebbed, white legged table, "do you miss Brent?" He asked.

He imagined Bear Kingsley shaking his head. *(No. I have you now.)*

Davey lipped a small giggle.

The sound of the sliding glass door brought his head up erect and alert as his heart lurched into the space in his mouth to gag his giggle. Nick leaned out of the doorway and smiled at him with a can of beer tilted in his fist. "Good morning," he gurgled to the boy who realized they hadn't been as sneaky as he thought, "are you talking to a stuffed animal?" Nick swigged from the can and as he swallowed the fluid, Davey swallowed his heart back down to his thumping chest.

The boy saved the bear from the table like a mother tucking her child behind her back from a potential predator, "no," he cupped a hand over the bear's eyes to shield him from *Nick, the Dick.*

Nick began to cross the backyard with bare feet, "Well, listen," Davey's hold on the bear tightened like he was going through a pre-mortem rigor mortis. The muscles in his shoulder blades cramped when Nick came within smelling distance and stopped, "I gotta call from your school," he said blandly with another swig from that white beer can.

Davey stared silently, his pulse beating heavily back up into his mouth.

"A guy named Ben Kingsley, or some shit."

Davey's eyes widened and he imagined Bear Kingsley kicked him, upset his eyes were still covered. "Brent called?" He gaped at the roommate, overwhelmed by the assumption that he was in trouble. *He shouldn't have skipped. Brent was scared for his bear friend.* He hopped off the seat and began to trudge towards the duplex, "should I call him? Am I in trouble??" His voice was high, "I didn't—"

Nick caught the worried boy by the arm and dragged him back to the front of him, "sure." He answered to no one particular question. His breath reeked from a layer of unbrushed grime, beer and an aging pack of cigarettes. "Are *you* trying to get *me* in trouble?" He hissed his words now and Davey twisted away from the heavy scent, "you and your sister banding together to *piss* me *off?*"

"No," his voice was a mouse squeak.

Nick's grip loosened and he went back to his dirty smile dusted with a dark, fuzzy scruff, "so you're skipping, huh?"

Davey thought: *Well, yes... but not in a bad way.* He said, "no," in his tiny croak.

Nick's eyes narrowed and he knocked Davey on the side of the head with his beer can, "sure looks like it to me, shithead," and his smile grew, "playing hooky!" He whooped as he patted his chest in a burp conjuring spatter.

Davey pulled his lip in, rather than reply. His head ached dully from the tin rim of Nick's drink.

"Don't worry, I'm proud of ya," Nick grunted, "show that Ben guy who the fuck's boss!" In other words: *stick it to the man!*

But Davey hadn't wanted to do that. It wasn't about Brent. It was about protecting Marilyn *from Nick*. His chin and lip began to tremble and his throat dried, "Brent is my friend." He tried to explain with a painfully stiff vocal box, "I don't want him upset with me." This type of consequence hadn't occurred to him as he'd turned away from the yellow school bus just a little while earlier.

Nick frowned distantly and his grip around Davey's arm tightened again, this time with a pull that lifted Davey's feet from the ground. He thrust the boy back into the wet lawn-table chair lopsidedly. It hurt Davey's arm in a hollow pinch kind of way and his tears began to well up into his eyes as the lingering sting began to grow and fester in the yanked muscles, skin, and nerves. "Listen –" Nick shook his head and ignored Davey's fight to keep from crying, "teachers aren't your friends, they despise little, filthy, snots like you." It was becoming physically painful to hold back the tears as Davey bit down on his lip and let one spill out over his cheek. He didn't have the heart to tell Nick that Brent *wasn't* a teacher. Nick's grin was back and he jabbed a finger at Davey's cheek to blot the tear, "you gotta stand up and say '*Fuck you, Kingsley!*'"

Davey let out a tiny gust of painful air through his running nose and the tears began to drop down his face freely. Sensitively. He hated that about himself and he set Bear Kingsley to his lap and rubbed open palms into his face to hide the salty streams with his stretched fingers.

"Say it."

Davey's hot eyes stared out at his roommate in confusion.

Nick swatted Davey's hands away from his face and spanked the boy's mouth with the tips of his fingers, "Say it." He commanded again. His smile twisted with something wicked now.

Davey cried and ran his tongue over the inside of his lips where his teeth had pinched from the hit. Nick glared and Davey shook his head with a hard no.

Nick dumped his head back into a roll around his shoulders and Davey covered his face again to shield the tears. When Nick's head came back a swinging hand did too, it crashed across Davey's temple—his ring finger and pinky crushed into the tip of Davey's ear. The boy's light cry became audible as his ear began to sting. Nick tossed his eyes as the cry was amplified by the child's cupped hands over his face, "you need to man up, dude." He grumbled. "Stop talking to *Teddy bears,*" he teased.

Davey's hands shot from his face and blindly reached out for Bear Kingsley but it was too late. Nick had the plush toy in his hands and his beer can dumped in Davey's lap, over Bear Kingsley's now vacant spot.

Davey screeched in panic as he rocketed out of his seat at Nick, "Leave him alone!" He punched closed fists at Nick's abdomen, "I promised Brent I'd protect him!" His tears swam off his face and now his wide eyes were only full of panic, determination.

Nick stumbled back away from the boy, the bear held up high by the neck in a shaky hand. Surprise dropped through his dirty face and he pressed the bear into his chest, "this is Ben Kingsley's toy?" He asked, suddenly intrigued and focused.

Davey sniffed hard enough to make the bridge of his nose feel like it might break, "no," he held out his hand, "it's *Brent's.*"

The foul grin was back, accompanied by a wetting tongue over his cracked lips, "this is good practice for you then, *smartass.*" Nick laughed and Davey's hand lowered, his lungs tight and his legs stuck, paralyzed. His hands braced flat out to the backyard breeze like useless fish fins. "Ready?" Nick hissed.

Davey hadn't heard the man, his imagination full of Bear Kingsley's cries to be free and his sensible mind frozen.

"Your Ben friend woke me up from a goddamn dream." Nick complained, "he was rude," he continued, "and I'm *sure* he thinks you're *just. The. Worst.*" He stabbed at Davey with his words until the tears were back in the boy's swollen eyes. "You ready?" He laughed the word this time. *Ready.*

Ready for what?

Nick grasped Bear Kingsley in both hands. A tight hold with one hand around the bear's chest and the other hand around his plush, baby arm. "Fuck you, Kingsley!" The man bellowed up to the grey sky as he began to tear the bear in separate directions. It did nothing at first, only stretching out and looking odd, so he persisted. He yanked with a grunt. This time seams in the right arm tore at the cloth and Davey felt his insides tear with it.

"Stop!" The boy shrieked as hot, blind tears began to plunder down his cheeks again. He shoved at Bear Kingsley's attacker jaggedly, his knees buckled and unbuckled like a small child throwing a tantrum. Cotton filling began to spill from the joint in the bear's shoulder like fat snowflakes and Davey's plea turned into a high, painful, shrill.

"Fuck you, King!!" The man howled over the boy's sounds of fear in a sung voice. *Maybe it'd be one of his next SoundCloud singles.*

Bear Kingsley was clawed out of Nick's crude hands from behind. The man jerked around with an inhale of air through his teeth to a one-eyed young adult. Her other eye swollen shut and her hand clenched firmly around a gimpy stuffed animal with a ripped arm that dangled at an odd angle. She was dressed in crusted blue jeans and a white *Billabong* sweatshirt. She'd dressed quickly– *her fly was down.*

"What are you doing?" Nick growled predatorily with an edge that made Davey cringe.

Marilyn held her hand up between them like a stranger might hold their hand up to a snarling dog, "listen," she tucked the tattered animal in closer to her chest and spoke softly in her opposition, "let me drive Davey to school…" Her words drifted as he took a slow glance around the man at her brother as he swiped tears away from his under eye. She glided her clear eye back to Nick, "then I'll come back." Nick tilted an eyebrow up at her and Marilyn took the gesture as an opportunity to step closer with the bear still held back, far enough away from the destructive roommate. "I will come back and we can work together to make you happy." She nodded as she spoke like her words were conducting a silk, seductive symphony, "make up for what's upsetting you."

Nick's eyes glazed over as the blood in his big head rushed to agitate the smaller, dangling, one.

Marilyn washed her lips with a gentle dart of her tongue to magnify what it was she was suggesting, "whatever it is you want to do." Nick's hand came into gripped contact around her upper arm and she made a noise in her throat as if to scold him. "After I drop off my brother." She promised.

"You'll hurry?" Nick panned like a half-charged robot, brainwashed and relaxed.

Marilyn's eye was on her brother now as she answered, "I will," the boy stared, frightened, back at her. His little heart still fluttering. She inclined her chin at him and he shuffled around Nick to grab hold of her.

They pinwheeled around towards the door and Marilyn nudged her brother forward with an overbearing fire in her stomach.

A *you-laid-your-hands-on-my-brother-you-are-lucky-you-are-still-alive* grimace on her face.

Once through the house, out the front door, and into the car Marilyn tossed a relieved sigh towards her brother and handed him his bear. Davey snuggled Bear Kingsley against him, "are you okay, Beary?" He whined at his friend. He imagined a sniffle from the toy as it wiggled itself into the warmth of the boy. Marilyn put the keys into the ignition and her car knocked before it spit a rumble from the hard-running engine.

Davey's attention was brought around to her, "Marilyn," his voice broke, "don't come back." He knew what she'd promised Nick, at least the gist of the gesture, and a solid pit had clogged his airway at the thought of it.

Marilyn cranked the car into drive and the car jutted forward, away from the curb it had been parked against, "I'm not," she chewed her lip, "and you're not going to school."

Davey buckled himself into his seat, "what?" He played with a string of stuffing in Bear Kingsley's ripped seam.

She removed seventeen dollars in crumbled cash that she'd recollected off the floor the night before, after being mauled by a fist, from her sweater pocket and flashed a dazzled smile at her brother, "I was thinking a *lot* of food and maybe we can catch a movie?" And by catch, she meant manipulate their way into a matinee.

Davey's tear washed face lifted into a wet grin under his Bambi eyes and he forgot about Brent and maybe being in trouble.

"It's a date." A sharp bolt shot through her molars as her jaw clamped down.

17

Brent drove silently through a tree-lined neighborhood while his molars bit down and tight balls of muscle pulsed from the sides of his jaw. He began to work the molars stiffly at dead skin in his cheek. His face ached from tension and he cocked his shoulders back to try to relieve it. The pressure built up and his spine made a light snap that leaked warmth up into the pockets in his neck and head. He dropped his lips into a frown and swallowed the bit off skin.

Davey never showed up and that Nick guy never called.

Brent slowed to let a father cross the street with his son in a soccer uniform before he milked his automatic steering wheel to the left. The 4Runner obeyed and the blinker slammed small clicks somewhere inside the dashboard.

His cheek was back into his teeth.

He thought of a holiday, Thanksgiving, the year before. He'd spent it alone with Winnifred. He'd come up the stairs with little hops off of his fancy shoed toes to her apartment door. He had been early that day, nine in the morning early, he had planned to help her in the kitchen. Afraid she'd burn down the complex trying to cook the turkey alone. He had been spruced up in a nice button-down that morning and carried his own kitchen supplies. He'd carefully set the pots and cookie sheets down at her doorstep and knock.

Brent took another slow cornered left.

The knock had been loud, crisp and fell off into a pattern like *Shave and a Haircut*, without a reply to follow. He had stood, hands on hips, and waited—not a stir from the apartment. So he knocked again. This time a three-pound rhythm of his knuckles, a little louder and a little more urgent. Tulsa had meowed from the other end of the door but a response from Winnifred was still absent. *She died.* He had thought that. Like a bell of a gong, it was immediately the thought that rattled through him. Then, something like *abandonment* began to liquidate his insides like he was still a little boy.

Brent took a final left onto a one way and slowed his SUV to a stop at a red traffic light.

He had knocked for a third time with a panicked tempo as his button-down had begun to collect prickling sweat from the back of his neck. Tulsa growled a deep moan and Brent's heart sank. He ended up throwing his shoulder into the door, once—twice. He'd lined up for a third when the door had jerked wide into the apartment's living room.
The fuzzy-headed woman had stood on the receiving end of the door with irritation sunk into her wrinkled, brown skin. The familiar emotion of abandonment struck at him then, like a slap to the back of the head as embarrassment took its place within him.

His face burned red now as he continued to drive through the main drag of town towards the store where they develop your photos. He could feel the same embarrassment he had that day and let out a captive sigh from his nose to try to relieve it. He supposed he hoped he was doing the same with Davey. *Overreacting.* He made a final left into a dead parking lot and slid his car into a space at the front of the store.

It was lit brightly with fluorescent strips and people with carts wheeled in and out of the automatic doors. Brent analyzed Davey's drawing that now sat, burnt, into the front of his mind as he zigzagged past shoppers to the photo counter. He chewed at what skin was leftover in his mouth as he thought of the purple noose and the X's in *dad*'s eyes.

There was a young clerk tucked behind the photo development counter with her back turned to the wide aisle Brent approached from, "excuse me," he spoke tenderly after he'd swallowed the last of the chewed cheek skin. She turned with a grin of top and bottom turquoise braces at him. He smiled a lip line back at her politely and discreetly assumed she'd just gotten them.

"How can I help you, sir?" She asked with a thick upper lip that worked sorely over the metal glued to her teeth.

Brent slid his phone from his pocket and flashed it at her unsurely, "I'd like to take photos off of this —" he trailed off as he felt a bit shy and unaware of how her eyes dilated at him the longer she looked over his solid, slim features, "— but I'm unsure how to. Could you help me?" He squinted his eyes at her curiously.

The girl, who's name tag read *Lili* in black sharpie waved her hands at him, "of course! It's super simple." He noticed the crescent of blush under her eyes then and stepped back from the counter a safe inch and a half. She opened a waist height, double hinged door and came around to the front of the counter where he stood. She pointed a finger out to a large computer screen at the other end of the kiosk as she strolled past him, and he followed. "This." She said, her finger still out. The computer was boxed into a counter and sold ads for photos on it's plastic sides

Brent nodded, his eyebrows furrowed and phone pinched in his hand.

Lili held her hand out to him as a request for the phone. He gave it over. Her fingernails were painted the same shade of blue/green as her braces and he thought it to be sweet. "Okay." She pulled a small cable up from the desk and jammed it into the bottom of Brent's phone, then handed it back.

"Okay," Brent mimicked and stared at the phone in his mitt.

"The computer is now hooked to your phone. You can go to your camera roll and select the photos you'd like to print and the computer will pull them up." She turned her head up to Brent and smiled, "like a flash drive." He nodded along with her and she continued along her explanation expedition, "Then you'll go to the computer," she pointed to it, "You can crop, resize and rotate your photos using the touch screen. Then—" her voice jumped with the word, *then!*, "you hit the big print button and it'll give you a time to come back and pick them up."

Brent had gotten the gist the second his phone met the phone cord, but he let her continue while he gave her an innocently charming smile.

"If it's a lot of photos it could take up to a few hours, just depending on what other orders are in front of yours, but if you just want to print off a few, I can have you out of here in thirty minutes." She smiled back at Brent and her blush seemed to deepen, "if you have any questions, just ask," she finished.

"I will, thank you," he nodded at her and she moved around him to get back to her station behind the kiosk counter. He felt funny with an ever-growth of embarrassment that washed down to remind him of that old feeling—*abandonment*—and he was pondering Davey's drawing again as he clicked the two photos he wanted to print with the side of his thumb. They popped up wide on the computer in front of him and he giggled for a raw, thoughtless, moment at Winnifred's crazed grin and Tulsa's uncomfortable deadpan. It was funnier blown up in front of him.

Brent rubbed at his head as a sharp peirce of a headache slid in from the side of his skull. His vision funneled out at the screen and he puffed his cheeks at nausea that slammed into him like a freight train. It continued to grow, like a sudden, explosive, tumor. He knew, somewhere in his sane part of his head, tumors didn't work like that but it was all he could consider as his vision collapsed.

The automatic store doors sucked open and at once the view of the room smacked back at him, his headache dissipated and his head snapped to the sound of the open entrance. He'd moved too quickly, he thought, because the room immediately began to spin and he fell forward. He crashed his hand into the touch screen computer to steady himself and blinked slowly to try to bring the world back into a steady pace. A numb spot had begun to form at the center of his brain like a hole had opened and shoved the neural structure tight to the walls of his skull. It reminded him of the fairground ride that forced you against its padded sides once it was moving fast enough. He released his air-fat cheeks and the room gave another swoop around him in a fluorescent blue.

With squinted eyes he watched a girl stumble through the doors with a hand at her forehead as if to check for a sudden fever. They made brief eye contact, he thought. *Maybe the room is spinning for everyone,* he considered it as the loops slowed and the numb feeling puddled around him. A nationwide case of vertigo. He dismissed the idea as quickly as it has come but couldn't shake the notion that the girl's vision had escaped her and ran a few laps just as his had.

The girl dropped her hand from her head, her hand swung down heavily past her hoodie side and she caught him with a sharp glare through one eye. Only one. The other swollen enough to hide her iris and pupil under a purple eyelid. The glare startled Brent and he lowered his eyes back to his phone. Perhaps he'd studied her for too long.

His phone blurred underneath him and he set it against the computer table disinterested as the fuzzy numb started into his ears. He found himself lifting his gaze back up to watch the swollen eyed girl. Through only curious glances this time, careful not to tip off her glare radar. She was walking steadily, carefully, down the aisle he had walked up from, her hips swayed in a stagnant rhythm as her head bobbed above her shoulders.

She was young, maybe only sixteen or seventeen, by Brent's quick judgment. She had thick, matted curls, hair that swayed heavily around her shoulders in messy puffs, her face streaked free of any kind of makeup. Her skin was an even mix of fair pink shades and olive tones. A band of lightly placed freckles across her nose and under eyes.

He watched her hagger a pace that picked up speed towards an old gentleman who stood and read the back of a vitamin bottle. He held a webbed plastic basket full of miscellaneous items clenched in his aged hand—items Brent couldn't pick out through the gaps in the blue plastic. The man shopped innocently and the girl beelined straight towards him. Brent had a fleeting thought to yell out a warning—like, *hey! Watch out! Speeding swollen eye girl coming at you!* But his auditory system seemed to shut down beneath the captivity of the pulsed gap within his brain.

The girl clipped her shoulder against the man and as the poor elder stumbled back her hand slipped into his Carhartt zip-up jacket pocket. It came back out with a retrieved billfold that she shoved into her own white hoodie. In, and out, fast. Like her arm and hand were a striking snake. *Poisoned.* The older shopper didn't notice the removal of his wallet, but Brent did. He, however, found himself still short for words, stunned and quiet as he watched the young con artist. Brent wanted to defend the man, *excuse me, young lady! I saw that! Give it back, now!* But his head was too heavy to think. He found it hard to just stand and watch, he honestly just wanted to lie down. Right on the floor in front of the big computer screen.

Was he experiencing the same sensation as a transorbital lobotomy?

The girl absorbed a sharp intake of wheezy store air as she grabbed the older man by both shoulders to help balance him, "I am so sorry!" she exclaimed. The disheveled and surprised man steadied himself against her double-handed embrace, "I am so clumsy!" She blinked at him through one good eye, "can't you tell?" She thumbed at the bruise on her face then winced as a demonstration.

The man gave a pity chuckle and a shake of his wrinkled head, "watch where you're going, young lady."

She gave him a sweet squeeze on his shoulder, "yes, sir!" She spoke with a pitched, ditzy voice that was so close to being real Brent almost believed it himself.

The girl turned back to the front of the aisle and walked towards Brent. His hand instinctively went to his pant pocket where his own wallet was held before it dropped back down to his side. She didn't notice and she stopped to scan the cap of the six-foot shelves. She was *charming* and good at what she did, he gave her that.

Ain't no rest for the wicked.

She reached for an Excedrin encased in cardboard on a middle shelf and ripped open the box calmly. The green migraine bottle slid from its rectangular package into her flat palm and she pocketed it next to the wallet with little rattle. Brent watched her rob a man, now a store, but all he could do was think: *can you share some of that Excedrin with me?* His mouth salivated with the remembered taste of the pill on the back of his tongue.

She passed him and moved smoothly back to the storefront, no longer interested in her own robbery. She hesitated in front of the automatic doors to remove the wallet from her pocket. Her shoulders hunched and she did a quick leaf through to pull cash out from its pocket fold. Then, before she passed through the open door and to the store's outside, she dropped it. As it fell she tossed a mischievous grin over her shoulder to Brent, as if to say, *"enjoy the show?"* She left and the doors slid closed behind her.

Brent's mouth parted as he stood dumbfounded. His head started to thump heavy again, the icepick leaving the top of his metaphorical eye socket, his frontal lobe fibers cut and separated away from the rest of his brain.

Thanks for the headache, Doctor Freeman.

He blew hot air from his nose and longed for that Excedrin a little harder.

He could still see the girl through the store's plexiglass window as she swaggered to her car parked next to his own vehicle. He watched through pinpoint migraine eyes as she wedged between their parked automobiles, her hand feeling her forehead again. Her car was old and a dark emerald green he noticed as she popped the driver door open with a grimace. Her cabin light flared a deep-yellow shadow against a Teddy bear sat in the corner of the windshield, displayed as if it were meant to catch his attention. *His* teddy bear.

The girl slid into the driver side of the car and a young, familiar boy rose from a reclined seat beside her. He began to chat at her and reached for the stuffed bear on the car's dusty dashboard.

Brent convulsed forward impulsively, "Davey!" He belted loud enough for the dry static air to absorb it, amplify it, and turn heads toward him. His cheeks flared up but he kept his eyes out the storefront window.

The girl started her car and began to back out of the white lines parking spot with her head turned back around her headrest to watch for passing cars. Brent yanked his phone from the computer cable blindly and pocketed it. He moved forward through the store to the doors, where the wallet laid on the ground. He took a quick, long-legged step over the older man's wallet as the doors whooshed open and he paused to study it. It was a brief pause where he thought: *I should give it back*. But then the thought was wrapped up by a Crayola drawn picture he'd seen earlier. He glanced back at the little green car now shifted into drive and following the exit arrows to the dipped driveway. *Abandonment.*

Brent moved through the doors into the bitter September air, despite the bill-less wallet that beckoned him to turn back and return it to the man. He nearly removed the black handle from his car door as he jerked at it to open. He leaped into his cloth seat and shook the keys maniacally into the little silver slot. *Overreacting.* The engine purred to life in front of him and he maneuvered the SUV out behind them. He switched his blinker to match hers, closer now and as their blinkers flashed in an unsynchronized rhythm he could see it was a Saturn.

She turned out onto the road.
He did the same.

18

The man in the store had been handsome, to say the least.

I should've patted him down for a wallet. Marilyn held a heated smile over her features as she thought back over the man's slender build and sharp jaw with a stir in her stomach. He was lab-made, a test tube result of John Krasinski and Francis, from *Malcolm in the Middle,*'s DNA swabbed together. Handsome like Michiel Huisman. From the bloodline of the Kennedy's. A young, stretched, and thinned out Harrison Ford. *Doctor Jones! Doctor Jones!*

She hadn't noticed the 4Runner that followed close behind, nor would she. She was too distracted by the thirsty thought of the attractive man in the store and the dilated pain through her head that faded in and out like a bad connection. The same damn headache that had shot a hot blade through her skull while she had been dropping Davey off at school, then dissipated once she left. It was strange then, strange in the store, and strange now. *It was like a sudden, explosive, tumor.* She knew tumors didn't work like that, but couldn't dismiss the idea as the Excedrin was ripped from her pocket.

"*Jesus,*" she hissed aloud as she steered the car clumsily with her knee and weighed down on the Excedrin cap with her hands greedily, "my head feels like shit." She grumbled with a glance at her brother who sat happily. He was full, from the pizza she mooched from a local shop, and his head was filled with images from the movie they snuck into. Some shoot 'em up she'd all but slept through.

A bend in the road approached and the green lid to the shitty white bottle was still attached, clung on to its childproof grooves. A frustrated grunt leaped from the girl's lips as she tossed the pill bottle to her brother and caught the wheel with both hands to guide the clunky Saturn around the corner, "Can you open that?"

The bottle crashed into Davey's lap with maraca *(Cha! Cha! Cha!)* sound effects. He scooped it into his hand calmly and pressed his palm into the top. The lid shifted down and he gave it a tight twist. The bottle opened and the cap escaped his grip and fell into the gap between his seat and locked door. *Oops.* He thought he should retrieve it, but maybe after his sister wasn't clawing through the air anxiously for the drugs. The plastic safety film stretched over the mouth of the bottle and he had to jam his thumbnail against it to create a small slit. The chemical powder-coated bottle air drifted into the boy's nose and he made a face.

"Get it?" Marilyn questioned while nearly foaming at the mouth.

"Almost." Davey stuck a finger through the gap in the sealant and jarred it back. The plastic and foil combination made a smeared stretching noise that vibrated against his flesh and made his jaw set into a clench. He tipped the bottle and four pills tumbled into his open palm like roly-poly bugs. He pinched two between his fingers and added the other two back to the maraca bottle. Marilyn's hand shot out flat and he dropped them into the center of it.

She smacked her hand up and pressed them one at a time through her lips. She worked the muscles in her cheeks as she conjured up saliva. The acidic pills began to burn the bottom of the bowl she made with her tongue and her muscles contracted to take the saliva and white pills down her throat. She could feel the lump work against her gullet and then pause in her chest like dry bread. She took another sip of saliva and pretended it didn't taste like movie popcorn.

Davey shook his head with amazement, he hardly liked to take the liquid stuff.

"What are you thinking for dinner?" Marilyn had found two twenties and a soggy, buttcrack one in the old shopper's wallet. *Cha-ching.*

Davey leaned himself back in his seat and patted an empty spot on his tummy before he grabbed Bear Kingsley and snuggled him in, "burgers," he answered with a definite craving. He knew Nick hadn't eaten the one he stole the night before. The burger had cooled and rotted in the kitchen trashcan next to a half-devoured apple and oily pizza crust. He sucked his lip in. He wasn't bitter about it—no. Marilyn was safe and that's all that had mattered to him... he just felt sad for the burger. It deserved a better way to go.

He would make it right with this next one.

Marilyn nodded agreeably and took a tight left underneath an abandoned train trestle. The car began to climb the landscape as the road hit the side of a hill and Davey tilted his head against the passenger window to watched tall, green trees pass their car. The Saturn climbed further like it was a roller coaster on a chain lift before they hit a peak and began to wind down the hillside into Grant. The car submerged itself in greenery from either side as the road steepened. Davey's tilted head was moved to be squashed flat into the cold window so he could look up and try to see the sky. The Douglas Firs around them stretched and swayed, their tops masking most of the darkened atmosphere. Fern branches stretched out across the woodsy floor to the right of them and he smiled, then thought of that old book, *Where the Red Fern Grows,* and reversed the expression on his face.

Marilyn thought of her father as Davey admired the passing shrubs, trees, and leaves. She hadn't been set up to think about her Dad, it just happened, suddenly. (As it usually does with the world gets a little quieter and a little darker.) A nostalgic grievance rocked through her and she pressed a palm lightly against her warm temple where the headache still twirled the walls of her drowsy skull. She'd need a third Excedrin. *Or fourth.*

The boy and girl sat in the silence of their rumbling stomachs and the cracked asphalt as it rolled under the Saturn's tires. The engine clicked as the car veered around a slight corner. Marilyn gripped the steering wheel tighter, not putting it past the car to randomly combust into smithereens. It was a piece of shit.

She glanced in her rearview, a routine check all drivers do consciously or not.

She was greeted by an intruder's face.

Elongated and torn, grey rotten flesh and puss-filled eye sockets. A head, attached to a body, leaned forward from her back seats and rested itself over her shoulder. Its beady eyes blinked slowly at her stuck, stunned stare through the thin rearview reflection. its hand slid the length of her arm and helped guide the car along under its grip. Marilyn's head dropped away from the mirror to its fingers coiled around her own dreamily, each one of her nerves depressed and dumb. A hairline slit in the intruder's wrist began to contract as insects emerged. The swell dumped onto Marilyn's own arm like an oozing wound.

Marilyn let out a low gurgle that came from deep inside her chest and flung her hands from the steering wheel to shake the tiny creatures free while she covered her face from the stretched, inhuman, body. Her foot came down, as solid as led, against the brake pedal and the car threw both passengers forward like a gag.

Davey made the gag sound as he collided against his locked seatbelt and Marilyn's low gurgle turned into a high pitched squeal. Davey's mouth opened one size larger than his wide eyes to try to say something to his sister, calm her down, unsure as to *why* she was so afraid –

Madness smashed into the back of their braked car and tore the back end apart like a vicious black monster. It smeared the metal into streaks and sent glass from the rear window up to blanket around the siblings like the teeth inside a rabid animal. The sound slammed through their heads like a firework and Marilyn's hand shot protectively out to her brother, only to be thrown forward towards the front windshield by the darkness that destroyed her car. She could feel her hand, and body, snap forward with the momentum of the blow then be yanked stiff against her driver's seat. Her foot had jammed into the pedal and her knee had hyperextended before her whole leg had lost its gravitational pull and lifted off. They were rag dolls, and without Marilyn's hold against the brake, the car was a self-driving missile. The Saturn chased down the rest of the slope as her muscles were stretched and her joints loosened from themselves to snap across tired tendons. She had a fleeting thought about the noise.

The road was so loud without the back end of her car.

Marilyn's head slammed forward into the rounded wheel as the car finished barreling down the hill and veered off between two Douglas fir for an impacted stop. An explosion, heavier than the imagined tumor, cracked through her for a tenth of a second before being snapped off abruptly by swollen unconsciousness.

PART TWO: MAGNETIC

19

Airbags.

Like clouds of venom set up to stimulate the sensation of breaking your face against a brick wall. If the crash dummies could talk they'd say the same, if not worse, about the airbag invention. *But it saves lives.*

Brent shoved the inflated material down and away from its suffocating hold around him. His nose burned with an acidic fire and his eyes leaked tears to try to put it out. He was disoriented and confused, his thudding headache now a solid lump that slid around his murky noggin. *Perhaps, perhapps... perhafs... you'd been following too close.* He thought drunkenly. His eyes slid closed as he laid his head back against the warm, red flow that bubbled from his nostrils.

Too close he thought again, *tooo close.* The words came to him like the jingle off an old commercial. Sing-songy, hyped, and familiar.

And it feels like I am just too close to love you. There is nothing I can really say-ay-aay. The song played in his head now. He wondered where he'd heard it. Maybe on the radiooo?

Too close.

Too close to what?

"The green Saturn," he mumbled as the taste of blood fell into his mouth and blazed new trails of iron against his tongue. "The green —" An electric shock stung his skin and his eyes were forced open as if he'd awoken from a falling dream. The front of the Toyota was shredded inward like stalagmite needles. It was parked off the road, pulled over neatly like he'd purposefully put it there, but he couldn't remember. The engine was dead and he could hear the hammer of his own blood organ against the inside of his ribcage in the silence of the wreck. *Too close.*

Brent strained his eyes out the broken windshield to a green sheet of crumpled metal wedged between two trees below the dip in the mammoth-sized hill. *Green Saturn.* Talons made of frigid fright jabbed him from every direction, "Dave!" His voice was smothered in bloody gravel. He bludgeoned his body weight into the driver side door and stumbled out onto the quiet road, "Davey!" Static waves rippled through his feet, legs, and hips as he stumbled down the hill to the metal, plastic scrap pile. The numb took over his skull as it had in the store, and he stumbled to the side as the world took a swoop out from under him.

The blood from his nose gurgled in thick strands down his chin and he wiped at it with the sleeve of his jacket. The red goo slicked the cloth material and soaked in. His legs started to shuffle down faster than he could keep up with and he fell pathetically on his butt. Leaves and twigs meshed with the blood on his jacket like an art project as he shuffled with his hands to push himself back up. "Please be alive, please be alive, please be alive," he whimpered as he skidded around the sandwiched car towards the passenger door. Towards Davey.

There was a shrill scream that wrapped his spine in dry ice (like the kind the kids got to see during the school science fair each year) as he reached the partly crunched green door. Brent's lead legs jittered and he fell against it—the world shot sideways, then rounded back slowly like a falling leaf. He groaned and cooled his forehead with the metal of the Saturn's roof. Wicked steam from the car engine bellowed around the man and stung his flushed cheeks like the grey perspiration was made up of wasps, all pissed he'd ran a car into their hive.

The scream hit him twice as hard then and adrenaline escaped into his leaky bloodstream. He dropped his head to look through the car window. *Please be alive, please be alive—*

The girl was slacked against the wheel. *No airbags.* Her head ran red from a rip in her skin and its stream wove over her closed, unswollen, eye. Davey was braced against the passenger door with his body turned towards her. The scream was coming from him, bouncing off her side of the car and ricocheting back to where he sat like a haunting echo.

Brent tore at the car handle with muscles that expanded and cracked like glow sticks.

Davey's head jerked around and expanded at the sight of his counselor as his wild shrieks turned into a name: *Brent! Brent! BRENT!* The boy's voice shook from the pressure he was forcing through his lungs and the man could feel his own vocal cords throb from empathy.

He yanked again at the handle and it pinched the pad of his hand as it snapped back like the mouth of an angry turtle. Smoke began to join the steamy fog in a thicker grey. Brent braced his free hand against the top of the car and ripped once more. The metal creaked but the door stayed firm. Aggression clenched his teeth and he cried through them in frustration. Davey's scream became raw and Brent dropped down so his eyes met the boy's directly with a stretched hand placed against the thick glass that separated them, "Davey!" He called for the boy through his hysterics, "DAVEY!"

The boy hit the window from the other side.

"Breathe!" Brent instructed beneath the exertion from Davey's throat, "Breathe!" He yelled again... and again. He repeated the demand like a broken record until the boy began to tire and cough. Tears boiled out onto his cheeks as he tried to gulp in air through a spasming chest. Brent kept his eyes locked with the boy and hoped they'd stay there. The girl in the passenger seat was fidgeting as she relapsed in and out of consciousness and Davey's panic would come back harder if he noticed. Brent nodded at the boy and tried to smile, "Good job, buddy." He didn't think Davey heard him but he stayed with Brent anyway.

The dark smoke thickened.

The boy feared fire would come next. Through the vents and onto his skin like a thorned tongue.

Thick bubbles of saliva grew and popped in the swollen arch of Davey's lips and his nose flared wildly. Brent could feel another swoop coming at him and he braced his feet against the ground as he focused his attention on each of Davey's bubbles. He tried to remind himself to breathe too as the vertigo spell slammed into him and his hold on the car went numb. He felt the world tip against his body and he forced his eyes shut as he took it on.

His eyes peeled when Davey began to scream again. He'd thought he'd seen that the girl was half awake and rolling her head around in her seat, but that hadn't been it. As Brent's eyes seared open he noticed he was staring into the back seat window. The vertigo had taken a physical hold on him and he had slid to the back, his feet still planted by Davey's door. He looked like he was doing bloody yoga. Davey cried for him to come back. "I'm here, Dave." He murmured against the car and streaked his way back to Davey's window to nod at him. He added, "breathe," to the end of his sentence and wondered how much longer the word would hold meaning to the kid. To himself.

He had to get Davey out soon.

The smoke twirled the inside of his lungs and he hacked into his elbow then fluttered his eyelashes against its sting with teary, red eyes. *Smoke follows beauty*. He grimaced and nodded again at Davey, "I'm gonna get you out." Davey nodded with him and worked on his hard, throbbed breathing. "Okay, listen," his voice quieted with fatigue, "can you get your arm around your seat to unlock the back door?"

Davey tucked his lip into his mouth and shook his head with a timid yes. He then began to turn his head towards the girl so he could crawl between the driver and passenger seat to move to the back.

Brent's hand slapped the face of the window, panicked, and Davey's head snapped back to him before he saw the girl who was now opening and closing her mouth. Brent swallowed to lube his heart back into a steady beat, "eyes on me, kid. Don't take your eyes off of me."

Davey stared at him, frozen.

"Reach your hand around this side," he tapped the door to indicate what he meant, he wanted the boy to slide his hand between his seat and his car door to the back, "keep your eyes on me," he reminded.

Davey obeyed and he kept his swollen eyes on Brent as he slowly turned clockwise and got up on his knees, his arm snaked between the small gap and he had to press his cheek into the headrest to get his fingers to the door lock. He looped the tip of his fingers against it like he had on the lock of the splintered fence and pulled.

The door made a pop and Brent lunged on it. It thrust open and he slid into the car frantically with a grunt of relief. Davey instinctively turned to leap through the gap of the driver and passenger seats, like he'd tried to before, but Brent was on top of him. He grabbed the boy's head and forced it away from the driver's side, adamant he didn't see the girl. "I got you," he promised, "close your eyes."

"Brent!" Davey shrieked against his hand as he tried to muscle his head the other direction—startled by the man's hold. He started to cry again, heavy and solid.

Brent's eyes were wide as he hushed the boy. He ran his thumb against Davey's red cheek to tell him he was trying to be gentle, "Davey, please close your eyes and I'll let go."

Davey hesitated, then shut them, still crying.

"Good," Brent encouraged, "promise to keep them closed?"

Davey squeezed his eyelids together harder.

Brent removed his hand cautiously and leaned forward onto the center console to grab the boy. Davey's arms looped around his neck and he did the same to Davey's lower back as he sucked the boy into him. He began to tip back and wiggle the boy into the back seats.

"Dave —" A female voice gurgled anxiously and a hesitant hand brushed his leg.

Davey's eyes snapped open.

Brent dropped back and tried to yank Davey out of the car before he saw her but it was too late.

"Marilyn!" He screeched into Brent's ear as he writhed against the man to get to her, "MARILYN!" His head bucked into Brent's broken nose and blackness filled his vision like ink drawn fireworks. Brent's hold loosened as pain poisoned his nerves and Davey fled to her, whimpering and howling like a dog.

"Are you all right?! I've called for help!" An out of breath voice bellowed from behind the wreak.

Brent's vision came back as he backed out of the car and turned to a distraught man in a greasy, orange electrician's shirt sprinting at them. The headlights of his stopped van splayed over the road and jabbed into Brent's eyes. He squinted at it, "the girl," he informed the man and pointed over the car, "get the girl out of the driver's seat. She's conscious."

The man looked flushed and frightened but he complied and jogged around the back end of the car, "Jesus Christ," he mumbled as he peered into her window, "oh, Jesus Christ..." Brent tucked back into the car and heard the man cry, "there's a boy!"

Brent nodded though the electrician couldn't see him, "I got him." The electrician opened Marilyn's door with just a few hefty tugs and Brent wondered if they were supposed to remove her from the car?—Then dismissed any concern as Davey's scream pierced an eardrum.

"I'm helping her," the electrician tried to promise the boy.

Brent looped an arm around Davey's waist, "Come on kid, it's alright. We're getting her out." Davey gripped her arm and Brent's free hand looped around the boy's white-knuckled fists, "breathe," he whispered against Davey, "breathe." He coughed at the smoke then reminded Davey once more to "breathe."

Davey twisted his head away from Marilyn and dropped it into Brent's shoulder with a sob.

"Good," Brent soothed, "just breathe." He began to back out of the car again as the electrician worked to remove the girl's seat belt as she watched him groggily, "breathe." He whispered again. He stretched one leg backward out of the car and rubbed soothingly over Davey's back, "almost out." Then added again, "breathe." He lost his balance against the boy's holding weight and braced a hand out against the backseat to keep from tumbling over on top of the kid.

A dark, long hand looped around his wrist like a silver cuff. Brent followed the arm of the holder up, puzzled. A face with broken and extended jowls pressed its rotten forehead into his with a deep internal hiss that turned into a heavy scream, like the screech of an owl.

The counselor stumbled out of the car away from *it* with his own version of a scream. His extended leg buckled and he skinned the back of his head against the door jam. He collapsed to a knee once in the outdoor air and fell against the car.

Davey grunted from the fall then cried out against Brent's neck.

Brent shuffled against the car, back to his feet, and continued to try to comfort the boy, tell him to breathe, but all that came out was distracted, "br-eathe... -eathe." Brent gulped at the world around them as he shuffled back, "bre–". He squeezed the boy against him and trembled his jaw into the kid's hairline, "–eathe."

The *thing*, the face with the jowls, it wasn't in the car any longer and he was in disbelief that it'd been there at all as he wavered to the center of the road. His back of his head throbbed from the lip of the door jam and his heart was beating a heavy echo into the boy's body. He wanted to ask Davey if he was okay, but all he could do was shiver into him and watch the Electrician remove the girl, Marilyn, *Davey's sister*, from the wreck.

20

It started with the sound. The high eerie ring that dropped, spun and gouged out into the trees with urgency. Different pitches but all from the same district. Then the purple, *blue-white-red*, purple line of lights stripped over the top of the hill and the ring became a blast of hot noise.

Davey burrowed his head into the crook of Brent's neck to hide his ears from the scream as the man continued to stare, paralyzed, at the car. The Electrician had stopped trying to get the girl out of her wreckage and had squatted beside her instead, talking to her and keeping her awake. That was good, *good.* Brent wet his lips, *good idea.*

An ambulance raced over the top of the hill first, then an SUV cop, then another, Dodge Charger, cop. Brent turned to watch them then and Davey lifted his teary face to do the same. The vehicles came in and parked in angles. A woman with a ponytail and a light blue jacket had rushed from the ambulance and had taken Davey from the man's arms.

Davey had removed himself from Brent easily and the counselor found himself feeling jealous of it. He followed the woman absently as he thought, *trauma, check him for trauma. You have to evaluate him.* The woman walked Davey to the back end of the ambulance by his hand. She chatted to him casually as they walked for a discrete concussion test. Brent thought: *I'm his counselor, I should help,* then stopped following at once and stood alone blankly.

Another ambulance came over the hill, this time accompanied by the fire department, and Brent wondered if that ambulance was for him.

He was turned around by the SUV cop then and his hand was grabbed for a firm shake, "Officer Hagen," the cop announced, "Brad Hagen. Are you alright, sir?"

Brent slid his eyes to the officer and shook his hand back dumbly, "fine." He blinked at the man a moment and the cold grip of fear from the face in the car started to clump behind his lungs.

Hagen pressed his shaking hand against his hip and eyed the man curiously. "What's your name?"

"Brent." He turned his head over his shoulder for Davey then and the cop cleared his throat, Brent looked back at him.

"And you're sure you're alright? What's your last name, Brent?"

"Fine. Kingsley."

The cop switched his weight and cocked a head at the white-faced man, "can I get a statement from you, Mr. Kingsley?"

21

The world could agree that there are types of nightmares that always seem the most chilling. The ones that still creep in and haunt you years after they were created. The ones that revisit and leave you panting into the dark of your bedroom. Make you question your sleep. *Zzz?* They let you know that you are the only one on God's green earth that understands it and remind you of your inability to explain it correctly. Strangle the emotion down deep in your chest where it burns.

They make you *confident* that you were born a psychopath and the dark, demonic has *finally* bubbled up to the flesh, porcelain surface of the half-built and understood exoskeleton you've made for yourself.

Nightmares and cold sweats that become normal to you. The ones you make friends with. Ones that make you feel the way Brent did when the odd question, "did you see who hit the Saturn?" Left officer Hagen's tight lined mouth. He had nudged his head towards the smoking car in the tree line as the words struck at the counselor.

Brent wanted to be a dick. Tired and distraught he had to pull back from actually laughing into the man's face. Laughing and curdling the blood from his broken nose out over his tongue and shrugging his shoulders sarcastically. Instead, he just stared at the man, dumbfounded, the way you'd stare at a wall after one of those *nightmares.* Officer Hagen tilted his head. *Me, Officer, I hit them.* Brent thought as he lifted his hand up to point across the double yellow line on the road to his 4Runner.

The bitter night wind seemed to absorb into him then stop as the gravity of Brent's pointing hand locked on the vehicle. His throat expanded painfully and his feet sank into the asphalt.

Officer Hagen followed the point and then looked back at Brent with a lifted brow.

Brent dropped his arm foolishly against his aching side and his eyes began to sting.

The Toyota seemed to point a mocking finger back at him from its spot at the shoulder of the road, under the lights of the fire truck and ambulances. Its own headlights on and the engine purred in idle. Its low hazard lights blinked at him and the front grill smiled.

Breathe, he heard his own voice murmur somewhere inside the numb, fairground ride, brain of his. He tried, the way Davey had tried, but his lungs didn't accept the air and it sputtered a gust of wind from his nose. He felt snot ride out with it and splatter over his top lip.

The vehicle didn't have a scratch on it.

"I...`` the thought of lying down. The ground was probably cold and perfect for coddling the hot flash that was beginning to seep through his exhausted body, "I don't know who hit them," He mumbled.

He had wanted to lie down on the road just like he'd wanted to lie down in the store... a night for anywhere naps.

"Did you get a license plate?"

Brent glared at his own three-digit, green tree, three-lettered plate, "no."

"Vehicle?"

Toyota. "I didn't see anyone," he promised the cop, "I'm sorry." But he had seen something. His vision spasmed as he glanced at the green wreck for *it.* That *something.* Like waking up from that nightmare, when you know it'd been in your head but you still stare coldly at the darkest corner in your bedroom for an answer. A reason. A *why*.

Officer Hagen patted Brent's arm sympathetically, "well," he sighed, "you did a great job getting that kid out of the wreck."

Brent looked back at the man with wild eyes. He had a brief thought that he now felt the way serial killers might feel before they took their next victim. Adrenaline buzzed and confused. Convinced of their own insanity. *Like they'd just woken from a nightmare.*

Brent shrugged off the officer's compliment with a red taste still on his tongue.

22

"What's your name?"

"Davey." He responded softly as two latex fingers split his eyelids apart and a thin light dilated his pupils.

"Just Davey, or David?"

The boy gave a double chin away from the light and blinked furiously, "Davey." He sniffed.

"What day is it, Davey?"

"Um...Tuesday?" His other eyelid was forced up by the purple latex and the light dug into it.

"How's your head feel, did you hit it?"

Davey's legs swung from the back end of the ambulance where he sat, "no. It feels sick."

The woman with the ponytail frowned, "sick how?"

The boy massaged his fingertips into his sinuses, "like I have crying snot plugging my nose."

She gave a gentle gestured smile, "but not like you hit it?"

"No." He wanted Brent then. Or Marilyn. His lip started to tremble.

The woman stood back from him and straightened her body, "Can you stand up, Davey?"

He sucked his lip in and began to shuffle his legs up beneath him. He stood shyly inside the ambulance box and felt his face turn red as he looked down at her where she stood in the dirt. He knew then, foolishly, that she meant down on the ground with her. He began to crouch to get on his butt and slide out of the metal box.

The woman shook her head and her ponytail flipped over a shoulder, "no, no, stay up there." She grinned as his eyes flicked to her and he hesitated in a half-crouch, "you're fine up there—in fact, I'll come join you." She crawled into the box and stood in front of the boy.

Davey backed up but his lip fell from his mouth. That had been nice—it was something Brent would've done.

"Can you hold your arms out like this?" She stretched her own upper limbs out horizontally like she was Jesus on the cross, or mimicking the belly of a plane.

Davey locked his fingers together in front of him and removed his eye contact from her.

"It's alright." The woman stepped forward and rubbed his shoulders with the palm of her latex gloves, "I'm just making sure your noggin is all good to go."

Davey looked up through his damp eyelashes at her and thought: *Noggin! Duuuude.* A light smile sprinkled his chapped lips.

She stepped back and stretched her arms back out in their airplane position and Davey copied her with a red face and his lip in his mouth. "Touch your nose with your right hand, like this." She bent her right arm at the elbow and tapped her nose with her middle finger, then stretched her arm back out.

Davey copied her and pretended it didn't show on his face that he felt stupid. His finger squished into the tip of his nose and he noticed for the first time how cold the snot clogged nasal cavity was.

"Good, now left?"

Davey did his left arm the same.

She smiled and nodded at him, "Again, right then left."

The boy paused as he thought about which arm was which, then did it again.

The woman opened her mouth to instruct further when a man dressed in a similar shirt as hers came around to the open mouth of the ambulance. The woman's ponytail whipped as she turned to him and he motioned for her to step down to the dirt with him.

She followed instructions and hopped down. "Hey," she spoke under her breath to him as she stepped closer, "How's the girl?"

The paramedic, Jonathan, glanced at the boy who stood in the box of the emergency vehicle with curious eyes on them. "Good," he positioned his body so the kid couldn't see his lips move, "she's stable. Just really confused. Worried about her brother –"

"Okay, okay," the ponytail woman whispered to show she understood.

"We have her sat up on a gurney, we'd like to wheel her in, but –"

"–her brother."

Jonathan smiled sympathetically, "right."

"I'll take him up front."

"Thank you, Ash." Jonathan gave her a wink and strolled back off for the girl on the gurney.

Ashley turned with her ponytail and stepped back into the box. The ambulance rocked and the boy looked up at her with worry tears bubbled at his water line, "hey Davey!" She chirped, "no reason for those," she pointed to the wet emotions.

Davey wiped at his eyes.

"Want to see something cool?" She asked as she knelt down to meet him at eye level. Ashley held out her hand to him as she heard the wheels of the gurney approaching over the loose gravel asphalt road.

Davey took it and she led him up through the little metal door to the passenger seat.

"Sit down." She instructed kindly and shut the metal door behind them.

Davey studied the electronic road map on the wide computer screen strapped into the Chevrolet ambulance dashboard curiously as he obeyed and crawled into the passenger seat.

"That's so we know where to go," Ashley explained, "someone called our dispatchers and they gave us a map to get to you." She tapped her forefinger into an electronic map pin that showed an animated picture of two cars crashed together.

Davey studied it with muzzled interest.

"And look," she tapped a grey box at the side of the screen, "that gives us a description, so we know what to do when we get here." The box was filled out like a college student's notes, "it says: Green Saturn S-series," she skipped over the line that described the wreck, *just in case,* "two bystanders on sight, two passengers in the car." She then again skipped over the line that suggested an unconscious driver and a possible need for a spinal board.

Davey leaned closer to the screen and began to stretch a hand out to tap it when the driver door popped open and a man slinked in. Davey shot back into the passenger seat like he'd been caught stealing candy and his face burned a cherry red.

The man looked from the boy to Ashley, to the boy again, "it's okay, you can look at that."

Davey side-eyed the heavyweight driver with the silver-rimmed glasses.

"Go for it," he smiled, "did Ashley tell you what it does?"

Davey nodded with his infamous lip tucked.

The man mimicked him, nodding and folding his bottom lip under his teeth, "cool huh?" He asked after his lip slid out.

Davey hummed softly to say it was and began to study it again.

Voices and the shaky gurney wheels neared the box of the ambulance and Ashley tapped the driver's shoulder urgently, "show him the lights and siren, Mike."

Mike adjusted his glasses as he looked back at his coworker with a common understanding, "sure," he said and adjusted his focus to a control panel of switches where a stick shift might be on a manual vehicle. He pushed his fingers into three lit up white switches and the red and white lights that swirled over the windshield stopped.

Davey's head turned and he stared out at the dark sky with interest.

Mike tapped the kid's elbow, "these are the switches for the siren lights, want to try?"

"Yeah," Davey croaked to himself and reached his hand out to press the white switches. The lights on the outside flipped on again and began to twirl overhead. They licked their red and white flicks out over the trees and Davey watched their methodic rhythm.

"Now do you want to try the siren sound?" Ashley encouraged as the gurney bumped up to the back of the ambulance.

Davey nodded.

Mike grabbed a thick gage that looked like a volume nozzle and began to twist it. The sirens whooped and Davey covered his ears and fell back into his seat with an amused smile pasted cautiously to his lips, his eyes wide. Mike scrunched his nose at the screaming red and white lights and waited until the gurney was wiggled up and secure into the box of the emergency vehicle before twisting the sound off. "That's pretty loud and crazy, huh?"

Davey nodded again.

"Want to try it?" Mike lifted his hand away and pointed to the twisty thing.

"Go for it, Davey." Ashley nudged then glanced through the tiny glass window back at her coworkers as they jumped into the box around the girl in the gurney.

Davey did, slowly turning the gauge and flinching as it hollered into the wooded road, but smiling as he did so.

The back ambulance doors pulled shut and locked as Davey played with the siren. Someone patted their hand against the metal door to signify to the driver that they were ready.

Mike shifted the key in the ignition and the ambulance engine rumbled.

Davey turned to Ashley with a wide, worried alert, "where are we going?" His voice peeled anxiously, "where's Marilyn." He began to leave his seat.

Ashley smiled at him nervously as Mike *"Woah"'d* and grabbed the kid's leg.

"She's in the back," Ashley explained, "but you can't see her yet."

"Why?!" Davey's face was flushed and his voice quivered.

Ashley glanced back through the glass window and watched Jonathan absorb blood from the girls head injury into pads of gauze while another EMT opened a sterile kit for stitching. *Bloody Mari.* She turned back to the worried brother, "because they're doing the nose touching test that I did with you, and she can't be distracted."

Davey's eyebrows furrowed and he opened his mouth to protest when Mike spoke up, "want to be copilot?" Davey's hard stare at Ashley turned to the driver as he steered the ambulance away from the side of the road, "control the sirens for me." He instructed this time, rather than ask.

Davey agreed slowly, "okay." He began to turn the volume knob.

Mike laughed and Ashley clapped at the boy, "so awesome! Good job!" Mike pressed the gas and the ambulance ripped down the hill's road towards the hospital.

Davey's smile came back as Ashley reached around him to feed his seatbelt down and lock him in.

23

"My brother." The newly stitched girl graveled from the propped up gurney.

Jonathan stretched his latex gloves off one finger at a time and smiled down at her, "he's up front." The paramedic bounced on his unlocked knees while the ambulance motored around a corner.

She glared from under her head bandage, "great, can I see him?"

She'd come fully to some time while he'd laced synthetic string through her leaky wound and cursed him out for being too kind. *Just fucking get it done,* she had cried at him while the EMT beside him let out a bit of a giggle. "We're worried how he'll take it," Jonathan explained then as he glanced to the front of the boxy vehicle.

The girl pointed to her oozy purple eye dully, "he'll be fine," she promised. "Let me see my brother." The room seemed to move slower than her body and she felt queasy as her eyes squinted. She thought that maybe if she looped an arm around Davey she'd feel better.

"Sure," Jonathan studied her, "how's your head."

It thumped differently than it had back in the store and it made her insides feel like jello. Marilyn grimaced at him and grabbed impatiently at his belt loop like it was the white collar of his shirt, "my brother, please."

Jonathan shuffled around her and knocked on the ambulance's metal door, "she wants to see him." He called against its cool, shiny surface.

Marilyn tried to twist her head around to watch the door open and the boy scamper out to her, but the twist made her vision darken and her tongue flick to the roof of her mouth like a vomit guard, so she just laid her head back instead. The white ceiling jittered above her nauseously as the vehicle bumped over grooves in the road and Marilyn blinked at it as her fingers began to buzz uncomfortably.

Davey's feet hit the ground behind her and she heard him gasp excitedly while Jonathan slid a hand behind her head, "head up girl, head up." He danced his fingers into the back of her skull until she lifted it back up onto her shoulders. The tingle in her fingers began to cool.

"Dave?" She asked and stretched her arm out.

The boy found it and wrapped into it, "Marilyn!" He chirped and nearly jumped onto the gurney with her, "Marilyn!!" He moved and whined like a puppy crying over their owner.

The girl squeezed his cheeks between her weak fingers and twisted his head side to side to check for bruises, or scratches, or stitches like her's. He was clear. Marilyn let out a whimper of relief but her stomach only knotted harder.

"He's A-okay." Jonathan told her as Davey wiggled his face from her hold, "no concussion, seems to be fine." He smiled down at Davey reassuringly, "we want him to get checked out in the emergency room, just to be safe, but I think you got the worst of it." He looked back at Marilyn.

She grinned wide at her brother as he kissed her hand, then wrist, then hugged her arm tight. Davey grinned back at her with the tall-tale smile he always gave when he was trying to hide that he'd been crying. His eyes looked weary and worried, he looked like their father when they were heavy like that. Marilyn's stomach and chest spasmed.

Davey's face dropped slowly, "are you okay, Marilyn?" He reached up and brushed her bangs away from her white face that began to dance the color green. Davey's head snapped around to Jonathan urgently, "she's going to throw up."

Jonathan scrunched his eyebrows at the boy, surprised by his certainty.

Marilyn's hand clenched her brother's arm and he announced it again, "Hurry!! She's going to throw up!!"

The EMT beside the parametric lunged for a pink bucket and shoved it under the girl's head just as she writhed into it with splattering brown liquid scented like acidic movie popcorn. Jonathan grabbed the back of her neck gently as another wave of puke pumped out of her.

Davey sighed calmly and rubbed Marilyn's hand as the EMT pulled the bucket away, "told you."

24

Brent rethought the feelings of a serial killer, certain that the way he'd felt before wasn't it, now was. The chaotic neutral that fried his nerve endings like one dense electrical current was being pulsed through him. Yes, that's how murderers felt before feeding their evil act.

He was in the 4Runner with the vents turned on him in a cool blast as his fingers bent around the pigmented vinyl steering wheel and his eyes pinned to the narrow, unmoving road. Firemen and officers paraded around the scene– Officer Hagen stood out of earshot as a tow truck pried the green wreck from the trees on a wide chain. The bed of the truck dropped and the wreck wheeled onto its black, greasy back. The procedure beep and motioning orange light rhythmically disturbed Brent's pulse and he began to feel frustrated. The *chaotic* in his neutral.

His head panned to the side and he watched the tow truck driver heave the mangled bumper of the Saturn through the broken back window. The window Brent had broken, with the *4Runner*.

His hand strangled his steering wheel and his SUV purred around him, alive even when it shouldn't be.

He'd seen it.

It had been totaled.

A whine began to boil out from the inside of his chest and he cleared his throat to silence it. His head dropped to a tilt against the cool SUV window and the side mirror outside his car frowned at him.

OBJECTS IN MIRROR ARE CLOSER THAN THEY APPEAR

His nose reflected back to him clean, clear and unbroken from above the mirror warning message. His eyes started to seep into a deep red color around the edges as tears paraded over his eyelashes. He was convinced he may need a real ice pick lobotomy, maybe even a straight jacket. A tear leaped out over his cheek and he struck a hand at it. "I'm okay," he tried to convince himself. His breath fogged the window and hid his uninjured reflection.

There was a sudden vacancy on the lively scene of the car accident and Brent's head lifted up to find it. The tow truck driver, a greasy man, stood under the tow truck's orange lights and chatted with Officer Hagen. The orange lights sat still and off and the hazardous beeping had receded. Brent chewed the inside of his cheek. The car was strapped into its place, ready for its graveyard. He studied it as the wind in the vents of his SUV fanned his cheeks.

When he was a teenager a boy two years his senior wrapped a car around a power pole and died.

Brent felt sick.

He had caused that wreck, he hadn't stopped in time. His Toyota had smashed into her Saturn and had sent her and his new student into a line of dark trees. His engine had compressed into the dashboard and his airbags had deployed. His nose had been broken. Frustration licked at him again and he jammed two fingers into the bridge of it and hoped for pain. The kind that made your vision blur and your insides erupt into hot discomfort. There wasn't even as much as a bruise. That whine came back as a low growl and he massaged harder into his nose. He wanted it to be broken. He wanted it all to make sense, but it didn't.

Brent looked out at the star-spangled sky and wondered if God was punishing him.

For what?

"Next time I ask you to do something, you will do it." Amanda's voice broke through his last black mental trash bag and stabbed into him. Brent's face twisted at the memory of her hand clasped against the back of his neck as he wheezed and sobbed over the ledge of wet porcelain. With the bag in his mind open old suppressed memories spilled and he remembered slinking out of the bathtub on his belly that day. He'd cried and crawled naked to her bedroom where his own bed was made up in the corner and had curled into it with Bear Kingsley held against his flipped stomach.

Brent's eyes fluttered to the wreckage on top of the tow truck.

He elbowed his SUV open and dropped out. The dashboard beeped at him to warn that his lights and engine were still on. Brent slammed the door to shut it up.

Davey had left something important to him in that car.

The greasy driver inclined his head at Brent as he walked towards the two chatting men, "can I help you?"

Brent grunted in the man's direction, not rudely, just unable to speak, his headspace fogged with an open foster care trash bag.

"Hey, pal, what do you need." The grease ball of testosterone stepped towards Brent as the counselor paced forward towards the tow truck.

Brent raised a hand at him without looking, like a courtesy wave, "nothing, thank you." He mumbled.

"You alright, sir?" Officer Hagen reached his hand out to the man and then drew it back as Brent dodged his shoulder around it.

"Fine, thanks." Brent reached the truck and wedged his foot into the space between the rusty nutted tire and its lipped frame. With a sturdy hop, his thigh muscles locked forward with heat and his body was propelled for the broken car. He grabbed, like a scrappy cat, at a chunk of metal to keep himself upright and against the tow truck's side.

"Hey!" Offended, oily mitts grabbed the back of Brent's slacks and tugged. His loose hold against the car slipped and the cold, hard material scrapped his palm as he dropped back down to the rough road. The driver stepped up against the counselor with drowsy, bright eyes and hot breath.

Brent slouched back, away from him, "I need to grab something out of that car." He informed the low-amusement truck driver matter-of-factly.

"It doesn't belong to you, bup."

Bup? How strange. A Bud-pup! Brent shook his head at the man who called him *bup*, "I know them —"

"Then tell *them* they can come get whatever they need from the pound."

Brent lifted a hand out of protest as he thought momentarily: *pound? The bup pound!* "It's important," he tried to reason groggily.

Greasy tow truck operator shrugged and clicked his tongue out from behind his rotting teeth. As if to say: *too bad, pussy cat.*

A fit of rage, out of place and not Brent's character, flicked the man's vision, "Hey! Don't be an ass!" He straightened back up to *Mator*.

Officer Hagen intervened then, "what's in the car?" He watched Brent's face as it shifted from painted red and furrowed eyebrows to a slack, embarrassed frown.

The counselor derailed his head off his sturdy posture to the cop, "A bear —" he scratched the back of his neck, "the boy's. I—"

Officer Hagen nodded, "get it."

Brent looked from the cop to the irritated operator, to the car. *Yeah, okay.* He pressed his foot back into the leveraged spot of the tire and launched upward with the same, familiar, burn in his thigh he'd had just a moment before. His hand held firm around the jammed handle of the passenger door this time and he hugged himself into what was left of the car. He stepped over the railing of the tow truck bed and rolled his forehead into the window to see on the inside. A plush foot and a green Excedrin cap poked from the underside of the passenger seat like a mouse and its homemade water dish.

He'd had a pet mouse as a boy, sort of. It was a nuisance to the family, vermin, a pest. There was a lot, in the walls and cupboards, but Brent had been convinced the same one visited every few nights. He'd wake up to it on its hind legs as it peered at him over the guardrail of his tiny, metal, toddler bed. They'd watch each other, frozen. The mouse with its hammering heart, and Brent with his steady breath blown into his pillow. He'd named it something but now couldn't remember.

Amanda had caught that mouse in a trap. She'd chased Brent through the house with it clamped between bar and wood. The trap hadn't killed it. The little thing had been squealing and bobbing its head. She'd made Brent kiss it before she put it out of his bubbly blood mouth misery with the heel of her foot.

Brent could taste the old tears and snot from that day in the back of his throat as he retracted his head back from the fogged window and discreetly shook it.

"Find it?" Officer Hagen called up at him.

Brent's head jolted down to the two men with their hands on their waists as they watched. "Yeah," Brent croaked and the memory absorbed back into a compressed compartment in his mind. "Thanks."

He slid his stomach along the car to the back door. The one Davey had unlocked and Brent had dove through. He took his time now. The handle popped beneath his fingers and the green siding creaked open. He stood on the outside of it and stared in. His eyes scanned the dark back seat littered in glass, wrappers, receipts, and a mangled green bumper. The inside of his cheek began to burn under the grind of his back molars as he searched the clearing, searched for a face.

You've lost it.

He frowned and dipped down into the car.

Glass dug into the soft spots of his hands and knees as he crawled in but didn't break skin. Just probed in a way he hadn't noticed before while with Davey. The cabin housed wind that whistled gently over the ceiling from the vacant back window. He waddled his shoulders through the front seats, over the center console, and dropped his elbows down into the seat Davey had been curled in. The hair on the back of his neck stood like the wind had formed a hand that ran smoothly over his spine. He worked to steady his breathing as his body goose fleshed and his eyes dilated. An eerie heat laid across his back as he snaked a hand down to the bear.

His fingers twirled numbly over its furry foot and he thought again of the mouse. The way its squeak stretched into a mangled cry when Amanda pressed it into Brent's tears and told him to, *"KISS."*

Brent blinked at the shifted floor mat, he wanted out of the car.

He jerked up and the bear came free from beneath the seat adjust bar and flopped in his gripped hand. He shrunk back out of the front and into the back seat like he had when he held Davey. His knees slid back off of the seat and he planted his feet steadily into the metal bed of the tow truck. His eyes flicked up at the back seat and he half expected to meet a foreign face again. The bumper reflected up at him instead, as he fully backed out of the car and slid the door shut.

He jumped down and took the impact of the ground in his knees, his face tightened then relaxed and he hoisted Bear Kingsley up for the two men to see, "thanks."

A sharp glare from the tow truck driver's direction burned Brent but he ignored it.

As he paced back to the 4Runner he brushed the interior stuffing that had snuck out from the bear's shoulder with the middle pad of his finger. He turned the bear over in his hands. *Had the wreck done that?*

25

The sterile green and white hospital walls smelled sick and made the lining of Brent's throat swell with paranoia. He followed plastered plastic signs with arrows to the emergency waiting area with Bear Kingsley strangled in his anxious grip like he was a little boy again. His head ached, the—*I'd like to nap on the ground*—ache and he squinted beneath the fluorescent lights against it.

The waiting room was small and the cushioned, green seats were vacant of patients. A nurse in purple scrubs typed slowly on a double monitor behind a hole in the wall where his desk sat. He didn't pay mind to the man that approached him in the silent, static room.

Brent cleared his throat, "excuse me?"

Distracted eyes met him and the nurse gave a half-hearted smile, "how can I help?"

Brent leaned closer and spoke below his breath like there were others in the room to hear him lie, "my niece and nephew... they were in a car wreck. I'm here to see them." He paused to roll his lips together, "I'm their... " he realized he didn't have to finish the sentence, that it was already implied, but he couldn't stop as the false word dropped from his lips, "uncle." The guilt of the fib set in just a moment later. He squeezed the bear in his hands and began to ring it like a damp towel as his face grew hot. He wasn't good at that, lying. *But she was.* He thought about the girl, how she'd pointed a jittery finger to her swollen eye and giggled an, *"I'm so clumsy. Can't you tell?"*

The nurse turned to the computer without hesitation, "last name?" His hands poised over the keyboard, ready to type.

Brent's eyebrows furrowed together, "Kingsley." They came apart as it took everything in him not to cringe. He was flustered.

The nurse typed, then shook his head, "I'm sorry. No King—"

"Matthews." Brent blurted from the force of embarrassment that had begun to build up in his chest like a bad cough, "their last name is Matthews, I'm sorry." He knew he didn't need to go further, but he did, "I thought you were asking for my last name." He laughed at himself despite the heat in his cheeks. Sweat prickled his underarms and hairline.

The nurse reciprocated the chuckle buoyantly, "that's alright, it happens a lot." He began to type again.

Brent doubted it but thought: *thanks.* And snorted another laugh to himself.

"I'm sorry —"

Matthews, their last name is Matthews, it's Matthews, right? Oh my god —

"Marilyn can't receive visitors right now."

Oh. Brent's face relaxed and his hold on the bear loosened enough for his hands to quit burning, "and Davey?"

The man began to click again, for a second, "David Matthews was checked out of the system already." He looked up at Brent thoughtfully, "My guess if he's with his sister."

"Davey," Brent mumbled to himself.

The man smiled at him with a closed mouth, "If you'd like to wait I'll let you know when visitors are allowed."

"Sure." Brent tried to return the smile, "thank you." He dropped his eyes to the old teddy bear with leaking stuffing, then found a seat.

26

"What spot is most sensitive?" A thick woman with a perm asked tiredly.

Marilyn was hunched over on a hospital bed draped in an incorrectly tied green and blue hospital gown as the specialist ran her fingers down each rung of Marilyn's tender spine. Davey watched from a seat in the corner of the room with their father's worried stare. Marilyn hid her winces for his sake.

"The most sensitive spot?" Curly-Q specialist repeated herself.

Marilyn thought: *All of it, you fucking hag.* But said: "the center of my back." In her ditzy voice.

The woman jammed her fingers under the central vertebrates and Marilyn had to bite back a yelp.

"Here?"

Marilyn's muscles contracted into a corset that made it too hard to breathe, "ye –p." Her breathing hitched and unwanted tears licked her waterline.

The woman stood straight and removed her fingers from Marilyn's spinal cord. Relief spiraled through the girl and cradled her aches. "Okay." The woman took a deep breath of her own, unaware that the action offended the sore girl in front of her, "we are going to get you an X-ray for your thoracic spine. I will have someone bring you a sample cup for urine." Marilyn made a face and the woman clarified, "we need to ensure you're not pregnant before we give you the X-ray."

Marilyn inclined her chin, "ah." She noticed Davey in the corner tasting *thoracic* on his tongue, his eyebrows knitted together in confusion. "I think the nurse lady here meant mid-back, Dave." Her brother looked at her, "that's what that word means."

The woman tipped back onto her heels, "I'm a specialist."

Good for you. Marilyn gave a snotty grin partnered with a nose flare.

The woman, unimpressed with the girl, turned and made her way for the door.

"Oh, hey!" Marilyn called after her as she scooted to the edge of her paper sheeted bed. The woman faced her again. "Are you only X-raying that one spot on my back?" She noted the way the white coat, finger poking, lady shrugged, *some specialist, huh?* "Because everything in my back hurts—and my ribs?" She took a deep breath in and held it like it contained nicotine, "yeah, they don't feel so great." Pain shifted through her like it was playing each rib bone down the length of her side.

The specialist seemed bored, "do your ribs hurt more than your thoracic spine?"

Marilyn exhaled and thought, "no." She answered.

"Then your thoracic is all we need to X-ray." She turned and left the room with her words dangled in the air like dull windchimes.

Marilyn tossed a baseball of concerned looks at her brother who returned it with a light giggle.

"Sounds like a dino." He whispered, "*thorashic-shaurus.*"

Marilyn snorted lightly.

Davey tucked his hands into his chest and stood with his fingers turned out like claws. He began to stomp his old man sneaker feet against the tile while he made aggressive growls from his closed lips. *Tears to T-rex.* Some boy he was.

Marilyn laughed her trademark wild laugh at her brother then held out a pleading hand as her stomach dove into a spasmed throb, "Davey—I swear to

Go—d. You can't ma—ke me laugh right now." She held her abs in the palm of her hand.

Davey stopped and flashed her his trademark shit-eating grin. The one that buried his adult front teeth behind the stretched skin of his lower lip as it stretched up beneath his eyelids.

Knocks hit the room door and Davey shot back into his seat with tense muscles and bones. He licked his stretched lip under his teeth and sucked on it.

Marilyn watched with a gentle frown, she really wished he'd stop doing that.

The door jarred open and a voice slid through, "Marilyn?"

The bandaged girl in an oversized hospital gown tilted her head at the talking door, "yes?"

A young, petite woman poked her head through the gap and smiled warily at the girl before she pushed all the way through. She sported a thin, blonde bun and blue scrubs with a pink *Long John* shirt rolled up to her elbows underneath. "Hi," the lady sighed in the doorway.

She was beautiful, the *natural* beauty kind of beautiful with lifted cheekbones placed like balconies for her sunken brown eyes. She was the type of tiny woman Marilyn imagined would follow a tall Mormon man around. At church, on a long Sunday, with a baby on her hip and three other children running laps around her while her husband caught up with an old *helmet, tie, and bicycle* friend.

Marilyn returned a smile like she hadn't judged the whole woman and a specific religion in a glance, "hi."

The petite woman with blonde hair, brown eyes, and probably a Mormon husband held up a wide twisty-cap-cup—it reminded Marilyn of a jumbo-sized pill bottle. *Xanax—Family-Sized.*

"You need my pee?"

She nodded, "there is a bathroom just down the hall if you'd like me to show you."

Marilyn shuffled to her feet like an old man from a *Lazy Boy* chair, grunt and all, "sure." She shrugged then gave a quick glance over her shoulder to her brother, "are you okay here by yourself?"

Davey bubbled his lip from his mouth and wiped the slobber with the back of his sleeve.

She took it as a yes and stepped out into the hallway.

A wave of vertigo spiraled her vision as a black headache swarmed her concussed skull and she reached out blindly. The nurse gripped her arm to help stabilize the girl as she blinked rapidly to regain her vision. "Jesus," Marilyn hissed while the fluorescent hallway lights beamed down around her like they were strobing.

"You alright?" The tiny woman asked.

Marilyn stared at her feet until the lights adjusted, "I'm fine." Her stomach was knotted again and she suddenly wished Davey had come with them.

"We'll get you some shades, to help with the lights, these fluorescent bulbs aren't the best for concussions."

Marilyn's lip curled. She didn't need *shades*. The headache wasn't from her concussion. It was the same damn one that had hit her at the store. She puffed her cheeks out and willed away the need to vomit.

The nurse that Marilyn depicted as a sad Mormon wife walked alongside her as her feet shuffled a slow pace.

"Do you have kids?" Marilyn asked, then winced at the split of pain through her head.

"Nah," the woman shook her head, "not unless you count cats."

Marilyn's Mormon mom theory withered away and an *Angela* type of petite blonde formed into its place. The girl smiled to herself.

The bathroom was hidden behind a wooden door with wires that stuck out from the top and a sign that read *Door Uses Low Electricity.*

"I assume you don't have children?" The cat-loving nurse asked as she stopped outside the door and turned her head to the hobbling, bandaged girl.

Marilyn made a face. *Quite the assumption, lady.* She snaked her fingers out for the family-sized pill bottle meant for urine, "I guess we'll see, right?" She took the bottle from the nurse with a short laugh.

The blonde gave a weak smile to the joke.

Okayy...

The nurse propped the bathroom door open, "Okay, Marilyn, there are instructions near the toilet on how to get a good urine sample. Do you need assistance?"

Marilyn shook her headache at the woman, "that's okay—I'm really good at peeing."

Still, only a half-smile was given, "alright," the nurse pointed behind her, "just head back to the room when you're done."

"Can do," Marilyn responded while she fought the urge to roll her unswollen eye at the woman. *Take a joke, Angela.*

"Great." The anti-humor blonde turned to leave and Marilyn dipped further into the bathroom. The heavy *low electricity* door clicked shut behind her and she reached a hand out to twist the lock with a *clamp*.

It was a dimly lit and spacious bathroom, which made it easy on her throbbing noggin. Marilyn took slow limbered steps through it, towards the oval toilet with a handrail and emergency use button. *"Push for assistance,"* a sign above it screamed in red lettering. Her hospital gown scattered around her ankles and tickled the top of her feet and she started to shiver. The room was a refrigerator.

Marilyn wondered how much of her backside was showing through the XL gown and who'd seen while she walked down the hallway with *Ms. Humor-Me-Not*. A smile poked her cheek as she decided she didn't care and hoped they had enjoyed the view.

The toilet seat sent jolts of ice through Marilyn's thighs once she sat. *An electric-powered door but not heated seats?* And *I'll be damned!* They really did have instructions on how to pee properly.

Marilyn unscrewed the cap of the canister as she read the laminated poster taped above the smudged, silver toilet-paper dispenser.

Urine Test—Vaginal

Marilyn skimmed the instructions in black printer ink, partnered with cartoon sketches of the process. *"Wipe with a sanitary cloth between labia from the urethra to the anus. With second sanitary cloth —"* Her eyebrows shot up beneath her forehead bandage and a childish giggle fluttered between her and the wall, "I'm just going to pee." She announced to the instructions.

She wedged the unscrewed bottle between her shaky, sore legs and moved her fingers to the grooved lip of the cup—as far from the center of her body as possible. She contracted her upset stomach and forced the pee to drizzle out in a scented burn. She paused every few squirts to make sure her fingers stayed clear of the urine.

Once she became comfortable that she wouldn't piss between her fingers she started to look closer at the room. It was bedroom sized. Probably to fit hospital beds and assisting staff members, she subconsciously glanced at the red button to her right as she thought of *assistance.* There was a white wheel cart in the corner piled with bandages, kleenex and unopened boxes of latex gloves. A broom with an attached dustpan leaned against the wall behind it. *Bathroom—slash—storage closet. Resourceful.*

She was done urinating.

She jiggled the cup out from between her widespread thighs and admired the brown liquid that filled it. "You gotta get more water in your diet." She coached herself.

She screwed the cap on and balanced it on the toilet-paper dispenser so she could wipe, after already considering to drip dry.

The silver-lined, rectangular bathroom mirror was not kind to her. It pointed out the way her coiled hair scruffed like a string through and over her bandage and how badly she needed to scrub the roots with soap. Paranoia slithered up her leg and she pressed a finger into the glass, *no space, leave this place.* Except, there was a space. She frowned at it like she was disappointed someone *wasn't* spying on her, then frowned at her own reflection. Her face slacked tiredly against the pressure of her downturned lips and she thought: *at least my swollen eye doesn't look too out of place now.*

She began to wash her hands in the lukewarm faucet water. She let her hands drop and the water slip around the surface and between her small, dainty fingers. It carried relief into her tight body. She dipped her head forward and groaned. She wanted to shrink herself into the sink and sleep in its warmth.

The walk back to her room was ignominious to most. She waddled with her open robe and urine as it bobbed against the screwed lid of the pill bottle cup. She kept her agitated head high and cheeks clear of red blotched as she haggard along past patients and nurses. If she didn't care, they wouldn't either.

"Hey Dave, want to hold my piss?" She cackled as she squeezed through her hospital room door.

Her good eye met the petite nurse who had been in conversation with her overly uncomfortable (and turned away) little brother, "that's really unsanitary," the nurse scolded.

Ah. So serious.

"I'll take it." She stretched a latex hand out to Marilyn who then handed it over with a pout. The woman shifted around her and left the room like her ass was on fire.

The door clicked shut and Marilyn gave a giggle to her brother, "who pissed in her cereal." Then ironically, Marilyn realized it was her, and it really was her piss.

Davey bit down on his lip and slid it painfully around beneath the clamp of his teeth until it was red, then it fell back in its place, "she was telling me about her cat named David. She thought it was cool that I had the same name."

Marilyn crossed to her bed and slowly sat, "lucky you," she moaned at the intense pain released through her spine as she sat, "did you *meow* at her to see if you and David had the same meow?"

Davey shook his red, smile swollen, cheeks back and forth.

"Good thing," Marilyn sighed, "she might have taken you to add to her cat collection."

27

A man in a grey polo t-shirt came into the room next, unannounced and wheeling a computer cart. His smell of gel deodorant and an outside break time cigarette brushed over Marilyn and a sudden craving for nicotine chased after it.

"Marilyn?" The man asked without looking up. His eyes and mind preoccupied with clearing the cart through the door without any collateral damage.

"Yeah."

"Hi," he gave one sharp glance for an acknowledgment before he dropped his focus to his computer screen, "I'm here to get some information on your motor vehicle accident." His personality was dimmer than the lady's before—his voice only one intonation. Low and lifeless.

This hospital had begun to depress her.

The man clicked through tabs on his portable computer a moment then cleared his throat, "Can you give me a description of the wreck, Marilyn?"

The girl deadpanned at the floor for no reason other than being annoyed by his voice, "yeah." She agreed, then looked up at him.

He stared back, his fingers poised on his keyboard, waiting for her to continue.

Marilyn shifted her gaze to her brother, "we were heading to *Layne's* —" The man tipped an eyebrow at her and she clarified with a wave of her hand and the best eye roll she could give, "The burger place at the bottom of the big hill in town." He nodded and she continued, " I was coming around a corner and I –" her voice dried up. Her lungs sputtered out air like she was suffocating and her vision fogged over in a thick black. The face, leaned forward from the back of her car engulfed her head and she gripped at her chest as the sensation of a heart attack sunk in. Her left arm tingly numb.

How had she forgotten?

The smell of the man in the polo was replaced by the sick stench of rotten flesh pungent and potent as it leaked from the hollow cheeks of the *thing*. The *thing* with the bugs. Marilyn felt as if gaunt arms tightened around her and were violently shaking her back and forth like a wicked porch swing.

The man in the polo said, "*Ma'am?*" But his words were swallowed by Marilyn's thoughts before she could hear him. His voice dragged down like it was anchored in the ocean.

Davey had crossed the room when his sister had silenced and now she felt his hand lock between her fingers. The black faded and her vision came back shaky.

"I can tell you," Davey shied from her side.

The man held a concerned stare on the girl before he turned his attention to the boy.

"We were coming down the big hill –" Davey began to speak. Marilyn pulled herself to his raspy voice to free herself from the face that gaped at her from the back seat of her car.–"A deer jumped out in front of us."

Deer? Marilyn's voice belched inside her head in its first clear and digested thought she'd had since the man walked in. It broke through the meshed poison and the broken pieces of the face seeped back into her deep tissue.

There was no deer! It was a dead THING! She heard herself gasp on the inside–a swallowed panic attack.

"Marilyn stopped the car in time," Davey continued with his story, "but the car behind us didn't."

The man clicked at his keyboard to record the information in the P.C. "And where were you? Tell me again."

"The big hill."

Marilyn's quaking vision relaxed in time to see the man give Davey a snarky look.

"Glen road." She answered tempered and amused as the man in the polo jolted at her bounce back from the trance she was in. She scratched her upper lip with the bottom row of her teeth while her droopy, non-swollen eye, found its way up to the man, "you know. The big hill."

He hovered his fingers over the keys in a delay with his lips perched in a prick pucker.

Davey's fingers sunk deeper between Marilyn's.

28

Brent had been massaging his iris' through his closed eyelids when the nurse in purple scrubs had called to him, "Sir?" He had said in a kind, careful tone. Brent used the same tone with children who weren't used to him. Children who were afraid. Children like Davey. It brought Brent's attention forward and he blinked the dark spots out of his vision to see the nurse standing behind his desk.

Brent's mouth was parted and he swallowed to replenish the dry pocket, then stood.

"Sir," the nurse grinned at the tall, weary man, "she can take visitors now."

Brent's stomach tightened and he contemplated a sprint to the bathroom.

The nurse took his seat and slid a pen and visitor sticker—pre-printed on a sticky stock card—through the gap between his desk and the walls that blocked visitors from the emergency hallways. Brent shuffled his feet to it and tucked the bear under his arm to scribble his name on the black line. He removed the sticker from its wax backing and stood in front of the nurse with the name tag stuck to his finger, its sides flopped over.

The nurse grinned up at the man, "you'll hear the door click—" he pointed an extended arm around the barricading wall attached to his desk to a wide door on Brent's end, "—then you can enter. She will be in room eight, just down the hall." His arm hooked back around to his side and he pointed his thumb over his shoulder at the hall behind him.

Brent eyed the door. It was a strong material of white powder-coated paint over metal. A yellow caution sign was plastered under a rectangular window and Brent could see the black letters on the circular sticker but couldn't pick them out. He imagined they spelled out a warning: *It's bad back here. Do you really want to enter? Man who lies about being an uncle?* Or something like that—if his conscience had written it anyway.

The visitor stick-on badge started to feel heavy against his finger, "thanks," Brent nodded absently to the nurse and stuck it to the top of his peck. His fingers rubbed it in and his pounding heart greeted them as a reminder that he really just wanted to sit back down. Bear Kingsley was dropped out from under his arm and he stuck his finger through the rip in its cloth shoulder. The stuffing was warm and he held onto it as he slunk over to the door.

His hand wrapped around its hooked metal doorknob. The door didn't budge and he relapsed back to getting Davey out of the car. Then Davey screaming. Then the face—*Oh noo.* His stomach pole-vaulted.

"After the click." The male nurse reminded him.

Right...

Click.

29

Brent doubled over outside room eight with Bear Kingsley held to his mouth as he tried to catch his breath. He pulsed feverishly and the hallway slipped gently from left to right. He grabbed the wall to stable himself and forced his eyelids over his vision. He'd had an inner ear infection once that had greased the world up and spun it on metal tracks but this vertigo couldn't compare. This vertigo brought tears to his eyes.

Brent fumbled madly for the door handle as his gut spindled inside of his body and his skin began to buzz in an opposite rhythm. He waited for a nurse or a doctor to rush up behind him and put their hand on his back. He waited for the touch, the flat hand on his spine, and the *"are you okay, sir?"* But it didn't come. Instead, his own hand made contact with the thin metal grip and he jerked it down with a deep breath into the plush toy's fur.

His head numbed and the world stopped spinning like a parent's hand would stop the back and forth of a toddler's swing. The ice pick in and the lobe detached. He stood straight and pried his eyes open to see a blurry image of a bandaged girl as she rubbed furious circles into her temples with the fatty part of her palms.

Her hands dropped as an icy relief washed through her like a needle had filled her with novocaine, and she stared at the disheveled man who'd just burst through her hospital room door with a stuffed animal pressed against his nose and lips. *A bear and a gas mask, all in one.*

The bear fell to his side, "I told them I was your uncle," he blurted while his wide eyes searched her single clear one. The colorless pale on his face began to fill with a cherry red as a heatwave scratched at his neck.

Davey leapt off the bed in a solid motion with an accompanied yelp of excitement as his little feet bounded to the door. His arms clamped around the width of Brent's waist in a strong-armed hug like he was a vertical bear trap. The man placed a hand between the boy's shoulder blades as an effort to hug back—but didn't remove his attention from the girl.

"Who are you?" Marilyn asked the man but was watching her brother with a bit of bewilderment as he snuggled into the stranger's body. Her head bobbed with the numb bulb that filled her skull and she tried to place his familiar face in her foggy memory.

The man looked guilty, "this hospital needs better security, they just *believed* that I was your uncle. Without question; I could be anyone, I could be insane," he rambled and as far as she was concerned, he was. *Insane,* that is.

Marilyn watched him, through jet-lagged vision, as he stumbled further into the room to let the door fall shut. The door made a solid slam as hinge met metal and the air became tighter in her lungs.

Her brother released the hug he had on the man's waist and lower torso and stepped back to look up at him, a stretched and bright smile drawn beneath his cheeks held up his wide, puppy eyes. She'd never seen Davey smile like that at anyone. *Who the hell are you?*

The man's tired eyes fell to the boy's and for a second Marilyn saw him relax. It was brief, his shoulders fell forward the red in his face softened to a less-harsh pink.

She recognized him then.

He had been in the store earlier—she had given him a daring, flirtatious show. Then she'd fantasized about his tall, handsome figure while she tried to rip the lid off the Excedrin. Then she'd thrown the Excedrin at Davey. Then, *the face in her back seat.* Marilyn's entire body shuttered and her mouth dried.

How do you know Davey?

Davey looped his fingers around the fuzzy jumble the man had been breathing through and pulled it into his own arms, "Beary!" He hugged the toy to his chest, "thank you!"

"Sure, bud," Brent whispered with a hoarse voice, "how are you doing?"

Davey grinned up at him, "breathing."

Breathe, Breathe, Breathe. Brent smiled, "that's good, good job." His eyes drifted back to Marilyn.

She noticed he wasn't as handsome now with his face flushed and his eyes dilated. (Granted, she wasn't a sight for sore eyes either.) She fought the urge to tug at the itching bandage around her head.

"Brent," he said, to answer the question she thought he had ignored, "I'm Brent."

Davey spun on his heel to his sister, "uhuh!" He nodded his head goofily like he belonged with the cast of *Little Rascals,* "Brent Kingsley! I told you about him yesterday!" Her brother hoisted the stuffed animal into her face.

Her head tilted back away from it and her chin doubled against her neck, "you said your best friend gave this to you."

"Yeah!" Davey turned his head innocently back and gave his grin to the man.

Brent watched Marilyn's jaw set forward and her eyes slowly slid back to him, her swollen one half-casted, but still potent.

Brent's hand shot out between them in defense: *No, stop! Don't think like that.* "I'm his school counselor." He explained with a rim of panic to his voice, *not a freak.*

She didn't look convinced, "how did you know we were here?"

Uh. I followed you.

"Brent got me out of the car, Marilyn." Davey spoke matter-of-factly for the man, "he got me and the electricity man got you. But he's not here —" Davey squinted at Brent, "right?"

Brent nodded slowly at him, "right. He's —" *I rear-ended you,* "he's not here. He went home." *You were unconscious and I was pulling your brother out of your totaled car because I was following you too close.* That song came back to him, just for a second, and he remembered he had heard it on the radio *—in 2011?* It was by that Alex Clare guy. *Too close to love you.*

Funny what comes back from the black pocket in your subconscious sometimes.

Davey shrugged then moved away from him, back to the hospital bed. He lifted himself up on the lip of it and twisted to settle down against the material on his butt. He scooted from there with his thighs, wiggled one-by-one until he was back against the hospital wall with Bear Kingsley in his lap.

Brent looked over to a chair longingly, his knees at a quiver, "may I?" He gestured the hand he'd just held out for moral protection to the green seat, hesitantly.

She nodded without following the gesture then watched him as he moved to the chair. He sat in it uncomfortably and tilted forward with his elbows on his knees and his fingers knitted together. The man glanced up into her eyes and his face said something strange. Inquisitive and mysterious. Something she couldn't quite pick out. Like his expression was as blatant as a sharpied question mark on his forehead but the reason was as foreign as tongues. The numb inside her started to tingle.

Davey patted her hand.

She looked to her brother and Brent dropped his stare to the floor, the space in his head vibrantly cool and warm and spinning, like a gentle tornado.

"Brent's favorite book is Super Fudge," Davey spoke as if his breathing couldn't keep up with his words, the excitement all too much, "do you remember when you read that one to me?"

Marilyn nodded.

Davey continued, "I told him Matilda was my favorite—do you remember when you read that?" The *"—one to me"* was implied that time.

Marilyn nodded again, this time with a slight smile that felt a little forced, "yes, I do."

"I told Brent that he's like Miss Honey."

Her eyes went back to the man and he met her with parted lips like he wanted to say something. She normally cared less about what men had to say, but at that moment, as his lips fell apart and his tongue met with his teeth to form words, she encouraged it. She wanted an explanation to whatever the fuck this night was. She wanted him to fix it. Fix it with the words that start with his tongue on his teeth.

A knock hit the door like a painful jab before petite—Catwoman—nurse walked in. Brent's mouth fell closed and Marilyn's temper fell angry. Her head pivoted to the woman who smiled at her unknowingly. "Are you ready for your X-ray, Marilyn?" She ignored the two males in the room with her words and with her eyes as she addressed the bandaged girl.

Marilyn felt cold as she responded, "sure." She held her breath as she slid her ass to the edge of the bed then let it out in short bursts as she stood. The nurse reached out a hand, and despite her irritation, Marilyn took it.

Brent stood too and ran his hands into his pockets. The sense of being unwelcome manifested in him and he cursed himself for coming back to see the siblings. In hindsight, he hadn't known why he did, or what answers he was looking for. He—

Marilyn's eyes pierced him from over her turned shoulder, "Stay here with Davey, *Uncle Brent.*" A demand.

His face dropped pale again and he slowly sat back down into the seat. He mimicked her response to the nurse quietly, "sure."

30

A wheelchair was parked on the other side of the door when Marilyn came out. *Right, because I didn't just walk to the bathroom and back.* She would've verbally been an ass but her thoughts were on the man behind her and her mouth wanted to stay wired closed as she contemplated him. She took a seat in its leather hammock bottom and dropped her arms over the cold, black, Twinkie-sized, armrests. The nurse kicked off the wheel lock and began to guide the wheelchair forward.

The numb in Marilyn's head faded and a wicked sting leaked into its place. It filled the seams of her twisted brain matter and her vision collapsed. Darkness filtered in, then the room bounced back into view, a darker shade—like it was hidden beneath a shadow—but there, all the same. "Fuck," Marilyn grumbled below her breath as nausea made a nest in her belly.

The wind that whipped around her as the nurse wheeled her tried to help by cooling the air that went into her lungs and body, but only seemed to strangle her instead. It was a familiar sensation. A car-sick girl in the far back of a hot vehicle with the air conditioning blasting through the vents onto her cheeks. It tried to help, but the artificial smell of car engine and dusty vent only made it worse. *Would someone please just let me put my head out of the window?* Marilyn knew that girl well.

The nurse stopped Marilyn in front of double wide hospital doors, windowless like boarded up French doors. She leaned around the girl and slid a key card against a magnetic strip. The doors lock clicked open and a green light above the strip flickered happily. Marilyn was then being used as a doorstop to prop the heavy wood open so both patient and petite nurse could get through the opening before it swung shut and locked again. She'd never felt more useless in her life than she did as the wheelchair doorstop with the swimming brain.

Petite nurse maneuvered the girl down the long hallway of fluorescent lights that poked her concussion and strange headache. Marilyn puffed her cheeks out and fanned a flat palm into the center of her stomach.

"You alright?" The nurse asked.

"Fine," Marilyn lied.

They wheeled passed closed rooms, different than the hospital rooms in the ER. They were windowless like the French doors. It made them more secluded in the long, unpopulated hallway with the mustard yellow walls and white trim.

Marilyn entertained the idea of what may go on behind the tall wooden doors. Maybe private test labs, or a porn studio. A smile tickled her dry lips at the honest, perverted, thought that came from deep inside the sexuality of her psyche. They stopped outside an open door to a dark room and Marilyn thought it was her turn to find out: *The doctor will see you now.*

The nurse pivoted the wheelchair, so both females faced the opposite of the door, then backed in.

"Hello!"

Marilyn twisted her head over her shoulder towards the voice.

A weighted woman with faded pink hair smiled at her, "I'm Janice, I'll be helping you with your X-ray."

Marilyn was turned in her seat by the petite nurse so she could give a weak smile to the pink dyed woman. She hobbled out of the chair, careful not to clip her ankles on the footrest. "Thanks for the ride," she sidelined to the nurse.

Petite–Catwoman–nurse nodded at the two females, "sure." She parked the wheelchair in the corner of the room and left without any more words to say.

Marilyn hated her.

Janice looped her warm, soft hand around Marilyn's wrist and unknowingly pulled the girl out of the mental funnel she was in as she led her to the X-ray, "I'm sorry you were in a motor vehicle accident," Janice spoke boldly, a thawing relief after trying to have a conversation with Catwoman nurse.

Marilyn eyed the machine as they approached it, "s'fine. Everyone is alright," she murmured towards the mechanical arm that slid on gears from the top of the ceiling. It reminded the girl of the handled light above a dentist's chair or an assembly arm over a conveyor belt. Like it might pick up her rag doll body, remove the dead battery from her back, then replace it with a new one– full of bolts and electricity. It'd drop her back to the belt and she'd be off, like the Energizer Bunny. But no, it was only a camera on a gyro arm in front of a radiation wave billboard.

"What kind of car was it?"

Marilyn turned her head to the woman who watched her kindly beneath the pink puffs of hair on the top of her head, "a stupid, green, piece of shit." Marilyn answered truthfully.

Janice snorted at the girl's remark, "I had a car like that, once," she smiled to herself and moved Marilyn between the machine and extended arm.

The arm stared at Marilyn with lights, sectioned into four, like it was an insect. A centipede. Snaked down to intimidate her–*it was working.*

Janice turned Marilyn away from the centipede arm and placed her shoulder lightly into the wall of the machine, "hold your arms out." She instructed.

Marilyn did, like a zombie.

"Okay," Janice tapped the girl's elbows until her arms were level with her shoulders, "don't wiggle or anything."

Marilyn closed her eyes and focused on her still body as the world twisted against her. The woman adjusted the arm so its four eye-like lights were adjacent to Marilyn's right rib cage.

"Okay," Janice said again as she scampered her curvy body to a desk hidden by the angle in the room, "Deep breath in," she instructed from around the wall.

Marilyn absorbed the air around her and her brain felt as though the pressure of wind into her lungs had crashed it against the front of her skull, she bit back a whimper.

"Breathe out."

Marilyn's lips parted and the air burst from them like a balloon popped as the four lights flashed and her body warmed.

The silence amplified the buzz of the machine as it worked to provide data to the pink-haired radiologic technician. The girl opened her mouth to say something, anything to kill the drone of the machine when a giggle filled the silent space instead. Janice's head popped around the wall, "are you still wearing your bra?" She had a smirk that said it'd showed up in her X-ray photos.

Marilyn glanced down at her chest, "yeah," she said then thought: *no, my tits are always this perfectly round and plushy.*

"Can you remove it?"

"Sure," Marilyn struggled to get her arms around to the back of her. Her tongue protruded from her mouth as her fingers began to tingle and her rotator cuffs burned as her hands crawled along to her bra buckle. Her fingers fought to loop around the material to squeeze the two stretched ends together. Blood began to pulse into her face.

"May I help?" Janice crossed the room to the eighteen-year-old gimp.

Marilyn huffed out a wave of frustration, "please," and as the woman's hands grabbed at the back of her bra she thought again of her porn studio theory.

Ms. X-ray will remove your bra now.

The bra bounced open and she tilted her shoulders forward to give it enough slack to slide to her elbows. The pads brushed her abdomen and her nipples went erect. She frowned at them as they arose through the material of the oversized sheet. Marilyn shrunk her arms in through the pooled sleeves of the gown and then again through the straps of the bra to free herself from it completely. It fell past her and landed against her ankles.

"Oops." Janice tipped over to collect the support material. As she dropped her pink ponytail flipped over the top of her and dangled across her forehead. On the way back up it whipped behind her with fanned air that smelled nice over Marilyn's face. She took the bra and draped it over a back handle of the vacant wheelchair. She side-eyed Marilyn kindly, "arms out, hun," she reminded as she moved back to her hiding spot behind the wall.

Marilyn extended her arms back through the hospital *blanket* with sleeves and held them out. She felt free, loose, and cold now. The breeze in the distilled room swept through the spaces of the gown and spun around the underside of her breasts. A chill rippled through her body and she stomped a dizzy foot against it.

"Stay still." Janice's voice called from the hidden desk.

Marilyn gnawed her teeth together to silence the quiver and the camera lights flashed again.

31

Brent lifted his head to watch his young friend sit cross-legged in the hospital bed while he played with Bear Kingsley's protruding stuffing. A smile held between his cheeks. He seemed fine, the last image of Davey hyperventilating as he screamed and vibrated now seemed foreign. Like a dream, or an old, old memory.

Brent leaned back into his chair and slid his feet out in front of him as he considered possible trauma or lack thereof. The purple Crayola drawing crossed the foreground of his mind and he felt pity. Not for the boy this time, but for himself. The fear of the drawing had driven to this moment. *Driven and crashed.* His jaw set forward and he bit down against the pink flesh blanketed around crowned molars. His head throbbed against the bite and he rubbed the bridge of his nose.

"Sorry," the boy's voice pinched him and he looked up despite the ache of the fluorescent lights. Davey held a ball of stuffing between two tight fingers and said it again, "sorry." He motioned towards the soft mess that rained from his index and thumb.

Brent's closed mouth spread into a pained, thin-line smile at the white airy fluff and he held his hand out for it, "It's okay, kid." Davey released the cloudy material and it floated gracefully into Brent's cupped hand, tickling his skin, "did Bear's arm get hurt from the car wreck?"

Davey's hand retracted and he tucked it beneath a thigh in his crossed lap anxiously, "no," his eyes passed Brent's like they had when they first met and his lip sunk into its damp hiding place behind his front adult teeth.

Brent nodded, "okay, that's good!" He wouldn't press.

Instead, he furrowed his eyebrows back down and rolled the stuffing around the defined lines of his palm. Its willow curls brushed each folded ripple and wrinkle and Brent remembered being in an old town chapel then.

He remembered being tucked in, next to Amanda. His hair had been parted to the side in thick gel and he wore a hint of Dad Onslows' cologne. It smelled woodsy and tart.

His vision darkened and he thought he could smell it then, at the hospital, under his headache.

Amanda had been playing circles into his palm to keep him calm and focused on the short, hairless pastor that walked the stage in front of the pews and the people.

"Relevance," the pastor had said, "we see what's in front of us, we see our places in the world."

Brent had surveyed the room in front of him and had thought: *I see church people.*

"Now imagine," the man had raised an open palm, "what you see, what you know—*everything* you know is a tiny, little, corner of a painting."

The church people focused forward, so Brent did too, though he hadn't understood.

"Imagine the *Mona Lisa*." The pastor closed his eyes and scrunched his nose, "everybody see it?"

The crowd nodded, their own eyes closed, imagining. Brent had nodded too, even if he couldn't see the *Monta Leeza* like the adults.

"Now imagine that you step very close to that beautiful painting. So close to it that all you are able to see is the iris of her right eye." He'd smiled and his closed eyelids smiled with him as he *imagined*. "You study every detail of that iris. Every brush stroke. The color palette. The history. Its reason. You are a *scholar* in the information and detail of that iris. That iris becomes your entire life. To you—the *Mona Lisa* is a painting of a right eye's iris." He'd paused to swallow his salivated mouth, "That's all you can see, that's all you know, that's what you believe." The pastor's eyes slid back open and he looked out over his people, "now, step back from the iris and take in each and every detail."

Nobody had stepped back, everyone was in their seats, Brent had cocked his head at everyone's stillness.

"Did you step back?" The pastor asked with excitement.

The crowd nodded and Brent had shaken his head no, they hadn't. Not in real life, at least, just in their heads.

The pastor smiled with achievement, "That's what our God sees."

There were hums of understanding that buzzed through the room, carrying the occasional *"amens"* on its back.

"We see only the smallest portion of God's plan." He nodded along with the crowd, "we say 'God, all you have given us is an iris?? I am bored with this. I have studied it, I have loved it, I have lived with it—is this it?!" The pastor had bitten down on his lip in excitement and shook his hands at the glory of God, "and our God says 'No, that is not it, child. There are eyelashes, and veins, and flesh, and eyebrows, and wrinkles, and tear ducts, lips, nose, ears, hair, clothing, hands, trees."

The crowd had leaned back in their chairs like they could see it all then.

"But you, you can only imagine and see the iris." The pastor crossed the stage as he prepared breath for his grand finale, "Be patient, have faith, and I will reveal to you the whole painting if you are willing."

The fuzz stopped being rolled against his palm and the man stared forward as the memory broke away from him. He hadn't understood that message then, but he wondered if he did now –

"Nick did it." Davey's raspy voice was held back and reserved.

Brent's attention was brought to the boy, "what's that, bud?"

Davey ran the ripped arm of the bear through his fingers, "Nick," he sighed, "I live with him."

Brent lifted his eyebrows and nodded as if this was the first he'd heard of Davey's roommate. *Who the fuck is calling me in the middle of the night?* Brent winced like Davey could hear the cuss word scrape through the man's mind. "Nick ripped his arm?" He asked gently and watched as Davey folded into himself.

"Sorry."

Brent shook his head and the room ricocheted around him, "not your fault." He held a hand out for the plush toy.

Davey hesitated and gripped harder to the stuffed animal, "are you taking Beary away from me?"

"No," Brent smiled soothingly at the boy and noted the nickname he'd given the bear, "*Beary* has a hurt arm and –" He studied the room through foggy vision, "– we're in a hospital, kid."

Davey watched his counselor as he brought his arms out and released the bear into Brent's stuffing-less hand, "They'll fix him for us?" Davey knew a hospital wasn't a toy shop—but maybe there was a secret deal the adults could work out?

Brent's soft smile spread into a wrinkled grin as he stuffed the plush innards he'd been balling around his palm back into the slit in the bear's shoulder like a quarter into the pocket of a pair of jeans. "No, but we can bandage his arm, and then I'll take him home to a friend of mine—she's a stuffed bear doctor." He meant Winnifred, she wasn't any kind of doctor, but she had skills with stitching. He tilted his head as he thought about it and his eyes caught a blue and purple counter with a line of drawers below it. He stood, "don't tell the nurse, Davey," he pressed a finger into a cheeky smile and winked at the kid.

He took the bear over to the counter and knelt to drawer level. His finger hooked around the thin silver bar served as a handle and flicked it towards him. The drawer slid easily against its rollers. The sound was a slight sensory overload to the aching man as it surrounded him and he grimaced to himself. His back hunched a little and his shoulders felt heavy in their sockets, he hoped Davey didn't notice as he straightened back up. The drawer was a surplus of bandaids, popsicle sticks, ear swabs, purple latex gloves, and brown gauze, the kind nurses wrap around a cotton pad after drawing blood. Brent scooped it into his hand and his thumb grazed the material thoughtfully, "Hey, pal?" He spoke at the drawer as he closed it.

"Yeah?"

Brent turned his weighted shoulders and moved back to his seat while Davey questioned him with his stare. He tuned into Davey's facial expressions and body language as he dropped down into his seat nonchalantly, "did Nick also hurt Marilyn's eye?" He tapped at the corner of his own as if he was pointing out a piece of food at the corner of someone's mouth. Davey's lip went in and his eyes squinted. Brent lowered his curious, kind stare to give the boy room to think as he unraveled the gauze slowly in his hands.

"Yeah," Davey's squeaked voice rubbed like sandpaper against Brent's sensitive skin.

He nodded anyway, cooly and matter-of-factly, "okay," he acknowledged. He worked his fingers against the edge of the gauze until it tore in a thin, diagonal line then looked back up at Davey who was using the backs of his hands to cool his flared cheeks.

"Please don't tell her I told you," the boy whined into a bit of a panic.

Brent wrapped the gap in Bear Kingsley's shoulder seam with the gauze as the pulse in his head beat hotter, "sure, buddy," he chewed his cheek without saying the words, *'I promise.'* It wasn't his business, but Davey's well being was. *Too close.*

Davey sighed and his rubbing hands pulled at his tiring eyelids as a yawn widened his mouth and flexed his tiny stomach in spurts of sucked oxygen.

Bear Kingsley's arm hung gimp and oblong against his potbelly side after Brent tied off a knot in the brown wrap. Davey scratched his own shoulder cuff nervously as he studied the gauze. It reminded him of a bad time, a bad time with mom. The bad time when she'd yanked him off of Marilyn's lap and accidentally broke his arm. The time that ended with Marilyn fighting for custody of him in a courtroom that had flags like the flags outside of Grant Elementary's library.

Brent had given the bear back without an idea of the thoughts that ran through Davey's head as the boy had yawned again. The man frowned as the boy's face settled with discomfort, "why don't you take a nap?" He suggested and wished he could do the same for himself, "it's been a crazy few hours, kid." Had it been a few hours? He glanced out of the shaded windows at the darkness that shielded the building and guessed that it *felt like* nine at night.

Davey had smiled at the man like he wanted to protest, but as his smile grew his eyelids drooped and his eyelashes seemed to curl into a sleepy mist. He'd laid down then and turned his back to Brent with Bear Kingsley between his curled arms.

Brent began to think back to the pastor... and Amanda's fingers that trailed over his young hand. The thought lasted long and was interrupted by a light puttered snore gurgled from the boy's nose. Brent smiled sympathetically at the back of him and tried to lay his own head back against the wall. His eyelids created a warm, clammy mask over his vision and a heavy stench spread under his lip. The face from the car painted itself into the black canvas of his closed eyes and something hard and fingered coiled around his ankle.

His foot was yanked beneath the chair and he shot forward with a sharp gasp that quivered his lips and pinned his eyes open. Like someone waking from a falling dream. The hospital room chilled and the stench vanished.

Davey stirred quietly against the paper sheets and Brent panted as his heart slammed against the inside of his throat and the skin on his face tightened.

The man tilted his head into the palm of his hand and caught his breathing between quaky fingers.

32

Marilyn's head popped against the tip of her spine as she stood from the wheelchair and stumbled into the room. Brent flinched and pinched at the flesh that held his temples as the vertigo passed and a numb spread through the both of them and filled their ears with cotton.

He met her concerned stare with collected certainty and she threw her gaze away from him, maybe out of fright. Her bra was secure around her chest again but Marilyn could feel the knot that held the gown together begin to slip. She focused on that, rather than the numb space that cookie cut its way into her brain matter.

Her head twitched unwillingly as she noticed Davey asleep soundly on the hospital bed and a warmth swooped in like a blanket around her shivering, revealing skin. His lips were mashed together, his hair flopped over into the pillow, and his eyelids flicked as he dreamt. She hadn't thought she'd been in the X-ray room that long, but noticed now that the window no longer showed orange sunset spots through the bubbled plastic.

The warm dropped from her as her eyes went back to Brent who was slouched sideways in his chair. He had been watching her when her eyes turned back and now they met. He held the stare and pursed his lips forward as his head shook to say: *no, I left your brother alone.* It was a slow shake, a determined, serious, shake. *Not. A. Freak.* He was adamant about it.

Marilyn crossed to the bed and slowly sat, careful not to wiggle her tired brother awake.

"Marilyn," The tiny nurse with the cat obsession noticed the sleeping boy as well as she spoke in only a high whisper, "you can get dressed now." She passed her voice to Brent, "you need to leave, sir. You can wait for your niece in the waiting room. It's almost time to release her."

"Sure." The man's voice was husky and dry.

The nurse left with the wheelchair and Brent stood after her, his knees cracked as his legs stretched and Marilyn watched as an uncomprehended glance from the man hit her brother. She watched him cross the room to the door that had fallen shut hesitantly and her mouth opened.

"Hey," she broke the silence between them, "what the fuck is wrong with your head?" She was a no-nonsense girl. Blurt it out and see what happens kinda gal.

Brent spun on his heel and stared at her like she'd slapped him in the face, "what?" He wobbled upright and she wondered if he'd gotten cramps in his stomach just then like she had.

She scooped a fingernail through her ear to try to clear out the numb buzz that filled it as she answered, "who in their right mind would lie about being a relative to a child they hardly know." When she'd asked she hadn't meant what was wrong with him *mentally,* she'd meant physically. *What was physically wrong with both of their heads.* They both knew that, too, but she admired as Brent stepped back to his seat and dropped into it to play along with her nervous mind game.

His arms rested against the arms of the chair and he shrugged.

Marilyn turned her head to her brother and trailed a tired hand over him to tug at the plush toy in his sleepy grasp. She smiled as his fists tightened around it. Brent could see her youth then, as she smiled, under the stress and bandages. Only a kid.

"Did you wrap the bear's arm?" Her voice was like a sheet of glass that slid straight through his skull and rested itself in the numb hole drilled between his own thoughts.

Brent scratched slowly at the shadows on his cheek then dragged his fingers to his neck to massage at its sore muscles as he spoke, "yeah, I figured it'd make him feel less anxious." Marilyn squinted at him, confused and unimpressed, so he made a motion to his own shoulder like he was removing stuffing from it, "he kept picking at the tear," he shrugged again and tilted his mouth to the side, "so I took the desire to do that away." His hand was done rubbing so he dropped it to his lap, "reduces his anxiety."

Marilyn tilted her head back and her dark swollen eye caught the light.

"It's stress-related," he pressed at his bottom lip, "just like Davey's lip sucking habit."

Her own, upper lip curled towards her pink nose, "you pay a lot of attention to my brother." She tilted back to intimidated him with her purple bruised stare.

Brent's own head inclined to match it, "it's my job."

"Right. *Counselor.*" Her eyes rolled back far enough to see her spine as she turned her head back to her brother. He studied as she pinched Davey's hair between her fingers while she stroked it away from his dreaming eyes.

"I called your house today—a man named Nick answered." *His sister is shit at keeping track of him.* Nick's voice teased in the corridor of Brent's internal thoughts.

Marilyn looked irritated, "yeah? He's my roommate."

Brent stretched his legs out, "that's what I hear," he waited until their eyes caught to continue, "does he have any kind of custody of Davey?" *Too close.*

Her eyebrows knitted as the question filled her with discomfort, "no."

"Good," Brent made a point to look directly at her injured eye. *Too close.* It caught him below a thin film of pain and for a moment he felt guilty as the air in the room thinned. He waited for an out lash, her to call him a quack and kick him out of the room she'd so nicely let him sit in for the past hour, but the out lash never came. Instead, she gave him silence. Brent respected her for it.

The silence dragged on and they both ended up watching Davey with weary stares and slow heartbeats.

"Why are you here?" She killed the silence, something Brent had begun to realize she was really good at.

His mouth opened, then closed, then opened again to dry as he just stared at her. He wasn't sure how to answer her question. His eyebrows now the ones that twisted with discomfort.

Marilyn lipped a hint of a smile that had begun to creep around her mouth.

"I'm the one who rear-ended you." His words dropped her smirk. Marilyn could kill the silence, but Brent could bring it back. Yin and yang. *Too close.* He bit his cheek as the silence grew and he felt obligated to continue, *try his hand in the killing,* "I don't know why I was following you, honestly. I had been worried about your brother —" he trailed off as he considered telling her *why* then decided that was for another time, "—I saw him in your car when you were at the store—and I don't know... I followed." He laughed at himself, "I don't know what I would've done once you reached where you were going. I probably would've kept driving." He heard the word *probably* slid from his lips and focused on it shamefully.

She waved her hand dismissively at his long babble, "you rear-ended me."

His eyes glassed over, "yes."

"Why did I slam on my breaks?" She had scooted to the edge of the paper bed and was leaned far enough forward for her hospital gown to slip down her shoulders.

Brent didn't pay mind to the soft, olive skin that stretched over her collar bones—his eyes kept at direct pace with her's, "I was hoping you could tell me."

She frowned, "what did you see?" He could hear the slightest pinch of panic laced in with her earthy voice.

"Nothing."

"Davey said I stopped for a deer."

Brent's nose flared as he shook his head no. *No,* there was no deer.

33

Marilyn shook her head 'no' along with him because she had known that. There hadn't been a deer. *Nothing* was on the outside of her car. *Something* had been on the inside. She lifted her fallen gown back over her shoulders and thought for a moment that she had appreciated that the man hadn't taken the opportunity to look. *To fantasize.*

Maybe she trusted him.

Brent pressed around his temples like he had been doing when she first walked into the room. She studied him and became re-aware of her own spacey brain. "What's wrong with your head?" She asked again, without the cussing, and with the true answer being sought: the physical one that included both of them.

She watched his cheekbones sink and his eyes broke away from her, "it's raw," he scoffed and rubbed his fingers into his eyelids until purple dots and green squiggles appeared before he looked back at the girl and shrugged like he was frustrated, "numb."

Her chest had been fluttering nervously until now. It stopped like a solid rock and its ragged edges dragged down her windpipe, "so you feel it too?" She spoke hollowly.

Brent's rubby hands found his mouth and massaged at his lips as his eyes drifted off again. It was what they'd both been waiting for—the connection—the other to say they had felt it too. He sucked at a pocket of air, "I felt it in the store, I felt it when I was following you and —"

"Now," she seemed relieved as a smile drifted up under her nose, "and when we're close, but not close enough it —"

"Hurts," he shook his head and laughed at how insane they sounded at that moment. A sad laugh, a gust of wiggly wind.

"Yeah," she tugged at the hair that was stuck inside her head bandage, "so what the fuck is that about." Brent mumbled something about an iris that she didn't quite catch, "what?" she asked almost irritable.

The man frowned like she'd pulled him away from an important thought, "nothing." His body shivered as she flared simultaneously into goosebumps. *We're seeing more than Mona Lisa's eye.*

Marilyn trailed a hand through Davey's hair again as she thought, "this is retarded," she decided with a whisper.

Brent gave no comment to her offensive complaint, only turned his head and surveyed a whiteboard that was pinned up behind him. It had a *'Rate Your Pain'* chart taped to the bottom of its whiteface, complete with cartoon faces seemingly uglier as the numbers above them counted up. He stretched his arm above his twisted head for a group of magnets collected in a corner of the whiteboard. He delicately used his nubbed fingernails to scrap two black, double-sided magnets away from the others in the corner. They clacked together as they flipped to opposite sides in the center of his hand. Ceramic Ferrite Magnets.

Marilyn remembered playing with magnets like that in grade school for a science unit. She watched as Brent removed them from each other like they were the chocolate wafers of an Oreo. He held them out in his open hand, away from each other. She tried to come off as disinterested but her stare was already locked in.

Brent held one above the other and began to press down against it. An invisible vortex held them apart like a clear ball of jelly was wedged between the two black circles. He increased his strength between the magnets and the top magnet started to throw itself from left to right. *Like poles repel.*

He released the resisting magnet and it flipped to attach to the other. *Opposites attract.*

"Try it, tell me what you think," Brent spoke in a courteous whisper to avoid waking her brother that she'd almost forgotten was there.

Brent held his hand out to her like an offering and she scooped the magnets from his palm. The tips of her fingers felt his calloused skin in that fragment of time and she felt dizzy from the touch, for a reason she thought might be different than their fucked up brain connection. She savored the touch, nonetheless, while Brent paid no mind and dropped his extended hand to his lap casually.

She pulled the magnets apart like he had, like they were sharing Oreos, and flipped them so like poles faced one another. She forced them towards one another and the top magnet twitched below the pads of her fingers, it wanted to turn, it wanted to connect with the other magnet badly. But the invisible ball and her hands wouldn't let it so it just quivered against her. Afraid, angry. She smiled at the sensation of resistance between the dark grey disks.

"Dad, try to push these together!"

Her father laughed as he picked up her two found magnets from their wooden kitchen table and began to force the two North poles together, "Isn't that the most satisfying feeling? Marilyn Mae," He batted his eyes at his daughter as her nickname left his mouth.

"I think," The memory absorbed and her adult voice spat out into the hospital room, "It feels exactly like the inside of my head right now."

Brent knew that. "Mine too," his voice was calm like he'd accepted it, but his heart puttered like he was soon expecting to wake from a bad dream. It was laid out in front of them and it still seemed to be only nonsense. A trip to the looney bin was sure to come about all of this. He shut his eyes as he sighed and the face from the car flashed across them like headlights, "you're right," his eyes pinned open, "this is retarded." He smirked at himself as he said it and an imitation of foolishness settled in around him.

A light exhale snort blew across Marilyn's upper lip and she smirked too. The silence was back, but this time it came with a sense of relief.

Relief that set in hard, until they both began to watch Davey sleep again. *Davey said it was a deer.* Brent felt his relief chill away by a wool blanket of fear. Davey saw only a deer. The man could taste the concern at the back of his tongue like it was a bubble of acidic vomit. His uvula danced around it like a witch around a sacrifice. It spilled over his tongue and through his lips, "we have to keep him innocent." The girl with the bandage and slippery hospital gown extracted her eyebrows as she tried to navigate what he meant. Brent pointed at the boy, "he saw only a deer, if we tell him about any of this he might –"

"Oh please," the girl's bitterness and eye rolls were back.

Brent's hand came up like a traffic cop stop sign, "–if we tell him about any of this he might start seeing whatever made you slam on your breaks."

Marilyn's face shot pale and green undertones spread just below her cheekbones.

"When I grabbed Davey from the car this person grabbed my wrist and–" he shook his head as the clammy hand tightened a phantom hold over his flesh, "its face –"

Marilyn's soft palate pressed down like a gag, "yeah, it was–fucking–," her dilated eye jostled hands with Brent as she shook her head, "– that *thing* was in my back seat." She yanked at her ratted hair then as stoned cooled her expression, "that was not a *person,*" her words hissed through her teeth.

Brent thought of its hung jowl, "we can't tell Davey."

She nodded, then swallowed heavily, her eye rolls tucked away again. The magnets in her hand folded together with a snap. They caught the flesh on her thumb in a tight pinch and she threw them at the floor, "fuck me!"

Marilyn wasn't the most elegant young woman Brent had ever met, but he assumed she'd never had the chance to experience elegance. He filtered a light laugh as he decided her sailor's mouth didn't bother him. She was spunky–like Winnifred.

Winnifred was probably home asleep, unaware of her good friend's absence. She had no reason to know his whereabouts or keep tabs, she was only an old neighbor he grew a liking to. However, the sense of her being so unknowing made his gut fill and boil with a type of grievance. The kind a heart tastes and reports the flavor to your mind without involving the taste buds or the tongue. She was in the dark, and Brent was in a hospital room with a young girl and a little boy, in his own kind of dark.

The hospital door swung open and an instinctual pulse sent Brent's arm to the floored magnets and he scooped them into his palm safely.

"Sir?" Brent hid the magnets between his fingers as he turned his attention to the pried door. The small nurse stood in its opening, "you need to go to the waiting room," the corner of her forehead lifted into wrinkles in a way that made Brent slightly uncomfortable–like a misbehaving child caught by a foster parent.

"Sorry," Brent stood and slid the magnets back onto the whiteboard.

Marilyn stood with him and her gown slid over her shoulders again. As she adjusted her clothing she asked calmly, "Uncle Brent, can you take Davey with you."

He looked to the boy, then back to her.

She smiled at his confusion, "I'll be out after I'm dressed."

Brent crossed the room cautiously and leaned in to wake him but she stopped the man with a cool look.

Marilyn made a cradle motion with her arms, "He's a heavy sleeper, you know that, Uncle B." She winked at him the best she could with her swollen eye and he was transported back to the store when he first watched the little con artist. She was good at her job.

"Right." He smiled at her as he suddenly felt bare and ridiculous. He carefully squished his arms under the sleeping boy and as they snaked beneath him Brent's sleeves jammed up past his elbows in an uncomfortable scrunch. Davey's body curved itself into Brent's chest as he pulled up like a weightlifter. Brent suddenly felt like he might drop the boy as he stepped back, the boy's body soft like a wet noodle, he clung Davey to his chest.

"Don't forget Beary," Marilyn warned as she picked the stuffed animal that had fallen from Davey's arms and tossed the fuzzy body about the two of them. It had crashed against the kid's horizontal chest and his tiny, dreaming nose wiggled.

"Yeah, thanks," Brent's voice was strained as he worked to support the dead, wiggle weight.

34

The two teetered down the hallway as the boy's weight sunk into Brent's long arms. Yesterday the two of them had laundered through a hallway hand in hand as they admired school art. Now, the boy snored into the man's chest with their stuffed animal balanced in the space between them.

Brent caught the eye of a grinning nurse and returned the smile with a kind, embarrassed nod as he passed her with the eight-year-old baby draped over his bent elbows.

Once in the waiting room, he noticed the male nurse who had let him in to see the siblings was gone, off shift for the night, back in early tomorrow. "Hi," he greeted as he moved past the woman who had taken the nurse's spot.

"You've got your hands full," she snorted after him.

Brent gave a good-natured grunt into her direction and rounded a jumble of chairs to a long cushioned, bench in the back of the room. He slouched forward over it and tried to find the best angle to lay Davey down. He decided that he could turn and sit back but feared the boy's weight might thrust against him and he'd stumble back against the hard window behind the bench. The orb in his mind stung and the upper half of his sore, aching spine begged him not to try it.

He blinked at the bench, his head was *so* foggy.

The idea to tip Davey from his arms onto the cushions did cross his mind, but the bench was shifting forward and back from the vertigo Marilyn gave him and the image of Davey being rolled out of his arms and missing the bench flipped over his head. He frowned.

This was a little *too* ridiculous.

"Hey pal," He wiggled Davey between his arms, "Davey, wake up." He spoke softly near the boy's ear.

His hooded eyelids gave a thick flutter but unconsciousness stayed hidden behind his snores.

"Davey." A little louder, "come on, kid."

Sticky hot lids popped open and sleep coated eyelashes brushed the red in the corners of the white.

Brent smiled at him, "hey, bud."

They slid shut.

"Wow."

35

Davey dreamt he was on a boat. It voyaged through a dark canal as tender waves guided it by kneading up on the back of it like the head of a purring kitten. The cool air grew warm against his cheeks and he heard a sharp crinkle of metal meeting stone. He ran his silent feet to the edge of the boat with strong fears of a leak. He stretched his neck over the rail to see the rock, stuck below the surface of the tepid water, *(hey pal,)* the voice tickled his ears. Was the rock talking to him? *(Davey, wake up.)*

Wake up?

"I am awake!" He told the rock but couldn't hear his voice, he waved his hands at the stone, "I am awake!" His voice swallowed beneath the mist and he frowned. The boat kept cutting water as it went forward and the rock seemed to ride along beside it. Davey began to stretch his hand out towards its rugged surface that began to break through the top layer of wavy water. The rusty rail jabbed into his stomach and his feet lifted off of the wet deck. They became overbearingly heavy like all the blood in his body suddenly rushed into his ankles.

(Davey!) The call of his name startled him and he stumbled off the railing and onto his back in a puddle of wet ship planks, *(come on, kid.)*

"I'm sorry!" He apologized to the rock as the cavern his boat was entering suddenly grew bright, so bright that it stung his eyes until tears began to sooth them. For a moment, in the bright, he swore the canal tunnel walls had old ceiling fans twisted on them. Like the windmills that covered the hills of *the Dalles*.

Then it was night again, *(wow.)* He heard the rock marvel as the walls darkened again, except this time he was sure there were windmills that generated air and waves around his swaying ship. He stood and began to move back to the edge to look over at the rock and ask what it wanted.

Giant arms snuck around the bow of his boat and grabbed his arms. They lifted and flung him through the air. His heavy led feet swung away from him and stretched his body like sea salt taffy.

Davey's eyes snapped open and took in the swaying room around him. Brent, who had him held bridal style had dropped his back feet and was hoisting the boy in the air by the underside of his armpits. The *arms*.

"Sorry, buddy," Brent's voice was quiet and smooth in the buzzing room, "I needed you to wake up." He set the boy to his tingling feet and held him by the shoulders as both staggered forward a little.

Davey reared himself to the bench and sunk onto it as Brent moved to sit next to him. " I was dreaming –" Davey spoke with a fuzzy tongue as his eyes worked to take in the room, "I think you were the rock," He mumbled.

The counselor juggled a laugh as Davey tipped against him with aching eyelids.

"Where are we?" He asked as he tried to take in the details of the chair filled room.

"The waiting room," Brent tucked the bear against Davey and Davey took it to press against his tired face without thought. "We are waiting for your sister. She's getting dressed."

Davey nodded into the man's stomach and began to shut his eyes.

The sound of the rushing water hits his ears first like a wet blanket. He could feel Brent's warmth pressed against his temple and could see the yellow waiting room lights against his eyelids that turned them a pink/orange—but he could hear his canal water as it lapped the sides of the green bellied boat. He was stuck like that, in the *in-between.*

Brent's jacket made a cloth crumble sound against the boy's ear as he draped an arm over Davey's shoulder. The light touch brought Davey back into reality for a moment. The liquid lap shockingly replaced by hospital white noise. Davey felt a pool of saliva collecting at the corner of his mouth and he slurped at it as he faded back into his dream.

He could see the boat now, under his feet. He moved back to the rail and peered over at the rock. He smiled at it without a reason. "Hi," he spoke to it and this time his voice was heard. He began to reach over the edge for it again.

"Okay pal," he felt the squeeze on his shoulder, "get up."

Davey forced his eyes to open and felt naked as the boat and water vanished.

Brent sat up in a straighter line, "Marilyn's coming out."

Davey stacked his arms beneath him to lift his groggy head up high enough to see over the hospital chairs. He frowned at the wide emergency door because Marilyn was not there. Maybe Brent had thought he saw her, Davey understood that. He'd done that once —when he'd thought a stranger was his sister and he'd grabbed their hands. He remembered how embarrassed he'd felt and didn't want Brent to feel the same so he smiled and nodded to the man who didn't notice him and continued to sit attentive to the door. Davey lowered his eyes to Brent's lap and noticed the circle of drool shamefully. *Whoops.*

He'd begun to lay his head back down into his saliva for a third attempt to sleep soundly when he'd heard it. The sound of stone and metal meeting in a drowned *'click'.* Davey's head pushed back up and he watched as the emergency door swung open and out stepped his sister dressed in jeans and her white *Billabong* sweatshirt.

Brent had a faint smile that lightened his features as he watched the girl pass the nurse at the desk. He'd felt her as she came towards the door, his head had pulsed along with her sneakered footsteps.

Marilyn's hair was nappy and a bandage no longer hid the black stitches above her eyebrow. Brent frowned at them, he'd done that.

"Hey stink!" She called happily to her brother who sat all the way up, his cheek imprinted in the wrinkles of Brent's clothing, "you're awake!"

"Yeah, sorry," Brent apologized from beside the joyful boy as the tingle of the novocaine numb set in between the male and female.

She gave him a coy grin as she moved around the chairs to her brother to give him a kiss. It was a light peck on the lips, but Brent looked away all the same.

His eyes squeezed shut for a moment and he cursed foster care for only providing two black trash bags as a memory tore through the last of his second mental bag and tracked around the inside of his lobe triumphantly.

36

The nurse behind the desk tilted her head at Marilyn with a bit of confusion.

Marilyn smiled back innocently, "I need to get checked out," she informed the front desk woman, "Marilyn Matthews." There was a silent stare between the two women and Marilyn wondered if the nurse had a hearing issue, she opened her mouth to repeat herself when the nurse began to giggle.

It was a mocking giggle. One that started as a boil in her potbelly and hightailed up into a whined nasal and the woman's eyes squinted and her tongue danced on her top teeth, "who said you could leave your room?"

Marilyn tipped back on her heel like the giggle had nudged her with its elbow.

Brent, who was still sat back on the bench with Davey, felt irritation nuzzle into the empty spot in his head. Not his own—hers.

"The little nurse with the bad attitude said I could leave after I got dressed," bitter vinegar rimmed her low spoke voice.

The nurse at the desk bellowed an ugly laugh partnered with spaced snorts. She shook her head at Marilyn like the girl had given her the best comedy material of the year. Marilyn responded with crossed arms and a popped out hip.

Uh-oh. Brent could feel her irritation begin to trickle into a hot pool of anger.

"You have to go back in," the nurse continued to laugh, "a doctor has to clear you, sweetheart."

That was a nice touch, *sweetheart.* Brent sat forward on the bench as he felt Marilyn's hot temper ripple through him at the use of the word, his own frustration meeting her halfway.

"Oh sure, *fatass.*" Marilyn's words spat out like a bad taste was in her mouth, "laugh at the girl with *fucking* stitches and a concussion."

The laughter stopped and the woman's eyebrows lifted like she was shocked at the outcome, "calm down sweetie." She reached for the release button that unlocked the emergency door, "I'll just let you back in," she smiled with her words, but it was pinched like she was smelling shit.

Marilyn shook her head with her own laugh, "no need to unlock the door, *honey.*" She spoke with bubbles as she pointed to the visible hallway behind the nurse's desk, "I can just go through here."

"Oh no," Brent mumbled.

Marilyn's knee was the first to make contact with the thin plastic desk and she lunged onto it, her hands splayed out in front of her as she fell into a position to crawl, like a dog through a dog door.

The woman gasped and slid her chair back away from the girl who entered from the cutout hole in the wall between emergency rooms and emergency waiting area. Marilyn's body knocked a pencil holder and it crashed to the ground, "I'm going to call the cops, I'm going to call security, what are you doing?" The woman was panting pathetically.

Marilyn pulled herself through the entire window and slid her feet to the floor on the nurse's side. As she stood she dusted off her knees and smiled with a corner of her mouth, revealing straight teeth and an angled canine tooth, "I'm not hurting anyone, sweetheart," she shrugged and straightened the hoodie to her sweatshirt, "just trying to get back to my room." She spun and strolled out of the open-backed office to the hallway.

The nurse sat, rooted in her spot, as her eyes sharply glided to the man on the bench.

Brent found it hard not to smirk at the rude nurse as Marilyn's satisfaction snuggled into his inner thoughts as it now pulsed with their proximate distance.

Davey yawned, already immune to hot-headed situations from eight years of life with Marilyn Mae Matthews.

Brent's cheeks were red. Brent, the red-tomato-fever-flesh. He sat back into the bench and let the pain in his head press down into the roof of his mouth. Like wisdom teeth, or new braces. Davey cuddled next to him as he stroked Bear Kingsley's gauzed arm, his thoughts back on the boat dream.

When Marilyn exited the heavy door a second time she came with papers folded in her hand and a head held high on her shoulders. Brent's legs gave a slight twitch with her hips as they swayed their way into the waiting room. Both of their heads relieved into a numb same-poles-repel wade.

Marilyn pointed to the boys, "I assume you're giving us a ride, Uncle Brent," she winked at him with her purple eye, "since my car is, you know, *totaled.*"

He stood with a nod, he owed her that much.

Davey joined him with a loopy, slow blink of his eyelids. He was still so tired and planned to let his clammy lids down in the car. It'd help him keep away from his worry of more wandering road-deers, anyway.

Brent picked his visiter sticker off and placed a light touch to Davey's shoulder as they moved to the stitched sister. Marilyn took her brother's hand and pointed to the hallway Brent had slowly moved through an hour earlier with Bear Kingsley being rung in his fists. She pointed with a look of curiosity as if to say *parked out there?*

Brent nodded.

The boy and girl began to walk but Brent found his feet stuck in their spot, the nurse at the desk window to his left. He could feel her judgment and sober stun being cast over them like a fog machine, her eyes darkly laid against Marilyn.

Brent pivoted to face her. His jaw was set tight, "miss," he addressed her with an alert stare, "a hospital is no place for a bully who snickers at patients. I would seriously consider finding a new job." He spoke in bitter storm swirls.

The woman sucked her teeth at him.

Marilyn had stopped her and Davey's leaving walk and watched Brent with a lifted eyebrow, "wow, you're so threatening, Uncle B." She brimmed with sarcasm and passed a grin from over her shoulder, one identical to the smile she'd given him back at the store where he'd meant to get photos developed, "but thank you, anyway." She'd actually meant it.

Davey, who clutched her hand and Bear Kingsley tightly was also smiling at his counselor.

Brent frowned, "okay, let's go."

He felt foolish and suddenly belittled by the Matthews' children.

37

Bitter and biting air coated the outer walls of the hospital like a well-swaddled baby. Darkness hung overhead but the parking lot lights gave a lit pathway that stretched around the parked cars and their creeping shadows. It was silent—the highway cars that passed made for a hollow mask of white noise. The air whipped colder around them, if at all possible as they walked. The fall humidity froze the raw skin inside their noses as tiny cloud puffs danced away from their faces with every breath. Winter would hit Oregon soon enough to kill the last of the surrounding state forest fires and fill the valley floor like a swimming pool.

"Where'd you park? Tim-buck-two?" Marilyn joked as she fought the need to clatter her teeth together.

A billowed puff of white air left the man as he exhaled, "sure seems like it, I'm in the back." He removed a hand from his front pocket and pointed. Marilyn followed the direction of his dry finger but lost it, she didn't know what kind of car she was supposed to search for. "Are you sure you're comfortable with me giving you a ride?"

There was a hesitation and their eyes met and Davey's breath was the only white cloud in that moment. Brent's face said concern, her's inquired.

"Yes," She gripped Davey's hand a little harder and gave him a reassuring grin. If she was honest with herself, and if she were alone with him, there wouldn't have been a hesitation. She would've sprinted to the man's vehicle with her clothes already half off. Like a skimpy one shot. But, with Davey, she hesitated. For him. Besides, the man wasn't interested in the girl half his age, not while she had stitches and knotted hair, that is. She looked away from him and watched as the parked cars to her right bobbed by.

"I can find you another way home, Marilyn. If you're nervous."

The idea sort of offended her, and Brent had felt it. Although, he wasn't sure if it was felt between the shared pull at their minds or if it was empathetic as he read it off her thinly pulled lips.

"I want to go with Brent," Davey added his two cents while he studied his sister from his tiny height.

"We are," she insured, "because he's going to take us out to eat!" She shot a smirk to the counselor.

"Sure," the man shrugged thoughtfully, "I can do that."

The boy gave a light cheer and skipped his old man sneakers over the pavement in an excited, hungry jig. As a child his age would, of course. Even a shy one.

The three of them rounded a row of cars and came face-to-face with the black 4Runner, tucked away at the literal end of the white-lined lot.

"This is us," Brent nodded to the silent vehicle. The vehicle's secluded location toyed with his gut and he couldn't imagine the flips that must be in her's. As he pressed against his upset stomach it occurred to him that she could turn it against him. *The man confused us and took us in the dark to his hidden SUV.* She could say anything along those lines and he'd have no proof of innocence. Hospital cams only show so much. Like him, walking children to his Toyota in the back of the parking lot.

The man peered over his shoulder at a security camera that watched from a light post. *You'd lose your job.*

She wouldn't do that. *The girl who conned an old man of his wallet right in front of the counselor bystander.*

Brent risked a surveyed glance at the girl then and the cool air pocketed against his expanded red pours. She had a twisted glare heat pressed into her expressions as she returned his glance with her feet planted still into the ground.

"You said you hit me," she whispered, but not kindly.

Brent dropped his head for a moment, then lifted it back up to study his black vehicle, "Yes, well... " He gave her a stare from the corner of her eye, "The *deer* wasn't the only strange thing to occur tonight, right?" He spoke below a mumble to avoid Davey's curious attention.

Marilyn sanded her lips together.

They proceeded to the 4Runner where Marilyn had to swallow a knot in her throat before nudging Davey into the back seat.

38

It was the drive-thru of the old burger joint that they ended up shuffling through, due to a young boy's groggy request from the back seat of the 4Runner.

Brent had taken the highway to avoid Glen road. For Davey, it was to miss the opportunity to see the smooshed deer decorated with red guts from its ripped skin. For the driver and bruised passenger, it was out of fear. Afraid of what might reappear to haunt them.

Marilyn chewed her fingernails as the car coasted from the lit menu sign to the waiting space just before the pick-up window. She'd only ordered a fry. Not too hungry. The truck in front of them had a lost tail light, the red shell cracked and the bulb shattered. Marilyn concentrated on it as the man beside her tapped his steering wheel. His car smelled like a tropical car freshener and soft linen. Though, Marilyn assumed the linen was the man himself. Clean cut and kind.

She spat a chewed nail out the passenger side window and imagined it twirled like a helicopter leaf from a maple tree. She wondered if the wind had caught and carried her nails against the black SUV and made Brent's car into a *Chia Pet* of nail clippings. She put another finger into her mouth, tore, and spit.

I took the desire away—reduces anxiety.

She dropped her chewed hand to her lap, no longer interested in the flavor of skin and nail. She *wasn't* anxious. The nails on the drive-thru floor, and possibly passenger side of the car, begged to differ.

The truck with the broken tail light budged forward, their order complete and received through their crank truck window. Brent began to follow the man for their turn to stare helplessly into the restaurant window as they waited for their dinner. The single tail light in front of them flashed and Marilyn yelped unexpectedly as Brent's foot jammed the break. Her whole stomach lurched forward with a full-body flinch as the Toyota stopped abruptly behind the culprit, braked truck. The sudden stop dominoed through the line like a bad rippled wave and Marilyn felt her temper beam through her forehead. *Fat fuck.*

Brent had put a hand out like a mother would when sliding too quickly into a red light stop and gave the girl a sad look, "I'm sorry," he gave an attempted comfort smile, "PTSD is no joke."

Marilyn glared back, annoyed.

Brent went back to the light finger taps on his wheel as he waited patiently.

The truck with the tail light finished its roll forward and took a sharp turn out of the curved drive. Not sharp enough, however, to miss the right curb as the truck bounced over it. Marilyn thought again: *fat fuck.*

The pay and pick up window slipped open with a bang and the wafting scent of burgers overtook the tropical air freshener car and Brent's clean linen smell. Marilyn's stomach rumbled hard and she knew that soon she would regret her single order of fries.

Brent retrieved his wallet from his front pocket and Marilyn noted which pocket exactly and how far it'd been lodged in. She did not plan to rob the man that made her head numb, it had just been a habit—to *observe.* He removed a red, plastic card from its second-to-the-bottom leather pocket and handed it to the young teen who leaned out the fast-food window. A teen Marilyn was thankful she didn't recognize—a teen without a southern drawl.

The plastic rectangle came back stacked on top of a pile of tan napkins. He took it off and held the napkins out to Marilyn.

"Your food will be out in just a moment," the teen with a large headset smiled.

Brent smiled too, with closed lips, "no problem."

Marilyn slid the napkins from his turned hand and began to distribute them as Brent brought his head away from the now shut window. She gave Davey extra and threw Brent's into his lap as he focused on his wallet to wiggle the debit back into its thin, leather slot.

Careful Uncle B, if your wallet gets stolen the perp could drain your bank account with that debit. It's safer to have a credit —

The window slammed back to its open position and Marilyn gave it a dirty look. A brown bag was thrust out into the air with a dark underside saturated in copper grease—easy to see even in the dark.

"Thank you," Brent accepted the bag and brought it through the car window.

"Have a nice night, folks."

Brent assembly lined the bag to Marilyn without looking, as he had with the napkins, and she took it.

"You too," Brent replied to the window clerk as they pulled away and his window was rolled up by an automatic button. A pair of car headlights took their spot at the window as they left the line.

Davey had been first to break into his burger as he took each bite and morsel as praise from God himself. He'd also been the one to eat the quickest and have the biggest tummy bloat.

Brent had slowed the car down at a stoplight as they all ate and had chewed a fry as the front end of the 4Runner grew increasingly close to a stopped Beemer in front of them. Without thought, and no real reason to, Marilyn slammed her hand into the passenger door and gripped furiously at the handle with sprawled fingers. She braced herself for a *bang.* For her body to be thrust forward and her head to follow on an awful delay. Except, she wondered if it happened in reverse when you were the hitter and not the *hittee*.

Probably.

Brent would know.

The 4Runner stopped smoothly at a safe distance from the vehicle in front and the man gave her another apologetic look, partnered with his own bit of panic, "I am so sorry, Marilyn."

Marilyn broke her hand away from the door and looked forward.

Davey had started to nod off in the back seat. The swoosh of tires on the highway and the rock of the SUV reminded him of the boat. *The boat.* His stomach worked to digest his inhale of food and his head began to drip forward on his neck. In his hand was a half-devoured box of fries he no longer could feel the pressure of between the pads of his fingers. His nerves had escaped his body and gone into his dream, where they waited for his consciousness to join.

39

Brent had noticed the boy asleep in the back seat first, his order of fries dumped into his lap, "tired kid."

Marilyn looked from the road, to Brent, to Davey in the back and gave a gentle smile—one that looked adult on her worn, tired face, "I think his response to stress is sleep," She looked back at Brent, "life's been pretty stressful for him lately." He'd sleep himself into a grave if he'd only felt half the stress she had piled onto her shoulders, but that's the beauty of getting older. You get stronger and can carry more—her nose flared.

Brent took a turn off the highway, pulled halfway over the white line so the cars behind could pass as he slowed his speed to residential. He let the car dwindle to a silent purr as he drove past an old graffitied park with lock and chain bathrooms, then a green Lutheran church. Marilyn had given him a general direction of her duplex while Davey had been dozing off in the back, *"by the ninth street market, you know where that's at?"* She had asked.

Sure he did. It was five broken blocks behind old Grant Elementary's brick building. In the *ghetto* of Grant. They were creeping closer to the market and he'd need more directions, but for now, they both sat silently.

He thought of the drawing in crayon, then the *Mona Lisa*, then Marilyn's bruised eye. All just a little purple in places.

"Take a right up here," the stitched sister instructed and he did. The turn was followed by another long road of silence.

He asked eventually, *had to ask,* "When do you think Child Welfare will stop in?"

Marilyn's face contorted hard enough to tug at her stitches, "what?" Her heart tickled her throat like she'd just been stopped by a cop.

Brent gave her a soft served look from under his brow, "Davey's social worker."

Marilyn focused back on the road, "a left on Buhl." She muttered.

He took it. The 4Runner curved an island of houses, set up like a reverse cul-de-sac. "Marilyn—"

"That was quite the assumption," she growled like he'd jabbed her in the ribs, "what if our parents died and I was just taking care of him, how insensitive you would be for assuming we were involved with Child Welfare."

Brent pinched his lips and nodded, "you're right, I'm sorry." He could've been insensitive, sure. Her response argued differently, however, as she seemed to know exactly what he was referring too. *Child Welfare.*

The 4Runner slowed to a four-way stop and Brent waited for instructions from the pin lipped girl with flared nostrils. She turned her head away from him to make the statement clear that she wasn't talking. So he sighed, then went straight.

"Which house?" He asked as they rolled through a neighborhood with a red and white striped dead end sign two blocks ahead.

"Pull over." She kept her voice low and masculine.

Brent did, tight to the curb. He throttled the gear shaft into park and turned to look at her cooly.

She had a sideways stare on him as her lips turned together while she bit the skin off of their pink surface. "Why do you care?" Her wall of *'how dare you!'* down and her thoughts curious.

He watched a porch light flip on through her window as he considered, then decided to follow up with his own question, "were you the Relative Custody option after a long trial of C.P.S. considering neglect or –" he paused as his throat contracted, "abuse." He knew, first hand, how long child protective services could take to clear a trial on neglect, the flow chart of decisions full of halts and trial-and-error nonsense.

Marilyn tilted back in her seat, "Yeah, it was something like that."

Brent nodded thoughtfully, "I care because I don't want you to lose him."

She watched him with a frozen expression.

"It's the Child Welfare System's job to make sure they placed him with the right care, they will randomly check up on you."

She shifted in her seat, "yeah, I was there for the trials, I know that."

It was a heated response and the change in her behavior fascinated the counselor.

He chewed his cheek and wondered if he should continue his journey into the dark swamp of the kids' personal lives, after glancing down and seeing he was already knee-deep he decided to open his mouth again, "pardon me for asking, but what are you going to do about," he gestured to his own eye, "*that.*"

Marilyn touched the sensitive skin around her swollen eyes, "you mean Nick the Dick."

Brent gave her a strange look for the nickname and she laughed solidly.

"I heard Davey call him that under his breath once"

Brent smiled now. Then it dropped off, back into the swamp, "Do you have a real job?"

The girl's smile was gone too, a wicked chase after his own.

"Or do you just pickpocket?" His hand instinctively brushed the leather bulge in his own pocket and he decided he could have asked the question more delicately.

"Wow," she snorted to herself and tilted her head to look out her window without an answer.

A knot tangled Brent's intestines and he bit down on his tongue before diving headfirst into her mucky swamp, "Look, I know it isn't my place, but I really think you have the odds going against you. You're –"

Her head spun back and she snapped at him, "What the fuck does that mean?"

Brent held out his hand, "You're going to lose him to foster care." He'd meant to add more to that sentence, to smooth it out, but had cut it off short to make the words more alert to her.

They *had* been alerting. They pinned her in the back with needles sharper than the leftover pain in her body from the car wreck. His words pissed over her. She smacked his extended hand away in a fit of random anger. The slap rang out through the cabin of the Toyota and her body ached from the twist and muscle use.

Brent retracted it back to his lap to sit on the red mark that was already swelling, "I didn't mean to offend you," he spoke calmly with a glance toward the sleeping boy to be sure they hadn't woke him.

Davey snored soundly.

Marilyn's face was a stone-cold glare as she massaged the sting out of her striking hand.

"I care about Davey, and because I do, it's important to me that you know that you need to find a real job. A full-time job, something with benefits." He spoke his words like they were his feet as they gently tiptoed through glass, "An employer's sign off will be crucial to you keeping Davey out of foster care."

Brent clenched his tight jaw to keep away from a shiver at the idea. He knew she had to of had a job when C.P.S. made the decision to make her the boy's guardian, they did their thorough research. He just wondered how long it would be until they found out she'd since lost the job.

Marilyn was silent to let him talk, so he took it and ran.

"Your home, I know you probably don't want Davey there in the first place, you're a good sister," he smiled at her and noticed the way her lip quivered up like she wanted to smile back but had fought it. "Don't wait," he whispered, "get Davey out as soon as possible. C.P.S will frown upon a *Nick the Dick.*"

"How do you know so much about all of this?" Her words no longer spat from her mouth, but slid out wet and absorbed, like she couldn't pinpoint her emotions.

Brent shrugged, "Work, and —" he paused as he considered continuing, "uh," he scratched at the hairline on the back of his neck, "personal experience." That could mean anything, right? *That could mean anything.*

Marilyn nodded like she understood and that smile she'd forced down started to come up. It made Brent nervous.

A small car, colored midnight blue, passed the parked 4Runner and they both watched it.

Her smile was a full toothed grin when he turned back, "Jesus," she hissed through it with a light giggle. Her arm tossed through the space between her and Brent's seats and grabbed onto Davey's knee as she turned to face the child, "hey, Dave," she'd laughed a little at his asleep lip that pouted forward, "wake up," she squeezed lightly against his thigh and knee.

The boy's thick eyelids cranked open and he threw his legs out into a stretch.

Marilyn rubbed gently into the skin she'd just squeezed around his leg as he finished his stretch, "hey, we're moving out tonight."

Davey's eyes widened as did Brent's.

"We have a new place to live!" She tossed her head back to Brent with a wicked grin lifted so high even her stitches seemed to smile at him, "you wouldn't mind sharing your humble abode with us kids, would you *foster boy?*" Brent's entire body tensed and she laughed lightly at it with a waving hand, "please," she dropped her hand and her smile along with it, "I don't need my psychology degree to know someone's *tell.*"

Brent stared with bewilderment harnessed to his face, neck, and shoulders when Davey queued in, "we're going to live with you, Brent?!" He'd leaned forward out of his sleepy state and his french fries jumped from his lap to the ground.

Marilyn winked at the man, "you know so much about keeping my brother safe, I had just assumed you'd open your home up to us. Help some kids out."

She was working to intimidate him, make him flustered, but he couldn't disagree with her. His home would be a good place for them to start. So he sported a shrug under his warm cheeks, "sure, I can do that."

She smiled a wide one again and Davey hooted.

Brent laughed at the boy as he turned the decision over in his mind, "I don't have much space –"

"We'll manage."

He smiled.

She gave her head a light shake at the road, "Okay, come on, Nick's house is one block up."

Brent thought: *this is a game to her,* then: *well played.*

40

He sat in the warm, idling Toyota as he watched the boy and girl play chase up the lawn of their aging duplex, their ankles swaddled in overgrown grass. The home was yellow and the gold accents of the aging door had all but rusted away. He frowned at the single-paned windows covered with stained blankets and each chip of paint off the window sills. He watched Marilyn reach the door then turn to Davey with a finger held to her lips, to say: *shh*. A warning.

It made Brent undeniably uncomfortable and he wrapped his hand around the handle of his driver's door as he contemplated a jog out to them to join. One pop of his door and he could be on his feet to protect them. But as he considered it he also knew that she was capable of handling herself, so he stayed and waited.

His head pulsed harder and a bright pain spread its way through him as she distanced herself.

The house door crept open slowly as Marilyn steered it with her hand to avoid the loud squeak of its hinges that required the attention of some WD-40. That of which they didn't have. Marilyn had glanced back at the man in the SUV to rub at her head and make a hard wince with her face. She could see, through her passenger door *(not covered in nail clippings)* window as the man nodded his head back to say he felt it too.

Davey slid through the opening in the door first and stared, overwhelmed, at the dark entryway hall. Marilyn had followed in behind him and nudged the boy forward. She left the door open in case a quick escape was needed, but somehow doubted it. A television screen lit the shadowed house and Marilyn expected to see Nick asleep with his head back and mouth wide for sunken snores as infomercials reflected off his dirty face. But the young man was not there, the infomercials played with ecstatic voices to an empty room. She nudged her hand into Davey's back and guided him towards their shared bedroom with a steady stare set down the hall, towards Nick's master bedroom.

They pushed through the door into the ice-cold room that smelled of burned candles and tobacco soaked wool. Marilyn could taste the nicotine that seeped through the wicker hamper and became overwhelmingly hungry for a Marlboro balanced between her lips. She imagined her light tugs of air on it until the stick burned down and the ashes fell and danced over her jeans to make white ash marks and warm her thighs. She sighed and the craving burrowed deeper inside.

Marilyn flipped the lid to her hamper and stared in at the pile of dirty laundry, mixed together with clean, like a leftover stew. She turned to her brother and surveyed the clothes, his and hers, scattered over the floor in unassorted piles, most of the clothes turned inside out. "Okay," she nodded at the ground as if she was in discussion with it, "collect all the laundry off the floor and jam it in the hamper, Dave."

She pointed to clothes, then hamper, with her instructions.

Davey obeyed and began to scoop dirty jeans, underwear, and socks into his tiny arms. He waited until the pile was above his little chin before dumping it over into the hamper with the flipped up lid, "all of it?" He asked as the clothes tumbled in.

Marilyn looked at the boy, then the carpeted floor, then the boy again with a carefree shrug, "try to." She bent and began to help him with a bit back moan from the ache in her body and the rushed thump in her head. *Icky Thump.*

They packed what they could into the wicker lidded basket, including two of their bed pillows and an old blanket. Marilyn swept a phone charger for her disposable store-bought phone with a drained prepaid plan and a lighter off their single nightstand and jammed them into the midst of the clothing. She crammed the lid over the overflowed items and heaved it into a hug.

Marilyn headed out first in a casual stroll to the door, Davey in toe.

The crisp air wafted in with frost that conjured up a sneeze in Davey. His head tipped back and he willed it away with watery eyes and a flexed nose. *What are you supposed to think of? Watermelons? Or are you supposed to say watermelon?* It was too late to make a decision for either of those choices as his head thrust forward and a piercing sneeze broke the sneaky silence in the duplex. Marilyn shot around and stared at him widely like he'd screamed.

Embarrassed, Davey covered his lips with a jacket sleeve.

Marilyn scrunched her own nose at the scent of snot, "bless you," she whispered.

A moment passed, then a drunken hand gripped and shook the closed door of Nick's master bedroom, "Marilyn, is that you?" His muffled slur stretched through the wood and sent the hair of the Matthews siblings' neck erect.

Davey shot a frightened look to his sister that she met with a smile.

"Last one to the car is a rotten egg!" She yelped then pivoted to bolt out of the open door. But really, it was: *the last one to the car has to deal with Nick and his drunken penis.*

As they both sprinted through the dewy grass the lid of the hamper bounced and threatened to spill onto the ground. Marilyn's arms heavied and her tongue began to feel too big for her mouth and she had a thought that *maybe* taking a jog with a concussion wasn't the brightest idea. Her stitches stung and itched against the wind and her legs wobbled against the whipped world—except—she was sure that was from Brent and not from the head injuries. *Except,* those were kind of from him in a way, anyway. She began to laugh, as the hamper bobbed in her weighted arms and her legs chomped against the grass. She was sure she looked insane. *Absolutely bonkers,* and that made her laugh harder.

Brent had removed himself from his spot in the car and jogged around the car with his brunette laps of hair waved into his face from his now numb head, "what?" He yanked the back door open and hoisted Davey into the back seat, "Why are you running?"

"You're a rotten egg, Marilyn!" Davey howled from the seat bench then collapsed into a trail of laughter.

Marilyn made a face at him, "No fair! You had your teacher's help!"

She turned to Brent to address his question then turned to look at the duplex for Nick's whereabouts. The house door was vacantly open and the front lawn was empty of any disturbance other than the sibling's matted footprints. Nick hadn't followed them, which had made the run seem suddenly pointless, and disappointed her down in her gut.

"We're seeing who was going to be the rotten egg," she told the man who's stone face relaxed.

"He's not my teacher!" Davey reminded her as she dumped the hamper into the back seat with him, "he's my *counselor!*"

Marilyn lifted the uninjured eyebrow at her brother, "oh yeah, well—" She looked from the laundry mess to the man outside of the car as she finished her sentence to Davey, "I hope your *counselor* also has a washer and dryer in his place."

Brent compressed a smile at her and gave a single nod to say he did.

Marilyn grinned at him as if to say *good,* and hopped into the back with Davey, no longer caring for the front where she could see the stopped cars in front of them as Brent slowed. She slammed the door and the stab of metal capping black elastic into place rattled her teeth hard enough to remind her of her throbbing body.

Marilyn had buckled Davey in as Brent turned off the block. Brent watched through glances in the rearview mirror while Marilyn began to collect cold french fries in their cardboard container until he remembered she had seen the *thing* through her rearview. The realization snapped his eyes forward to the route. A prickle of sweat at the base of his neck threatened to roll down his back and his stomach twisted into a zeppelin knot as the idea of something rotten leaning up behind him and breathing hot air against his ear crossed his mind.

They coasted down a steep hill and Marilyn's stomach flattened into her spine as her hips jutted forward to brace themselves against oncoming trees that weren't really there, her face stretched down into a pained expression. They came up onto a level plain again and her stomach settled. She let her face relax into a dull expression.

Brent took a sharp turn into an asleep parking lot with parked vehicles, damp and friendly, in every spot. The apartment complex wasn't large—you could see the end from the start—but it scattered itself with towering apartment buildings, all three stories and painted olive green.

"Which one is yours?" Davey asked with a sweet voice while Marilyn thought: *apartment? Jeez, you are a millennial.* Her and Davey were Gen Z, she was entitled to judge.

Brent pointed a steady finger towards the back apartment building, "the middle one," he answered, then his finger jerked up as the SUV tires rolled over a girthy speed bump.

41

The front door spat them into the living room of his tiny apartment where a light brown couch deadpanned at them. Brent, who'd heaved the hamper up the concrete flight of stairs let the children in first, then promptly moved passed them to the coffee table as he dropped the hamper in front of the now-closed door. He turned back to the girl once knee level with the rectangle piece of furniture and gave her a look of concern, "are you okay?" He asked and seemed to study her like an X-ray, "do you need to sit down. How's your head?"

Marilyn, who'd been judging the room she stood in the corner of, looked at him steadily, "numb," she responded with a smile.

Brent flared his hand from his wrist and shook his head, "no, I mean, with the concussion. Those papers the doctors gave you, where are they, you should read them."

Marilyn wanted to roll her eyes at him but she saved the gesture for a later time, she was grateful he was allowing them to crash in his bachelor pad and didn't want him to think otherwise, "I left the paper in the car. It just said to avoid screen time and stuff. I'll be fine," she laid a hand above her breast, over her silently beating heart, "I'm fine. Thank you."

He chewed his cheek as he surveyed her held up head before he dropped his own back to the table, "okay," he lowered himself and wrapped his hands around the table to shove, "I have an air mattress —" he puffed his cheeks out as the industrial coffee table popped off his black rug and began to scrape loud and echoed noises against the hardwood. His thighs were engaged and his glutes clenched as his feet stayed and his upper body thrust.

Wow, Marilyn thought as she tilted her head at his bubbled out ass, *the neighbor's downstairs must love you.* She meant, sarcastically, for the noise, but they might also like his butt too. It was absolutely a plus for her—and the hormones that swam her bruised body.

Brent stood back up with the table half moved from its original spot, like a cookie jar lid balanced on the lip of its container, "I could sleep on the air mattress, you two could take my bed," he looked from Davey to Marilyn, "I would change my sheets first, of course."

Marilyn crossed her arms and studied the floor plan of the living room, "No, we can take the air mattress."

Davey caught her eye and she smiled at him.

Brent tipped his weight onto one leg and scratched at his chest, "are you sure?"

Marilyn would love to eventually share the bed with the thirty-something-year-old, her lips parted as the desire fermented, but she nodded anyway, "We don't mind, thank you."

Brent sucked in air through his nose and his upper body extended, then he dropped the wind from his lungs with innocence, "okay, sure."

He lowered back to the table and began to shove again.

Davey pranced forward and caught a paperweight before it dived off the table and slammed headlong into the hardwood. It was a grey metal that resembled a dog knelt to a bell like a man kneeling at an altar. Davey turned it over in his hands curiously.

"Thanks for grabbing that," Brent said to the boy in one exhaled grunt as he jammed the coffee table into the wall.

Marilyn began to trail her fingers along the inside wall of the apartment, past the boy and man, as she took in each detail of their new temporary home. There weren't frames or decor that accented the white walls but she had to step around a bookcase stuffed full, one she'd return to, to scavenge through later. The white wall covered with spray sand spoke a braille conversation to Marilyn's extended fingertips. The wall guided her to a dining table fit for a family with its long legs and oak four-by-fours. It sat horizontally to curtainless windows covered with thick drops of dew. Beyond the water speckled panes was a beautiful view of the mountains. A view admirable even in the dark.

To the left of the wooden dining table with black metal dining chairs was a cove in the wall, Marilyn crossed to it quietly. The kitchen stared back at her in the enveloped dark. She placed a flat hand against the paperstone countertops painted to look like brown granite. She traced the blotched patterns as she walked slowly through the shadowed room. It was clean, a magazine cover of *Country Cottage* cleanliness. She stopped at the sink and peered in. It was a silver two-compartment sink, deep and empty of dishes. She tossed a glance at the matching stainless steel dishwasher with silent sticker buttons before she moved along, further into the kitchen. She stopped at a stacked row of drawers that stretched from the lip of the counter to the beige tile floors. Her hand came loose from the counter and her forefinger flicked at the black handle of the top drawer. It slid open easily like it had been greased the morning before. A silver mesh tray shot forward and crashed into the front board of the drawer with rattling contents. *Forks, butter knives, and spoons! Oh my!* A plethora of spoons, actually, piled into two separate mesh compartments.

"Jeez Louise," Marilyn mumbled PG to the empty room, "someone likes soup."

It was actually cereal.

She pushed the silverware drawer shut with a satisfied *thwop* of cork wood sealing into counter stock.

Marilyn toyed open the second drawer to reveal napkins, white squares bought in bulk from a grocery store. The next drawer was filled to the brim, with *junk*. Junk too ugly and random to be welcome in foster boy's pretty palace.

Sounds of shuffled feet and vocal chatter as Brent asked Davey for a hand swam through the living room and into the tiny kitchen where Marilyn stood and peered into the third drawer down. She paused at their noise and searched over her shoulder for signs of the man to come charging in and spray her with a million questions, *are you snoopin' on my spoons?"* but the kitchen staid undisturbed and the noise contained itself in the living room walls.

She turned back to the full drawer and began to leaf through it. She lightly tossed batteries and a broken watch to the side. If it had looked valued she may have clung onto it a bit longer but the watch was black and digital with dirty rubber. She wasn't entertaining the idea of robbing the man... hell, who was she kidding, she definitely *was*.

She shook her head.

She knew better.

Deeper in the drawer she found an old wallet and she flipped through it anyway.

Marilyn shut the junk drawer three drawers down and wandered out of the kitchen, past the dining table sized for a middle-income family, and through the back of the living room. Davey sat on the tan couch, which had been shoved back at least three feet, as he watched Brent pump a queen-sized, blue mattress up. The man fought with a black motor and the air mattress tab silently. Marilyn paused her stroll and watched the almost comical act for a moment before she proceeded down a hallway. It was a small, boxed in hallway, Brent's bedroom on the left and a bathroom on the right. She stepped into the bathroom and flipped on a *too bright* florescent light that ignited the restroom. It was a clean as the kitchen, the scent of wet porcelain and *Men's Suave* shampoo tied the tiny room together. She moved further into the room and shut the painted wood door behind her. The lock clicked into place and tingled the inside of her palm.

The motor in the ceiling fan pulsed louder and rattled each of Marilyn's joints from the floor up. She moved to the mirror that reflected the image of her upper body. She looked worse than the night before when she'd stopped in a mirror after grinding on *Jerr-bear,* however, the girl that looked back at her reflected kinder than the one who'd greeted her in the hospital bathroom/utility closet. Her hair was frizzed in curly grease and knotted at the nape of her neck still, but it looked better without the bandage taped over her black high E-string stitches. Marilyn gave a coy tucked smile to her own reflection, "cute."

She turned to the toilet and threw the lid up in a solid motion, suddenly overly aware of how bad she had to piss. The porcelain bowl was spotless, pubic hair and dried urine free, something she wasn't used to in Nick's duplex. The foster boy was the hygiene king! It occurred to her, as she squatted to the cold ring, that maybe foster boy was also a *homo* boy. The consideration invited a frown against her cheeks as her pee tinkles blended with the buzzing ceiling fan. Her eyes slid over the tub in front of her with the black striped curtains. The image of Brent, tall, naked, and scrubbed in white foam splashed through her mind and her frown flipped over. Perhaps he was so clean because of his past—ol' foster boy had to stay clean, it was all he was in control of then... her face tossed back into a frown. She'd seen the way his eyes had glazed over when he asked about C.P.S—she knew then it was personal—it was in the way his cheeks shuttered while he spoke. It was a copy and paste image of herself when the memory of her father, wrapped by a belt and hung from the ceiling fan, resurfaced and swung behind her eyelids.

She stood from the toilet and moved back to the mirror as pee dribbled down her leg and caught in the jean hammock around her ankles. *Yes.* She poked her pale cheekbone. *That's the look.*

Marilyn came out of the bathroom without washing her hands and nearly slammed face-first into Brent's chest. They both stepped out of each other's way and made the strangely universal "*Oup!*" noise, then both spat a, "sorry!"

Marilyn tugged her bottom lip with a canine and her cheeks blushed.

Brent jammed his hands behind his back and took a step and a half away from her, with his eyes wide, "hey," he smiled and wished the hallway wasn't so tight in space, "you're welcome to use the shower."

Marilyn's smile withered and she lifted a hand to twirl at her dirty hair, "thanks, I'm gonna do that."

Brent bit against the tip of his tongue with a slight nod—thankful that she would.

42

"Wow…" Marilyn stared in awe at what was left of Brent Kingsley's living room as her hair dripped lukewarm water onto her sweatshirt and her stitches stung in the cool air. Her hands rested against her hips which were now covered with soft, oversized pajama bottoms. Courtesy of Brent, *kind of.* They were in his bathroom, in a cabinet, next to his folded towels. She'd found them happily after being reluctant to put her jeans back on.

The living room had been stripped of its original design to welcome the blow-up mattress, now draped in white sheets, a thick, blue quilt, and two fuzzy blankets. Their pillows from home were thrown out at the top of the bed and Davey had wiggled himself beneath it all. His head was sunk into a red race car pillow and Bear Kingsley was being tossed gently from one hand to another, his eyes on the ceiling.

Marilyn shuffled around the couch and plopped next to Brent, who'd been sitting on the sofa with a decorative pillow fallen over in his lap as he played with the seams of it. She had sat a half cushion too close and the man seemed startled by it.

"I know," he responded to her as he put the pillow back and stood like he was being cautious not to offend her, "It'll do for now, right?"

She watched as he noticed her legs in his pajama bottoms. She tried to share a look with him for it but his eyes had already slid to her hamper as if to secretly ask, *didn't you pack your own pair?* That eye roll of hers was short-fused and came back at that moment, thankfully without catching his attention.

"Definitely," she mumbled.

Brent looked at her now and put his hands on his hips to mimic the way she stood when she first entered the room, "tomorrow we can get you more blankets if you'd like." He lifted a finger to point at his ceiling, "my neighbor has plenty," his finger dropped like a door across a castle moat to point at Davey, "she'd fix Beary's arm for us too."

Davey's head tilted back against his pillow and his eyes rolled up to see Brent and his sister, "Beary would appreciate it," he sucked the bear against his chest.

"Your neighbor sounds like a gem," Marilyn had picked the decorative pillow he'd been holding up and was toying with it now.

Brent sighed and changed the subject, too preoccupied with the night growing late, "I have to go to work tomorrow, at least for half of the day. Then, I can help you get situated—we can do a grocery run, and pick up anything you two might need, I noticed you packed lightly." By that, he meant that he had thought about how much they could've brought out if they'd each had two black trash bags as they ran through the front lawn to his 4Runner.

"Am I going to school too?" Davey kept his head tilted back, "I want to," he added.

Marilyn looked to Brent and Brent shrugged. It wasn't his call, it was her's.

Marilyn tipped her chin back to her brother and gave a hollow smile, "how about you go with Brent, have half a day."

Davey agreed with this and curled further into the sheets with a smile of his own against Bear Kingsley's neck.

Brent agreed after a silent glance to Marilyn that asked: *are you sure?* And was met with a reassuring nod.

"Okay, Davey –" Brent crossed his arms and pinched absentmindedly at his bicep, "– get sleep, you'll have to be up early with me, I have to get to work before school starts. Okay, pal?"

Davey was already fading into a sleepy dream, but managed a whisper of the word, "*yes.*" before he burrowed his head further into the fluff of his stuffed animal and withered off further into sleep.

Brent watched him doze with a bit of guilt as the sensation of his Toyota barreling into the stopped girl and boy rushed through his body like a heatwave. He moved against the feeling, back behind the couch and let out a shaky breath as he leaned into the backboard of the long seat, "do you need anything?" He asked the girl, "maybe an ice pack?" He pointed to his own neck and back in reference to hers, "I have–*maybe*–frozen broccoli?"

He squinted his eyes awkwardly which forced a laugh from the girl.

"I'm fine," she assured him and moved to join Davey one the wobbly air bed, "goodnight foster boy," she cooed as she slid beneath the blankets and his pajama bottoms bunched up around her thighs.

Brent's hands clenched. He'd tell her the nickname wasn't appropriate, but not tonight.

He was too tired, and she was too new to him.

"Goodnight," he responded in a low toned voice as he crossed to a light switch and flipped it off. The living room dropped into shadows and the moon beamed in over the dining table.

43

Marilyn hardly slept that night. She had laid and thought of her father, then of her mother. Her mother who gave up a little boy who now stirred softly against Marilyn's side on the air mattress. She thought of Nick next, and the home they abandoned.

Brent had fallen asleep, she knew, because her head dropped a little heavier into her pillow, like Brent's Pavlov Dog paperweight had been deployed into the open space they shared in their brains.

She knew when his dream had started too. She could feel it, gentle brushes over her body, like small insects, or wind that ruffled her sheets. She laid and felt, and tried to understand what he was dreaming. It was uncertain for a while until a beating in her chest picked up, like a heartbeat, but not her's.

It was his heartbeat that rattled over the top of her own that pumped a normal pace for her size and health. She put a hand to her chest and held the flutter that belonged to him, like dragonflies with cannonballs strapped to their paper-thin wings. His dream was a nightmare, she became sure of it.

She wondered if he dreamt about the creature with the face as she held his heartbeat. The one that had stalked her in her own stupid, *dead,* green Saturn. The gentle brushes on her skin now full of evil energy and electrical currents. She turned, beneath the quilt and fuzzy blankets, and sucked her brother into her arms.

44

Brent didn't think of Amanda as his morning shower rushed around him and pooled against his ankles—not today, even with his mental trash bag destroyed, she didn't come out to play. Instead, he thought of Nick. The trade wasn't better, but at least it wasn't as *personal*. His lips arched down and the water dropped from them as he felt pity for his selfish thought. It was personal, he cared about the Matthews children. He shifted his head beneath the water to feel the pressure of the drops massage his hair against his scalp.

Brent scrubbed the lasting soap in his hair down his neck, onto his shoulders, and under his arms as he hummed lightly. It was an echoed hum of a tune he'd thought of the night before. The one that he was sure now that he'd heard on the radio. That *Alex Clare* song.

—But I need to breathe.

He bent and scooped up his shampoo to dump into his palm and rub down the rest of his body as the hum passed another line of the song.

At the end of it all, you're still my best friend.

He dropped the bottle and it bounced against the tub floor before it bobbed to the top of the water like his toy boat once had, and was forced to swoop around his ankles in the idled water.

Which way is right?

Which way is wrong?

He moved his head under the faucet again and his soapy body followed.

You know we're headed separate ways.

Soap-suds made races down in streams on his face and into his parted lips to wash his thoughts and hums away. The song was gone from his head with soap and water as he spat it from his tongue.

It had come back, while he brushed his teeth, to remind him of the chorus as he brushed the beat against his back molars.

And it feels like I am just too close to love you.
There is nothing I can really say.

He stopped humming and brushing to stare numbly at his reflection with toothpaste smeared out of the sagged corner of his lips. His nose had begun to burn and thin tears began to force themselves from his dry tear ducts. He bent and spit the potent mint from his tingling mouth into the sink where it stuck and began to bubble. He scrubbed the minty residue away with his hand and the cold faucet water that ran. His hand limped into the sink and spots of red started to fall over the skin that stretched the top of his palm. Brent's head lifted frantically and his reflection looked back with a bloodied nose, broken at the bridge, and sharp pain spread from the impact sight through his face like a virus through an ancient town. He jammed the palm of his toothpaste-residue hand against the flow and dropped his head back to the sink like there was a sudden led ball dropped into the center of his mind. His head exploded into a migraine that sent his vision spiraled and threatened to kick him to the floor.

TOO CLOSE

The song screamed in his head like a radio that fed back a dog whistle screech. Except, it wasn't the song at all. The tune was gone and the words no longer came with familiarity. It was a demonic adaptation of what once was something he'd heard on the radio.

TOO CLOSE; it screamed.
TOO CLOSE
TOO CLOSE TO A GREEN SATURN.

Brent exerted a pitched whine that came out in pain, almost louder than the shrieking between his ears.

Then, as quick as it came, it was gone. Tears spilled from his eyes as he regained himself and wiped at them with the backs of his hands. He straightened his spine, out of the existential crisis crouch, and took his reflection back in. His nose was pink and happy. The broken bridge fixed and his skin clear of blood.

Brent blew a mint-flavored breath through his lips. *Post Traumatic Stress.* He rubbed under his nose until it began to sting. *Just a little Post Traumatic Stress.*

Davey was on the floor under the kitchen entrance as he entertained himself with Bear Kingsley and his bandaged arm. He stood up when Brent exited the bathroom. The man walked slowly and adjusted his brown belt over clean blue jeans and a tucked-in, white, button-up with rolled *(just below the elbow)* sleeves.

Brent glanced up from his belt buckle and gave a gentle laugh to the young boy who bounced jubilantly on his sneaker toes, "Hey, pal," he whispered to the boy.

Davey was in his clothes from the night before and a large cowlick pushed the right side of his sandy hair up over his ear.

"How are you feeling?"

Davey gave a shrug, "fine," he said and sounded like his sister.

Brent grabbed the back of his own neck and gave a light massage to it, "your neck hurt?" *From the whiplash after I wrecked my car into the back of yours.*
TOO CLOSE.

Davey's tiny eyebrow lifted in sudden understanding, "oh, a little, but it's okay!"

Brent passed the boy into the kitchen and Davey followed close behind.

"Like a sunburn, kinda, but one that doesn't hurt that bad. One you'd still go swimming with."

Brent appreciated the clever analogy the boy gave him and returned it with a wide smile as he leaned over the boy to his red coffee pot, "yes, I understand," he was still low in a whisper, "is your sister sleeping?" He crossed to the sink as he asked to dump old coffee into the silver drain with the black, plastic, teeth shaped flaps.

Davey's feet slapped the ground behind the man, "she just fell asleep, I think,"

Brent turned with full attention on the boy, "oh no," his voice fell into a lower, breathy whisper to be extra careful that he didn't wake her, "she didn't sleep at all last night?"

Davey shook his head no, innocently enough, but it made Brent's stomach hurt, "she fell asleep when you were in the shower."

Or brushing my teeth, the man thought but was unsure as to why he thought it.

He stepped from the sink and bent his long torso out of the kitchen entrance, coffee pot still in hand. Marilyn's body was contorted against the deflating air mattress and wrapped furiously around the blue quilt he'd lent to them. Her hair was still slightly damp and clutched in curls to her forehead and shoulders. Brent could almost see the drool that leaked from her lips and soaked into her bed pillow that had been turned sideways and jammed into a hug between her arms. He worried about her sore muscles as he studied the way she slept.

Davey watched Brent curiously from a few steps behind him, his little hands collected into his pockets as his mouth moved slobbery circles around his bottom lip.

Brent's body came fully back into the kitchen, his face a featured mix of caution and complication as his eyes passed from the coffee pot to Davey, to the coffee pot again. He then opened his mouth to present a new idea to the boy, "how does fast-food breakfast sound?" He asked as he wiggled his eyebrows gently at the kid in front of him. He sat the coffee pot back into its holder, already set on the idea of getting coffee and food from somewhere to avoid waking the girl.

"I love –"

Brent shoved his finger against his lips and Davey ripped his hands from his pockets to cover his mouth.

He understood the attempt to stay quiet now and whispered gently to the counselor, "*I love that idea.*"

Brent nodded with a smile then pointed to Davey's backpack, propped up against the couch that was shoved halfway into the dining area and said, "okay, let's go; get your bag." Davey bounced past the man on light toes and scooped the bag into his grasp.

While the boy shoved Bear Kingsley into the top of his American rucksack Brent wrote a note with a half paper and a blue pen he found in his junk drawer.

> Plenty of food in the fridge and cupboard,
> Help yourself to whatever?
> Davey and I will be back around noon.

He set the note beside the red coffee pot that had leftover sink water dripping from its glass bowl and set the pen against the corner of the page. *Hopefully, she'll be up before noon.*

45

Brent and Davey strolled into the small elementary building side by side. Davey observed the way their steps echoed against the hall in the absolute silence of the calm before the storm. The smell was different too, pulped and almost sweet without the other children there. He nibbled off a hash brown patty Brent had bought for him at the drive-thru window. He decided that he liked the school quiet, absorbent to him and only him, he wished it could always be like that.

Brent had begun to think clearly again with a fair distance between him and Marilyn, her presence not currently blocking up his mind space. The privacy gave him a sense of relief and security, the blinds behind his eyelids shut and blackout curtains draped. In his hand, he held a disgusting cup of black coffee, watered down and instant, but he sipped at it anyway.

The office adjacent to Brent's left shoulder was heaved open. Debra, today dressed in a cotton purple skirt and blue diamond-studded glasses, stepped through the doorway and waved her flabby arms, "Brent, did you —" she stopped in her black flat tracks and stared down at the side of Brent where Davey stood. Her eyes lifted up above her glasses to look back at the man, her head still down, highlighting her double chin covered in dark powder foundation. Her purple lips drooped to a gravitational frown. She planned to ask if he'd gotten ahold of Davey and could see now that she didn't need to.

"Good Morning, Mrs. Garcia!" Brent gave her his award-winning morning smile that she always referred to as *handsome* and *cunning*.

Davey shrunk behind Brent's lumber legs as *Mrs, Garcia's* eyes fell back to him. He continued to nibble on his hash brown patty in replacement of his bottom lip as she searched him.

"Good morning Mr. Kingsley and David," she responded without a waiver of her blue glasses eyes.

"Davey," Brent corrected her and reached behind his back to gently grab the boy's shoulder.

"Davey," she repeated in courtesy to the child, "my mistake." Her dark skin played with a paler shade and she tossed a concerned expression to the tall man, "I was just going to ask about that *thing* we were worried about yesterday."

Brent gave a dismissive shake of his head, "all is good," he smiled at her, "but hey, if I have papers that need to be filed or attendance issues I'll be sure to include you." It was a jab, or a push, back into her lane. The one she knew she needed to stay in.

There was a silent stare down between the two as Debra's color came back, redder then it had been to begin with, "*Ei.* okay," she pivoted back to her office without a quick draw and Brent continued on his way with Davey shuffling beside him.

They turned at the library and strolled the fifth-grade hallway so Davey could admire the drawing by *Alexis Adams* again. He considered asking Brent about Debra—but kept his lips occupied with collecting hash brown for his teeth to chew instead. He was smart enough to know that *thing* they had been worried about might have been *him*. Brent's silent glare might have been saying: *Don't you dare. Don't you dare bring him up right in front of him.* Davey frowned at the thought and hung his chin to his chest.

"You don't have to hang out with me," Brent told the boy once they reached his burgundy office with the tiny table and *Kelso's Wheel* poster, "you can go to the playground," where other kids would soon collect and play.

Davey slunk into a plastic chair, "I'd like to stay here," his voice had thickened.

Brent's eyebrows lowered over his brow bone, "great," he said with a soothed tone meant to mix in and fluff up Davey's thick, sad drawl.

Brent had left the door open and he took a seat to click through his morning emails. He was surprised to see there hadn't been a response from Ms. Gus yet, then immediately nervous she'd be saving it for verbal interaction.

There was a secret about boredom and silence that made all of God's creations curious. Something hidden while you twiddle your thumbs as your friend clicks through emails that drives you to stand and look for something, anything, because you crave to be curious. It was the case for Davey who had found himself a deck of cards from the same shelf he'd discovered Bear Kingsley and spread them out over the tiny table to study. He wasn't interested in a card game, but maybe some simple sanity. Once he'd organized each card into its rightful suit he began to catalog each card numerically. Ace counted as one, that's what Marilyn always said, anyway. The stack of spades was first to be complete, straightened and placed on Davey's left. Hearts were next, each card face down as they counted from Ace to King. It was diamonds then, the pattern a steady red, black, red from outside left to his centered right.

The stack of spades counted from ace to six then skipped to eight in the last pile on his outside right. The missing seven set something feverish off under the boy's skin like itchy organs, internal and unreachable. He began to count back through with narrow fingers like a drug addict would pick at spots on their skin. *He'd seen that before.*

Spades, then hearts, then diamonds. They were all there, none with an excess card that belonged to the clubs. *That damn seven.* He went back through the piles a second time with his bottom lip warm and salty under his dragging teeth. Davey grabbed at the tattered box, thin from years of use, and shook it against the table like a cereal box to a bowl. Three cards rimmed the tilted cardboard and Davey clutched them between his fingers. Two jokers smiled from the top when he flipped the cards over and he frowned at them before putting them into their own pile, above the divide between hearts and diamonds, still faced up, unlike the rest of the stacks. The lingering card in his hand glared at him with a wicked evil as the fever inside turned up to a boil between his ribs and he wiggled uncomfortably in his seat. It was a card of words. Instructions. A card of disappointment.

Brent had been able to hear the anxiety as it steamed off the boy while he scrolled through endless emails. Unable to bear the empathetic anxiousness that overtook him he finally swiveled around to Davey with his hands folded in his lap, "are you okay, pal?"

Davey looked at him as if his flesh was deteriorating and he was in agony, "the seven of four-leaf clover one is gone," he whined before he turned back to study his piles, the closest stack to Brent a seven of *four-leaf clovers* too short.

Brent tilted back in his chair with a nod and watched the boy curiously, his morning had turned quickly into a psychological study as if he'd hid the card and meant for this to happen.

Davey tapped at his chest and rocked in his seat, his lip slobbered raw. He looked as if he'd smelled something rotten.

Brent took a deep breath he hoped Davey would hear and copy as he sat forward in his chair to study the situation closer, "What options do you have?"

Davey looked at the man, then the cards, then the man again. The man who was praying that the bell wasn't close to ringing.

Davey shrugged and the hard muscles in his face seemed to mimic the movement of his shoulders, up high, then dropped way down low were they stayed sagged.

"Don't give up," Brent encouraged and pointed a slack finger back to the cards, "what can you do to make the bad feelings go away."

Davey looked back at the cards and his hand that poked his chest began to rub it instead, "I could cut the box."

Brent tilted his head, "why would you do that?" He noted the way the boy spoke when he was anxious. Like he was years younger, with a gurgly, slurred, baby voice. Like he no longer had energy as he tried to mimic a toddler.

Davey grabbed at the box and held it into Brent's face with the same young attitude that his voice carried, "it has a picture of a card on it, I could cut it out to match the other cards." The hope in his face diminished as he considered the cardboard replacement, "but it wouldn't match. It'd be too thick."

Brent nodded, "and you wouldn't have a box to put it away in."

Davey was poking his chest again and his lip had turned a deep red.

"What else could you do, kid?"

Davey's head pouted forward in defeat and he hobbled out of his chair blindly. He wanted to cuddle then, smother the burn between his lungs in a safe hug, and Brent was safe. He reached the man and his slack head dropped sideways into the man's shoulder. Warmth spread from his temple into his neck and he could feel the heat locked down below begin to wither into a chill as he nuzzled closer.

Brent smiled for a moment before he let the facial expression deplete and gently nudged Davey away from him. Davey began to tantrum as the bad feeling came back and Brent held him away from his warm body where the boy wanted to be.

"Davey," he spoke gently, "think. What else could you do?" He remembered then, the boy he'd seen the night before who screamed his name from the crumpled green metal, the boy he told to *breathe*. He let his hands drop from the kid as guilt washed between his toes and fingers and expected the boy to rush back into him. But Davey stayed put. This surprised Brent.

Davey ditched the pout and had started to think again, long and hard about his options. Then a bit of a smile crept over his anxious lips. "I could print a new one... and glue it to the instruction card." The baby voice was still there, and his hand still tapped, but the color in his face had begun to resurface.

The guilt left Brent as quickly as it came and he grinned at the boy, "what a brilliant idea," he glanced back at his computer, "I'll let you use my computer and printer."

Davey nodded and started to step to the man's monitor and keyboard with hesitation.

He wasn't logical. No, logical would've searched for the card, deeper into the shelves, drawers, other decks of cards. Logical would've searched until they found. Davey didn't consider that because Davey was creative. Stress was put into motion and he sprung straight into thinking outside the box—*or cutting it right out of the box*. Brent tucked a smile, he liked that. Creative meant he'd be an author, or a songwriter, or an artist. The man's vision glazed as he thought of Davey's drawing now crammed in his drawer surfaced, then tucked itself away again.

The bell had rung as Davey carefully glued a cutout paper card to the worded side of the instructions card. The high vibration of the metal hammer to metal bowl burnt the tips of Davey's ears. Brent watched as the boy flinched at the noise and wondered if he flinched at the noise of metal fought against metal when the $_4$Runner hit the green Saturn.

Nancy, with her magnifying glasses, had hopped into the office at her usual time to tell *Mr. Kingsley,* "Hi," then didn't skip a beat as she turned and said, "hi!", to Davey too. She then turned and flapped her oversized jacket wings back down the hall.

Davey stood slowly from the little chair and rolled his tongue over his bottom lip as he stared out into the trafficked hall and slid the crafted card through his fingers.

"It's pretty crazy out there in the morning," Brent explained to the boy who didn't give a response as he stood frozen with rattled eyes.

Brent tipped forward out of his chair and looped a palm around the lip of his open office door and guided it shut. He kept his hand at the door and his lightly crow-footed eyes on the boy, ready to pop the door back open if Davey showed any signs of discomfort or hesitation. He didn't in fact, he relaxed the second the door made its sealing click. It didn't surprise Brent as he tilted back into his chair, away from the door, Davey was used to the man's presence alone now—like they'd known each other for ages.

"I'll take you to class once the hallway quiets down," Brent promised.

Davey nodded and sliced the outside right stack of cards between the six of clubs and the eight to slide the card he created into place, "thank you," He sighed to the man and the bad feelings released.

46

Mrs. Engels' face widened into a surprised smile as the small, shy boy walked into her classroom with Brent in toe like a security blanket. The man returned the smile to his coworker as he studied her lifted cheeks and her bright, smokey eyes that stayed on the boy.

"Hey, Davey!" She clapped her hands together and her rings collided with a *tangy* sound, "we missed you yesterday!" Her thick black hair was curled towards her face, half of it pinned back in a barret.

Davey glanced back at his counselor who looked soft in the face and felt sad, again, that his teacher's name started with a *MRS*.

"Why were you gone?" The boy Davey saw pick his nose on Monday asked as he butted his way into the conversation out of boredom. Like a *nose picker* would. Entering into things he *shouldn't*.

Davey frowned, "I was with my sister."

The booger boy scrunched his booger nose, "yuck, I *hate* my sister."

Davey's face went red and his bottom lip went wet as it fell under his teeth. The heat in his cheeks clawed their way to the back of his neck as it went from embarrassment to frustration smoothly and without explanation.

"Sorry to hear that, Sai," Brent crossed his arms at the booger kid and Davey let his lip free into the classroom air with a dry swipe against it with his jacket sleeve.

Mrs. Engels pointed Sai in the direction of his booger boy desk, "why don't you take a seat?" Her voice carried kindly but her eyes pinned.

Davey could feel children stares on him and the shade in his face went from frustration red back to an embarrassed shimmer.

Brent nudged Davey with a soft knuckle to his little shoulder blade and smiled softly as the hot face turned around to him, "meet me in my office at lunch, like Monday."

Davey's face creased at the forehead and he made a quick glance at the class that watched the teacher, counselor, and mysterious new kid.

Brent felt the hesitation grow between them and nodded, "I'll send a note to excuse you from lunch," he whispered to avoid the ears of the other children.

Davey avoided eye contact, "sure," he mumbled then sunk away from the center of attention and slinky'd his way to his desk with his head down.

Brent frowned in his direction, then brought his attention to the teacher, "can I see you in the hallway, *Mrs. Engles.*" He slanted her name with his voice to make up for the slip of her first name in front of her class the day before. *So taboo.*

She flashed him a line of beautifully straight teeth, free of coffee stains, "you lead the way!" She chirped like a bird then dismissed him for a brief moment to turn to her class, "please get out a pencil and paper and practice your cursive letters!"

There was a wave of children groans that watered down her smile and she ran her hands through the air to quiet it, "ohhh please," she sighed melodramatically with a slight giggle, "just think of those cool cursive licenses you can all have when you complete this unit!" *Pink, paper printouts. Laminated and taped to the top of each kids' desk like a certificate. Kids went wild for them.*

Brent gave a double thumbs up to the kids in their desks from behind the woman to help her out, like an impromptu hype man, before he dipped out into the hallway.

Emily Engels was the first to speak once the door fell shut and the quiet of the hallway closed in, "Is he alright?" Her arms folded over her chest and her jean clothed hips tilted. Brent opened his mouth to respond but the woman unintentionally cut him off, "you seemed very upset yesterday."

Her brow lifted, removing the shadow from her glistening eyes.

"Yeah, Em," Brent bit at the corner of his mouth as he began to feel uncomfortable with the way he'd acted the day before, it all seemed so silly now, "he's alright."

"Oh, good!" She melted into her words with a grin and a straightened spine.

Brent shook his head slowly, "except —"

Her lips dropped and the shadow cast back over her eyes.

"He was in a car accident last night."

Emily gasped and her eyebrows shot up but left the shadows against her eyes as a hand came out of her crossed arms and covered her lips, "oh no," her voice was a whispered, empathetic cry.

Brent rocked back on a heel, "he's alright," he reminded, "I just wanted you to know so you can be cautious with him." The man waved a finger at his ear and squinted an eye, "I'm worried about loud noises, I can imagine," *he knew,* "that a car accident is loud. So, just be courteous of that when you deal with him today." He knew she would be, she always was gentle with her students.

"Oh sure," she nodded with him, her hand that had been at her lips pressed against her stomach, "was everyone okay?"

Brent stared at her.

"The car wreck," she clarified, "is everyone safe?"

The man rubbed at his nose, "yeah, yeah," his cheeks started to burn, "as far as I know."

Emily nodded like she was *sort of* comforted by his response, "okay," she searched him for more information with her wide, round eyes.

"Don't say anything to him about it," Brent warned as he pocketed his hands.

Emily looked offended by the idea, "of course not," she smiled at him then, "thank you for letting me know." The hand at her stomach lifted and grabbed at a silver necklace to rub the charm across its chain.

"Yeah," he sighed, "thank you."

He turned then and everything in him wanted to turn back.

In the classroom Daisy's blonde hair was crafted into two braided pigtails that whipped around her shoulders and slammed their secure hairbands into the hollow center of her back as she turned to Davey, "are you in trouble?" She asked with her bubble gum mouth and bored stare.

Her question sparked the attention of other children and they all tuned in for Davey's answer.

Davey wiggled uncomfortably against his cold plastic seat, "no... " he hesitated because he hadn't thought he was. Unless Mrs. Engles was mad he missed yesterday, he realized bluntly that he shouldn't have mentioned he'd spent the day with Marilyn. *Yuck, I hate my sister.* "I don't know." Davey finally decided.

"Oh," Daisy shrugged and popped an imaginary pink bubble between her lips, "because you came in with Mr. Kingsley, I thought you were in trouble."

A girl a few seats up in a blue sweatshirt nodded her head in agreement.

"Maybe he's crazy," someone at the front of the class suggested.

"– that's why he's with Mr. Kingsley a lot!" Someone else added.

Davey had begun to sink low into his chair with his eyes stuck to his desk, his vision shaking from forgetting to blink above his rosy cheeks that spread to his ears and hairline. Davey's toes stretched out as he slid down and his sneakers began to stretch below Daisy's seat as side conversations about his mental health carried from one curious friend to the next.

Daisy's braids slapped back around, away from him as she turned with anger towards the class, "mind your own business!" She demanded from her classmates, "don't *Eve's-drop*!"

"This doesn't look like cursive," A woman's voice stung through the air and little heads retracted back to their own desks, away from it, to allow Davey to breathe comfortably again.

Mrs. Engles crossed from the shut classroom door to her desk as she eyed her class. She gave a moment to pass a sweet glance to Davey who sat back up with his shoulders tight and a cog in his chest.

47

Brent found himself in the front office with his spindly fingers toyed around the linen in his jean pockets, his headspace still empty of the numb vortex but full of thoughts of the teenage girl. He wondered if Marilyn was sleeping alright as Debra gave him dirty glares over her blue glasses while she talked on the phone.

Mr. Olmstead, Grant's principal, excited his back cornered office into the main office and gave a paced nod to Brent.

"Joel," Brent caught his attention as he sidestepped in front of the man.

In *Matilda,* the principal had put fear into her employees and the school's attending children. Joel Olmstead, however, did nothing like that—he did nothing, really.

Brent wasn't even sure how the man stayed employed in the district, "I need to leave at noon today," he explained to the barrel-shaped man, "are you alright with that?"

"Sure!" Joel Olmstead gave Brent a wide smile and patted him on the shoulder before he moved around him and out of the main office door.

Brent nodded a 'thank you' after the man. He started to believe Davey's *Matilda* theory couldn't be applied to their situation, not unless Marilyn and Brent were both Matilda Wormwood. He pulled a hand from his pocket and pressed it lightly to the skin over his temple. He decided he didn't like not feeling Marilyn taking up space in his mind. He'd begun to itch for it, like a mother itches to check on her children at all times. Like he was already addicted to the magnetic pulse with the dizzying side effects.

TOO CLOSE TO A GREEN SATURN.

Brent flinched.

"What? Am I that bad to look at?" Debra's voice erected him from his thoughts. She was off the phone and stared into eye contact with him.

"Sorry," he apologized as he blinked to wet his eyes, "bad headache."

Debra sucked her front teeth and her purple lip bulged over her tongue unattractively. Her passive-aggressive glare a hint to the hurt feelings he'd given her that morning.

Brent exhaled, and as the air lowered from his lungs his eyelids mimicked them and fluttered down away from her, "look," his voice was a hollow smooth as he gently approached her desk and patted it with the hand that stayed out of his pocket, "I apologize if I was short with you this morning, I appreciate your concern for the kid–it's just,"

She batted a hand at him and her tongue returned to the pit of her mouth, "It's fine, handsome. What do you need?"

Brent let his mouth close to chop off the sentence he didn't finish then reopened it to begin a new one, "can you call Marilyn Matthews and have her confirm that I have permission to leave with Davey."

Debra stared at him.

"Davey's guardian sheet didn't have her number on it, and you have an updated version on your computer?" Brent gestured his head at her double monitor.

"I do."

"Great," Brent bounced on the balls of his feet and tapped his hand over her desk.

Debra's slit eyelids batted to the beat of his fingers into the wood like it hurt as she turned and began to click at icons on her screens. The reflection in her glasses showed highlighted hyperlinks on gray backgrounds as they grew into excel sheets. She filtered and typed with a weighted sigh, "a landline is listed."

"Nope," Brent's playing fingers stopped their tap dance as he trumped her sentence, "don't call that number." He let Nick cross his mind as the woman looked at his phone number and felt a heated lasso brush the back of his neck, "is there a cell phone?"

She popped her lips apart, "yes."

His hand tapped again and his eyes winced, "call that, please?" He smiled reluctantly and hoped that number belonged, personally, to Marilyn.

She smiled back, reluctantly, a carbon copy of his own, "sure, handsome," she picked the phone up like it was stiff roadkill and threw it to her ear with a sour twist on her lips.

Brent gave one final tap to the desk, a flatter, louder, tap before he excused himself with a whispered, "thank you," and pressed at his temple again.

48

Marilyn's eyelids, shrink-wrapped to her eyeballs, snapped open dryly as soon as the space in her head closed with the absence of the adult male. Her back and shoulders cringed like taffy stuck molars against the dipped blue mattress and she threw an arm out to grab at Davey for comfort. Her ball and chain hand and arm slammed into the cold, empty sheets on her brother's bare side and as her body stung. As the back of her head burned she thought: *oh yeah. School.*

Marilyn groaned into the lonely apartment and cupped her palms into her eye sockets. Her hospital bracelet scraped at her cheek as her sleep struck hands rubbed at her skin and the night before crashed into her chest. The slam of short term memory propelled her deeper into the sheets.

Fuck me.

The stretched face and the throw of her body as her car's back end obliterated into a sculpture of twisted metal scraped her spine just as the bracelet had to her cheek and she released another, more guttural, groan. She tumbled off the half-mass mattress and landed against the area rug on her hands and knees, the sheets tangled around her ankles like shackles and her hips tilted off-center like a broken sail. Her hair had fallen forward in its moppy mess and her bangs tangled into the small line of stitches.

She stood like she was low on battery juice and kicked the spilled sheets back to the air mattress while she ripped her hair from the deep cut. It itched and sprouted wires poked at the sides of her fingers as she attempted to ignore the slick sensation of the wire and hair separation. The laid bones in her feet wrinkled against the joints in her toes as they sprawled and her body convulsed into a full stretch of cracks and sore screaming muscles.

She began to teeter forward off the area rug and onto the cold hardwood floor. The calluses on her feet let the chilled ground seep in as energy distributed the ice through the rest of her crooked posture. She yawned and a quaking shiver chased after it. The apartment was dark, the only light in the room from a grey Oregon blanket draped in from the curtainless windows spread behind the wooden dining table. Marilyn stepped sloppy boned feet past the couch, then the table, then windows to the cutout kitchen, the one with the spoons and the content cleanliness. She found herself still with a naked twist on her face as she glared at green numbers displayed on Brent's microwave. *9:45*.

She groaned for the third time since her eyelids singed open, and this time it came out more like a pinched whine. Had she even slept an hour? Marilyn pulled at her hair with a closed fist as she turned and noticed the note, scrawled out in ink and laid out delicately against the counter for her to find.

> Plenty of food in the fridge and cupboard,
> Help yourself to whatever!
> Davey and I will be back around noon.

Marilyn smiled at the paper as she scooped the pen into her morning claws that had begun to feel intoxicated as her concussed brain worked to focus. She slid the pen to the edge of the paper sheet and scribbled with unfeminine, bold chicken scratch:

> thanks, fosterBoy

A deep hum from the hamper in her new living room rattled her nerve ends and she dropped the pen to the counter. Wide steps were taken out of the kitchen towards the bug buzz of a prepaid phone jammed below her *packed* clothing in the wicker basket. A groan came out for the fourth time just before she answered.

49

Brent had stopped in the cement stairway to exhale stringy breaths through partly parted lips as Davey jogged up the flight ahead of him, towards the apartment. While Brent crouched into the railing and massaged his eyeballs with their eyelids he wondered why he'd missed Marilyn's presence back at the school. With a final gust of centered breath, he straightened back up and fought against their vertigo up the rest of the stairwell.

Davey bounced anxiously in front of Brent's apartment door, "come on!" He cried with an *I'm-so-happy-to-be-home* grin.

Brent tried to nod but it only threw his vision and caused him to make an unhappy grunt as the view boomeranged back. He stepped around the boy when he reached the cool door that he craved to put his forehead against and jingled a key into its lock. The door swung and then two males stepped through it to find Marilyn sat up, Indian style, on top of the quilted air mattress with her curly hair pulled up and her hands folded over the keyboard of Brent's laptop.

The illuminated screen of the thin, handheld, computer cast from under her chin and gave her face a spooky, stretched overcast of pale hollowness as their heads numbed into a vibrant sting.

"Hi, Marilyn Mae!" Davey called and collapsed forward onto the bed.

"Hi," she responded with rasp sweet in her voice left from the nausea she'd had just a moment before. Her swollen eye had gone down and her skin hid the last of its discoloration as she looked up at Brent. She danced the pads of her fingers over each key on the laptop's board without actually pressing them down, "I registered your address as my own online for my license." *Her real one.* She told him with a breathy burp that released the brew in her stomach.

"Proactive," Brent responded in a mumble, afraid the vertigo would sneak back up on him if it heard him speak. He shut the apartment door gently and leaned his back against it, "I thought you weren't supposed to have screen time."

The girl made a face at the man who suddenly sounded like a strict aunt, "I'm not." She shrugged with the words carelessly before running her tongue under her top teeth to smile, "My tongue feels pretty swollen, actually." She then laughed, a burst one that was out of place and dramatized.

Brent frowned and flipped off the apartment light; the room destroyed the yellow hew and a cool, cloudy grey settled in, "you need to sit in the dark," he smiled, "but I appreciate that you took the opportunity to get some stuff done," He walked around the edge of the floor bed and reached a hand out for the laptop.

The girl closed the lid on the silver electronic, "I did try watching TV but you don't have cable," she passed a stupid look to his television, the size of a computer monitor balanced on a tiny end table against the wall by the door, "and your TV is so goddamned small."

Brent lifted the laptop from her held out hand and pressed his fists into his hip, "size doesn't matter. It's a TV ain't it." He smiled then with an innocent wink of his eye.

So innocent it made him seem stupid.

She smiled back and wondered if he said that about other things too.

The innuendo hurtled itself over his head as he turned his attention back to the laptop in his hands, "Where did you find —"

"Your nightstand drawer."

Brent's lips parted uncomfortably, "okay, but how did you get into it, it has a password."

Marilyn rolled her eyes so hard that the muscles in the back of her head burned, "It's 'Pavlov'," she strangled a tight giggle, "not hard to figure out." Her hand pointed towards his Pavlov Dog paperweight at the edge of his rearranged coffee table but her eyes searched his bookshelf of Psychology books.

Brent tried to hide the unsettling chill she gave him behind his red cheeks and bewildered stare, "wow."

She bowed her head, "Ms. Con artist." She wore it like a medal of honor.

Davey intervened then with a quiet voice that drifted up from the pile of blankets that he'd wiggled himself into, "I want to watch a movie," he pointed to the tiny monitor sized television on the wire legged end table.

Marilyn looked at Brent and Brent shook his head, "your sister needs to stay in the dark for a while."

The girl flapped a drowsy arm at her brother, "like a vampire!"

She hissed and showed her canine teeth as Davey laughed and dipped deeper into the sheets.

Brent had gotten her that bag of broccoli from his freezer and clenched his jaw at her written response back to him on the note as he did so. *Foster boy*. He'd asked her to lay back and close her eyes, the bag of thawing broccoli under her lower back. She'd obeyed and had fallen asleep. He noticed, as she snored, the way his head dipped forward like he'd strapped a weight to it.

They had left for the store around four-thirty, once Davey had luck getting Marilyn to wake from her coma.

They now meandered down the wide, main aisle of a superstore. Brent handled the cart, wheeling its twisted, hair tangled, wheels towards the hygiene department with his sights set on the side aisle of toothbrushes. Marilyn strutted beside him and laughed at Davey as the boy helped steer the cart from the front, sometimes steering wrong and making tiny *oops!* noises every time it almost collided with something.

The adults had started to get used to each other's invasive *numb* and the cotton that filled their ears started to feel normal, welcomed, accepted. Marilyn stepped too close to Brent and the cart nose dove for an aisle cap as the man tried to distance the space between them. She side-eyed him, as Davey made his *oops!* Noise and centered the cart back on track.

She cleared her throat and trotted up to the front of her cart to walk alongside her copilot brother.

"Don't ram into us," She instructed the man cooly from over her shoulder as she wrapped a hand around Davey's side.

Brent stopped and sucked the cart handle to his abdomen as his face shadowed into a green translucent skin. Marilyn laughed at him as he thought of how he'd rammed into them the night before. Her head bobbed and the fried curls tried to bounce with it as her cheeks heaved up over her bottom eyelids. It was a hoot, using touchy subjects to get a still, solemn reaction from the grown adult.

Brent squinted and began to move the cart forward again. A stuck wheel skipped and hiccuped over the polished store cement and he decided to try his hand in her little game, "don't stop for the *Boogie Man* and I won't," as the words came out chills released against his skin, despite his smile, and he hoped Davey didn't catch that he didn't say, 'don't stop for a *deer.*'

Marilyn's lips spread with the widest laugh he'd ever seen humanly possible as she collapsed her shoulders and rippled a few snorts between the wide chuckles. She had to lock her knees and stay in place as she let the laughter out and Brent, unable to stop in time as he watched with amusement as she laughed, bumped into her. *Accidentally.*

Brent gasped and yanked the cart away from the girl who stumbled forward with a hand to her back. She turned slowly and the hand came out to grab the cart for stability as she threw her body forward in an echoey fit of laughter.

Tears threatened to spill over her piled-up cheek muscles as she vomited the belly laugh.

She stood back up with the wet in her eyes and tried to speak to Brent, her face red, "what," she chuckled wide, "are the *fucking* odds." Her voice was watered down and muddy inside her tight, gurgly throat as she wheezed at the irony.

She screamed another laugh and dipped back forward as the tears finally burst down her cheeks. The odds that he'd crash into the back of them, again, *accidentally.*

Brent, who'd watched her with a hollow horrification began to chuckle himself. He couldn't pinpoint the source, however. Whether it was her crazy, chaotic and contagious bursts of giggles and snorts, or from the embarrassment. He dropped his head and chuckled a contracted breath towards the ground as he decided it was definitely both.

Davey had laughed, a slow confused giggle that had trailed off due to being accustomed to his sister's humorous outbursts. He covered his lips to muffle his chuckles. Both male's focus was on the girl who utterly lost herself within the laughter. Davey had turned his head over his shoulder and shrugged with a smile at his counselor. Brent had winked back and gave a similar shrug.

"That's some funny shit," Marilyn ended her laughter with the words and began to strut forward again while she wiped tears and shook her head of nappy, shoulder-length hair.

In the dental aisle, as Davey scanned rows of toothbrushes for his favorite, Marilyn reapproached the side of the man—this time far enough away to keep him from startling, "I cannot believe you hit me," she whispered and bite her tongue to keep from busting out another laugh like a chest cough.

Brent felt sick, but well enough to joke with her, "which time?" He cocked the corner of his mouth as she muted the cough like laugh with the back of her hand and her eyes watered again.

"With the cart," she clarified though they both knew she didn't have to, "I didn't even stop for —" She used her fingers to drag her bottom eyelids down over her cheekbones to reveal the whites of her eyeballs and the pink, layered, underside of her eye sockets, "*Boogie Man.*" She snorted and released her skin.

The look scared Brent, but he smiled along with her laugh as he leaned forward and pulled a pink toothbrush off of a hook and handed to her, "I can't believe you guys didn't pack toothbrushes," He joked as she continued her laughter and took it from him to hold against her heart.

Her shoulders began to bounce in pace with her wiggled eyebrows and she lifted the packaged brush up to her lips and began to sing through clenched teeth, "*Brusha, Brusha, Brusha, get the new Ipana!*" She mimicked Jan who sang *Bucky Beaver* in *Grease* the movie.

Brent shook his head and tried to mimic one of her eye rolls but had only looked like a tired, middle-aged dweeb, going into epileptic shock.

She tossed the toothbrush into the cart with a smile and continued her wide shoulder bounces.

50

They'd arrived home with the back end of the 4Runner stacked full of superstore grocery bags. Toiletries, food, and a new backpack for Davey. Marilyn hadn't protested the school bag as Brent offered to buy it for the boy. *Free shit was free shit.*

As they soldiered up the cement stairs with plastic bags in their fists an elderly woman haggard down the highest flight with an overweight cat teetered in her frail hold. Brent had seemed disturbed by this as he scolded the woman under his breath and set his bags on steps in his footpath to jog up to her. He wrapped a long hand around her crooked elbow and assisted her steadily down the rest of the steep flight to the outside flat that led to his apartment.

The woman was dark and her eyes had faded a cataract blue from under her white hair eyebrows that fuzzed-out, slept on and scraggly.

She greeted Brent and his helpful hand with a "stop! I can do it on my own!" then, "What are you doing home early?!" Then, "I was going to tape a note to your door again," her hand jutted from the underside of the cat's belly like a broken bone to show him a pink sticky. She waved it through the air the best she could without dropping her pet. She then asked: "who are they?" Her voice a brittle whine.

Brent let out a deep breath from his puffed chest and braced his hands to his hips, "Winnifred, this is Marilyn and Davey," he gestured to them then swooped the gesture back to the elderly woman, "Kids, this is Winnie and—" he pointed to the tail flicking creature in her arms, "Tulsa."

He smiled at the stubborn woman and cat as the woman danced the feline against her chest.

The backpack and plastic bag of toothpaste, socks and, deodorant in Davey's hand slacked against his side as he eyed Tulsa. His face a cornucopia of positive emotion, "hi kitty," he whispered, careful not to startle the woman's black pet.

"Hi," Marilyn nodded to the elderly woman and the bags in her fisted hands rustled.

Winnifred narrowed her bad eyesight at the siblings, then passed the same look onto Brent. He gave her his gentle smile and rubbed a hand over her arm, then over Tulsa's back, "they live with me," he explained then quickly added, "temporarily," to keep Marilyn comfortable. He scratched behind Tulsa's ear and wondered if he was capable of doing such a thing as making Marilyn *uncomfortable*. He'd begun to fear he couldn't.

Winnifred shook her head, "okay? Children of yours I didn't know about, abducted children, what?" Her under eyes smiled at him but her old, wrinkled lips drooped with concern.

"Friends," Marilyn interrupted and Davey backed her up with a nod, one he became unsure about as it weakened and his lip fell into its wet dome of teeth.

Brent picked Davey's nod up where the boy had dropped it and carried it on, "Davey is one of Emily Engles' students."

Winnifred's jowls grew light at the name and the blue cloud in her eyes brightened, "ohhh," she smiled at the man, "Emily."

Brent's face reddened as Marilyn's head tilted in his peripheral and her grocery bags slacked. The girl intimidated him. A ball of sexual emotions that couldn't take her attention off of him.

His stomach knotted as he willed an acutely stubborn memory of Amanda away.

Winnifred's eyes cascaded to her cat who'd begun to try to paddle her back paws out of the woman's hold.

Brent took the opportunity to divert the subject completely and dropped a smile to the boy on the steps, "Davey, Winnie is the one that can sew Beary's arm back together."

Winnifred's head tipped back, "Uh, I ain't sewing shit. Not with this arthritis infestin' my bones." She tried to show her hands but Tulsa's bucking body made it hard for her as she clawed the cat back to her chest.

Brent wavered in his spot and pierced his lips together, "alright," he said with a stretched corner of his mouth, "then *I* will sew Beary's arm back with *her* sewing kit," he smiled at Davey who braved a tiny smile back.

Winnifred clapped her lips together and continued on her arthritis spiel while Tulsa moaned distastefully, "My hands aren't good for anything, just petting my cat and this." She freed an old woman claw and swung it behind Brent, her palm and stiff fingers making a cupped connection with the underside of his ass cheek.

Brent yelped like an injured puppy and swatted at the woman as he bounced away from her, "Winn!"

The old woman teased him with a shit-eating-grin and giggle that threatened to spill her dentures out of her slippery lips and onto the cement landing.

Marilyn snorted the last of her laugh from the store at the startled man.

Davey thought to laugh too but had swallowed it as he studied the change in his friend's face; from a sweet smile to a pale, stone, sweat. Davey realized that it was nothing to laugh at, and his sister had missed that. But that was okay, she missed stuff like that the most.

Brent moved a sad look along with him as he went to his apartment door and un-pocketed his keys to jingle them into their slot and twist until the lock snapped open, "are you coming in, Winn?" He asked with a dull voice as he carried the door open to the messy living room.

Winnifred cheeked a grin knowingly at the man and walked past him in a waddling stride with Tulsa now halfway hung out of her arms.

Marilyn entered next, her grocery bags pulled back up into a comfortable carry, "I like her, foster boy."

Brent's muscles chilled and his neck strained—he knew she would. The two women were spitting images of each other's personalities and he now wondered if he could handle two of the same, "hey Marilyn, please don't call me that."

Davey watched with a sad rock against his stomach as his sister turned a proud face over her shoulder and flashed it at the man without any words.

Brent's jaw set forward.

Davey knelt and tried to wrestle up a few of Brent's grocery bags from the steps along with his own light bag and backpack. He'd done it to make the man feel better but Brent was on top of him too quick. His smile back and his skin to a healthy shade of tan again.

"I got it, Kiddo!" He chirped and began to scoop his arms through the plastic handles, "thank you for your help."

Davey stared at him without response as an empathetic meter spiked somewhere inside his body. Brent's feelings were hurt, but he'd been good at hiding it. Davey gave half a frown, maybe someday he'd be good at it too.

51

The next morning Bear Kingsley's arm had been sewn with dark brown string and needle courtesy of Brent and Winnifred's sewing kit. Davey dressed in clean clothing in the steam of the bathroom and studied the bear that sat on the bathroom counter where he'd set it before his shower. His clothes from the night before laid across the floor with matted black fur in between their seams like a gorilla suit.

Brent worked to straighten his button-down beneath his deep blue sweater in the center of the kitchen while a pot of coffee brewed in front of him.

Marilyn staggered in and popped the refrigerator open—the cool breeze from behind the sealed door of the six-foot-tall unit spread out and clawed through the cloth of the pajama bottoms she stole from the counselor. They'd bought blueberry bagels the day before and she groped hungrily at the closed bag.

"Good morning," Brent shook an arm to straighten out his sleeve, "did I wake you?"

Marilyn tossed her head back and forth to say, 'no', as she removed the plastic bread tab from the clear bag of blue bagels. She had felt Brent fall asleep again the night before, except she'd been pulled down with him into a blanketed dreamland. Then, their eyes had popped awake at the same moment this morning, both their eyelashes tickling eyebrows in unison, but *no* he hadn't *woke* her. She theorized the possibility of their psyches becoming accustomed to a synchronized schedule like a group of women and their periods as she untwisted the bag and slid a cold circle of dough and dried berries out. The edge of the sweet bread was between her lips before the rest of the *boring bagels* were returned to the fridge twisted in their bag, but no longer with the bread tab.

Brent watched the girl frisbee the plastic tab to the counter and she gnawed against the breakfast and gave her a half-hearted smile.

She flashed a cheek stuffed grin at the male like a fat squirrel, "worked up an appetite from teasing you last night," her words were muffled beneath the dough that coated her moist throat.

Brent lifted a side of his pressed lips and crinkled the corner of his eyelids at her before he turned his attention to his finished pot of coffee. She *had* teased him the night before—Winnifred and her pinging jokes off of him like a pro-tag-team, both laughing their asses off when he'd wiggle uncomfortable, or drop his head.

"Yeah, yeah, yeah—" Brent poured a cup of black coffee, "you two make quite the pair."

Marilyn smiled against her bagel as she revisited Winnifred doubling as far as her frail body would allow in cackles when Marilyn had spilled that she'd considered *foster boy's* sexuality when she'd first been introduced to the cleanliness of his apartment.

Davey had snuck into the kitchen with his wet, shower-hair and stitched up Bear Kingsley with a craving for a bagel like the one that hung from his sister's mouth. He beelined behind her back for the refrigerator and dove in to grab the bag of bagels for himself.

Marilyn's hand swooped in from above him and lifted the food out of his hand, "did you brush your teeth?"

Thick, yellow front teeth showed when he sucked on his bottom lip like a pacifier and Marilyn tilted her body disapprovingly.

Davey's head ducked into a pout.

"Go brush your teeth, that's disgusting, Dave."

The boy turned with feet that slapped against the wood floor as he sulked.

Brent sighed out of his nose and leaned into his kitchen counter with a belted hip, "*Brusha, brusha, brusha,*" he sang quietly as Marilyn bit into another bite of bagel and watched her brother mosey through the dark living room with a weighted head on a weak neck.

She turned and laughed with a closed mouth to keep salivated crumbs from a spill down her chin.

Brent had pointed a finger to his coffee pot as an offering to her.

Marilyn nodded gratefully and balanced the rest of her bagel between her teeth and lips to free her hands for a mug, "*shank yoo.*" She said through the pores in the bread.

She'd stopped him at half a cup of dark roast to fill the rest of the mug with milk before she stirred the two liquids together with a dipped in middle finger.

Brent made a face at the young woman, "would you like some coffee with that milk?"

Marilyn set her bagel to the counter and ignored the way the bread dripped soggy at the spots that had been held in her mouth as she sipped the hot drink, "I *loooove* milk," she drooled from a steamy tongue and gulped another mouthful of coffee down her throat. As she gasped against the heat that sunk through her chest she gave him a tilted smile, "someone once told me milk is the reason Americans are fat." Another long swig of the heated milk with a little bit of coffee flavor, "she had slanted eyes and an accent." She whispered, then winked.

The man's lips parted like they wanted to laugh but were too P.C. to let that happen.

Davey had trotted back into the room and stared longingly at the refrigerator. His sister stepped out of the way, closer to the man who instinctively backed up, to allow Davey access to his bagels. His minty-mouth watered and his tongue flicked his taste buds.

"Davey, do you want your bagel toasted?" Brent asked the boy who now had his breakfast in hand.

Davey considered.

Shrugged.

Then chomped a bite of the top layer of bagel, "*Nah,*" he answered with his mouth full. Bagel crumbs spilled down his chest and settled around his socked feet.

Marilyn watched Brent as Brent's eyes followed the crumbs to the floor then snapped up and away. *'He's the cleanest person I know. Mr. Clean!'* Winnifred had joked the night before about Brent.

"Davey—" Marilyn warned softly, "please get a plate." The Matthews' children might drink lots of milk and not eat their bagels toasted, but *we aren't animals!* She thought as she pulled her own drool infested breakfast off the counter and chewed at it.

Brent's eyes had followed her crumbs to the floor as well.

The man had waited patiently until Davey had gone to the front of the living room and creased his hands around his shoelaces before he asked, "can I get you a job?"

Brent walked around Marilyn as the question dangled overhead and leaned into the entryway of the kitchen, still with a distance between them for his safety. *For her safety too*, even if the girl had been standing with her fingers crossed that he'd take just a step closer.

"I got one," She leaned her shoulder into the freezer door with an expression only the cockiest thefts used.

"Pickpocketing isn't a job."

"Yes—"

"Pickpockets' don't pay taxes and pickpockets' lose their brother's to the foster system."

The words had weaned through the air with a harsher sting than what he'd meant to give but she shrugged them off anyway.

"Or to my mom."

Sure, Brent thought and avoided asking.

Purple Crayola noose.

TOO CLOSE TO A GREEN SATURN.

He flinched.

"What kind of job?" The girl then inquired as she straightened back up, away from the freezer, and crossed her arms.

Brent chewed the side of his cheek slowly, "the school?" He asked her as he considered it himself, "you'll be close to Dave."

She smiled and tapped her noggin' with a forefinger.

52

Brent had waited until Thursday to stand in front of Debra and pitch the idea of Marilyn working alongside her—filing papers, making calls, taking notes and cubby mail to teachers, *etcetera*. He presented the idea without strings too attached to the girl and hoped Debra wouldn't ask too many private questions.

Her lips twisted as her mind motored around his opposition like the sidecar of a Harley Davidson.

Brent watched the white panel office ceiling as he waited.

"Why can't she be your assistant?"

Brent's head dropped down to her.

He had considered it earlier in the week but kept coming around to the way the young girl looked at him with dilated eyes and had dismissed the idea prematurely—afraid of it, "I don't think it'd be appropriate," he answered honestly.

The woman's lips parted, then, "ei, I see. *Handsome,*" she winked and without attempt gave him a perfect example as to why Marilyn couldn't work directly with him, "why are you helping her?"

Brent gave her a side-eye, disappointed that it hadn't taken her long to get around to the *personal questions,* it never did.

She frowned at him, then shrugged like her bra straps were too tight, "I wouldn't mind the help."

Debra was like a green light—he breezed through her with both hands in his pockets. But now, he cautiously approached a yellow light, *Olmstead,* with two hands on the steering wheel.

Olmstead's yellow flipped to a green and Brent had dropped his hands back into his pockets casually. Surprised.

He stood, now, over the lazy grey-skinned man as he wrote an email to the district office as a *request for approval.* A new, thought up job, for an office assistant.

"Can you copy me into this email?" Brent asked and tapped the CC line on the screen.

His boss nodded and typed *Bkingsley* into the line for the computer to autofill the rest of the email address.

53

Marilyn had mounted herself on Brent's bathroom counter and crossed her legs into the sink to let her ankles dangle with their boney nubs rubbing uncomfortably against the white porcelain while she shifted weight. She glared into her medicine cabinet reflection at the high E-string stitches that stared back like bulbed insect legs that cursed a pink-flesh slit in her olive skin.

Her back molars ground together as she tried to imagine a job interview with a school. She couldn't foresee an outcome that considered her hired if she walked in with guitar-string insect-legs crawling around her forehead.

She picked the wound with two fingers like it was a pimple and pressed dry lips together every time the stitches shifted beneath her brittle skin like a crackling spine. She poked the end of the black lines and watched them move against her forehead. She placed a finger on either side of the split and tugged her skin away from it. The stitches shifted again but the wound stuck still, a healed seam of flesh.

Her hands dropped to a pair of scissors balanced like a playground teeter-totter on her bent knee. She'd found them in the bottom of Brent's junk drawer, *three drawers down.*

With a steady hand, like a surgeon, she lifted the packing scissors to her forehead and dug the pointed tip between the first strap of stitches. She slowly snapped each connecting strand of wire between the mouth of the scissors, then stopped. She inspected the fragile plastic as she lowered the black-handled scissors back to her lap and balanced them against her knee where they wobbled back and forth. She used her fingers to pull at the wound again.

The sensation of a tear startled her as the stitches spread out below her itchy flesh. She paused and watched, her fingers at a limbo against her oily forehead. There wasn't a sign of blood or the pink underside of flesh so she tugged a little harder to test that her skin wouldn't split into two halves. *Nothing.* Just a red itch below a white crease surrounded by black legs stabbed through tiny holes in her skin like a butterfly on its back.

She pinched an end of the E-string stitch reluctantly between thumb and finger and gently began to wiggle it free. The stitch slid from under her skin like an internal paper cut. Her lips parted and her tongue punched forward against the back of her bottom row of teeth as her stomach swelled into a dark pit. Her skin moved with the string as microfibers clung to its latex coating. It slipped from the man-made pore and Marilyn's skin snapped back to absorb into itself. She glanced at the plastic laid out on her finger like an eyelash and swallowed a gag.

The next stitch fell out with an easier glide and crumbling dry skin that quivered her dilated eyes as it sprinkled out around her. "Fuck," she hissed with cold air between the unflossed slits of her teeth.

She bit the tip of her tongue until it bulged red as she removed the last stitch with a pop, pull and puss bubble.

Her nails danced across the new, fragile skin as she scratched at the scar tentatively. A feverish tendency had been set and all she wanted to do was to reopen the wound with a long scrape.

Marilyn dropped her hand before she could.

Fresh air was comforting against her body and frigid against her new scar now hidden by falling bangs that brushed into her eyebrows as she paced a cracked sidewalk in the *forgotten side* of Grant. She skinned the corner of the block and found herself outside of a dirt, dust, and spider web infested convenience store with a red ninety-nine cent painted to the cataract window. *Ninety-nine cents for what? An STD from the toilet seat?*

She'd left for a walk to ease her wavy stomach and fluttering eyelids after deep breaths through her nose failed to help. She now caught eyes with a toothless man leaned against a graffitied bike rack and gave him a nod. He reciprocated the gesture with a jumble of words and pushed a cigarette from his fingers into the space between his gums like it was a sucker.

Marilyn's mouth glazed over with thick saliva like a salivating dog and her tongue flicked over the rough of her mouth. *Pavlov dog.* She frowned at the thought and the nicotine drinking man before she beelined for the Market entrance with craving.

She entered beneath a dinging bell and stepped from solid blue tile to a marbled, dirty tile. Mismatched, filthy shelves lined the thin walkways of orange tagged items hung lifelessly from chipped hooks. She flicked her foot across an astray, outside leaf, and ducked behind an aisle of single-serving chip bags. An Oriental woman, behind the smudged glass counter filled with gambling *scratch-its*, called an accented *'Welcome!'* to the girl who lifted a hand over the chip rack and gave a spread fingered wave before she shoved both hands into her front pockets. Her youthful fingers coiled around cotton currency like a snake around a mouse and her lips peeled from their snarl to a smirk. She walked the length of the aisle without interest to round the end of it and head up the second to the counter.

The Oriental woman stood against the glass case and blinked boldly at the girl as she approached with a steady eye on the tobacco wall behind the middle-aged Asian.

"Hello," The woman greeted without any facial intuition.

"Hi," Marilyn's dry lips smeared together and her scar stung beneath the fluorescent shop lights.

The woman's eyes glistened off of the white line on Marilyn's forehead, then went dead, "you gamble? What do you need?" Her accent was thick and she stood beside a tacked up sign: *After January 1st, all tobacco purchase ages will be moved to 21. NO EXCEPTIONS. Thank you—The State of Oregon.*

Marilyn made an arched bow with her lips and her eyebrows creased, "Marlboro," she jogged a shoulder to the rows of cancer sticks behind the clerk.

'Which?" The woman pointed over her shoulder to the colored packs.

"Reds."

The woman turned to the dispenser shelves and slid a pack from its sleeve of identical cardboard boxes with wrinkled fingers. Her shoulders stayed relaxed against her spine and her head swiveled her straw hair against her thin neck. With pack in hand, she turned back to the counter without acknowledgment and jammed the cigarettes beneath a handheld laser scanner. It sounded a pitched beep and a digital green price registered on a black, rearview mirror sized screen that faced Marilyn. The girl ran a pocketed thumb over the robbed money she held in her fist. The woman crossed her hands together and lightly sucked her wrinkled cheeks in as she waited for —

"this too."

that.

Marilyn tossed a small, black lighter to the counter from a little shelf stood next to the register. The lighter spun like a top over the showcase glass and stopped against the woman's folded fists.

She picked it up and ran it through the scanner, the numbers on the *rearview mirror* screen flashed to a different price. She put the black lighter on top of the Reds and glared at the burdening girl, "seven, ninety-eight."

Marilyn pulled out the conned twenty from her pocket and slid it between two fingers to the clerk.

Ms. Oriental took the bill into a closed fist and jammed a single finger into keys on her register until the drawer popped out and socked her in the abdomen. "ID," She spoke like an old machine.

Marilyn's hand pressed further into her pocket, then pulled out to tap it and the pockets on her ass for the thin, plastic card. Her head dipped back and she bounced a balled fist off her thigh as her pants came up ID-less, "I'm sorry," she grumbled at the woman with a tongue that began to ache for the nicotine taste, "I left my ID at home. I–"

The woman flipped up the plastic tab that clipped down a stack of twenties in her register and put Marilyn's on top like she was bedding an infant. The drawer was then shut, without any change taken out, and the cigarettes were offered to the coily haired customer.

"Good Day, come back."

Marilyn's mouth twitched until it held a half-smirk as she took the items into her own hands, "thanks," she purred towards the clerk that avoided eye contact before she bounced away from the counter and pocketed her tobacco and fire.

54

Marilyn lit an unboxed cigarette and puffed the filter to guide the spreading embers towards her lips as she walked. She paused her steps to focus her energy on an inhaled gulp of heat that danced down into her lungs and her entire body shuddered with goosebumps that flared beneath her skin. The black mass swelled her throat and mouth and the back of her tongue fuzzed as her chest gave a gentle contraction, like a hiccup. She held in the nicotine and gently shut her eyes to keep the smoke from coming out of her tear ducts.

As the relief of a fed addiction rubbed warm circles into her nerve ends she thought of her late father. The way his bottom lip would hide half of his top teeth when he smiled, she smiled herself to mimic him in the streets of Grant with her eyes closed and a cigarette balanced between two fingers as the sudden memory stretched a soft picture across her forehead. She'd gotten her laugh from him. The wide, crazy one that came out of the strangest situations and spilled tears from their eyes.

The thought of him laughing hurt and her lids opened to get away from the image—she exhaled the smoke through tight teeth with a heavy chest.

The cigarette was to her lips again and her legs were wading a path over cement sidewalks again, back to Brent's apartment as she forgot the abrupt memories of Dad.

The sun had begun to poke out of wet clouds and stabbed bedazzled lines into the exposed flesh on the smoking girl as she rounded a hedged sidewalk corner and grimaced into it. The sun shrunk back into the clouds and removed the pinned glare from her constructed vision so she could see what was in front of her. She winked up at it. What a gentleman, the sun was. *"You are really a peach, Mr. Sun!"*

Marilyn's head dropped back and her chest cramped as the cigarette she'd been sucking on fell from her lips.

A figure, at the end of the long sidewalk, mimicked her stance with a drooping face and bead black eyes. It hunched its back and its skin wilted until it swallowed the tiny, round eyes into their grey slits. *The Boogie Man.*

The embers of Marilyn's forgotten cigarette flicked around the toe of her shoe and died against the cold cement as the creature swayed, and she stood, paralyzed. Her lips froze parted and the muscles in her neck strained and pulsed in thick strings that bulged from her skin. They mimicked being strangled and she mimicked a human without lungs.

The lower jowl of the creature sunk past its strained tendons to reveal a black mouth and paper-thin tongue in the forefront of a hole that deepened further into its esophagus, like the belly of a snake. The stench of the creature fastened around Marilyn's dry muzzle like a hot rag that she whimpered helplessly against as her neck continued to contract and her lungs begged to breathe. Her chest caved against her pathetic cry and her eyes began to burn.

Its body swayed counter to its wind caught jaw and the frightened girl was hypnotized by it, her own body set into a sway.

Then the creature was moving. Fast, then faster, and Marilyn's eyes blinked rapidly like she'd caught something in them as the thumps of its feet grew loud, then louder, its body moving at in unrhythmic pace towards her.

Marilyn's palms pounded into her cheekbones and her fingers webbed out over her eyes like tobacco scented nets to keep out the morbid monster.

Her knees went watery against the sensation of its jaw clasping around her and she buckled into the ground, her ass skidding into ember, ash, and cement as her fingernails dug into the tops of her eye. She let out a wet cry and laid her back on the sidewalk with a twitching head that bounced against the hard ground. She could feel the being, the *Boogie Man,* on top of her like a taloned bird on top of prey. Its scent a wool blanket she was smothered beneath as she writhed into the pavement.

Another scream curdled against the inside walls of her throat and a cold sweat broke through her twitching body as the wool lifted and fresh air forced itself into her sobbing lungs. Speckled magenta lines sliced against her eyelids as her nails tried to cut through and her lips whimpered against her forearms. A final scream and aftershock sang through and out but only through her nostrils this time as her knees sucked up into her chest.

(It's okay, kid.) A voice comforted from a deep, weary spot. *(Open your eyes and join me.)* She wanted to spit at the voice, nash her teeth at it, growl like a territorial dog until it backed off. It was lying, she refused to listen. Her fingers crawled like spider legs up her tense forehead and into her hair where they entangled. *(Join me.)* The voice, a man's, cooed and she began to tear at her matted mane. Her scalp screamed in sheer pain that rocketed through the rest of her bones and made her elbows tingle but she continued to pull.

She pulled until she was back to the night she'd found her father.

Tiny and on the unpolished hardwood floor of Davey's nursery with her ten-year-old hands ripping hair from its follicles. Davey happy in his crib, her father's socked feet hung at eye level to her, his belt supporting his lifeless body in it limp, *swaying,* hang. She could hear herself moan *"Daaaad!"* In a guttural cry that was streaked with sharp stabs that cut into the fleshy insides of her cheeks like prison razors. She sucked a breath in and the razors turned and sliced the back of her throat until she coughed and gagged thick saliva and screamed for him again. As her hair fell out into her fists she dared to glance up at him, his purple, bubbled face.

But the memory was different this time.

This time her father stared at her with a faded smile on his blue lips and relaxed, bloodshot eyes.

Marilyn's eyes snapped open.

Grey sky greeted her as a cool breeze danced the tangled hairs from her cramped fingers. *It was gone.* The cool cement became known against her jeans and backs and she lowered her palms down into it. *(Join me.)* The voice came again through her thoughts and she blinked at her Boogie Man-less surroundings.

The *human-less* surroundings. Not a soul in sight or a hand held out for help. She was alone.

Marilyn blubbered a deep, panicked, chuckled that rattled her shoulder blades against the sidewalk as fat tears rolled from her eyes and into her ears.

55

Davey was the first to notice Marilyn's missing stitches as the Matthews' siblings and single Kingsley sat around the dining table with pork chops and steamed potatoes under their noses. He'd pointed it out with a finger and eyebrows that tightened closer together with every chew he took against a piece of pork in his mouth, his voice making a hum to catch her attention.

She looked up from her uneaten meal and felt her scar with the soft pad of a finger. A light shrug off her shoulders followed, "Yeah, it'd gotten pretty itchy."

Brent lifted an eyebrow, "Did it hurt?" He asked, then dismissed the question with a buoyant shake of his head, "I'm surprised the wound didn't reopen," he chuckled to himself and pushed a slice of potatoes between his lips to chew on thoughtfully as he studied the girl's forehead.

Marilyn nodded at her food and shuffled the pork into her potatoes.

Brent frowned as his studying dropped from her forehead scar to her body language and his tongue removed a bit of potato from between his teeth to swallow it.

"That makes me feel sick," Davey announced through a mouthful of food and watched as his sister gave him a twitchy lip in replace of what would normally be a wide, mischievous grin.

Brent leaned back into his chair and stabbed his fork into a pork chop so it stood up straight, "How'd you get them out, Marilyn?" He continued to suck at his tooth for reassurance that he'd gotten all of the left behind potato.

Her eyes lifted and met his with a hollow flatness that prodded at him, "the scissors I found in your kitchen."

She mumbled her voice over the full plate of food below her. She wanted to hide, excuse herself to the bathroom and flip the faucet on to mask the sounds of her whimpered screams from the sidewalk earlier that day. The ones that now rang wild in her head and made her face feel cold as the creature's presence haunted her like the tickling residue of a bad cough.

Brent met her cool, settled stare for a moment, mimicking it as his own. Then he smiled, his face spreading into a shade brighter and happier than hers, "you mean the scissors I used to prepare our dinner?"

Davey's head whipped from Marilyn to Brent with a scrunched nose and a giggle.

"The scissors I cut the *pork chop bag* with?" His voice was high and his smile was higher.

Marilyn fought to match it with her own smile, unwilling to give it to the man who was making it annoyingly obvious he was trying to make her laugh. Her eyes crinkled and her nose flared, but she dropped her head before the full expression could go into effect.

"I cut the potatoes open with those!" Brent's mouth gaped and his eyes stayed wide—despite the lie, he hadn't cut anything with the scissors.

Davey, susceptible to the humor, began to laugh and poke at his dinner.

Marilyn's head came back up like she was a tired dungeon prisoner held by the wrists against a damp wall, "added extra flavor," she flatlined her punchline.

Brent threw his head back despite her dull delivery with a palm to his forehead, "Oh my God!" He laughed dramatically, "I'm throwing them away!"

The smile, the one she'd been working to hide, revealed itself and she quickly covered it with the back of her hand like she was about to sneeze, "sorry."

Davey, who still laughed and stabbed his food, scrunched his nose, "yuck, Marilyn Mae!"

The girl's eyes brightened for the first time since the males had gotten home, "Mmm, delicious, Davey Niles."

The boy snorted a laugh and Brent shook his head, "I'm serious, you guys. I'm going to throw them away."

There was a silent lull that had made their breathing and Davey's gentle giggles crisp in the apartment and Brent tried to make eye contact with the girl across from him. She avoided it and Brent rubbed his lips together like he was using them to put a pin into the subject matter before he changed it.

"How was your day, Marilyn?" He asked with a voice that now nestled down to normal level, no longer pitched and fun.

She shrugged and he held back a sigh.

Davey stabbed at his food aggressively like he was auditioning for the part of *Mowgli* in *the Jungle Book*. Brent leaned forward and grabbed Davey's plate, "want me to cut it up for you?" He asked the kid.

Davey looked at him sideways then smiled, "yes, please."

As the plate scraped along the wooden table Marilyn's head came up. Brent grabbed her eyes with his and loosened his lips, *"what's wrong?"* He mouthed to her. He'd begun to feel nervous, *had Nick found out where she was, did she get a call from C.P.S.? What was it?* Brent scooped a steak knife into his mitt and began to cut diagonal lines over Davey's dinner while his eyes stayed at pace with the girl's, afraid he'd lose her attention.

Her face narrowed and something pale took over her normal olive glow as she brought hands up to her cheeks, slowly, like it was a stickup. Her fingers were placed below her eyelids and she used them to sag the lower lids down. Her skin stretched and the red underside of her eye sockets was revealed to the man, the same way she'd done it in the department store.

"*Boogie Man,*" She mouthed back to him before she returned her tingling fingers to the crossed space between her thighs.

The knife Brent had been holding broke through the meat and scrapped a grey line into the dinner plate as his muscles spasmed and his eyes dilated at the girl. The hiss of metal and glass smearing over one another made them flinch and he wet his bottom lip with a shaky tongue.

Davey, unaware of the tight chests and chilled faces the two adults shared back and forth, reached for his dinner, "thanks, Brent."

His sweet, kind voice brought Brent out of his paralysis and he turned a fake smile to the boy.

"No problem," he spoke beneath graveled breath and slid the plate back onto Davey's placemat.

The heat in the room had evaporated and goosebumps tightened his cheeks as he turned his head back to Marilyn with a mouthed question formed on his lips. *What do you mean? You saw him? It? The Boogie Man.* But she was scooting back in her chair and her eyes were lost in thought.

"I'm full," She stood and turned her back to them and her untouched food. Without pushing in her chair she slumped to the bathroom and slipped behind the door to bury her face in Brent's running faucet.

Brent had wrapped her plate in Saran wrap while Davey danced around the living room in an imaginative world with Bear Kingsley held out in his arms.

The man stared at her wrapped food with his cheek as a substitute for flavorless bubble gum against his gnawing molars.

"Beary! You're the pirate coming to steal my ship!" He heard Davey yell at the stuffed animal.

Brent opened his fridge and slid the plate onto a cold wire shelf. Why had she seen it, but not him? The *Boogie Man*. He closed the fridge and leaned his head against it with a selfish fear that it'd be his turn next to experience *oogity boogity*.

"Boom! Beary! I shot you with my canon!" In the living room, Davey collapsed to the blue blow-up mattress and wrestled the toy that posed as the pirate.

The man patted the fridge like the back of an idling van and stepped back away from it to straighten his back and walk into the living room.

56

The Boogie Man hadn't come to take his turn with Brent—and had left Marilyn alone by the looks of her warm cheeks and easy glow when Brent and Davey had gotten home from Grant Elementary Friday afternoon. She'd been laid out on the couch with her hands folded under her hips to keep them upright as Davey barreled through the door with two ice cream cones and hyper, jittering limbs.

"Guess what!!!" He screeched with the ice cream cones held above his head as he ran over the wobbly air mattress to his sister's side and passed her a cone of *vanilla and chocolate swirl.*

Marilyn took it from Davey and toasted it into the air as she gave her best guess to *'guess what!!!',* "You and Brent stopped for ice cream."

Davey let out a long, loud laugh and shook his head, "No!" His face scrunched to contradict himself, "I mean, we did…" He trailed off into a distant thought then came back around to slam into her with his smile and words, "but not that! Something else! Something WAY better!"

Marilyn shuffled an elbow below her back to sit up and took a lick off the chocolate side of her cone, "what then?"

Davey tossed his head to Brent who was leaned against the closed apartment door with one hand in his pocket and the other around his vanilla ice cream cone. He'd been smiling at the boy and now paired the smile with a nod for him to continue sharing, "Go ahead, pal. You can tell her."

It was like he'd added baking soda to vinegar as Davey spun back around to his sister and erupted, "You're gonna work at my school!!!" His free hand shot into the air and his fingers spread to whip around like a celebratory flag.

Marilyn stared at her brother blankly, then turned her stare to Brent. *Had she skipped the interview process?*

Brent shook his head as if he'd read her mind, "there will still be an interview, but the position was opened up for you," he shrugged with the corners of his mouth.

Marilyn slouched back into the fluffed couch cushions, "wow..." Her eyes glazed as she tried to imagine herself pushing papers in loose office blouses with bubbly fake women around her. It revolted her and she noticed her lip had been curling to her nose at the thought.

Davey climbed onto the couch beside her and cuddled his warmth into her sore body. His untamed hair tickled the underside of her chin and soothed the skin-crawling, *vomitile*, repulsion the job offer gave her as he slurped melted lines of ice cream off his hand.

Davey then popped his head up high enough to clash her teeth together, "aren't you so excited?!"

He chirped as Marilyn made a double chin to get his head out from under her.

She brought an arm around him and patted his back, "I am," she lied. Sort of lied, she was thankful, but dreading all in the same. A wrapped ball of confused yarn and conflicting emotions. She kissed Davey's head, her eyes as tall as the man leaned against the door, "thank you."

Brent had been watching her with amusement like he *knew* she was terrified of the idea, "sure," he said and straightened out of his lean, "they're going to call you."

They (some woman in the district office named Tami Beagle) did call— around five while Davey took a bath and Brent vacuumed around the air mattress in his living room. She had apologized for calling so late in the day and Marilyn had apologized for the noise in the background as she plugged her phoneless ear and walked into the kitchen. The call was quick and Marilyn hung it up with the basic understanding that they'd scheduled a meeting at the district office for eight in the morning, on Monday.

She'd put the phone down against the counter and let out a pressed sigh as Brent, who'd stopped the vacuum to eavesdrop, came around the kitchen corner and congratulated her with a, "woohoo!" and a, "you'll do great!"

The girl frowned at him, "I'll fuck it up."

Brent's body tensed like a startled cartoon character, then settled gently with a thoughtful grin, "you won't." He spoke in a soft tone that made his vocal cords purr in a way that meant, *'I can tell you're regretting letting me set this opportunity up for you, but I'm proud of you for at least trying to act like it's worth your while.'* Because it was.

Marilyn's head tilted and her vision pulsed over the view of his abdomen that lay below his shirt, then over his arms, then the angle of his jaw tilted over his limber neck. A wicked smile had stitched into her skin and she flexed her toes inside her socks as an opportunity arose like a teenage boner. An opportunity to touch him. She cheered, "thank you!" Like she actually was excited and crossed the kitchen in a leap to wrap her arms around him. She fell into his body and buried her nose into his chest of warm oak and rose scent.

Brent startled and his feet shuffled back against her, his hands restricted in his pockets.

Marilyn pinched a happy moan and trailed her hands between his shoulder blades to suck him in close and feed the horny pool in her stomach.

The hug ground their flesh together like they'd been sealed as one by hot wax. A magnetic field of dizzying decay boxed them in together, *a Christmas package mailed to hell*. Brent gasped as he felt his lungs collapse into his back and Marilyn's arms fought to un-attach from the pressure that'd been put around them. The floor dropped from under their feet and the room began to spin against them, harder than it had ever spun for them before. Both of their visions lost as the pain of their bodies being impacted together and thrown through vertigo tunnels intoxicated them.

Brent was able to free his hands from his pockets and shucked them between the two of them like the flat end of a crowbar. He let out a muffled cry full of saliva and shoved the two of them apart. Marilyn stumbled back, her eyes fluttering as she regained step, space, and sight. Brent sidestepped the girl and fell two steps to the sink where he doubled over it and dry heaved. His vision clotted and came back in black specks that mimicked mold.

Marilyn steadied herself against the fridge at the entrance of the kitchen and the floor that now felt solid below her feet with puffs of nauseated air. "Holy shit," she panted, "that was some *Freaky Friday* shit."

Brent sobbed a pained laugh into the bowl of the sink, "no more hugs," he wheezed as he stood back up and glanced at her with pale under eyes. The pale turned to seaweed green and he dropped back into the sink. *It was some* Freaky Friday *shit.*

He flicked the sink faucet on and ran the cold water over his buzzing fingers, then pulsing wrists, then burning forearms. His head dropped against the top of the faucet until the motion sickness passed and the pit hardened and fell to the bottom of his stomach.

TOO CLOSE TO A GREEN SATURN.

Brent cupped his hands under the faucet and caught water to toss into his face and rub down into his cheeks that had started to stubble. Marilyn's eyes plunged into the back of him and pinned him against the counter with discomfort. He turned the sink off and stared into its silver bottom as the girl rubbed the sore spots of her breast bone where he'd shoved.

57

Brent had lent his black Toyota 4Runner and a folded stack of cash to Marilyn on Sunday morning with precaution and a, "take it easy," as he evaluated her concussion with skeptical scrunched eyebrows.

The girl now fought the church crowd on the main drag through town. She leaned her head against the car's rattling driver window as she inched through the traffic. Marilyn was terrified of the rumble and speed of Brent's black highway machinery after the wreck and the white knuckles over her hands promised the new fear was real.

A family van cut her off and she raped the horn with a heavy hand and hard glare at the church wife who flipped her off.

"God bless," Marilyn grumbled and waved at the woman with the French tip middle finger held in front of her rearview mirror for Marilyn to see, her toddlers sat innocently in her back seats. "Enjoy your day at church, asshole," Marilyn hissed to the mom who couldn't hear her before she took a left into a lightly trafficked parking lot of the department store where Brent had bumped the back of her with his cart. Marilyn's bottom lip folded against her teeth as she decided she wished Brent would bump into the back of her with other things. *Maybe she could go to church and pray for it.* Then the jolly Santa in the sky would *make all her dreams come true!*

Marilyn was cranky, for no reason at all, and mad at the God everyone believed in. Maybe because of French tipped, bird flung, church woman.

She had found a spot up front and steered the 4Runner to it with a sharp corner, taken too wide. The vehicle centered itself on the white line and made her feel foolish as she backed it up to correct her misjudgment. *God mocking her.*

"I'm not used to driving bigger vehicles," she justified to the empty Toyota that seemed to laugh from its stitched seams. She knew, as she blew hot air from her nose, that she'd always been an awful parker, and the SUV had nothing to do with it. She killed the engine with a sharp twist of key and ignition and chewed the skin on her lip as the 4Runner puttered to sleep and the dash lights faded into interior lights.

The store was ten degrees cooler than the brittle air that hugged the outside of the building. Air conditioning in the fall, it set the girl's teeth on edge. Marilyn narrowed her eyes at a woman in a motorized chair like it was her fault as she crossed her arms and thought: *We wouldn't need air conditioning if fat asses like you didn't overheat under your rolls.* It was a crude, uncalled for thought that the woman didn't deserve, but Marilyn felt zero regret for it. Her eyes pinned to the fat that waterfalled out of the woman's lap and dangled against her bent, kicked up, feet. *Wunderbar.*

The familiar, feathery craving for a cigarette signed the back of her tongue as the tip of it flicked against her teeth. Marilyn pressed two fingers to her lips like they contained the nicotine stick between them and turned towards the clothing department. It was a beeline, past the obese woman, as Marilyn felt the hot reminder of why she was here spark against her heel: *clothes for her interview.* Her stomach cramped and her fingers pressed harder into her lips until her teeth made little indents into the wet back of her soft mouth. She passed a rack of cardigans and scowled at them reluctantly as their long, bellowed sleeves scowled back.

She would've continued past them but *shit.* If she was going to get the job she'd have to look the part, *right?* She grabbed a grey cardigan by its hanger and almost completely hated Brent for it. Marilyn knew it was downhill from the moment she folded the cardigan into her abdomen. She might as well begin saying stupid, bubble gum phrases like, *"good deal!"* and, *"oh, absolutely!"*

She thought hastily of the man she called *Jerr-Bear* that she let grope her for basically nothing and some bad condoms. She frowned at the wool draped over her arm and thought that maybe this job would be good for her. She could handle smiling and stapling papers for eight hours a day. Sure! Her tongue flicked for a cigarette again.

She had found a business casual suit blouse that made her stomach look lean when she did slow turns in the department store mirror with it held up against her chest. She snagged a brown belt and imagined she'd pair the belt, shirt, and pre-owned black jeans. The style reminded her of something Brent would wear, which in turn, was most likely why she liked it so much. She ran a hand down the blouse material on her stomach and felt horny like she had when he'd hugged Brent on Friday night before they dizzy danced.

She swallowed against her hormones and dared a smile at her reflection. Her period had to be just around the corner, she was sure by the reflection that started back in heat. *Maybe I'll sync up periods with the bitch teachers.* Wouldn't that just be dandy?

"Good deal!" She squealed to herself, then gagged at the mirror.

Marilyn left the store without shoplifting, the cash Brent had given her a little thinner and a few quarters heavier. She unlocked the driver door with the F.O.B key as shopping bags slushed back and forth over her extended arm. The Toyota's front lights flashed and the sound of metal pulling out of metal bounced at her ears. She reached for the black, dust-coated handle, and her stomach cramped.

A figure, seen through the driver's window, stood at the other side of the SUV. It moved as soon as Marilyn's eyes flicked to it and her body locked into a paralyzed statue. A grey shoulder on the exterior end of the passenger window dipped out of sight like a silent whale dropping further into black water. *The Boogie Man.* The image of the creature slithering to its knobby hands and knees to slide its slick body under the belly of the 4Runner stuck like a knife into the center of Marilyn's forehead and she instinctively shuffled back, away from the vehicle.

Her mouth had dried and her knees felt springy as she stood with her chest erect and her eyes bulged at the lip of the Toyota's belly blind spot. Her ankles began to itch as she imagined a long hand dragging against the ground to wrap around her bone and foot. Her feet stumbled back further until her back flattened up against a warm, recently parked truck in the next spot over. She whimpered at the carbon fiber shell on wheels that restricted her from a backward run escape. Tears, familiar to the ones she'd given on Thursday, dropped from her eyes as the waterboarding rag of *the Boogie Man's* scent engulfed the lower half of her face.

"Boo, Marilyn Mae!!" A young, shrill voice screeched as a large movement was flung at her.

Marilyn's whole body shut down in a code red attempt to save herself as a shriek ripped from her throat like a wild raven from a wire cage. As her lungs drained of breath her fists gripped to grocery bags shot up and beat at her temples. Her eyes seized into shut quivers and her face burrowed into her brought up forearms.

A small, uncalloused hand softly rubbed her jittering arm as the young voice spoke again, familiar to her this time. "Oh, Marilyn," her brother sighed and her eyes relaxed open to watch him teeter off his toes, "I'm sorry if I scared you too bad!"

His massaging hand loosened her shoulders and her fists and bags slumped back to her side.

"I was trying to be funny," his eyes watered sorrowfully as he studied his sister.

Marilyn shook the tingle in her head, "no," she croaked with a sore throat, "you didn't scare me." She cleared the gravel behind her tongue with a cough, "you're okay."

She searched the parking lot wildly rather than joke with him, or pull a punch against his shoulder, which made the boy suck his lip with concern.

"Where's Brent?" She asked as her searching eyes dropped back down to study the underside of the Toyota.

Davey peered around, "he was right behind me," he spoke sheepishly, "I ran when I saw you. We were on a walk."

It didn't occur to Marilyn how far they had to have walked to make it to the store she shopped at, or how her brother's hand no longer stroked her arm. Her heart sank as she considered the creature no longer being below the SUV but rather had slithered out and run after the tired man who jogged in a panic after the boy who'd sprinted away from him through a parking lot. The same way it had run after her on Friday. Her lips tightened and she lowered herself to her hands and knees to see.

Her hand swept behind her to grab at Davey for comfort.

Except–

She couldn't.

Her hand brushed out for him but his body slid back, away from her, like he was peppered water propelling from a soapy finger. His eyes flicked at her like a hologram and his cheeks hollowed.

"Dave," Her flesh grew cold as she breathed his name. The underside of the 4Runner *was* empty, but the creature hadn't run anywhere after anyone. "Dave –" she whined to the boy who shuddered like a flag in the wind beside her with a dead stare.

Her nose flared as tears kissed her waterline and the curly hair on the back of her neck stood straight, the way a dog's hair might when they felt threatened by a nearby predator, their body lowered and a brewed rumble growing from the lowest pit of their chests. She needed to get into the car.

Davey, in turn, was the one reaching for Marilyn now. His hand enclosed her wrist with cold fingers, "you okay, sissy?" He asked with a glazed mouth.

Never, *ever* had Davey, in his eight years of life, call her sissy.

Marilyn stood slowly towards the boy then began to step forward like she was attempting to cross the length of a tightrope. Her eyes super-glued to the 4Runner as she stepped, toe-heel, towards it. Davey's grip tightened around her wrist until the joint burned. A sensation, like tickling, came next–above his grip. Tickling like the frail legs of insects.

(Join me.) She remembered the voice from the sidewalk. The one that whispered it's body like a serpent into the blank slate of her mind. She was sure now that she absolutely *knew* the voice.

The insect legs spilled onto her stimulated skin and fat-bodied walked along with them.

Marilyn's free hand swung out for the 4Runners black handle and coiled around its gripped plastic. The department store bag in her hand rattled against the driver door with a sound that sliced at her ears. Insects had begun to push below her sleeve on the arm the boy held and rushed to the pit of her elbow.

With conjured fear and shaky bones she ripped at the door handle. It pulled out with a pop, then snapped back into place, the door sealed and immovable. She screamed through pinched lips and yanked harder at the locked door as the bugs began to spill down her back.

Her jaw broke open and the muted scream slid from her lips at full, siren pitch.

Something weighted slammed into the center of her chest.

58

A pile of soft grocery bags rolled from Marilyn's panting breast to her lap as she shrieked and sat out of her napping position on the couch. Brent, who had set the bags on the sleeping girl stepped away from her as her eyes peeled and her hands sprawled out like claws.

"I'm sorry," he apologized, "I didn't mean to startle you." He'd been trying to be funny, somehow to him, putting shopping bags on the girl's chest while she slept would be just that: *funny*.

Trying to relate with the kids.

The girl winced and batted at her forehead with open palms. "Ohhh god," She groaned, "It's fucking haunting me in my dreams now!" Her voice was a stretch away from a vocal suicide. She stood and the bags in her lap tumbled to the air mattress laid out in front of the couch.

Brent stared without words at the girl.

Marilyn kicked at the air mattress that'd never gotten sheets from Winnifred's, irritably, "The fucking *Boogie Man* or whatever." She gave herself a double chin and shook her head as she threw her fit.

"I'm sorry, Marilyn." Brent nodded at her like he understood, but he didn't. Boogie didn't bother boys. Not since the car wreck, anyway, "you alright?"

Marilyn still felt like she had insects running against her skin as she let her eyes fall into a glare at the man in casual jeans and a zip-up hoodie, *Sunday clothes*, "no," she had sweat at her temples, "where's Davey?"

Brent frowned and Davey's head slunk out from behind the man, his features wide and curious. He'd been standing there, beside Brent, the whole time.

"Oh shit," Marilyn sat back on the couch and rubbed a heavy hand across her chapped lips, "sorry Dave."

Davey shrugged and wobbled past Brent, to the couch with his sister, "sorry about the bad dream," He said.

He felt warm beside her, as he always did, and Marilyn felt comforted that he hadn't called her *sissy,* or try grabbing her wrist.

Brent flipped the car keys in his hand around his finger—the sound of them as they impacted into his catching palm stabbed sharp and firm at Marilyn's ears. Her eyes watched the F.O.B. 4Runner key hypnotically and her arms felt heavy from the memory of yanking, but the door remaining locked. Marilyn dropped her head and stared with dewdrop eyelashes, at the rolled bags that now laid on the air mattress, "what is that?" She pointed a long finger at the bought items.

Brent shifted his weight.

She had been awake when Davey and he left. She'd been awake when he told her where they were going, what they were doing, and when they'd be back. Yet, now, as he looked her over, he could tell she didn't remember any of it.

"Clothes," he answered and thought of times he'd woken just as confused and dazed from nightmares.

His head always spinning and his gut asking where he was as he panicked in his bedsheets. That'd always been as a kid, though, that he'd have a nightmare that bad. When he was moved onto other foster households after the Onslow's didn't want him anymore, *after Amanda didn't want him anymore.*

"I picked up a few things for your interview tomorrow." The air between the two of them tightened and he shifted his weight back, "I hope that's okay?"

She bent and strangled the bags into a shaky grip to bring back to her lap, "it's fine, thanks," She unwrapped the first bag like it was an anniversary present and pretended the thin plastic crinkle didn't make her feel sick. Her hand slid in between the stretched handles and a warm blanket of yarn ignited her senses as her sleep stricken hand stroked it. She gripped at it and removed it from the bag. It unfolded itself against her extended arm like a cobweb. A cardigan, with its long, billowing sleeves stared at her. *The cardigan* she'd picked out in her dream. It immediately felt hot with electrical currents in her hand and she dropped it to her lap with an urgent panic.

"Sorry if it's ugly —"

Marilyn shook her head at him, "it's fine," she mumbled and stretched the second bag apart.

"Oh! I like this shirt!" Davey admitted, knowing what she was about to pull out—he'd held it up to his own body in the department store mirror and did a few twirls. It reminded him of something Brent would wear, but just in a girl, *sister*, size.

Marilyn could taste the thick apartment air and Brent's warm oak and rose cologne as her lungs expanded to accept a terrorizing dry breath. She brushed her hand over the grey button-up, and brown belt, she'd bought in her dream and her heart seemed to seize up against her chest. Her chin recoiled and her neck throbbed.

Brent chewed the side of his cheek as he surveyed her body language and noticed for a moment that it was Davey sitting in front of him, ruffling through the shopping bags. Tired and anxious. Then her guard was back up and she flicked a smile at him, though it seemed physically painful to do so.

"Thanks," She said.

59

It was a straight spiral downward that propelled into a steaming pile of shit. The heavy man across the table with the last name Olmstead thankfully ate the shit with a spoon, but the woman who sat diagonal to the girl kept her curveballs sharp, her nose lifts sharper, and her dining plate *shitless*.

That *fucking* woman.

Marilyn had begun to feel pissed off.

She was in the cardigan that had appeared in her dream before it'd appeared in the real-life shopping bag Brent had laid on her sleeping body. A concept she no longer found terrifying after a solid nights rest to process the fuckery of her nap time nightmare.

She milked the sleeves of the cardigan over her wrists and up half her palms and found a sense of comfort in the warm, blanket-like texture.

The interview room occupied by the principal, the woman (*Ms. Important District Woman—some bitch that joined the interview*), and Marilyn fell silent. The silence, quiet enough to hear the buzz of electricity in the cubed fluorescent lights above their heads, resurrected Marilyn from her internal thoughts about the sweater and the dream. She parted her lips and stared dumbly at the man and woman who stared back, less dumbly. *Fuck.*

She missed whatever retarded question the woman threw at her that time and resorted back to shoveling another spoonful of steaming shit to feed to, *at least,* the principle. She had maybe heard the woman's monotone voice squeak something about school so Marilyn gave a less than prideful, "I graduated with a 4.0."

The man, Mr. Olmstead, leaned back into his chair and rubbed his cotton clothed, bloated belly, with delighted enchantment like he was impressed with the girl's answer and perhaps *hungry?* The way his hand caressed his stomach as if nurturing an unborn child, or maybe a digesting burrito gave Marilyn the Willys and she made it an effort to keep her eyes away from him.

The snobby woman, who had introduced herself as Ellen, had her face pierced down into Marilyn's resume. The biggest pile of steaming shits out of all piles of steaming shits. A lactose intolerant shit with corn and Taco Bell in its murky brown fluid. Eaten and farted out on paper the night before using Google Docs and the provided resume template.

Ellen ran her finger over each line like she was a first-grader sounding each word out slowly and precisely.

Marilyn felt the need to stand over the woman's shoulder and help with the big, tough words. She practiced a smile: *feeling teacherly already.*

Ellen pursed her lips and tapped the lip gloss on them with a long finger, "you graduated from Elliot Edwards High?"

Good Job! Marilyn nodded slyly, *that's a hard name to sound out. El-EE-ot ED-WURD-s.* "Yeah," she affirmed out loud, "graduated early." She had.

Ellen dipped her grey bobbed head, "good."

Marilyn sat further back into her seat and sucked on the inside of her cheek. The idea had been to graduate early and leave, taking Davey with her since she was old enough to be his guardian in November. The courtroom, however, had changed that plan for her as they took their time to argue, evaluate, argue, consider, and argue more. The granted custody of Davey wasn't given to her until the end of summer. Her gut burned with bitterness at the memory that felt almost completely foreign now. All she'd been worried and upset about then now overshadowed by the *Boogie Man* and the handsome man with the magnetic mind.

"You opted to miss out of senior prom?" Ellen's dull voice once again aroused Marilyn from her tunneling thoughts with a question Marilyn would've spit at if at all acceptable to do in an interview.

Something she assumed was *not*.

"Not a prom fan," She answered with a polite smile. She didn't see a point in waiting on a boy to make some fucking stupid poster that basically screamed *YO HOMEGIRL. I'M A GAY ASS FAG* in cheesy puns and taped on candy bars. The idea of then finding a dress painted repulsive colors of the rainbows and then actually WEAR IT out to an adult-supervised party with a bunch of sweaty, hormonal, pimple-faced teenagers sporting hard-ons... No thanks.

Her eyebrow lifted as she thought about it harder. She may have considered the whole prom fiasco if she'd known Brent then. In a perfect, fantasized while she masturbated, world the thirty-something year old would've gone with her to prom—and nobody would've been there. Just the two of them. And that fucking prom dress would've been so repulsive and heavy on her shoulders he would've had to take it off of her.

A perverted smile replaced her faulty polite one as she then realized it may be better if everyone was there, make it more risqué...

"Shocking!" Ellen presumed with a voice that obliterated Marilyn's fantasy where it stood, "you look like a prom queen!"

"Flattered," actually revolted. But then her fantasy came back and masked the woman and fat man sitting in front of her. Instead, the image of Brent, pantless, with the prom king hat tilted against his head cradled the idea of being a prom queen and made it a little less disgusting. A little more erotic. She wiggled in the conference room seat as the space between her thighs got a *little more* wet and a *little less* ladylike.

She'd have to stand under a lawn sprinkler to snap herself out of her horny trance, she knew, as soon as the interview was over. Her glazed eyes unglazed and she became re-involved with the man and woman in front of her and she thought: *hopefully soon.*

"Tell me your strongest quality."

Marilyn squinted her eyes at the woman, then slid the irises in her pressed slits to the heavy man named Mr. Olmstead. How the *fuck* was she supposed to know. She hummed as she thought, then said the first thing that came to mind, "I'm a critical thinker."

Her nose scrunched and she wondered if they could see the shit oozing from her teeth.

"Can you give us an example?"

A fire had begun to spark internally and Marilyn concentrated to keep the embers off her cheekbones with a smirk that lifted her fatty cheeks into balls of olive muscle. "I –" her eyelashes flicked over her watering eyes, "well," *shit.* Could she go back and change her answer? What the hell had she said: *critical thinker!* Like a Goddamned idiot. She'd opened her mouth to say: '*This interview.*'—Snarky. An unusual defense mechanism of hers, when Ellen waved her hand.

"That's okay," she said and Marilyn curled her tongue in her mouth against the defeat, "I believe that you are."

Bull.

Marilyn waved her hand back, "No, I uh, I'm really good at evaluating. I see what's around me and always evolutionate the best outcome through problem-solving and creative thinking before—you know," she paused as she became sure now that she'd said *evolutionate* rather than *evaluate.* The word hung in the air then swooped back to crash into her face, wanting to go back to safety because it definitely had not belonged in that sentence. "*Doing,*" She finished her sentence weakly and noticed the internal flames *had* made a warm appearance to her forehead and neck. She hadn't made sense and if either Ellen or Olmstead believed or understood anything she said they were no better than whitey-tighties stained with shit streaks.

Marilyn's nose flared as if she could smell the soiled underwear.

Ellen's face was a dry expression, "okay," she said and clasped her hands together over Marilyn's resume as she turned her head to Mr. Olmstead with a pinned up eyebrow, "do you have any questions for Marilyn, Joel?"

Marilyn prayed to God she wasn't sure she believed in that he didn't. She could taste the interview coming to an end, right next to her stimulated craving for a cigarette. Her mouth parted slightly and her tongue flicked a dry corner of her lips.

An action Joel Olmstead's hungry eyes noticed before they diverted themselves back to the cranky woman, "No! I'm peachy!"

Marilyn felt rejoiceful like it was a spiritual experience.

"Do you have any questions for us, Ms. Matthews?" Ellen's grey bob haircut faced Marilyn alone.

The girl did, or was told she was supposed to by Brent in the car ride to the district office that morning. She wiggled her lips in thought. She had assumed she'd be able to pull the question from her ass when/if the time came but now, found herself completely bull shitted out. Her bowl of spooned out shit empty and licked clean. Brent should've been a *doll* and given her a question to *ask* them. *Prick.*

"That's alright," Ellen, even less amused than usual concluded before she stood and adjusted her chair below the lip of the table, "It was a pleasure to meet you, Marilyn," Her boney hand extended out from her elbow.

Fuck, fuckety, fuck. Marilyn thought as she stood on her own accord and took the woman's hand in her's with a tight shake, "and you."

Joel Olmstead fought to stand and gave a curdled grunt as he did so. Marilyn turned and took his hand after Ellen and gave it the same tight handshake that he'd held onto a second longer than the woman had.

The room had suffocated her and she had broken through the doors into the hallway to escape after they had all spent a moment too long staring at one another in the silent room. It had begun to feel less like an interview and more like an interrogation. *Lamp on, 'Where's the money?!'* Marilyn stomped her feet down carpeted steps and out the front district doors to the sidewalk.

She then reconsidered the idea to stand beneath a lawn sprinkler but no longer because she needed to cool off from sex fantasies. She thought of jousting herself in the face with the iced hose water rather for capital punishment for being the worst interviewer in the history of *FUCKING* interviewers. She clenched her fists around the long cardigan sleeves and thought of banging them into her temples like ammunition from a gun.

The shame grasped and tightened like a corset just below her breasts, its laces being wrenched and its material gutting her. A pitiful frown wet her lips as she glared at the sidewalk and the back of her neck tensed and spasmed. She *knew* she didn't get the goddamn job. Brent would be disappointed and possibly frightened for Davey and all that C.P.S. garbage. Marilyn's glare heightened to a sneer as she thought: *whatever. It's not his business.* She shook her head and felt sad as her hair fell forward to cup her cheeks like strung-out cotton swabs.

At least Joel Olmstead had seemed to like her, in the way most liked her, but that was okay—that was how she'd always gotten what she needed. She thought of the way he'd watched her as she slapped her feet into cement, his hand at his belly, his lip tucked out in amusement and *hunger.* Like he could have jumped (*no, flopped*) over the table and eaten her whole. At least she'd managed to jingle his jollies.

She'd made distance as she traveled the ground by foot and her thoughts by brain wave. She was now only a block and a half from Grant Elementary and focused her eyes on its tall glass top that glistened like the fucking Northstar in the cold, overcast sun. A faint pounding had started inside her head as Brent's mind worked its way through her skull. It was a lagged signal and would've gone completely unnoticed if she hadn't been so stuck in her head as she pouted down the sidewalk. She bit a lip as she hit the next block and hoped Brent wouldn't mind the sudden surge of her dropped in presence. *Destination Dizzy Town! One ticket for Brent Kingsley and his plus one, Marilyn Maeeee Matthhheewwws!* She smiled despite her disappointment and thought: *Oh, won't you take me to...*

She'd stop in and say her hellos to the boys so she could later say, "sorry Davey, I really messed up that interview and can't work at your school now, but HEY! At least I got to see the inside of her school that one time!" And hope it'd make it up to him, or something.

She had reached the parking lot and walked a wide circle around Brent's black Toyota, eyeing the belly of the machine as she did so. Her head made a saggy swirl and the song she had thought came back: *Oh, won't you take me to... Dizzy Town!*

60

Davey tilted his head forward into his palm as Mrs. Engels switched from her lesson on Harriet Tubman to asking the children to practice their cursive. An anxious prick inserted itself into his elbows like a shot in the doctor's office as he decided he was sick of the cursive unit, but pulled his notebook out of his desk like all the other students anyway. The room quieted as the children took their pencils into artistic swoops and crosses. Practicing *Penmanship.*

Davey looped the word "Tonka," and tried to forget about the anxious poison that slid vertically from his elbows and into the rest of his body. He started to swirl "apple" in graphite with Daisy whipped her blonde hair, today in a single ponytail, around to face him.

"Hey, Davey!" She whispered like a snake over his sheet of bound lined paper and into his face.

The boy, who'd been concentrated on his second 'P' in 'apple', ignored the girl as he circled the bottom of the line and brought it up to connect with a backward 'c'.

Daisy got impatient and tapped a frantic finger against his composition book like an urgent message in Morse Code.

He looked, his head dipping up and his hair drooping over his forehead.

She smiled a bucked grin, "I have a question."

He brought his head up further like maybe he was interested in what she had to say but kept his shoulders draped forward towards the desk. He knew if the question had anything to do with a tree and K.I.S.S.I.N.G. he'd drop the pulley that held his head up and continue writing like he hadn't acknowledged her persistent presence in the first place.

"Do you want to come to my birthday party?" Her bubblegum voice popped sweetly and decorated the air with pink scents as her cheeks balled into happy clumps below her bright eyes and see through eyebrows.

Her question had stunned Davey. And she giggled as he stared with a heavy bottom lip that wavered as it decided if it wanted to be in his mouth or the open air. It chose the latter.

He'd never been to a birthday party before and hardly counted his own as *parties*. Marilyn had always tried her best, but without friends or a willing mom, it was never a party of more than him and Marilyn.

Davey managed a, "when?" Then immediately felt immensely adult for his choice of question. Less excited and more concerned with what existing plan it'll interrupt. *Can't be when I need to do my grocery shopping or house cleaning. What an inconvenience.*

The girl accepted the question with an adult-like smile and a flip of her hairstyle that was more her age, "Saturday!" She wiggled her shoulders in beat with her nose, "at my mom's house!"

Davey counted on his fingers five days until *Saturday!* He hoped her mom's house would be a pleasant place for a party as he imagined a living room like Brent's filled with pink streamers, balloons, and a humongous 'Birthday Girl!' sign stapled to her mother's wall.

"Sure!" He smiled under his breath, "but I have to ask my sister."

Daisy grinned with her teeth and her rosy cheeks shaded down two shades rosier, "I'll make you an invitation!" Her hair nearly made an erect 360° spiral as she spun back to her cursive practice with a new excitement ignited against her. An excitement that made Davey feel suddenly important, more important than anyone else in the class, and he let his tucked smile grow as he thought about his friend. *Friend.* Someone his age that might just like him a lot.

Daisy and Davey sitting in a tree!
K.I.S.S.I.N.G.

The boy's smile turned into a hard scowl at his school work as the rhyme played through his head. He sucked his lip into his mouth to cushion his clenched teeth and thought:

Davey and Beary sitting in a tree.
P.L.A.Y.I.N.G

He liked that rhyme much better and repeated it in his mind.

Davey and Beary sitting in a tree.
P.L.A.Y.I.N.G

Davey was light hearted again and began to practice the word *playing* in cursive on his paper. It wasn't a part of the list of words that Mrs. Engles had given the class to practice, but he hoped she wouldn't mind the extra scribbles.

Emily Engles had watched it all, from her corner desk with her foam apple being squeezed between her fingers like a stress ball. She watched Daisy fling her hair around to Davey, she watched the boy ignore, then respond after the girl's persistence. She admired as Davey went from unsure, to wide-eyed, to curious, to gently smiling. She watched the girl try on different shades of red on her cheeks, then twirl back to her work with a happy tapping foot, then surveyed as Davey's polite smile grew, then dropped into a glare, then lifted back up as his hand worked to twirl the alphabet together on his page.

Emily set her foam apple down on her table and tipped back in her seat with her own mirrored smile.

61

Marilyn stood at the front entrance and stared in. She could make out the library and the tan tile floors through the scratched front door windows. Her cardigan sleeves kept her palms warm as she let an arm out to shrink-wrap around the cold metal door handle and pull. The door budged forward like an old piece of farm equipment before it hit a bar lock and stopped its moving altogether. She fell into the locked door and emotions from her nightmare sprinkled hot shivers down her spine. She hissed a hard vowel and rolled her head over her shoulders to pop the air pockets below the skin and release tension.

A single-camera eye above a silver keypad grabbed for her attention and she sidestepped to it with curiosity. It had a small speaker like the buzzers you see outside of brick apartment buildings in New York, New York movies. She wondered what it was doing strapped to the outside of a school building in ghettoville, Oregon, *ghettoville, Oregon* as she jabbed a finger at the doorbell shaped button at the bottom of the keypad.

A buzz sucked through the pencil poked speaker. An actual buzz that set a giddy, childish excitement off inside the girl that she hid behind a hollow, stone stare. She waited for the response patiently as she teetered back on her sneakered heels. *Fucking sneakers!* She threw a hindsight glare at them as she became overly aware that she hadn't even worn nice shoes to the interview.

Baby hair bangs fell forward and looped into her eyelashes to give her something to swat at with frustration and tuck behind her ears.

There was a heavy metal *'chunk'* as the school door unlocked and set Marilyn's irritated snarl into a heated frown. There hadn't been an answer through the buzzers intercom like in the *New York, New York* movies. Not a *'who is it?'* or *'come back later'*. Which saddened the girl much deeper than she'd admit as she yanked the once locked door open. The breeze of finger-paint scented youth whipped around her and freed the baby hairs from behind her ears in a contemporary dance as they fell back into her face.

It had made sense, the more she thought of it, someone in the office probably looked through the camera and determined that she wasn't a predator to the school full of children and *'chunk'* pushed a button to unlock the door for her.

It heightened her nerves with unsettled fear as she considered it harder and stepped into the yellow-lit building. How had they known she wasn't a predator? The question had sparked a fire of debate inside of her twisty straw noggin that could feel Brent's presence completely now.

She could've been anyone hiding anything under her cardigan. They buzzed her in their school with the New York, New York movie doorbell based on what? *Her vagina?* Like the sex organ between her legs was a prepaid function that didn't come with mental issue side effects and the need to feel superior?! She made a finger gun under her cardigan sleeve and scowled down the main entrance. She could be a *PSYCHO!*

Her baby hairs fluttered against her temples again as the door fell shut behind her.

The flesh gun under her sleeve retired to a limp fingered hand as she entered the main office and scowled at the woman behind the long desk.

"Hello," The woman gave her a strange glance that made the young adult feel bare below her cardigan that now felt as if it pooled against her like a large bed duvet.

Marilyn lifted her lingering glare and gave the woman a nod, "Hi."

The woman eyed her a moment longer than smiled, "Marilyn Matthews?" Her lips were glossed and strings of sparkles smeared against each other as she spoke the girl's name.

Marilyn kept still with furrowed brows and hesitant feet.

The woman winked, "you look like your brother."

The girl inclined her chin, then dropped it, unsatisfied with the woman's explanation.

The office woman swatted at the air like there were flies, "Debra," she introduced herself with a slight roll on her tongue, "we've talked on the phone."

Marilyn nodded like the conversation no longer interested her as she stepped up to the front desk, "I remember." She gripped the lip of the counter and slid her eyelids over her expanded pupils as a gentle wave of nausea pressed at her like a wading water wave.

Debra frowned as she watched the girl sway steadily in the dead static space between them. She had met the girl once before, on Davey's first day. She'd stood in the doorway with that same strange sway and scrunched face as she held onto her brother's shoulders. She'd been worried about the bus, Davey had to get on it, and Debra promised that he would. Marilyn's hair had been in a greasy bun that morning and the scent of sex and cigarettes had spread to the walls of the office like a sticky paste. Debra's frown hardened and her Hispanic cheeks hollowed. She wouldn't bring it up–she'd refrain.

Marilyn sighed and Debra acted as if the Crayola noose drawing hadn't begun to surface in her head as the girl steadied herself and relaxed her face until her eyelids slid up like wet lizard skin.

Marilyn pressed her weight into the ground through the balls of her feel like a dancer preparing for a plié and tapped the desk with her fingers as if she'd been waiting for something from Debra.

Debra blinked away the hypnosis the girl's dizzy movements had, had her in and gestured to a booklet of name tags, "are you signing in?" She asked, "I assume you're here to see Dave?"

Marilyn tilted her head at the book and bounced a heel off of the other foot's toe, "both *Davey* and Brent," she answered and gave an amusing grin as the woman's mocha skin reddened like dark cherry.

"Please sign in," Debra shook a finger at the booklet and licked her eyes back to her computer screen.

Marilyn stared down at the sign-in booklet distastefully. It wasn't fancy moleskin like you'd maybe see in a New York, New York movies, but rather a dollar store binder put together sloppily by a half caffeinated, underpaid, school employee. She thumbed through it like something exciting might pop out at her before she turned back to the original page and scooped a pen from Debra's pen holder.

The woman stood and cleared her throat as Marilyn filled out her name, date, and time in.

Nine, thirty-two.

That was what the wall clock had said anyway. Marilyn removed the flimsy sticker and patted it above a breast as Debra eyed her.

"I can take you to Mr. Kingsley," she said, then seemed concerned she'd used the wrong name with Marilyn.

Marilyn looked up from her chest where she rubbed in the white name tag and surveyed the woman with her black hair pulled back into an iron curled ponytail. "Sure," Marilyn said but would've preferred to weeble wobble down the hallway on her own to avoid any kind of judgment as her and Brent's brain synced painfully.

Debra had walked a half pace quicker than Marilyn with high heels that stabbed the hallway floors hollowly. The girl admired the walls as they passed for a moment, then became uninterested and dropped her head down to focus on her shoes as a heavy wave rippled through her and made her vision spot.

She was sure she would've been able to locate the man's office just by sensation and vertigo waves like echolocation but was now glad she wouldn't have to. The sooner she got to Brent, the better. The girl ran a finger over her pulsing forehead as she walked a step behind Debra.

The door to his office had been closed but his blinds had been turned so you could see clearly through the cracks in their off white plastic. The counselor was sitting Indian style on the floor with his hands limp in his lap and his back to the window where the two women stood and viewed. Marilyn's head filled with lukewarm novocaine and she watched as Brent's tilted slowly like the numb was being squeezed through his ear and he was trying to distribute it evenly. She mimicked the tilt.

A girl sat in a little yellow chair in front of him with crocodile tears bubbled below her eyes. She had wide, oily cheeks and hair that stood erect from grease, her teeth a crusty yellow as she pleaded pudgy words over her counselor. Marilyn's lip curled as she imagined the girl's filthy stench. If she were Brent she would've keeled over already.

Brent's head bobbed as he spoke gently to the low hygiene fifth-grader. She sniffed at his words and rubbed dirty fingernails at her tears that spilled trails down her swollen cheeks.

As her head dropped away from the man in sniffles he turned his own over his shoulder to look at the two women in the hallway. His lips were pulled into a tight line and his eyelids drooped with something empathetic for the little girl.

He winked at the women and held up a finger to say *"wait a minute"* then dropped the appendage to point back down the hall.

"He wants us to go back to the office," Debra translated.

Marilyn's cheeks puffed out as she considered going through the dizzy walk back.

Brent's eyes held her single attention for a moment as he played his dropped finger into his temple sorely as an apology.

She kept his eye contact with her cheeks puffed out and her chest tight until he broke the connection and turned his head back to the obese girl.

Debra started her way back down the hallway with the assumption that Marilyn would follow. She did. Debra tried to make small talk but Marilyn ignored it, her responses generic.

It wasn't until Debra's mouth peeled with the words, "he loves your brother," that Marilyn became interested in the conversation.

Her woozy skull turned towards the woman with dilated eyes.

Debra smiled gently at the girl, "Brent. He's been attached to that boy the moment he met him."

Marilyn kept her stare at the swirly pace with the woman as they walked and her head pounded.

"He sees something special in Dave," she shook her head and her curled, black ponytail bounced, "he's a good man."

Marilyn felt vulnerable as she looked away from the woman and frowned at the hallway, suddenly overwhelmed with a weak emotion. It was a dose of love she wasn't expecting to feel and she quickly killed it with a sharp drawn line of her eyebrows.

Back in the office, she sat. The pounding in her head still painful, but tolerable, like the mental hammer moved from sharp cobblestone and now worked gentle knocks into wood. Debra typed at her computer and would occasionally stop to glance and smile at the girl in the old waiting room chairs.

Her nipples had hardened under the cool office vent and she wondered if Debra had noticed as she leaned forward to rest her folded elbows over the tops of her knees in a *shitting-on-the-toilet* kind of pose.

A cramp started at the dimples of her back and stripped to the bottom of her hip bones like tacky wax paper. Her lips pressed as the cramp turned into a hot iron pressed into her asshole. Her eyes flicked up to study the room and get her mind off of the sudden (period-is-soon-to-come) cramp when the man (*the myth, the legend*) entered the office, no longer with a thin line of lips, but with a dimpled smile.

"Hey!" He greeted Marilyn with a bright look as both of their heads cooled, "how'd it go?" He meant the interview. He'd known how it went, he'd gotten a call from Joel Olmstead as the man drove back from the district office.

He wanted to know Marilyn's side, though.

Marilyn frowned at Brent's handsome smile and doe eyes as another cramp, except this time a stomach cramp, blundered through her. She shrugged dully and gave him an "'s good."

His head tilted up, then sideways with a soft sigh, "you want to talk about it?" He straightened his light blue sweater over the white button-up it covered for a moment, then put his attention back on her with a gentle, one-sided, smile. A lanyard was draped over his chest and his name and a kind mugshot dangled off of it, against his flat belly.

Marilyn shrugged again, disinterested and suddenly exhausted. Her brow stuck in a deadpanned line.

Brent gestured for her to stand, his lanyard swinging with his arm movement, then turned his smile to Debra, "thanks for keeping her company."

Debra returned the smile less convincingly, "surrrre!" She tried to chirp but her voice hit a pothole and popped, letting all the air out in a dramatic breath.

Once in his small office that had aired out from the little girl's stench, Marilyn had let out a long, pressured sigh of frustration and palmed at the door to shut it. Brent had stopped the swinging door with his foot and pushed it back open—all the way open. His hands were in his pockets and his styled hair fell forward out of its slightly gelled hold as his foot came back to him. His face gave the exasperated girl a relaxed look that *almost* convinced her that he wasn't opening the door because he was scared of her.

Brent slacked down into his office chair and the girl copied his movement to crouch into the pulled out yellow chair the little girl had been sitting in. She shifted uncomfortably as she imagined the grime left on the chair from the girl, her face twisted with a little bit of disgust.

Brent removed his hands from his pocket and dropped them to his lap, "So, how'd it go?" And he meant for real now as his eyes searched her innocently and the warmth pooled back between her legs.

Marilyn sunk into the back of the chair and hoped she wasn't relaxing her back into dandruff, "it was embarrassing," She said honestly, fresh out of shit to shovel.

Brent's lips lifted into a grin that he covered with a finger as he rested his cheek into a palm to be polite.

She scoffed at his poor job of hiding the smile and continued to complain. Long lulls of doubt and frustration that she poured from her sorry lips. The man listened, and nodded, and smiled. He'd smiled too much at a girl who was *very* upset and she began to feel belittled by him. Her eyes narrowed into dark triangles and lava'd anger began to bubble between her cramps. It was the same flavor of anger she'd been induced with at the hospital when the nurse had laughed at her. She stopped her pity puke cold, "what?" She snapped at him, "what's so funny?!"

Brent sat back in his chair and his cheeks dropped the smile like it was suddenly scorching his face.

"It's your fault I had to do the interview!" She went on, her vision pulsed and pierced on the man who's smile came back fuller, and wider.

"Marilyn," he spoke short and calmly with that smile that seemed so wicked to her.

"It was *so* embarrassing. I—"

Brent's hand came out as he said her name again, "Marilyn." He looked like an officer directing traffic with his hand out, all he needed was the bright vest and a whistle, "you got the job."

I got the job?

The girl's thoughts and words went into a wind tunnel and for a second the world was silent. Then the world came back and every sound pierced at her all at once, "Bull–*fucking*–shit!" She moaned, still frustrated.

Brent's face contorted as if she'd slapped him with her words and he made a hissed "*shh!*" As he reached out and swatted a hand against his door to shut it, "no bull," he'd answered with a slight laugh as the door clicked closed.

He then stood and turned his back to the girl who watched with a dropped jaw and harsh eyes to open his blinds completely for a clear view into his office.

Marilyn felt in a trance as Brent worked the off white plastic lines up the window with the pull of the yarn string.

"Joel called," he explained, "before my appointment with Kristen—"

Marilyn assumed Kristen was the dirty girl who'd been crying and she tilted her head at the way he had said '*appointment*'. Like he was a doctor or a *real* therapist.

"He said you were great, they are happy to have you a part of our staff," Brent turned that same smile he'd been giving her over his shoulder.

"No," Marilyn glared at him like it was some sick joke he was playing with her.

Brent's whole body turned and she sat back into his seat with a sigh, "yes"

"Well, I'll be fucked!" Marilyn yelped as a bright light lit behind her eyes.

A streetlamp after the sun goes down.

Brent's face fell victim to his disapproving glare again and Marilyn covered her mouth with a warm hand and a giggle. He cleared his throat then his smile came back lighter, "you have to act surprised though," he winked and her insides jello'd, "I wasn't supposed to tell you." He prepared for more foul language but she'd just smiled, nodded, and stayed foul free. He nodded back and popped the door to the hallway open again.

She'd done her best in a full vocal and body performance to act surprised when Joel had barreled himself into the office with the news. Brent had done his part with a "congrats," and an "I can't wait to work with you."

She had shaken Joel Olmstead's hand, then paused with her hand out to Brent. They stared at each other for a moment as they both remembered the world spinning and Brent dry heaving into the sink the last time they'd touched, then she dropped her extended hand. She thanked him verbally and Joel Olmstead said she'd start Wednesday.

62

Wednesday.

Marilyn laid against her sore back and adjusted her eyes to the ceiling cloaked in apartment darkness as she thought about *Wednesday*. What it entailed—and otherwise meant. It meant, she thought, that she'd matured and had begun to pursue a better life for the Matthews siblings. Except, she wasn't pursuing anything—the job wasn't her idea—yet here she was, lying in bed, dreading *Wednesday*.

The tips of her fingers began to feel led against the bed sheets and she clenched her fists against the sensation. She'd stayed up late enough to see Monday seamlessly glide into Tuesday as Brent fell asleep and her head bogged down with him. She stayed awake against his sleepy pull to think, dread, mourn *Wednesday*.

She unclenched her fists.

Marilyn rolled to her side, away from the center of the bed where Davey slept sprawled with Bear Kingsley pressed into his face. She glared at the bookshelf nudged against the white apartment wall and tried to pick out a title. Her vision broke off in the dark and made the white words on book spines look like askew heartbeats—unpatterned beats like Brent's heart that tapped lightly above her own as he slept. It began to bother her, his fluttering valves tickling her chest, like insects. Insects that crawled into her sleeves and down her back.

Her fists clenched again.

If she were alone, (Davey's light snore a constant reminder that she wasn't), she'd get up and flip on a light, the yellow one that'd smother out the darkness. And alone, under the illuminated ceiling bulb she'd pick out a book and read it. *Alone.* The idea of never being alone again began to fester into a jab at the back of her neck. A cattle prod of restlessness. In the morning it would be her last day of *Me, Myself and I*–after the sun went down she'd begin working eight hours a day for five days a week like a real, depressed, adult.

Then she'd come home –

Her fists unclenched –

And she'd spend the evening with Brent and her brother until bed. Then she'd wake up and do it all over again. Like a *real, depressed, adult.*

This time her hands seemed to swell into tightly sealed balls that suffocated her nerve endings as an imaginary fire sparked against the flat of her back and throttled her from the tangle of sheets and to her feet. Her sheets recoiled from her flailed body and fell back into the air mattress lifeless and leaving her shivering. She folded her arms and tight fists against her chest and memorized the cold flick of apartment air on her legs. *What now?* She thought as her eyebrows snarled at the dark. She turned flat steps to look down at the shape of Davey's sleeping body in the spot next to her vacant imprint. *Leave.*

Her eyes shot to the door like it had screamed her name as she considered. Not forever, no, just *leave* for the night. She twisted her lips beneath her nose as each design of the door crept into her line of sight–the darkness melting from its rectangular frame as she stared.

Hot anticipation began to twinkle below her eyes and her body twisted to her laundry basket of clothes.

Her fists unclenched.

63

A bar on First and Archer named *Voodoo Lounge* looked less than a pleasure from its street view of webbed, blackout windows and painted over brick. A lit sign with a tossed clown mask around it like shoes on a telephone wire gave light to a group of homeless dressed men that shared cigarette smoke against the entrance of the bar.

Marilyn released her hands from her jean pockets and straightened her shoulders as she lightly trotted around the group of surveying, sunken eyes. She anticipated a voice, the way a light sleeper may anticipate an alarm clock, as she passed the tobacco scented men. Her head bobbed as she waited for them to call after her or ask *"what's a pretty young lady doing out all on her own?"* But their mouths had been too full of dark clouds to speak or call out.

She sucked at the fumes of second-hand nicotine with her nose as she reached the bar entrance. Her hand reached around the curved door handle that seemed to drip with flakey dead skin and grime that made her cringe as her limbs pulled at its metal. The spill of accompanied chatter and jukebox music slapped her in the face like a concrete barricade as the door slivered open. She squinted and smiled at it like she'd smile at a drunken hit from her mother as she slithered through the space between door and frame.

There was a tiny wooden platform, built as a stage, against the wall to her left that she studied as she passed. It was naked of any talent or karaoke at the hour, one AM karaoke on a Tuesday morning wasn't exactly *small-town*

Oregon heard of. Maybe in Portland, but not in Grant. In front of the plank stage was a green-carpeted floor dressed in round tables and black painted chairs that skirted around them. Marilyn waltzed through the spaced hallways between tables as she avoided eye contact with the older men and women that had found a kicked back spot in the black painted chairs.

The floor stretched on to a pool table and a half wall that heavy dressed, middle-aged, men and women leaned and laughed over. The sound of billiard balls rattled together over felt tingled the crowds' vocal conversations and made Marilyn's nose flare like she was smelling a nostalgic scent.

Past the pool table, the floor dropped a step down onto a hardwood, scuffed surface that naturally pathed to the bar. A single bartender scrubbed a stained white rag over the glass countertop and laughed occasionally at a man in his sixties who told jokes through the stripped strings of white mustache that hung below his nose. A waitress, the young mother type, passed Marilyn with a kind tilt of her head, a tray of tall drinks balanced on a flat palm above her shoulder.

Marilyn passed the felt pool table slowly with head up and fried hair curls down, her bangs draped against her new scar. She dropped a foot onto the bar floor that needed to be swept and smiled absently to herself. *The Voodoo Lounge*—a dive bar to say the least—and it was just the way she liked it.

She swallowed a thigh around a bar stool like a cowgirl mounting a saddle as she took a seat and thumbed at a smudge on the glass countertop. A flyer laid out in front of her, laminated and taped to the glass with clear packers tape, *The Voodoo* it said in white chalk letters layered over black sky background. *Live Music*, it continued in smaller letters at the bottom, *Fridays and Saturdays 6– 8. HERE!* The word *"here"* was bolded and the exclamation point was drawn on with paint, like an *Uh-Oh, Too Slow! Should've added me before you printed, sucker!* afterthought. There was a picture of a smiling moon, sketched in white strikes, between *The Voodoo* and *Live Music*, that seemed to know all of Marilyn's secrets as it studied her with dead, drawn eyes.

She frowned and thought in a tired, sing-songy voice: *The cow jumped over the moon...*

Her thought stretched out into a drowning hum as she tried to remember the children's rhyme, her fuzzy head begging to finish it with... *To fetch a pail of water.* But she knew that wasn't right. She shook her head as the children's rhyme persisted to jumble together other rhymes and sing lowly into her brain: *The fork, the spoon, jumped over the moon... to fetch a pail of water... The cow fell down and bumped his crown... And didn't wake up in the morning.*

Marilyn's elbows slid against the glass top of the bar until she was sat into a head hung slouch that stared at her laced fingers, "how am I supposed to work at a grade school?" She mumbled at herself like her tongue was a tiny knife, "I can't even remember a fucking nursing rhyme."

Her lips shut and her head corrected her: *You mean Nursery Rhyme.* It spoke up shyly and she scowled at her hands.

The stained, white rag she'd seen being used to scrub the counter as she walked through the tables slapped near her arm to mop up a ring of alcoholic condensation.

"Minors not allowed, doll," The owner of the cleaning rag spoke above her in an earthy, obtuse tone.

Marilyn's eyes see-sawed up to meet a half-lidded stare from the overweight bartender with snake bites and greasy hair. Her lips were spread with a thick purple coating that smiled at the girl to reveal a gray front tooth.

"I know," Marilyn answered with a lick of annoyance while she reached in her back pocket for her fake I.D. The plastic card slid between her index and middle finger like it was made to be there and she slipped it out to the bartender like a magician would flip out the magic card, a finale to their act.

The bartender took it like a chip from a restaurant basket and examined it under one eye, the other eye squinting into folded fat with eyelashes. She then set it against the counter and slid it towards Marilyn, her body moved with the card until the woman and girl were close enough to share smells. Her cheeks stayed pulled like botox had stuck her purple lips into the smile she beamed into Marilyn's face, "Listen," she swiped the card under Marilyn's resting arm to hide it, "you in any kind of trouble?"

Marilyn's head recoiled back from the bartender like the woman had blown hot breath into her face and her eyebrows furrowed into deep creases, "what?" *The cow and the spoon jumped over the moon... to fetch a pail of water...* Marilyn blinked rapidly.

The woman backed off and shrugged as her posture straightened, "keep your drink covered, doll," She mothered as she grabbed her rag and rubbed a dry line across the counter, "Best faux I.D. I've seen in a while."

A weighted glare fell onto Marilyn's young face like a picture falls into place when the trigger of a View-Master is pulled.

The bartender laughed, her voice a smooth growl of chuckles, "so, what will it be, babe?"

Marilyn didn't answer.

The woman popped a hip out and clicked her tongue over her teeth in time, "let's see," she winked at the unasking girl, "Shirley Temple, out on her own in the middle of the night," she paused to think then addressed Marilyn directly, "*Daddy Issues?*" She hissed the question all too knowingly.

Marilyn bowed her head away from it.

The bartender in purple lipstick laughed again, a sad laugh this time, and turned her back to the girl, "I'd say you need something hard, kid." Her head dipped back over her shoulder and watched Marilyn frown at her, "but you're just that—a *kid.*"

Marilyn's lip curled, "either kick me out or leave me the fuck alone," She snarled quietly enough that even her own ears rejected her crackled voice and ignored her. *Or help me figure out that goddamned rhyme,* she thought irritably.

The woman pocketed the rag in a waist apron and winked at the girl then went on with her job. Marilyn watched with a cool breeze trailed over her upper lip from her nostrils as the woman collected liquid ingredients and mixed.

The girl dropped her head back to the poster for *The Voodoo* and thought: *It's off to the moon we go... do dah, do dah... the cow, the fork, fetched the moon... all the do dah dayyyyyy.*

A tall thin glass of cold fluid was slid to the girl over the wiped glass counter, "Tom Collins is the drink, Tammy is the gal," The woman, named Tammy, thumbed at herself with her stuck smile beamed at Marilyn.

Marilyn took the glass between her hand and let the condensation chill the wrinkles in her palms as she brought its black straw to her lips and drank it like water. The drink bit at the back of her tongue and made her throat tingle but not harshly, just enough to let her know it was there.

Tammy passed a white napkin towards the girl whose drink swirled its ice cubes like a shipwreck in a whirlpool. "Be safe, princess," She said and gave a nod to the hardly alcoholic beverage.

Marilyn watched her strut away, back to the man with the untamed mustache to laugh with him over his drink. She pushed the drink away from her and ran her tongue across the roof of her mouth slowly until it hit the back of her teeth. Dominante-Bartender-Tammy wouldn't let her get more than tipsy, Marilyn knew that.

But Tipsy wouldn't cut it tonight.

Tipsy was fucked.

She finished the drink hastily and slid from her seat without paying the bill. *It's off to work we go... high ho, high ho. The cow, the moon, the fork, and spoon,... all the do dah dayyyyy.*

64

Davey had awoken to Marilyn's bursts of anxious movement and irritated sighs through the dark apartment as she dressed for her sudden night out. He'd laid still and played asleep with Bear Kingsley in his face and his eyelids fluttering as he forced them to stay shut. He'd continued to snore lightly with a sleepy chest until the front door had shut behind the girl and her feet made an echoed beat down the concrete steps that descended to the parking lot.

He sat up then, fully awake and a little bit more alone—Bear Kingsley now nestled in his lap. Davey tugged at the air mattress blanket until it was up around both boy and bear like a warm shield and imagined Bear Kingsley batting his beady eyes until they fell shut and comfortable sleep took him into dreams. Davey cradled his plush friend against him and smiled shyly at the sleeping toy, he knew he wouldn't sleep as well as his friend. He couldn't, actually, because Marilyn had left, and he had to wait up for her, an obligation he'd felt deep in his gut and couldn't avoid.

Marilyn had visited his classroom just before lunch after she'd been told she'd start *Wednesday*. Her and Brent snuck into the back of the classroom and stood quietly until it was appropriate to interrupt the third-graders' math lesson. Davey didn't notice the two adults who stood behind him as they waited. His head had been hung low towards his paper and his mind had been a man on waves, surfing over dreams he'd had in the past. One, in particular, bobbed clearly like a tsunami wave above all other dreams while he scribbled misunderstood equations on his paper with a sharpened-until-it-was-too-small Ticonderoga. The tsunami of a dream was the one he'd had at the hospital the week before, the smell of the boat and the ocean sea waters still fresh and crystal clear in his mind.

He let a muse take him back to the dream with its waking waters and deep canal as the classroom floor had begun to sway against his feet as he stood on the deck of his boat. He immersed himself into the memory and his eyes blurred until he could see the metal, rusted rails and the dark, rock walls of the cave. He was tucked so far into the daydream he hadn't noticed when Mrs. Engles' voice had trailed off strangely in the middle of her lesson like she'd been caught off guard. He hadn't noticed when Daisy had whipped around to look at him and behind him with her large eyes and bubblegum mouth.

He hadn't noticed anything until his face began to heat beneath the prod of classmates' eyes that watched him through the water of his daydream. His head had aroused from the drifting wood and thoughts and the cool classroom swung back into view. The whole classroom had been watching him with light smiles and curious eyes. Eyes that lifted to the wall behind him and stretched their smiles then fell back to him.

Davey became hyper-aware of the extra body heat that seemed to trickle against his back as the hair on his neck stood erect like porcupine prickles. Davey studied Daisy's face for an explanation as she giggled close to him, her eyes above him.

"What is it?" He whispered to the girl who responded with a high giggle that she quickly muted with both hands.

His curiosity outweighed his frightened resistance to look and he ended up spinning around to match the rest of his class. Brent had been leaned back against the back wall with his hands in his pocket and a mirrored cheek smile hot-pressed into his face. Beside Brent, and directly behind the boy, was

Marilyn. A finger had been pressed to her lips to quiet the class (Emily Engels included) as she attempted to sneak up on him. She dropped her finger helplessly and stared at Davey wide-eyed like a bandit caught red-handed as he turned to face her. Then she'd grinned. A pure, shit-eating, grin—meant only for him.

Pure excitement and surprise melted any bit of introvert Davey held on to in his veins as he rocketed from his seat like his ass was on fire to grab her and hug her, "Marilyn Mae!" He cheered into her, his feet jittering in little jumps as his class broke out into chatter, their silent staring spell broken.

"Hey," Marilyn hugged him back with both arms and smiled down at the top of his head. Her voice had been a rasp of motherly love that coated over the top of him like a cough drop over pain.

It slid against his nerves in the shape of a warm coat that made his insides settle. It had protected him, then, from caring what everyone else thought. He hadn't cared how big he smiled, or how red his face was, or how watery his knees felt. He hadn't cared as Brent excused him from the class and had to lead him to the hallway so they didn't disrupt any more of Mrs. Engels' lesson.

He wanted to show Marilyn everything. She'd seen Mrs. Engels, and his classroom, and where he sat, and she'd even seen Daisy. But he wanted to show her the library with the flags, where he'd found Matilda on the shelf, the childrens' artwork on the walls—especially the drawing by the fifth-grader *Alexis Adams.*

One of the most astounding artists of this time, Brent had said as Davey admired the girl's blue sketched springer spaniel on his first day, he'd said it was a wink and a playful smile, one Davey planned to imitate once Marilyn was admiring the drawing as he had.

He hadn't cared when Marilyn had frowned as Brent told them Davey couldn't give her a tour, not yet, he still had class to attend, but maybe sometime later. He hadn't cared that he forgot to point out the graphite fingerprints along the walls of the school where children dragged their hands as they walked. He hadn't cared about anything—he was just happy to see her.

He hadn't cared until his classmates had.

It was at lunch, after Marilyn had left, that the questions had begun. Zachary, the boy with the small face, threw the first paper airplane question as Davey squeezed the edge of an *Uncrustable* between his raw lips, "is she insane too?"

Davey hadn't understood the question so he'd dismissed it and assumed it hadn't been for him as his eyes trailed off across the cafeteria and his mouth worked slowly against his lunch.

Sai, who sat at the same table bench as Zachary began to giggle and waved his hand in Davey's face, "earth to David!" He beeped like an alien-robot and Zachary snickered along with him.

Davey had blinked at them and swallowed his mouth full of food, "what?"

Both boys had laughed and a girl down the table a few seats had joined in with the giggles that had seemed to stab into Davey's ribcage and pry the bones apart to his heavy thumping heart.

"Your sister," Sai implied, "is she crazy too?"

Davey still hadn't understood as he stared, red-faced, at the boys with his food stuck dry in his throat.

Daisy slumped into Davey from their shared bench seat and turned her head to just him with a gentle whisper, "they're asking because she was with Mr. Kingsley like you always are."

The bright red striped below his eyes and across his nose deepened to a bloody amber as he understood, "no," he squeaked defensively to Daisy rather than the asking boys, "not one of us is *crazy.*"

Daisy looked at him with sad eyes and a flared nose as the boy's lip propelled into his mouth and he took his eyes off of her and put them back on the two kids across from him.

"But you *are* always with him, Davey," the girl down the table, named Jessie, pointed out.

Davey looked at her like she'd thrown something at him, "no—".

"Yeah, you are!" Zachary stabbed.

"You are *always* with him," Sai backed up, his eyes wide like he was explaining something to a child with autism.

Davey's heart was sputtering out of rhythm and his leg started to shake as he felt overwhelmed, "no—".

"Stop lying!" Zachary acted offended, which had been the final stab that brought tears to Davey's eyes.

His fists balled against the blurry liquid at his waterline, "it's because I live with Brent!" His eyes widened and his mouth dry like sandpaper, "I mean Mr. Kingsley," he mumbled with a rough tongue that scraped almost bloody lines into the roof of his mouth. The warning Brent had given him on his first day, *just don't call me that in front of your peers,* branded his burning cheeks and trembled his lip as he realized he failed to obey his friend's request. The image of him leading the unwanted children to the boat peer flicked against the inside of his eyelids like a bad taste in the back of his throat.

His classmates hadn't noticed that part as they all leaned closer and became more interested, their full attention towards—"you *live* with him?!" Jessie's voice pitched as more kids tuned into the conversation with wide eyes.

"Why with Mr. Kingsley?!"

"Where's your dad?"

"Yeah, what about your mom?!"

"Did they give you up for adoption?!"

"Guys! Maybe Mr. Kingsley really is his dad!"

"No! He isn't married!"

"Did you run away?"

"Is Mr. Kingsley your uncle?"

"Is he your brother?!"

"Maybe his parents died!!"

"Maybe he killed his parents?"

"Davey, were they in a car accident?!"

"Maybe Mr. Kingsley is his God Parent, I have one of those!"

Davey had burst into tears as the overstimulation of voices stung him like hornets and Daisy began to scold all of the asking voices around him.

He cried now, in the dark apartment as he reminisced unwillingly on the earlier confrontation. His head spun and his tears turned into chest quaking hiccups that he muted with Bear Kingsley's back as he stared at the blurry door in front of him. He prayed Marilyn would walk through soon with a smile. She'd kneel beside him and tell him the anxiety would pass and he'd curl into her arms and cry himself to sleep over overwhelming feelings that he didn't understand.

It was a prayer that went unanswered.

65

Marilyn stumbled down the cracked sidewalk towards a dive bar called *Lumps*. Her feet fumbled not because she was drunk, the Tom Collins not enough to do any damage, but because of the woman that rubbed up against her with a red face and intoxicated movements. A woman with a dike haircut and a dog paw tattooed on the back of her neck, directly where skull meets spine. She'd laid into Marilyn at *The Voodoo Bar* and had introduced herself as *Topaz*. A bleach blonde, dike cut, lesbian named Topaz—Marilyn had laughed at the stereotype and wished the bitch had been kidding.

She'd never spent the night bar-hopping with a lesbian and had looked forward to collecting her mental badge of honor to say she had by the end of the night. She'd hoped they'd maybe get wasted and spend a long time letting Marilyn experiment with her tongue and lips. Then, she could be a Katy Perry cliché.

I kissed a girl just to try it,
I hope Brent Kingsley don't mind it.

Topaz tripped on herself and pressed a little further into Marilyn's side with a hand that used the small of the younger girl's back to stabilize herself. Marilyn smiled at the sidewalk because of Topaz's rubbing touch and swayed her hips a little wider as they walked.

Lumps was darker than the other dive of a bar and held a room capacity of far fewer bodies. Topaz squeezed into an empty booth furthest from the front door and watched Marilyn closely as she dropped into a plastic and foam bench seat across from the woman. Marilyn leaned back into the booth and studied her—the wrinkles set lightly by her eyes and thin lip mouth suggested she had peaked into her thirties.

Topaz patted a ringed hand against the booth space beside her with heavy, drunk swings, "Come sit on this side with me," she purred. Her thin lips pulled apart and revealed sparkling white teeth with stretched canines that looked like they'd feel good being dragged in light bites across Marilyn's flesh.

Marilyn scooted to her open end of the booth and stood out of it to cross to the woman with a bit of curious fire in her belly. She sat down next to Topaz and scooted close. Topaz looked softly at the girl who leaned into her before she removed her wallet from her jean pocket. It was a billfold, crafted for a man, and had leather cracks that decorated it tiredly. Marilyn's muscles tightened as she watched the woman flip it open. Her tongue flicked out over her dry, eighteen-year-old, lips as the woman leafed a fifty out and placed it between the two of them, under the dim booth light.

Jesus. Marilyn had thought as her eyes bugged at the green paper and an internal timer began to count down how long it would be until she *had* to feed her conning impulse. She let her now wet lips jump into a heated smile as she nuzzled a little closer to the woman and hoped her wallet had more of the big bills, and not just ones for strippers.

"Get us something heavy, will ya?" The woman murmured into Marilyn's ear as she delicately plucked the fifty from the table and slid it into Marilyn's palm.

Marilyn watched herself close her fingers around the cash and nodded slowly as the soft currency brushed her skin cells.

66

It wasn't his alarm that woke him but the dryness of his mouth—his tongue a flopped, suffocated fish on his shrunken, cracked lips. Nausea hit second as Brent adjusted to his side with a groan. He tried to ride the acidic boiling in his stomach as his knees contracted up to his chest and his toes flexed against the waves of sickness. He breathed deeply through his nose and concentrated on the way his water-deprived tongue felt as it entangled itself with his mouth and teeth.

As the heated pain in his gut hid itself behind his constructed breathing the notion to be curious tapped him on the shoulder. He obeyed and peeled his hot eyelids open to read the time. The neon red numbering on his black nightstand clock was a gut punch and metal hammer to the head. The red smeared as an explosion of discomfort hurdled the man from his bed and pushed his tired feet towards the bathroom as he cradled his abdomen in both hands.

He didn't vomit.

But the wet flashes of diarrhea made him wish he had. The more his body emptied the harder his head pounded behind his temples. He dropped his sweaty forehead to his clammy hands and released a frustrated whimper.

He was resurrected from his silent groans and contractions by the sharp stab of an alarm. His alarm, as it screeched from the nightstand of his bedroom.

It split into the space between his eyes and cracked slivers from his skull. He had to turn it off.

With one hand suctioned to his ear and his shoulder jammed into the other he muted the piercing screams from the little machine and hobbled back to the bedroom to shut it off. His hand came down on it hard and it strangled off into silence as he collapsed back into bed in a state of fatigue. The sheets of his bed felt like sweaty pine needles against his hot skin and offered little comfort as he curled into them. His breathing thickened until his stomach cooled and he stood to dress reluctantly.

He bypassed his usual morning shower of wading ankle bathwater as his muscles preemptively ached from the thought of the pounding water against his neck and shoulders. His stomach curled again and he doubled against it.

Davey had fallen victim to Brent's sudden sickness as the man gave him a look of pure grieving as Davey chirped a "good morning!" He frowned at his counselor's response and followed Brent silently as the man staggered to the coffee pot and pressed his fingers against his lips like an expecting mother as it brewed. He looked pale and sickly—which twisted Davey's stomach sympathetically as the man kept his back turned to the natural light that leaked through the apartment window and into the kitchen nook.

They both stopped and surveyed Marilyn who was twisted and drooling into her sheets. Davey had felt guilty as he looked her over and thought of how he dozed covered in dramatic tears the night before. He'd meant to stay up for her, and he had failed. Brent scrunched his eyebrows together to release pressure on the ache in his head as he thought of how uncomfortable she seemed, sleeping twisted that way, and instantly his head throbbed a rod of pain down through his neck to remind him he must've slept in a similar position. He'd also noted the faded red lipstick stuck to the side of the girl's mouth and had a fleeting thought of how he'd never seen her in makeup before, completely unaware that the lipstick wasn't her own.

Brent's stomach tightened and he felt the few sips of black coffee he'd forced down begin to slide back up his throat, still hot. His analysis of Marilyn now replaced with the repeating command to *breathe* and *don't puke*.

67

Her mind was fogged as her limbs stretched out over the mounds of mothball scented sheets and pinched her nerves between muscle and bone. She moaned into a pillow saturated with whiskey drool and sucked her legs up through the lapping sheets. Her thighs rubbed and squeegeed off one another like fat inner tubes in a public pool. Like she was wet. She rubbed her legs together again as her groggy mind worked to place the familiar, slimy sensation. A slime warm and fluid as it rolled up towards her back as she shifted on top of the bed. Warm like blood.

Her eyes sagged open and she poked a hand into her tense abdomen with a panic. "Oh god," she croaked with a strained voice and the veins in her neck strung out. She rolled from the sheets to her knees and yanked the blankets away from the mattress. She threw them to the ground and studied the fitted sheet for a murder scene, but it proved to be clear of red. Fresh or old. She shifted her weight and noted the way her underwear felt as it cradled a muddy red swamp that leaked like candle wax down the inside of her leg. She stood and the mucky waters spilled from her laced panties faster. She waddled to the bathroom as she felt the thick liquid begin to wet the back of her knees.

She ripped at the shower handle and the pipes rattled and screamed, like tea kettles, to life for the first time that morning. The sharp iron scent of blood pushed up around her patted her cheeks as she dropped her pants and soaked red lace to the floor. She stood over her jumbled pants and stared into a shower for a long moment as she dripped like an unspayed dog.

She then flipped the shower nozzle and the bath faucet switched to the showerhead, the water jetting out and ricocheting off the porcelain tub at a godly pressure. She stepped delicately into it and collected shower water into a parted mouth to then spit it out over her chin as she dipped her ratted hair into the industrial waterfall. She became aware that she was *missing* something as she rubbed hot water over her stomach that crinkled like it was full of eggshells.

Marilyn was sure that she felt *robbed* of this feeling.

It wasn't until she lathered Brent's shampoo into her matted mane that it occurred to her what was absent—a hangover. A deathly one, at that. She washed the frothy soap from her hands and rubbed the tips of her fingers over the wax texture smudged against her mouth. A wicked grin revealed against her touch and she thought:

I kissed a girl and I liked it.

Leftover, Red Mac lipstick.

She rattled her head around and waited for the rush of nausea. But it never came. No hangover, "fucking sweet!" She cheered against the rainwater that guzzled soap into her moving lips. *Fucking sweet* was right, considering she'd drank enough to die.

The shower ended and she dried quickly before she rolled toilet paper into a deflated rectangle and jammed it between the lips of her vagina. She wattled, bare, back to the living room, her ass clenched to keep the two-ply in place. She rummaged through clothing for a clean pair of underwear when a thought had popped her head up like whack-a-mole.

She stared out across the cold, empty living room and thought: *Money.* Topaz's money, had she successfully pocketed some of the woman's cash?

She bounced on the balls of her feet, with her arms crossed under her breasts to make a flesh bra, back to the bathroom where her bloody pants laid.

She dove for them and inserted curious fingers into their jean pockets. A laugh began to rumble through her as she removed the item from a soft pocket. She had stolen Topaz's whole fucking wallet.

68

Brent slid further back into his chair that had been chosen for him in the tiny, main office, conference room. He cupped a hand over his brow and groaned with hot breath to himself as it shaded his burning eyes from the fluorescent panel lights. He slid his eyelids shut to take his attention away from Joel's droning speech to the room of staff. His head pounded harder than it had when he woke up that morning, and his stomach was in threads with coffee vomit that wanted to spill through his nose and onto the oval conference table. A statement was made by the principal and a moment of silence followed it. Brent had begun to enjoy the silent stocked room with a soft, feminine hand tapped his arm.

He made a *hm?* Noise from his chest and reluctantly peeled his wet eyelids away from his stinging eyes to take in a room of faculty that looked at him curiously. He locked sight specifically with Emily as she retracted her tapping hand away from his arm and relaxed back into her chair with a shy smile.

"Sorry," Brent mumbled to the room then cleared his froggy throat–the phlegm flicking down the back of his esophagus with a metallic sting, "I'm not feeling so good this morning."

Joel Olmstead nodded, "flu season is just around the corner–go home if you need to."

All coworkers seemed to lean away from Brent like he had contracted the plague, all coworkers but Emily, who was adjusting a ring on her index finger.

Brent waved Joel's offer off with a weak blink, "just a migraine."

Emily's eyes came back up to his, but this time with a bright, quietly laughing smile underneath them.

Why?

"I was telling everyone about our new staff member joining us tomorrow," Joel's voice brought Brent away from Emily and sharply back to the rest of the room that stared at him coldly.

He cleared his phlegm flicking throat again, "yes, she's a young friend of mine. Joel was kind enough to make a position for her, and Debra —" he nodded with his sharp, light-sensitive, head towards the Hispanic woman who smiled reluctantly and dropped her eyes to the conference table, "was kind enough to allow Marilyn—*my young friend*—to work alongside her."

Debra shifted in her seat as coworkers turned their heads to her.

"Thanks, Deb," Emily addressed the woman.

"We're excited to work with her," Joel concluded.

Brent tried to smile at the man but the action only sent a stab to his gut. So he instead grimaced and applied pressure with two fingers to the joint in his jaw.

It would be spread around like a rumor that Marilyn was Davey's older sister later, but that hadn't mattered. He had no reason to explain or justify, so he just sat and let his coworkers converse like birds.

69

It was like desert explosions behind his eyelids, all sharp, bright and sweet. Not the lovely sweet either, but the sweet that signal chills into your bones and electricity into your teeth. Like biting aluminum foil. Brent laid his head down onto his desk, forehead first, and blew an electric breath from his lips. He wanted to honestly die then. Heart attack, stroke, mallet to the back of the neck? He hadn't cared—he just wanted an abrupt cut off from the pain. His full-body sweat and sour temples twisted his lips and he groaned heavily like a tired jungle animal. The echo of the low whine bounced off his desk and cocooned around him to rattle the back of his wisdom teeth and lock his jaw. He sat his head up and cracked his jaw open reluctantly, sure he was going to vomit as his TMJ joints crinkled near his eardrum sorely.

 A light tapping of a woman's knuckle against the metal door frame of his office brought his head up the rest of the way and he turned to face the sound despite the fire that bolted into his tear ducts and made his stomach swim.

 Emily Engels starred from under her dark eyelashes with a shoulder pressed into the door jam, her body leaned halfway into his office, "party a little too hard on a school night?" She asked with a delicate giggle.

 A greasy scent had waltzed in behind her and decorated the stiff air of Brent's office as he furrowed his eyebrows, his face paled as he quizzed her with his facial expressions, and he feared he might puke on his coworker.

Emily tilted her head at him as if studying the way his nose flared as he noticed the smell in the room then revealed a fast food bag she'd had hidden behind her back. It swung through the doorway in her fist and the scent thickened, "I got you something —" she bowed her head with embarrassment, "actually no, it's my leftover breakfast —" she sighed, "I think it's greasy enough to help."

Brent tilted his head to mimic her as she came fully into his office and ran his clammy hands over his pant legs. He was confused.

She fluttered her eyelashes and looked up at the wall behind him, then dropped her eyes back to him, "bacon and egg breakfast sandwich," she explained, except her voice seemed a little more unsure then it had been before, "the grease —" she wagged a finger at her head, "I heard that it helps with—you know," she laughed nervously, "hangovers."

Brent bit at skin on his lip as he contemplated how he was going to tell her that he didn't have a hangover, "Emily,—" He'd started, but then a chill in his body stopped him still, as Marilyn, that morning, twisted in her sheets with a smear of red lipstick over her chin and cheek nestled against his frontal lobe. It was like a neon sign and he parted his lips at it, a finger lifting to his temple and tapping at his flesh like the obis in his head was a fishbowl full of sleeping flounder. "Thank you," he'd finished and extended a hand out for the bag.

Pleased with herself, Emily handed it over, "drink lots of water," she told him with a wink.

He nodded, already drifting away from her into his own thoughts. He tapped his head again and the image of Marilyn vibrated like a bell.

70

Marilyn had leafed her fingers through Topaz's wallet and helped herself to the cash and a *7/11* rewards card without much regret. The remainder of the billfold was discarded against a sidewalk as the girl left her favorite Oriental-Owned convenience store with a box of tampons and a box-shaped bag of night-time pads. She'd been right about Topaz, the rest of the wallet had been mostly ones —*and* two beautiful twenties. She sighed happily as she sunk her fingers into the two large bills and a thick stack of ones. Fifty-three dollars total, Marilyn classified that as a *win*.

Someone would find the thrown out wallet and return it to Ms. Topaz P. Lutz. Her full name highlighted on a license in a clear wallet pocket. Marilyn contemplated what the *P* might have stood for as she walked along the sidewalk. *Patricia? Prim? Peggy?* The possibilities were endless—*Possibility?*—especially with the idea of it being a male name. *Peter? Parker? Pablo?* Marilyn had smiled to herself: *That's it for sure,* she thought, "Topaz Pablo," she'd snickered as the name left her mouth and the wad of toilet paper fell from her vagina and halfway down her pant leg.

She arrived back to the apartment and slid a tampon into where it belonged with a relieved toss of wet, red toilet paper into the trash can. Marilyn then went to Brent's bookshelf and plucked a random title for its size and the texture of the outside cover—glossy. She dropped to his couch and flipped to a random page where she began to read from the middle paragraph with not much more than mild enthusiasm.

Marilyn eventually kissed boredom and dropped her head into the back of the couch to stare sadly at the apartment ceiling. The window behind her illuminated the tip of her nose with a beam of Oregon mountain light and she went cross-eyed as she studied it, the book whopping to her lap and closing. She could almost feel the cotton tampon tube blossom as it absorbed her hot body fluids. She shifted her weight against it and ignored the way it turned inside of her to stab momentarily into her shedding uterine wall.

Her head began to buzz—distance and deep buzzing that reminded her time was almost up. The bell buzzer ring inside her head began to sting like hot wire and she cursed it. Marilyn's life of being alone and free was depleting as the pain in her noggin began to climb the cement stairwell outside the apartment door. The hurt spread feverishly to the outer lining of her skull and she scrunched her nose like she had a brain freeze. She could hear their voices now. *On-my-own* was over. She set her eyes forward into a glare on the door.

The door opened and the pain subsided to a cool cough drop sensation as Davey and Brent entered the apartment. Brent still had a wince on his face from his side of the pain pool they both swam reluctantly in.

Despite the defeat that burned internally like her stomach was a hot plate, she smiled and greeted them.

Davey leaped onto the air mattress and gave one good pump of his legs to launch to the couch and hugged his sister who grunted as the book in her lap fell to the floor.

Brent had smiled back at her with flushed under eyes, "hey kid."

He felt better, compared to the man he'd been that morning—the greasy food and jugs of coffee he'd drank finally swooped in to save the day. Now he just felt bogged down and clouded over—like depression of the eyes. His bed invited him to collapse into it and give up for the night, but he couldn't.

His day wasn't over yet, *he had questions,* "Marilyn, can you help me with dinner tonight?"

She didn't want to, not even at the slightest, but she nodded anyway and stood. Her tampon string tugged between her thighs and the blossoming cotton in her bloody canal shifted down harshly.

Davey's high cheekbones lifted even higher and his wide eyes brightened, "I'll help too!" He imagined Bear Kingsley rustling against his back from inside his new school bag and added, "Beary wants to help too!"

Brent had spoken over the boy, "you should take a shower instead, Dave," and his words hung strangely in the air as Davey quieted and his lips found his slobbery mouth, like Brent had hit him.

Marilyn's chest cramped slightly and her eyes seemed to dilate like an animal smelling prey. *Brent wants to be alone with me?* The real question was *why?* But she was too distracted by lust to ask it.

Brent tilted his head at Davey and looked at the boy with hurt in his eyes, "I'm sorry pal—but after you, your sister has to shower for her big day tomorrow."

She didn't, but she let him continue,

– "and then I'd like to shower after that." He shrugged at the sad boy, "then we have to go to bed, right?" He became aware of Marilyn's eyes as they watched him closely with a gaze that set his nerves on edge, "make the shower quick." He added in a half mumble and winked at the kid.

Brent leaned his back into the kitchen counter once Davey's shower was pouring into the porcelain tub and crossed his arms at the girl who stood with her head cocked in front of him. The ingredients for dinner, *shepherds pie,* were laid out behind him and Marilyn's attention was laid on him.

She admired the sturdy thin of his stomach and the way his shirt laid buttoned against it. She admired the width of his hips and how snuggly his brown leather belt hugged them. She let her eyes flick lower for a brief glance to notice the way —

"Did you go out last night?"

Her head jerked up to his red cheeks and irritated scowl with a hollow stare, "maybe," she licked her top lip with a flexed tongue as flash memories of Topaz moving against her painted her insides with a wet warmth. Their lips *had* felt *real good* together. Her smile at Brent thickened.

A hand of one of his crossed arms traced lightly over a seam in his shirt just above his bicep as he thought. Marilyn watched it like he was a hypnotist, "it's okay if you did."

She focused back into his moving lips with a bit of a glare—of course, it was okay—he wasn't her father and she didn't have an obligation to fear disappointing him. The idea came with anger that she shook away.

"I'm just curious because," he moved his tracing hand to his face and pressed at his drooping eyelids, "I'm sorry," he shook his head like a shaggy dog, "did you drink last night?" He felt hot under the kitchen lights.

Marilyn giggled behind closed lips, "enough to drown a village—honestly." *No obligation.*

Brent pulled his hand from his eye sockets and pressed the back of it to his forehead with a moan, then a laugh. His laugh came in three short breaths as he blinked at the ceiling, then dropped a relieved sigh back down to the girl, "yeah well," he shook again, but this time with a bit back smile and hair that tickled over his brow bone, "you gave me your hangover."

His smile came fully as he realized how ridiculous he must sound.

Marilyn's face scrunched as she processed his words, like a frozen computer as it processed data beneath a spinning wheel of death. Her eyes slid to the corner to think for a split second then came back to him almost aggressively, "no fucking way?!" She stepped towards him curiously, "did I really?"

Brent stepped away from her kindly, "yes," *short laugh,* "you did."

Marilyn's chest expanded and she used her arms to cross a barricade over it, "damn," she exhaled as she continued to process the *ridiculous* information. She had been wondering where her hangover had run off too, obviously not far, she concluded. "So what —" her nose flared, "—our brains share sicknesses now, too?" She wasn't sure she classified the hangover as a *sickness* but couldn't decide on a better *classification* for it. *Maybe stupidity?*

Brent shrugged, unsure if he'd even began to understand the half of it.

"Do you think if I punched myself in the head you'd feel it?" Marilyn lifted a fist to the side of her head and laughed at the way Brent flinched his own head back, one eye squinting closed in a wince.

"Please don't," He put a hand out to stop her.

She turned her fist upward and flipped up the bird with a wink.

Brent bit the inside of his cheek and brought his hand back to cross his arms tighter than they had been before, "funny."

Marilyn nodded, dropped her *fuck you* finger and cackled her famous witch cackle.

Brent gave a closed-lip smile without making eye contact before he turned to his dinner ingredients, unimpressed with her joke.

Gee, what's with the sudden stick up your ass? Marilyn thought as she stepped a foot back from him.

Brent squinted and wrinkled his nose as the plastic around the raw ground meat tore at his fingertips and squeaked against the blood-stained styrofoam tray it sat in. Once the squeaking stopped and the meat was free of its packaging he sighed.

"Marilyn?" His voice dragged her name out on gravel as he studied the meat. It was spoken softly despite the growl his voice gave it—a feathery cushion to catch the *thud* of her heart against her ribcage.

"Yeah?" She matched his soft voice with her own female version and wondered if he could feel her heavy, anticipated heartbeat the same way she always felt his when he fell asleep first.

Brent tipped the styrofoam tray of meat into a matte black frying pan, "don't sneak out again, please." He looked at her as he spoke this time, then dropped his focus back to the ground beef that sat like a block of pink fat in the center of the cold pan, "I know you don't need to take orders from me—you're an adult —" he crossed the kitchen to the sink and dropped the empty, bloody, styrofoam into the trash can beneath it. He paused his monologue to stick his hands under the sink faucet and scrub them with soap under hissing water. He flipped the bubbly stream off and dried his hands on a draped kitchen towel before he turned his full body towards Marilyn.

For the first time that night she noticed the red in his eyes from her hangover and a five o'clock shadow that highlighted his wrinkles.

"— But, I care about Davey," Brent crossed back to the raw meat and put it, pan and all, on the stove.

He turned a dial and began to stab the block of ground beef into tinier blocks of tinier ground beef with a plastic spatula.

"What if you'd gotten yourself in trouble with the law? Drinking underage?" The food sizzled as the burner heated up and Brent continued to stab like he might be angry at something, "or something happened to you. What would Davey have done?" *Stab, stab, sizzle.*

The girl flexed an eyebrow, "lived with you," she answered simply.

"Marilyn!" *Stab,* "The fact is —" *stab,* "you're walking a dangerous line." He turned fully to her again and his hazel eyes seemed to wet as he looked down his nose at her, "you obviously worked really hard to save him from something," he thought of the purple Crayola noose, "don't be stupid and screw it all up."

The girl's jaw set forward as she leaned back on a heel and popped her prominent hip out. *It's okay if you did,* he had said as his hand rubbed the seam of his shirt. She knew now that, that had been bullshit. Fine, but why can't he, "talk to me like I'm an adult."

Brent flattened the meat into the pan and stared at it as the sizzle became a low hiss, "if something happened to you I'd have no chance. It'd be foster care for Davey. Or back to your mom."

Marilyn's vision flicked with sudden irritation, " no way!" She hissed like it hurt, "my mom broke his fucking arm because he sat on my lap and not *hers*. No way they'd give him back to her!" Her face was wide and she swung her hand in the air as she talked. A heated reaction, much like the one back at the hospital when the nurse had laughed at her.

Brent turned, spatula jammed out at her with conviction like he was an old-time TV detective and she was handcuffed to a metal, interrogation table, "you *saved* him from that! Don't screw it up."

There was that word again—she wasn't going to *screw* it up. She wasn't an idiot. She scowled as the sensation of blood soaking the line of her underwear began to make itself prominent.

"Don't do anything to mess up your chances to be successful," Brent continued past where she'd wished he would've stopped. He went back to stabbing and flipping the cooking beef, "foster care —" he shook his head.

Marilyn, who was fed up with his soapbox speech, cut him off, "you have a pretty shitty attitude towards foster care—who touched you without your permission?" She'd meant to offend him but hadn't meant to make his whole face goes pale, like it had, like she'd socked him in the gut with an iron fist. *Oh... shit.*

Brent bit the inside of his cheek as the color in his face continued to drain and he tried to act like he hadn't heard her.

Marilyn shifted her weight as embarrassment started to turn her cheeks red. An Embarrassment that she decided to flip into anger, "whatever," she said to the man who wasn't looking at her, "I need to change my fucking tampon." She turned and left the kitchen with a weighted speed like she was anticipated to be hit from the back by the man.

Marilyn leaned into the bathroom door and bumped the base of her palm against it, "Davey!" She yelled through the plaster wood, "hurry up!" She could feel the blood begins to pool like her panties were a poreless hammock. A tiny, "one second!" came from the other end as Davey dried off and Marilyn felt the weight of what Brent had said. Admitting it or not, she knew she had to be more careful with the little boy on the other side of the door. Her lips sagged.

In the kitchen Brent continued to stab mindlessly at the meat in the frying pan as the purple Crayola noose was shoved aside to welcome a new image—Davey's mother, snapping his arm in half out of jealousy. The man's hangover headache was back and his stomach curdled with it. He squeezed his eyes shut as the idea of Davey's arm snapping played like a movie through his head. It was vivid like he'd been there to see it himself. His mother's hand squeezing down and biting the flesh around his wrist to *yank!* The same way Amanda's fingers had bitten his bony shoulders as a boy, bitty and in the bathtub.

His eyes opened and revealed charcoaled bottom meat. He dropped his head and pressed air harshly from his lips.

Burnt beef would have to do.

PART THREE: MILK

71

Marilyn stood in the mirror of the teachers' lounge single-use bathroom. She stared at her young cheeks that hung in a tired sag and seemed a little less youthful than the last time she had counted her flaws. There were freckles on her left jaw that had infected themselves into tiny moles sometime in her early teen years and her eyebrows needed to be plucked. Her body reflected more bloated than usual, her curves fitting themselves into her hips and spreading themselves to the back of her legs where her black jeans hugged snuggly and she frowned. She was in the same cardigan she had interviewed in and now—in the heavy yellow light—she realized it didn't pool off of her as much as she thought it had. The tail of it hung low and hid half her heart-shaped ass from view and the sleeves drooped long past her fingers—forcing her to roll them up—while the rest of her fit tightly in it. The knitted grey, black and white material stretching suffocatingly over her elbows, biceps, and boney shoulders. Its open front draped strangely over her breasts and she spent a full minute adjusting it until her '*C' cups* looked decent below its cotton string and her old black tank top.

Marilyn's hair was in a bun and, despite her best efforts, revealed the sprouting baby hairs that curled up from her pale scalp. They feathered out like ferns and bowed over her oily forehead. She pushed them back, flat against the rest of her tugged and combed hair just to watch them spring back up and sway in the distilled bathroom air—like there was a breeze.

The door handle to the locked bathroom was tugged from the hallway and the door jiggled loudly from the force. Marilyn had started at the sound of the lock restricting them to enter and had whipped her head around to the solid wooden door of the ugly painted, orange, single-use bathroom to ensure the lock did its job. The door was unbudging.

With her eyes away from her bloated reflection she was able to relocate her confidence. She turned back to the mirror, feeling more like herself than she had a moment before, and saw a girl on the second day of her period. *The deflated and depressing day.* She straightened her shoulders and gave herself a half-cocked smile, "get over yourself," she mouthed to the unmasking and shameful reflection as it tried to remind her of everything bad.

She pivoted from it and thrust the bathroom door open. The office hallway air crashed into her and sprung more baby hairs out to dance in its breeze. A woman she hadn't met yet was leaned into the hallway wall as she waited for the bathroom to free up. They gave one another an American-friendly smile before Marilyn passed the woman who slid into the open bathroom doorway as the girl stepped out of it.

Debra had given Marilyn a note to deliver, *an Excuse Slip,* to a teacher named *Mrs. Mack in room A02.* She walked with it down a long hallway and fanned herself as she went. As her shoes (flats—not tennis shoes) slapped like little fly swatters against the polished tile floor the school building smells and their corresponding emotions decided to reveal themselves.

She was aware that as a child the building would have smelled like peers, her school supplies rolling in her backpack, sneakers. It would have smelled like faux warmth and fake welcomes and fear as her parents rolled away in their car and waved goodbye for the day—leaving her on her own accord. They would've provoked the emotions of submission and claustrophobia. At least for her as a child it had. School meant you were stuck and the classes were controlled and the lessons were selected for the majority—not the creative minority. Something her father had always said as he encouraged her to be creative with her free time.

On Monday, when she had visited the school it had smelled not like peers, but like little children, strangers to her and much smaller than she had remembered. The emotion was nostalgic yet unconnected to the walls around her.

Now, the smell was important. Like paper, and folders, and the musk of adult perfume and cologne around her, mixing with crayons and floor wax. The emotions provoked responsibility, and importance, (oddly enough.) In a few months, she would be accustomed to the strong scent and would blend it. Only remembering the strong aroma and connecting emotions when she came back after summer and the building was new and fresh to her again... Marilyn puffed her cheeks like she was sick.

She rounded the corner to the fifth-grade hallway and the scent of mop cleaning fluid replaced the school's otherwise suffocating stench. A tall janitor with slicked back white hair and a mouth like a horse lapped up spilled juice with the dreadlock hair of a mop. He dipped the wet broom into the yellow rolling bucket and glanced at her as she passed.

"Hello." Marilyn nodded.

"Who are you?" He talked with a slight lisp given by his large bottom teeth that faced inward. He asked as if she was a lost child in a place she didn't belong. *Tricky*—because she wasn't sure she did yet. *Belong.*

"Marilyn," she introduced herself and stuck out a hand.

He didn't take it, "Rick," he responded, then his underbite dipped into a frown and his eyebrows furrowed. He towered over her in a lean stature and she could see the spot of hair he missed when shaving under his chin, just before his Adam's apple.

Rick stared at her, inquisitive, so she stared back in the same manner—her outstretched hand falling to her side. He placed a folded fist against his hip and shook the white hair out of his eyes, "Smile, please. I bet you'd look good with one."

Marilyn's body and face twisted into an appalled snarl, a belch of sudden anger pitted like a fire on the inside of her ribcage. *What the fuck?!* She thought as she tried to comb through his words like a calculator would comb through an extensive equation before erroring out.

Her head broke into a numb chill as it'd suddenly been dropped on ice, and her anger was thrown for a moment.

"Hey! Good Morning, Rick!" Brent, who had been an earshot distance from the janitor and girl while reviewing evaluation sheets in his office, chirped as he swooped in between the two of them with a wide set smile and his hands in his pockets.

Rick looked at him with a glazed stare.

Brent nodded at the man then tipped his attention to Marilyn, "Hey, I'm glad I caught you, I need your help." He glanced at Rick then back to the red tempered girl, "super urgent."

He turned back towards his office and stared wide-eyed at her until she turned two. They began to walk and he watched hesitantly as her scowl grew deeper.

"Who the hell —"

Brent whined through his throat loud enough to cut her off, "just wait 'til we're back in my office," he mumbled under his breath once she quieted and glanced back at Rick.

They crossed into his office and he scrambled around her to get the door closed.

"He was so rude!!!" The girl swung her arms wide with her words and the excuse slip crumbled in her fist, "is he the school's RETARD?!"

Brent dropped into his office chair—satisfied with himself for getting her into a detained spot before she exploded—and waved his pocketed arms out like his elbows were floppy, featherless, bird wings.

"*Smile, please. I'd bet you'd look good with one.*" She mocked the janitor through a thick gag, "Fuck off, horse face!"

Brent squinted his eyes at her and licked the corner of his mouth before smiling, "I know right, doesn't he know who he's talking to?" He took a hand from his pocket and pointed to the young, panting adult, "miss Hot Head Matthews!" The night she'd crawled through the reception window at the hospital coming to mind.

Marilyn glared, "right."

At least she agreed with him.

She blew hot air from pressed lips and her baby hairs swayed in it.

Brent leaned out of his chair and propped the door back open, "In all honesty," his nose scrunched and his voice dropped into a whisper, "nobody likes Rick. He's rude to us all."

This was true, Rick was worse than I.T. in most cases.

"And the smile thing... I wouldn't take it personally. He's told me to smile before too."

"I'm gonna smile as I rip his throat out."

Brent flexed his face in one swift movement, like a flinch, "just avoid him," he suggested.

Marilyn dropped her hips back against Brent's door frame and scanned his office like it was her first time seeing it before dropping her eyes back to him, "rip it the—" she widened her stare and lowered her speech into a hardly audible whisper, "*FUCK,*" smile, "out."

Brent clenched his jaw at her fowl mouth like he was going through rigor mortis.

She laughed and waved the crumpled note in her hand through the air, "gotta take this to Mrs. Mack. A girl named Laurel is getting picked up by her mom at noon." She straightened and rapped her knuckles against the door frame, "thanks for saving me from Rick."

His jaw relaxed and he nodded as she turned to go to room A02, *Mrs. Mack's*.

72

The electric buzz of television newscasters woke her with their friendly voices. A scripted banter between the weatherman and lead anchor livened her living room. An elderly arm reached out and flipped off the white stand up fan by her bedside. Tulsa entered into the bedroom and gave a girthy meow. Winnifred laid her head back against her pillow and willed the stupid cat away. Tulsa meowed again, then, *umph*, jumped into the bed. The mattress rattling against her weight.

"G' morning Tulsa."

With the drowning white whipping fan off Winnifred could hear the newscasters better.

"Well Todd, it is 8:21 am on a Thursday morning and I am feeling great. Do you know why?"

Todd said he didn't.

"Because the sun is shining with a high of sixty-five, not too hot, not too cold —if you were to ask for my opinion. But folks if—"

Winnifred tuned out their voices from there. Preoccupied with Tulsa's flicking tail.

"What the hell do you want, fat ass," she slurred to the cat with her toothless mouth.

Food was probably (absolutely) the answer.

Winnifred pressed a frail hand at her right hip—it stuck forward against the bed, misaligned with the left that laid flat and not-as-inflamed. She didn't remember when or how she got old—it was hard to keep track because *black don't crack*. If her body didn't hurt and her teeth hadn't gotten pulled she would think she was no older than fifty-five.

The woman rolled to her side and flipped the sheets past her swollen legs. Her purple comforter flicked out the furthest and landed on the Maine Coon. Tulsa growled and jumped off the bed, slamming front legs first into the ground. Winnifred tried to do the same by pushing into a sitting position. Her head swayed at the sudden movement and the higher elevation made her dangling ankles ache like pinned shackles were weighted against them. Really, she didn't remember getting old. She had just gotten there one day.

As she hobbled to the bathroom Tulsa wove between her feet, "I swear you're trying to kill me," Winnifred admitted to her cat. "You'd starve."

Starving would be good for her. She'd lose some weight and gain some manners. *Meow.*

"Oh, that's right. You could eat me," she entered the bathroom, Tulsa tried to follow but she kicked her out gently before shutting the thin apartment door made of Lewan board. She knew from memory exactly where the light switch sat on the wall—upper right, bicep height, half an arm's length away, in the corner snuggled with the door. She blindly reached out and *flicked* it on.

A dark, thick object bombed the woman's head as the light hit the surfaces of the bathroom. Winnifred ducked and it recoiled back up and to the three-way intersecting corners of two walls and the ceiling. Winnifred crept backward to the closed Lewan board door with her eyes on the black object braving out of the corner and walking, six-legged, across the wall, towards her vanity bathroom lights. She squinted with curiosity and shuffled a foot forward to get a better look, her eyesight fading in and out.

"What are you?" She asked it and as if hearing her the insect stretched its dusted wings off its back to showcase under the bathroom bulb. Its wings mimicked an orange autumn leaf speckled with nature's self-inflicted beauty marks and veined wrinkles. Under the elongated arrowhead-shaped wing was a fuzzy mocha brown body striped with sections of its torso. Winnifred's back hit the closed Lewan board door in sudden fright as the large sphinx moth pushed off the wall and dove for her again.

In the bathroom, where Winnifred had blindly remembered the exact location of the light switch, the old woman panicked and fumbled her hand around the wall and door for the doorknob. Her mind scrambled and left arm flailing at the creature as it bounced off of her just to loop around and come back. The cold knob pressed into her searching hand with a force that said, *hello Winnie, I've been in the same spot forever, you idiot.* She yanked the Lewan board door open and squeezed her body through the crack nearly tripping and breaking that bad hip over Tulsa trying to push her way through.

"NO!" she yelped at her every bit deserving cat and slammed the door behind her, entrapping the moth that was trying to kill her like a kamikaze pilot. She could hear its heavy body collide with the Lewan board door three more times before retreating up to the vanity mirror lights. Winnifred gave an unmasculine squeak of terror and turned her body away from the bathroom. The mottephobia woman relapsing to being an impish little girl in her apartment hallway, Tulsa as her witness.

In a half an hour she had regained enough courage, through slow pacing and verbal reassurance, to open the bathroom door back up. This time with Fat-Ass-Tulsa in both her thin arms. The oversized steroid injected insect bombed toward her again and she tried to hold Tulsa up in front of her as a swatting barricade of death to the moth. Except Winnifred failed to hoist the cat up—the muscles in her shoulders and the joints rolling in her elbows screamed for her to stop the second she started to lift. The cat then turned, frighted from the insect herself, and climbed her owner, using Winnifred's back as a launching platform back to the hallway ground. Winnifred let out another weak squeak and sealed the Lewan board door, the sphinx moth bouncing off of it a few more times before retreating, again, to the vanity lights.

"You stupid fucking cat!!"

Me-e-eow.

She swatted her foot at her pet and her hip popped.

Tulsa dodged her dry skinned foot and then turned to strut down the hallway with a wide swinging ass and a smug upright tail.

Brent stopped by after a call from his neighbor rescued him from a counselor class lesson he had been planning. He walked out of the vacant bathroom now with the moth inclosed in his cupped hands. Its frantic wings and dangling legs bouncing off of his skin in an attempt to escape before settling down and trying to find a way to crawl out.

Winnifred backed up as he walked closer to her, "Don't you dare!" She gag spoke her dentures in her mouth now.

Brent let out a chuckle and lifted his closed hands to eye level as if inspecting the terrified little creature, "I wouldn't." He then lowered his hands to inspect his terrified little neighbor, "I have never seen you exert any emotion other than hard-ass, I didn't know *squeamish* was in your personality's vocabulary."

Winnifred glared with her bad eyesight at the handsome man, "A moth flew into my mouth when I was a little girl," she explained blatantly.

Brent wiggled an eyebrow as he walked towards the apartment door with the furry friend still in his grasp, "Pathetic excuses? Didn't know you were capable of that too!" He bounced on his toe with a bit of excitement for his smart remark and the old woman cursed behind him.

Once the moth was released outside he promised his friend a peaceful pee– the enemy had escaped.

"I'd rather the *enemy* be destroyed!" She told him, a sneer in her voice echoing off the bathroom walls as she entered the room for the third time that morning.

Brent made a face of disgust, "No thanks, that's like squishing a mouse with wings."

The door closed and he could hear his friend release a loud scoff then an *ahhh* before the trickle of urine. Brent retired himself to the living room until she was done.

"Gettin' out of here?" She asked as she walked into the living room, hands wiping dry onto her pajama bottoms.

Brent smirked, "I am getting out of here. My job is done—now I have to go back to my real one. I have a lesson to teach using puppets today!"

He was enthusiastic—a quite appalling opposite to the elderly woman's expression.

As he neared the door, he added, "maybe I'll hire you a full time, in house, nanny," he was joking, but not entirely.

"Cunt, you wouldn't." She growled at him— *cunt,* her favorite word to call people, her pet, and inanimate objects.

The male felt honored.

"Besides," She waved him away, "You can't afford to save *everyone.*"

Everyone as in Marilyn, Davey *and* her.

He nodded, "right, okay. Love you."

He left at that and sagged his hands into his pockets as he descended the stairs, hoping not to trip. *Everyone.* That burned at him, rattling his bones and poking his sides as he succumbed to a frown.

He wasn't trying to be the small-town hero.

73

Brent had treated the two Matthews' children and the elderly woman to *Mexican cuisine* on Friday night in celebration of Marilyn's first week of work. As they sat in the red laminate booth Marilyn worked the skin off her lips. She was only sometimes a fan of Mexican, and never a fan of positive attention.

A waitress with black curled bangs and a greased back bun approached the table with a checkbook sized notebook and a ballpoint pen. She introduced herself quickly with a liquidy accent, then blinked at Winnifred, who sat on the inside of Marilyn, "drink?" the waitress asked with a customer service smile.

"Margarita," Winnifred answered way too quickly.

The waitress giggled, nodded, and scribbled the order down before turning and pointing a pen at Brent who sat across from Winnifred, on the inside of Davey, "you, sir?"

Brent stared at Winnifred as if the word *Margarita* had come out of her mouth in bold, *Sesame Street* letters. His eyes said *tequila* and as he slid them to Marilyn they translated to *payback?* He smirked and thought: *Hangover receiver becomes hangover giver?* It would be a science experiment on their minds' connection, or, not so nicely put: *revenge.*

Marilyn met him with a mirrored smirk that said, *I dare you, Fosterboy.*

His smile parted and his tequila eyes dragged up to the waitress who waited patiently as they had their silent conversation, "water," he said with a held back laugh, "please."

"Agua," the waitress scribbled her pen into her paper with a nod, "okay," she then bobbed her head at Davey.

Davey sucked his lip into his mouth and watched the accented woman with wide eyes as he slunk back into his seat.

Brent immediately shrunk in closer to Davey, "What are you in the mood for, kid? Soda? Lemonade? Water?" He whispered to Davey only, with his shoulder and head dipped down to the boy, "Oh!" His eyes brightened, "they have something called a *Virgin Margarita* which is just like a really yummy smoothie."

Davey made eye contact with the man.

Brent nodded, "you want that?" Davey's lip came out of his mouth and Brent nodded again, "you have to ask her yourself, bud," he pointed from Davey to the waitress as he leaned away from the boy.

Deer in headlights. *Or*, Davey in headlights.

(No, it hadn't been a deer, it'd been a thing *inside her car.* The Boogie Man)

Marilyn tapped the toe of her shoe into Davey's leg, "you can do it," she encouraged.

Davey turned his head to Brent for backup, but Brent shook his head no. The boy frowned and looked back to the waitress, "um, a *Margarita* please?" His voice was full of froggy cracks and it made his face turn red.

The waitress laughed politely, "Too young for alcohol, *virgin?*" She had only been joking, but it had made sweat stab out of the boy's skin as he nodded at her with a dry mouth. She used her pen to make the note, "strawberry?" She said in her heavy accent and smiled as Davey nodded again.

Brent nudged the boy gently, "nice job, pal," he spoke with a wink.

"I didn't mean alcohol —" Davey explained nervously towards the man's ear as his hand picked frantically at his jeans.

Brent pressed the boy's hand until he relaxed it into his tiny lap, "we know what you meant, don't worry," he whispered back to the kid whose face cooled slowly.

"You, miss?" The waitress faced Marilyn.

Marilyn chewed a piece of dead skin from her lip, "do you guys have milk?"

The waitress looked puzzled as the rest of the table snorted at Marilyn. "Leche?" the woman smiled as if she didn't understand a joke, "no, no leche."

Marilyn shrugged and popped her lips apart, "a coke then, thanks."

The woman wrote the order down and left.

"Milk?" Brent laughed at the girl as the waitress rounded into the kitchen.

Once again Marilyn shrugged, "I have a craving."

"There's some at home," Davey chirped with his socially tired voice and Brent smiled at the word *home*.

"No," Marilyn scrunched her eyebrows at Davey like a brat, "we ran out this morning."

Brent snorted, "oh no, could you only fill up half your coffee mug with milk today?"

Marilyn rolled her eyes into a glare pinned at the man, "barely."

His snort spread into a full laugh as he turned his attention to Winnifred to explain Marilyn's milk versus coffee ratio as the girl scowled playfully at him.

74

Davey had failed to mention Daisy's invite to her birthday party until Saturday morning, the day of. He did right by at least waiting until Marilyn's teeth were brushed to bring it up. The crumpled invitation that had been wedged in his backpack now in hand, for proof. His sister starred groggily at him and despite his half thought out plan to calmly bring up a very last minute thing her eyebrows began to scrunch and her stare hardened.

"David Niles," Marilyn, who was exhausted mentally from her first week of being a real *depressed* adult, scolded. She took the invite from his tiny hand and tried to ignore his bottom lip as it folded into his moist mouth, "I don't even know who this Daisy girl is!" She handed the invite back to him, "no. Sorry little bro," Though, she was flattered that he was making friends. Perhaps, *Daisy* wouldn't end up being an adult, this time.

Davey took the stock card invite back and stared down at it with blurring eyes. It was blue with a hot pink picture frame edge, YOU'RE INVITED printed at the top in yellow bubble sans font, "that's okay!" He tried to sound more enthusiastic than he had felt at that moment.

To make it more believable.

He wanted to feel relieved—he now had an excuse to not show up to a socially exhausting party for little kids. Except he didn't feel relieved, maybe because he owed Daisy—*for standing up for him at the lunch table.*

He looked at his sister who's eyes had softened into a soggy mop of eyelashes—he knew by the look that if he tried to push the idea any further she'd steam into a blown gasket.

Brent, who'd been dusting his bedroom moments before, stepped in from the back of the room, "I know who Daisy is," he looked from Davey to Marilyn with a bright face, "she's a great girl."

Davey blinked at his sister and thought he could actually see the steam begin to precipitate off her forehead and side temples.

Brent leaned his waist into the back of the couch and braced his arms into its upright cushions, "I could take him. If you're okay with that, of course."

Marilyn's mouth parted as she thought and Davey began to feel the heated tinkle of high hopes against his lower back and inner chest.

"It wouldn't be a problem," Brent insisted, "I'll even talk with Daisy's mom and make sure he's in good hands before I take off," He grinned lightly at her from the comfort of his Saturday clothing and loose, gel-less hair.

"Sure," Marilyn nodded and pretended to not care for the way Davey bounced excitedly on the balls of his feet, "thanks, Brent." She thought then of having time *alone* once the two boys were gone and almost laughed. *Alone,* something she'd so melodramatically thought would never occur to her again, but here it was, stood directly in her face—an old friend.

Davey's rapid bouncing blurred the beam of teeth on his face into a spread strobe light, "thank you!" He cheered. Marilyn sighed and pointed Davey in Brent's direction—understanding the boy spun and threw the same, "thank you!" at the man.

Brent shrugged in a *'sure thing'* kind of way and moved forward to take the invitation into his own hands. He was in a casual, dark green shirt with the sleeves scrunched to his elbows and the veins in his hands and forearms twitched as he slid the invite between his fingers, Marilyn noticed.

The ink scribbled in Daisy's mother's handwriting had been smudged from living in Davey's backpack for too long but the date and time still showed through. Brent lowered the invite and stared at the top of Davey's night time sweat and greasy hair with a tilted eyebrow, "Hey," he waved a hand at the waft of stink that came from the young child, "you have enough time for a shower, you should take one." He winked as he spoke, first at the boy, then at Marilyn.

Brent had gone back to pick up dusty, used rags and make his bed while Davey showered quickly and with enough energy to charge a car. When the man had come back from his bedroom Marilyn had been laid out on the couch with a bag of frozen peas shoved into the center of her twisted, car wreck, back. Her hand covered her face as she gently willed away the sore muscles.

Too close!

Brent's eyes shot away from her as the internal scream rocked against his spine and internal organs.

Davey, who'd been drying his hair on a bed sheet rather than a towel perked up from the deflating air mattress, "are we ready?!" He asked Brent hopefully.

Brent returned with a nod, "sure, kid."

Marilyn's eyes peeled open and she twisted at the sound of his voice behind her, winced against the sharp shoots in her spine, waved the car wreck pain away, and lassoed snaps over her head to grab the man's attention, "Hey, hey," she pointed to the kitchen, "I left a note on the counter for you."

She had indeed, next to the fridge.

Brent slid the note between his fingers and lifted it into apartment lighting to read her abrasive and sloppy handwriting.

I can't do it anymore
Please pick up some God Damned MILK.

She doodled a cow at the bottom of the note in leaking ink. It side-eyed Brent beneath a wig, curled and short like her own hair. Brent laughed and shook his head dismissively at her strange sense of humor before he wiggled the note into an empty card slot of his wallet.

"You really want milk *that* bad?" He questioned as he rounded the corner, out of the kitchen nook.

Marilyn, without opening her resting ice pack eyes, twirled a hand to her forehead dramatically and moo'd.

That must mean: *yes.*

"I'm on it," His wallet fell nicely from stretched fingers into his back jean pocket as he crossed the room to Davey to rustle his partly dried hair, "probably should stop at the store to get Daisy a present anyway, huh?"

Davey shook off Brent's hand and shrugged, "Oh, *yeah.*"

Brent scrunched his nose at the kid, *"yeah,"* he mimicked as a joke.

Davey knew it had been a joke but had found his lip in his mouth anyway. A sad expression passed the man's aging face and Davey spat his lip out, sorry that he had made Brent think he had hurt the boy's feelings. He hadn't. *Really.* Davey could take a joke. *Yeah.* The boy scrunched his nose back at the man until the sad look left.

75

Davey didn't struggle to find a present at the store. His eyes immediately scanning aisles as the two males came in through the sliding automatic doors. He'd nearly tripped on himself as he beelined to the toy aisle with shelves of pink objects. Without hesitation, the boy had swiped a Barbie from the shelf to show Brent. It was a young modeled Barbie with a bright pink capris and a white, sparkly heart decorated t-shirt. Her hair was horse hay blonde and braided down the back with a silicone bow to tie it off. The doll *looked* like Daisy. Both boys' had thought so and it had been easy.

Now they sat still in the idling 4Runner against the driveway of the addressed mobile home on the invite. Davey's eyes were paralyzed and wide as they dilated and blurred out the Barbie that sat in his lap, now in a purple, present bag with white paper filling. He was lost in thought and paranoia. Brent pretended that he didn't want to ask about the boy's sudden anxiety as Davey pretended the anxiety wasn't because of Brent. Davey tried to sign some of the pressure in his chest away as he looked at the double-wide trailer Daisy lived in and thought of the kids at his lunch table.

"Did you run away?"
"Is Mr. Kingsley your uncle?"
"Is he your brother?!"
"Maybe his parents died!!"
"Maybe he killed his parents?"

"Davey, were they in a car accident?!"

He felt tears begin to well in the sockets above his cheeks and he decided he didn't want Brent to go inside with him, he didn't want anyone to see them together, and he didn't want any more questions. *Why didn't Marilyn want to take me?* He thought, suddenly sad and lonely.

Brent had been watching Davey, who was too small for the front seat, through the rearview in short glances—but now let his eyes stare out past the nose of his Toyota, "we're early," he pointed out quietly, hoping his voice wouldn't startle the child in thought, "No one is even here yet, gives you time to get adjusted to Daisy's house and family before the others show up."

Davey gripped at the bag in his lap and dared a glance to Brent—he thought maybe the man could be a mind reader—but knew Brent was really only good at reading facial expressions. It was his job.

Brent nodded as if Davey had said something, "ready to go in then?" He asked as he unbuckled himself and killed the engine.

Davey shrugged and popped the back passenger door open.

Both boys had walked to the trailer house and it had been stomach flips the whole way.

76

Marilyn slid back against a dining table chair and watched out the apartment windows, the mountains a white overlook in the distance. She wasn't looking for anything in particular but kept her eyes outside of the pane glass anyway as her mind wandered. Perhaps there'd be a bird or a fallen leaf that she could follow until it went on, past the window of the apartment, but so far there had been nothing.

    She arched her back to narrow her hips forward and looped an index finger into her front jean pocket. It fish hooked around her favorite cardboard box and she sighed inside her throat as she slid her finger and the cigarettes into the open. She lowered her hips back into the seat and flicked the lid of the cigarette box with her thumb, a salivating appetite on her tongue. She delicately rescued an unlit stick from its package and pressed it between her lips before trading the box to her cloth-in-jean pocket for her lighter. She kept her sight unfaltered from the frosty windows as she cupped a fist around the cigarette and opened a flame against it. The embers sparked and she sucked against the filter to spread the heated oxygen through the cold tube. A tongue of smoke slicked down her esophagus and made her body tingle. She held onto it for as long as her hungry lungs would allow before blowing the charcoal gray air through her nose. She smiled and her eyes wetted like she had yawned.

Her meltdown in the early AM on Tuesday, *Topaz Tuesday,* began to feel silly to her. A *drunk, lesbian* episode, all because she thought she'd never be alone again. But here she was, enjoying a cigarette and an Oregon view–alone. She tapped the sagged end of the cigarette off onto the table, "I'll just clean it up when I'm finished," she justified to herself, "what Brent doesn't see doesn't hurt him."

The burnt dust fluttered through the air and collected in a smooth pile on the laminated wood table.

Work wasn't bad. She could admit that. Delivering notes for Debra was the extent of it and she would be getting a nice paycheck for doing so. Plus–she wiggled her hips to enjoy the dry sensation between her legs–her period was over. *A fortunate girl,* her mother had once told her, *three day periods.* She dragged her lips against the cigarette and tilted her head back to release the air. It billowed up then crashed back down around her in an atomic nicotine cloud.

She sat up as a sliver of light appeared in a reflection on the window and she squinted at it. It fanned out, a wide transparent slice of light. *The door.* She spun in her seat with sore muscles and her cigarette teetering between her dry lips.

Brent.

He smiled at her from the open doorway of the apartment, the stairway cement lights illuminating his tall body and casting through the apartment to reflect off the large window.

She looked at him with worry and he dropped his smile to cock his head and return the worried stare, "I can't feel you," she told him as a hand came up to knock on the outside of her skull.

He closed the door, the fan of light shrinking to a sliver then cutting off entirely. He brought his smile back up and crossed the room to her, "the nicotine probably has something to do with it," he waved a slow finger at her lips as they sagged in awareness.

"Shit," she mumbled and removed the stick from her mouth. *Busted.*

Brent let a corner of his mouth slip into a mock frown, "I can still feel you," he tapped a knuckle into his temple the way she had a moment before to confirm it really was the nicotine that was throwing her off. His hand folded down from his head and held out like he was receiving an offering.

Marilyn's eyes rolled away from the man before unenthusiastically placing the cigarette to his fingers. He took it between the pad of his thumb and index and inspected the orange cherry of ashy fire that seemed to breathe on its own. She waited for him to jog to the kitchen to put it out beneath faucet water before coming back, heated and scolding her for the residue on his table. *You're irresponsible!* He'd probably tell her. Her eyes made a full roll and came back to him with a scowl. A scowl that was quickly dropped as her face paled and her eyes dilated at the man who'd slid the cigarette into his own mouth.

Brent's eyes fell to her as he took a deep chest drag off the stick, he winked and the corner of his mouth lifted in a cocky smile. He blew the clouded air out over her head slowly like a fog machine. He then grabbed his own dining chair to pull out and sit in. As he lowered down next to her he continued to watch her wide stare as the smoke curtained against her. *A skeleton's wedding veil.*

He looked to the table and fingered the small pile of white ashes curiously before lifting his eyes back to her to pass her half-smoked cigarette. She took it in disbelief and he turned away from her, both elbows rested on the table and sight fixed on the distant Oregon mountains.

Marilyn chuckled and shook her head before she placed the stick in her dry mouth to vacuum smoke into her black lungs. The filter was wet with Brent's saliva and her tongue flicked against it as a warm pooling in her lower gut made her legs cross. She released the smoke over the dining table, "you forgot the milk, ass."

His head tilted up and his eyebrows knitted together, "Whoops," his voice was a gravel growl that made the warmth in Marilyn's belly swim deeper, past her ovaries.

She flexed her crossed legs.

He stretched a hand out and slid the tips of his fingers over hers as he tried to get ahold of the smoldering tobacco stem. It laced between his forefinger and middle finger as he plucked it from her hand that twitched involuntarily from his touch.

Chills disguised as pins and needles ripped through her body and her cheeks hollowed. Brent placed the cigarette into his mouth like a lollipop and let it dangle on its own as both hands lowered to rest back on the table. Marilyn let her crossed legs relax into a slight spread as she watched the weight of the stick drag his lower lip down into a raw pink dip.

"It's nice not having Davey here," his words were swallowed with a cigarette induced speech impediment as smoke fell from his nose. He puffed against the cork colored filter, "don't you think?" He inhaled the words with the smoke, held it in his chest, then blew out slowly.

Marilyn nodded at him even though he wasn't looking, "sure," she said.

His eyes flicked to her and he smiled into the cigarette with his nose in a high scrunch, "definitely."

"Definitely," she mimed with her mouth.

Brent looked away from her to kiss one more drag from the cigarette before removing it from his mouth and crushing its ambered tip against the table. A line of dead smoke left it like a spirit from a body and danced up through the air.

Marilyn's attention fell to the crumbled, white cigarette with a slobber shared brown filter and she thought: *I wanted more.*

Brent's eyes came back but this time hung low in a hungry droop. His tongue stretched out over his bottom lip and his teeth followed to drag a light bite against the pink flesh.

All of Marilyn's thoughts silenced as his lip swelled with a light coat of saliva. He began to lean closer to her and she let him. Her neck and jaw tensed so tight it firmed her breasts as her heart racketed and made her dizzy, her vision convulsing.

Brent braced a hand against her knee as he passed the front of her heated face to place his stubbled cheek into her soft, young cheek, his lips parted in her ear.

The nicotine is working, Marilyn thought disorientedly as their bodies stayed still, no swirls like when she'd tried hugging him.

Brent's thumb was massaging into her knee as his breath touched her ear and his cheek scrapped her own, softer cheek, "*I hope Davey never comes back.*" His top lip nipped at her earlobe.

Marilyn's breathing audibly hitched and her hands came out to knead at the bottom of the blue cotton t-shirt he was wearing as she felt him smile into the side of her face. She forced her eyes shut and tried to work her lungs at a normal pace as her skin quaked with overstimulation.

Brent's cheek gave her whisker burn as he smeared it back to push their noses together, his breath as intoxicated and flaky as her's. A static, one they hadn't felt before, was bouncing between them like a cell tower signal and frying the nerve ends in Marilyn's face, neck, and chest.

She wanted to grip him and yank him into her, but she couldn't. She was stuck, paralyzed, so tense that she thought if she were to move her muscles would explode and her body would become a sack of jelly.

Brent's sneering smile had dropped and now his lips sat half open and plump near her lips as he shut his eyes to work through the radioactive thoughts that made his hands sweat.

Marilyn wrung his shirt between her fists as a pressed whimper pouted out over her tongue. Brent's lips went back in a canine bearing smile, the girl could tell as his breathing spanned wider over her face.

"*Can you just—*"

Brent's hand at her knee tightened and he tilted his chin in to slide his top lip over the bottom of her's.

Kiss me, her sentence finished as a drunken thought. Marilyn hiccuped a second whimper before sighing into it. The space where ribs separated and the human soul lived began to spin and heat as their lips locked deeper together and she could smell his sweet skin that mixed purely with her favorite raisin tobacco scent. One of her tight hands escaped the hold she had on his shirt and elevated to his neck. Her thumb rested at his cheek as the tips of her fingers entangled into the soft hair at the nape of his neck so she could work him in even closer to her.

Brent opened his eyes as he bit gently against her lower, wet lip so he could watch her shut eyes scrunch harder above her red cheekbones and her eyebrows furrowed deeper. His hands went to her hips as she leaned in and kissed him vividly, their touches to each other intoxicating and saturated in a lustful flavor. His eyes shut again and it was him this time that let a low moan leak into her mouth. He could feel the girl vibrate against him as her kisses became quicker and their teeth clattered together.

Brent moved back away from her hungry kisses, "*slow down.*" He purred. *Purred.*

Marilyn could've cried.

His hands gripped at her sides until she was sure she'd have hand-painted bruises. They then began to tug at her until she shifted from her dining chair to his lap, her legs quaking as she straddled him. His hands rubbed softly at the sore skin he'd left behind, then began to trail down. They ended up below her ass so he could stand and pull her up with him.

She locked her ankles behind his back and her lips at the corner of his jaw so he could see as he walked them through the apartment. He braced her weight with one arm that stayed firmly tucked against the fat of her ass as his other arm came up to hold her lower back, his fingers sprawled for support, his index against her spine.

Marilyn's tongue lapped out and she ran it from his jaw to his neck, to his earlobe.

Brent grunted at the wet warmth from the young girl as he rammed them through his bedroom door and dropped her to his white linen mattress. She stared up at him from where she lay, sprawled out, and ran the skin of her thumb through her mouth like a pacifier. Brent's pupils swallowed the color in his eyes like he was an animal smelling fresh blood and she gave a mousy giggle as he crawled on top of her, his face flushed. He gently moved her arms until they were above her head and pinned together in his fist. His other hand researched her goosebumped skin below her damp t-shirt. He kissed her and she bucked her hips against him. His lips broke away from her and he stared at her with his wide eyes as he used the weight of his own hips to force her down onto the bed.

"Oh -mygod." Marilyn breathed towards his ceiling.

Brent kissed the corner of her mouth before flipping to his back, the duvet on his bed, sighing as his body flattened its feathered weight. Marilyn took it as an invitation to reverse their roles and climb on top of him, her hands braced out over his firm chest and her ass lightly glided over the bulge beneath his pants zipper. His hands groped the bruised spots at her hips again and helped guide her in a sweaty rhythm. His head arched back into his bed and his lips pinched together as he hummed. The girl shivered against him as inaudible words left her mouth.

Brent exhaled and brought his sight back to her, "cold?" He asked as his hands found the underside of her shirt again, this time on her back.

She shook her head as her neck flexed beneath it, "no," her lips shuttered like they should've been blue and her breath should've been white, "just–"

Brent's hands had moved up from the dimples above her hips to the back of her shoulder blades, "excited?" He asked, his voice smooth and mature.

She paused her dry grind to study him. She'd forgotten his age until now, as she looked down at his cocked eyebrow and hinted wrinkle lines. He wasn't a horny teen looking to *fuck,* he was an adult man, and he chose *her.* Marilyn's heart rate lowered into a solid *whack* and the inside of her brow raised. Her hands elevated off his chest slowly and lifted above her head, they held eye contact as he used her position to remove her shirt, his hands on her back working it up over her head and raised arms.

In just her bra she bent down and kissed him softly, lovingly.

He kissed back the same, his warm palms braced into her bareback as her hair fell into his face. He gently scanned her back with his fingertips before sliding his thumbs below either side of her bra buckle. Her breasts ballooned around the plush support material as he stretched the buckle together to then hang heavy into her bra as he popped it open.

She'd never been in love before, but if there was a difference between lust and passion, she was convinced this was it. It was a sobering thought she melted into as he guided her back onto her back. The cups of her bra spread oblong and her straps slacked while Brent laced his fingers into her hair and kissed her collar bone.

Marilyn wrapped her legs around his waist and grinned as his lips continued to work into her flesh. His mouth moved to her neck as his long fingers removed her bra and dropped it to the floor. Her nipples hardened as his shirted chest brushed her bare breasts while her fingers tangled into his sweat prespirated hair.

Brent sat up to look down at her naked upper half and doe eyes that beat soft eyelashes up at him. His nose flexed and he ran a hand from her hip to her breast and gently twisted a nipple between the webbing of two fingers. His breathing wisped thickly from his parted lips as she reddened and squirmed below him. He liked that. He used his other hand to force her legs that hugged his waist into the mattress. She flexed her stomach and arched her back beneath him as her muscles continued to quiver. The hand at her breast stroked further up, to her neck. He pressed the flat of his thumb into the soft space at the center of her throat and tilted his head at the way the skin swelled around her eyes and her nose brightened at the tip. He leaned back on his heels and gripped at his belt.

Marilyn massaged her palms into her eye sockets as the sound of Brent's belt bucket coming undone made her head convulse. She tried to breathe steadily while his leather belt slowly left his belt loops in a slow static sound, her mouth and neck twitching with each anticipated exhale.

"Relax," he said as the belt slid from its last jean rung and dangled out in his hand.

She nodded and removed the pressing palms from her face but kept her eyes closed, still focused on each breath and each tiny muscles tighten.

Without her knowing he'd fed the belt back through the belt buckle, a leather noose now in his hands as he stared greedily at the soft skin laid over her throat.

She hummed to herself innocently as her eyes drifted and trailed against her closed, feverish eyelids and her hair puffed out around his sheets in curls.

His belt wrapped around her neck then, and he yanked it tight to seal her airway.

Marilyn's eyes widened and sudden spots flicked around her vision as oxygen was revoked from her. Her hands came up in slapping attempts to try to grab him, her mouth gaping to scream at him, tell him to *STOP!* He straddled her kicking legs calmly and swatted her clawing hands away, back to the mattress.

Brent leaned to her ear mellowly as he had in the dining room except for this time his brushing stubble rigged her with panic rather than hot prickles as she struggled for air, "do you think —" he stopped as her hand caught a handful of his hair and yanked. His voice trailed off smoothly as he removed her fight from his head and slammed her wrist into the headboard of his bed, her lips spreading out in a silent cry. "Do you think —" he started again, "—this is what your dad felt as he hung from Davey's ceiling fan?"

Marilyn began to wrath against him, a tight scream squeezing from her throat and her nails ripping through the air as her heels kicked and her hips bucked.

He sat back up, away from her flailing limbs and tightened the belt, a smile flickering at the way her skin puffed up around the metal buckle. "Sh, stop it, kid," he cooed above her, *"your daddy issues are showing."*

77

Marilyn had managed one connecting swipe of her nails at him and had left red crescent moon marks on his cheek before she'd been dragged from the bed by her noosed throat. An explosion of lights fire rocketed past her vision as her spine, curved between her bare shoulder blades, took the impact of hitting the ground. She'd bit her tongue when she hit and now blood foamed from her mouth as she flexed her lips like a fish. Vomit curled into each space in her lungs and her fingertips clawed harshly at her neck and skin and her muscles steamed and popped below the surface.

Brent fed her body along, her skin smeared raw against the hardwood as he pulled her to the living room, unimpressed with her kicking legs and elbows that slammed hard into the floor. "You're just hurting yourself," he tried to explain.

She smacked her fatigued limbs to her fat, swollen face as her vision pinned into a view through straws. She'd started to give up. *You're just hurting yourself.* Did she agree?

"Stop, kid," his breath sighed, "give up, and *join me.*"

The voice—the voice from the sidewalk, from her dream. She knew, even in her panicked delirium, that she'd known that voice. *(Join me.)*

He'd been stopped just outside the dark kitchen nook when he dropped her.

Her head violently cracked into the floor like a bag of wet sand as the belt was released. A bloated sob sliced from her vocal cords as it expanded against the slackened leather and buckle. A blue flamed fire pumped through her lungs as she worked her fingers into the triage around her throat and loosened it all the way. Her tongue jutted out and she gagged coughs while weakly rolling to her side to let the blood and saliva drool to the floor. Her heaves for air jolted bright cuts of lightning through her as her esophagus clicked and spasmed.

A scent, musky like underwear and summer heat, engaged with the air that she grappled for and her red face shaded a light, olive green. It was a thick scent that coated her like a rag of chloroform and reminded her of her car wreck. She sobbed through bitten tongue blood and forced her vibrating eyes up to see.

Brent's face hovered above her, where it smiled like a painted clay mask, his eyes glazed in doll like eye sockets. Beneath his face was a neck, shoulders, arms, torso, and legs that made watery creaks as they stretched and broke under grey flesh.

Marilyn choked on a gasp and sat up, the stench and sound now beating senselessly at her like a swarm of sparrow. *Boogie Man.*

It dropped to all fours.

Marilyn's scream pissed out like a whistle as she scrambled away from the creature with Brent's face. *Not Brent, Not Brent, Not Brent!!!!* A siren blared pitched squeals between her ears as her elbows hyperextended against her scrambling weight. Her spine collided with a dining table leg and she whimpered out like she'd hit a brick wall— like she was cornered by the shape-shifting.

It rushed at her and induced a bubble of short sobs from her tender lips as she crumbled back against the table leg. Brent's mimicked mouth tried to latch to hers but her trembling hands stopped it. She folded her left hand's fingers into his mouth and tore at his jaw to try to *hurt* him. Soft, pebble teeth sagged into his greying gums like old tombstones. Her hand came back in disgust as her lungs pumped. A front tooth had caught against her nail and fumbled out onto her lap. It wasn't Brent and it never had been, she understood that as saliva spilled from her lips like tears.

It let Brent's jaw sag until it hung like a snake who's face had been stomped on. Puss oozed like breast milk from the elongated tears in his cheeks and dribbled to his chin that concaved like a cavity.

Marilyn's whistled screams became nothing but broken air as she closed her eyes against a run of tears. She kicked her feet helplessly as the broken face and long body crawled closer.

"Join me," she heard Brent's voice hiss from somewhere deep inside the creature's fleshy chest.

She blinked forward with hot fluttering eyelids that worked to open like she had chlorine drying out her sight. They opened and saw Brent's human eyes begin to erode into shriveled pockets of white membrane and pink blood. They flattened like egg yoke and pinwheeled backward into his doll face eye sockets. There was darkness below the oval bone where Brent's eyes had been, and then there were *its* eyes. *Boogie Man's.* Beady, black, bug eyes sat at the balcony of Brent's cheeks. Watching her.

Marilyn's lips puttered around a cry as her hands came up to tear the image away. Her nails dug furiously into the hairs on her brow line and clawed at her skin. The sharp stink and metallic grind against her skull dully reminded her, as it always had, of the day she had found her father. Her silent cries came harder into the palms of her cold hands.

There was a tisk of disappointment from the creature as its gnarled hands gripped the wrists of her's. It pinned them into her lap, its fallen Brent Kingsley tooth dug a slit into her left thumb and she threw her head upward as its breath danced against her face like a fan of hot air.

"Join me," she heard Brent's voice command again, this time like his mouth was full of fluid.

There was the buzz of something thick and soft as a gentle tickle began to decorate spots on her bare skin. Again, her eyes flared open. Moths had begun to swarm and pop from the rips on the creature's flesh to cover her body in insect feet and wet, triangular wings. She shook and squirmed to try to get them off but couldn't move against the monster's pressure that held her arms into her numb legs. Her eyes bulged as she watched and felt the termite head of a moth burrow into the flesh in her arm, its powdered body sliding beneath the surface and entangling into her nervous system. Her head threw back and a pain-racked sob broke from her lips and tears spilled down her swollen purple cheeks. Another fat moth worked its way up her abdomen and to the breast *Boogie Man* had been playing with. Snot blew from her nose and tears fell harder down her cheeks as she kicked useless kicks and watching the insect insert itself beneath her nipple. Its termite blackhead pulling the skin apart and its wings folded against its back to slip through. Frothy saliva rolled down her chin and neck as the tearing pain of the insects burrowing rippled through her.

She began to beg. Beg for it to stop. Her body tired from fighting and her face swollen from tears, snot, and spit. But its hands continued to pin her down and its body continued to ooze moths. The insects pushing into the space behind her kneecaps, her arms, her stomach, her breast. Each tear of skin and incision more sickening and painful than the rest.

The air from her throat that came out in cries began to quiet and her eyelids began to fall as she fought consciousness. Then boosted wide open again as a fire started in the center of her head like an icepick disconnecting her frontal lobe. She cried out through gasps of air, she knew now that the real Brent was near. The *Boogie Man* seemed to know it too as his unhinged jaw looped into a sneering smile and its long hands released its hold on her. She swatted weakly at it without any connection. The creature already gone, deep somewhere in shadows.

Marilyn felt something shift beneath her skin and stared down in horror at her forearm. The designed wing of a thumbnail-sized moth traced an outline through the top layer of her flesh as it rested from its journey into her body. She doubled from her slouched position to her hands and knees, then to her feet and blindly sprinted to the kitchen, her hip striking the dining table to throw her in a limp and her jowls stuck in a tight downward position.

She yanked the kitchen silverware drawer and cried at the sound of disconnecting cork board from counterstock as it rolled open and the metal utensils shifted inside. She threw a hand into it the drawer as her line of sight stuck with the nestling insect below her skin. A tight fist closed around the first metal object it came in contact with and frantically retrieved it from the drawer, the silverware inside clanking away from it. A spoon.

She laid the bug budded arm against the counter like a landlocked fish all ready to be gutted as her vision wobbled and dipped. She sunk her feet into the ground the best she could as vertigo tipped her equilibrium and stabbed the sharp end of the spoon into her flexed forearm. A blood-red moon formed on her broken skin as she groaned in agony and stomped her leg into the kitchen tile. She jammed the spoon at her arm a second time, this time not breaking skin. The moth spread its tiny wings and shifted deeper into the webbing of her skin as the spoon lifted and came back to collect a small chunk of her muscle like ice cream from a paper container.

78

Brent backed into his spot in the apartment parking lot and killed the engine of his black 4Runner. With an effortless grunt he scooped two chilled milk jugs with light blue lids and a tray of cookies from the passenger seat—because cookies went well with milk, *right?*

He climbed the cement stairs with the small load of groceries cradled in his arms and his thoughts on Davey. He considered methods and conversations that may help the boy release whatever he was keeping trapped in his little shell. *Dad on a noose, mommy and my broken arm, what else?* It was possible that neither of those incidents related to his quiet personality, that maybe it was nature, rather than nurture. It also occurred to him that maybe Daisy would be the key to unlock the shy child. He smiled to himself and knew he'd find out when he picked Davey up from the girl's birthday party. He'd liked the girl's mom, she'd been easy to talk to and hardly any less bubbly than her daughter. *Kim* was her name. Kim and Daisy just might be exactly what Davey needed. He smiled hopefully, then frowned.

At five steps from his apartment platform, Brent had to stop, his body weight leaned gently into the stair's rail. Vertigo spilled through his veins and his tongue swelled against the roof of his mouth as his eyelids fluttered into the dizzy spell. He puffed his cheeks against the nausea that pounded at him in increasing swipes before continuing up the stairs.

He hummed as he balanced the milk and cookies in one arm to unlock his apartment door. It swung open gently into a still apartment as he re-pocketed his keys and spread the groceries out between both arms again. He stopped in the doorway and peered into his home that suddenly seemed foreign to him now. His head numbed but a strange ache continued to bully his stomach as he studied the silent living room like it was his first time seeing it. The air mattress laid against the ground in its usual lost air sag and the couch rested behind it. He bit the inside of his cheek and his jaw tried to lock as he continued to feel unsettled. He tilted his head up at the dining table in the back of the room and felt an itch at the back of his skull. The table had been nudged off-center and two chairs were pulled out from beneath it. A lighter sat upright on the surface of the table near a small pile of white dust and a crumpled cigarette. *What had she been doing?* Brent thought as he stepped through the doorway into the apartment. He shut the door behind him with a foot and opened his mouth to call for Marilyn when a noise out of the eerie silence caught him off guard. He paused and listened.

It was a breathy sound, like air broken free from a pipe. It hissed and he imagined white steam billowing out of a rusted apartment duct. But, what duct? He furrowed his eyebrows and listened harder, his breath held quiet between his lungs. His head turned like a compass dial to his kitchen nook and the whistle of air grew louder. *A teapot?* He didn't own one.

The steam scream hiccuped and became a human sob. His heart slammed against the inside of his throat, "Marilyn?!" The milk jugs and cookies dropped from his arms in consequence as he sprinted forward towards her ripped vocals. The opaque plastic containers cracked against the ground and milk projected across the apartment like blood spatter.

Brent turned into the kitchen to find Marilyn degrading the skin on her arm with a bloodied cereal spoon. Intense fear harpooned through him as he dove at the young woman's bent backside to pull her arms away from one another like she was Jesus of Bethlehem, nailed to the wood splintered cross. She screamed through cracks in pitch and arched her back against him. Their limbs started to wilt together as the room spun like when she'd hugged him a week before. Brent tried to close his eyes and hold out against it but the shifting bones in her body stabbed against him unbearably and he eventually had to break away. He wheezed as he fell back away from her and caught his thrown vision on sea legs.

She turned to him with the spoon lifted weakly above the self-infliction site on her other arm. He blinked at her, unconcerned with her bare breasts as he sorrowfully studied how deep the cuts in her arm were and how hard her purpling throat was working to force almost silent cries from its oddly shaped stretch and strain.

Brent took a hesitant step towards her and felt panic at the way she flinched back away from him, "*it's alright,*" he murmured as tears slid in thick lines down her cheeks. A hand slowly came out, his fingers trembling, "*can I have the spoon?*" His voice was barely audible and his eyes didn't waver from her's.

She discarded their stare to look at his hand, then the spoon, then her arm, "it's in me," she gagged. The spoon lifted then jutted back down, deep into her flesh.

"Marilyn!" Brent rushed her to rip the utensil from her grip as she screamed and swatted at him.

He stumbled back, his fingers looped around the bloody silver, and watched in horror as she collapsed back into the kitchen counter. Her feet shuffled out in front of her and she sank slowly down the wooden cabinets to the cold floor, "it's in me," she cried again. Her nails went to her arm and clawed at the cut skin.

Brent discarded the spoon into the kitchen sink as he dropped to his knees in front of her, "stop!" He scolded. He groaned at the way she ducked away from him as his hand came out for a kitchen towel draped over the counter above her. He gripped it flat in his palm and used it to grab scraping nails from her open wounds. The thick towel material worked as a stopper and kept his touch from sending them through a spin tunnel. "Stop," he said softer and then used the rag as a bandage around the incisions that bubbled out drops of blood.

"In me-" she sighed into a twisted mouth, her usual olive glow now a pale green.

Brent nodded like he knew what she was talking about as he held the rag to her with both hands, "okay." The world, slowly, mutedly, began to swirl again as her warmth seeped through the towel and the man was forced to let go.

Marilyn stretched her wounded arm out and looped her fingers into the bottom of his shirt. She rubbed the material with her thumb and began to whimper, "you're wearing a green long sleeve," she cried aloud to the man who stared back at her with widened eyes, "*green.*" She should've remembered that. She should've remembered the green shirt, she'd liked the green shirt. He hadn't been in blue. She should've known it wasn't him—he wasn't in blue. "Blue." She blew snot from her nose as a full cry took over her body. She let go of his shirt and crossed her arms in front of her face to sob into the crease of her elbow, her eyes open and burning against the thick tears brushed by the stale apartment air.

Brent's head hurt, "Marilyn —" he tried to speak above her bawl, "—is someone else in the apartment."

She shook her head no.

"*Was* someone?"

Her eyes pierced him in a cold, red-rimmed, stare.

He nodded to himself, "Marilyn?" He glanced at the rag around her forearm then watched her other hand carefully to make sure she wouldn't go back to pick it, "was it," he moved both of his hands to his voice slowly, keeping direct eye contact with her in an attempt to not spook the clearly traumatized girl. In his expression were empathetic pains and an abundance of fear. The kind you'd see in a child as they watched their first horror film, a blanket tucked up around their chubby, adolescent face.

He placed two fingers on either side of the apples of his cheeks and began to pull down. The skin pressed below his fingertips and the pink and red blended underside of his bottom eyelids began to droop down the length of his face. Their sign language for *Boogie Man*.

Brent's stretched face sent a sheer internal scream from the girl and she covered her eyes like she was now the child watching their first horror film.

"Was it?" Brent said again in a whisper that slid off the linoleum and scrapped each one of her nerves.

She nodded into her hands.

He stayed silent, frozen in his spot, unsure of what he could say or do to comfort her. Selfishly, he felt bitter that these things continued to happen to her while he lived his life normally. "Your arm?" His voice slid over the floor again and this time hung itself on her nerves like she was a coat rack. Her body firmed and her mouth tightened into a thin line. An answer she wasn't ready to give. He understood, "I am going to stand up, okay?" He warned her so she wouldn't be frightened by his quick movement, "and I'm going to give you some space." She stayed still as he stood and his knees cracked. *("my knees pop too," the boy confessed.)*

Marilyn lowered her hands and kneaded the kitchen hand towel into her sore arm. The frayed strings feathered into her cuts and made the raw incisions sting. She winced with watering eyes and a burning nose. Her bit tongue lapped at metallic saliva that pooled against her clenched teeth before it could drool out over her lips. She stood on jittery legs and leaned her dressed hip into the counter for stability, "I'm going to clean this up." Her voice was strangled and she had to force air against her vocal cords in thick strings to get the breathy sentence out.

"Okay," Brent stepped back to give her room as he studied the strange dangle in her neck.

Marilyn couldn't see or feel the moths any longer and thought it may have been a delirious illusion as she massaged at her arm through the rag.

"Do you need my help... Or -"

"No," she moaned while keeping her head low, "leave me alone, please." She stumbled forward and sucked dripped snot back into her nose.

He leaned to the side to let her pass and glanced at the bloody spoon in the bottom of his sink as she did so—an unsettled knot formed in his stomach like cancer. He then watched her bareback move leisurely through his apartment to the bathroom. Her head turned to glance into a dark corner of the living room as she passed, then lowered to study her injured arm below the kitchen towel. Brent followed her stare but didn't see anything other than a familiar shadowed wall, free of anything threatening. His headache was getting worse.

The man had done a perimeter check for the *Oogity Boogity* before going to his knees with paper towels, carpet cleaner, Pledge and a small bottle of lavender *Febreeze*. He jumbled his sleeves up over his elbows and lapped up milk, with his mind somewhere absent and his hands doing all of the busywork. It was splattered up over the air mattress when it had fallen and he now tried to mask what would soon start to smell with doses of the *Febreeze*.

He sat back on his heels and stared at the pile of damp towels in front of him with his hands stacked into his thighs. His eyes lifted and he found himself stuck in a glare with the blank corner that Marilyn had glanced at as she walked sadly to the bathroom, "leave her alone," he threatened foolishly as if the creature was there. Then his face painted a deep rose color and he dropped it back down to study the milk soiled paper rags.

Brent had finished cleaning and gone to his bedroom next, he wasn't sure why, maybe to lay down and recalibrate as the shower ran in the next room over. *Yeah,* maybe that had been the plan. But he couldn't remember now as he stood in his bedroom doorway and stared in while sickness thickened against the back of his throat. Marilyn's bra and shirt laid lifeless against his bedroom rug and his bedsheets had been wrestled and compressed by body weight. *I suppose she'd lied when she said nobody human had been here,* he thought with a shrug to himself, "that's okay." *But, did she have to use my bed?* He shook his head, there wasn't room for negativity inside of its thumping corridors, *I guess it would've been awkward to use the half-deflated air mattress.* "That's okay," he sighed again to himself as he stepped over her discarded clothing to grip his bedsheets in two tight fists.

He undressed the bed from its linen and walked staggered with the pile of white in his arms to the washer and dryer stacked in his hallway closet. There were faint sour scents that brushed off the sheets and into his face that he wished he hadn't noticed as he jammed the fitted blankets into the cylinder washer spindle. The cancerous knot returned to his stomach and nestled deep into his nerves and skin cells.

Brent hoped Marilyn wouldn't mind as he folded the cups of her bra together and laid the black support undergarment on top of her shirt that he'd also delicately folded. He walked her clothing to the bathroom and sat them outside of the door. He stood and stared at the white bathroom door, hyper-aware of her whimpers that steamed past the shower water. *God,* he hoped she wasn't picking at her arm again. *It's in me,* she had cried.

Brent shook his head as he turned away from the door, *what's in you?* He stepped with soggy socks to the living room with the bottom of his shirt gripped in his own fist, *you're in green.* What was she talking about?

Too Close to a Green T-shirt.

79

Davey followed closely behind Daisy with his hands cupped in front of himself and his shoulders laid forward. The girl was dressed in a pink shirt completed with hot glued rhinestone diamonds in the shape of a heart. The outfit was completed with a white ruffled skirt and polka dot leggings from Goodwill. Her feet patted along in front of Davey in dirty, mismatched socks and her hair swung solidly against her back in a large, single braid, of wet, blonde shower hair. Drops of water from the tail of her braid darkened her t-shirt into magenta drops down her back, but the girl hadn't cared or seemed to notice.

Davey, however, did. He studied them despite not really wanting to. One drop of water, in particular, was an oval of water rather than a perfect circle like the rest. It set his teeth on edge and he had to force himself to look away.

Daisy glanced at her Disney Princess birthday cake on a Dollar Tree table clothed table as they passed it. Davey looked at it too, its battered white and hot pink frosting and plastic Princess toys stuck out the top to stare back at him maliciously. His birthday present to her, covered in its purple bag and white paper stuffing, sat behind the cake like a tower. He kept his eyes from it, afraid that acknowledging the gift he brought her was being self-centered—self-indulging. Emotions beyond his age, but not unfamiliar. So, he kept his head low and tried to forget that he'd picked out a present for her in the first place.

Daisy swayed her wet braid as she walked happily, a new nine-year-old showing a new friend around her mother's double-wide trailer home. A mother,

Kim, who watched the boy follow the girl close behind with a gentle smile plastered on her lips like paper mache. Something Davey also tried not to notice.

Daisy and Davey sitting in a tree.

"This is our kitchen," Daisy's voice dazzled as her fingers stretched out to the half kitchen with pull up plastic tile.

Davey nodded and acted interested even though he'd already seen it from her front doorway as Brent chatted and laughed with Kim.

"Mom is making everyone sandwiches for lunch!" The girl added with a genuine smile that Davey returned with courtesy—through the effort nearly put him out completely. His mental enthusiasm tank was running on fumes at this point.

Davey could feel himself turning inward, like a self-imploding star, lightyears away and hardly glowing anymore. *Why did I want to come?* The sleeves of his jacket held the palms of his hands gently as he twisted his fingers around its material.

"Look," Daisy commanded so he looked, actually watched, as she backed herself into the kitchen, her eyes a blaze of excitement.

Davey's head tilted like a curious puppy as she swiped her feet against the faux tile like gum was stuck to her foot. She then sprinted out past the lip of the glue on tile and leaped to the trailers recently mopped hardwood floor. Her feet glided into the wood and she slid like an ice skater in her dirty, mismatched socks.

Her hands tossed up as she came to a slippery stop and she turned to giggle at the boy, "our floors are great for sliding, do you want to try?"

Davey stood hesitantly and wiggled his own dirty socks like his toes were waving at him.

"Come on! It's duper fun!"

Davey blushed at her. *Duper.* What a funny word.

Without speaking he'd begun to back himself up into her kitchen counters, his socks collecting fake static as they shuffled backward like tiny Swiffer mops. He imagined lights, bright stadium stand on thick black poles, all around him. Lights and *Cameras*.

His fingers untwined from his jacket sleeves.

He imagined an ice arena. Marilyn was there, her hands clapped together in the stands and her teeth beaming into the white lights as she grinned the biggest smile he'd ever seen. Bear Kingsley was in her coat pocket, his narrow, matted head leaned out to cheer on the boy. Brent was there too. His hands cupped into a tan flesh megaphone to amplify his hoots of: "*Go kid! You can do it!*"

Davey revved his feet into the floor.

"Here goes Davey Matthews," an announcer's voice blurred in an oval echo over the arena's intercom, *"attempting the long slide."* Bear Kingsley cheered in the distance.

Davey ran three strides and leaped, as Daisy had, and landed with his feet planted sideways like a blonde beach surfer. He glided fast and only wobbled a little as he skated up to Daisy.

"He sticks the landing!" The intercom judge hollered and the crowd went wild!

"See Davey," The girl's bubblegum voice popped in his face and yanked him from his daydream, "fun!"

He smirked to his eyes, "again."

This time they went together, both shuffling a moonwalk back to the trailers kitchen cabinets.

The daydream was back and the announcer cheered in a boom box over the crowd: *"Daisy and Davey, now attempting the team slide!"* The crowd silenced in anticipation and Davey's heart thumped dully in his ear.

They revved, sprinted, and leaped.

Daisy coasted further than Davey but stumbled at the end, her hands sprawled out to catch herself in a lengthy yoga pose.

"Ten points!! A little wobble but she regained it!" The crowd went *wild!*

Daisy danced in her stopped spot, her cloth skirt whipping into her leggings, "One more time!" She had retired from her bubble gum drawl for a bright pink lemonade squeal.

Davey raced back to her kitchen for *one more time!* Giggling in rhythm with Daisy.

A knock on the tin, screen door of the mobile home broke through their imaginations and Daisy instantly forgot the game. A birthday girl, too excited for her *big day* to feel sorry for Davey, ditched him to skip jubilantly forward to her mother who peeled the screen door open to welcome a new guest. A tall girl with blonde hair like Daisy's. A *cousin*. Her mother, a heavy woman with a modern cocoa brown mullet kissed Kim on the cheek and winked at Daisy.

"Happy birthday!" She said with a cigarette growl, "how old are you now? Twenty?!"

Daisy laughed with her head back before shaking it heavily, "I'm nine, Aunt Jan!"

"Oh, that's right." The woman, Aunt Jan, winked again.

Davey frowned to himself shyly and held the sleeves of his jacket again as the ice arena vanished and Daisy's kitchen filled its place. It was a darker, dirtier room this time as he stood alone on the stick on linoleum like an outsider people watching. A ghost in the walls. His shoulders fell forward again and his toes patted the floor.

80

As the mobile home filled with unfamiliar, happy, celebrating children Davey shrunk. He slouched in a dusty corner with his lip rested numbly beneath his top teeth. A kid with a shaved head glanced at him and he lowered his eyes and stayed stuck in his own, echoing tired mind. The one that promised to always stay hyper aware of his shy self. So introverted that if he were to let on a little more to the loneliness he'd be so within himself that he'd simply disappear and not exist. It came as a comforting idea to him. To *not exist*. Not forever—like dad. But for a day, or two. Blip off into another realm of nothingness and come back when the time was right. Come back when he felt better and felt like talking, walking, smiling.

He'd come back dapper and his day would continue from there, and questions wouldn't be asked about where he went. Others would just know, and accept, that he was gone—and then he's back—and that would be okay.

The corner of his mouth slacked against his folded lip and his eyes shut in a long blink.

The waters lapped against the boat wall that swooped, swept, and swayed. The smell of the sea salt ocean coated his tonsils like a wet napkin.

He removed the eyelids from over his droopy eyes and watched Daisy laugh with her cousin. The boat dream he had at the hospital rocked horizontally in his memory. He could feel the cold mist of the foaming canal water against the backs of his knuckles and the very tips of his fingers, under his fingernails. He blinked again and saw the rock, briefly, over the edge of the boat.

"Time for cake!" Kim waltzed in from the small kitchen with her TV host smile and her long blonde hair brushing down over the tops of childrens' heads as she leaned over the young crowd to grab a lighter and candle from the pink clothed table. Her split end locks made the children giggle and Daisy almost knocked her mom out as she sprung up in a sugar rush dance. Davey blinked at all of them like he might fall asleep in his dusty corner in the house.

Disconnected suddenly from the other children was Daisy—her face isolated to only the boy in the corner, "Come on Davey! I want to hear you sing happy birthday to me!"

He crossed his arms across his chest and walked to her, careful to ignore the way her mother grinned down at her daughter—proud of her for taking care of the *shy little one*.

Daisy made Davey sit in the chair to her right so he could be real close when he sang and she could hear it. And he had sung—a very quiet happy birthday to a sweet nine-year-old. She had liked it and he had been awarded the second slice of cake—the first cut for her of course. He supposed that made him her Vice President, or number one. That placed him above her cousin on the friendship totem pole... and... that made him nervous.

Davey had only picked at his piece of cake. He'd put a vanilla crumb in his mouth only when he'd zoned out and his body instinctively tried to feed him. *What had happened to the sandwiches?* Wasn't Kim supposed to make sandwiches?

He took another nibble of his cake.

It turned out, sandwiches were the dessert today, and the cake was the meal. An adult may have been upset by the order the food was fed into the childrens' mouth, but this was Daisy's day and Kim made it about the kids. That had been cool—maybe Davey liked Kim, even if the sandwiches had been plain bologna and cheese and he'd only eaten the bread from the top.

Brent had come just after the presents were opened, which had made Davey thankful. He'd hugged Daisy and said good-bye to her mother with the first toothed smile he'd shown since getting to the girl's house. Brent had stayed in the car and gave a gentle wave to Kim from behind his windshield. Kim had wiggled her fingers back before turning clockwise back into her home that buzzed with sugar-high children.

Davey skipped down the steps and to the car buoyantly and didn't think twice about rearing the back seat door open and leaping in. He melted into the seat cushion with a sigh and felt his cheeks warm from the Toyota's blasting vents. As he sat up and buckled he'd noticed a potent chemical aroma that made the bridge of his nose tingle into a small sneeze that he released into the palm of his hand.

Brent turned with a tired, narrow side-smile, "Hey kid, sorry—I probably smell like bleach, huh?" His eyes dropped a half-inch from Davey's and glazed over, "I was cleaning."

Davey scratched his nose and blinked his eyes, "cleaning what?"

Brent turned back around and scrunched his own nose before rolling the windows on the vehicle down to let the stench out into the open, "milk," he nodded to himself as he pulled away from the curb.

Davey cocked his head and noticed hair curling out from the front passenger seat. He leaned up and around and made a gentle gasp—*hua*—at his sister who sat silent and slouched in the seat with her hands tucked between her thighs, "Oh hi, Marilyn Mae!" He giggled childishly, "I didn't even know you were there!"

No response.

Brent frowned at the road that jittered under them as Marilyn stayed still and muted, her hands harshly scrubbing together in slow strokes between her legs like she was a cricket. *Jiminy Cricket!* The man brushed his eyes up to the rearview and caught Davey's concerned stare, "I spilled your sister's milk *everywhere,*" he laughed like it had been a funny story, "so clumsy of me. I totally tripped coming into the door and both cartons *exploded!*"

The image painted a cartoon scene over the boy's imaginative mind and he snorted, "that *duper* sucks!" He looked at his paralyzed sister, "Is that why you're mad, Marilyn?" The girl didn't answer, again. Davey lifted his head back to the rearview and expected to catch a glance with Brent, but the school counselor was studying the road with furrowed red eyes and his upper lip stuck under chewing teeth. Davey considered, then said: "*don't cry over spilled milk, Marilyn.*"

His sister rocked up from her slouch like an erect fist, "I swear to God, asshole!" Her voice was wrecked like broken glass.

Davey dropped back into his seat, startled, and Brent sent a hard look to the girl as the 4Runner swerved against Main Street, "Stop."

Marilyn tightened her jaw and slouched back into the grey Toyota seat with tears in her eyes that made the world around her bubble into a blurry view.

Davey shot another look to the rearview to meet Brent's stare, but the man was focused on the road again, his face a deep shade.

Davey wanted to go back to Daisy's.

PART FOUR: MARILYN MAE MOTHER MOTH MATTHEWS

81

Had she recovered?

Define recovered.

Her voice had come back but the muscles in her neck seemed stringy like fucking spaghetti noodles cooked a little too long and made a little too soft. And it was bruised. A nice dog collar of moth kissed hickeys. Except there was nothing *nice* about it and its leather belt marks.

Marilyn scratched awareness to her throat, mostly covered by her naturally curled hair and the front seam of her shirt, with her chewed short nails. It warmed beneath her touch as her face cooled like she had stuck it against an air conditioner's vent. She opened her mouth and let a wimpy cough fall out—a cough that tangled her noodle strung muscles into a thick ball of cotton against her esophagus—and her waterline became moist.

Monday morning had passed and had begun to trickle into Monday afternoon and still, Debra had not noticed. Or at least, if she had, she didn't pry. Marilyn flipped a black office pen through her free hand's fingers and eyed the Hispanic woman as she typed an email across her screen. Debra should've noticed and should've cared—*that unobservant cunt.*

Marilyn sighed distastefully and dismissed the way her ribs shivered against her heavy lungs. She'd decided the moths infesting her body had probably been an illusion and she probably hadn't needed to deface her flesh with a spoon like she had but she *knew* the rest of Saturday had been real. The *Boogie Man* had been real.

She scraped her nails down her bruised neck again and winced at its tender lines.

Brent, the real one, had bought her band-aids and white gauze to doctor up her arm on their way back from Daisy's and Davey hadn't asked as the girl proceeded to *fix* her crescent moon cuts in her arm on the drive home. Marilyn suspected it was because she'd called him an *asshole*. The boy had shunned her for the rest of the day for it. *Fine,* Marilyn thought, *he was being an asshole.*

She sighed again, this time with a little rattle from the back of her throat as the spaghetti muscles flexed like acoustic guitar strings.

She supposed she was *angry*.

(*And rightfully so, you were raped and strangled by —*) A deeply internal voice justified for her—but even it, her drowned conscience, couldn't bring itself to say it. Say: *a monster.*

Because that was stupidly *cheesy*.

Marilyn dismissed the idea anyway with a twitch in her jaw. She hadn't been *raped.*

Her fucking waterline reddened under clear tears again and she grimaced like she'd been slapped in the face. She glanced at her wrapped gauze arm that stayed hidden, nestled under her shirt sleeve.

Sh, stop it, kid... your daddy issues are showing.

Debra, *oh little Debbie*, piped up then and resurrected Marilyn from confused and harmful thoughts, "hey girl," she spoke with her nose still narrowed at her computer, "could you —" head turn, eye contact, smile, "— deliver an office note for me. It'll need to go to Ms. Gus." Maybe it was the delayed blankness in Marilyn's face as her wandering thoughts brought her back around like a boomerang that made Debra feel the need to go on and explain, "Ms. Gus is kindergarten. A right at the library and straight back.

White-haired, cranky lady," she scrunched her nose for a silent laugh at her *taboo* comment.

Marilyn scrunched her nose back in a sorrowful imitation, "sure, I can do that." Her dull fingernails quit scratching at her neck and she let her hand fall like a dead weight into her lap.

"You're a doll!"

Am I, Deb?

Debra puttered her hands around her desk in quick mice like taps as she searched for the correct slip to give Marilyn.

Ms. Gus. Kindergarten. A right at the library. White hair. Is a bitch. Marilyn thought back as the woman looked stupidly at her desk. The girl had eyed the note a moment before and had locked eyes with it like a hint. Like her irises were a compass.

"Oh!" Debra's hand clasped down on the note as if it might run away from her, "here you go!"

Marilyn dragged herself to Ms. Gus' class to be interrogated by the woman's eyes behind wire-framed glasses. The young adult lifted the note, which she'd been folding over and over in her hands as she'd walked the long hallway, into the air and waved it, "for you."

The white-haired woman shrugged her off like a careless comment, "put it on my desk."

"Fine," The girl crossed the room without paying mind to child stares that cast

like ghosts across her. She slid the folded note from her fingers and to the wood desk and watched it as it spun into the teacher's keyboard. As she did so she felt a tickle, like you'd get in your throat just before coughing rudely over your covering hands, except this tickle was low. It brushed, like baby hair, at the inner wall of her stomach. Marilyn spun, startled, away from the desk and thought horridly of the moths. Her forehead beaded sweat as she considered them, *burrowing* into her, and she made an almost audible cry as her face heated. Her hand went first to her stomach, like she was massaging a cramp, then to her bandaged-below-her-shirt-sleeve arm. She pressed her thumb vigorously into the healing wounds beneath the cloth and gauze and found herself whirling with the bitter pinch that shot up into her elbow. She stepped past the children as she squeezed her arm and willed the memory of moths and lingering sensation of *nerve wading* away. She was haunted by it–like a bad taste hanging onto her mind's pallet.

She exited the room without acknowledging the old woman or her classroom of small people and let out a hard gust of cooped up air as the door clunked shut behind her. She listened to the clip-clop of her shoes as they banged out the post images of insects from her mind. She withdrew her black office pen from her pocket and began to work the trigger on it up and down in high clicks. *Open, close, open, close, open, close.*

Click, click, click, click, click.

Rick, the dickweed janitor, had caught her before she'd turned the bend– back to the main hall, back to the main office. Instead of his mop and yellow wheel bucket he'd held a roll of blue rags and a murky squirt bottle of green fluid, "Hello," he greeted with his odd set jaw and his bulged eyes.

Marilyn gave a nod back and refused a smile, her lips crumbled into a deep-set line. He didn't deserve a smile, not after his comment before. They had made eye contact accidentally despite her best effort to *just ignore and move past.*

Rick slipped the paper towels into the crease of body and armpit to free his hand so he could point it at her. A held out sausage finger jabbing only inches from her face, "smile, woman!" He barked then laughed like it was a joke. Like he was funny. Like–he *owned her.*

Sh, stop it, kid... your daddy issues are showing.

Marilyn's face hardened into a red ruby stone and her fists clenched into knots. Her thumb triggered her black office pen *open* and the sound of it seemed to swallow her.

Click.

Rick's face balled up smug and thin, his horse mouth plunging outward as if he didn't have teeth in the top row of his square face. Marilyn could feel the tickling again, internal and entwining. It contracted through her like heat waves as it spread through her abdomen and up behind her breasts. Her vision became foggy in a whirl of bright specks that danced to the rhythm of the pulsing itch beneath her skin. Like their *legs* brushed her from within.

They weren't real.

A wing brushed the deflated milk glands behind a perked nipple.

It was strange, the way the world seemed to cave and corrupt around her for a moment as the weight of the pen became all she could focus on, like sensory tunnel vision. Its black plastic smudged into her skin and her vision quaked. And, the wing brushed again, her hand lifted and she swung it out.

Her pen arrowhead through tan, aftershave flesh and into the underside of Rick's trapezius muscle and the skin around his neck seemed to swell against the digested plastic instantly. She stepped back, stunned and afraid, and watched as his neck regurgitated blood in lazy clumps of red.

The tickling inside her stopped.

Marilyn watched as the cleaning bottle in Rick's filthy hand was squeezed and unsqueezed and chemical mist from its spout drifted like distant snowfall through the air. The paper towels that had been nestled in the crease of his arm and body hit the ground with the sound of a muted basketball and rolled a significant distance—a left trail of blue absorbent cloth behind it.

The tickling started again and Marilyn could feel herself laugh. A *Tickle Me Elmo.*

She snickered at the man and the comical attempt he was making to clean up his mess as he bled out. Muscle spasms and a bobbing purple jaw with a swaying swollen tongue was no way to clean a mess but the idea and show on display were enough to rig her full of schoolgirl laughter. She covered her mouth with a sleeved hand and laughed wildly into it. She felt her stomach tighten and she laughed like she'd laughed in the store when Brent had bumped her with the cart.

She pointed her free hand at Rick and snorted into the hand around her mouth. Tears had begun to swell into her eyes and her face was beating red with her laughter.

The pen jumped and danced against his tight, dying neck. His eyes bulged and his clothing began to decolorize to a deep, sticky red. The blood seeped across the school's floor like an overflowing tub. Marilyn giggled as the thick lagoon paced towards the underside of a classroom door. Soon it'd sweep under and curious children would be peaking out at the murder scene.

A Kool-aid slip and slide to play in!

She doubled over in laughter.

Rick collapsed against the ground like he was in a low-production action movie, knees first, then the rest of his body—a solid weighted dump into his own red, pooling filth. His long arms slammed, like silverware against a kitchen plate, into the ground. The sound of his bones colliding with dewy floor made Marilyn's teeth tighten and laughing stop.

A caved and corrupted world lifted and the pen was back in her hand. Closed.

Click.

Marilyn blinked horribly at the janitor who stood, *alive,* in front of her with a cleaning bottle and paper towels in his hands. She stumbled away from him and grabbed at her stomach as if she could make the itching go away from the outside. Scratch the dead skin cells around her hips and belly button and it'd go away. But the itch was too deep within, swirling and swiping, like the mouth of a forest fire. She had begun to pant like a winded dog as she stared into the eyes of the skeptical and confused janitor.

"What's wrong with you?" Rick asked the girl who had zoned out in front of him.

She shook her head at the man who talked through a clear mouth, clean of blood, his Adam's apple bobbing healthily beneath his chin.

"Sorry," Marilyn mumbled and pressed her hand harder into her stomach. Through her thin shirt material and thick layer of skin, she could feel fluttering. Wings. Dancing and hopping off if the inner wall of her body as if they were celebrating. Or performing a ritual. "They're real," She whined to herself as fear sunk deep into the calcium pockets in her joints.

"What?" Rick shook his head at her.

The girl dove around the man and rushed to the main office.

Debra popped her head up to the sweaty girl who flung the office door open and tripped onto the mushy office carpet. The woman tried to say something, maybe *ask* something, but Marilyn was too quick. She ran frantically to the employee bathroom in the back and jammed a thumbnail into her swirling stomach as she did so.

The heavy door heaved open and she almost released a cry as she lurched into the empty bathroom. The door droned shut slowly on a stopper spring and she threw her body against it to shut it faster, unnaturally. It slammed like a fallen tree and she used her same jamming thumb to engage the press-pin lock.

The overhead fan buzz rattled the walls and her teeth and the insects inside danced like Indians with large, feathered headpieces that stuck into her innards like tiny needles. Marilyn began to pull at her shirt, her trembling fingers fighting the sweat that tried to hold the cotton against her skin. The shirt eventually peeled from her body and was flung to the ground in a panicked crumble. The girl watched her stomach in the mirror but did not see the signs of the internal intruders. She could feel them thought, heavy near her lungs and behind her breasts. She wrestled with her bra and a strap snapped her against her collar bone as her finger slipped out from beneath it. The insects fluttered away from the strap as if suddenly startled then settled back down to turn their antennas and stretch their dusty wings.

The bathroom doorknob was yanked and someone laid their body weight against it, but the lock held them back. Marilyn whipped her head towards the echoed sound of someone trying to break in before they had a pee accident in the hallway, then whipped it back to her upper-half naked reflection. Her eyes were on her left breast. A dark triangular smudge, just to the right of her dime-sized nipple, reflected dully under the yellow bathroom light. She was trembling as she leaned closer to the full mirror–her eyes first watching the reflection then dripping down to her bare flesh chest below her head.

The doorknob was yanked again.

She lifted her breast upward to turn the triangular object into the overhead light. Her fingers cupped around her nipple for a better hold as they shivered barely against its pink flesh. The object looked brown beneath the hard layer of skin that stretched above it.

The doorknob yanked.

She braved to poke around it. It warped as her breast bent and she thought it looked like a dirty fingerprint now and decided to just rub it off. Her thumb pressed gently against the shape.

A moth retracted its wing away from the outer skin barrier of her sensitive breast and began to burrow its fat body deeper, away from her touch.

Marilyn pinched back a scream as it disappeared and lost itself in milk glands. She twisted her body and collapsed to her knees against the floor to crumble heated flesh and bones over the lip of the public toilet. Her body coiled together like a kinked hose then vomited hard over someone's unflushed urine and floating, used toilet paper. Her, Marilyn, the exoskeleton to their fuzzy, insectual lives. *They're real, they're in me, they're real, they're real, they're real.*

The doorknob yanked.

82

The air mattress was flat.

Flat, not all the way, but flat enough to make it wibble and wobble slowly like a deflated, blue whale. Which is precisely what Davey saw it as in the center of Brent's cultured, well lived in, living room. The counselor was hunkered over it in an old graphic white t-shirt and his Saturday jeans as he jammed an air pump into its whistling, plastic hole. The bed wheezed and groaned and then the electric pump was motoring along in the man's hands.

Davey sat down criss-cross with his back to the apartment door and watched as the whale he'd slept on the past few weeks slowly came back to life. He kneaded Bear Kingsley, who sat in his lap, and tilted his head gently as the pump fell from the hole and Brent grumbled something as he shut the machine off and began to work the nozzle back into the whistley gap.

Marilyn had gone for a walk, proclaiming she needed to get out of the *rotten* apartment in a high whine and dead, irritated eyes. Davey had watched as Brent gave her a concerned look then nodded. He'd offered her an iPod attached to blue, drug store headphones, "My workout iPod—if you want music," he had said. Davey's sister had ripped the offering out of the man's hands and had left the apartment with a spit out, *"thanks."*

Now it was just the two males. And the sheeted whale.

The motor popped through the mattress hole and Brent flipped its switch. It began to run again in a steady low hum and Davey shut his eyes. He tried to remember the boat, and the sea, and the talking rock, but couldn't. All of it was foggy and distant. His eyes reopened and his lips frowned at the polyester whale.

Brent balanced the electric pump on the ground without accidentally removing it from its frugal mattress seal again. He pivoted his body and gave a semi sweaty smile to the boy, "how was school today?" Small talk.

Davey shrugged and pinched at the fur under Beary's armpit, "Daisy and I both had chocolate milk with our lunch," he trailed off momentarily then came back with a lined smile, "she called us 'twinsies'."

Brent rubbed his brow with the back of his hand and sat back on his socked feet, "you should invite her over some time, bud." He admired as Davey's face slacked, then brightened, then drifted away to stare blankly at the man's bookshelf. The boy's lip wavered and his mouth opened to accept it, then closed. His lip had stayed on the outside and he sucked his cheeks in to cushion his molars instead. Brent made an observational note but kept it to himself. He shut the air mattress pump off and sucked his own cheeks in—his molars gliding gently against their jelly sides.

Davey's attention came back to Brent to watch him wrestle the plastic cap back over the hole of the mattress before all the motor generated air escaped. Brent dropped a flat hand into the back end of the mattress to test the air pressure and watched with amusement as the opposite end bounced up, "hey kid-" He looked to Davey with an intriguing smile, "go sit on the other end of the bed."

Marilyn stabbed her feet harshly into cracked sidewalk as she paced, earbuds rammed deep into her ear canal. She was going to the beat of eighties rock and clenching her fists tightly inside her pockets. *My work out iPod,* Brent had said. She tried to imagine, as she stormed through chilling air, the man jogging lightly into the conveyor belt on a treadmill with his eyes set forward and his mouth parted. His hair curled from his sweat and matted thoughtfully into his forehead as *Burning Heart* by *Survivor* thudded nostalgically against his eardrums—his toe and heel jogged steps kept in beat. At the chorus hit his head would tip forward and a salty drop would fall against the black ever-rolling floor.

The girl shook her head and changed the song.

In the burning heart, just about to burst, "shut up."

I Love Rock 'n' Roll—Joan Jett and the Blackhearts shuffled and began to play. The chugs in the guitar set her eye level with irritation, but she kept it anyway and locked her jaw.

The moths, her lovely little moths, were asleep. The bobbed below her skin like led pills. Pills she was forced to swallow and keep down like a bad trip to the doctors. Or asylum. Nurses in white bowed hats and button-down dresses pushing a white Dixie cup into her trembling fingers and forcing the horse pills down her gullet.

Rick's words stung her in the face as she rounded a corner, *"smile woman,"* he had boomed as his finger circled her glare. She began to feel queasy again and her head started to pound in a sore offbeat with *Joan Jett and the Blackhearts*. The occupants of her internal organs began to wake as if she'd called and stretched their wings tiredly, the dusty surface brushing the wet side of her skin. She walked faster, with heavier feet and their tiny bodies shook and drew insect breath and mourned for *food*. A *feeding*. Anger suddenly demanded to be felt and hot flashes of Rick's body convulsing demanded to be seen against her achy eyelids. His lips puckered and digging the air for oxygen, her laugh, her giddy smile—it all pulsed past her as she stomped down the tilted street sidewalk. The song crackled against guitar strums and a bass line as Marilyn hissed unhappily to herself.

The song —

...and we'll be moving on and singing that same old song

Yeah with me

— Cut out into static.

Marilyn stopped walking and rolled her tension headache back on a stiff neck, "what the hell," her voice was pinched as she brought her head back forward to the silver iPod laid flat in her palm. The screen was lit and the soundbar continued to move as time passed and the song played silently. It blinked at her, the CD track flipping across the screen with an electronic health. *I'm here,* it seemed to say, *did your headphones break? Why can't you hear me?* She twisted the headphone jack irritably and frowned at the sharp crackle in her ears.

Then it began to moan. A low, robotic moan that vibrated the headphones. A moan that slowly grew and became human. A male, human moan that pinched off into a sexual gasp. Then, "Hello, kid." Brent's voice, thick and dominate. Like he was drunk on a power trip, or horny, or both.

Marilyn's stomach cramped and she almost doubled against it as her breathing became strangled.

"I was wondering how you were doing since I last saw you?"

She could hear the smile in his voice that was followed by his tongue rubbing a wet line against his lower lip.

"You were so pretty," he hummed into a happy sigh, "I can't believe we advanced our relationship like that, so quickly, you know? So passionately," that happy sigh again, "*wow.*"

She should've taken the headphones out—thrown the iPod down a street gutter—but she didn't. Instead, she stood and listened with horror pierced into her body like metal rods.

"Makes me hard just thinking about it—thinking about you."

"Stop it, just stop it," Marilyn whined to herself below her earbud plugged ears.

"Goodness, and when I went inside you," his voice growled and he clicked his teeth together.

Marilyn's body triggered into a tight clump of nerves and her vision blurred. *It* hadn't gone inside her—that hadn't happened. Her eyes dropped to her bandaid and drug store bandaged arm and her tongue dried like a dead fish—because it *had*. In mini, dusty, triangle forms it sewed itself to the inside of her body. She cried shallowly and clenched at her stomach.

A long, *happy* sigh broke through the earbuds again, "Anyway," Brent's voice trailed off and almost seemed to giggle, "how are they?"

The moths.

"They must be so hungry."

She was shaking.

"Can you *feel* how hungry they are?" He grunted distastefully, "my poor babies."

There was a twisted tickle from inside her.

"Feed them soon, *Mama*."

What did that mean?

His voice broke off then and *Love in an Elevator - Aerosmith* stabbed through her ears in a pitched volume that made her jump back from pain. Marilyn ripped the earbuds from her ears harshly and began to whimper. Out in the open with her blurring vision set on a sidewalk tree. Her shoulders bobbed in wet cries and her hands dropped helplessly at her sides.

Back at the apartment Davey's airborne body crashed into the blue whale mattress and bowled down the length of it into Brent's side. Both males were laughing as Davey threw his fists up, Bear Kingsley clenched in one of them, and cheered, "again!" His dimples burrowed deep into his cheeks as he shimmied his young body back to the far end of the blowup bed.

Brent stood, his breathing a bit heavier and his smile wider than Davey had ever seen it, "okay, okay," he huffed, coughed, then chuckled, "ready?"

Davey animated that he was as he hooted and gripped Bear Kingsley tighter.

Brent dropped his body onto the opposite end of the mattress and Davey launched into the air with his head back and arms panned out. The boy and bear both crashed into the center of the bed and rolled into Brent's side again. The man laughed hysterically and clapped his hands as he did so, his head leaned back into the blue felt, "that was the farthest you've gone yet!" The farthest out of *twelve* times.

"Again!" Davey cheered and tried to stand, but Brent's hand grasped the back of his shirt and the boy fell to his butt on the wobbly plastic.

"Hold on kid, let me rest," he was panting comically.

"Again!" Davey hollered like it was the only phrase he knew and began to giggle fiercely as he stood and was pulled back down again by the back of his shirt.

"No!"

"Yes!"

"Noo!"

"Yes!" Davey's nose was scrunched into his eyes and his laugh was snorting out through a lightly bit tongue, "yes, Brent, yes!" Brent had opened his mouth to protest but was stopped by the boy who, despite his argument, gave up and flopped onto his back against the man, "yes, but in a minute," he'd decided.

Brent smiled at him thoughtfully and cupped his large arm around the boy. Like two buds on a bleacher, "okay," he sighed and relaxed into the half pumped mattress, "yes, but in a minute."

Davey nodded at the ceiling and cuddled Bear Kingsley closer into his bent elbow.

Brent noticed and suddenly felt a twang in his chest. Something tight and nostalgic. The warmth of the boy's body cradled into him and the nostalgia was thickened until it didn't feel like nostalgia at all—but longing. Longing for a family of his own, someday. His hand gently gripped Davey's eight-year-old bicep as he thought distantly.

The boy squirmed, "okay, again!"

Brent's eyes bulged, *my goodness, kid,* "in a second," he smiled reluctantly as the boy looked at him with large, frowning eyes, "your sister will be home soon—we should wait so we can show her how high this thing throws you!" He snickered. *She'll be home in a few seconds, actually.* His head was aching heavily and his vision was full of dips and dots—swirls and strings. She'd walk through the door with her head bobbing to his running music playlist at any moment.

Walking through the door with her head bobbing was the wrong idea entirely.

The door jerked open and regurgitated a narrow-eyed young woman through its entrance.

"Marilyn! Watch this!" Davey squealed and stood. Brent's hand fell from his shirt as the boy moved to the opposite edge of the bed and dropped down to his back.

Marilyn's eyes pinned on Brent, her chest heaving up and down like an engine valve. The pop in their heads held in her stare and built pressure between them. He could feel her weight and anger as they held eyes and his own chest heaved nastily in rhythm with her's. Under her stare, Brent suddenly felt like he could break like she had sized him up and won.

Still giggling Davey wiggled against the blue mattress, "come on Brent, can we show her?" He asked giddily, unaware of the strange, silent showdown between man and sister in front of him.

Marilyn's eyes creased up to Davey then, held a moment against the boy's smile, then dropped, hurriedly, back to Brent, "stay away from him."

Brent's capsized thoughts swooped and he sat up on his elbow, his hair flopping over his ears as he observed fear hollow out her cheeks and under-eye,

"Woah, hey," his voice was soft but accused her of being looney, "*kid.* What's-"

She screamed.

It was a slow and guttural scream that boiled her vision into a slow-cooked stew of irrational frustration. She seemed to drop back away from her sound as the two adults' heads finally popped and the cold numb filled in. She regained herself, as Brent sat up further, on his ass, wide-eyed and *oh-so* concerned like the good *therapist* he was, and she darted forward.

It was quick, heated, and resulted in Davey pinned tightly in her fists by both his arms. The boy let out a sudden gulp of confusion as his smile and laugh cut off into oblivion. It was brief, both males' split second of uncertainty, and then it was chaos—all at once.

Marilyn yanked Davey from the mattress by the hold on his arms, "stay away from him!" She commanded to not one male in particular as Davey's head snapped back from her hard, unexpected tug and the boy let out a shrill cry, "stay away! Stay away! Stay away!" She was shaking Davey as her vocals chortled out her strange plea.

Brent, horrified, threw his hand out to grab the boy, or her, or both and he missed. He missed like he had thrown a punch in a nightmare. His hand fell lamely to the air mattress and his insides subdued to terror. Why had he missed? Bear Kingsley fell from Davey's hands and crashed like a wet towel into gravel next to Brent's tired limbs.

The boy began to throw his legs out in a tantrum as his body was hoisted high enough in the air for Marilyn to begin to drag him away from Brent, "Stop!" He pleaded through his sudden, hot tears, "I'm sorry, I'm sorry!" Except he didn't know why he was sorry, just that she was mad, and he was in trouble. His feet skidded into the ground and his knees buckled helplessly as he tried to stop his sister, but she was determined. Her face stone as she jerked him along. "Marilyn!" He submitted to his crying and let out a bellowing moan like an upset toddler as his feet continued to kick and his shoulders burned from her pull.

Marilyn, who'd been bullying Davey towards Brent's bedroom turned back to him and bundled the cloth of his shirt into one of her hands, the other hand running a red ring of Indian burn around the crease in his elbow. Her face was dark and heated the boy's face as she lifted him to it, "You stay away from him!" She scolded and Davey bawled with his eyes closed and wet tears racing down his cheeks.

Brent had found himself on his feet dizzy and had lunged out towards the altercation. He'd gotten his hand to make contact around the kid's shirt this time and had ripped him from Marilyn's ugly hold and snarling words. The boy's shirt stretched and the seams creaked as he stumbled back into Brent. The man realized with the disgusting sound and Davey's gag of tears that they were playing tug-of-war with the kid, like two dominant dogs fighting over a rope chew toy. He stepped between the two siblings with confused sweat pricked at his brow, "Stop!" His voice was high and hurried and panicked, "What are you doing?!"

Marilyn stumbled forward and Brent stepped back, pushing Davey with him. The girl, as quickly as she'd begun to scream, began to cry.

Brent had turned away from her and picked up Davey without effort, and without asking. In his socks he walked out onto the apartment landing and up the flight of stairs to Winnifred's, his hands firmly held to Davey's back and his eyes set forward. He had expected for Marilyn to protest and run after them, but she hadn't. It all reminded him of something so chaotically similar and if he hadn't known better he might have called her *Amanda.* The idea made him shudder a bit inside and a frowning scowl set in against his jaw and his lips around it.

Davey cried hollowly into the crook of Brent's neck, "I–I'm, I'm –" a short release of air, "Mm–sorry," his voice pinched off the 'y' in his sorry and it trailed on in a high squeal.

Brent shook his head and took a hand off of Davey's back to knock softly on the elderly woman's door, "It's not your fault, kid."

Davey coughed out louder cries as he sunk closer into Brent's body.

Winnifred's door opened and the woman stood concerned in its frame.

It became clear to Brent that she might already know why he was there. Apartment floors are thin, "Winnie."

"Come in," she nodded and scooted frayed slippers backward to get out of his and the crying boy's way.

"Thank you," He stepped through the door and slowly lowered the kid to his feet.

Davey landed on them reluctantly and tried to keep his burning arms looped around Brent's neck as the man knelt.

"Hey," Brent gently removed the kid's limbs from his stubbled neck and looked him in the eyes, "it's not your fault, right?"

Davey stared with tears and snot engulfing his face.

Brent began to kindly rub against the spots on Davey's arms that Marilyn had tugged, "right?"

Davey nodded.

"Okay," the man gave a half-smile that hadn't reassured either of them.

They held eyes for a moment before Davey's face twisted hard and he submitted to glossy tears again, "she's so mad at —" he croaked with high pain in his throat before releasing a pressed, "me!" And blowing snot from his nose in the burst of sorrow that fled him. His head dropped shamefully and he covered his leaking eyes and nose on his sleeve.

Brent glanced up at the elder woman, too tired for drama, then down at the large cat that rubbed into Davey's leg for comfort.

Davey tilted his head down at Tulsa and let a small giggle, drowned by facial fluids, out at the cat.

Brent took it as an opportunity and lifted Davey's chin back to him, "she's not mad at you, Dave. Marilyn is super stressed out and I just think it's affecting her behavior," he thought of what may have happened on Saturday—she still hadn't talked about it. "I think it'd be best if maybe you stayed here tonight, with Winnie and Tulsa." He glanced at the woman and she approved with a nod.

Davey shook his head, "she's mad at you too," his lips quivered in thick, red lines as he spoke, and as if he couldn't take it any longer, he collapsed into Brent's arms.

Brent sighed and hugged him, "I'll be fine, bud."

Winnifred excused herself to find blankets and pillows to make Davey a bed on her couch and Tulsa followed slowly.

"Beary," Davey's voice was muffled into Brent's neck.

"I'll get him for you, it's fine," Brent confirmed as the boy's chest contracted in unkempt, wet heaves against him. His hands gripped the cloth t-shirt on the boy's skin as he drifted away from the situation and into his own thought process, like getting stuck on an innertube in a lazy river.

He was thinking about what Winnifred had said when he'd rescued her from the bug in her bathroom: *"You can't afford to save everyone."*

"Okay," he'd decided Davey had cried enough, "okay, come on." He nudged the boy back away from his shoulder and thumbed a tear away from his cheek.

Brent had wandered back down the steps, noticing this time how cold the cement slabbed stairs were beneath his socked feet. His shoulder was damp with saliva and snot that he tried to ignore as it stuck unhappily to him against the stairway caught wind.

"Marilyn?" He spoke her name softly as he rounded the railing and stepped through his open apartment door.

She stood with her head hunkered where he'd left her and her hands holding her elbows across her chest. Her head bobbed up at his voice and her lips pressed into a long line, "his arms, are his arms okay?" Her nose flared as she spoke and her eyelids fluttered as their heads expanded back into numb obis'. She was thinking about the time their mother yanked Davey from her lap with a wet pop and Davey's shrill screams.

"What was that, Mari?"

She stared at him long and hard before looking off to the wall behind him.

Brent sighed, "his arms are fine."

She looked back.

"His head though?" Brent crossed his arms across his chest, "he's confused, kid. He's all messed up, up there because he doesn't understand what the hell just happened. I don't either, to be honest with you. I –"

"Don't call me *kid.*" Each muscle below the hot skin on her face trembled as she held a rough grimace.

"You're not listening to me."

She shook her head harshly, "no, you're not listening to *me!*" Tears swelled visibly against her waterline. *Makes me hard just thinking about it—thinking about you.* She moaned a fragile cry and looked away from Brent as tears bubbled out.

"Okay," Brent said gravely as he shut the apartment door, "Marilyn, you need therapy." It was the best option, she needed to talk about what happened on Saturday—he'd begun to expect it'd been more than just the *Boogie Man.* His thoughts flashed back to his sheets and her discarded shirt and bra.

She'd abandoned pity in front of him like a butterfly abandoning a cocoon and let her trembling muscles relax into a solid stab of anger, "fuck *you,* and fuck your therapy." A moth slipped its wing against her internal wall of skin and she gritted her teeth: *feed them soon.*

Brent stepped back as her eyes suddenly flirted with him, "I think it'll help." He spoke quietly, unable to remember what they were talking about, for a moment.

Then she faded back into her sad, sickly self, "I need to lay down," she whimpered. The tears were back.

Brent scratched the back of his neck, "take my bedroom." He watched her put a hand to her stomach strangely and turn for his room with a twisted face and chokes of tears. He'd take the couch, that was fine. And Marilyn... needed *therapy,* yeah, therapy would help.

He grabbed for Bear Kingsley and went back to the stairway with the old, familiar friend in his hands. Would therapy help?

Would therapy have helped you with Amanda, Brenty-Boy?

He rung his old bear by the neck anxiously as he walked with socks back to Winnifred's one bedroom. Then he unrung it and tickled his thumb into its plush jawline with a distasteful sickness in the pit of his stomach.

84

Marilyn had twisted against Brent's bed in low, moaned cries. The moths inside slick with her bodily fluids like lubricant as they dove, and slid, and touched between each of her intestines. She was a fun house to them. They filled each gap between her bloody guts with salivated foam cocoons that crinkled and popped like bathtub bubbles when she moved.

She stilled and her heart rate slowed to a weak murmur like a washed-out bass to the moths' unwelcomed party. *Wuh bum... wuh... bum—...—wuh.* She thought for a moment that it might stop—a young, healthy, heart attack—but below her softening cries, it was still there. *Wuh bum... Wuh bum.* She bit against the tip of her tongue and the fatty back of it jerked in small, unsettled twitches like a rat stuck hopelessly in a snap trap. She released it and it coward against the roof of her mouth, away from her chomping teeth. *Wuh bum... Wuh bum...*

She lay still on her side, the left of her body elevated and chilled, and the moths moved away from it unhappily, their bodies dropping into her right side like raining .22 long rifle bullets. Her right side weighted between them and Brent's white sheets.

Her pupils flexed like a camera lens until the wall of Brent's bedroom blurred into nothing but a feathery background. She stayed like that, watching what light was left of the night disintegrate into dark shadows on the fuzzy, out of focus wall. She didn't sleep—or blink. Her body absorbed into a state of paralyzed hibernation, her mind carried off by the tiny insects. Saliva trailed down her cheek slowly.

A second heartbeat began to thump over her slow *wuh bum* lively. *Brent's*. Still, she laid against it without movement. Like her mother used to do in her own bed. A depressive episode of frozen insomnia. Her mother. *Am I my mother?*

Davey's face, crying into her's as she scolded wildly beat into her mind and she pondered it for a moment. The fear that had been in his eyes, the 'sorry's' that had fallen like panic from his lips—she saw it in slow motion now.

Marilyn's right hand twitched into a fist without her telling it too and dragged across the sheets to her stomach. It pressed into her gut as she felt a lick of misplaced terror spark in the back of her chest like a brewing cough. She could feel the moths as they began to attack the pressure applied to her stomach. They were upset. They were hungry.

Feed them soon, Mama.

A little past three in the morning she came, dazedly, out of her comatose to find herself standing. Her knees hyperextended against the suddenly aware weight of her upright body. She swayed and her feet flexed into her toes to keep her body steady. *She was too tall, she was too high in the air, it was too much.* She lowered obediently against the aches in her stale body to her hands and knees—like a wobbly toddler. Brent's area rugged floor tangled against her dry palms with limp cotton strings and she stroked it for a moment, her head low and her eyes glassy.

She began to crawl with her lips rolling over her dry teeth and cottonmouth at the same tempo of her limber limbs, grappling across the floor like a wounded bug. She came upon the closed bedroom door and clawed mindlessly at the handle with stiff, sleep swollen fingers. It triggered and bounced towards her against flashes of window moonlight cast across the bedroom.

She had a moment of sanity, pure bliss clarity, but it was only a moment. Gone like a quick breeze or a sleepy thought. Then she began to crawl again.

She crawled into the hall and paused at Brent's light snore from the living room. She glanced, with a swiveling and haunted head at the couch and admired the puffs of lapped hair that bowed up over its armrest—like coconut conditioned common wheat caught in wind. His forearm was rested dead against his forehead like he'd fainted. *Poor poor me, oh goodness my.* She smiled, turned her head forward, and crawled to the bathroom.

The bathroom light illuminated her skin and the moths within began to work their way back through the tunnels they'd created to face it—like metal towards a magnet. She welcomed their sensation with a light, guttural chuckle as she stood to face her reflection in the mirror. She was pale and unfamiliar with herself. Hidden from reality behind fogged sight and a strange, strange urge to *kill herself.*

No—no. That wasn't it.

She stared numbly.

Kill someone else.

Was that it?

Marilyn's legs wobbled slowly as the moths seemed to chant and buzz from within her. Perhaps shedding skin? Do moths —

Do they do that?

Her stare was dead but unfaltering with her reflection. Her eyes shineless— like the black pit of a grave or a dried-up well—too deep to hear the pebble hit bottom when a child flipped it off his thumb and counted as it fell to find the distance. How far down? *Too, too far down.*

She smiled again, with creaking lips that strung up in a way she'd never seen. Like the lips were not her own. How *strange—strange.* An urge.

Feed them.

She stared at her scar, the one from the car wreck. She'd removed the stitched from it sitting in the exact same position she sat in now. Except, that memory seemed old, and grey, and no longer reality. Like maybe she'd dreamt it—far off in another life. The memory only a mere mirage at the bottom of that dry well that swallowed the thumb slipped pebble like a last drawn breath. Marilyn began to press at the white line of healed tissue with the rough pad of her finger curiously.

She felt nothing, she felt nothing, she felt —

Pain. Present and bright suddenly behind the socket of her right eye. Like a Pop Rock explosion from her tear duct. She winced away from the sharp stab with a young baby like whine. A pout and a slap to her face to try to get rid of it. The frisky sting became a hot, irrational, burn and she'd begun to cry against it. Cry. Blankly, without emotion or reddening lids, just tears spilling salt-lessly down her washed-out cheeks.

Then, at the source of the pain, came an object—red and puffy like a developing pimple. The strange cyst began to move, oddly like a waddle to her brow line. It smeared below her eyebrow and her raised flesh pricked the coarse hairs into erect positions. She watched with amusement. *Like a baby's foot it a mother's womb.*

Her same wondering finger pressed at it with its pad like it'd pressed at her new scar. The object crunched. *It is a moth* she thought with a sudden wave of coherency. Her skin flattened in a saggy crater against the squashed body. It was dead.

It was dead and it was stuck above her eyebrow like a cancerous lump. She pinned her finger against it again, harder this time, and felt a shiver in her spine as its wings separated from its callused back. The fur grown from its body brushing her skull under the pressure. Another beach wave of coherency crashed across her psyche's shore and she felt a slice of panic wedge into her.

She began to claw at the dead creature beneath her skin and grimaced slightly at the sound of its dissolving and crushing body like deep, internal surround sound. She scraped downward in red, puffing lines and the crumpled body rolled towards her eyelid like toothpaste in a thin and almost empty tube. Blood began to surface in each microscopic pore dimple from her dragged nails but she continued to work it down, towards her eye.

Marilyn's vision went dark in her right eye as the body dropped down and its jointed, limp legs jutted out from under her lumped eyelid like brown eyelashes made of string. She gently pinched her eyelid and lifted it like a tent to inspect her darkened eye. The crinkled bug stuck lifelessly to her wet eyeball like it was a car windshield in the rain. Its wings had been torn away and just its webbed wing cartilage was left, almost blending to her eye like the red running veins on its white surface. Its head was shaped oblong and its antennas were bent like a zig-zag zipper. A tight stream of air released from Marilyn's lips in a deflated whistle.

She gripped its mashed body between two fingernail tips and removed it from her wet eye. Her vision cleared and she stared at it in her soft palm.

A full tsunami of complete coherence snapped up around Marilyn and plunged her away from the numb, crawling body that possessed her. Clearer and immediately terrified, she began to cry. Hard heavy tears covered with crippled emotions.

85

It was his week for recess duty. The chilled air nipped around the front of his nose like premature frostbite and reddened his nostrils. The early September afternoon heat had finally dwindled and the October mountain breeze had begun to roll down into the valley. He smiled thoughtfully against the icy air that stuck around.

He'd slept well the night before contrary to the darling drama they'd endured. His worry has melted into the firm seat cushions on the couch as quickly as his spine had and he had slept dreamlessly. His arm had laid weighted against his forehead all night and his head felt fuzzy from light compression, like a slept on hand.

Marilyn, you need therapy. He'd wished he'd said it differently. Had he been too blunt? It didn't matter. The girl had hardly spoken to her brother or him that morning as they drove to the elementary school. Davey hadn't talked much either from below his bedhead from Debra's couch. Brent had sat in silence and wondered if he'd messed up, he wondered the same now.

Brent shifted his weight and the first aid bag, a mandatory dress code for *recess duty* (along with the orange vest), repositioned against his thigh. A boy with golden-brown skin ran towards Brent then stopped. His eyes stared from hooded lids at the man as Brent watched, playfully, back. The boy whooped a call over his shoulders to a huddle of same-sized friends and they all began to sprint in different directions.

The boy continued to run past Brent while squealing, "I've been spotted! I've been spotted!" His alliances hollered it back in an echo as they all dove to individual hiding spots.

Brent passed a closed-lip smile onto a teacher to his right, a blonde middle-aged woman, and she shook her head back. The children thought they were clever, but the staff knew the orange vests meant they were the bad guys intruding on the youths' secret spy world. Brent stepped back further onto the playgrounds lining cement sidewalk and laughed to himself as the boy with the hooded eyes dove wildly behind another, unsuspecting, student.

Davey's hands stung like he'd washed them in mouthwash as he climbed a cold barred play structure in toe of Daisy. His nose had begun to run and he sniffed the leak back into his nostrils absently as Daisy's sneaker kicked out and missed the side of his head only by inches. He glanced at it as it passed his temple and noticed the dark, wet bark dust that flung out like splinters from the circular shoe prints.

"Hurry Up, Davey!" Daisy demanded as she shuffled her knees off the climbing bars and onto the brown play platform.

Davey nodded up at her and climbed faster.

He made it to the top powder-coat brown level and joined Daisy to lean against the blue painted guard rails and look out over the play structure. He watched as Brent, orange vested and in the distance, stepped out of the way for James, a strange boy with dark skin and slanted eyes. Davey then let his eyes fall to the bark chips below them and noticed they looked like a skyscraper view of a German Village. The ones with the wooden huts.

Daisy smiled harshly at the boy as a mischievous thought spindled in her mind like a rapidly spun tire swing, "We're like king and queen! We rule the world!"

Davey nodded at her with a smile only half the size of her's, but joyful nonetheless. He thought of the ice arena and the overhead announcer again:

"Daisy and Davey are going to rule the world!" the crowd, now further down—amongst the bark chipped huts, cheered them on. His smile grew.

"I wanna be king, though," The girl admitted casually as she looked out over her kingdom.

Davey nodded again, his head had started to ache from doing so, "King Daisy and Queen Davey!" Daisy turned her mischievous grin back to him with approval. It reminded him of his sister which reminded him of the night before. His head dropped away from Daisy sheepishly.

Groups of children came and went on the play structure as the two friends looked out over their kingdom. They came and went so often, most of them diving down the slide to their left, that they hadn't noticed when some of them began to stick around. A small collection of children stood back and still to giggle at Daisy and Davey as they *ruled.* King and Queen. "Daisy and Davey sitting in a tree K.I.S.S.I.N.G." one of them finally blurted out. An aftershock of laughter rippled through the crowd as the boy and girl turned around startled. Zachary stood at the front of the group with his lips pulled up as he sang it again, "Daisy and Davey sitting in a tree —"

"Oh, stop it!" Daisy swatted at him and the group of young kids spread back like a wading school of fish before joining back together to watch and listen.

"You're the *queen,* David?" A buzz headed fourth-grader with deep dimples laughed from behind Zachary. The kids seemed to shift closer like a nightmare, cornering the friends between the balcony and twisting slide.

Daisy stepped in front of *David* and puffed her pink, sparkly chest out at them, "you don't even know us," she spoke past Zachary and to the fourth-grader, "his name is DAVEY. D.A.V.E.E." She glanced back at Davey who had shrunk himself into the metal corner of the playground structure and tilted her head delicately at him, "right?"

Davey shrugged, because it wasn't, then nodded anyway to say it was.

Zachary scoffed at her, "we don't care about your boyfriend's name," his voice pitched into a high, nasally whine that turned into a laugh as his nose scrunched and lifted his upper lip above his teeth.

"I'm not her boyfriend," Davey piped up and the fourth-grader lifted an eyebrow to say: *oh yeah? You're a liar!* Davey's face filled with red fire and he looked away. His eyes swept back to the fourth-grader as the boy began to laugh. His laugh was a key deeper than Zachary's but entirely the same. Davey realized they were brothers then and frowned. *Poor parents.*

"Davey, did you kill your parents?" A girl, the one who'd asked the same question at the lunch table a week before, asked again. Her cheeks were round and puffy and her eyes sunk deep into her skull.

"No," Davey mumbled as Daisy took a stomped foot towards the tiny crowd of tiny children to try to drive them off. Davey thought: *you really are a King* as the children scattered back like landlocked birds.

"Then *why* do you *always* hang out with Mr. Kingsley?" Sai asked like he might have been offended as the kids came back around, closer and giggling louder.

Davey glanced out over the German village bark chips for Brent at the mention of his name. The man was standing straight with his orange vest, red first aid bag, and head turned a different direction. Watching Sydnee Joseph concur the monkey bars it seemed.

"Because him and Mr. Kingsley are friends!" Daisy defended humbly.

"Why?!"

"Is there something wrong with him?!"

It was a repeat of last Monday at the lunch table.

"His sister works in the office, maybe they need to keep a close eye on him or he'll go crazy!"

"Like nutty hospital crazy?!"

"Yeah!"

"I'm scared —" A girl's voice trailed slowly from the back of the group.
"Or he's a monster! Like a werewolf!"
"Or Frankenstein!"
"Guys! Stop, I'm really scared!"
"No! Maybe he's DRACULA like from *Hotel Transylvania*!"
"But then he'd be afraid of light!"

Davey shut his eyes and imagined he was on the boat from his dream. The waves crashed and the old cedar planks creaked against the pressure. He could feel the mist of the water on his face like starlight and the hollow breeze that danced through the canal. The boat groaned against the water, mimicking a tired old dog lying against his paws before falling off to sleep. A low sigh and breathy growl. The boat slammed into a hard, jutting surface, before bouncing back like the laughing kids had. His head jerked back against the impact like it had when Marilyn had yanked him off the air mattress. His arms burned in memory of the grip she had, had on him. His cheeks felt raw and his eyes felt clammy.

He'd forgiven her.

Sometimes people just get angry, it was okay.

Davey ran to the edge of the dreamboat and threw his torso over the rail to look down at the familiar rock that anchored the small ship in the water. *(Hi, Davey.)* It spoke in a low, drowned voice that softened the wax in his ears in short bursts of frequency, *(I'm glad you're back!)* The boy smiled lovingly down at the rock.

"Hi," he greeted.

The water began to rush past the boat in foamy waves again but the rock kept up, its grey bolder surface seemed to smile right back at the boy.

"Stop guys! You're being mean!" Daisy's voice came through Davey's daydream like it'd dropped down from the sky. It bounced endlessly through

the caved canal and Davey glanced away from the rock momentarily to follow it. Then he was back and the rock continued to smile.

The boy leaned his weight into the edge of the boat's rail with his arm stretched out to the rock. He wanted to touch it.

(Be careful) it warned.

He was being careful.

So careful.

His sneaker tiptoed over a wet, eroded board and his ankle rolled out from under him. The edge of the boat's rail knocked into the bottom row of his rib cage and his gut punched unpleasantly against his spine. Davey let out a gust of pain pinched wind and spread his hands out to catch himself clumsily. His hands grappled nothing but wind-whipped air as he toppled forward over the boat. His heals turned over his head and his back leveled with the approaching water and jutting rock.

Davey's legs shot out against the play structure and his eyes snapped open, away from the falling dream. He stared, frightened, at the bullies that taunted Daisy as the sensation of falling still held a firm grip on him. His stomach stung in suspension and his back arched against the playground railing as water still seemed to slap up around him from the dream. Davey tried to rid the sensation with movement, but his body stayed frozen inside the dream as his eyes looked out into reality. Daydream sleep paralysis.

Daisy took another stomped step towards the kids, "back off!" She threatened. Daisy wasn't *just* the king of the world, but the *warrior*, Davey thought.

Zachary lifted his arms like a forklift and braced them against her, "no, you!" He shoved.

Daisy stumbled back.

Davey's neck muscles strung through the surrounding skin as he tried to yell: *Don't!* But the paralysis kept him still as the misty wind thickened with the dreams approaching canal water.

Zachary shoved again and Daisy stumbled to her butt.

Davey slammed his eyes shut and he could see the sea's sky above him as the rock pierced through his back and out the front of his chest like a bloody arrowhead. The falling sensation blew through his chest with the rock and his arms dangled back into the laps of cold water. The boy gasped in small dashes of painful air as the rock twisted deep against his spine and lungs.

His eyes opened back up to the real world.

He could breathe peacefully as the playground came back into view and he stumbled forward out of the paralysis, his hands jutting instinctively out to help Daisy up as the haunting daydream evaporated. But Daisy wasn't there anymore—not on her butt that is.

She was standing.

Her eyes wide and her hands clamped over her ears as a high pitched alarm began to ripple through the air. The girl who had said she was scared was knelt beside Daisy with a cold, green, queasy face and a hand to her stomach. The other kids were scattering across the play structure frantically without plans to return this time. Davey made eye contact with his friend and thought: *Wait a minute? Where's Zachary?*

Daisy dropped her eyes over the side of the playground railing as if she'd heard his startled thoughts and pressed her hands harder into the side of her face. Davey crossed to the edge and looked down. His chest began to cramp against a stammering young heart as he realized the high squeal of an alarm wasn't an alarm at all, but a continuous scream.

Zachary was sprawled out on his back with his arm jammed un-naturally behind him. His lips had drowned into a thick, plump shade of purple-blue and they worked tirelessly around his never-ending shriek of pain. His brother was hopping around him with his own panic dosed cries for help. Tears streamed out of both brothers' eyes as other children joined in to scream at the broken boy on the ground.

Davey glanced up over the playground for Brent. Brent was running—no *sprinting* alongside other teaches, like a stampede of *Orange Vested* heroes.

Then Daisy was gripping Davey's arm and helping him down the play structure's stairs to the bark chips below, her legs jittering in wide wobbles as she hopped along the metal staircase.

What happened? Davey thought.

Young eyes began to bounce off of him like reflections of wicked light and he began to feel himself cower away as his name started to get passed around the hysterical group of children surrounding Zachary.

86

Joel Olmstead lounged casually against the reception desk with his arms spread across its countertop surface as he talked lazily towards Debra. The woman would laugh and Marilyn would join in on the laughter—a lullaby to her baby insects as they slept soundly in pockets of her skin. Joel let his eyes fall over to Marilyn as she kept her head down. She doodled slowly against a scrapped excuse slip in black, office ink.

"What're you drawing?" He asked the girl with his lips that sat along fat jowls.

"Moth," Marilyn mumbled to herself before swatting a strand of curly hair back behind her ear and tilting her head at her artwork. It looked back at her with 2D eyes and she smiled a little. It was the moth she'd removed from her eye—its antennas broken into jagged lines and just the boning of its wings left on its dull, ink back.

Joel shook his head and flab from under his chin wobbled, "I hate those buggers," he admitted.

Marilyn glanced up at him and as her eyes took in his heavy face her nose took in his scent. Like a clean trash bin full of rotting roses. It set her teeth on edge and a low stir as a led pill bug baby woke up tickled her large intestine. Its wings stretched and she found herself saying, "yeah, I hate them too." The moth knocked its wing into a ball of nerves and her body flexed in pain.

"Then why are you drawing it?" Debra piped in. She was nosey, Marilyn had come to find out.

"I dreamt about one," she spoke as the moth jittered inside her to remind her it wasn't a dream at all, though, she wished it had been. She stared dazed at Joel as he tilted his chin at her, probably enjoying the view of her looking up through her eyelashes at his pudgy face.

A loud ball of chaos burst through the far end of the hallway and bowled towards the main office door like an Indiana Jones boulder of swarming teachers in orange vests and two crying boys. Joel's head whiplashed to the sound and visual disorder as the walkie talkie clipped to his hip crackled to life, "Joel, there was a fight on the playground," Brent's voice spoke through the static on the man's hip and Marilyn's attention perked to it, "Zachary and Abe Steele are coming your way." As if queued for ripe appearance the crowd burst through the office door and the sound of Zachary's wailing—once warbled by the office window glass—broke through in a pure pitch.

"Oh boy," Joel's voice stumbled through the noise clumsily as he tailed behind the recess duty into the nurse's office. His arm extended out towards Debra and his head turned to follow it as he instructed her to get ahold of Zachary's emergency contact. The woman, however, already had her ear to the office phone and her finger dialing rapidly against the phone's round keys.

Zachary's arm was bent like a coat hanger against his chest and his wrist twisted sickly in the opposite direction. Marilyn studied it as the shaking boy passed. Her lips parted thoughtfully and her head tilted on her neck.

Joel Olmstead's voice boomed over the crowd this time, "What happened?" The question was let out for anyone who was listening.

I know what happened, Marilyn thought blandly as she shut her mouth and pouted her lips out, *that kid broke his arm. In two different places. I could hang a t-shirt on that mess of a limb.* She shrugged carelessly and began to turn her attention back to the doodle on paper in front of her.

The older boy, *Abe* was his name, began to twist in frustrated agony—his face purpling as his eyes widened and his fists balled, "THAT NEW DAVID

KID! HE –" He shook his head violently as a teacher knelt to calm the angry boy, "–HE SHOVED HIM!"

Heads, first Debra's, as she talked hushed and quickly to the party on the other end of her phone line, then Joel Olmstead's turned to Marilyn. The girl who was now up on her feet.

Any kind of cold hold her sleepless night had, had on her singed off her to fire as her heart thumped the community of insects within her awake. Marilyn was no longer staring blankly or boringly at the world around her, but feverishly, her jaw clenched wildly as an inhuman emotion dwindled through her body.

Feed them,

Feed them,

Feed them.

She shook her head at the boy named Abe harshly, "shut the hell up, you liar." Her voice was low, like the growl of a rabid dog. Or a wolf.

"Marilyn!" Someone scolded to her right. *Debra?* It hadn't mattered. Marilyn's vision was speckled with bright lights as the internal fire of thick winged tickles washed through her in sparking electric waves. An identical sensation to the moment before she'd daydreamed Rick's murder. Her mouth dried and the lights flickering in her eyes grew brighter.

"Olmstead? You there?" Brent's voice broke through the Walkie Talkie again and Olmstead's hand jumped down to the electronics on his hip like it was a gun in a quick draw.

Marilyn's heated head snapped to Brent's voice and she felt the same heaving chest terror she had the night before as his voice groped through his jogging headphones: *hello, kid.* His voice had sighed into a heavy moan. Her insides melted and the moths seemed to lap it up joyfully.

Feed them soon, Mama.

Marilyn had moved around the desk to the office's entrance with blurred memory of actually doing so. There was a noise and scolding, and disapproval shot through the mouths of adults. Someone grabbed Abe and shuffled him away from her, into the nurse's office with his brother. Someone took Abe from her like Brent had taken Davey away the night before. Marilyn broke through the office door into the main hall and pounded her running legs towards the playground.

Feed them.

87

Brent stood close to Daisy with his brow-line peaked like a large tent that stretched across his forehead and his lips glued together in a thin line. He was studying Davey who now stood where Zachary had been lying as another teacher talked at him sternly. A sight that boiled something protective within Brent like a mother bear catching the scent of wolves on the breeze.

The man feared that it was true—Davey pushed Zachary and the boy fell through an opening in the guardrail for the playground fire pole and to his back, where he landed on his arm. Was it a directly linked result of the night before? Should he have stayed longer at Winnifred's and talked with Davey? He swallowed and there was an audible click in his throat. Had he *abandoned* Davey?

Even more horrifyingly he'd feared that it wasn't true. This fear dwindled from the girl who stood in front of him with her newly nine-year-old blond pigtails. Her head slowly shaking, left to right as she looked out at the gathering children and at the teacher who sternly pressed her words at Davey, who stood pale and frozen beneath her. Davey's name popped out of the mouths of the children, *Davey,* it rushed through like the hush of winter wind. Then Zachary's name came through the crowd. It carried itself in a sadder, empathetic tone and then died out like campfire smoke. Then the verb came: *pushed.* It rippled from mouth to mouth like wildfire before shapeshifting rapidly among the children to *shoved,* and as that spread a new beast formed from their lips and soon the word *threw* was bouncing around the children, clearly audible now, *"Davey THREW Zach over the edge!"* Still, through it all, Daisy stood still with her blonde head shaking *NO*.

What had that meant?

Brent took a step forward, around Daisy, "alright kids, go play!" They all turned and looked at him. The man waved his first-aid bag at them and opened his mouth to repeat himself when sickening dizziness set in. He shut his eyes and felt the world swipe aimlessly against his feet in spells of familiar vertigo. *Dammit.*

The school's side-door to the west of the playground swung open and anger began to fill the gaps in Brent's temples, along with the cool numb. Not his own anger, but her's. Like he'd borrowed it as their minds exchanged dizzy spells and ice-pick lobotomies.

He turned to face Marilyn with steady legs and tight muscles as the last of the novocaine dripped into place and their vision cleared. The girl he saw resembled the girl he'd seen the night before and stood furiously in the apartment's doorway as Davey laughed unknowingly against the half-inflated air mattress. Her face was a solid mask of terror and vexation as she panted. He could feel each full pant run its course through his own lungs as his chest syncopated with her's.

Brent began to pace towards the girl. His strides were nervous and full of a heat that was not his, "Marilyn," her name swooped through him like a painful cough as he tried to grab the girl's attention, "Marilyn!" Her eyes pinned past him and grasped tightly to her little brother.

She hadn't cared much for the orange vested blur that moved at her and barked her name, "Let me see him!" She punched the words through her teeth with a venomous tongue as she collided into the man that was using himself as a barricade between her and the school children.

Brent shook his head against the heat that radiated off of her and through his scrambling brain, "I don't think you should be out here." Her anger pulsed through him like stained wasabi on his tongue and throat, "You're upset." Her eyes, dilated and beady, stabbed into his and reminded him that, that may have been an understatement. Brent took a slight step back.

"Let me see him." Her voice, low and gravelly, slurred with saliva, made his hair stand up on the back of his neck like the hackles on the back of a dog.

"Let me take care of it," He met her with the same dominance in his voice as he searched her strange, strung out eyes for a sign of rationality. He came up short—and disappointed.

Marilyn took a dodge around him and tried to run herself towards the play structure where Davey stood with his head down. The teacher who'd been scolding him, however, now stood straight—her mouth sealed shut as she watched Brent try to control the eighteen-year-old with a hot temper.

"Marilyn!" Brent snatched her wrist and spun her back around to face him. His hand seemed to melt into her flesh as they touched and their vision spiked into a fast thrown spiral. He bit back a pathetic, nauseated whine as he peeled his fingers off of her bony arm and broke the connection.

Marilyn ripped her tingling wrist to her chest and held it in her other hand, the one on the bandaged arm, as the playground steadied again beneath their feet. The moths had begun to chant within her darkly. Their micro-mouths chomping into bits of her nerves and their wings scraping at her stretched guts. They rumbled to remind her they were hungry.

Feed them.

"Let me see my *fucking* brother!" She hissed her voice from the pit of her stomach as the moths danced around it.

Brent grabbed her and yanked her close to him with a look that reminded Marilyn of her father, the few times he'd scolded her in his life, "This is *EXACTLY* why you *CAN'T* be out here!" The man's eyes glazed and Marilyn noticed how the world had begun to slide by sideways. Brent let go of her again, this time with an audible groan as he steadied himself against motion sickness.

Marilyn turned away from him towards Davey again and Brent ran around her this time to stop her–avoiding direct contact, "I need you to go," He puffed.

She mocked him, *"I need you to go,"* and her voice was high and nasally as she did so, her face twisted ugly.

It was so childish. All of it was. They were two school children themselves at that moment. Playing cat and mouse on a playground that didn't belong to them.

Brent wanted to hit her.

No.

The man's head tossed back and forth as the disturbing thought rolled from one side of his skull to the other. It whorled around within the chambers of his thoughts and he felt sick against it.

That wasn't his thought. He didn't want to do that.

His head jerked again and his eyebrows furrowed harshly into the bridge of his nose. The foaming fury passed between their mental connection had spread like cancer through him. It was a dictator, puppeting his mind with impure ideas.

Hit her.

Brent squirmed in his own skin uncomfortably as a fragment of his own sanity glitter though: a crystal flake in a shadowed corner.

No! His conscious fought back to the boiling anger that did not belong to him. *No!*

He stepped back, away from Marilyn.

Brent didn't know it was the moths who were talking with him. Their tiny commands flashing thought, the beaker signals between man and adolescent–

like a phone riding a long strip of stolen air radio. He didn't know the moths, *the anger*, were telling Marilyn to do *much* worse.

Feed them, mama.

Marilyn's twisted face sprung into a smile.

Frightened, Brent stepped back up to her, "leave," he threatened, "go home."

The smile dropped from the girl as an explosion of radioactive frustration passed in waves from her to Brent, "with what car?!" Her breath sliced through the air as she gasped, "you fucking totaled mine! Remember?!" The knife-edge in her breathing turned into a silver sword that dragged heavily against glass in the man's ears.

Brent's jaw tightened. *Saying fuck every damn minute doesn't make you cool. It doesn't look good. You're trash, you're trash, you're trashy*—He took another step to her against the evil words that thundered down his mind's mountain range and grabbed her one final time. He grabbed her lightly despite the borrowed madness that pulsed in his bloodstream. He hissed between his teeth as his hands absorbed into her with a bone-crushing weight. He then turned her and let go to regain his balance, "Then walk!" He spat closely to her ear before nudging her off with two fingers to her back. The playground somersaulted around them then rested still.

Marilyn, to his surprise, walked. She walked away with upright shoulders and her hips in a strut. Her hand was pressed into her stomach (to greet the moths) and her neck and head popped with veins as she went.

Feed them.

She walked faster.

Once out of direct face-to-face conflict the moths seemed to calm—for a moment. It was a quick breather, a sideline cup of water, but it was enough to liberate Marilyn and give her a slice of her own thoughts back. She thought, tiredly, of her father. *"Good show,"* he used to always say through a chuckle.

Marilyn let out a long sigh as she passed through the playground gate to the school's parking lot. *Yeah, good fucking show. Now what?* But she knew what —*Feed.*

Brent watched her walk out and her growing distance had made the fenced lining of the park feel more public as the signal that had been caught wickedly between them broke. He realized then that he had forgotten where he was in all the excitement: stood out at his work, in front of children. He slowly turned his body and took in the teachers and students who all stared back at him. They looked the same, all of them, a sea of open mouths and shifting eyes. Brent's face heated and the red suddenly on his cheeks violated his vision. Davey was turned sideways and his face was laid into the scolding teacher's side, *Ms. McGail.* Brent began to helplessly walk towards the boy, the red in his face cherrying darker in acknowledgment of all the eyes that followed him.

"Hey, kid." He knelt slowly next to Davey and Ms. McGail, who had her arm swooped around the boy's shoulder for comfort, "let's head to my office."

Davey's face smeared out of the teacher's side and glistened in the clouded playground's white light. Covered in tears and colored blotches, the kid shook his head 'no'. He folded his lip in his mouth as Brent's face fell sad.

Brent was reminded of Daisy, shaking her head 'no'. *What had that meant?* Brent turned from the boy to find her. He saw Daisy who stood pale behind him, her hand grasped around a pigtail and a deep pain washed through him, "Davey." He croaked the boy's name as he swooped his head back to the crying child, "are you sure you don't want to go back with me?"

He was met with Davey's blank, lip in mouth, stare and knew that meant *no.*

No, Davey did not shove Zachary.

No, Brent would not hit anyone.

No, Davey would not go to Brent's office.

The man wet his lips and felt sorrow ooze out with his wetting saliva. The sorrow was in everything in him now—he was sure to *piss* it the next time he used the restroom. Just sure of it. He stood and kept his eyes low, away from Ms. McGail. He then wheeled his head to Daisy, "Daisy?"

Eyes of children watched her like weasels as she nodded, "let's go."

88

"Mr. Kingsley?" Daisy's voice squeaked up from his side as they shuffled through the silent hallway towards his office.

Brent looked down over his cheeks, that still balled up in red streaks, to the girl. They made eye contact and Daisy decided what she had to say wasn't important as she turned her head back to the floor. Brent nodded slowly to himself, "Daisy?"

They crossed into his office and she looked up at him from the doorway, "Yes?"

Brent motioned for her to come in further and take a seat at the tiny table where he and Davey had shared lunch on the boy's first day. He tossed the orange vest he was required to wear at his desk as he crossed the room and sat with her, his legs up to his chest in the tiny yellow chair, "Did Davey push Zachary?" He folded his hand against the table and smiled sadly to himself as he remembered the boy's big eyes across from him as he munched on grilled cheese and grapes.

Daisy shrugged and looked away from him. Brent let the silence pass through them calmly as the girl studied her shoes. Finally, she looked up, "Mr. Kingsley?"

He smiled softly at her, "Yes?"

"The kids make fun of Davey because of you."

Brent thought, looked away from her, back to her, then nodded, "Oh?" The sorrow that filled him head-to-toe swished through him and reminded him of its existence painfully.

She nodded her blonde head, "They make fun of him because of his sister too. They think you have to take care of them because they're crazy or scary or something."

Brent bit into his lip until it hurt, "Thank you for telling me, is that why Davey pushed Zachary? Zach was teasing him?" His voice was steady despite being billowed from a tight, hurt chest.

Daisy tilted her head and her brow-line shrunk into itself, "Yeah but —"

"Davey didn't push Zach?"

Her head shook, "The bullying is why Davey didn't want to come with you to your office, Mr. Kingsley." She scrunched her nose, "He might be embarrassed," her words rode a whisper and the man had to lean in to hear it.

"Of me?"

"Yeah."

Brent nodded to himself. Tough news to receive from a nine-year-old, "Okay, who's bullying him, kiddo? Zachary and who else?"

She listed names off then slid lower in her chair sadly, "it seems like the group gets bigger every time. Everyone always asks him bad questions and more people get curious and then they ask worser questions," She sighed dramatically, "I try to hold them off but," she shrugged.

"Bad questions?"

Daisy waved her hand through the air before sitting on it, "*Is your mom and dad dead? Did you kill them? Are you a monster? Like Frankenstein?*" She looked disturbed, "He doesn't even look like Frankenstein, Mr. Kingsley."

Maybe, as a little boy...Frankenstein was the doctor—not the monster. Brent blinked the thought away then grimaced slightly at her, "That's not okay, you're right." He thought of the purple Crayola noose and his frown deepened, "Thank you, again, Daisy—for telling me. That was very brave of you."

"Yeah, I know." The girl laid her head into the crook of her elbow that rested on the table and looked blankly at Brent's wall for a long, solemn moment before lifting her eyes to him, "Have you ever seen *Matilda* the movie?"

Brent sat up straight, his eyes wide. Had that been the answer? *Did Davey push Zachary?* Was that it? "Yeah..." *I think you're Miss Honey - and I think I'm Matilda.* Davey had said to him the day they met, "Why?"

Daisy looked like she might puke as her lips pulled apart to answer him.

That's when Joel Olmstead entered. He bent his head at Daisy, "Ms. Norberg," Daisy blinked at her principal as he addressed her by last name, "Mr. Kingsley and I need to chat. Can you head to class?"

She looked at Brent as if asking for his permission and he nodded for her to go on, disappointed in Joel's timing.

The men watched the young girl go then Joel shut the door behind her. Brent stared for a moment at the closed office entrance then forced his eyes to his boss' large face. He smiled a wearily closed-lip, polite smile at it and stood.

Joel shook his head, "Take a seat, Brent."

Brent looked back at the yellow kids' chair then crossed his room to slouch in his adult-sized office chair, "Alright." He exhaled and laced his fingers together in his lap.

Joel leaned against the adjacent wall with his arms folded and his teeth clacking over his tongue, "I need you to write up a suspension report," The man continued to chew on his tongue and sucked his teeth as Brent's face began to prickle into an irritable sweat, "for Davey," He clarified as his tongue folded down from the front of his teeth with a *pop* that sent Brent into a spiral of overstimulation and needled skin.

The counselor leaned back into his chair, offended, "We don't know if it was actually Davey who shoved him." If Zachary was *shoved* at all. Brent felt uneasy as the hum to *Little Bitty Pretty One* slowly rocked his thoughts in a curious lullaby.

"The kids all say it was," Joel shrugged at his weak excuse.

Brent stood, no longer feeling the need to sit, or the will to continue to look up at Joel's wobbly chin as the man continued to roll his tongue through his mouth, "Daisy said it wasn't and she was standing right there."

"Daisy is his friend, Brent. Friends do a lot for each other," *pause to suck slowly at his teeth,* "especially at their age. You know that."

Brent pinched his lips together and tried to ignore the way his stomach flipped at Joel Olmstead's stench of sore flower and rotten attitude, "are you saying she's lying for him?"

"I'm saying I need you to write up that report for me."

Brent shook his head, "you should talk to Daisy, we should get her back in here. You're basing it off of kid rumors."

"And Teachers, you might not have been paying attention, but other teachers were: *Mr. Kingsley.*"

"I want evidence before I —"

Joel leaned forward off of the wall and his tongue flicked down over his fat lower lip, "this isn't a courtroom, Brent. Write the report, okay?" He eyed his defensive employee until Brent dropped his stare with frustration. Joel flexed his crossed arms tighter into his chest, "besides, Davey's suspension is *seriously* the least of my concerns right now."

Brent lifted his eyes back to the man and crossed his own arms, knowing what was coming.

Joel clicked that stupid tongue of his, "Marilyn."

Brent's shoulders dropped forward and he let his eyes fall behind a slow blink, "I know," all defenses were down, "I'm sorry. That was *so* uncalled for."

Joel leaned back into Brent's office wall, "I'm going to be getting a lot of calls from parents concerned about the lunatic office girl their children tell them about at dinner tonight."

Brent frowned at his choice of words, "She's not a *lunatic*. She just..." He trailed off shyly because he knew Joel was right. Joel hadn't even been on the playground and he'd already been briefed on it. The story was being spread rapidly and would continue to spread and reshape like a virus the rest of the night. Maybe the rest of the week. *Month. Year??* Not often kids get a front-row seat to an adult fight at *school.* It might go down in those kids' history forever, Brent realized. *Come 'er grandchild. Lemme tell you of the time my school counselor got in a fight with a young office girl on the school playground. Times was crazy back in my day, no respect.*

Brent felt ashamed.

Joel stopped playing his tongue inside his mouth and gazed off thoughtfully into the corner of the small office room and his hand came out to rest against the closed doorknob.

Brent waited.

Joel's mouth clicked open finally and his eyes slid back to Brent's as he spoke slowly, "I don't know if we can keep her around, Brent." He pressed his fat hand into the handle and the door popped open.

Brent's hand came out and nudged the door closed again, his eyes steady with his boss. *Was Olmstead just gonna drop that bomb and leave?* He thought as his heart pittered against his ribs nervously, "No, Joel. Listen," he paused with a dry mouth as he studied the unimpressed, fat man in front of him. Brent sighed and shook his head at himself, "She needs this job." He hated how pathetic he sounded and let his held eye contact fall to his shoes.

He could feel Joel glare into the top of his head.

Brent lifted his chin, "She needs it," his voice was stronger, "suspend Davey—that's fine. But give the girl another chance." A chance he prayed she'd take seriously. Her head was a storm keeper of black spiraled clouds currently and he had to find a way to break through it. A task as easily compared to yelling over a freight train's rumble, he knew.

"I'm worried for the kids' safety." He was worried about bad press more, honestly.

Brent stared at the principle like he was hurt. His mouth opened slightly, suspended for a moment as he processed, then it helped him say, "She's not dangerous." His face hardened sternly to prove he meant what he'd said, but his insides seemed to melt in protest. *Was she dangerous?* No, just unstable–just needs help–he can help her–it's fine–she's fine–no danger. His strong expression weakened helplessly as he heard the lie leave footprints through his head, "just," his face flexes again, "give her one more chance."

Joel shifted his weight from one hyperextended knee to the other and his scent wafted up into the room potently. He chewed on his tongue, slow to answer. Finally, he sighed, "One more chance."

Brent's heart jerked against his throat, "one more chance," he repeated in a nervous stammer before biting back a smile of relief.

Joel stood off the wall and Brent scooted back to make room for his body, "an outbreak like that again and it'll be *your* job we're discussing." The door was forced back open against Brent's hand and the counselor retracted it back like the door was suddenly stovetop hot. It swung and threw fast air into Brent's stunned expression. "Write the suspension report and bring it to my office when you're done," Joel stepped from the room with a grunt and shut the door behind him.

Brent studied the pattern on the back of his door for a prolonged moment, his hands finding their way into his pockets to sit slacked against the cloth lining. He eventually turned from it and sat at his desk to write Davey's suspension.

89

Brent walked to Joel Olmstead's office, tucked deep behind the main office, with the suspense slip gripped tightly in his two hands. His shirt had begun to feel tacky against his chest, the buttons digging into sensitive spots in his skin and the seams at his armpits felt tough like leather. He cleared his throat and lifted his head higher, aware now that it felt as if the collar of his shirt was trying to strangle him.

He passed Debra without a glance as he felt her eyes dig into him. Concerned or maybe disappointed? He didn't know. He didn't care. He passed the nurse's office second, its yellow walls and ripped patient bed empty. Zachary was probably at the hospital by now. He and his brother, Abe, probably chauffeur off by an upset mother. Brent tilted his head as we walked. He remembered meeting their mother once, she was high strung—he could recall that.

He began to feel thankful that Marilyn had come to the playground and targeted him. If she'd stayed in the office Zach and Abe's mom may have gotten the blunt end of the young girl's temper tantrum. What was her name? *Megan?* He shook his head.

Brent stepped into Joel's office with his breath held tight in his chest. A snotty-nosed and puffy-eyed boy glanced at him through globby eyelashes. He was curled up in a plush seat with his arms locked tight around his knees.

Brent tried to work out some breath from his lungs but it clogged at his throat and his stomach contracted nervously instead, "Hey kid," he said to Davey, "how are you holding up?"

Davey looked away from him.

He wondered about *Matilda* fiercely then. Why had Daisy brought it up? He supposed he could figure out how to believe it, Davey having some sorta superpower? Yeah, he could believe that. Given the circumstances, that is. He could believe that he'd wrecked into Davey and his sister and broken his nose. He could believe that something grey, rotten and lanky grabbed him as he tried to remove Davey from the car. He could believe that when he'd talked to the cops he'd seen that the 4Runner had been sputtering idle on the side of the road—healthy—and the broken bridge of his nose had suddenly been replaced with a straight bridge of cartilage and bloodless nostrils. He could believe Marilyn was visited by the *Boogie Man* maybe twice now since the wreck... So, why couldn't he believe *Matilda*?

He bit the inside of his cheek until pain stung through his whole face like pepper spray.

Joel sat back in his wide office chair that creaked against his weight, "Close the door, Mr. Kingsley."

Brent obeyed.

"Take a seat, please," Joel motioned to an open chair beside Davey and Brent followed his instructions. As he sat beside the quiet, distant boy he studied his reluctant signature at the bottom of the suspension report: it seemed to burn a hole straight through the page of paper. Disgusted in it and heavy-hearted, he handed it across the desk to Joel Olmstead.

Davey was suspended then. Three days.

Brent felt foolish as he reached back across the table to take the slip back into his own hands, Joel's signature now added at the bottom with his.

"Please take that home and have Marilyn sign it." Joel's voice was steady against the siren wave of Davey, crying shamefully into his jacket sleeve.

Brent nodded but wanted to throw it back in the man's face. *An outbreak like that again and it'll be your job we're discussing,* Joel had said. Brent considered then how important his job was? What would it matter if he'd gotten a different job?

He pinched his lips together. He knew he wasn't thinking clearly. *One more chance,* he was taking a gamble on Marilyn, *one more chance.*

He folded the paper and slipped it into his pocket, "If you don't mind, Mr. Olmstead, it'd like to take the rest of the day off to get Davey home."

Joel lifted an eyebrow, "that's fine."

Davey gagged a cry.

Brent felt like an asshole.

90

She stood still.

The moths flopped enthusiastically inside her, diving and swimming into the darkest corners of her body, but Marilyn Matthews kept still.

She had walked aimlessly for a half-mile, then walked purposefully for the second half—sure then, at the half-mile mark, of what the moths were asking of her. What they meant, *it* meant when it said to: *Feed Them.*

She had stopped outside of a familiar duplex and pivoted towards it. Now she just stood and studied it, her eyelids sagged and her lips loose against a distant smile. It was Nick's and formally, but never officially, Davey and hers as well. A broken walkway below her feet led through the overgrown grass to the cement step her and Davey had sat on the night she'd come back from Portland short on cash. Beyond that step was the creaky door framed by chipped wood and a dirty, yellowed paint home. She cocked her head at it—as if it was her first time seeing the duplex—and her jaw fell at the angle of her tilted head and her smile went askew. The house had single glass windows and the largest (*the living room*) had a Bob Ross blanket draped across it to block the sun from blinding Nick as he slept a hangover off in his single living room chair.

Just a pretty little curtain replacement.

The girl, not much of herself any longer but more of a puppet meat suit full of unwelcome insects, began to move her legs forward. She crossed over cracks delicately, careful not to step on a single one. *Step on a crack, you break your mama's back.* And the moths didn't want that to happen, *Nooo. Not that.*

She stopped at the door and swayed for a long, dizzying moment before knocking against it gently. She straightened up righteously as she waited for a response and tried to remember how she'd gotten here. *Walked.* Yes, she'd walked, but why? Where had she been? It all seemed so foggy at the moment and her last clear memory was of pulling the crushed moth off of her eye. *Was that last night?* She couldn't remember.

She knocked again, still at her same gentle rhythm. It went unanswered again, which made her lips droop shallowly into a frown. She massaged the door handle open as silently as she could and slid in at her own accord.

The familiar reek of grease surrounded her like a wool-lined coffin and she gasped through her nose at it, "Nicholas?" She spoke his name without an incline in her voice, like a slow spoken statement. The front door groaned shut behind her and her moth hostage mouth coined back into a smile.

The house was dark and her sight involuntarily shifted to Davey and her old bedroom. It was open and she could see Nick had pawned their left behind things. *For drug money,* she knew, as her tongue flicked against her upper lip to wet it. It was sweaty and for a moment she couldn't remember why. Not until she took another step further into the house and felt the fatigue in her upper calf. *She'd been walking.* Or *they* had been *walking her.* Yes, she remembered now. She was at Nick's. Formally, but never officially, her *home*.

The creatures buzzed like locus below her soft olive skin.

"Holy shit! Marilyn?" A scrawny, tattooed adult-boy stood in the doorway of his bathroom as the scent of shit wafted, warmly, out behind him. The ceiling fan buzzed above him obnoxiously until he flipped off the bathroom light, then it just slowed, sputtered, and died in the darkness of his dirty bathroom. "Where the fuck have you been?!"

The moths fluttered in her stomach like excited butterflies—poisoned in sore anger and sharpened wings, "out," Marilyn answered. She'd been *out*.

Nick stepped from the bathroom and the shit scent followed him, "you owe me, lady! Rent is almost due!" His face twisted with his words and a hiss snuck from the tip of his tongue.

The girl shrugged over her shoulder as she looked back at her old bedroom. It starred back bare and lifeless, "you sold all my stuff," her head turned back to him and her shrug relaxed, "isn't that money enough? Or did you spend it on *necessities.*" Her nose scrunched mockingly and she felt the smile on her face grow wider like the Cheshire Cat.

He eyed her, curiously, his teeth working to chew dead skin from his lower lip. He was dressed in basketball shorts that hung from hip to knees and a blue, crusty, *Metallica* t-shirt. "*Ride the Lightning,*" it said.

Marilyn stepped towards him in a slow, careful strut. Like she was walking a tightrope in lingerie clothing. She pressed nearer to him and his hands drifted up to catch her shoulders. His stubby, unwashed fingers knitted around her skin in a weight that made her neck ache splendidly. She could feel a fog of heat rising from his close body and her smile darkened. *He was in heat like a bitch dog.* "I missed you," she cooed through a formed bubble across her lips and watched eagerly as his eyes dilated.

She hadn't missed him. Hadn't thought about him at all—since Brent... but she needed something from him. *They* needed something from him. Her fuzzy, winged babies. It was primal.

Instinctual.

She thought it was sex.

She thought it was sex that they were so hungry for, that they ached for, that they buzzed against her bones for. So that's what she'd given them. Her back arched into Nick's bed as her hands gripped the back of his neck and her fingers yanked against strands of his greasy hair. Nick had been too lazy to pull his shorts all the way down and the polyester material had begun to rub a raw spot into Marilyn's ass, but she hadn't minded, the pain almost seemed soothing.

She began to think of Brent. Her mind wandering over his tall build and brown, soft hair. She thought of his jawline and the stubble that had flawed it beautifully the past few days. She thought of how she suddenly wanted to kiss his whiskered jaw, suck on it, pant against it. She imagined Brent the night she'd been *impregnated* with the little moths. She knew, as Nick thrust into her, that it wasn't really Brent that night and she wondered why she'd been so upset by that. Sure, it hadn't been Brent–but hadn't it been *better* than Brent. She thought so, now. She thought of his flushed face, and brushing lips, and dark eyes. She thought of his hands around her neck, then his belt.

Feed them soon, Mama, she heard his voice spread over her.

Little moans began to press from Marilyn's throat. This excited Nick and he fell stupidly out of rhythm with her. She grimaced and gripped his sweating face between her fingers and thumbs to squeeze it. His lips sagged forward between his squished cheeks and she nipped her teeth into his bottom lip as her mind drifted back off to Brent.

She thought of the Brent she had confronted on the playground. His pressed face, his redirecting grip that had stuck to her as the ground spun up and around them, his two fingers that had jabbed into her spine, *walk* he had demanded. And she had. She had obeyed.

The moths seemed to settle in her belly then, their wings suspended out like Chinese fans. Marilyn had a clear thought for only a moment: like a hint of a familiar scent you can't place. *What am I doing with Nick?* Then the thought was gone and she was dipping her hips into him and smiling. The moths collected together, then in unison, burrowed. Deep down into her spine.

Marilyn yelped and Nick took it as a personal challenge, his throat unable to mask the tight grunts that he worked to keep in. She needed obey again. The moths directing her from within to *obey,* "hey," she mumbled against Nick as her hand caught a clump of his oily hair, "rollover."

He didn't.

Unsatisfied, Marilyn groaned and pressed her legs together, making eye contact with him as he sighed at her, "roll over," her voice was more stern.

He studied her for a moment before flopping to his back beside her. Marilyn brushed her hand over her stomach and the moths weaved forward to rub against its pressure. She giggled to herself as they did so then climbed on top of Nick, straddling him with her olive thighs.

She knelt her head down and kissed the corner of his mouth while keeping her breath held firmly behind her mouth and nose. As she knelt her eyes drifted up and she caught sight of his nightstand: scattered with miscellaneous shit on top of dust and grime. He bucked against her and tried to kiss her lips straight on but she pulled up and away from him before he could. Nick took the opportunity of her arched angle to slip himself inside with a jittery motion. She let him work against her like a rabbit as her eyes continued to search the nightstand. Only an arms reach away.

A pipe with a burned bulbed end, an unplugged digital alarm clock, a broken necklace, a twenty-dollar bill, three pennies, a dime, a Dollar Tree pair of wire-framed reading glasses, and a tiny screwdriver. A sticky, tiny screwdriver, made for screwing tiny things but used for packing weed into his little burned pipe. She knew then, at the exact moment, that the moths had not been hungry for *sex*.

Flashes of her *pen in neck* fantasy with Rick absorbed into her frontal lobe and she bit her lower lip into a red, rubbed smile. A small whimper dancing through the gaps in her teeth. They needed something *else*. She *knew* that now. It's what they *always* needed.

Feed them, Mama.

She turned her face down to the sweaty young adult and let her smile grow into something sinister as the moths spun dusty wing webs inside her. Her hand traced up his chest, dabbled across his neck, chin, lips, then finally came to rest across his eyes like a blindfold.

Nick protested with a small, irritated moan and reached a hand to pull her away.

Marilyn swatted at him, "No," she tightened her cupped hand over his eyes and whispered over him, "*Trust me. You'll love it.*"

His curiosity overweight his impatient personality and he left her hand there, over his eyes to keep her actions hidden, making himself vulnerable.

Feed.

Marilyn reached out gently with her free hand and gripped the screwdriver by its handle as she let loud moans stream between her lips to hide the sound of scraping screwdriver over dirty nightstand wood. The moths galloped within her and made her feel useful, loved, obedient. She straightened back up, the metal screwdriver grasped tightly in her hand.

Nick, still blinded by her left hand over his eyes, slid deeper inside of her, taking advantage of her arched hips.

Marilyn dropped her lower lip away from her smile and side-eyed the screwdriver. Then, the puppeted grin slithered back into place and she squeezed the tip of the screwdriver into the side of Nick's neck, just below his jawbone.

The moths dove forward and she felt the skin in the front of her body stretch to accommodate their flailing bodies. They danced eagerly to the sharp screams that barreled from the man like a startled car horn. His hands spasmed outward as he tried to grip at Marilyn's face then at the screwdriver that had now pierced a half-inch into the fat of his neck. The fat that bulged around the shiny stem of the tool the same way she'd imagined Rick's neck would've bulged around her office pen.

Nick's hips thrust rapidly into her, not for pleasure, but because of the pain. His legs stretched in convulsions against his dirty bedsheets and his toes worked in and out like they could grab hold of something.

Marilyn giggled to herself and tossed her head back—it was like a carnival ride.

His hand struck her chin before it clasped around her throat and began to flatten her airway. His thumb scrapped at the soft center of her neck and made her laugh come out moody and deep. The poor bastard kept his nails chewed to the nub which, despite his efforts, left nothing but a pink blemish that would clear in only an hour's time. Nothing to say he'd been there in an altercation with her.

Marilyn pouted at him, "do you think," she rasped from within his grip, "if you'd worked out rather than done heroin," she shucked air in and it sounded like a bathtub drain sucking out the last of its filthy water, "you'd be able to buck me off." His eyes widened and the driver jiggled in further, now a full inch.

Nick's hand loosened around Marilyn's neck and for a moment she felt sad—it had reminded her of Brent's belt. *Or...* (*Not*) Brent's belt... she couldn't remember anymore. *Anyway.*

She watched blood pool from Nick's flexed and twisting mouth in gurgling bubbles. It made red river streams down the sides of his cheeks and into his ears as it frothed between his teeth. It reminded her, honestly, of blended strawberries, and she thought to taste it but knew she'd be disappointed if she did.

The moths built pressure inside of her. Unbearable pain from her core that forced her to jerk the screwdriver its full length into Nick's neck. It went in at an angle and came out beneath his tongue like a pole under a fat, pink tent.

Then, Nick died.

A sour smell seeped around the girl like nectar as she threw her head back to let out a long moan. Her body shook with tremors of pleasure as she traced the blood from his closing mouth with her sunken eyes. The pain in her body subsided and the moths relaxed. They were satisfied. They got what they needed.

Marilyn let his dead sex organ slide out of her as she unstradled him to stand. She turned thoughtlessly and delicately away from the murder on the bed and danced lightly across the floor on her tiptoes. Her hand came down and rubbed soft circles into her belly as she balanced against her toes and swayed lightly on her feet, "I did what you wanted," she whispered to her grumpy tummy, she whispered to the moths inside her. "Are you happy?" Silence and comfort met her from the other side of her flesh.

She tipped her head back and let out another naked moan of relief. It was done. Over.

At least, they let her think that as she showered the sex and death off her body in Nick's bathroom. They let her think she was free, free of a curse, of a burden, of their grasp.

They let her believe her thoughts were her own as she strolled down the sidewalk in one of Nick's button-up plaid shirts matted to her wet, showered skin and thought: *I don't feel guilty yet, when will I feel guilty? Will I ever? I'm free.*

They let her believe she had Free-Will as she *"chose"* to walk the mile and a half back to Brent's apartment with a sad smile on her face and a warmth in her belly.

Freed.

91

Brent had invited Winnifred over for dinner that night as a thank you for watching Davey the night before. And also, less admittedly, as a third mouth since Marilyn hadn't made her way home yet. The elderly woman sat at the dining table with her cat in lap and talked quietly with Davey as Brent strained the boiled, soft noodles for his spaghetti.

Davey's face was sponge swollen and his head throbbed from the tears he'd been fighting since getting home that day. He scratched behind Tulsa's ear and nodded slightly at Winnifred's soft, wrinkly voice as she told him stories. His lips twisted and his eyes blinked at he fought the urge to cry for the *hundredth time* that night.

Brent stirred sauce and noodles together in the drained pot and decided that he wished Davey would just cry it all out. The crying, stopping, crying, stopping, crying was going to make the kid sick. His head began to pulse and he held his breath against the dizzying spins with his hands braced into the kitchen counter until the front door opened and the center of his head cooled into the familiar numb that spread rapidly through his body.

"Hello, everyone," Marilyn's voice came from the living room entrance in a calm, steady pitch.

Her anger no longer dumped into Brent's body and he felt grateful for it. He left the noodles to pop his head out of the kitchen, "just in time for dinner," he said and her eyes hit him sharply before they bounced off to her little brother, whose tears came freely and shamefully now.

"What's wrong, D?"

Davey dropped his head to his hands and cried into them.

Winnifred stiffened uncomfortably and Brent went back into the kitchen to finish preparing their dinner and grab a fourth plate for Marilyn. She was wearing a man's shirt that Brent didn't recognize and her hair hung in damp curls from a shower. It wasn't his business, but—a frown deepened into gently aging wrinkles on his cheeks—he hoped she didn't go to Nick.

Brent and Marilyn sat at opposite heads of the table with Winnifred and Davey sat on a shared side, the side that looked out at the mountains. Davey sat closest to Brent, Winnifred closest to Marilyn, Tulsa beneath the table—closes to food scraps. Their plates were decorated with swirled spaghetti noodles and slice garlic bread. They all poked at their red sauced food, the three Grant Elementary goers replaying the day through their heads into their own perspective. Their elder guest, who's spaghetti was cut into small bits of noodle to accommodate for her dentures, sat silently as the sense of cold tension between the other three washed against her. Tulsa waited to eat as well, since there were no scraps to purr at before slurping up on her spiked tongue. She meowed from under the table impatiently and flicked her fuzzy tail into Winnifred's ankle.

"Why have you been crying, Dave?" Marilyn asked her brother as her eyes pinned into Brent like a thumbtack into corkboard.

Davey kept his gaze steady with his plate as his lip quivered.

Brent looked away from Marilyn and watched the boy with a concerned expression and slouched shoulders, "hey Marilyn," his eyes slid back to her and met a dead appearance—something sober, thoughtless, in her eyes, "can we talk about this after dinner, maybe?" He squinted at her.

Marilyn tipped back in her chair and scooped the first bite of the night off her plate. She sucked the noodles slowly, cleared her throat, wiped sauce from her lips, then shrugged, "why?"

Brent continued to stare sternly at her, trying to tell her to back off with only his expression, *now is not the time, kid,* it said.

Davey bobbed his head, "it's okay, Mr. Kingsley. You can tell her."

Brent jerked his head to the boy, startled, and was met with a kid who kept a still, paralyzed stare with his food. *Mr. Kingsley?* Brent thought bewildered.

Marilyn bit down on the tip of her tongue and snickered lightly through her nose, "yeah. It's okay *Mr. Kingsley.* I don't bite. I just want to be informed about my brother's emotions. Care to brief me?" Her fingers swirled out and pointed like insect legs at her brother, almost playfully.

Brent pinched his lips together and tilted his head at her. *Brief me?* He suddenly felt like he had no idea who she was. His jaw tightened and he rolled it around in its socket until it popped sorely.

Winnifred shifted her fragile weight, "for God's sake, what the hell happened? Stop with the silent conversation you two are having with your eyeballs," She waved her clean fork in the air, "I want to be included."

Brent mimicked Marilyn's tilted back stance in her chair and ran a cupped palm over his lips, his facial hair darker and less kept at that moment. Noticeably longer, "Davey got suspended today for shoving Zach off the play structure." *Have you ever seen Matilda the movie?* As Brent watched Marilyn he noticed Winnifred's posture droop out of his peripheral and he felt guilty. *Let's talk about it after dinner*—that had been what he wanted. Why are they talking about it right now? A tinge of panic flicked against his ribs and he coughed a small burp of air.

Marilyn's overbearing anger suddenly flooded straight into him, probing his mind and swallowing brain matter into chewing gulps. Her eyes widened and as the heat spilled from her to him he noticed, for a moment, that she didn't look angry, but scared. Terrified, actually, as her relaxed stature tensed and her hand rushed to her stomach to tend to it like a mother to an unborn child.

"Why –" her body seemed to vibrate and her head dipped low, hiding her expression from the man, then her head drew back up and what Brent saw chilled him to the bone. Her olive skin now a deathly pale and her eyes predatory, "you are a fucking quack." The girl from the night before, from the playground that morning, she was back.

Brent leaned forward into the table, "that's not appropriate, Marilyn, I don't know –"

"You're supposed to protect him from this kind of bullshit! Why was he suspended?!" Her voice, God, her voice. It was high and buzzed like hornets.

Brent shook his head at her, "I'm sorry. I -"

"Oh, shut the hell up. Oh my Jesus. You –" A snarl twisted across her lips and distracted her as she let her eyes flick to Davey like vertical eyelids on a lizard, she looked at him with disgust. "What's wrong with you," she hissed towards him as her lips trembled at the boy who had begun to whine out strangled cries.

Winnifred waved a bony hand at the girl, "back off spaz, what's wrong with *you.*"

Marilyn spat a response at the woman that was cut off by Brent's hand smacking the table, "hey!" He barked at her and her head whipped to him as silence vacuum sealed the room. Brent dropped his hand to his lap and pretended it wasn't stinging. "Hey," he said again, quietly, as he fought her anger that tried to tell him to scream, "this is not the time for a breakout, kid. If you need to talk lets wait, okay?"

"Oh," Marilyn rolled her head back and the whites of her eyes gleamed over the table, "what. Talk later so you can tell me I need therapy and need to talk about my feelings, and need this and need that and need, need, need. What I got isn't good enough."

"Marilyn, I never said that."

Now it was her hands slamming into the table and making the silverware jump. Her body throwing back forward so she could jab him with her looks, "shut up." She laughed at the man, "you're not good at what you do, Kingsley. You're a *quack.*"

Brent tilted his brow, unintimidated.

Marilyn's hand fanned out to point accusingly back at Davey, "the kid carries a goddamned teddy bear around with him in his backpack! And you're just like '*oh yeah, okay, that's fucking normal!*'" Her face was darkening into a red devil as she shrugged to mock him, "you don't see anything wrong with that?!"

Brent's brow had dropped into a defending scowl, his lips parted in disbelief, "What are you doing?"

Marilyn grabbed at her hair to work it between her fingers in frustrated yanks, "The kid is a FREAK! And you're enabling it!"

Brent was on his feet, the anger that she'd tipped into him now boiling into a mixing pot of his own, owned fury, "What are you doing?!" His voice cracked against a growl as Davey collapsed into the crook of his elbow to sob wildly.

"*Jesus,*" Winnifred mumbled to herself and tried to pull Davey into her arms, the boy fought it with an audible upset tantrum as the woman's frail arms popped back, away from him. "*I didn't know I was coming over to a goddamned soap opera.*"

The last of the air in the room seemed to evaporate as Marilyn's hands tossed in the air to make a runway for her infuriating yelp–a long, drawn-out, sharp sigh that made Brent's hair nip upward on the back of his neck.

"Kid."

"Shut up!" Her shriek broke through a young female body that had been flung up, out of her chair, her hips thrust harshly into the wooden table, "Shut up!!"

"Marilyn."

"You are useless! You have done nothing, *nothing* good for us!"

Brent shook his head at her words and at the radio signal between them that had been chanting *hit her, hit her, hit her* came back again like a demonic carnival ride.

"You're a —"

"Stop!" Brent's neck began to heat into the visible red that had claimed his face.

"Davey is fucked up because of you!"

"Davey is old enough to speak for himself, Mari! He's FINE! He's normal! He's healthy!"

"He's psychotic!"

Winnifred reached back out for the boy and this time Davey caved into her without protest: *he's right in front of you guys'* the elderly woman thought. Then, *I'm too old for this shit.*

Brent pressed his hands into his face as he visibly shook against their shared signal, "Davey —"

"—Is fucked up because of you!"

"Stop saying that!" Brent cried, "Davey would be stuck in the system if I'd let you take care of him on your own!"

"Oh, my hero!"

Brent felt Winnifred glaring into him and dropped his head to her and the crying boy. Reality crashed into him like a car wreck and he fell back into his chair suddenly, his face softening and his heart pulsing a rhythm into his hot ears, "Dave," he whispered to the child who wouldn't look at him, "I'm sorry, bud. I'm sorry." He lifted his head to Marilyn with defeat, his nostrils flexing, "Marilyn, please sit down. I'm sorry. This has gotten out of hand."

The girl shifted her weight.

"Let's just talk about it after dinner."

"I'm not hungry."

His temper quaked, "Marilyn, sit."

The girl locked him in a cold stare, slid her plate above her fingers and lifted it into the air like a diner waitress. The plate balanced on her fingertips for a long, still moment, before she tipped it. The spaghetti crept off the ceramic dish and splashed like a wet rag into the tabletop, red sauce flicking across the wooden dinner space as the plate bounced back up and the girl studied its empty surface. Brent's lips parted slowly and as they did she lifted the plate higher, then threw it down. It clipped the table and shattered in a waterfall around her. Shards of white glass powdered up in the aftermath of the crash and Brent's hand shot out to try to protect the young boy and elderly woman from it as he got up to his feet again.

"Seriously?!" Brent barked as his temper capsized.

Tulsa bounded from under the table and into the kitchen, frightened by the argument.

"No please," Marilyn's features blanked into a misused canvas, "please sit down and tell the dinner party about how: If it'd been up to *me* Davey would be rotting away in foster care," Her words had been spit out with wet speed but now she seemed to take a second to lower her voice and steady her breathing, her stare with him unfaltered, "probably getting *molested* by some foster sister." She smirked knowingly then pivoted towards Brent's bedroom with the words hung on imaginary meat hooks in front of the man.

Brent's throat tightened and his body paralyzed. *How had she known about that?*

She hadn't. The moths did. They spoke from the parts of her bones they'd hollowed out and puppeted her feet carelessly over the broken glass.

"Marilyn!" Brent yelped woundedly as he came out from the table after her, "Marilyn MAE!" He had lunged forward to catch her arm but found it stuck in hesitation as the name he'd called echoed back to him. His hand retracted as quickly as it'd come out and he thought: *Why did I say that?* He hadn't known where it came from, the use of her middle name, he'd heard Davey say it before, but why had *he* said it. He had a split second to think that maybe it was because of their theatrical *fatherly-daughterly* argument they were having, then: *that's not good* before the girl had whirled a full hundred and eighty degrees and her open hand had slammed into the side of his face.

The slap snapped crisply in the room and his jaw cracked out of a tight clench, "Don't you dare call me that!" Marilyn gagged as she stumbled back from him.

Her hand had clipped the corner of Brent's eye that now stung and dropped watery tears against the cold air as he blinked, stunned at her. She looked horrified. Traumatized. *Human.* Like it was really *Marilyn* staring back at him and no longer the angry face that belonged to the girl that had yanked Davey off the air mattress and made a scene in the school's playground. The anger he'd felt dusting off of her like the desert floor caught in wind.

Then her brow-line darkened and a gust of her frustration blasted into Brent as she hardened back into something heartless. She pivoted back around and strode to his bedroom to slam the door behind her.

Brent ran after her, to his bedroom, unable to stop himself as resentment pulsed into his bloodstream. The door seemed to mock him as it blocked him from the tantruming girl and he suddenly felt as though he couldn't breathe, "Marilyn," he spoke against the barricading door frame and then tried the knob. It jiggled in his hand but refused him against a lock. Panic, *abandonment,* struck a nerve and sweat beat from open pores as Brent shook the knob below his fist, "Marilyn!" His voice bounced off the wood and cocooned a web around his face to stab harshly into his ears without a response. Rage burst out of the center of his suffocating chest, "GODDAMMIT!" He bawled and tilted back to throw the heel of his foot into the door. The door bent on its hinges then slung back solidly, the lock making a bitter *hammer into plaster* pound against the forced movement. He rammed the base of his palms into the temples of his head that ached against rushing blood and let out a cry of frustration as his anxiety beckoned, (*No, it forced*) him to face flooding memories of Amanda.

He broke away from the hallway and dribbled his feet numbly back to the dining room as Amanda's smile whipped across his imagination. He kept his hands at the sides of his forehead as his eyes welled blurring, wet lines through his vision and small seizure gusts of breath strung sticky saliva from his swollen lips, "*Winnie —*" he croaked like a child and buckled his knees to keep from falling over as his breathing continued to thicken in panic.

The woman, who had Davey's head tucked into her shoulder and her hands around his ears to mute the fight as much as possible, turned her eyes to the sorry sight of a grown man. He had a visible hand welt kissed across his cheek and lower eyelid that she frowned at as his nose reddened and he struggled to keep tears from dropping down the length of his face. She gave him a brief nod backward towards the apartment door. It was a green light, a *"go, I got this"*.

So Brent went. His lungs gulped at the fresh air as he yanked the apartment door shut behind him and dropped his back into it. His lungs then rejected the fresh air and he saw tunnel vision for a moment before it was replaced by vertigo from the distance between him and the girl as he ran down the stairs. His knees bounced up as his feet jabbed into the cement steps and created that musical echo between the painted walls of the apartment building. He could see his 4Runner gleaming at him from the parking lot and he moved to it with no intent to drive it. The hood reflected a tired-looking man with a tight, twisted face and cord-like ropes bulging from his neck.

Breathe, breathe, breathe. A memory whispered against the inside of his skull and he nodded to it.

He stumbled over the sidewalk and knelt beside his vehicle and leaned his shoulder against the wheel well. The pressure of his thigh pressed firmly into his abdomen forced a long sigh from his chest and relief began to warm his throat and lungs as he swallowed in air to fill its place. Out again. In. Out. In.

He forgot to release the breath as he quivered and became distracted by the cool air around him, his mind drifting along with the breeze and his breath pinched back inside him. *I just wanted to help.* His thought came back like a boomerang and the breath in his chest became caught by another anxious clot. He laid a hand against the cool metal of his Toyota and began to pant against the pain as the thoughts continued to come unwanted. *You failed her. You failed to protect her. What happened on Saturday? You weren't there to stop it. This is your fault. All you wanted was to fix her. She was a project to you, not a person, and you failed.* He thought of the look she had, the afraid panic in her face as she gripped at her stomach. He thought of her discarded shirt and bra in his bedroom. He thought about *the Boogie Man.* "I just wanted to help," He whispered to himself. His pathetic, tight voice startled him and he stood up, away from it. The 4Runner reflection shaped his body like a funhouse mirror that mocked him and he walked away from that too—down into the parking lot to follow the lines of cars to the complex driveway. He felt sick. Disgusted. *TOO CLOSE.*

Breathe, that memory plundered back—sweaty against his soaring imagination and for a moment, as his face scrunched, he thought he might start to sob but then it passed and he was left panting and walking and trying to *give himself a break.*

The break came eventually. Like out sweating a fever, and he was able to breathe steadily again. His boiled thinking dialed down into a low simmer.

92

Marilyn was propped up against the side of Brent's bed with a clump of his sheets between her lips and teeth as she let out guttural cries from the foamy walls of her stomach. The wicked haze she'd been swaddled in had lifted and she'd begun to realize what she'd done. Full, pure, Marilyn pre-moth possession was present in her headspace as the moths napped inside her joints and nerve nettings. Full, pure, Marilyn was now seeing Nick's death, feeling Nick's death, smelling Nick's death.

Her body trembled tirelessly and her eyes poured thick, stinging fluid as her teeth tightened down into the blanket and she screamed again, her scream pitched off into a shriek then broke off into a convulsion of sick coughs. She cried again at the pain and shut her eyes to try to mute the memory.

Nick's face twisted and the blood draining from the gap in his flesh displayed in full color against her dark eyelids and she flung them open with another bawl against the slobbery sheets.

What had she done?

She imagined his body sprawled in the empty, cold bed. Left there until someone found him. Would anyone find him? Would his corpse rot into a shriveled scent of oozing fluid and eroded bones?

A laser-like surgical burn began to darken her senses and she bared her teeth into Brent's sheets. She knew then that it was them, the moths, trying to take their spots back into the driver's seat of her psyche. She punched a fist into Brent's bed mattress and felt the insects protest inside her. She wouldn't let them control her any longer. It was over.

The moths began to burrow a hole somewhere deep within the lining of her stomach as a threat. The girl released her teeth from the sheets and sobbed sharply into her hand that clasped tightly around her slobbery mouth as the contraction of insect teeth rippled through her.

Her imagination played back over Nick's bloodied face, then Davey's as she'd screamed into it, then Winnifred's as she waved a wrinkly arm at the asshole girl, then Brent's. *Molested by some foster sister.* There had been hurt in his eyes that tunneled down into the foundation of his soul as she'd said those words. A scar that she'd pride open with a crowbar. That *they* had pride open. That she *let* them pry open.

Marilyn punched her closed fist into her stomach and reminisced on the shallow pain she'd felt from it. Pain she'd felt by choice. They attacked it from the inside and she ground her teeth together until she could feel the bone rubbing agony in the top of her skull.

"Leave me alone!" She cried hoarsely into the palm of her hand. She leaned into herself and her fist that still pressed into her stomach and began to sob uncontrollably, *"please,"* she muttered as her slobbery hand that had been over her mouth ran shakily through her hair. *"Leave me alone, please."*

Nick's face liquified in her mind and rolled courses down her cheeks as she cried.

Her mind then silenced into a grey whisper that steamed like ground fog across a blank plain and Marilyn became hushed. Still. *Waiting.* She waited for a twitch in her hand, or a tear from her eye, or a *thought.*

And that *thought* did come—riding in on a black horse through that steel fog that had made her skull into an empty cavern for this thought to rest.

Suicide.

It was silky as it wrapped around her brain matter and tangled like baby skin into dark, unclean places she'd forgotten existed. It had a satin towel that dusted her chaos off and polished her sanity. It wore a velvet mask and danced around its feather smooth hair that hung to its knees in wavy, tangled strands of flowing, liquid brunette.

Suicide.

Marilyn surrounded herself with the fine cotton thought and found comfort in its presence. Still, sleek comfort. But then it faced her and she saw its eyes. Sunken and beady below black shadows, its jaw unhinged and smiling. She began to whimper to herself as it continued to lace its silk dress around her in delicate weaves. Her feet stung in the still air of Brent's bedroom and she wondered if she'd cut them as she'd walked across the glass. She hadn't even *cared.* The moths had dulled her down to something lifeless.

Suicide.

She pressed a hand to her fevering forehead as she considered it. Considered taking her own life. Her face purpled above a belt triage as her limbs hung damply below her—like a potted plant drooping from a porch awning. Then her dead face was replaced by her father's and Marilyn was ten years old again, looking up at him with clumps of her pulled out hair in her hands.

The girl in Brent's bedroom became sick with grief.

Suicide?

She could *never!* She would never do to Davey what her father had done to her. Her dad was a *coward!* Her dad left her because he couldn't handle it anymore? Couldn't take being a father to a newborn and a little girl. *A selfish coward.*

Marilyn began to feel angry as she remembered that she *hated* her father for what he'd done. Her temperature spiked and she climbed up onto Brent's bed where she'd once laid shirtless.

She thought of the *Boogie Man's* belt that had stolen the air from her lungs and sealed off her airway and shook her head at Brent's ceiling, "I would never." *I would rather rot in a cement box then kill myself.* It was what she deserved. Her eyes shut and she saw Nick again as the moths bathed in her self generated fury at her father.

Never, she thought as the silky darkness tried to beckon her again. The idea of suicide frightened her into trembles.

Never.

She began to cry again.

Brent came home sometime later, his head fuzzy and his limbs light from being walked too long. There was a knot abnormally lodged in the pit of his stomach that still worked in anxious twists, although his urge to cry had long since passed.

He stood beside the empty air mattress and studied the dining table, now in front of a black window, untouched plates of food laid across its surface like bloated carcasses. Brent huffed painfully and moved to the table. Winnifred and Davey were gone and a note swooped in fine ink, laid ghostly against the front of the elderly woman's plate. Her food had looked like jello after being sat out to cool and stale—Brent glanced around the table—all of the spaghetti looked like that. Even the pile of upturned sauce and noodles on Marilyn's side. That painful huff came again and his chest sagged with it.

The note Winnifred had left stared up at him, its ink fresh:

I'll watch D.
See you after you get off work— Tomorrow.

Unlike the note Marilyn had left him to beg him for milk, Brent didn't keep this one in his wallet. Instead, he slipped it into his hand and walked it to the trash can. Then he retrieved a broom from his small, half-door pantry, and walked back to the shattered glass around the floor to sweep.

He'd showered after that, the plates and untouched food left for him to clean up the next morning. Left to stale from jello to tiny mounds of rock in his dimly lit dining room. He didn't care.

Brent waded his feet in the shower and thought of Amanda.

"Don't be so quick to anger," Mom Onslow had once said to him sternly as she pinned his young body in her lap, "It makes you look foolish Brenty-boy." Her voice had been loud next to his ear and he remembered flinching away from it. He'd been older then, maybe seven, and Amanda had touched him –

Brent stood under the cold, trickling water in his shower and scraped his nails along his skull like he was washing it. "Bad," he mouthed against the stream of water that crept through his lips as he thoughtlessly talked to himself.

Amanda had touched him *bad.* Wrong. It had scared him. Her disgusting hand that grabbed for him, the smiled snarl in her face, the suffocating fear of being trapped there by her.

Brent began to pant against the cold water, lost deeply in the memory, and the cool water felt good against his cotton tongue.

He remembered he'd lashed out at the girl and scratched her, drawing blood across her plump cheek. He'd been spanked for that by Dad Onslow's callused worker hand. Then he'd been handed off to Mom Onslow who'd spoken instructions into his ear as he'd cried, *"don't be so quick to anger."*

Amanda had gotten away with what she'd done. She'd said she'd tried to hug him and he'd reacted like a spooked cat. Brent remembered wondering if it had been just a hug, then feeling guilty for his overreaction. He wondered why he'd panicked like she had been doing something naughty as he sat in his foster mom's lap against his will. Was his mind dirty? Was that something he'd gotten from his biological parents?

It hadn't mattered what he thought, because Amanda had come to his bed that night —

Brent turned his head up and let the icicle shower water stab him in the face. He opened his eyes against it and hoped it'd pressure wash the memory away as he felt vomit build in his throat with an always familiar acidic burn.

93

Something stroked along the side of Marilyn's cheek. Something smooth and slightly wrinkled with age. A finger, perhaps. It conjured her up out of deep sleep as it brushed down towards her chin. She strained her neck to lean into it, her eyelids still blanketed over her conscious eyes, she felt comforted by it. It trailed back up her waking skin and started its path back down to her chin once again.

Marilyn's sleep drunken mind warped her back into her childhood to put the touch in place. Brent's bedsheets had washed away below her and her twin-sized, baby pink, bedsheets took their place. She smiled and felt drool rub into the cheek that was smashed into her *Lisa Frank* pillowcase. She knew what the touch was now, the gentle brushes of leathery skin, it was her Father. His gentle knuckle of his forefinger running a silky line down her face, her hair that'd been mopped over in curls now pushed back behind her ear.

He always did this. On the nights he'd get home late from work, or the nights when Mom wouldn't show up after an argument and he'd get restless. He always would come into her room. Sometimes Marilyn would never know he'd stopped by, her father, Vaughn, had been good at sneaking in and kissing his daughter's fuzzy head without tipping off her radar. He'd kiss it, and pray for her, then kiss it again. Sometimes, however, as he'd pray his finger would stroke her cheek—as it was doing now. Usually, when he did this she'd wake up, sometimes to flutter her eyes open and tell him, "*hello*" before he whispered for her to go back to sleep.

But Marilyn had gotten good at pretending his touch hadn't stirred her from a dream. She'd feel it and wake but keep her breathing low and her eyelids drawn. She'd started doing this so she could lay for a long time and hear her father's whisper to God without Vaughn knowing. Her visits with him seemed longer that way because instead of him telling her to go back to sleep and leaving, he'd just stand there—over his daughter and talk. He'd talk for a long time, like a silky lullaby over the girl's tired ears. That'd been Marilyn's favorite. His voice like rain falling into her dreams that would eventually take her away again.

Tonight, however, she couldn't stay still—she couldn't just lay and listen. Tonight she was too excited to see him. Too excited to bring her eyelids into her head and reveal her red-rimmed eyes to him. She had missed him, all though, at that moment as the drool on her pillow seemed to cool against her, she couldn't remember why she missed him—or how long it'd been.

"Hi dad," she mumbled and her voice sounded odd, loud in her tiny room that sat across the hall from Davey's new nursery. It wasn't a voice she'd been used to hearing come from her body at the age of ten, it was deeper and older—mature. But it seemed to be hers?

Marilyn reached a heavy arm up and tried to grip at the wrist of her father's gently painting hand over her cheek. She missed and her hand flopped down against the bed. She tried again and missed again, her hand swiping through cold air and past the hand on her cheek, "Dad?" she croaked as she peeled her sticky eyelids open.

Brent's bedroom rushed her at a horrific speed and crashed against her to make her feel sick and misdirected. A headache stung awfully at the base of her neck and her eyes gauged the man's walls.

Marilyn was an eighteen-year-old again.

But the hand—*it brushed down the clear peach fuzz on her cheek*—it was still there. She strained her eyes and tried to see her father standing beside her—her brain still halfway submerged in a dream. He wasn't there. *Dad's dead.* But the pressure of the hand...

Marilyn scrunched her chin to her neck with muscles that protested at the back of her head and tried to see it—try to see the hand. It was there, suspended out with the finger that'd been against her paused in its movement. It seemed green, ghastly, glowing. Her brow furrowed together as her eyes continued to adjust like camera lenses. The hand—was just a hand—*nothing more.*

No wrist, arm, elbow, bicep, shoulder, or body seemed to come after it. Just a hand.

A hand? Just a hand? Just a hand?

Marilyn used her elbow to wedge herself back, further away from it, to try to get a better look. But it moved.

Marilyn drowned in a sharp inhale of shocked breath as the fingers and palm came at her face, spread out like a jumping spider. It dropped away from her wide expression and clasped to her neck, then slid to the center of her chest, then quickly down the remaining length of her body. It hesitated for a split second at the bone of her ankle to grip tightly and yank. Marilyn's paralyzed body was shifted down the bed and her leg burned from the gripped jolt of the hand.

She sat up against the tug that had wedged the bedsheets against her in thick balls of fabric and began to moan half-developed screams from her tight, clammy throat. Her eyes bulged and she slammed her open palms into the empty bed around her, her fingers striking into the sheets half a moment later, like tiny whips. The first awake thought that came to her came like a blunder of birds into a window: someone else was in the bed. Someone had snuck through the apartment and had slid into the bed with her. Someone.

She yanked the sheets off her legs and kicked furiously against the sweat wet mattress. But there was no one. Nobody but herself inside the boat of a bed. The king for Kingsley. She ran a hand along the edge of the mattress and tried to regulate that pumps of air coming from her lungs with a distant thought: *I actually think this bed is only a queen.*

She pressed the back of her hand to her mouth and groaned into it.

There was nothing.

Nothing.

The hand was a nightmare.

There was —Light.

Brent's bedroom fixture, shaped strangely like a salad bowl, illuminated and brought the sleeping room to life. Silence rang through her ears in a static that laid only on the floor of her ear canal as her eyes flinched and ached against the glare. Her heart hammered heavy and her breathing had sunk into swallowed gags as she continued to study the room. Her sight caught the flicked up light switch at the edge of Brent's closed–*locked*–door. She stared at it without blinking, afraid to look away. Afraid to move. Her hands contracting and collecting bits of blanket in their fists absently.

She thought then that she wanted to yell for Brent, she knew he had come home, she could recall that now, she'd heard the scrape of glass as he swept up the mess around the table and the run of water as he showered. Yes, that's right: She'd heard the shower head spit unhappily against the water that always pooled up around her ankles as she showered. Yes—she remembered. He *was* home. She remembered. So she sat there and contemplated yelling for him.

Her chest tightened and she knew, as the hair on her neck and arms pricked up under goosebumps, that if she did yell for him it'd come out more like a scream. A shriek even. A shriek that would tear her throat open as she began to cry and shiver. She knew that would be what would happen, but at the moment all she could do was sit and stare without blinking, her body completely frozen.

She wished he'd just walk in. To check in on her, like her father always had. Pray over her, slid his finger along her cheek in a slow, kind rhythm as she tumbled back into a dream.

Really, she just wished she wasn't alone. That's what it came down to, yes. She wanted Brent to step through the door, his husky voice lathered with sleep, his eyes wide with concern, *"I was worried about you. Are you okay, Marilyn?"* She imagined he'd say and she'd say: "yes, I am okay." She mumbled the words out loud to the lightened bedroom as she thought over the scenario in her head. "I'm okay."

But then he'd say he didn't believe her and he'd say he would sleep on the floor, just beside the bed, to make sure she stayed safe, "thank you," she said aloud to the fantasy. "I don't want to be alone in here."

"You're not."

Marilyn's head snapped around to the familiar voice that broke the sting of silence in her ears. The *rotten* voice. He was there, crouched at the foot of the bed, just his eyes poking up to hold her vibrating vision. Hold it like he owned it.

He was in that blue cotton shirt he'd been in the day they kissed, she noticed, as he crawled his tall body onto the mattress with achy limbs and a dark smile that stretched his cheeks into strained muscles. His brown, lappy hair flopped over his forehead in whisker whisps.

The shriek she'd been afraid of before tore through her esophagus brightly now, like the white of a flame, or the bleeding claw of nails from the inside of a closed coffin. Her legs twitched and kicked and he crawled over them, his hands working up the length of her skin as that broken, long smile only seemed to stretch wider, farther, until the corners of it were separating his ears. So wide she could see where his teeth ended and his cheekbones started. His lips peeled the skin back from his face.

He purred at her pitched cry, "Hey, *Kid.*"

94

Brent had fallen asleep on the couch after his shower, his leg draped over the seat cushion and a stiff fabric pillow stuffed against his face. He'd woken up slowly to the heavy flutter of Marilyn's heart against his own chest. He shifted his weight against the couch and dropped the pillow that'd made imprints on his forehead and cheek beside the deflated air mattress that took up the rug space of his living room. Marilyn's heartbeat continued to interrupt his sleep and *finally* calm breathing. Brent pinched his lips together and assumed it was a nightmare she was having as his large hand glided across his chest and held her heartbeat below it. His flesh was hot beneath his shirt from the friction and his stomach had begun to upset against the rapid pulse. He had laid still for a while with Marilyn's heart, above his own, cradled in the palm of his hand.

He thought: *I should get up and make sure she's okay,* but his eyes had begun to feel weighted and he'd let them fall shut against his better judgment. Sleep had begun to trace itself over him again when he'd been spurred awake by a gut punch of terror and the undeniable, never-ending, blare of ripping human vocals.

It had startled him to his feet to the hall and to his *door.* His locked bedroom. His cheek had spasmed against the inside of his mouth in a fight against his biting teeth that he hadn't realized he'd been using to *pinch*, blood now drifting across his taste buds and filling the back of his throat with the aroma of copper. *Iron.*

"Marilyn!" Her name had drowned below her racks of sore breath that came out of her body like peeling paint from the other side of his bedroom entry, "MARILYN!" Sleep had fallen from his voice like phlegm from a hard cough as he rammed his foot, for the second time that night, into the door. It fought back against him and his hip throbbed into his lower back as he stumbled a step away from it. The white wooden door. A slender, bullying barricade.

It palmed panic back into his chest. Tight anxiety. *I am between you and her* it seemed to remind as it loomed against him in a moonlit spotlight.

No, Brent thought as his foot came back up to kick, *was the moon even out tonight?*

Marilyn's shredded vocal chamber broke like chains against Brent's skull and he collapsed forward with a girthy kick into the center of the white wooden frame. His heel felt as if the skin had begun to splinter and curl away from its bone.

His hand went to the handle and felt the cold of its metal against his trembling fingers—he hadn't noticed he'd been trembling until then, "Marilyn!"

Her strained voice broke off at the door and the apartment fell silent, an eerie end to the sound of her anguish. Brent's ear was wedged into the wood to try to hear her through its thick panel but the silence of his bedroom on the other side met him with a long, horrid hiss of distilled bedroom air.

Brent backed away from the door, far away, his face flushed and his heart hammering a beat against Marilyn's now slow steady pulse. He planned to rush the door, his head bowed and his knees bending to embrace the ground with the flat of his feet for a solid lunge. He was going to throw himself into it. Yes, that was the plan. It would work, he was sure.

He was stopped from running at his bedroom by a flick of light across a *turning* doorknob. He straightened up and watched the silver knob carefully, unsure if he'd seen it clearly. It twitched again, slightly, as if it was being unlocked.

" Kid?" He mumbled through his tightened down jaw that had been grinding his molars together.

His bedroom door popped open from its latch and a sliver of bedroom light joined him in the hallway.

"Are you okay?!" He asked and couldn't help but hear how frantic his voice sounded in the sleeping apartment and he rushed through the now unlocked, partly open, door. He had expected to run chest to chest with the girl, who'd unlocked the door for him—*he thought*—but instead found himself stopped against the inside of his room, panning his eyes from the base of his bed to the ceiling.

Marilyn was there, awake, and standing. She was standing at the center of his bed, her spine stretched in a straight posture line and her head tilted back to stare up. Her neck worked as she made tiny gasps from her jittery lips like she was being suffocated.

For a moment Brent could see his bedroom without his bed in it, Marilyn's feet two plastic school rulers from the floor, a *purple Crayola noose* tied tight beneath her chin. The vision came so clearly to him that he'd stumbled back into the door that had slammed solidly closed again against his falling weight, "Marilyn!" He yelped as a dull ache sobbed at his spine. Her head tilted down to him and as it did so his bed flicked back into his vision and the noose evaporated into the dark parts of his thoughts, away from the light.

She stared at him for a long moment before she dropped her knees and landed with a tiny bounce on his bed. Her legs folded in *Indian Style* and her arms placed in her bowl-shaped lap. The blankets seemed to wave up in warm, slept in mountains around her and her face sagged slowly into a fearful expression.

She looked so young like that, young like Davey. Brent stepped away from the door, he wanted to run forward and scoop her into his arms where he could rock and comfort her. He wanted to, but he knew he couldn't, and he also knew that right then—at the moment—he was afraid of her. Terrified.

"Please stay away from me," She vibrated harshly as her eyes welled into tears.

"Marilyn", Brent felt certain as he watched her flinch away from his voice that she was just as scared of him as he was of her, maybe even more scared.

"Get out."

Brent teetered on his feet like he was caught in a breeze. The girl's lip lifted and he thought he could hear her *growling*.

"GET —" Marilyn rushed him from the bed, her feet tripping over the floor as she ran at him, "OUT!" She was stabbing her nails at him in swipes, swats and slaps as she came at him, "GET OUT, GET OUT, GET OUT, GET OUT!" Her head jerked and spasmed against her stringy thought as Brent staggered backward into the door, away from her foaming lips, "GET OUT GETOUT GET GTOUTGET GO GETOUT OUT!!!!!"

Brent's hands had found their way to his chest where they gripped at his static skin from above his shirt, his breath caught beneath the pressure of his working fingers. He was curling away from her just as his hair had begun to curl just the same up against the sweat off his forehead.

She threw a fist at him and he sidestepped away from it as she screamed.

"What are you doing?!" He felt his lips form in the shape of the yelped words, but his voice had been lost within her thrashing void, "kid!"

He'd fallen from the door as he stepped away from her and found himself shuffled into the closest corner.

Her snarl widened, "GET —" the snarl dropped. Everything in her— dropped. She was a hollow shell held up only by a stiff spine, everything else saggy and darkened from life. From free will, from thought, she stared to the side of him with dull, doll-like eyes. Like a blind dog. A hand lifted from her side and she rubbed gently into the bottom of her dropped lip until it turned into a dry, slobberless red.

Brent drank a line of breath in through his clamped chest and stepped out of the corner, his back wet with itchy sweat.

The door to the bedroom beside them opened. Brent's eyes flexed at it and for a moment he thought he saw a third person in the room, leaned into the frame of the door, its hand against the open door's handle. He fluttered his eyelids at a tempo three beats faster than his pulse and the person shadowed against his sight.

Marilyn cleared her throat, "Brent?"

Brent turned his head back to her and met her dead eyes, "Yes?"

"Yes, sweetheart?" A second voice answered, cutting the man off.

Brent looked back into the shadows but the tall body was no longer there. *Was that my voice?* He thought as he suddenly felt exhausted, like all the sleep he'd shaken off while trying to get into the room had come back heavier now. His mouth dried and his eyelids tightened over his sight.

Marilyn shook her head against the response, "*I want him out.*" She looked directly into Brent as she spoke.

Brent burrowed his brows and he felt comatose stick his back with a sharp finger against his spine. Like it was striking a match along the bumps of his vertebrates.

The man woke up on the couch slowly and noted, as he rolled to his side, the fat ache on either side of his throbbing head. His eyes peeled open against grey daylight and met Marilyn's calm, awake face. She sat against an edge of the air mattress as she worked a pair of shoes over her socked feet. She smiled gently at him, "good morning," she blinked and her eyelids seemed to stick to the surface of her eyes for a moment, "we're going to be late for work."

Brent sat up with a gasp and the room spun in cloud-covered Oregon light, "I had a nightmare," he hissed. He looked into Marilyn's eyes as the image of her standing in the center of his bed skated itself across his hot fleshed forehead, "a bad nightmare." As he said it he watched her slow blinking eyes pale and distance themselves from meeting his gaze slowly and he *knew*. He *knew* it wasn't a nightmare. He closed his eyes and remembered the sound of his voice *Yes, Sweetheart?* He'd heard it say.

"Yikes." Marilyn said like she was bored and Brent reopened her eyes to watch her casually shrug and loop a shoelace around another bunny ear lace, "that sucks."

He pinched his lips together and nodded, "what happened last night?" He wasn't sure if the question was to her or just to himself, but had met her unimpressed stare anyway.

"We got in an argument."

He shook his head drunkenly before grimacing to himself as he thought: *How did I get back on the couch?*

Marilyn smiled distantly as if she'd heard his inner turmoil, "bad nightmare." She confirmed.

Brent hissed a breath in over his tongue that he bit sharply, he felt like he had the flu then, his body sticky with cold sweat.

95

Davey's legs stretched against purple bed sheets as he curved his back into a squishy bed pillow that'd been propped up behind him like a couch cushion. The sheets held his legs in warmth and he curled his toes against the comfort.

He felt sick, *or,* at least felt as if he *should* feel sick. The boy nodded to himself and the thought. *Yes,* if he was sick—maybe with a bad cold or the flu—he wouldn't feel guilty for being home while everyone else was at school. A frown cast across his lips and he stretched his legs again until the back of his knees felt strung and sore.

He'd slept against a pool of tears on the couch the night before and had been woken by Winnifred, who had given him a denturless smile. She'd helped him from the stiff seat cushions and walked him to her bedroom, *"how about a good ol' day in bed?"* She had said as he climbed her sheets to sit across the mattress, *"stay here, I'll bring you breakfast!"* And she had, ten minutes later.

The boy glanced to the nightstand where a half bowl of eaten oatmeal and an empty glass of milk sat. His stomach cramped and he thought that maybe he would've enjoyed the oatmeal better if Winnifred hadn't emptied her entire sugar jar into it. He could still feel the gritty white against his tongue as he smiled distastefully at it.

Winnifred had also brought him a rusty clipboard of browning printer paper and stale wax crayons—he looked at the stack of pages and Crayola in his lap now as he thought about her quick waddle into the room and her irritated foot that kicked at her cat as she put the antique art supplies into his lap, *"draw me something pretty, boy,"* she had instructed kindly with a compressed smile wrinkled against her lips.

He'd drawn Marilyn. Her face a circular set of scribbled lines and her hair curly-Q'd like pasta noodles down past the circle's chin. Her eyes were hard-pressed dots in brown, dusty crayon and her lips had been drawn in red—a thin, stick figure smile. She was happy. He held a pink crayon tightly in his fist now as he colored blotches of pink at her cheeks. *Happy.*

The last time he'd seen her happy—

His thoughts trailed off as he tried to remember against white wisps of blank memories.

Her loud, boisterous laugh rang at his ears then to remind him what *happy* sounded like, but still, he had to fight hard to remember the last time he'd heard it? At the store? When they first moved in with Brent?

Davey bit at his lip nervously as he set the drawing of his sister aside to stare at a blank, browning printer paper canvas. He thought to draw Brent but had dismissed the idea quickly before he could even lift a crayon. The thought of Brent made the back of his neck ache and he ran his tongue through his teeth and over his lips and felt the creamy residue of milk against his parched skin.

"Davey would be stuck in the system if I'd let you take care of him on your own!" Brent said the night before.

Brent didn't have faith in Davey's sister—and that was that.

Davey frowned, hurt by the idea, hurt inside the feelings that wanted to protect Marilyn.

It was Brent's fault, really. Davey wouldn't get bullied of Brent didn't exist, or pay such close attention to him. Brent wasn't safe anymore. It wasn't safe to have Brent's name branded over the kid's head, made him a sheep among mean hunters.

He began to draw absently as his jaw tightened and his throat burned. He was drawing Daisy—strong, the *Queen and King* of the world to him.

If Zachary hadn't pushed her, if he'd just left them alone, Davey wouldn't have dreamt of the boat.

He slid the paper with Daisy drawn against the center of it off his lap and reached for a green Crayola crayon. He then began to scribble a green boat. He didn't understand it—the boat, the dream, the rock.

He closed his eyes and worked hard to remember the cave tunnel that came up out of the water like a gaped mouth of a fish. His eyes stayed closed like that, crayon tightly held in his fist, until he could feel the damp boat wood below his feet. He began to imagine himself walking the length of the boat, along the railing, and the sound of his muffled footsteps and licking ocean water began to fill his senses. It was becoming clearer now. He walked to the lipped railing of the boat and peered over it to the water.

(Hello again, Davey.)

Davey's body jerked and his eyelids flapped back open to take in the silent warmth of Winnifred's bedroom. The rock's voice, low and gurgled, distanced itself from his hearing with a trail of pulsed sound waves.

Davey widened his eyes and leaned harder into Winnifred's propped up bed pillow as the memory of Zachary's body lifting by itself and tumbling over the rail of the play structure presented itself to him. The rock in his dream had done it. It had crashed through Davey's chest and Davey had felt his eyes turn hot inside his eye sockets, and then Zachary had been thrown without anybody touching him.

It had been the rock.

(Hello again, Davey.)

He shook his head until he was sure his brain would pour from his ears like a blended drink, then he glanced to the side of him. Bear Kingsley sat beside the boy with his glossy eyes peering into his face from matted honey mustard fur.

"*– the kid carries a goddamned teddy bear around with him in his backpack!–You don't see anything wrong with that?!*" Marilyn's voice hurt Davey's head and he glared at the stuffed toy before grabbing it by the top of the head and tossing it to the foot of the bed with disgust.

"*– He's fucked up –*"

Davey felt the heat of tears on his waterline.

Tulsa had trailed in through the doorway as Davey finished the sketch of the boat, now with a rock added below its side surrounded by blue waxy lines of water. She made a *rmph* noise in her throat as she lunged herself at the mattress and clawed her way over the edge to then wattle her way to Davey. She was a black mass of fur with a tail that stuck directly into the air like a puffy feather duster.

"Do you dream about a boat and rock too, Tuls?" Davey asked below his breath as the cat lined up with his thigh and plopped down against it.

She turned her head to him and blinked lazily.

"No?"

She meowed then head-butted him before turning over to her back, her black paws bent tiredly in the air.

He nodded: *Just me, then.*

Davey discarded the boat drawing by tossing it to the pile where the Marilyn and Daisy drawings rested. It floated casually into them with its paper edges curled up. The boy frowned at the pile of three papers and turned his head to yet another blank page. He began to sketch Tulsa.

He'd made three full-colored sketches of her, all in separate positions before she's woken up from her nap and fought back to her paws.

"Morning!" Davey said to her as she lowered her stomach to the bed and stretched her neck out. She scurried like that to the edge of the bed, her head low and her shoulder blades spurred up behind her spine like bat wings. Davey tilted his head at her and felt the stiff ache of sitting hunched over for too long, "what's wrong kitty? Bad dream?" Her ears twitched backward and her tail flicked against the bed comforter below her as she kept her stare attentive to the open doorway. A low moan began to spill from her throat in dampened drags as her back arched timidly into the air.

Dread rose through Davey like floodwater as he rolled from his butt to his hands and knees, the mattress topper squishing down against his readjusted weight. He didn't know what he'd expected to see as he crawled up behind the disturbed cat—maybe a ghost, a dark shadow, the sneer of a clown mask. The haunted possibilities were endless.

The girthy chest rumble came again from deep inside the cat and Davey peered over the edge of the bed nervously, his breath coming in small darts of wind from his nostrils. There was nothing. No ghost, no strange shadow, no *IT*. His heart lightened and he stared out across the room to the empty doorway, empty hallway, and a slivered sight of the brightly lit living room.

"You're being silly," he whispered to the cat with a voice that seemed to quake against nervous air.

Tulsa lunged from the bed and scuttled against the area rug like a cartoon, all four of her fuzzy legs pumping against the ground that continued to slide out from beneath her. Eventually, on the third swift drag of her paws, she caught her claws into the rug and gained traction that catapulted her forward. Her dashing legs threw her out of the bedroom door sideways and her body slammed into the door jam to turn her in a pivot before she hurried off out of sight, into the hidden side of the living room.

Davey hesitated at the edge of the bed, unsure if he should laugh at her or continue to feel the fright that pinched him in the fatty parts of his arms. He slid his legs through his braced front limbs and bounced from the bed to his feet cautiously. On his tiptoes he leaped to the edge of the room and leaned into the doorway, his lip folding against his top teeth. His head turned back to the unmade bed and studied Bear Kingsley, who laid face down in the corner of the mattress. He teetered against his feet and his lip flexed inside his mouth. He'd forgotten he'd felt disgusted by the bear only moments before and lunged at the bed to grab it, his feet sweating as the thought of something grabbing him from below the bed surfaced in his head.

Bear Kingsley was nabbed into his arms and he ran quickly from the room like a hot iron had been pressed into his spine. In the hallway he smothered the bear into his shut mouth and felt comfort in the way his plush fur drug against Davey's dry lips, *"Sorry, Beary,"* he said with a mousy whisper, guilty for tossing the plush toy away from him earlier.

He could see Tulsa's tail from the back of the hallway as it dropped heavily and repeatedly into the floor of the living room, "Winnifred?" Davey called her name and felt cold air respond silently and his flesh flexed into goosebumps. He walked slowly from the hallway and turned to see the full living room where Tulsa hunkered.

There was a fort, made of bedsheets and knitted blankets, at the center of the living room. Right where the air mattress was in Brent's version of this apartment. Right where he and Marilyn slept a floor boarded layer below.

Davey tapped his toes into the floor, "Winnie?"

There wasn't a response. Silence seized the air in his lungs and he closed his lips to feel the last of his breath beat around against the slimy insides of his cheeks before tumbling from his nostrils. He glanced down at the cat and watched her tail thump hard into the ground again as a deep moan slid from her body.

"It's just a fort, Tulsa," His reassurance to the feline was breathless and sounded stale inside the empty walls of the apartment.

It was strange—the fort.

In all fairness, it was nice of Winnifred to build the fort for Davey, but he hadn't heard her move the furniture to make room for the fortress of cotton and wool. He frowned at the woman's couch and armchair that had been shuffled to the edge of the room, against the wall. He hadn't even heard the tiniest scrape. It had been quiet. Like it was now.

"Winnie, are you hiding?" He smiled, "I don't like being scared, please don't jump out, I don't like it." He swallowed hard, "really. I promise. I don't like it at all—ask Marilyn." His rambling went without response and he suddenly felt as if he might need to pee. His thighs flexed together and he pinched his lips, "where are you?" He whispered against his chest, his eyes tied to the still fort.

Winnifred was hiding inside the fort, that was it, that was where she was at.

Davey scrunched his nose and took a step towards it, "please don't scare me!"

Tulsa hissed and Davey jumped away from the harsh, teeth bearing, noise. Her paw swept into the air and struck claws through the empty living room space as her hiss died into a high cry.

"Tulsa!" Davey scolded, "s'a fort!" He gestured his hand out to it as if she'd understand.

The cat ran her tongue over her nose and her upset groan distorted, like she was trying to talk to Davey, protest even.

He frowned and took another wobbly step forward. He lifted Bear Kingsley back to his face and memorized the thread count of the old bears matted, cotton fur against his upper lip and nose. The urge to urinate was stronger now as the boy furrowed his eyebrows and took yet another step as Tulsa moaning warnings from behind him. He thought he'd been wrong about the fort being made of bedsheets and knitted blankets as he got a closer look. The sheets were a pasty grey and seemed hard, see-through, crisp—like cowhide. Stretched, dry skin.

He stopped hard, halfway between a step, and swallowed against his sporadic heart. He noticed something new as Tulsa hissed again. Veins. Green tunnels that wove from one side of the opaque blankets to the other in twisting and knotting streams.

"Winnifred," his voice croaked into Bear's fur and stuffing, and his face reddened. As he stared longer his eyes became aware of the movement. The slight quiver of the fort that made it seem as if it were breathing on its own. In, out—like a fleshy lung. Saliva clung to the back of his throat like led and he felt as if he might cry, or puke.

The fort began to collapse into itself —a structural concave into something meaty and alive.

Terror bloomed through Davey as Tulsa hissed again, her paw swiping through the air, audible to his tingling ears. The fort shapeshifted. What once was a tent of sheets now stood at the center of the room, a tall—strangled—stretched—grey *monster*. Its limbs draped down with long bones and tight flesh and its eyes gleamed at Davey from hollow sockets.

The boy's legs collapsed and his tailbone collided into the ground to send a shock of rattled anguish through his spine. His vision blurred against the fall and he felt the warmth of pee glide into his underwear and against his tiny thighs—even wetting the space between the little cheeks of his butt.

The creature smiled at him with a jaw that sagged far along its body in a wet, gravitational pull. Drool coated its grey lip and drained out like lines of webs, or oily rain. Tulsa was screaming, and crying, and hissing beside the boy, her back pulled into a high arch and her pupils thinned into wild slits.

Winnifred was there, on the ground, laid out on the area rug that the *fort* had been hiding. Her dark skin was devoid of health and her eyes bulged. Her throat was a thick, boiled purple, and swelled up against her chin. Her face pumped full of blood that had begun to cool and freeze her mangled expression like stone. She had been suffocated. Strangled. Smothered. *She was dead.*

The creature swayed with satisfaction above her lifeless body.

Davey used his arms to drag himself backward as his pee smeared along the floor in front of him—his mouth a tight, broken frown as he tried to scream, tried to yell *"no!"* At the grey, smiling monster as if it would listen. It'd turn its back and leave him and the ownerless cat alone. He squealed. *"Nnnnn!!!"* The

'N' to his plea stuck like sand in his throat and shredding into his vocals, *"nnnnnn -"* he sobbed and Tulsa charged forward at the ghastly thing, her claws turning through the air. It picked the cat up—the thrashing cat—in its strange taloned hand. "– *Oooo!*" Davey screamed, "NOOO!" He shoved Bear Kingsley over his eyes and willed it away. The cry of pain from the cat, the scent of his pee and the scent of the creature, Winnifred's dead eyes.

His feet kicked into the ground and he propelled backward some more until he hit the corner living room wall that led into the hallway. The room died into a silent burn, Tulsa's low moan cut off and gone.

Davey buried Bear and head into his knees and snaked his hands to his ears, his fingers locked behind his skull. He tried to remember the rock, remember the boat, the ocean, but he couldn't.

His brain on Winnifred, Tulsa, and the monster.

Dead, dead, dead.

96

Brent's inbox was dramatic that morning as it filled with electronic mail—each delivery ding deafening and hate inducing. He ironed the butt of his palms into the bone of his eye sockets and groaned—the dinging never-ending. His eyes began to throb under his eyelids as his hands forced into the soft space below his brow bone—making his headache even worse than it had been moments before.

Ding.

He thought of Marilyn as diminished chords banged through his drained, energy-less brain and felt heartburn against the bottom of his throat. His hands left the sockets of his eyes and he felt a rush of dread fill his tight stomach as he ran them through disheveled hair, "she had woken up fine this morning," he mumbled the words to himself with a pinched expression.

Marilyn.

She had woken up just fine. Her usual distant and dewy—but not disturbed.

The way she'd stood at the center of his bed, her spine stark straight, her lips bobbing opened, then closed, as if they were gasping for air. Then her broken words *GET OUT, GET OUT* as she ran at the man…

Brent grimaced at the thought that begged to feel like a dream. Begged him to sweep it back into a little nightmare box in his brain and turn out the lights.

But he wouldn't. *Couldn't.* Because it was not.

It was not a *bad nightmare.*

It was real.

Ding.

He slowly moved his head back and forth, against his neck—his hair tousling forward against his forehead in slow swipes as his hands came back down to stroke against his cheeks, then lips. She had said his name and *his voice* had responded, he remembered that. He remembered and felt sick—because he couldn't remember what came after that. The next event that had led to him waking on the couch.

Ding.

Brent dropped his hands to his desk with a hard slap and he bit a line into the top of his lip.

Ding.

He let his head flop back against his neck and let the fluorescent bars on the ceiling of his office singe his eyesight. He wanted to run down to the main office where Marilyn was. He wanted to find her, and grab her by her shoulders, and shake her. He wanted to shake her until her dead eyes brightened and he saw *her* again. The girl who'd laughed wildly at him in the store, who referenced *Grease*, who was *such—a—smart—ASS!* He smiled despite the throb in his chest and brought his head back forward to watch his computer monitor. He wanted —

Ding.

— He wanted to bang his head against a wall.

"Hi." A voice, just as pitched and buzzy as the ding of his computer, bounced from behind him.

"Hello, Nancy," the counselor sighed to himself. He hadn't heard the bell ring against the hall corridor and thought that maybe he was better off for it—his shoulders felt heavy and he probably would've broken something at the sound of the metal ring against the wall of his office. He clenched his teeth and his jaw crunched like the sound of stuck taffy on molars.

"Hi —" she said again but then seemed to trail off.

Brent glanced through the blinds of his office window to the side of him and noticed the empty halls, deprived of good morning children. The bell *had not rung. Why are you here so early, Nancy?*

"Mr. Kingsley," her voice was a whisper, "are you hurting me?"

Brent's eyebrows knitted together hard and made his headache spiral on pins and needles, "what?"

The door to his office beat itself into the door frame with a thundering slam and he jolted around in his chair to the little girl behind him, his eyes wide and stale lips parted. Nancy glanced at the now-closed office door curiously then repeated herself, "are you hurting me?" Her voice seemed to melt into a deep howl and her eyes broadened behind her strapped on, pink rubber framed glasses.

Brent wheeled his chair backward, away from her, as her skin seemed to swell her pores into open wounds that ooze oil and blood. The mixture of bodily fluids seeped against her skin slowly at first in bubbles and sprinkled streams over her infecting flesh. Then the oily yellow texture seized into small droplets and the blood erupted from her body with a *whoosh.* Like her body was a cracked mason jar of cherry filler—*a milk carton dropped to the floor to break and splash wildly.*

Brent choked on a frightened cry as his hands rushed out to her, to help her. His hands went to her face and neck to try to plug the pores, stop the bleeding. His cry pitched as the blood fell thinner and smeared through the spaces in his fingers to turn his hands a deep red. The fluid spilled down the sleeves of his shirt and bathed against his forearm, elbow, bicep, and armpits—it clung to thick, deodorant dampened, hair in thick liquid balls of crimson. He continued to try to seal her back together with his palms and long fingers like she was an inflatable boat. Like they were going to sink.

Blood splashed into Brent's face.

Nancy was smiling as her body crumbled below his touch, her lips drawn into an inhuman grin that sagged against her extending lower jaw. Her eyes dividing to make room for beady dots that stared through him. Her body bloated, creaking against its ripping seams and his hands. Blood washed from her in thick waterfalls that now coated his office floor in stewed liquid.

The small body stretched until it burst and a hellfire rain of hot, chunky blood washed over his seated frame like boiled Gatorade at a football game. *We won, coach!* He stood against the red rain and stumbled forward on weak legs as his feet tried to wade against the pool that filled his office. Waded like he was in the shower at home—in the calf-high tepid water. But now the water was red and thick.

It continued to grow from the floor, the small room *bleeding* on its own, seeping in through the corners of his walls and crashing with warped, rushed, gurgles into the pool around his ankles. Then his shins and knees. It soaked through his pants as it continued to roll up his legs to his thighs. Then his hips. It squished through his zipper and made him feel as though he soiled himself. He moved towards the door but was forced back, like he'd been trying to swim against a wicked whirled wave.

It was over the peak of his hips. Dread heaved itself into his throat and came out his nose in hot streams of panic as the blood washed thickly through his shirt and licked at his navel. Brent gagged as his hands stroke the hot mess in a swimming motion, he could taste the drenching scent of iron at the back of his tongue and wanted to vomit. Wanted to scream, quake, cry.

He thought of his 4Runner—the way it had jerked as the engine block was smashed into oblivion. He thought of the way it had gleaned at him as he spoke with the traffic cop, untouched and unscratched. The way it had purred into the driver's seat he had sat in and then showed him a clean-shaven, healthy reflection—his nose unbroken, his face free of blood or pain.

It was all so *insane*. He was *insane*. Wasn't he? It was the only plausible answer. Wasn't it?

He tried to fight his way to the door once more but was forced under.

Like a giant, disproportional, Godly hand was shoving him down. Down below the surface of the liquid, crimson copper. The blood filled his tear ducts like soap and clogged his nose and lungs from breath. His body slammed with a muffled thud into the carpeted ground of his office and he was held there, held below the pressure and the hot red. He had his lips pierced closed but could feel the fluid work into the back of his throat and lungs from his flexed nostrils. The pain was searing and slow. His eyeballs ached in cramping waves against the thick darkness that stole his eyesight.

He was suffocating. He was dying.

He didn't want to die that way—shoved down below iron muck where even his skin couldn't breathe. Smothered below a torrid, black mass blanket until his lungs expanded too far and his ribs harpooned holes through them. He didn't want to die that way just like he hadn't wanted to when he was four years old. Underwater, under Amanda's grasp.

Brent began to hemorrhage against the heavy molasses night-time-wine that drenched him. His legs kicking and his elbows digging into the floor. He lost his shoes.

Still, something fat held him against the moppy carpet.

He thought suddenly of his boat. The toy *cruise ship* with a green belly and plastic portholes. The one Amanda had bought him that same day she'd tried to drown him. He remembered he'd been able to see it as she held him below the bubbly bath water—its almond shape distorted in ripples as he convulsed against the porcelain tub bottom.

He was convulsing now. His body tight and full of pumping, sucking spasms. He was going to die, he understood that now. There was no longer an

Amanda, a *someone* to lighten their hold on him and let him up to the surface before he lost consciousness. No one to spit words in his face about *not listening. Misbehaving.*

His lips opened and his tongue boxed the blood away helplessly as it killed him. His thoughts began to shrivel into flashy warning signs, his bodies last fighting attempt to keep him alive as the muscles in his neck worked the blood down into his stomach in long gulps. *A miscommunication from his brain, perhaps.*

He'd forgotten what his fingers felt like, if he even had any, as his arms numbed and bogged helplessly into the red seafloor. The concentrated goo bore into his ears and met his brain to make him deaf. Deaf, blind, and dumb.

And dead.

Almost, anyway.

He heard something, through the bass of hearing loss that beat into his head like a drum, the sound slow and distorted. Like the boat had been under his waterboarded eyes. *Too close,* it seemed to say, *you got too close.*

97

The office door opened. *Burst* open. Backward on bent hinges against the pressure of building, *pooling,* red liquid texture. Blood. It sucked Brent and the swept-up contents of is office out into the hall like a vortex and sent him spiraling over the crimson wave and across the freshly mopped hallway floor. He flopped over like a fish out of water and his chest hit the red, muddy ground with a hollow *thwap*! He gagged then vomited blood out over his tongue and through his nose.

His body was needy, deprived and desperate, for air—it forced him to gasp in—but his mouth was still full of the humid copper drink and he only sucked it back down into the windpipe, the suffocation worse and deeper now. He tried to cough but only made a sunken spewing sound as his lunged pumped in a sporadic rhythm.

He heaved himself up onto his elbows with fatigue and his sounds of strangulation became cleaner, real coughs. Coughs that were muggy, and bright, and painfully sharp. His eyes cried to drain his vision of the dark red and the blood drizzled from his nose in pissing streams as his hair dripped from fallen, dampened laps of brown.

His body twitched and another breath of air was forced to be felt. His throat gurgled against it, his chest cramping and his stomach suddenly full.

A paper—untouched, unsaturated with blood—clean, crisp, colored, slid across the blood *Slip-n-Slide* and nested beside him patiently. *Hello, I am here, notice me when you are able,* it seemed to say. His eyes blinked and focused against the ooze and tears to take in its details. Its *purple Crayola* details. Drawn with familiar purple, waxy strokes. A noose. *No,* a belt. Looped through itself like a snake eating its tail to make a noose. Purple. Crayola. Noose.

Guttural, wet moans the color of dark red escaped the man as he fought to his knees, *"Dave!"* His voice was drowned and inaudible as his hands and knees slipped against the blood and he spread himself out like a fawn on icy ground. He coughed and wheezed in iron air, *"Davey!"* He dragged himself to his feet and immediately doubled over against the agony in his gut as his stomach contracted at a fraying, tearing speed—his body back in tremors. The drawing continued to float along misdirected now, its purpose no longer useful.

Brent carried his aching body through the hall under the weight of the weeping blood that dropped from him like shower-head rain. His legs pressed fast but his socked feet, soggy and slick, kept him from sprinting. He slipped past the artwork by Alexis Adams, stapled to a mesh board, and spared it a glance. Her blue-penciled Springer Spaniel seemed to glare at him with its furry smile. Snarled and mocking him. Its canines dug down into its doodled lip.

His head dragged away from it and he continued down the hall with a new sense of *fright* somewhere inside him, bloating his belly along with blood that sloshed around as he ran hypothetically against his red set footprints. He was near the turn in the hallway—the one that led to the main office—when a girl exited the bathroom to his left, her head low and bobbing as if she had music playing in her ears and her feet dancing along in light-up sneakers. Brent came to a stop, his socks making an ugly *thud* into the ground as his feet came down against the wet cotton and blood between his toes. His arms flailed to keep balance and his lips pinched to keep from making a startled noise. She must've come in from the playground to use the restroom. Someone must've let her in and now she was dancing to herself in front of what looked to be a murder scene with a lone survivor—Mr. Kingsley.

The girl, her hair cut in a short pixie and her small sweatshirt stained with grass and dirt, lifted her eyes.

Brent knew her. Her name was Madison. She was a first-grader who sat in the front row of Mrs. Pattenson's class, *"S'okay!* It's —" blood beaded from his lips as he hunched over and coughed hard, his lungs on fire.

The girl—Madison—sat down on her butt and began to sob.

Brent sucked at air and it absorbed into his lungs with a choppy whistle, *"Maddy* —" he spat up over his chin and shook his head as dull knife-like pain contracted against his chest. Blood flung from his hair like a sprinkler and he dropped to his knees to help the crying girl. Her face swelled and her eyes shut, her hands over her ears. His dark cherry hands made contact with the sleeves of her dirty sweater to try to help her up but she only screamed—shrilly, like a broken siren lost out in the fog, somewhere down the road. Her head was vibrating.

Brent removed his hands hastily and stared in horror at the dark, satiny handprints he'd left on her sweater, *"Oh god."* He hadn't meant to do that, why had he grabbed her? He must look like a monster to her, his figure mopped in crimson colors and his hands the size of her skull alone, "I'm sorry." He gulped and his throat glugged against the thick flavor. He could *feel* her scream now—crushing his insides with steel traps—turning his stomach.

Brent stumbled to his feet clumsily just as a teacher hotfooted through her classroom door to address the uproar in the hallway. He heard her yelp words in distress and panic as he continued down the hallway to the turn. His feet slipped and he grabbed at the wall for stability as the woman made awful sounds behind him and the little girl bawled helplessly.

A bloodied, disheveled man had broken through the silence in the main office moments later and no one had known who it was. No one knew it was

Brent who was quivering under the cardinal paste as Debra's head came up from her computer and then jerked as she was startled backward by him—her gawky voice caught in her throat. She'd eventually made some noise, an odd, dreadful whine that fluttered in her chest as her hand shot out for her office phone.

Her weird cry had caught the attention of the young girl who'd been organizing a filing cabinet to the back of Debra. The girl stood slowly and turned to face Brent, a stack of papers gripped lifelessly between her two fists. She made eye contact with him and stared with overwhelming dullness—incomprehensive. Her heart a steady rhythm against his, which beat frantically below a layer of her skin.

Debra had jammed the phone to her ear, then dropped it as she found her voice, "sir! Do you need help, are you hurt, are you hurt?!" She was shaking wildly and her fingers jabbed the numbers on her phone pad: *9-1-1*. It rang slowly in her lap and she hoisted it back up to her ear.

Marilyn tilted her head as the man slammed a palm into his temple. the whites of his eyes stained red, his irises dilated and locked with hers. He seemed to say—with the pound of his palm to his skull: *You can feel me, you can feel me right?!* The girl nodded solemnly to herself as her gaze shifted to the woman who was babbling into the phone to a *911* operator, "it's Brent." She said calmly.

The phone dropped for a second time and the muffled voice of a male dispatcher played through the dotted earpiece from Debra's lap, *"Hello - hello? Ma'am?"* He must've been saying. Others, staff members, had begun to emerge from their back offices to the main hallway—Joel: fat and foreignly scented among them. *"Brent?"* Debra's voice singled itself out from the low mumble from the group of people, "Honey - what did you *do?!"* Hysteria began to peel the paint on the walls as it steamed up from the growing crowd of coworkers.

Brent's eyes flashed to her momentarily, a groan caught in a bubble of blood.

Joel stepped up through the crowd then, "Brent."

His voice, deep and demanding, punched Brent in the gut and the man's eyes rushed back to Marilyn as awareness brought him back into trepidation, "Marilyn," he croaked and shook his head heavily as blood smeared out from behind his teeth, "Davey, S'Davey!"

The girl teetered carelessly on her feet, her eyelids low.

Someone had come out of the crowd of Grant Elementary morning staff and tried to grab the man but he flung his hands out against them, his face now hot and wild, "MARILYN!" Her name broke through him like a knife through a mummified corpse, hollow and flaky as he rushed forward to the front desk to beat it with his hands, "WAKE U-" he whooped a cough and leaned into the counter heavily, "-p". His legs were weak but he pressed back up on them, his body tight and determined, "Wake up, Kid!"

There was a moment of pure, crystal silence as Marilyn watched him, her face blank. But then the comatose hold the moths had around her throat was felt and she began to fight against it–Davey's name bundling up her consciousness in a warm blanket until she was able to think clearer, for herself, her body moving forward.

"Wake up, wake up. It's Davey, wake up!" He was moaning the miserable cries as someone else tried to strong-arm him from behind but he threw them off.

Marilyn could remember the night before then. She could remember Nick, remember her tears. She, again, could see through the veil that the moths had slid over her bridal style. *It's Davey.* Her eyes widened and she came up over the desk frantically, *"I'm here - I'm here!"* She could hear herself screaming at him as the moths tried to take back the reins. She dropped to his side and grabbed a fist full of his shirt to yanked him out of the office, away from their coworkers, away from Debra and the *9-1-1* call that sat in her lap. She gritted her teeth and willed the moths away, willed to think for her own, "what's wrong with Davey?!"

Brent doubled over and breathed hard at the ground, a ripe cough blundering speechlessness from his beat red face and hot veins.

Someone was opening the office door, coming after them. Marilyn let out a frustrated cry and began to run towards the entrance, Brent followed.

The 4Runner was parked tightly between a white lined space in a row of cars just beyond the student drop off lane, its headlights pearly and wide-eyed, ready for the flick of light to glisten through them.

Grass stabbed through the spaces in Brent's dress socks and split the sticky blood as they sprinted over the curb to the Toyota.

Marilyn was the first to reach the vehicle and she spun on her heel as she did so, her hair fanning out around her in poisoned curls, "I'm driving!"

Brent stepped back from her and felt the tug of drying blood against his leg hair that now sat snug and stale to him. He didn't trust her then. He realized it bluntly as fresh air from the trees above them helped him cough the last of the blood from his lungs. "Davey," he sighed hard as his hands laced tightly into the soaked cloth of his shirt.

"Yes! Fuck! Davey, I know!" Her face was hot and her lips melted with her sharp sprung words, "Give me the keys!"

Brent shook his head.

"HEY!"–Joel. The fat principle man had broken out to the parent pick up lane, his face bloated and beaded with sweat. Joel was now jogging towards them and Debra was emerging behind him with her hands clutched to her chest.

Marilyn shoved Brent into the side of the 4Runner with a solid, absorbent motion, "GIVE ME THE GODDAMNED KEYS!" She screamed at a pitch too high for Brent to hear through the low wubbing heartbeat in his ears. He had to read it off her lips as her hand dove down the length of his bulging front pocket and grabbed for his key ring.

He let out a startled cry as her hand sealed to him from inside his pocket and the earth quaked around them. *Grabbing hand bad, her hand was bad, was aggressive, was not in a good spot.* "Don't, Amanda!" He sobbed. *Amanda?* He tried to rub the blood that fell into his eyes from his eyelashes but only smeared more in from his hands. His face scrunched.

Marilyn gripped the stuck with blood keys in her hand that was now stained in the crimson and jerked back away from him, away from his pocket. His soaked wallet came with the keys and without a second, unplanned, thought the girl pocketed it. Habit, perhaps. For a sliver of a moment, her face reflected confusion at the name: *Amanda* but then her eyes dug through Brent as they passed him and took in Joel, now only strides from them. She bounced around Brent to the driver's door as her thumb pulsed against the key F.O.B, "get in the car!"

Joel's voice was close, hollow, "what are you doing?!" His eyes had been on the keys in Marilyn's hand—the way they looked like keychain'd surgical tools as the clouded sun shimmered against the red that'd begun to crust like rust around them.

Brent turned to the back door of the 4Runner and flung it open.

The girl slammed her door and speared the ignition with the soggy key as Brent collapsed in the back seat and slammed his own door. "Jesus," she hissed at him and threw the 4Runner into reverse as Joel Olmstead ran in front of them with his hands out.

He was yelling, telling them to stop, come back. And then he was running his hands across the top of his oily head and shaking it at the back of the Toyota and Marilyn whipped from the parking lot.

Debra had turned back around and gone inside with the lingering staff that watched from the front entrance windows. The police and ambulances would be there soon.

98

Marilyn steered the 4Runner into the apartment complex and wedged it between two parking spots sideways. Brent hadn't waited for the gear to shift into park and had bounded from the rolling-to-a-stop vehicle to sprint to the staircase and Winnifred's apartment. His legs pumped across the concrete lot as Marilyn came up not far behind him, nearly beating the man to the steps where they skipped stairs as they ran. Brent skimmed three or four steps occasionally with his long stride and Marilyn kept behind him with tinier, mousy high steps. She could feel the pulse of her heart behind her brow bone and realized she'd been holding her breath in the compact compartment of her throat. Holding it in the shape of a scream.

She had run a red light on the way over and blew through a crosswalk scattered with just-missed pedestrians, yet—Brent hadn't said a word about it from the back seat. Instead, she'd felt him lean up against the cloth behind her, his warm scent drowned away by the coppery tang of blood. She could feel him press with his right leg—press hard into the floor of the car—like he was exhilarating as well, driving just as reckless.

Something *had* to be really wrong with Davey. She knew that then.

They passed Brent's small home without a glance at it as they belted for Winnifred's one bedroom. Brent hit the top flat that led to her door and was met solidly by the urge to collapse and cover his eyes because what he saw punched thickly into his their sockets and sent explosions of lava tremors through him—to the bottom of his spine.

The door was shut and innocent nonetheless. But the doorknob—

Brent could feel his feet sinking against the cement corridor slab like it was made of quicksand.

— on the doorknob, hung like a *Do Not Disturb* tube sock was a fat line of fur with a cascading tail. *Tulsa.*

The curved knob was knitted through the lining of her fur throat like a coat hanger and her eyes reflected lifelessness through transparent glimmers of green like the retinas of an insect. Her jaw was broken open and her teeth bared helplessly out at the man.

Marilyn came up behind Brent and gave an unnerving pinched groan that filleted the man's flesh. The burn of Marilyn's low rumbling terror propelled him forward towards the apartment, his mind fully geared for Davey again. The dead Maine Coon seemed to hiss at him from its broken bottom jowl as he approached it hurriedly and tried to avoid noticing the blood that pumped down the hole in its throat like guzzled streams of water down to the concrete— the wound still fresh, the death still new.

Brent reached for the door handle instinctively and felt the naked crunch of Tulsa's skull below his palm and fingers. It slurped like a drink as he threw the knob down and burst into the apartment entrance with a swallowed gasp and watery knees.

As the door swung into the home and collided with the plastered wall Tulsa's body was flung, she flopped and rolled like a sack of flour against the apartment hardwood and made the room feel tight and queasy. Marilyn shoved past Brent to find her brother—stumbling into the apartment and shrilling the little boy's name over her tingling tongue.

Brent, on the other hand, didn't move. His vision was spiked and stuck wistfully on a lump of wrinkly body at the center of the living room. A wrinkly, dark-skinned, mangled body with grey puffs of tangled hair.

Brent did collapse then.

His hands and knees caught him in a sticky puddle of gooey blood and he began to crawl across the floor to the body like an infant, drunk on terror and a high dive of dread. *"No, no, nono, nonono,"* Brent whimpered into salivated, cherry bubbles that formed between his lips as he approached her. He vomited the word as if he said it enough it would become true. *No* this wasn't happening. *No,* her cataract blue eyes wouldn't be bulging out at him. *No,* her throat wouldn't be swollen and her face wouldn't be a stone pale. *No, no, no, no.*

Brent moaned an arched, painted cry and slid his hands over the sides of her head to lift it like a hollowed melon and cradled it, *"Winnie,"* his voice was grouse as he brought his novocaine legs around to the front of him and sat on his butt, *"Oh - Winn,"* He laid her head in his lap and stared blankly over her frail body as he stroked her hair that felt waxy and fake against his dirty hands.

It hadn't been hard for Marilyn to find Davey. He'd backed himself into the darkest, dustiest corner of the hallway—the scent of piss cascading up around him from the wet streams in his pants. Choked sobs of relief shattered from both of the siblings as they saw each other and Marilyn toppled into a crouch to collect her brother into her arms.

Davey wedged his bear in between the two of them and his face down into the crevice of Marilyn's strung neck. His tears burned like acid into her exposed skin and his mouth wept incoherent words against her collar bone.

Marilyn nodded her chin into the top of his head and lifted with her legs to hoist him up into a firm hold. His words barked clearer as she stood and she heard him slur, *"big jaw,"* before she tuned out the rest.

She felt personally offended. Davey hadn't seen it before the car wreck, or in his dreams, or on a sidewalk, or lurking in the corners of Brent's apartment. Davey should've *never* seen it. The *Boogie Man* was supposed to leave the boy out of it. "It'll be okay," she tried to promise as she walked them forward out of the hallway as something small and fluttery twisted sickly against the walls of her stomach, "everything will be alright." The flutter came again, streaked in poison, and she felt oddly aware that she was lying to Davey then. She kissed the side of Davey's head absently and looked up into the living room for Brent.

She saw it for the first time then. Saw *her*. Winnifred. Parts of her body stiff and bent strangely like a neglected barbie doll. Marilyn cupped Davey's head down into her shoulder firmly to hide him from the scene. Brent was twisted over the woman's head that he'd shifted into his lap and was crying silently, his mouth parted in a pathetic frown and his body rocking in soft convulsions.

"Brent," the girl's voice croaked as she stepped closer to him and passed her eyes over the murdered body, "Brent, we need to go."

Glazed, absent eyes looked up past her as the man choked back a sob. Then, to Marilyn's horror, squeezed the head in his lap.

Winnifred's dead eyes bulged further and Marilyn stepped back, "Brent!" His grip released and he stroked the elderly woman's hair—unaware of how hard he'd actually gripped the skull with the dead brain matter on the inside, "oh god," Marilyn gulped and balanced on her feet nauseously. "Brent," she said again, smoother and softer, "it's not safe. We have to go. Now."

Brent looked down at Winnifred and the muscles in his neck and shoulders flexed.

"Now," she repeated and Davey let out a slow cry that ricocheted through her and to the upset, swimming moths that nested in her gut.

Brent didn't move.

Marilyn knelt slowly against wobbly legs - her face beat red from the weight in her arms, "hey," she let out a tight gust of air as Davey repositioned and almost knocked her off her feet, "we need to leave." Nothing. No response. The girl grimaced and laid her chin into her little brother's shoulder, "Brent," her voice came out in a wide, hot-wired warning, "she's dead. *It* got her. Let's go before it gets us, okay?"

Brent's eyes rolled to hers and he pinched his lips together as a sloppy whine rumbled inside him.

The flutter in Marilyn's stomach came again, sharp like razor blades, and her eyes darkened below the shadow of her brow bone, "man the fuck up, dude," her teeth collided with a dull *snap* sound, "let's *go!*" A kindled irritation lit her body with a flickering flame and she braced her legs to get up and leave him. Walk out with her brother and the 4Runners keys and let him stay to weep feebly over the elderly woman until he too met the same fate as her. Whatever. That was it. Fuck him.

But Davey hadn't felt the same.

The boy had wiggled from Marilyn's hold despite her bruising grip protest and flung himself at Brent—not concerned with the crimson crust that stuck itself over the man. His arms slamming around the counselor in a heavy hug against his neck. His knees swung forward and collided into Winnifred's lifeless head in Brent's lap and he let out a small cry into the man's ear, disgust mournfully swelling up from the base of his knee caps where he'd felt the wet smack of her skull against him.

Bear Kingsley was in Davey's fist against Brent's back and the boy imagined the stuffed animal kicking its feet to help him wake the adult from his trance.

"Please, let's go," Davey moaned against Brent as tears fell down his cheeks and slid below the collar of Brent's bloodied shirt, "*me and Beary want to go.*"

Brent's hands came off of Winnifred and came up around the boy to embrace him back, "Davey," he sighed.

Marilyn nodded at them as irritation continued to swell up through her— happily bathing the moths in its leaking heat, "okay." She stood and clapped her hands hard together, "let's go! Let's go! Let's go!" She turned for the door and began to leave them behind.

Brent hesitated until Davey nestled further into him. *Boogie Man.* He was reminded of it just for a moment as he slid out from under Winnifred's head and stood with the boy. The elderly head bounced against the floorboards like a deflated basketball and Brent felt any coherent thoughts the boy had reminded him of flood out the back of him with the noise of his dead friend's dropped skull. It made him a zombie, a walking meat suite of damaged emotions.

He followed Marilyn drunkenly to the 4Runner and glided himself into the back seat without purpose or reason, Davey still slung around his neck and scented like chilled pee on jeans.

99

Brent was somewhere deeper and darker than under the mounds of blood now. Somewhere evil, numbing and forgotten. Somewhere that frosted over him like a snow glacier as side roads and afternoon traffic passed him in damp globs.

Davey was laid out in his lap and Bear Kingsley was being held in the man's own hand—his thumb massaging a familiar patch of stuffed animal arm where the fur had long since begun to fade into balding puffs. Brent's eyes and nose burned and his throat was full of risen yeast and heartburn as he stared blankly at the rolling road.

Marilyn's foot revved harder into the Toyota's pedal as she changed lanes to box around a silver Mazda then boxed back into her original lane posted at fifty-five that she drove at seventy-eight. She glanced through the rearview mirror at the silent man and was reminded of when she'd glanced back for the last time in her green Saturn. Brent's blood clogged pores contrasted with his pale green skin like something from a nightmare.

Something from her nightmare.

The 4Runner swerved slightly and she slammed her eyes back onto the road as her hands strangled the soft plastic black wheel.

She remembered the insects that had slid from the slits in the creature's skin as it reached around and grabbed at her in the Saturn. She'd thought then that maybe they were slugs, or silkworms, or maggots. But now she thought differently—it had been moth larva. She understood that now, and as if to confirm her theory, the moths nested inside her gushed against the walls of her intestines. She bared her teeth and let the road blur in her eyesight.

"Hey," her voice was falsely balmy as it projected against the windshield in front of her and coated the man in the back in a layer of wool, "how are you holding up?"

Brent's lips parted and his clumpy eyelashes fluttered down as he squinted out the window.

"Sorry about Winnie," Marilyn sobered as she slowed to a camera surveillance intersection and scanned the tall traffic poles for the speed sensors, "and Tulsa." The 4Runner coasted through the four-way going fifty-two, then sped back up against Marilyn's led foot. When Brent didn't answer, the girl thought: *At least she was old—would've died soon anyway. And Tulsa's a cat. Cats die.* The thought was dark and it brought a miserable frown to her lips.

She took a hand from the wheel and rubbed it into her stable stomach for the moths to brush up against, the sensation strange and intoxicating.

They had driven in random directions for *perhaps* an hour before Marilyn made a last-minute decisive swerve into a single level motel parking lot, just off the main drag of highway that c-sectioned an unfamiliar town in half. The parking lot squared itself out like the front of an 'L' shaped strip mall and she pulled into a center space, below a black pole street light, not yet on. The motel shared its large square parking lot with a *Walgreens*—the nose of the 4Runner pointed at the sliding store doors.

Marilyn popped her lips and tilted her head at the cursive 'W' of *Walgreens* that flickered sporadically against the grey cement wall of the store. *A motel and a Walgreens?* Her teeth skimmed over her lower lip to collect dead skin and her eyes shifted out her side window to study the almost completely vacant motel. The sides were a faux sandy cobblestone, spray-painted on and detailed by a cheap commercial contractor. The door a honey orange, aged and dirty with yellow trim windows arched at the top, white curtains over their spiderwebbed glass. The trim around the main room windows an off white, or perhaps pure white with a layer of coughed up highway tire dust.

Marilyn's nose scrunched.

The Toyota's muttering engine died as Marilyn twisted the key her way and removed it to drop in her lap, the stuck blood making the metal clash of keys to keyring muted and crunchy. She turned her head over the seat to the boys' in the back - Davey's face buried in Brent's red crusted stomach and Brent's gaze distance into somewhere empty. He hadn't noticed her watching them, he hadn't noticed anything. By the looks of it, in fact, Brent was more vacant than the faux cobblestone motel beside them.

"Stay here," Marilyn instructed to the two bodies in her backseat without expecting a response.

Still, however, when her voice wasn't met with acknowledgment from either boy nor man she felt the steady tug of annoyance at the base of her hairline and she smacked a scratching hand against the back of her neck with a weighted sigh.

She turned back to face forward then popped the door open, swinging the keyring over her finger before holstering it into her pocket. She slammed the heavy black door behind her and straightened her shirt, investigating its clean material for any sign of blood.

None. Nada. Nothing.

She smiled, satisfied, and swept a distracted hand across her strangely rough jeans—her smile then dropping. She glanced down again and noticed the blood-smeared handprints that ran across the blue material on her thighs, left there by her after each time she'd touched Brent. Once in the office when she'd gripped his shirt to pull him from the crowd, and once against the 4Runner as she'd dug through his pocket for the keys *and wallet*. Each time she'd cleaned herself of the iron paste by dusting her hands onto her jeans. *Fuck*.

She laid a hand over her stained handprint for a long moment before shrugging. She could pass that shit off as a period accident. *Uh, yeah, my tampon string broke and I had to go diggin' through my vagina to get ahold of the cotton tube I'd jammed up there.* Good excuse. *Yeah.* Besides, would anyone really go out of their way to ask?

Her smile came back and she proceeded towards the motel with slappy sneakers.

The silver guarded door with smudged window glass and a black *'Push'* sticker labeled as the *Motel Office* caught up with the girl and she wedged herself through it, startled by an old fashioned ring of a bell as the door swung into the room. A woman with a botched bob cut colored platinum blonde sat behind the motel counter with a ripped book spread in her lap, the nail of her thumb being run through her teeth like dental floss as she read.

The woman's head came up at the sound of the bell to take inventory of Marilyn, stood in the entrance, then dropped back down for a moment to bookmark her ratty bound book—her brow scrunched together above her wrinkled blouse as if she was disappointed to see the young woman in front of her.

She stood and braced herself against her side of the counter—her blue eyes crystal and transparent as if they were glaring straight through Marilyn's dirty, moth dusted soul, "hello," she said.

Marilyn had a funny thought as she studied the woman: *Norma Louise Bates?* It had made her insides tickle with the slightest giggle, but as the woman's mouth opened to greet Marilyn the girl had seen that maybe *not*. The lady's front chompers were rotten to yellow slivers of bone. *Maybe if Norma had been a meth addict.* Marilyn thought and the giggle erupted through her lips.

"How can I help you," meth-head-Norma-Louise sighed at the giggly girl.

Marilyn ran her fingers over her mouth to rub the laugh away, "I just need a room," her voice came out stripped and chuckle-less.

The woman nodded and moved to an old, moaning computer and monitor. Her actions inviting the girl to step up closer to the desk and accept the stale mold scent the office had to offer.

The woman's index clicked, her head back to crack her neck, then she clicked again. A moment of silence placed itself against the room until the printer behind her warmed with a chugging whine. It swallowed a sheet from its bottom paper tray and buzzed loudly as ink transferred to it.

It silenced and Marilyn shifted her weight.

The long quiet pause passed and it regurgitated a single sheet of white paper. Meth-head-Norma-Louise pivoted with graceless feet and stole the sheet from the machine without much effort, her blue eyes interrogating it as she walked it back to the counter to flatten it out in front of Marilyn.

Marilyn tilted her head at the black inked contract.

"I'll need you to fill this out, please." The woman coughed into the crook of her elbow and Marilyn's eyes flicked up to her, "And give me a copy of your I.D." Her voice was gruff from the cough and she smiled sorely at the girl, "sorry." Her hand went out and gripped a glass of water sat beside the book-marked book she'd been reading.

She gulped the cough away as Marilyn pinched the white sheet between her fingers, "sure," she said—ignoring the woman's apology for the sick sounds, "do you have a pen?"

The woman extracted a blue ballpoint pen, with a *Dollar Tree* flower roughly taped to the top of it, from a dark gray vase at the edge of the counter. She shook it out at Marilyn like a feather duster and the girl took it, then turned and took a seat in a raggedy armchair near the entrance.

Marilyn had chewed her cheek as she considered a fake name for the sign in, a dictionary of possibilities toggling through her thoughts. She squinted until her eyelashes restricted her line of sight before quickly scribbled in the name:

Amanda. She smiled suddenly, remembering now that Brent had called her that. *Amanda.* She bit her lip: *Who is Amanda, Mr. Kingsley?* Little brown winged insects rushed up behind the skin of her breasts at the notion of the name and Marilyn straightened her spine, "Whoever she is, they like her." She snorted to herself while the moths settled back down.

Last name?

Easy.

Marilyn wrote the name *"Kingsley"*.

She considered the risk of putting Brent's last name after she'd written it–reminded suddenly of Debra with her ear pressed to the phone dialing *911*. The name blurred out from beneath her and she interrogated it without blinking. *911*. Would they follow them? The police, that is. She blinked, the name came back into focus, then she dismissed the risk entirely.

Age. Date of birth?

What age was Amanda Kingsley going to be? Hm, twenty-three? She nodded and her curled hair twisted against her cheek. Old enough to rent a car –old enough to rent a motel room.

Marilyn moved past I.D. number, phone number, and email–each one a bullshit answer. She then stopped and scowled hard to the *Credit/Debit* slot–perfectly laid out for sixteen digits. Four–little–slots–of–four. She shifted her weight as a frown pressed through her and felt the bulge of a square trifold against her thigh. Brent's wallet making itself known against her and she slid a finger into her pocket to retrieve it. Her lips parted to make room for a mischievous toothed grin. Thankful then for her sticky fingers and habit reactions to wallets in pockets.

Marilyn froze while more blood made cold bubbles out onto the stains on her jeans as she flipped the billfold open in her lap–the fluid still a liquid base from being deprived of drying wind while inside Brent's, *then her's*, pocket. Her head twitched upward to meth-head-Norma-Louise but the woman hadn't noticed the trickle of red across Marilyn's seated legs, her face bent down, back into her book. The girl in the seat puffed her cheeks out and widened her eyes momentarily before slipping Brent's debit from a fronting pocket, blood now smeared in her fingers like she'd pinched the nostrils of a bloody nose.

She sprinkled her fingers over dry jean material to clean the blood from her hands then continued to transfer each sequence of numbers on the man's plastic card to the paper. *You gotta be careful, Mr. Kingsley,* she considered with a quiet sing-songy voice stuck just between her ears, *Debit is wired straight to your bank account, someone pickpockets you and you're shit out of luck.* Her eyebrows raised as if she were honestly talking to him out loud and her hair stroked her face again as her head bobbed.

Expiration date. *CVV.* Applicant's signature.

Marilyn licked her tongue over her lips at the half-assed, elegant, scrawl of *Amanda C. Kingsley.* At the bottom of the page. *'C'?* Maybe for Chelsy, or Catalina, or Cathy. Her tongue returned to her mouth and she bit against the tip of it as she returned the smeared card back to its wet leather trap, then to her pocket.

The girl stood against the hungry shift of moths inside her and walked back to the counter, fanning the paper out in the air for the blonde to take it. Marilyn waited patiently as the woman pushed the debit card's numbers into her junky computer system then stopped and squinted at the female's chicken scratch handwriting.

"Your name doesn't match the card holder's name." Meth-head-Norma-Louise blandly spoke.

Shit.

"Oh!" Marilyn tilted back on her heels, "it's my husband's!"

Blue eyes slid to the girl carelessly, "I can't give you a room with someone else's card."

Marilyn pouted her lip forward, "oh–please," she laughed, "he's asleep in the car... I would really hate to wake him to have him come in here just for you to verify us," she shook her hands through the air, "that's ridiculous." Her hand went to her stomach and she felt the steady kick of raving moths within her.

The woman stared coldly, unimpressed with the girl's good-mannered excuse.

Marilyn bit against her lip as she leaned in closer to the counter, "look," her bit lip curled up into a pinched smile, "it's our honeymoon, actually." She snorted a scrunched nose laugh and tipped back away from the counter, "of course this isn't our final destination but –" she trailed off as her eyes dilated, she laughed again, "well, you know."

Meth-head-Norma-Louise lifted an eyebrow at the girl as if she didn't know, or *didn't care.*

Marilyn continued, "ugh, you know, he's just –" her face reddened under swooning heat, *"he's so good in bed,* right?" She made a settled smirk to the woman, "me being the horn dog I am, I just, woah," pause to laugh giddily at herself, "I can't wait."

"Congrats," the woman slid the registration back across the counter to the girl, unamused with her story, "please get me your I.D. and *your* debit card. Or," she met Marilyn with a mocking, intoxicated expression, "bring your *husband* in here."

Damn. Marilyn reeled back from the counter as if the oak top she'd had her hands against set on fire. Those blue eyes really could see through to her soul. Like little, crystal grave diggers–or big bluff bounty hunters. "Sure," the girl said with a scowl, "I'll be back soon." She turned with her words as the moths hunkered down against her disappointment and offered a nasty solution to her dilemma. A *nasty... bloody...* solution.

No. Marilyn scolded them as she exited the little, stale office.

They seemed to protest within her then as they flew in tiny, bug flocks down joined tunnels of nerves and tissue.

The girl grimaced at the parking lot and gripped a hand into her gut, *No...*

They fought harder within her and she began to *crave* their control. Their demand to be obeyed. She almost *wanted* it.

"Not now," she urged out loud.

100

Marilyn had flashed a cautious look through the smudged entrance door as she buckled her knees against the cold exterior air around the motel. The blonde Norma woman had her head tipped back down into her book—her hair cocooning around her hollow cheeks—her attention fully away from the girl.

Marilyn hissed against a mischievous smile and scampered along the fake cobblestone wall of the building to the first creamy, cobwebbed motel door, her hand finding its handle solemnly and yanking. Nothing. The plastic metal of the curved doorknob burned cold streaks into her palm as it refused to even jiggle. She sighed and moved to the next room and fought its closed-door—again, nothing. The knob stuck solid in a lock. She slumped into the door, "dammit."

She slung her eyes out over the parking lot and stuck them to the 4Runner, sat like a sleeping black cockroach below the street light. She felt thankful then for the vehicles tinted back windows: keeping bloody red Brent and piss pants Davey hidden from the outside world—like a body bag tightened over the human remains of a crime scene.

Her insides swelled in salivated moth nests and celebration as she studied the black machine on wheels and thought: *I could just drive us off a bridge.* It was a semi-comforting thought, there would be no more oogity-boogity–Boogie Man...for any of them. She brushed the tips of her fingernails over her stomach's stretched flesh—*no more moths.* They kindled within her as her thoughts train-tracked suddenly to Nick and her skin paled.

Two doors down from her left a couple exited the motel with a ripped, green duffle bag and a children's backpack slipped over a burly trucker man's shoulder. He shuffled along with a redheaded wife with older, sagged features. *Sagged everywhere but her melon-sized breasts.*

Marilyn's back left the door as she stood straight and grinned gladly at the couple. The way you'd grin at a free bathroom after standing in line with shit cramps.

She jogged bouncy, joyful steps towards the couple, "hello folks! Did you enjoy your stay?"

The saggy woman's head snapped over the girl and her cappuccino brown penciled in brow line furrowed, "hi. Who are you?" Her voice was drenched in cigarette tar and her husband seemed more spooked by the gravel growl than Marilyn's approaching bubbliness.

"Tami," the name came out easy and wet, "the manager's daughter." She glances back at the office where her '*mommy*' sat with her book then turned back and squinted at the riddled couple, "been trying to help mom out around her as much as I'm able!" Her hand came out and her palm faced the sky, open and accepting.

Trucker husbandman shifted his weight, "what's that for?" He readjusted the strap to the children's backpack and frowned at her.

Marilyn laughed a ditsy southern chuckle and ignored the swirl of wings beneath her skin, "your room key, sir." She danced her shoulders above her breasts and shifted her eyes from him to his wife, to him again, "It's this new thing mom wants to try! For hospitality!" Her eyelashes fluttered and the redheaded wife sat back on her heels in Marilyn's peripheral. There was a dragged pause so Marilyn went on to continue, "I take your room key and make sure you get all checked out with my mom and *you guys...* " She addressed them with emphasis, "get to mosey on outta here without worrying about it." Her eyebrows elevated and pulled her smiley cheeks up with them, "sweet, simple an' nice!" Her southern hospitality voice peaked at a twang and she became aware of it for the first time: *where did you come from?* She asked it in plain Oregonian thought. As if to answer her the southern voice came back with a: *Ma'am!* And she was reminded of the curly-Q grease cheek girl at the burger shop. Her fake, nasally, customer service resonance as Marilyn had stood in line.

How may I help you today, ma'am?

Marilyn's smile had started to falter into a grimace.

"Not sure I believe that, miss." The man with a kid backpack scoffed and Marilyn's smile was pulled back up in full attention.

The redhead swatted at her husband, "Give it to her, Len."

Len frowned as he interrogated the girl in front of him with dark eyes inside greasy eye sockets.

Marilyn's hand twitched out for it.

"For god sakes babe—give her the key. She's a nice girl," The gravelly voice of the woman gurgled.

Marilyn thought: *Yes, nice girl, Len.*

Len's truck grease fingers sausaged down into his pocket and he cast the key out to her—not wanting to upset his woman.

Marilyn's hand gripped for the metal-ribboned-to-plastic key hungrily and her feet flexed into a tiny, happy bounce, "thank you!" She squeaked, "you have a fantastic day now! I hope you enjoyed your stay at —" her eyes saucered into dinner plate pupils as the name of the motel came up blank in her mind. She didn't know its name. She hadn't looked, "our motel," she finished with a suave wink to hide her hesitation.

"You too," redheaded melon breasts said with a long-nailed wave.

Len seemed less satisfied as his perky chested wife dragged him away, his tired eyes digging back at Marilyn suspiciously as the mustache over his upper lip quivered in the wind. He lowered into his car with a grunt after his wife and Marilyn was sure she'd heard him voice his opinion of her: "*The girl is a thief or something, I'm telling you. She —* "he shut the door and his voice broke off.

Too bad, so sad. Marilyn thought as she waved them goodbye from the curb then turned to head for the office, the key flipping in her hand like a little golden gymnast. Their car backed out and chucked along the pavement until its nose peaked out into the town's highway, its blinker flashing orange streams of light into the grey air. It then turned and was gone.

As it left from sight Marilyn pivoted away from the approaching office and patted herself on the back as she gleamed at the motel door she now held the key too. *Too easy.*

"Should've listened to good old Lenny, miss," She murmured as she skipped off the curb and scampered her way through the motel parking lot to the *Walgreen's* parking spaces like a drain rat.

101

She side-shouldered through the *Walgreens* front door with her forehead tightened against the distancing pain between her and Brent, who still sat with Davey in the 4Runner. She'd begun to rethink her careless idea that the police wouldn't be searching for the bloody man who'd road off with his much younger, female coworker.

Bloody man... Where had the blood come from?

Marilyn pondered this as she passed under the yellow fluorescence to the back of the shop while she studied the aisle caps steadily. An aisle of cheap cotton clothing shared strangely with boxed elderly walkers, caught her attention and she passed to it.

Surely the cops had arrived thanks to lovely Debra and surely they'd found the source of the blood. Or at least long trails of the blood from where Brent had run.

She snaked an extra-large, black long-sleeve through her fists and folded it to stomach as she wandered down the aisle way.

The cops would probably find Brent's apartment, and it wouldn't be long after that before they found the cat and the elderly woman upstairs.

She bungeed back into the main aisle and started her study of aisle caps again—looking for... *wipes*. A satisfied hew came over her as she noticed the plastic packages of wet baby cloths. She crossed to them and collected a bulky pack to hold against her stomach with the t-shirt.

Would they notice Davey's absence? Debra would tell the police the boy was suspended and at home. She would tell them Brent had sirened his name like a tsunami warning through the confined box of the office.

Fuck, Brent. Marilyn through at she squeaked sneakers to the front of the store because; *Fuck,* they'd go back to the apartment, see Winnie, see Tulsa, but see no Davey.

Her nerves suddenly felt stripped by razors as her body prepared for the pitched buzz of electronics breaking through with time stopped *Amber Alerts.*

EMERGENCY AMBER ALERT

GRANT, OREGON / BLACK TOYOTA 4RUNNER / LICENCE PLATE#-

Marilyn stopped her imagination there—because... she didn't know Brent's license plate.

If the cops found Winnifred and Tulsa, and the blood, it was clear to her that they wouldn't find the *Boogie Man.* No, he saved himself for her, for Brent and now for Davey. They wouldn't know the story, they wouldn't know the danger, they wouldn't know that Brent and Marilyn were victims.

She thought again of the alert, what it might say.

EMERGENCY AMBER ALERT

GRANT, OREGON / BLACK TOYOTA 4RUNNER / LICENCE PLATE#-

An aisle cap of hats addressed her politely as she made her way to the cash register, their black beanie masses of cotton promising to hide the blood in Brent's hair from any bystanders who might notice them as they walk to their new motel room. She nodded at the aisle cap as if to say 'thanks' and snagged a label-less beanie into her chilled fist.

Walgreen's hadn't minded that she'd fed Brent's card into the open-mouthed chip reader rather than her own card. They hadn't batted an eye, not at her, not at the card, not at all. She'd stood calmly with her hip tilted into the side of the counter and memorized the lumpy agitation in her abdomen left there by napping moths. Their conscience at rest and their wings at bay, tucked tightly into their furry backs to shape them like submarine missiles against her intestine walls.

The chip reader saluted completion with a squeaking beep and the girl removed the card–the card that she'd quickly thumbed blood off moments before so the chip reader would accept its plastic taste.

"Receipt?" The old man behind the counter droned above his hearing aid.

Marilyn's head tousled 'no' as a smile licked up like a blue flame across her cheek, "no, thank you."

The man crumpled the wax white paper between his wrinkled fingers and tossed it to a small bin at his feet, "have a good day." The bag with a red 'W' cursive over its front was shifted across the counter to the girl and Marilyn took it graciously.

"You too," she mumbled and the contents of the bag bounced against her thigh as she lowered her arm to her side and began to walk out.

The elderly store clerk told her thank you from his spot at the register and let her leave. He didn't try to stop her. He didn't say: *"Hey, have you seen a black 4Runner around? A boy is missing!"* He didn't wince at the electronic bang of an Amber Alert breaking through all systems, he didn't do anything. He just let her leave.

Maybe that was because an Amber alert hadn't come through, and maybe would never. Maybe they were safe...

Her stomach cramped like a contraction and she bit a moan into her lip.

102

The 4Runner was cold in the back seat, an icebox of dead emotions, left without the engine idling to keep it incubated in vent warm air. Marilyn hugged Davey into her arms as she sat wedged beside Brent on the icy mesh bench seat. Davey was burrowing to her neck as she studied the silent man, his bloody lashes open and his gaze stuck out the tinted door window, the Walgreen's bag neglected in his lap.

"Brent," The girl's voice was an antiseptic surgical tool through the dead skin of silence in the vehicle, its sliced sound even irritable to her, "change." Her finger flicked out and rustled against the bag in Brent's lap.

His head turned and his eyes met her then, his lips parted, "it's getting foggy out here," he sighed across the car with a heaving chest and flexing nose.

Marilyn glanced out the window at the white-lined parking lot for low clouds of mist and was met with only light sprinkles of rain across the thick glass window, "okay —" she pretended to agree. "You have to change out of the bloody shirt."

Brent's eyes were glazed in grey, murky fear.

Marilyn tasted chunks of cheek skin as she dined on the wet flesh with her molars and squeezed Davey a little tighter into her. She tried tirelessly hard to remember how she'd felt after she'd found her father dead—she tried tirelessly hard to sympathize with Brent—but she couldn't. The insect bombed laced into her body's matter had cut off that part of her. An exoskeleton bullet wedged into that spot of her brain that linked empathy with past emotion. Her thoughts were cold with robotic data that instructed her to feel frustration.

It fed on her, the flavored irritation, and she began to feel angry with him.

"Come on," her hand broke the bag in his lap apart and she hook and lined the beanie from the thin plastic. It came up in a ball of soft material and she tossed it unhappily at the man. "I got us a motel and you can't go walking to our room looking like *Carrie*." Her words were bit back inside her throat to keep the sharp edges from spitting out into the cold vehicle space like blades. She reached for him again, this time her fingers dampening into an oily button on his shirt and lacing it through the tiny button-up slit near his collar.

Brent startled a whine and swatted at her hand as his back wet into the mesh seating, away from her, his lips working against a word. A word. A word. "*Amanda—*" he broke off. A name. His lips had worked against a name.

Marilyn kissed a frown across her lips as she watched the name tumbled from his mouth like dry vomit. There is was again. *Amanda.* "Okay, what the fuck?" Her tongue sizzled the accusing sentence like grease in a frying pan.

The man looked at her steadily for a moment before dropping his gaze and using his own hands and fingers to feed the buttons through the secure sown slits of his shirt. His white undershirt mopped in crimson below—forming to his muscles across his chest.

A moth woke from its nap and bit Marilyn from within. She grunted into the pain of the nibble and neither hugging boy nor delirious man seemed to notice. *My heroes.*

Brent's button-up smeared down his arms as he shook it off and studied his undershirt numbly—his hands crossed over the front of his body and tangled into the wet bottom of the cotton to hoist it up over his head like it was an adult bib absorbed with soggy food. It flopped onto the floorboard of the Toyota and Brent's head bent to inspect it as his body paralyzed against the sound of its slap in the quiet car. The sound was deadly, ghastly, haunting.

Marilyn bent her head as well, but rather to admire the abundance of blood painted across Brent's bare flesh. His body kissed in small moles, black below the dark red. He'd frozen too long and she'd become angry again as her hand went back to his lap—to the bag.

Brent made a moan with the back of his throat and scolded her with dark eyes, "I got it," his voice puppeted from his emotionless body. He groped the baby wipe cluelessly and pulled them from the mouth of the plastic sack.

"To clean the blood off your face," Her instructions pinched through her vocal box like bee stings.

He stared at it as his hand strangled the corner of it between thumb and finger.

"For god sakes, dude!" Marilyn braced a hand into Davey's back to keep from dumping him as she bent forward to grab at the plastic package in the man's hand. Her fingers came out like cat nails and stole the item from his dumbed grip to then tear open. Wet cloths oozed from the side seam and she ripped them into the open air, slamming one like a slap to his cheek and scrubbing.

The blood caked to Brent's stubble only seemed to spread and darken with each heated swipe of the white rag. More moths spread themselves into awareness and began to snack on her body, "fuck!" Marilyn yelped and dropped the rag as they wiggled within her. Her heart hammered steadily and she realized there'd been intoxicated vertigo between man and woman as she'd tried to clean him.

Davey whimpered against her as he resisted her hold, "you're hurting him," he groaned and she released the boy. Davey scooted back from her lap without meeting her eye and climbed into Brent's. His legs straddled around the man's thighs and his hands tucked the man's hair behind his ears thoughtfully, unconcerned with the crisp blood that crinkled against his tiny fingers. Brent's lower lip quivered and Davey acted as if he hadn't seen it as he found the cloth

Marilyn had been using and began to streak the sticky liquid away from Brent's face.

Marilyn sat back from them with her lips pulled tight and her sight narrowed, "alright, fine." There was an entrail of laced pain in her sneer, "hurry up Romeo and Juliet, I don't have all fucking night." She broke the seal to the SUV's door beside her and fell to her feet on the pavement, unaware that as the bottom of her sneakers smacked to the concrete the moths took back over, the buggy legs back on the reigns of her actions.

Marilyn was an unknowing puppet now—her actions dependent on buggy brains and what they *needed*. They ciphered her blood through their possessing insect filters and worked her legs to walk heatedly to the other side of the 4Runner. The girl ate the back door handle where Brent and Davey sat with her hand and cranked it open widely, "get out," she commanded.

Davey's eyes shifted to her as he scrubbed blood from Brent's forehead.

"Come on."

Brent took the wet wipe from the boy and swiped it over his face sparingly before dumping it to the floor of the SUV where his shirt slept. The black long sleeve was then worked over his torso to hide the blood on his chest and arms and then the beanie absorbed the sight of his bloody hair.

Davey nodded, "all hidden." His hand went down and rescued Bear Kingsley from Brent's side before his eyes flipped back to his sister who stared hollowly at them.

Brent kneaded Davey's sides until the boy stepped out to the parking lot to join his sister, then he followed.

Brent tailed the Matthews siblings through the parking lot at a wide berth, his cheek shoved between his teeth to work his tight molars apart from one another, his mouth salivating in warm iron. His stride stayed behind, far behind, consciously that way because he could feel it again. That feverish anger that misted from the girl into their mental radio signal and made his insides quake in its intensity. Whatever it was, it was back.

The girl who yanked Davey from the air mattress, who'd verbally fought the man in the playground at Grant Elementary, who'd come home dressed in a man's shirt and wet with shower water, who screamed awful things about Davey, who'd looked as if she'd been hung from Brent's bedroom ceiling, who'd talked to the voice that sounded like Brent's, who'd glazed her eyes past Brent as he'd burst, bloody, into the main office that morning... Yes. That girl. *That girl*—was back.

103

The motel room was under kept and messy—or was that an understatement?

Marilyn glared below a line of heat at what was in front of her.

The motel room was a graveyard of shadow cast insects and Len and his lady had left thrashed linen in their wake. That was *not* an understatement. *Lovely*.

The girl's lip curled to her nose like steamed hair as Davey pressed in behind her to see the room with the double beds—both sweaty and under kept with haunted images of Burly-Trucker-Man and Redhead-Wonder burning beneath Marilyn's stale eyelids.

"Gross." She mumbled as moths puppeted her to step aside and allow her brother in.

Brent came from behind her as well, hardly missing her shoulder with a brush of his arm as he steadied himself around Davey—who'd stopped at the first bed to study it—and paced into the center of the room without acknowledging the scent of sex, or the girl in the doorway.

"I don't bite," she promised him with something deep inside the smear of vocal cords and breath that challenged that statement.

Brent had heard it, the blazed growl from within her, and chose to ignore it. Stay tucked beneath oblivion with his sight fogged out of focus and his head turned away from her. His mind stuck swimming in a distant, faded atmosphere.

The body of the girl was twisted onto one hip as she blew air from her lips to press at the man that he'd pissed her off. He didn't notice.

A 'Do Not Disturb' door tag greeted her from a desk at her peripheral and her hand slipped out for it. The motel door was then met with her aggressive attack to get the sign to hang across the outer handle before she slammed the dirty door and locked it.

The sign hung the same way Tulsa had hung, lifeless and like a warning. The girl's stomach would've churned at the thought but the moths had eaten away the discomfort before it was felt, the memory of Tulsa smashed away from her by their dusted wings in an attempt to preserve her. Keep her theirs.

Ignorance was key now.

Marilyn began to stride to the bathroom in an ass flexed strut, "you should take a shower," she sung lowly as she passed Brent and flipped her head back over her shoulder to him, "get the blood out of your hair." She scrunched her fingers through her mopped, curly hair.

Brent caught her with his eyes and heard that noise again, that low buzz deep inside her feminine voice.

"Come on, *kid.*" She encouraged as her feet pivoted in a kick and she pushed through a half-massed door to the steam captive bathroom. Lenny and his lover had left a pair of underwear splayed out on the hair swept tile and Marilyn made a face at it. "Awesome," she murmured as she shuffled the soggy cloth under the bathroom sink with the toe of her shoe.

"What —" Brent's voice was a barfed out whisper from the doorway of the bathroom.

Marilyn jolted within her skin at his sudden presence, then turned to milk the faucet into life. The water broke from the rotted silver pipe and shattered into the floor of the porcelain tub like china glass. She straightened her spine and sliced her eyes into his, "what?"

But Brent was gone again, his head tilted down to the sound of the water, his lips parted and his tongue pinched between his teeth.

"If you were gonna ask what I think, then I think," she rocked forward and squinted at him until her vision was only a dark line of eyelashes, "you need to take a shower." Her hand flapped down into the water faucet and flipped drops up at him like reverse rain, "get in, get the water coming out of the showerhead, sit under it—it'll help you clear that big, dumb noggin'."

She smiled as he shifted his attention back to her.

Her smile wiped off like a bad taste as he turned and sat against the lip of the tub. He dropped his head down to study his folded hands in his red lap. His chest heaved in the heat that puffed from her like radiation and his heart rate thickened beneath both their chests.

"Get undressed."

Brent didn't respond.

"You will feel better."

He twitched at the buzz that had begun to sound like a whistle as it traveled through her throat.

"Get in the water, asshole."

Asshole, it struck gravel as it blurred from her lips and sounded broken, and sharp like it could cut Brent, but he still did not react.

Her hands balled at the collar of his black long sleeve with venomous white-knuckled fists and shoved him backward into the tub. Her flesh grip stuck to him like tacks as his body landed bluntly against the plastic bottom of the bath and his head scraped into the corner of the rusty faucet. His arms fanned out in a panic as his lungs broke a gasp from his rib cage and his legs tipped up around her. Her hands broke the seal from his shirt and came to her chest momentarily before collecting his hair greedily and forced his face under the boiling blue tap water. Crusted blood from his hair streamed over the both of them in pink flurries as her grip fastened to him and the ground began to turn below them.

Water blundered paths down his nose and lungs and Brent had a clear image of Amanda puncture holes into the soft skin around his temples, the holes themselves burnt into erosion as the water steamed against his numb flesh. He sprawled his limbs out and struck her hands away from him and away from the tipsy grasp they had against him. His eyes peeled open in shock against the clear flames of water and his lungs blew it from his nose while he picked himself up from under the stream to sit back on the ledge—his body tense in sneezy convulsions to release the fluid from his lungs. *"Don't—"*

The girl came at him again, her head lowered and her back arched in an ugly stance.

Brent caught her hands in his this time and bucked her. She tripped and crashed spine first into the bathroom floor, hauling the man with her by their magnetically knitted hands. He caught himself on his knees and yanked his grip away from her before the room could sweep around them in a full ferris wheel spin. His head shook pulses at her and his hair dripped cherry blossom water at the ground, "Don't you dare! Don't you DARE do that!" His voice reverberated the startled sob over the bathroom tile like wounded nails over a brick sidewalk as he continued to shiver in front of her.

Marilyn sat up against the oval toilet bowl to wheeze fluttered breaths back into her knocked breathless lungs. He was coherent again, all there, *better*. A cool look settled over her panting face and her lips lifted to coo, "welcome back." She sucked at the air that left with her words, "told you, you'd feel better." She laughed from her achy chest and the sound of flapping wings bubbled out with it.

Brent widened his water wet eyes and scooted back away from her, his hands pressed into his lap and his thoughts constricted around fear.

"Are you okay?" Davey's voice slapped into the room as he teetered into the doorway with Bear Kingsley pressed below his chin, "what happened?!"

Marilyn's head tilted up from her spot against the grainy toilet and she palmed at her nose, "your turn to shower, pissy." She tugged at his soiled jeans with the same hand that had been at her nose and admired as the boy's face reddened.

104

Marilyn had laid her head into a mashed down pillow and shut her eyes with her lips twisted up into a frozen smile. There'd been a red hair coiled along the pillowcase surface that she had swiped off with her forefinger—the hair spiraling a gentle snake-like tickle down her finger as it sunk from her hand to the floor.

She didn't know what time it was, maybe only noon? One? Surely, it wasn't too late. There was no real way to know, she supposed, everything looked so dark below the dictation of the moths. Her smile deepened and she played footsie with the used comforter that she'd snuggled up to her chin. It didn't matter what time it was, really, sleep wanted to come and she was willing to let it.

They hadn't eaten, the three of them that shared the motel room.

Marilyn hadn't even begun to think of food, her stomach too full of moths and menthol cravings to feel the low rumble against her abdomen. How many hours since breakfast? Had she eaten breakfast? She didn't eat the night before, did she? It didn't matter. She wasn't hungry, not for food.

The boys had forgotten food as well, as Brent made the bed beside Marilyn's so Davey and he could rest on the top, hopefully clean, cover. Their heads were too full on haunted thoughts for them to consider filling the empty spot below their chests. Neither sure they could keep it down anyway.

Davey was dripping with water from the shower but still smelled of urine with his soiled underwear and jeans back on. It was the only clothing he'd had for the lower half of his body. Marilyn, who'd begun to snore in the bed over from them, hadn't thought of that while in *Walgreens*, he supposed. He crawled above the sheets as Brent finished tightening them to the headboard and sunk against the itchy comforter—feeling un*comfort*able. His face was hot like he'd developed a fever from the sulfur scented shower water and he pressed Bear Kingsley to his lips to filter the air from his chest cavity.

Brent had knelt beside his half of the bed and studied the heated boy as he twisted against the flu sensations that rotted the insides of his stomach, "you okay?" Brent had drifted his question to the boy over the comforter like it was a cursive letter across an old oak desk.

Davey had rolled and met the man's hurt stare as it peaked over the lip of the bed with his knelt body, "are you?" The boy returned, his voice barely above a whisper and his cheeks sore with red warmth.

Brent had looked away for a moment as he stood back up, his upper lip being worked against the bite of his teeth, "Yeah, bud," he'd croaked without conviction before meeting the young stare again.

Davey had frowned as he noticed the wobbly quiver in the man's voice and lip.

Brent shuffled onto his side of the bed and lowered to his back, his eyes at the ceiling and his hands lose against his strained chest.

The man's aged stuffed animal laid against the center of his chest where the tips of his fingers rested. Davey's voice, low and sweet, danced to the man from his side, "I think you need Beary more than I do, right now."

Brent had begun to cry then. Tears boiling up from pulses of pain in his throat. He kept his lips sealed, silent, and hoped the boy wouldn't notice as droplets slipped down his face to collect in his ears.

Davey's head laid into Brent's tight, quivering shoulder.

"I know you and Marilyn didn't want me to see her." He bit at his bottom lip as the man's nose flared against a crater in his breathing, "but I did," the boy's vocal cords squeezed and he nuzzled further into Brent's shoulder, "I saw her in the living room, I saw her."

Brent's hand cupped around the back of Davey's head and cradled the kid against him as his silent cry peeled into something thick and audible behind his clenched teeth.

Davey wrapped his own hand around the wrist of Brent's hold, "there was a monster, Brent, and I saw Winnie, and —"

Brent held the boy harder as his nostrils flexed deep cries. The stuffed bear slipped between them as he had turned into Davey and lowered his pulled lips against the top of his head. His eyes shut against the wet pool of oily grief and his body quaked against a held in sob that made his head burn at the base.

Davey silenced and let them man mourn.

105

Marilyn had woken to the light brush of a long, thick hand against her abdomen, its spindly fingers collecting the cloth of her shirt and bunching it up to the tip of her showing rib cage.

The motel felt hot against the spread pores in her cheeks and she lapped her tongue out to smooth the grainy, dry skin on her lips as she stirred in bed.

"Hey, *kid,*" a voice—murmured and silky—purred against her ear as the hand continued up to the wire lined bra she wore. Its rough palm igniting trails of patient pleasure down the length of her stretched stomach.

An inquisitive hiccup hitched against the back of her throat and she tilted her body into the slender warmth beside her. Her cheek increased the burn it felt as it smeared along his facial hair then stopped at the corner of his mouth—a soft spot where deep brown whiskers ended and his bit lips started.

He opened his mouth gently and danced them over her flesh as he played a kiss into her blush and laughed, the laugh quiet and tickling, "wake up."

A single eyelid had been spread to study the darkroom as the lower half of her body squirmed into him, *"Brent?"*

That slow laugh touched her again and his hand slipped below the wiring of her bra to lace her nipple between two fingers softly, "how are my babies doing?"

She smiled now, that dead grin she'd dozed off with back to spread her dry lips until they bled. She smiled because she understood he'd meant: *the moths.* And the moths were just fine. Happy, healthy, in control.

He dragged his lower lip over the tip of her jaw and she let him, her breath short and spine quivering with electrical buzzes. His upper lip joined in a gentle kiss and his hips rolled into her as his stubble scratched along her ear.

Marilyn opened her mouth to let out a whimper as her hands balled into fists against the sweating sheets but he stopped it with a *tisk* against her ear lobe: a warning to stay quiet. She pinched her mouth together and felt the bright burn of pressing pain in her lips as his fingers twitched tighter around her breast. Her head tilted away from his kneading kisses and she saw Brent–*the real one*– asleep with her brother cocooned across him in the bed beside her. She saw him and felt nothing. Felt nothing except for the liquid pooled between her legs as she turned back to the Brent that laid beside her.

"Shh," his teeth hissed the whistle and she leaned to kiss at it.

He let her.

Her breast repositioned in his hand as she flipped fully to her side and gripped at the waistband of his pants that extended over his hip and to the small of his back. Her slobbering mouth kept her intoxicated as it pressed against his lips.

His cradling hand slid out from beneath the cloth of her shirt and snuck up to her throat to lace itself around it. His kisses spreading with a smile as he gripped and felt the soft churn of moths below the surface of her smooth flesh.

Marilyn traveled a finger below his waistband and shivered as it dipped off the point in his hip and found the shallow stubble of pubic hair. Her hand cramped into a tight ball and she felt his squared belt buckle against the soft of her palm. It sparked a memory that the moths quickly smothered and left her with only one thought: *take the belt off, oh please take the belt off.*

She whimpered then–unable to contain it.

"Shut up," he'd suddenly pinned the words against her as his thumb stabbed firmly into the front of her neck.

Her head spun from the grip below her chin and she apologized by removing her hand from the lining of his pants and drifting it up to the indent of his navel.

"Do you know what I want you to do?"

She stilled and felt him lower his hips into hers.

"Marilyn?"

She nodded then.

His breath darkened and thrummed within his throat with an audible note that made the hair on Marilyn's arms prickle pleasantly, "then do it."

She was cold now. The warmth of his body evaporated and his touch only a silhouette of a dream. She was also standing now—and shivering, between the two beds as her drowsy eyes trailed the sleeping man who cradled her brother closely to him.

His hair was draped back with grease against his scalp and his face was shiny from too many tears. It had swelled beneath the watery salt: pink and puffy. Marilyn looked at him with disgust as she crept closer to the bed. It was not the man she'd just been cuddling with, kissing with. No, it wasn't. The man laid below her was the weaker—*softer*—version.

The *pathetic* Brent.

Then do it.

Feed them. The way Nick *had fed them.*

Marilyn leaned her legs into the worn mattress and stroked the tip of her middle finger up the length of Davey's spine. The touch was gentle and aroused more prickled hairs at the base of her back. She cocked her head sterilely as the boy sighed and gripped at a handful of Brent's shirt like a safety blanket.

Then she got on the bed. Her movements were slow, and limber, as the bed sagged below her weight and rocked the sleeping males. A leg perched up to her side and she arched it over the width of Brent's hips to straddle him. As she sat and wiggled her ass over the top of his jeans his eyes opened. *A light sleeper?* The tears that winked at her from his reddened eyes suggested that he hadn't been asleep at all, but only in the process of crying himself to sleep. *Pathetic.*

"Marilyn?" He removed her name from his throat in a hushed croak as he shifted beneath her.

Her weight locked into him as their bodies were sealed and the vertigo started like the crank of a roller coaster.

Brent whined and shut his eyes away from the twisting-like-candy-canes motel room and tried to arch his back away from her. His arms came up to shove at her but she'd grabbed them and forced them back down to his sides.

Marilyn knelt and laid over the top of him, her chest to his and her hands tied at the nape of his neck.

He groaned as their chests tightened together and the bed felt as if it had washed out from under them. Davey rustled against Brent and the man became aware that the small boy was smashed between them—the crease in Marilyn's elbow hooked around the back of the boy's neck and keeping him joined to them. Davey's eyes opened against agitation and his face paled around motion sickness.

"Dave," Brent's voice was smothered through the weight of their suctioned bodies.

The boy cried against Brent's chest as Marilyn's body continued to lock to the man's as she laughed drunken giggles.

It had been the longest her and Brent had touched then—and the three of them felt it. They felt the room pivot, then pivot again, then flip out from beneath them.

106

They'd been suspended in reverse, their hair drifting in spikes above their heads like they'd been hung by their ankles. Then the room shifted again and gravity made itself present. Their sight was stolen and darkness was given to the three of them as the sensation of falling expanded the spaces between their held bodies and separated them.

Marilyn's fluttered giggle stretched out and held hands with the absorbent yelp of fear that Davey gave. It wrapped itself around the sob and broke its neck, silencing it at once.

Their feet flattened into a concrete hard ground and a shock waved through their shins like they'd jumped from a high spot. Brent buckled his knees against the impact and had felt the blow in his hips, his tongue pressed to the back of his teeth to muffle his moan of pain.

The darkness was an unbearable blanket then as invisible heat sweltered into their faces like a broken car vent—or like a ghost-shaped anxiety attack.

The man's arms fanned out against his blindness until he felt a tiny, vibrating frame, and brought the boy into him.

Davey sunk his face into Brent's abdomen, "where are we?" He spoke breathlessly through beads of sweat.

Brent had shaken his head under the sightlessness, convinced they had wedged themselves into a dream. Where had Marilyn brought them? A 'Stevie Wonder' world, he supposed.

His eyes had begun to adjust and he'd sent them out to find her. The top of her frizzy head blurred in his vision at the front of the two males as it bobbed like a shadow. She was *excited.* Jittering. It made his stomach cramp.

"Moths," Marilyn's voice trailed along a circular path that globed around them.

Were they stuck in the bottom of a cylinder? The bottom of a black bottle?

Brent parted his lips to ask her what she'd meant: *moths*. His lips scraped up the silky surface of his front teeth before clamping back down into a tight line because he thought he could see it now. *Moths*. They moved in a wall around them, their dinner plate sized bodies capturing light and swallowing it before the three humans could get a taste. Like a black hole.

Brent knelt steadily and hoisted Davey, who'd been clung to him by his nails —tightly enough that the man thought he may have drawn blood from his arms. He made out the soft glow of Marilyn's wet face as she turned towards them and stilled, her face ghastly as the darkness welcomed its smile.

"Have you ever wondered where the —" her sentence suspended itself in the air as her hands crept up to pull her lower eyelids down over her cheeks, "— *Boogie Man comes from?*"

The man's muscles firmed to his skeleton as her smile became clearer to him.

The girl danced forward and began to walk away in a waltzed strut with her hands at her stomach. She patted at the flat skin below her shirt and felt the settled bodies of her sleepy babies. They were happy, home, healthy. She let a held breath break over the surface of her tongue with a quaked laugh that chased after it, falling dull into the lightless space. She felt relieved. The mothership her little moths had invaded had brought them *home,* they could evacuate her rotting body and grow to be big, *strong*. They could spend their adult lives living as *walls*.

Another giggle tickled the back of her throat as she reached out and brushed her hand through the thick swarm of reddened wings. They shrunk away from her and revealed endless darkness behind them as a strict warning before shaping back into a nineteen-fifties wallpapered cylinder. She tilted her head back and hummed curiously. The moths in her body stirred against the vibration and the wallpaper moths shifted into a long hallway for her. *Like Moses parting the sea.*

Marilyn turned the smile back over her shoulder to Brent, aware that it was a clear smile to him now as their eyes developed to the dark. It was a smile that aged her face and made her vibrant eighteen-year-old stare sag below loose eyelids, "put Davey down," she commanded through the grin.

Brent clutched the boy, whose body heat almost seemed to cool the man down, tighter into him and breathed harshly into Davey's hair, "I'm fine holding him."

She pouted, "he can walk, Brent."

His name had snapped out of her with a bad taste and he felt a shiver load against the base of his back—ready to fire up his spine with her next movement.

She turned her full body to him to study his hesitation under her sunken sight, "put him down."

Marilyn's skin trembled above bullet-shaped objects that ran beneath it, the larva sized welts swelling under the flesh on her face. Brent widened his eyes like it would help see it better. Help him determine whether he'd succumb to hallucination or if he was really seeing the girl's skin quiver like sand. "No," his voice was hard as he took a step back, away from her.

Her creased smile dissolved into a buried frown that sunk far into her jowls, "yeah," she sulked beneath her expression, "you have to." Moths began to swell away from their wall position to swarm and seal his sight back into darkness, their wings brushed and batted against his face with a webby, soft flesh finish, like powdered silk.

Brent's arms began to relax away from his chest and Davey's weight altered into the man's wrists as his small body fell down the length of the man's extended arms. Brent's neck roped hard muscles into his chest as he tried to fight it—tried to pull Davey back into a tight hold—but the cloud of insects continued to beat at him and dampen his senses. His body was flattening into a dull, numb matter. Useless and large like a pillar of flesh.

Davey began to cry out desperately as he clawed red lines down the length of Brent's arms that fell like dead tree limbs to the man's side. The boy's feet kicked into the ground and he tried to leap back up around Brent's body, "pick me back up! Pick me up!" His scream was shrill and caked with frosted horror as the moths continued to thicken around Brent's head, his face no longer visible to the boy.

Davey spun to his sister and saw her darkened face, now full of a pearly smile again, and began to sob through the humid heat.

"Pick me up!" He threw his arms out for Brent and felt them racket through the storm of moths like fisted baseball bats. He spun back with a gasp stuck in his throat and saw nothing. No Brent. Brent wasn't there any longer.

Just an empty space of heat and moth wings.

Davey jerked his legs in a tantrum as a final bawl dragged from his mouth and nose then collapsed to his butt. Defeated in the dark.

107

Listen: *I Don't Wear Glasses—Brique a Braq*

The sun materialized through branches and decorated his sight with a yellow spirit that he squinted against curiously, his eyelashes fanning down into a knitted umbrella over half of his vision. His hand brushed up and shaded his forehead as if he was sneaking a kind wave 'hello' towards the sky. The trees. The branches of leaves above his head.

He followed the bark of the trees down their fronts, to the roots, and noticed they all grew from a *rock*. All of them, from a single—*rock*, its pores grey sides wet with sprinkled condensation from the dewy grass.

He could hear laughter—Davey's. It was caramel flavored and whipped like cream. Warm like the yellow and pink dance of sunlight across tree bark and cut grass. Yellow and pink sunlight that painted the hot goosebumps away from his skin like a loving kiss.

The laugh first only existed in his head, like a nostalgic memory, then became real and loud. It spread up from behind him and he turned to it with weightless, bare feet.

A glimpse of the boy's wide eyes and floating, clean hair as he ran caught the man like a passing stranger's smile. Brief and gentle. He stepped back into the silky grass below his feet as the boy dodged around the man's legs and tumbled about in vibrant thumps towards a dip in the ground. He noticed a small hill of daisies across the park. Pregnant with vibrant color and smiling blooms.

Someone was chasing behind the boy now. They came closer with their unique patterned stomp of running feet. It was a man, a young man, and he scared Brent. The hand of the sun unable to evaporate the fear that nested between the counselor's shoulder blades. He wanted to reach out and grab the running adult, stop him, protect Davey's caramel laugh. But as the man grew closer Davey's whip cream chuckle echoed louder and Brent let himself understand that there wasn't any reason to feel fear. Davey and the young man were *playing*.

Tag, perhaps.

The young man stopped and faced Brent breathlessly, his eyes grey and cheeks blushed from the sun, "thanks for the picnic, Brent." His mouth moved with his words but the sound of his voice only existed in the coating of Brent's brain. The grey-eyed man's timbre felt in his own chest like he'd spoken the words for himself.

Brent's eyes hooded from the man and the sun and fell to his feet. Still bare and no longer padded in grass but the cold fabric of a quilt. The blanket was stitched in patches, white, then black, then white again—otherwise patternless and simple.

A bee—bumbled and striped, glided in buttery jerks around his ankle—butting into his skin to inspect for pollen. Brent shook his head at it and lifted his foot to warn it off. It bounced back from him, inspection complete, and traveled down the length of the quilt to a small stack of half-cut sandwiches. Each slice dripped with warm jelly and tanning peanut butter.

A wrinkled, dark hand came into view casually and stole the top sandwich slice with the pluck of two shaky fingers.

Brent's mouth parted warily and he followed the arm back to its owner—an ornery face with bluing cataract eyes. *Winnie?* His thought rang through his head with a hitched cry before falling into a quiet crater of disbelief, *you were dead.*

The elderly woman tore apart her sandwich and presented a corner of bread and jelly to the black cat sunbathing from her lap, "no I'm not, asshole." Her eyes sparked against the soft sun like flint wood and her dentures popped out in a mischievous smile.

Brent accepted this—and accepted she'd heard his thoughts. Like God—hearing prayers.

I was so... sad.

She winked and snagged a crumb of bread into her own mouth to chew thoughtfully.

A dainty hand spread into the space in Brent's back where fear had originally rested. The touch to his spine healing and placed for comfort. He turned to it, slowly, with feet that fell in love with the tenderness of the blanket he stood on. The face he met raised its dark eyebrows up to its dark hairline, pulled back into a fluffy bun, and smiled at him.

"Emily?" Her name scraped raw from his throat in a sticky lipped mumble as his chest contracted above his ribcage.

She cocked her head slyly at him with a toothed giggle—her canine's prominently out of line with her white teeth and beautiful, *(Yes, love?)*

Her voice echoed with its lightly enveloped joke through his head and he let the muscles in his face lift in trembles of sun-kissed happiness. It seemed okay to have her voice slide through his thoughts without a flex in her lips, it seemed normal.

"Come on," she spoke aloud this time and her hand moved from his back to his forearm, "sit." His arm followed along in her hold as she sat slowly to the silky quilt across from Winnifred and Tulsa.

He shifted to the blanket, the ground wobbly below his weight as he followed her instructions to sit and he folded his legs beneath him. The sun warmed his cheeks as it gleamed through the trees on him in a new angle.

Emily's hand trailed lightly across the top of his forearm without thought and welcomed itself into his hand to squeeze feeling into his limp fingers.

Brent watched its tan surface stroke into him for a long moment before he squeezed back. He expected the woman to pull away, but she hadn't. Instead, she looped her hold in deeper to his and talked casually above their lunch to the elderly woman.

She held his hand up in her's to greet it with her lips before placing it down on her stomach, her voice still laughing outwardly at the cat and elderly woman.

Her stomach.

Her bulge, watermelon stomach.

Her baby carrying stomach.

Her hand caressed calmly over Brent's—which laid flat against the top arch of the balloon belly—then slid down to massage gently into the bottom half of her abdomen. He watched her hand stroke the surface of her pushed out dress material and noticed the way the sun colored her wedding band.

A wedding band he'd never seen before, plated with gold and vintage. It was classy. Different than the one he'd learned to know in her classroom setting.

The hand left in his lap twitched and he spared a glance at it. A wedding band, golden like hers, met him with a graze of light from the sun. Like the sun was holding it up and showing it to him for the first time under its rays. The ring strapped to his left hand like it was a part of him. Like it was meant to be there.

"We're married," he mumbled towards the ring and both women turned their heads towards him.

Emily met his darkened pupils with a grin that seemed to make her belly bounce against his holding hand. *Mrs. Kingsley*.

"You're going to have a baby soon," he stated it like a badly read line from a play script.

Emily nodded, "we are," her hand guided his down the front of her to get a better hold on the child that kicked inside her, "William—Come out soon!" She laughed playfully at her belly, "dad and mom are dying to meet you!"

"William," Brent repeated with a wax tongue that peeled between his teeth, "a boy?"

"Yes, you knew that," she reminded and he nodded along with her–like he *had* known that.

"I did," he tried to wet his mouth as he stared hard at her stomach, "I did that?"

Emily and Winnifred's laughs mixed like a harmony inside the man's head and he felt tears warm his eyes.

"You did that, babe," Emily's voice cooed like honey, "you did that good."

He locked eyes with her and she winked beneath the sun's comfort.

"Hey, Brent!" A curly-haired, young woman chirped to him from Winnifred's side of the quilt as Brent lifted his head to her voice.

Marilyn.

Her hair was pinned back and her curls were grown out, past her breasts. She had a pair of reflected, frameless, sunglasses balanced over her nose that showed Brent's image back to him like a neatly set mirror.

His hair had greyed, at the sides, and he'd grown his beard out. The man's hand moved up to scratch it–the hair prickling below his fingernails.

She moved the glasses up and placed them at the top of her head in her soft hair to reveal mascara licked eyelashes that cascaded above awake eyes, no longer sagged, no longer deep inside grey, sleepless sockets. She wore a tank top that flowed out like a blouse over a pair of lace shorts and her shoulders were tanned from a sunburn as she squinted at the man, "sorry I'm late." Her hands pressed at her hips and her feet slipped from dirty sneakers as she stepped onto the blanket.

S'okay.

The man with the grey eyes jogged up behind the girl and kissed gently into her cheek, "how was work?" He's asked just her at that moment but Brent felt like the question was for him.

"Good," the counselor mumbled as Marilyn's chapstick soft mouth shaped the word.

Emily looked at him sideways and he let his lips close into a narrow line.

The bee was back, swaying delicately around their food like he had been invited to the picnic too. Brent decided that he had and thought to the bee: *you can stay awhile.* The bee flew to him with appreciation before lifting above their heads and exploring further into the park for pollen.

Marilyn sat and the grey-eyed man followed. He reached for two sandwiches and handed one off naturally to the girl who's hair looked much different long and weighed down. Much more velveted and sleek. Gorgeous. She took the food and kissed into the man casually—the sun setting a ray between their foreheads.

Brent knew who he was then—as if he'd known the stranger for ages, "Conner," he addressed him, "pass me a sandwich?"

Marilyn's grey-eyed boyfriend nodded and reached over the tower of bread to hand a grape jelly slice to the man. Brent ate at it, but couldn't taste it.

How long had it been? How old was Marilyn? How had she met the man named Conner?

He could feel that he'd know the answer somewhere deep inside—but the sun kept it incubated below the surface, just out of reach.

"Food!" Davey bellowed as he panted a long stride jog up to the blanket, "Yum!"

His voice was lower, Brent noticed now, and his teeth shared braces with his mouth. *You're in sixth grade.*

Davey knelt and brought a sandwich up in his hand as he eyed the aging counselor, "going into seventh," he corrected and Tulsa meowed at him.

"Going into seventh," Brent repeated.

(Brent,) Marilyn's voice smeared through his head like a horsehair bow over an untuned violin, *(look.)*

He looked at her but didn't remember looking.

The picnic was gone.

The sun was gone.

They were in a boxed room now.

Brent's skin tightened under a cooling vent above his head—surrounded by dirty fluorescent lights that had been shut off. The room they shared dark and frozen.

It was a hospital room—the hospital room—where he and the young girl had met formally. The scent was sterile and pure as it stung the back of his throat.

Marilyn's hair was short again, scraggly under a tightly tied bandage that hugged her forehead. She sat on a hospital bed, Davey asleep beside her, eight years old again. Winnifred was gone, Tulsa, Emily, the baby: it was all gone. Connor didn't exist, the name no longer belonged to Brent in a familiar way. C.O.N.N.O.R. just faded away into a list of stranger's names.

He was sitting back in a mesh hospital chair with his elbows rested out against the arms of the uncomfortable seat. He tilted his head and shrugged at the girl as she'd said something.

What had she said?

The girl shook her head at him and he noticed the purple swell once again around her eye. The purple swell from *Nick*. N.I.C.K. it came like a sharp cut down Brent's spine and he wished he could replace it with C.O.N.N.O.R.

She continued to let her head shake in the dark shadows of the unlit room. Why was it dark? It hadn't been dark the first time they'd been here.

No.

What was she saying 'no' to?

Brent's head was moving too: *No.*

"Davey had said I stopped for a deer," Marilyn's voice tugged from his memory like a dead, dragged body.

No, there wasn't a deer.

There was a *Boogie Man.*

Brent could feel his heart pick a hyper pace as the creature materialized inside his skull.

Marilyn's hospital gown had slipped, the corner of the sleeves down her olive shoulders the same way she slipped her lower eyelids down when mimicking the *Boogie Man.*

Brent had looked this time–studied her skin as the material sank around it. He remembered he hadn't looked the first time it had happened, his sight keeping direct pace with her's as she'd scooted to the edge of the paper bed– but he looked now. He looked and he saw rot.

The flesh that hid her collar bones had begun to erode into deeply, sand pitted holes, and moths had begun to eat their way out. Their bodies stretched from the slits in her body and their wings extended as they shook her skin off like *puppies* shaking away water.

Brent reclined further into the hospital seat.

"Brent, look." Marilyn's voice came again.

Her hand was held out to him, in it: the two magnets he'd used to describe what they felt inside their heads' the first time they'd sat in these spots. The globe of gravitational pull that separated their brain matter. A metallic cookie cutter wet with novocaine in their psyche.

Hadn't it been him who grabbed the magnets the first time?

He'd reached up and collected the black ceramic from the whiteboard behind him, the one with the *Rate Your Pain* chart taped to the bottom of its glossy surface. He twisted his head around to the whiteboard now–the *Rate Your Pain* chart exactly where he'd remembered it, but now it seemed to laugh at him. Each scaled face enhanced with black, sunken eyes. The mouths of them dropping further down the chart, the last unhinged and dripping towards the floor. *Dripping.* Like fresh ink.

He turned back to Marilyn and the magnets in her hand.

His hand was in her hand now.

He didn't remember how he'd gotten it there, on top of hers like they were shaking hands over a demonic deal. A crossroads.

Brent could feel the pulse of the magnets against his flesh, hot and wubbing, as they distanced from one another in a magnetic repel.

He could feel Marilyn's touch, calloused and fragile.

He could feel the room gyrating through them as his vision darkened and his stomach ached.

The magnets in their hands folded together with a snap. They caught the flesh on his thumb in a tight pinch and he threw them at the floor. Her hand broke away from him with his burst of movement.

The magnets never hit the floor. The magnets had never left their hands, actually. One welded into his palm, the other into hers, like *Joy Buzzers*. Brent turned his hand over slowly and studied the matte black slice of a cylinder that'd sunk into his skin.

And sunk.

And sunk.

Until it wasn't a magnet at all, but a hole.

A keyhole.

A slot.

"Brent, look."

He did—despite the quill of hair at his neck that stood as Marilyn's voice crept on spider legs from the spaces between her teeth, its pitch deepened below a growl.

In her hand was no longer a magnet either, nor a hole, but a key.

Black, beady-eyed, key.

Her hand was in his again, suffocating his hold on her. Brent felt the key slide into him and he dipped his head to his chest with the wave of squeezed pain that hiked through his body like an electrical current.

It slipped deeply and parted the dark veins in his wrist like a split in cedarwood.

Brent bit into his lip and withdrew from her as the souls of his shoes scuffed into the unmopped hospital floor. She held harder, the grooves in the key shifting into his flesh like teeth and keeping him there, stuck to her.

The man could feel the ink faces behind him—the *Rate Your Pain* chart—as they smudged their jaws further towards the floor with their broken smiles. He could smell the fresh, black ink as it oozed like Nancy had oozed and he began to whimper.

The whimpers were plain, colorless, flavorless, and raw. The whimpers were female.

He looked for Marilyn again and saw her pinned eyes wild on him. Brent was not whimpering.

It was her.

Her lips sealed together like she was fighting to keep something in. Her mouth trembling behind each static whine.

The key licked deeper into his body and the girl's mouth steadied against the tremble.

Then it opened.

"We're special, Brent." She cried his name as her jaw began to sink towards the ground, "we touch and the world opens." Her jaw stopped like a hiccup in an elevator, stuck as far as the bones in her face would allow. Lockjaw.

Then it broke.

The snap echoed from her and through Brent like an atomic bomb that needled his stomach with radioactive fluid. The fluid crept and he could feel it heat the back of his throat as the girl's flesh stretched to lower the bottom half of her jaw further towards the floor.

She glanced to her side, "Look—Brent." Her voice came to him with prominent dictation despite the tongue that lapped in a gray, dead form between her bottom row of teeth—now hung near her chest.

He looked.

"Like a lock and key, Brent."

An image, held up like a magic mirror, greeted him from their side. It'd opened with a fog wisped fabric, like a curtain, or a mesh veil. Through it he could see the alive moth winged wallpaper of the deeply blind world he'd been stuck in with the siblings not long before he showed up in the park, then the hospital.

He remembered it now, he remembered holding Davey—and then not holding Davey. Why had he let go of the boy?

He detoured from the frame hole they'd opened with their touch and searched for the sleeping boy on the hospital bed. The bed was empty beside the decaying body of Marilyn that sat at the tip of it.

"Davey," Brent heard himself slur.

The girl pulsed her fingers against his grip like morse code and Brent's head was forced back to stare at the black world through the veiled hole. He could see the boy sat on his butt in the darkness, like Brent was watching a TV screen capture of a live play: *Davey and the Darkness*. The kid was small and out of focus on an unlit stage.

"Davey," Brent said his name again and the slur became harder inside his chest, like a sleight of rain.

"We open the world, Brent."

He faced Marilyn with a clear mind, "I want to go back."

Her head tilted and her jaw made a wet slap against her lap as the skin from her cheeks continued to stretch into spaghetti noodle strands.

"I want to go to Davey," his free, keyless hand pointed out to the space that reflected beside them—the two-way mirror into a *Stevie Wonderland*.

The jaw that no longer belonged to her face seemed to sneak up in a smile—in some odd way—Brent could see it. A grin with her bottom row of teeth tilted forward and her eyes squinted.

The ink behind him dribbled against the floor in stormy drops and began to roll towards his ankles where they could grip. Grip like hawk talons into his pant legs and fleshy bones. "I want to go back," he repeated coldly against the hold that made his feet harden.

The smile continued to tilt on the girl's broken face as the strung-out cheeks that held her lower jowl into place like swing ropes quivered against her ragged breath, "look, Brent." Her hand-extracted from his then.

The key hollowing out his hand and lined pieces of his tendons out on its hooked face. The man cried out as a soft, chunky stream of his blood speckled his pants—clean pants—his *picnic* pants. He cradled the throb in his arm to his chest and *looked.* Again, against his will.

The black-framed veil was gone, Davey was gone.

"Wait, no!" He yelped as his body whiplashed forward towards the empty space where the curtain they'd opened had been.

"Stay!" He heard Marilyn's gruff voice demand as her dead body rushed at him. Her hands attacking his shoulders like she had when he'd sat at the lip of the tub. Like Amanda had when he was four—exploring the world of *Boat Kingsley.*

He fell through the backing of the hospital chair and his back slammed into a dirty sock scented carpet.

108

Brent's spindly fingers dredged into matted synthetic curls of wool as he was projected violently from his dream. His back arched against the itch of the floor while his lungs gargled against motel air and he peeled up his fever painted eyelids to study a fogged, distant ceiling.

The arch in his back peaked into a pinch and he rolled from it to his side, as a moan warned him of hot vomit in the back of his throat. The man tried to swallow against it but was forced into a cramped, ugly dry heave despite the efforts. He could feel his stomach crumple like a paper bag from within him and he brought his knees up to try to comfort it as another retch rocked through his frame and made his body tremble in cold sweats.

It had been a nightmare.

He was on the floor of the motel room.

Winnifred really WAS dead.

Winnie was dead, Winnie was dead.

Winnie—was... DEAD.

He sat up against the wet infection inside his weak person and pressed the back of his hands to his clam skin eyes. As the darkness flat ironed into his eyelids and enclosed him inside his head he was able to feel the hospital room again, *"Brent, look."* He mumbled as his hands came down to his lap and his eyes rejected their forced upon darkness.

He stared at the motel room in front of him. The motel room. Motel, "Brent, look." He said to himself again with a bare voice. His name felt foreign as it swirled from his lips like a drunken fly.

He could feel the importance begin to trickle between his breast bone as he scowled at the motel wall across from him—*motel.*

We are in a motel.

We.

An inclusive word that triggered a muscular response: *We.*

The man stumbled to his feet lamely and scoured the two motel beds for *we*. Empty. The sheets were spat up into slept in bunches but the children were gone. *We.*

"Brent, look," he muttered again and could hear the leftover residue of Marilyn's ragged voice inside his head.

He looked further, to the ground, where he'd woken up and felt the oxygen in his body shrink away as his tongue swelled. Beside him, like the lined up bodies of deceased soldiers, were the children. Davey and Marilyn, both unresponsive vessels laid out flat on their backs on the carpet. He'd been laid out beside them, like the three of them had been prepared to be zipped into black body bags.

Brent choked on a chest full of panic as he moved to drop over Davey, sweat from his brow distracting his attention as it plopped against the comatose boy, "hey kid," his voice drowned beneath a rippled wave, "wake up, kid." His hands gripped at the boy's moist, cold shoulders and kneaded into the pale flesh. He could feel the lame roll of Davey's bones below sleeping muscles as he tried to gently shake the boy awake.

The man lifted Davey to his ear and listened for the soft exhale and intake of air as he held his own breath. The boy was sighing softly and the man hugged him into his chest with relief as Davey's head limped back away from him. Alive.

Davey was alive.

Winnifred was *not*.

Snot blew in a webbed line from the man's nose as he memorized the hitching, asleep, breath against his eardrum. As he cradled Davey he thought of the nightmare he'd woken from, bits of it coming to him like sun reflections off broken glass; bright, hot and gleamy. He remembered Davey sat in the dark world, sat like a small actor on a large stage that faced a crowdless theater.

"I want to go back," the man said into the boy's greasing hair.

Go back.

Go back the same way he'd come, to the moth wallpapered space Marilyn had taken them.

He turned his head to the silent girl laid out on the carpet with her cheeks hollow and her grey under eyes prominent.

"I want to go to Davey," his lips turned with the words but his voice staid smoothly within the nightmare, where he'd originally spoken those words to the girl as they watched Davey through the opened veil.

(*We touch and the world opens,*) the girl had said.

The man could hear her voice now, like frosting decorating the inside of his skull and making his brain sticky with cane sugar, "Like a lock and key, Brent." He spoke the words before the cavity nightmare could and felt the water riptide scoop away his insides with a grappling hook. His skin a numb carcass as he laid the boy back onto the carpet and crawled to her.

He tilted over Marilyn's silent body and understood. The space cratered into the center of their heads, the *ice pick lobotomy*, was where the lock and key sat. When they touched, the hook, line, and sink of key to lock created a vortex. A black hole, absorbent of all light, that sucked them into an *open world*. The 'Stevie Wonderland' of sweltering blindness and moths.

Where the *Boogie Man* came from.

Where Davey was now.

Where she was now.

Where Brent was *not*.

"I want to go back."

His hands slipped down his tight, knelt on thighs and tucked around the girl's face where he was devoid of sensation. He streaked his thumbs across her stoned cheeks and craved to feel the steel breeze of a musky Ferris ride swirl– but nothing came. His skin glided along her's without pain and his head felt clear and cloudless.

Brent's mouth tightened behind his teeth as it dried and his heart forgot to feel its beats within his chest, "Marilyn," his posture broke into a low hunch as he winced her name from his sandy tongue, "oh, kid." He lost his voice somewhere inside the pit of his stomach and nothing but a whistled whisper gave life to his words. She'd pulled the key out of him. *(Stay)* she had demanded.

He was stuck here.

Davey was stuck there, with a ratted, leather version of his older sister.

The man's brow-line shrunk as he laid his forehead into the girl's, her curled bangs wetting into his sweat as he did so, "I want to go back."

(*Brent, look.*)

He stilled into the girl and felt the creep of liquid darkness smear towards him in clawed lines of shadow. He felt the notion of company and was reminded of the stretched, ink, faces that had melted behind him in the dreamt hospital room. The ink that had rolled beneath his feet and grew along his ankles. *Rate Your Pain.*

(*Brent, look.*)

The lingering air, pinned like a button into his chest, left in a slow, twisted, exhale as he brought his head away from the girl and *looked.* As his head shifted over his shoulder with a strung, owlish neck he was able to notice it. *It.* Hidden in the shadows.

The *Boogie Man.*

It watched him closely through lifeless, pebbled eyes.

"I want to go to Davey," the man whispered to himself as he rose to his feet unhurriedly with his arms dead at his sides—eye contact kept steady with the creature's gloomy stare. He could feel his guts shift with his slow elevated movement and the bones in his knees begin to feel stale. Pink sweat dripped from his hairline and streaked paint down his nose as he challenged the creature with his posture. The same way you might with a bear. Solid and statued.

Except, with a bear, you're meant to back up, talk calmly: apologize for being in its way and slowly back step your way to safety. At least, Brent had heard that's what you do—heard it as a child somewhere and decided to carry it along with him in case he ever did *run into a bear.*

But Brent did not back up now, he did not apologize, the *Boogie Man* was not a bear unsuspectedly on the same woodsy trail as Brent. *No.*

The Boogie Man had mastered its shape shift, for Marilyn it had been Brent, for Davey it'd been a blanket fort, but for the *real* Brent... for the real Brent, it stayed pure. Pure creature. Pure monster. Purely decaying.

Brent could feel his chest thicken with a wet snarl in the base of his throat. Like a dog, warning off a much larger predator. He knocked the human growl out with words, "take me back."

The creature clicked its jaw away from its joints and its skin trollied its lower jowl towards the ground.

Brent flexed his nose at the scent of rot and the falling jaw that reminded him of a dumbwaiter as he stretched his arms out as if he were being crucified on a cross, "take me back." His arms ached and he decided he didn't look like he was hung from a cross, but like a suicide jumper, "take me back."

The creature seemed confused, pondering, *drunk* on death and bodily debris.

Brent wanted to spit at it as he banged the flat of his hand into his chest: like an ape. Each slap of his hand to his chest a catastrophic explosion that rattled his teeth and whooped the terrified words from his lips, "Take me back! Take me back!"

The man advanced toward the lanky, grey creature with anger so sharp it seemed to piss from the center of his body like a wire blade. Anger so suddenly placed into view like the red line of a sniper's laser.

Anger rinsed out with regret as the *Boogie Man's* talons strangled around him, a high strung shriek breaking from the inside of its body.

It had unzipped him from his intestines.

Its black fingers boring into the man and stringing his guts to the floor as blood boiled in gurgles through the man's teeth. *Rate Your Pain!*

Brent's arms caked around its head as he felt ice stack itself inside his legs and the blood from his stomach made his pants feel muddy. Everything flopped in a long drape of pink down the outside of his body.

The creature pitched its shriek louder, in competition with the pained cry that sparrowed from the ripped man. It dug deeper, to the man's spine, and used it as a handle to pull the man along with it.

Brent's head sunk back lifelessly against his neck. His sightless eyes bulged at the motel wall behind him.

109

Bear Kingsley was bound into Davey's stomach as the boy's free hand retracted back into his hair and tugged at loose strands of grease, collected at the roots of his skull like wax. The bear's legs dangled like a limp pendulum as the boy shivered through a cry and dragged his knees to his chest and pinched the animal between them.

The bear was stroked through tingling fingers as Davey strained his eyes into the moth swarmed darkness, "he's gone," the boy had whined as the stuffed animal's fur stuck to the sweat on the boy's flesh. *Brent* was gone.

There, just a minute before—gone the next.

Where had he gone?

The bear swung lowly through the air as the boy stood with its arm clenched in his hand. He spun and the bear did too, crashing featherdly into the boy's knee.

"Brent's gone!" He skinned his voice through the hot, swarming air to his sister, the yell tasting like antique sandpaper and sawdust.

Dust. Like the dust on the moth's wings.

The boy could feel his baby pulse hammer-like sludge through his forked veins as he scanned the darkness for his sister. He could feel the darkness enclose over him, congregated in webs of fluttering wings. Each wing pricked with hairs that stabbed at the boy like tetanus shots. He'd begun to scream and swat at the insects—their fat bodies pelting off his striking fingers. They were trapping him like they trapped Brent, before he disappeared, before he was *gone*.

Davey began to nurse on the humid air, forgetting to release it, trying to inflate his lungs. Still swatting and suffocating.

"Stop."

Stop.

The word had traveled under Davey's scream and met him like the bite of a dog into the side of his streaked cheeks.

Stop.

The moths receded then, away from him. Receded like the hair on an elder's head. They frilled wickedly amongst each other, dropping and flipping to their backs as they fought through the air together to make a cylinder hallway shape once again. Returned to their posts. Like soldiers.

He could see again, his sister stood with her hands at her face. Her lips pursed forward, suspended after her spoken word: *"stop."* The moths had listened. The moths were obedient to her.

Bear Kingsley was jerked along the side of the boy as Davey stumbled forward to her, his hand pressed into his chest as he gagged air, his stretched out palm and fingers looking like the hand of a traffic cop for a congested airway. Or, like he was *Pledging Allegiance*. Or making an oath. "Marilyn!" He'd bawled like a child much younger than his actual age. Her name tumbling from his lips like a toddler down a steep set of stairs. *Crash, burn, babies learn.*

Marilyn's eyes rolled back into her head, bounced like they'd kissed a spring that was cork-screwed into her brain, and flashed back forward to him to hold his wide, frantic stare. Her eyelashes flicked up high to keep her vision clear and crazy.

The boy stopped and the bear in his hand was tossed up to his mouth like a blanket would be pulled up to the brim of someone's eyes as they watched a horror movie, the music anticipating a *jump!* A startle!

The bear masked Davey's nose and upper lip and his feet burned as he flattened them into the ground in a hollowed stance.

A bear and a gas mask...

The hands at Marilyn's face began to streak down her skin as if she were applying sunscreen. They moved slowly, dragging her cheeks down with her palms. It left red, painful Indian burns behind each slide of her sweaty hand that once fell from the peak in her jaw moved back up to her eyes and slid down once again. Then again. And again.

Her skin was swollen pink and her eyes seemed dead as they drifted along with Davey's. Like bobbers in a lake. Bobbers to catch a fish and bludgeon it to death with the back end of a garden shovel.

Her nails curled in and skin began to collect beneath them, spotted blood collecting in their stiff cuticle wake. Her hands slapped into her hair and grabbed strands of that too. Yanking it out like strings of hay.

Davey hadn't known that the girl in front of him had done the same thing the day their father died. The day their father dangled socked toes and saggy pants from the ceiling fan in Davey's nursery. She'd clawed and her head had gone bald in spots.

He hadn't known that their mother was forced to cut the girl's hair short just to hide the split ends and frayed patched.

She'd never told him that part when she told him about that night.

They had talked about *that night* only a few times, Davey bringing it up when he had questions—Marilyn bringing it up when she was pouting about something and needed to hold it over his head. *Dad died in your room and you're lucky enough you don't remember. I found him.*

She'd always made it seem like it was his fault, at least, that's how he'd felt. It *was* his fault. Dad died because Dad didn't like Davey: *or something.*

He'd always been very sure of that. Even mom, through her sneering drunk words and greasy lips, had made it seem that way to Davey. Made him seem like he was the culprit that pushed a man to *suicide.*

Suicide.

Davey understood what it meant but always wondered if it was a secret. Only certain people in the world knew about the word and its meaning, perhaps. If more people knew, more people would talk about it: *Right?*

Just like everybody talked about car crashes and the Holocaust.

Suicide.

His lips mimed the word into Bear Kingsley's stuffed side as he considered the *secret* that he knew.

Marilyn tilted her head and her limbs clanked like weighted chains to her side then, Davey's body responding with frozen goose flesh and tightened fists around the bear still held to his face.

The girl's cheeks swelled outward like she had a kiss face full of air and her eyes squinted into small, half almond slits.

Squinted at the boy and for a second he thought he saw *his Marilyn,* the sister he'd grown up with. The one who read him books and let him ditch school for movie matinees at the *Regal Cinema* in the town over. The one who twisted around in her sleep and sometimes accidentally kicked him, or stole his blanket. The one who did what she was able to see him healthy and smiling. The *happy Marilyn.*

It was brief, a blink of an eye maybe, but as he stared at her he'd sworn he saw it before her cheeks melted back into slacked skin and her eyes bulged at him.

Davey's thighs flexed in his piss pants and his knees quivered consequently as Bear Kingsley collected snot in his matted fur.

Bear Kingsley was a good friend. A good bundle of comfort when the boy needed it and an even better snot rag, as it turned out. Bear Kingsley, however, was easily forgotten then, as his fuzz plush was dropped to the ground. His bead sack arms slapping into vantablack darkness in front of Davey's toes.

Dropped because Davey had become unable to *hold on* as he saw a *thing*, the *thing*, creeping up behind his red-cheeked sister. His hands becoming cold and caked in what felt like chalk. Or dried cement.

The *thing* stared through Davey with its dead, black eyes.

The *thing* that had camouflaged itself over Winnifred as a child's fort—made of blankets and wrinkled bed sheets.

Davey wanted to warn his sister, her name stuffed into his mouth like a dirty sock, "*Mm—Mm—M,*" His throat bulged against the stuck stutter, like a cat working up a hairball, "*M— Mm —*" he pressed hard with his tonsils, but it wasn't coming. Her name was stuck as if it were dry cotton, painful and ripping. His bottom lip folded in and his tongue jabbed at it: *get out of my way!* Its pink budded surface seemed to say to the cracked flesh bitten between his teeth: *I need to say the girl's name!* But the lip was stationary now, locked between jagged front teeth like a limb pinched between a dull guillotine. Or the half rung neck of a bird.

Stuck.

I'm Stuck.

The *thing*, the horrible beast that it was, caught up to Marilyn's backside and snaked a bloodied talon hand around her wide, crooked, hips. *Always crooked because the girl would sleep twisted on her side with one hip jammed all the way into her stomach.*

"*Mm—!*" Davey thought he could feel the veins in his temples begin to expand through his bones as he tried to force the name from his clamped mouth.

Marilyn's own hands lifted from her side and trailed delicately around the holding, rotted arm that had hiked the cloth of her shirt up unknowingly. Her eyes left Davey as her head tilted back and they rolled up to study the creature's head as it popped over her shoulder expectedly.

Expectedly?

What was it expecting?

She puckered her lips and kissed it. Kissed the devil on her shoulder. Rot and meaty stench licking into the rim of her mouth as she kissed and its skin wriggled below her loving touch.

Davey gave up on the stuttered name and let a high whimper jiggle from his nostrils instead.

The creature's hand trailed the inside of Marilyn's shirt and rested onto her breast, one side of her chest now looking plated with pipes where its fingers laid.

The girl's eyes rolled back to Davey and for a moment he thought she looked partly *embarrassed*, the way a parent may look when they get stuck watching a sex scene with their child: guilty even. But then the monster hand below her shirt flexed and she gave a smile to her little brother. A deep, gum and tooth smile.

He wanted to look away, to shield his eyes, but he couldn't.

He was *stuck*.

The thing laced itself against her the way a human male might to a small woman he loved and Davey wondered if it was doing *camouflage* again. Like it had with the living room blanket fort. He could see a *monster*, Marilyn could see *love*. Was that it?

The creature nipped at an ear that sat nested among Marilyn's curly hair with lightly whispered words. Words that sounded like the scream of an owl from Davey's paralyzed stance.

The girl's hands clawed into its loose flesh like a kneading cat and her mouth parted. Her eyes stuck to Davey like an invisible string tied her irises to his.

Stuck.

Something behind her tongue began to move, to flick, to twitch. *Something.* It twitched like the stem of a cherry–or *antennas*. Antennas and stringy legs and *wings* crawled out onto the flat of her tongue. A moth.

That slow, tightened, "*Mm–m–m*", started like an old car motor in the boy's throat again.

Marilyn's whole body began to quiver. Quiver with the ripples of insects racing below her flesh. One dug from her collar bone in the same fashion a blackhead would expand from a dirty pore. It flew forward at Davey as the rest of her body crumbled with crawling, winged insects. Like an anthill.

Bear Kingsley was forgotten entirely then–left to sleep against the sweltering floor as Davey's paralysis broke and his body spun to sprint. His legs pumped wildly and he could hear the deep *thwomp, thwomp, thwomp* of his heart from the backside of his ears. His legs burned above the back of his knees with each press off the ground and he thought horribly that the *thwomp, thwomp, thwomp* was not his heart at all, but the creature following with mucky swamped slaps of its fleshy feet.

The boy screamed through the letter 'M', "*Mmmmhh!!!*" Because that's the only sound he could make as he swore *IT WAS* chasing him with his sister towing behind it like a popped sandbag.

Like something he'd seen in *Coraline*.

(The mice want to give you a message. They say, 'don't go through small door.')

Through the small door, the mice were RATS. Rats with sand-filled in their bellies and stitched sacks for their skin.

Davey's knees puckered as he ran like they might give out as his fists swung like Cheney Hammers through a wall of moths and he felt needled splats of wings against his fingertips.

"Mmmmhhhhh!!" He cried with an open mouth and clenched teeth, his tongue slicking the roof of his mouth as the back of it bore down towards his throat, like he'd eaten peanut butter, or super glued it to the back of his top row of teeth.

Davey fell then.

Tripped, actually, *most likely.*

Like *ink* had leaked up his soiled jeans and YANKED his ankles out from under him.

A bellowed yelp broke from the boy just before his head broke his fall, his clumsy hands coming into contact with the hot dark bottom after his forehead had already bounced up, then back down again. Excruciating pain was there for a blinking second, *(like the one he'd seen the happy Marilyn in),* just before his eyes drove upward into his skull.

The sound like a golf ball being slugged into an ice-topped lake with a meaty *CRACK* lingered in his ears for a long moment after the pain, then the low hiss of static took its place and he felt, for a moment, comfortable.

He blacked out after that.

110

Brent, *the Brent she liked,* walked with webbed feet in front of her. His hand was back behind him and entangled into hers, like a roped knot. He led her that way through the boiled oxygen heat with her arm lying loosely behind him and his grip.

She felt tranquil, felt inhibited by a darker force and *nothing* like Marilyn. She walked, heel-to-toe, behind the tall man for an eternal hour, her internal clock ticking and soothing the moths that had stayed within her.

Her head sank against her shoulders as her knees bent and stomped and her eyes rolled back behind her to see the wade of darkness the two of them left behind. She'd seen the tail end of a running boy that way, his shirt fading into the darkness, then soon his whole body too. *Gone.*

Who was that boy?

A foreign object of tangled short hair and baby eyes. She guessed she'd somehow *known* him. A sensation of familiarity really making her chest fucking ache.

She knew he'd been horrified as she'd kissed Brent, the man's hand on her breast. She'd seen the expression so clearly it'd made her insides tingle like the static of a lost T.V. channel. Made her want to reach out and fucking *squeeze* him. Squeeze him until he popped and oozed yellow, frothy disease. Oh, but he'd run. He'd run and now he was gone.

Marilyn's head sat back up and balanced itself on a stack of vertebrae. She thought about *kissing* now. Kissing Brent. His sweet taste that had fumed into her mouth and candied over the caps of her teeth like fluoride.

She wanted to kiss him again.

"Where are you taking me?" she'd asked and her voice had died in the air with a flat drone.

His hand had tightened around her, then he'd removed it. His body stopped and turned to study her.

Marilyn blushed as her arm dropped against her side and clipped the peaked corner of her hip.

His eyes were cold on her (beady, even) as his chest lifted and fell slowly, a smirk set kindly into his cheeks, "do you know what I want you to do?" Unlike her words, his had flapped through the air like soft wings and landed delicately on the girl's shoulders.

She pinched her lips to keep from smiling.

He winked, able to see her humble holdback, "Feed them, mama."

His request the same as it had been before, but this time seemed to sparkle in a way that lit small fires inside of her. Like her body was the map of a *campground* just before sundown.

He slipped back into the shadow then, invisible from her eye. *Gone.* Just like the running boy was *gone.*

In front of her, on the black ground, was a body. *His* body. The *pathetic* Brent. The one she *hated.* Yes, she didn't remember the boy—but she remembered the man.

An animalish snarl set in as she stepped towards the crumbled body, "*Mr. Kingsley.*" Saliva slipped from the front of her barren teeth and fell into the pink ravine of her dried lower lip.

111

He was alive.

The guts that had been unzipped and dangled like pink jewelry down the front side of his body had somehow recoiled back into their moist, warm home. His stomach sewn shut by jagged scars that puffed out in grey flesh. He could feel his intestines shifting back into their original pose as he lay with his eyes shut against the ground, their texture like wet sand.

He was thinking about the young clerk at the photo kiosk, from when he'd met Marilyn, informally. Her blue/green braces that'd matched her fingernails and her thick upper lip that'd swelled over the metal on her teeth. *What had been her name?*

A line of gut splatted into the inside wall of his abdomen and his toes flexed unhappily against the pain.

Lili. That'd been her name. *Lili.* He could see it scribbled across her plastic white name badge in delicate strokes of *Sharpie*.

Had he thanked her for helping him with the photos? Or had he been too intoxicated by the vertigo that'd made his heels feel as if they were sinking below the earth—like quicksand.

The sweat that precipitated against his forehead in swelled drops seemed to dip across his cold skin in the shape of her name. Like it was twisting in a small, theme park roller coaster.

"*Thank you for your help, Lili.*" He mumbled, although unsure if his voice had come out of him at all.

He thought of the braced girl, perhaps, because he'd felt guilty for failing to give her gratitude. Or perhaps, because he really only wanted to think of Winnifred, but Lili kept falling in the way.

She *had* come first, hadn't she?

First Lili, then the flat screen kiosk, then the slow download from his phone, then the hour wait you'd get while the digital pictures printed.

Then, Lili would've given the photos to him. *The photos.* Of the elderly woman and the weary cat.

"*Are you all finished with your shopping?*" Lili would've asked sheepishly from beneath her red cheeks—elastic with widened, crater pores.

Brent would've said, "*yes!*" and she would've rung up his total with the click of nails that matched her wire-metal smile.

Would've.

But he'd never gotten that far.

Or, maybe, he'd gone *too* far—*in the wrong direction*—and now he was here.

Here.

Where was here?

"Mr. Kingsley."

Brent's breath made short hiccups against the dark and dusty ground like Morse Code, all probably spelling *S.O.S.* as the rasped voice trickled down over him in pin needled rain.

Mr. Kingsley.

The man triaged a palm to his freshly scarred stomach and made a grunted effort to roll up to his knees, "Marilyn." Her name warned from his crisp lips as he didn't quite make the knelt position and landed, tripoded out, with his free hand braced into the ground and his head bent down against his chest. His guts slid in swallowed lumps against the front of his abdomen and he clenched his holding hand as if to grab them before they could fall *further*. Fall threw him, even.

The sound of a slap carried only by gray tones answered his call of her name.

Brent filleted his hand over the deeply shadowed and sweaty ground until he felt stability in his knees and rose up in the two-legged crouch he'd originally tried for. His body swayed sorely on a soft spine and he thought, for a moment, he'd lose his tied in guts out the back of his pants as his weight shifted.

Spots flicked across his vision in the color of dead flesh and his nose warmed familiarly with the sweet residue of orange vomit, "*Hey-heh.*" He bit his lip until the dried skin split sideways.

"What was that?" Her voice was tangy and *smart* from above him, mocked from the back of her throat like a smooth exhale of skunky smoke.

The spots in his eyes began to dissipate into deep holes of sight that he stared at her through. Her face was red and puffy, cut dully by long strikes of her nails that pulled the blood to the surface where it speckled like bee stung beauty marks. Her body seemed rotten, below the swollen face. Rotten like she'd been in the hospital room from Brent's dream—he could remember that now. The craters on her skin picked like leprosy.

Moths moved in and out of the bloodless abscesses like busy workers, building a nest. A moth hive. A joined cocoon. An anthill. Brent watched with taxed nausea in his rearranged gut as the small insects carried small, bitten off, pieces of Marilyn on their damp, hairy backs. Chunks of flesh—creamy with bodily residue and infection.

"Oh, Kid," The man whined with a block of built-up breath that dwindled into a depressed sigh. Ejected from him like an oozy bubble of disappointment.

The girl, meticulously puppeted by the hungry bugs, swung her head into a dramatic shake, "*Kid,*" her hiss muffled by the mop of sweat wet hair that swung around her as she continued to shake, "I hate that, I hate that name. We hate that name."

"We," Brent repeated without the incline of a question in his voice and watched as Marilyn, *(what was left of her)* glanced down at the moths that fluttered against her and through her. Brent nodded with understanding.

The girl began to mumble with a low sound of smeared latex tied in with her voice, *"...ed, em."* She danced lightly around her half-heard words as she repeated them like an echo, *"ed, em, ed, em, ed, em."*

Brent shuffled forward against the friction hot ground and the latex in the girl's words became *gritty*—gritty enough that he could feel each of her breaths and pronunciations grind through the valleys of his own molars and send sparklers of bright pain to the backs of his eyes.

Her words became audible, blubbered from a deeply stretched smile, *"feed them, feed them, feed them."*

"Who?" Brent knew who, but he'd asked anyway. He knew who, or *what*, as he watched a moth string skin from the bottom of Marilyn's tongue—*the moths*. She had to feed the moths. That's what it was—and it looked like she was already succeeding.

"Them," Marilyn giggled carelessly as the moth dropped from her mouth and her uvula tapped the back of her tongue in small, punched out clicks.

Brent's back spasmed as he straightened his spine to angle his tired eyes up into hers, "how?" Stern disappointment was a train that took his single word from his lips and delivered it to the girl on metal tracks. He'd spoken it from the grave, his voice buried below steady soil to keep it out of the arms of a quiver.

"I'm-gonna *fucking* kill ya!" Her eyes bulged with the words as her fingers jumped beside her like spiders tied to the end of her decomposing arms. The grit that'd been in her voice now smeared down her chin in a mucused drool as she gurgled her giggle.

As simple as that.

A made-up, theatrical performance plagiarized off the back of Jack *I-Said-I'm-Not-Gonna-Hurt-Ya-I'm-Only-Gonna-Bash-Your-Brains-In* Nickolsen himself.

Unamusment made an overcast of dark lines in Brent's face before he shifted away from their cheap horror film dialog, "Where's Davey?" That's what he'd really wanted to know, wasn't it? *Davey.* That's why he'd begged to be brought back.

An opaque glass, muddy with clouds, slid into the hollow of Marilyn's eyes as her face slacked, "Dave," she spoke as if she'd been hypnotized. Hypnotized by the memory of the small human that had run away from her. *Davey.* "Fuckin' —" The cloud in her vision dissipated to reveal incubated moths within the layers if her eyeballs, "Davey!" His name barked with a sliced cheek smile.

It occurred to Brent, as he watched her study thoughts inside her own head, that she wasn't associating herself with the name. She did not know *Davey* personally any longer. His spine erected straighter then, and he began to choke on his steady, concentrated, breathing.

"He ran away from me."

Brent's mouth opened and the saliva that had coated his tongue like hot candle wax evaporated into the dark air.

Davey had run—Davey was alive.

The man's mouth shut with a stone jaw that crackled against the drums in his ears.

Marilyn's teeth snarled down toward him, the spaces between them bleeding out a silver giggle, "I'm-gonna *fucking* kill Davey!" She spun with her wolfed words toward the direction she remembered seeing the boy last.

Instantly, Brent's body crumbled forward as a foot stacked beneath him to stand, "No!" The hoarse holler peeled the dried-white wax from his tongue and bolted nails into his eyes, like train yard spikes to hold his eyelids up and wide.

The girl stopped and her shoulder blades pinned out of her back that now faced the man who shrieked at her while on one knee.

A proposal gone bad, perhaps.

112

Brent knew that his tangled yelp, *"No!"* Had not been what stopped the deranged, decaying girl. Hadn't been what made her turn back to him and reconsider who she'd *fucking kill* first. He, in fact, had *nothing* to do with the way she'd slumped around and studied him like a child who'd been told to go back to the dinner table to finish their greens on their supper plate.

But he knew who *did.* Or, *what,* had stopped the girl.

He could see it.

Its body slinking out of the shadow to block Marilyn as she'd turned to find Davey. Its jaw painted down into a smeared frown. *Like ink.*

Rate your Pain —

—And the steady ache against the crisping carcass of Brent's chest told him: *six.*

The creature had clicked at Marilyn. Small, spitless gleeks, from the black tongue that sunk deep into the pit of its jaw. It had *communicated* with her that way—and she had nodded. She'd nodded and turned back around, and studied Brent like a gross meal. Like it'd told her to. Like she'd understood it.

Despite the cold pulse that froze against Brent's flesh like sewing needles, he found himself beckoning her with a nod, "me first."

Her finger twirled up in the air, "you tried to trick me," she contemplated as her finger then dove down and plunged into the waistband of her pants, "you tried to send me after the boy."

Brent let his face cast directly towards her as his eyes trailed around the edge of her to watch the *Boogie Man,* "yes." He agreed.

Her finger wiggled and her jaw sets forward with an antique creak that shifted the man's eyes back to her.

"Yes," he swore again, "you're absolutely right." *Be angry at me,* he thought desperately as the foot he'd planned to use to stand sunk back behind him and his knee came back to rest by the other.

The longer she was angry with him, the longer she'd be occupied with him. The longer she was occupied with him, the longer Davey had left to live unharmed.

That was why he'd been brought back anyway, wasn't it? To be a sacrifice from the *Boogie Man.* To *feed them.*

"I tried to trick you," he added and sunk his teeth into his cracked lower lip while letting his eyes drift back to the creature. An ugly thought: *Davey was being harmed, not just by his sister*—scraped through Brent's brain like an ax through gravel. The man winced and searched gravely through his mind for bits of old, torn, black trash bags. Ones he'd use to keep his foster care memories tied away.

"You did." Not a question. She recognized his honestly and flicked her darkening tongue out to taste it. To taste the *honest.*

Brent forced his eyes back to her and tilted his chin towards his chest, convinced that what he'd said *had been* honest. Velcro peeled at the back of his sinuses and he blinked harshly at her, feeling stupid—yet again, how he'd felt the moment he'd extended his arms out in a challenge towards the creature. A challenge he'd lost.

Rate your pain.

"Do what you have to do, *kid.*"

The word peeled itself against her skin and her head thrashed forward violently, her moth wombed eyes bulging as her nose and lips vibrated against teeth. The sound of clanked oral bones like a roaring freight train.

Brent let his guard drop like an upturned tree as her cold and clipped nails dug out at him, collecting the fat in his cheeks below them. He knocked back against her—tree roots stripped from the ground—and rocked to his back against the curve of his spine.

The Boogie Man stepped forward with anticipation as the girl straddled Brent, its beady eyes finding contact with the man as Marilyn's fingers crushed at the sides of his head like a weak Venus Fly Trap.

The girl's hips bucked backward into him and Brent's knees jumped reactively, his stomach sucking in and his heart dropping low inside of it as his sight was pin-balled back to her. Moths curled like hardened pus from slits in her face and caterpillars dug deeply into the reds of her eyes. Brent's lips skinned apart with a hesitant groan.

A groan that the moths' puppet noticed as her nails slid backward towards his ears in infecting scrapes. Brent's eyes flicked back to the monster behind her and noticed a quiver of something new in its face—like a picture laid transparently over another picture. Something colorful and familiar shaped over its melting grey flesh.

The girl's nails pierced deep into Brent's ear canals with bright, exploding pain that set hot pink bonfires off behind his eyes. His vision was sent into star beams and his hands braced around her wrists to pull her away as her pantsed vagina slid lower down his abdomen, over his waistband, and her fingers plunged deeper.

His hands clamped over the dead pulse in her wrists and he felt the joints expand as his grip tightened, bone rolled beneath her puffy skin.

She laughed, mutedly, and her nails sunk—gauging the tight tunnels to his eardrums.

Brent cried out but let her wrists go. His hands falling to the ground with sweat pooled in his itchy palms. He wouldn't fight back.

The sacrifice was meant to do just that—be sacrificed.

Do what you have to do.

Through the electrical current that pulsed freely across his headspace, he was able to remind himself that he couldn't feel her, or the vertigo. That part of Marilyn was dead.

His short vision went back to the creature that now—

— seemed human.

Brent's body twisted reactivity against the ground and Marilyn's thighs tightened to keep from getting thrown, her upper lip spreading over her front teeth like a Rottweiler.

Her hands released, away from Brent's face and ears, and he gasped as if he'd been holding his breath as an internal doorbell ring wubbed away any other sound. She lowered her cheek to his and braced a hand over his eyes as his hands came up to the small of her back, wanting to collect her shirt in his grip and yank her away.

Her free hand curled gently around a collar bone and began to knead her sharp, bitten nails beneath it.

Dull agony gnawed from the bone to the back of Brent's spine and his legs kicked out, his hands tightening against her shirt material.

Marilyn kissed his cheek then spit against the ground beside him, her chapped lips dissatisfied with the scruff on his skin.

Then her hips slid further, over the zipper in his jeans, and she *moaned.* The hand across his eyes squeezing in a climax as she thought of the way Nick had thrust below her—his neck pierced with the skinny, silver tool she'd taken from his nightstand.

Brent convulsed against her, his hands jerking against her shirt as his senses of protection and responsibility went blind.

The collar of the shirt bruised a line into her sagging skin and Marilyn made a startled belch against the strangling line of cloth as she was dropped to her back, the man's hands trembling against her shoulders to keep her down.

"Don't!" He'd hollered with a high, cracking voice.

The voice of an adolescent.

Her shoulders peeled back like broken bread and moths evacuated from the webs in her skin.

Brent's hands bailed back, "Why would you do that?!"

She scowled at him and the bugs in her eyes broke out with quiet *pops* before crying down her sinking cheeks. Running from something.

"WHY WOULD YOU DO THAT?!" Crass and carried as his head bounced against strung muscles in the back of his neck.

"You did it to me first."

"I–what?" Brent sat back, away from her just as the moths were doing, slowly evacuating their host.

A human hand brushed through his line of sight and he glanced up, towards the monster.

Like a record—the day he'd found Marilyn with a spoon half jammed into her arm played with little static through his head: "you're wearing a green long sleeve," Marilyn had sighed through a sore throat and glossy tears, *"green."*

The monster stared back at him like a reflection in the mirror, its sun fleshed hand waving gently.

Brent remembered he'd discarded her *green shirt* epiphany and had asked: "was it –" and had pulled the lower lid of his eyes down. She had nodded.

Brent slid his sight down the creature's familiar frame as it dropped its spindly hand. His eyes eventually fell and rested back to Marilyn's. The moth infested (*it's in me. In me!*) girl now pushed up on her elbows.

113

His hand had sunk around her own and dragged her forward, away from the fleshy clone of himself that stood and watched with hawk eyes and a grin. Marilyn frowned at the sweaty man.

"It's been me this whole time, hasn't it." Brent marveled quietly, afraid he'd spook *it:* the creature that had taken his form.

Marilyn tilted her head back to it and they held eyes.

Brent shook her until her head popped back up, "the day I found you in the kitchen…"

"You're the pathetic Brent."

The man gripped her tighter and looked at himself in the eyes, "I'm the only Brent." He spoke slowly, pointedly, towards the creature.

"No, you're not." His own voice replied like an echo.

Marilyn's head snapped back again, like a trap door on weak, dismal hinges.

The man pinched his fingers into her skin as his teeth bore into the deepening slit on his lower lip, "Marilyn," he begged. His free hand came up to her linked arm and thumbed into a scabby, crescent, spoon stabbed crease in her skin, "the day I found you in the kitchen —" he tried again.

Her body jerked and her head snapped upward again.

"— You kept saying something was in you." A moth waddled over her arm, across their held hands, and onto him. Brent glanced at it, then back to Marilyn, "were you talking about the moths?"

The glassy glaze in Marilyn's eyes faded into a murky cloud, and more moths pressed out of her to run down her skin like villagers escaping a trembling fault line.

"Did *it* put the moths in you?" He glanced back up to the snaky version of himself and saw Marilyn yanking Davey away from himself in its eyes.

Stay away from him. Marilyn had demanded as she stood in the doorway of his apartment. Brent had then called her: "*kid.*" And she had screamed.

The man let his lips fall at the corners until it hurt before he corrected himself, "Did *I* put the moths in you?"

"*You're the pathetic Brent,*" Marilyn's lips mumbled like she was now trying to convince herself of something, "*you put them in me.*" Her brows furrowed and two small moths climbed out from the stretched neckline of her shirt, "I was wondering how you were doing since I last saw you?" She began to speak like a puppet, her voice thrown and lassoed around Brent as her tongue wet her lower lip, "you were so pretty," she hummed, "I can't believe we advanced our relationship like that, so quickly, you know? So passionately–" she sighed, "*wow.*" She was a record player. Replaying the words Brent's *iPod* had crackled to her as she had walked the day Davey had been yanked off the air mattress.

Brent's fingers bruised into her slimy skin as the eyes in her head rolled back.

"Makes me hard just thinking about it–thinking about you." She continued with a slow, melodramatic drawl, "goodness, and when I went inside you –" her mouth snapped together in a primal, toothy *click*.

Then Marilyn became afraid. Her eyelids fluttered and her lips tightened down like she was being electrocuted, foam kissing the corners of her mouth as her nails dug into Brent's hold on her.

"I don't want them in me, I don't want them in me, I don't want them in me, get out, get out, get out." She was growling through the froth on her lips and Brent was pulling her towards him.

The moths that'd crawled out and covered her arms, chest, and legs began to fly away from her like tiny bead-blasting bullets, their wings pumping drums past Brent's face and body.

"I'm so sorry," he should've paid more attention to her. He should've listened to her, "I messed up ki-*huh,*" his throat hitched, "*I messed up.*"

Her eyes rolled forward and tears colored them red as her face screwed up like a rung rag, "I did bad things, Brent." The froth on her lips slipped down her chin in streaky drool. "I let them make me do bad things."

He told her it was okay as her hand went to his throat and she pressed her finger against the side of it while imagining Nick's neck and the screwdriver. She pressed until Brent pulled back, his eyes wide above his flared nostrils, still promising that it was okay.

The monster paced up beside them.

It wasn't okay.

A claw, crafted into Brent's own hand, glided low like a bomber and collected hair from the top of Brent's head between its fingers.

The Brent dressed Boogie Man dragged him away from the girl as the man kicked his feet, his hands twisting up to tear at its grip on him. Brent's heels drug like brakes until they caught and he tore from its hold, tumbling to his back to then flop over like a fish. He scuffed to his feet and stared hard into his three-dimensional reflection—his head a whirlpool: *pick on someone your own size.*

"You've been torturing her in my skin!" Brent spat at the dreary, dangly mimic of himself.

It laughed (his laugh) and stepped at him with a stride that was meant to only belong to the man, "Please," Brent's voice snotted towards him, "she loves it, loves me, loves *you.*" A full-face smile possessed its human expressions, "You could own her if you wanted."

Brent frowned with a simmered disgust.

"But you don't want—right?" His voice growled low from its chest, "so I had to." Another step towards the man, "She was so wet for you, it was easy." Brent's voice began to melt away and become the monster's slithery hiss— like losing a loosely practiced accent.

"Fuck off." Brent's face reddened as the statement left his dry mouth, the curse word feeling staler and out of character then he'd thought it would while rehearsing it in his head. It was meekly and came out of him the way cursing stumbled out of young, insecure, middle schoolers. He thought of what Marilyn had said: *you're the pathetic Brent.*

Is that how she categorized the two twin appearances in her life?

He was the *pathetic* one.

Weak, whiny, unable to protect her.

"Oh, ho—hoo!" The creature used the muscles attached to Brent's modeled face to scrunch it into a smug, surprised expression. A look Brent had never made with his real face, "look at you, big guy."

Brent wanted to spit at it. But instead, he turned, back to Marilyn. His hands bridging down for her to grab.

She didn't take them.

Brent said her name.

She didn't take that either. *"Get out, get out, get out."* She continued to mumble.

The creature's human arms trapped around Brent and sucked him back, "you lost your chance," it sighed into the man's ear with a renewed version of his own voice before knocking him to his knees.

A gasp of pain locked itself behind Brent's puffed cheeks as a shock wave bolted up from the grimy ground, through the caps of his knees, and to his hips. He didn't have time to stand.

Brent's wrists were bound in hands that copied his own and he was wrenched forward until his palms smacked flat into the ground. His body a poster child for *Cat Pose* yoga.

The hands that were duplicated from his DNA began to skin themselves, like a shedding snake, to reveal the grey undertones of the monster's flesh. It began to click in Brent's ear, using his tongue and his teeth.

The man tried to retreat, Marilyn's name overflowing from his mouth as he fought against the gnarled hold.

She didn't answer.

The creature's hands pricked out from the flesh glove of Brent's hands in long birdish talons, its nails black and polished below body grease.

Brent fought to keep from squirming as the creature traced talons across the boney centers of Brent's spread out hands, and then the creature smiled a sweaty smile against the man's temple and —

—Brent began to scream.

Broken jagged saber-toothed talons stapled both of Brent's hands into the black ground like the holy pegs through Jesus' palms. The creature stood over him and studied the now missing index fingers on its own hands as Brent bathed himself in tears and drool, his arms tight with twitching muscles and swollen veins while blood slid out from beneath his fingers like a dissolving bath bomb.

114

Davey's head pounded back into consciousness and his tongue lapped curiously out onto dry, dusty lips. His arms clamped around empty space, void of any comfort, and tightened. Void of Bear Kingsley. His eyelids slipped open and the muscles that grew from his brain flexed against the clearance of lightlessness in front of him. The boy winced at the black nothing and palmed his hand into the soft bridge of his brow-line.

His lips were pursed, the letter 'M' still molding them in place and making his breath wheeze out of his nose in a low hum. His heart fluttered back into a runner's tempo at the back of his throat and he twisted onto his back and bridged to try to catch more airflow.

Bug bodies bounced off of his elevated stomach like a swarm of bees, homeless and busy, as they passed and he dropped his curved spine back into the ground, startled. The swift movement knocked a gust of air from his tight mouth and the letter "M" burst and splattered into lines of saliva around his face.

Moths.

The boy swiped a peach arm across the spit on his chin and muffled a cry into it as it passed. The cry said: *Moths,* and *Marilyn,* and *he remembers running and why he'd been running.*

The thing. *Thing!*

Davey sat up rigidly, his hands hot across the sweat wet ground where his back had laid. His fingers curled until his dirty nails scrapped and he thought he heard its owl screech—the *thing's* owl screech. *Had* heard it.

Davey pivoted on a pocketed cheek and clamped his lips into a thin line to keep from making a noise. *Brent.*

Davey could see them. The man; sat forward with his hands locked onto Marilyn's arms, Marilyn; Sacked backward with hollow, white eyes as her mouth mumbled, the *thing*; clicking its tongue across its long jaw behind her. He could see them as if where-ever he'd run too had been a big race track loop and he'd tripped at the finish line—his body lowly laid into the ground just in front of the three beings.

Brent, *(oh Brent, you're back!)* spoke softly to the comatose girl.

Davey bit into his lip as the sandbag version of his sister let a silent cry peel apart her sore, red face.

He wanted to call to them and make his presence known—the idea bold and exciting—and his lips looped to make the holler. His tongue lifting then clamping back down between his teeth with a startled snap of oral bone.

The *thing* was moving. Up behind Marilyn. Its hand umbrellaed out. Umbrellaed into spikes that combed back Brent's hair and clawed into it like it were a handle to yank the man back.

Davey clamped his hands over his mouth with a clammy slap and dropped against a shoulder as Brent cried out. Davey compressed his eyes shut and kneaded into his lips with shaky fingers as the counselor writhed against the clicky creature's pull.

Don't see me, don't see me, don't see me. He was praying.

Mist began to kiss his cheeks and an internal grown of moist ship wood met him at the center of his sudden dream drowned ears.

Davey was in the wheelhouse. His hands groped out against the wooden pegged helm of the boat as the water on the outside crashed against the green belly in muffled wades.

The mouth of the canal gaped at him from the smudged windows and the helm turned slightly below his hands like the boat had *hit something.*

(Davey?)

The rock!

Davey spun, sneakered squeak across fishy floorboards, and lunged for the cabin door. The aglets of his shoes ticked the narrow, metal staircase as he descended down towards the lip of the boat but he did not notice. Just as he did not notice the black boat scrawl of words across the wheelhouse side as he jetted past them, letters leaking down the sea kissed wood: *BOAT KINGSLEY.*

Able to speak again and no longer stuck on the 'M' sound Davey bellowed, "MMMy sister! Brent! I need! I need —" he thought: *to save them!* His gut met the rusted rail of the boat and he was slapped across the throat with the hard hand of nausea. His vision a queasy line of sight down towards the rolling water.

He'd fallen the last time he'd bent over the bar.

Davey's arms hugged around the cold hurdle and his feet bore into the ships siding, afraid.

The water licked around the grey stubble of the rock below him and the boy threw a quick wave at it before bearing his arm back around the rail, "What do I do?!" He cried toward it.

(What do you mean?)

Its voice was a mellow comfort that the boy had missed despite the panic that drummed at the nape of his neck, "the *thing!* I have to help!!"

The rock forgot to answer, or ignored the boy altogether, its ragged top starring in animatedly up at the boy.

Davey trembled against the rail as his hand jutted out once again to wave at it, "Remember, I had magic the last time I was here, I had this dream and then Zachary fell!" His words were drowned out by the wade of water and he scrunched his nose up into shut eyes, willing to do it again. Willing to wake up startled and find the *thing* flung across that dark place with its arm broken behind its back.

The rock sighed against the water and Davey's eyes jerked open again to study it.

"Remember?!" He cried and shut his eyes again: *magic, do the magic thing, wake up.* He thought in jumbles that admittedly meant he didn't know what to do, how to do it, or even what to hope for.

His shoulders throbbed from the tight hug he had against the boat.

"I fell!" He recalled, "remember I fell and then I woke up and Zachary was hurt!"

(Then fall.)

"Fall?" The boy repeated as his knees became fluid and his calves quivered consequently.

END: THE PURPLE CRAYOLA NOOSE

115

The skin that mimicked Brent began to melt, no *crack,* off of the creature as the man yanked against his broken bloody hands in front of it. The skin below—pink, fleshy and aged—glistened at the same tempo of Brent's hyperventilating gasps and deep groans.

Brent's skin suit slipped off of it like a dirty coat and it trembled triumphantly in front of its hand-kept prisoner in its new, pearly outfit. It mimicked another man, now. A man wrinkled with ten years of age more than Brent and peppered stubble across his chin and cheeks.

Brent's eyes rolled up to the new man, then continued to the back of his head as his mouth broke apart with another, *pathetic* groan.

"Dad?" Marilyn's slouched voice cradled under Brent's chin and he plunged his eyes back down in their sockets to look at the manly fleshed creature.

"Marilyn Mae!" It answered, its voice a canvas of hysteria.

Brent shook his trembling head and the muscles from his neck tightened the grip of his hands into singeing fires. His teeth clenched and his jaw bulged at the sides.

Marilyn was standing, her slitted body wavering on unsteady, swollen ankles, "Dad!" She screeched. Her voice suddenly louder and purer than Brent had ever heard it.

"No!" The man warned as his nails spooned up lines of his own blood.

The creature, dressed in her father's body, scooped Marilyn's head into the crook of his shoulder, her tears bending down the fat in her cheeks and wetting the cotton sweater it wore.

Its head tilted away from the blubbering girl and showcased a deep, red rash and greening stripe around its carbon copy of the man's human neck.

A dangled stick figure memory met the man who was stapled to his hands and knees and he felt hot sweat prickle against it. *The purple Crayola noose.* "Marilyn!" Brent cried.

The girl had ignored him as she tightened herself against her father's body, her hands squeezing around the back of it in a lung compressed hug.

The creature's man hand rubbed into the back of Marilyn's hairline to grope her closer to it, "I am very disappointed in you, honey."

Marilyn had a sad moment to make a question with the hum of her voice before her father's hand tore her away from his soft shoulder. A startled yelp coughed from her chest as her neck ached and her eyes stared widely into his stern face.

"I've seen everything, Marilyn. You grew up to be quite disgusting."

Her hands kneaded at his strong-armed hold as the hair at the back of her head began to tear from her scalp in burning snaps. Painful tears began to well up and outrun the tears of joy that still stained her puffy cheeks.

Brent shifted his hands back towards himself, then fell forward into his cry as a needle-thin shock wave of agony reported up through his body and out the tops of his feet. He shook wildly against the puncture wounds at the center of his palms and his eyes dodged upward again, towards the back of his skull while Marilyn's name rested on his parted, drooling lips.

"Dad?" His name was said in disbelief, in fear, "Dad!"

"Shut up!" The hand dropped her and she stumbled back, her nails peeling against the cloth of his shirt before losing grip.

Brent's eyes came back down and his vision pulsed.

Marilyn sobbed into the cup of her hand.

"Stop crying, Miss Mae." Her father's voice sweetened, then his hand slapped out against the side of her head and the voice hardened again, "stop!"

Brent rocked from side to side and watched through gripped eyesight as the bones in his hand spread to accept the thick ends of the talons, blood boiling heatedly away from the center of the wound in chunks. "That's not him!" He bellowed, "That's not your dad!" He felt pale, cold, feverish.

"They made me do it, Dad!" Marilyn pleaded, "The bugs!"

The creature gripped tightly at the front of her and snarled at her with her father's face, his voice booming, "They made you fuck like a disgusting whore your whole life?! Like you weren't alive unless your pussy was wet and her tits were popped?!"

Marilyn was released from his slobbery hold and fell back to her ass with a teeth-chattered sob.

"Like candy buttons! Right, Marilyn Mae?!"

Brent's throat tightened into a stripped, grunted scream and threw his shoulders harder and felt the skin on his hands begin to tear.

The girl choked horribly on her cries, "Daddy–!"

Her father's body lowered and his eyes held onto her, "but you're right, love," his voice was sugary again, smooth across her heart wounds, "the moths did make it easier to do bad shit, right?"

She whined in response.

"Such a fucking victim." He rolled his eyes and stood back up to tilt his nose up on her, "I didn't raise a victim."

"You left –"

The toe of her father's shoe hooked out against a hanging breast and Marilyn collapsed away from him. Her arms crossed over her front and her shoulders quivering in trembles.

"You're guilty."

She nodded.

"You're weak."

She nodded.

"You're a piece of shit."

She stared still as lines of his saliva splatted out over his disgusted face.

"I am so disappointed in you."

Marilyn nodded. She understood. It was her fault. Her hands fell from her chest and she felt asthmatic as her brain seized up into a constipation of dreaded emotion.

She had too big of an ego.

She carried too much shame.

Too much self-doubt.

Too exposed.

Too much sexual drive—she was a fucking pervert!

Too much regret!

Too much HATE.

She hated herself.

Her head began to bob along with the thoughts as her father stood above her, spit wet at the corner of his frowning mouth, she hated herself. Hated herself bad.

"Marilyn!!!"

She twitched in the direction of Brent's yell then fell back to her head bobbing slouch. Unable to empathize or identify his appeal.

"Marilyn Mae."

She blinked at her father as all of her attention sunk back into him.

"You're pretty peony and helpless, aren't you?"

"No!" Brent's voice tried to interject before it was absorbed into a dark, muted hole.

"Yes," Marilyn answered her father.

The creature with the features of the weepy girl's father knelt once again and the rough of his finger nicking the underside of Marilyn's chin. "You need them."

Marilyn's face puckered curiously, then glazed, "need?"

"Your *buggy* friends, yeah?"

"Yeah," she spouted without understanding.

Her father's hand slid down the length of her arm and tightened around her wrist. It lifted the arm then, straight out to their side—pointing at the struggling talon–hand man. It leaned into Marilyn and they both looked down her arm as if it were the top barrel of a gun. Her father's face waxed into a smile, "see this?" Her father's thumb thumbed the crescent moon that had begun to heal. The spoon inflected crescent moon that Brent had used to try to pull her from the fog.

"Yeah," she answered, now craving that *fog*.

Her father's thumb pressed into the moon shape until it popped. Marilyn's voice popped with it in a loud howl of pain and she dropped her face down into her father's chest. The thumb worked her scaring flesh down like a cardboard box tab and opened her arm out to the sweaty, stale air. "Look at it."

Marilyn looked at the open door in her arm and smelled the scent of decomposition and human debris.

"You need your moths to make you feel better?"

Marilyn nodded.

"You're so fucking pathetic without them, aren't you?"

She nodded.

"Do you want them back inside you?" Her father's nose pressed into the side of her face, "you always want something inside you, don't you?"

"I want them inside."

Brent had writhed his full body forward with thick thighs that jittered like post-workout shakes. His hands had become searing objects of obliterating suffering and he held in his scream as he tore forward, further, against them. The feeling in his fingertips gone and bloodless.

"You want them?!"

Marilyn caved into her father's chest, "I want them!" She cried.

The creature fired a cheer from its raisin lungs and the moths swarmed up, out of the darkness. Their bullet bodies glistening with like wants. The creature rejoiced.

Rejoiced.

The swarm dove and the hole in Marilyn's arm was bottlenecked with fuzz, guts, and wings.

The girl seized against the hold of her father as the bodies slipped deeply within her, back into their *nest*. Bodies returning to the womb.

Dark red flicked out in squirts as Brent's dying appendages escaped their spiked captivation. He was free. His palms gouged out to the rim of his hands in broken purple as his arms convulsed and he pulled the bloody hands up to his chest. Brent stood and his blood drained down his forearms to rest in the dip of his elbows before shooting off the boney tips. His feet washed against the spraying as he ran forward into the moths.

His body was used as a shield to block Marilyn's body from the storm of insects, the rest of the swarm cut off and angrily pelting into his back.

The creature dropped Marilyn and she fell to her back, Brent bent over her and continued to hide her from the bugs.

Marilyn's eyes had begun to cloud back over, almost hollow and puppet, "get off!"

Brent pressed his knee into her open arm to stop the runway for moths and she kicked beneath him, "stop!" His body trembled and he could feel the bone of her arm roll below his bent knee, "you don't want them, kid!" *Kid.*

"I need them!"

"No, you don't!"

She spat out the blood that fell from Brent's body to her face and her eyelids pinned wide open against the wet tears at her lash line, "I deserve them."

The moths had begun to bite into Brent's back, arms, neck, head but he kept sturdy, "you don't! Marilyn please!"

"But dad —" her eyes drifted over Brent's shoulder.

"That's not your dad." Her lips tightened. "Marilyn! Marilyn, look at me."

Her eyes continued to stare past him as Brent's blood made red freckles on her cheeks.

"Look at me, kid."

Her eyes came back to him.

Brent nodded and hid a hard wince as a moth pelted into the soft behind his ear—they were coating his body now and drinking from the holes in his hands—, "you don't deserve them. You didn't do anything to deserve —"

"Yes, I did!" She screamed, "I'm disgusting, *pathetic!*"

"So is everyone else!"

Her head slammed back and she cried out of frustration.

"Breathe!" Brent instructed, sounding like he had the day he'd rear-ended the Matthews' children. *Just Breathe, Davey.*

She subbed in breath and her eyes leaked tears across Brent's blood on her face.

Brent grit his teeth against the speckles in his sight, sent there to inform him he was losing too much of the chunky, red fluid as his stomach suspended below his fever flesh, "Kid."

"Alright, cute salvation moment is over." A voice behind them growled as arms locked beneath Brent's armpits and hoisted the man up, off of the girl.

The swarm of moths plummeted and absorbed into ever space of Marilyn. The crescent slit in her arm, the burst holes across her skin, her mouth, her wet eyes, her runny nose, below her waistband.

Her body was a sock of rice as it twisted and slithered over the ground, the white of her eyes like strobe lights in the darkness.

Brent's scream slid over the back of his own, thinly putrid, milky vomit as the girl rag-dolled up and plopped whole clouded eyes into her sockets. Her body no longer a keeper of freewill and her lips a dollop of smiling, frothy teeth.

116

Brent's arms were jacked straight out and the creature's *father-like* hands laced at the back of his stiff neck. He was a real image of *Jesus Christ* as he stood in a holy-hand 't' with his shirt riding up the sweat on his belly and his chin drizzled in acidic waste.

Marilyn stood straight in the man's line of dwindling, blood loss, sight and her dumbed expression dug glazed fear into him.

Brent's feet kicked in loose stomps that toed weakly into the ground, "Marilyn!" Her name a repeated record in his emptying vein repertoire, "Kid!"

No response, other than a half stretched Pitbull snarl across her front teeth.

"You know how I hate it when you call me *foster boy?!*"

Her hollow eyes brightened at the familiar name and Brent continued, hurriedly.

"I never told you why and I'm sorry for that." The arms that strapped him up tightened and his shoulders creaked, he moaned, "I was in foster care for a long time, kid. And unfortunately, my case wasn't too good. The Onslows—" *tighten, creak, moan*, "I lived with them the longest. They even fought to adopt me!" He side barred, "but they weren't great and they had a daughter, Amanda."

Marilyn's face tightened and bug bodies danced beneath the folds of her skin. *Amanda.* She remembered the name. Brent had called her that *name.*

"Yes! I accidentally called you that. I called you Amanda, and I'm so sorry." He was very apologetic, but he wanted to be *VERY LOUD*. He wanted to scream information at Marilyn until the face scrunch turned into clear-eyed bewilderment and she no longer wanted the moths in her. *Get out, get out, get out!* He craved to hear her say those words, but had stuck instinctively to his hushed story instead, "anyway, Amanda really looked after me a lot. She looked after me and bathed me and loved me. Sometimes too much."

The fog lasted in her eyes, still, and Brent continued on. Despite the loss of feeling in bled out, led arms and his vomit heavy tongue.

"Amanda did bad things to me, Marilyn. Things I'm still," *scarred from*. His whole head dipped and he thought for a moment he tasted blood on his *vomit heavy tongue*. Metallic brights, and *man,* his vision was to a pinhole now, "Marilyn, Amanda killed herself!" The blurt burst from his lips and blood did dribble out, red dye across the milky chin and t-shirt vomit.

Marilyn's eyes blinked. First one, then the other.

Brent's arms were slacked and his shoulders squeaked forward slightly. His hands now bobbing at his sightless peripherals like swollen, red *buttholes*. "I found out in my–twenties." Drowsy drizzling red from his tongue, "She hung herself with a belt." *Couldn't handle what she'd done to me when we were kids.* "Is that what happened to your da –"

Brent was discarded and the '– *d*' landed hard into his clamped jaw as his body stumbled, then collapsed into the ground.

He sighed sleepily and his head swam and his body floated to its back. His greasy eyelids folded open and there she was. *Amanda.* Her blonde, scrunchies ponytail and narrow eyes glaring down at him. All there just to confirm his theory.

"You talk too much, Brenty-boy." Her voice was a sing-song of irritable vowels and cursing consonants but still somehow–*male.* Gruff. The creature had shimmied skins but hadn't shifted voices. Its radio dial flicking back and forth until Amanda Onslow's voice spoke through one clear vocal wave, "don't you?"

Brent waved his hand up to his neck then let the holed pouch of bones slap back into the ground like the stomach of a dead fish. "Your neck." His two squawked words drowned and he coughed heavily, his lungs filling with the red, dark clumped of crimson copper.

Her neck was belt buckle bruised and rashed around the sides.

She bent and straddled him, her face pudgy and only in the eighth grade. Strands of her hair wet and plastered to the sides of her round cheeks like sideburns. Like the day he'd splashed her when he was only four. The day that had started all days.

Brent hummed hard into his rattling teeth and ignored the pressure of her hips over him—*a much more petite weight in his sternum now that he was grown and his body was adult-sized.*

Her hand strangled fingers into the joints of his jaw until his mouth popped open like a puckered *fishy* and she, *the creature,* smiled. Her other hand looped into his lower teeth like a rake. Very salty, fat fingers brushed down into his tongue to pin it against the low floor of his mouth's bad breath and blood. It pinched and his heavy eyes watered consequently. "Can you taste *me* on my fingers?"

A gurgly gag groaned from the pit of Brent's stomach and he clenched his jaw, biting her fingers like rolled, jelly carrots between the front of his teeth. He couldn't bite hard, his energy gone with the blood from the holes in his hands that he attempted to lift—the muscles in his arms a dead demolition crew. Useless.

Amanda's beady, buggy eyes flicked up above Brent's head and her lips curled towards the flair in her nostrils, "would you like to help me, Miss Marilyn Mae?"

Brent blew choked, frantic air against the creatures wet, Amanda fingers, and his pupils expanded as his eyes gleamed tiredly at her extended double chin above him.

Marilyn's hands came from behind and ground strands of his hair into clumps in her fists to pull and hold on to. Brent's eyes rolled up but could only see the flattening curls puffed around the girl's head through the dark line of his eyelashes.

"Marilyn is a lot like me, isn't she Brent?"

Brent's tried to bite again but Amanda's hand jerked his jaw down towards his neck as air hissed from his lungs.

"Always very hot for you, huh? It's what you get for being so handsome, I guess. Bastard" Shoulders shrugged and fingers pinched deeper into his tongue.

A *bastard* was the President on the T.V., a bastard was the car when it didn't work, a bastard was the bad thing that you were *mad at*. HE WAS NOT A BASTARD. It wasn't his fault. He knew that. He reminded himself of that as salty-sweet fingers pierced the taste buds on his fatty, dry tongue.

Marilyn tightened the hold in his hair with a *purr* and the eighth-grade body of Amanda Onslow jerked back against Brent's lower jaw. Her hands bending his teeth down into his gums until pink saliva squished out.

He tried to cry but that was worthless energy used as the back of his throat filled with bodily fluids like a coroner's soup bowl.

The joint of his jaw resisted like stale gum or fossil tar, and his eyes jutted further back into his head, sinking deep below the soft surface of his eyelids. There was a sick sizzle of ground bones and cartilage that exploded with slivered off white pain that thrashed claws through his mind. His jaw dropped, unhinged inside of useless skin and his tongue stretched out against it.

His face broken and bubbles of blood waterfalling in cascades out of each, sagged, corner of his forever open mouth.

Lillian Rose

"Like I said," Amanda's voice sighed, "you talk too much, Brenty-boy."

117

Davey's back lined vertical against the horizontal bow of the boat's railing. The rock below the rail directly across from the boy now. He'd backed himself up to here. Revved wearily until his spine sank into the adjacent cold metal bar.

His eyes narrowed and the boat swung him.

The rock wanted him to fall… didn't it?

His old man sneakers bounced forward, weakness and fatigue lining his legs as he skated for the railing with the rock below. Just like he'd skated in Daisy's double-wide trailer kitchen. *Here goes Davey Matthews attempting the long slide!* He'd fall. He'd fall. Oh, how he'd fall if he just leaped —

And he did leap. Legs blundered into the sea kissed guard rail, eyes connected with the point of the rock before his body splayed over and his arms spread in a free fall. Mist flew against him and wind caught beneath him and the rock burst through him.

118

Brent had been slipping deeper into his own darkness when the light hit.

A glint of red that bridged to orange and then expanded into a white beam all at once, *the big bang*. It barraged and bustled heat across the man and the other two who stood over him, blazing life into their dark sight.

The heat singed like fire then froze over them in a stillness—ice crystallization in its white strobe.

Amanda's eyes sunk into beady holes that locked with intoxication on the frozen flash, her jaw sliding on putty skin in a low unhinge that mimicked Brent's broken mouth. Her skin slipped like paper maché and chunked heavily pasted splats into the ground, the creature emerging from the inside of her eighth-grade carcass. Its hands twitched and its chest heaved drunken breaths.

Marilyn's body rumbled.

Brent's wet eyes blinked in jabs as a silhouette brought forward the light. The silhouette was small, a child, a *boy*, Davey.

Davey.

Brent's body ribbed him onto his stomach as a visual migraine pumped colors across his eyelids and his open, dangling jaw bucketed the leaking blood from his mouth. His tongue rolled through his lips to help scoop the choked red away from his lungs as he coughed and wheezed.

Have you ever seen Matilda *the movie?* Daisy's voice recalled through him.

Marilyn continued to twitch and vibrate above Brent. The moths running track, frantically, within her. Some of them tumbling from open wounds in her flesh and flying hastily towards the silhouetted boy and his rim of light.

His light that burst like an explosion from his chest.

Like it must've burst on the playground, too close to Zachary, too explosive to keep the bully on his feet. The light had blasted Zachary off the play structure, the light had broken his arm.

Have you ever seen Matilda *the movie?*

Yes, but Matilda didn't glow, Daisy.

Moths, like bullets or buckshot, disintegrated Marilyn's Tourette induced frame and flew for the light at one. Pelting it, trying to dim it–hide it. Her eyes popped and melted down her cheeks and her blown through body deflated into the ground, beside Brent.

Brent's jaw muscles contracted and tried to pull a round mouthed moan from his lips as her body crinkled like a dead pile of leaves. His shoulders tossed bare feeling, holey hands out to the girl and he watched them slap into her unresponsive stomach.

He belched and coughed blood around her name that he wanted to form in his deeply destroyed mouth.

The moths attacked Davey and his light but–

119

He stood still.

The moths flopped maniacally against him, diving and smashing into the lightest corners of his body, but Davey Matthews kept still.

The light had not lasted on the playground, he'd only fallen then, but now it beamed on. He'd leaped *faithfully* and it showed, *shone*. His pupils had digressed and only the clean whites showed as his sister's body jerked to the ground before him. He watched as Brent's hands made weak efforts to grab at her, before falling back and painting against the blood from his lungs.

Davey shifted his body and the light followed smoothly, tearing the seal between this world and the one he'd been born in as it sliced. White eyes met black and beady and he threatened the creature with his little boy stance. Its body stock still and its low jaw swung, talons *(minus two)* rested like gorilla knuckles against the ground.

Moths, even those that had created the thick obis wall continued to thwomp against him and sting with stingless bodies and he let them.

My lights too bright to be full of fright! He thought, poetically. *My light is TOO BRIGHT to be FULL of FRIGHT.*

Davey stepped at the creature, like stomping away a rodent.

It flinched, then drooled.

Brent shifted, back to his back, and watched Davey's light ricochet into diamonds off the creature's saliva through the glints of his weary vision. He glanced through the shards of crystal streams and studied the boy who stood erect against the chaotic wings that punched and bit him. *Was Marilyn dead?*

The man coaxed himself onto his numb elbows and flinched at the way his jaw sunk back against his throat with a full-body gag. The gag thrust him forward and he sat up against the pull in his abdomen. *I failed. Marilyn is dead.*

The creature began to circle Davey, stalking him with its low jowl leaving a wet trail on the ground. The boy watched steadily and shifted again. The light floated behind him and the veil between two worlds widened.

Brent could see the hole now.

Beyond it, the motel's carpet and their laid stiff bodies.

Brent's head jammed over his shoulder and his spiraled eyes caught glimpses of Marilyn's lifeless build, torn and wet with bodily fluids. He tried a sob, but the funnel his broken jaw made produced only a small, shriek like noise. The gargle sent goosebumps through his overheated body and snot lined his nostrils in long watery drips.

He needed to stand.

Davey's white eyes brought themselves to Brent and encouraged him to do just that—*stand.*

The boy could feel the light begin to face in towards him. Turning in to self indulge and go out at once. The burst of rock was no longer enough, "Brent!" He continued to keep pace with the creature as it circled but his pupils had begun to resize inside his eyes and his heart began to race against the metaphorical stone tip through his sternum. *My lights not bright enough. My lights not bright enough.*

(Keep at it, Davey).

Brent worked himself to his feet, his eyes dragging between boy, creature, and open veil. The light casting shadows across his footpath as he began to trudge forward. Slow, stumbling steps at first, then longer strides all together. Strides he felt in slapped vibration through his knees.

The creature closed in as the light slipped back, closer to Davey and dimmer in the darkness. The veil began to swell shut and the moths lined each side of the tear, trying to sew it shut with their buggy legs.

Brent reached Davey and slid behind him, a limp hand casting down over the glowing boy's shoulder. Blood from Brent's jaw globbed into Davey's hair as the man tried to pull him back towards the thinning veil slit.

The light evaporated further into the boy's flesh as Davey stepped forward, away from Brent and closer to the approaching creature with three talons and a thumb at the end of either arm.

Brent could feel the tear in both worlds' taste his back and he made a jawless cry for Davey.

Davey turned, his eyes wide, "you gotta go!" A moth pelted against his lips and he swatted at his mouth with the back of his hand. The light was going, the veil was closing, the creature was creeping, "go!"

(Three in, only two out.) The rock's disintegrating voice whispered to the boy.

"Three in, only two out," Davey repeated without understanding.

Brent tried to step forward to Davey but their motel room world sucked him back, towards it.

"Three in, two out."

If Brent could scream he'd grab the boy and shriek away the kid's mumbled nonsense. *Three in, two out?* What did that mean?

The light had faded back and rested only inches from Davey's feet now, its beams unable to reach any further and the creature's jowled face resting just outside the shadow in a low grin. Davey's eyes widened as if he'd heard a whispered secret and his hands swatted out of the moths, towards Brent, "Go first! Three in, two out! Three in, two out! Three in, two out! Three i–"

Brent was buckled against the veil's vortex that slithered around him and tousled him backward into pure, real darkness.

His back slammed into dirty sock scented carpet.

120

Brent had regurgitated off of the motel floor faster the second time, knowing the Boogie Man was not there to take him back again, it was with Davey. His knees quivered below his tight thighs and clenched lower back as he pivoted and pasted his hands through his crispy dry hair. They laid where he'd left them, *lined up like they were ready for body bags.*

Three in, two out! Davey's voice screamed internally.

His fingers curled and dragged strands of hair against the bloody undersides of his nails.

His fingers curled.

Brent dropped his open hands to the front of him, startled. They were healed. His fingers wiggled and jerked on his command and his palms stared up with swollen scars at their center. The pass through the veil healed him, just as it had healed him when his guts had been long necklaces on the outside of his filleted stomach.

"Three in, two out." He whispered with an intact, creaky TMJ jaw. His tongue free of blood or pain. He lowered to Davey's comatose side, "What the hell, kid," his voice creased inside his throat, "what does that mean?!" The light had to be gone, now. Davey was on his own with the creature.

Brent bit the skin off his lips and tried to keep from convulsing in small, nervous shivers.

His hand scraped up onto the motel bed sheets and blanket material shook his hand with tiny, cotton limbs. His eyebrows furrowed, "I'm out." He sighed. *Three went in, Only one has come out.* "I have to get you out too, kid." *Three in, two out.*

His head carried itself over his shoulder and studied Marilyn, as asleep and cold as Davey.

"Marilyn can't come," he'd stated it but kept a question mark close, like he'd made a promise with his fingers tied together behind his back. *Three in, two out.*

He let his muscles lead his head back to Davey and tears began to swell on his swollen lash line, "how?"

His bed clenched hand dropped to his side and he followed it wearily with his eyes. His belt buckle smiled grimly into view and the leather around it stretched uncomfortably over his hips as if to answer.

Purple Crayola noose.

His breath hitched with an audible click.

Three in, two out.

"I can't," He spoke aloud as he turned his body and crawled to Marilyn, "I can't do that," but he knew better—he didn't have time to waste, Davey was alone with the creature. *Three in, Two out.*

Marilyn seemed peaceful now, the closer he came to her. Her eyes gently shut and her skin washed of color. Her hair laid in clumped tangled over her cold ears and her chest danced silently with each slow breath.

Brent sat back on his heels and dropped his head, the belt smiling at him once again, "Jesus Christ," he whispered, then began to cry. Fragile and weak weeps. The sorry sobs of a *pathetic* man.

His tears dropped first to his flexed stomach, then—his belt—snaked into the loops of his pants like a poisonous python, tightened so the blood in his body could no longer pass into his legs. The lowest joints buzzing small alarms to warn him of the lack of blood.

Brent rolled his hips forward on a *whim (Three in, Two out)* and his hands went down to fumble around the belt buckle. The silver clanked vocally in bitter stings as his arms shook and his eyes quaked into a blur of tears. The leather tongue of the belt with puncture holes slid against his finger and he pulled it up, away from the metal tab that penetrated the third hole. The belt tightened and he straightened his back against the stiff, unwelcome rawhide. The lapped tongue slipped from the buckles bar and frame and he clenched both ends of the belt in one fist each. The material dug into his fresh palm scars rottenly.

Brent dropped the two ends into his lap with a sweet rattle of metal against loose jeans and he punched the bottom of his palms into his eyes.

No time! Three in, Two out.

Brent rubbed at the tears in his eyes, palm versus eye socket making deep suctioning calls like wet mud below bare feet.

He groaned over the sappy sound and threw his hands back into his lap to loop around the belt. He jerked it and it unsnaked itself from his pants with friction hot against his back on the way out.

Brent straddled Marilyn.

Brent looped the belt around her neck.

Brent tightened it to her cylinder soft skin.

Frustration began to prod the backs of his arms and he clenched his jaw, "Moths!" He screamed into the girl's face, "kid," the scream echoed back in a ragged sob, "I tried to tell you—you," breath, "you didn't need them!" His head tilted back on his rolled forward shoulders and his thighs pressed into her sides. His Adam's apple caught dusty motel light and for a moment he wished an arrow would be shot through it, "why didn't you listen to me."

He brought a white-knuckled fist around the black leather end of the belt and flattened a hand against her chest to keep her body against the floor. The belt was stretched up and Brent's eyes were squeezed shut. The sound of hide being stretched against skin and short breath bashed into his ears like Amanda's open hand slaps. Brent's face began to pulse red as he held his own breath, squeezing it down inside his throat until veins showed.

It exhaled from his mouth in a broken sob as his arm brace up higher, triaging Marilyn's airway. Her body convulsed below him in tiny movements and still, he didn't look.

Look, you coward.

Brent pinched his lips and his face began to beat red again.

Look!

Her chest felt soft and compressed below his hand.

Brent, look.

His head tipped forward and his eyes peeled wide open with another explosive exhale, spit flicked out in mucus strings as regret met him instantly. A cold rush through his body like ice water.

Marilyn's eyes were open.

Purple rimmed and half popped from the socket they stared past Brent into a space he'd only know when he was dead. When he was strangled from life like Marilyn.

The man dropped the belt like it'd come to life and bit him and the buckle slapped hollowly to Marilyn's forehead. Her dead eyes were unresponsive and dry. *Three in, two out.* Brent choked air into tight lungs and swung his attention to Davey, who still laid in comatose.

Had he been wrong? He'd thought if Marilyn died on both sides of the veil Davey would be able to sink back into their real world. *Three in, two out.* Isn't that what the kid had meant? Brent muffled his mouth with the back of his wrist and his body began to clench and unclench in painful, quiet sobs.

He came back to Marilyn and her lifeless eyes and began to peel the belt's waxy hide from her imprinted, swollen skin. His *"I'm sorry"*s tripping fluidly over a block of dough in the back of his throat.

Coarse, blistered, gritty gasps.

Brent jerked around to Davey and watched the boy rise from the wool ground with coughs and gags. Tingles shot down Brent's back and he clumsily unstraddled Marilyn to rush Davey in friction shuffles on his knees. The unscathed, glowless boy. Davey fell into his arms easily and his body molded warmly against Brent as the man embraced him. Davey's head dipped against the crease in Brent's neck and his eyelashes blinked tickles against the man.

His head lifted and studied his open-eyed, lifeless sister.

Brent felt Davey shift and sat upright with his hands embraced into Davey's shoulders, "*m'sorry,*" the man found himself croaking below a wet whisper.

Davey firmed his eye contact with Brent and he nodded. His lip did not slip into his mouth, tears welled in his eyes but did not fall, his cheeks hollowed in aged lines—too deep for the face of an eight-year-old, "Three in, two out."

Brent's shoulders rolled back and his face hardened.

Davey began to weep then and Brent scooped him into his arms with guilt that cradled the boy's frail weight on its own. The man stood and crossed the room, his car keys splayed out at the end of the bed Marilyn has slept in. They hooked around his finger and he slinked towards the door.

The outside air couldn't touch the cocoon of shame that braced the man like a hot cast as he slipped out into the dawn with Davey in his arms. Awareness catapulted against him as the cars in the parking lot smiled sleepily at him, they weren't alone. The cold carcass behind him was in a single room surrounded by warm-bodied rooms of sleeping strangers. Some maybe already up, on a morning run perhaps. *God, he wanted to go on a run.*

The thought that maybe his cries had woken these strangers startled him and his arms quivered around the boy as he staggered for the 4Runner. The 4Runner: Sat obediently like it always had, a loyal dog on its hinds, waiting to serve its master.

Brent grimaced at it as he pressed the key FOB and its headlights flicked. If it were really a dog he thought he might kick it. Tell it to find a new home.

The back door swung against his pull and he tipped to let Davey fall into the seat. The boy slid from his arms before being swept back up against Brent. The man's eyes were wide, "Jesus," Brent marveled at the back seat with bloody clothes, bloody baby wipes, bloody seat material. His stomach filled with acid and he closed the door and turned his back to it wearily before crossing sides to the front passenger door.

That's where he'd left Davey.

In the seat that Marilyn normally sat.

Marilyn.

Brent went back to the motel room, his eyes hardly holding contact with the motel building as he staggered. Cold carcass, cold carcass, cold carcass. She would become a game children played in front of the bathroom mirror in the dark.

The motel room welcomed him back and the door faded shut behind him as he stood and studied Marilyn's body, his belt dropped over her, her eyes pockets of sightless goo.

Brent crossed the room and retightened the belt to her neck before gently lifting her by the underside of her armpits. His sight a teary blur as he dragged her back towards the bathroom. Once the carpet digressed into fake linoleum the man hoisted her up towards his chest with a tightened grunt as her body flopped against him.

He stumbled into the still wet belly bathtub and stared hard at the showerhead with an overbearing rush of exhaustion. Brent ruffled his nose into her neck and let out the rest of his tears for that night. Those left for Winnifred, those aching for Marilyn, those guilty for Davey. Her shoulder, neck, and hair soaked in his grief and saliva as he choked his final sob and found it too painful to continue to sob.

He lifted his blotched cheeks and shifted Marilyn's weight to one arm. He then, with his free arm, looped the long end of the belt over the thin neck of the plate-sized showerhead. *Neck to Neck,* he thought. *Cold carcass, cold carcass, cold carcass.* He twisted the belt tightly in his free fist and gently let Marilyn's body go. The belt jerked against her weight and the leather smeared burns into his fisted hand as her body swayed and her face planted softly against the tiled shower wall.

Brent looked away horridly and used both hands to work his end of the belt over the neck of the shower like a pulley block. He worked the belt towards him until Marilyn's toes no longer reached the bathtub floor. Her body twirled against the leather belt noose and her back flanked against the wall. Brent tied the belt around the shower neck and glanced at her lips that'd begun to swell into a bright purpley blue.

Brent tripped and grappled from the bathtub while Marilyn's swaying, and knocking body haunted him down into his core. He kept back vomit and beat his fists against his temples. Sweat rolled down his back and anger flamed up his front where it caught his own neck and made him double over in hyperventilation.

Once straightened back up Brent took steps. One foot in front of the other, and made it back out to the motel room. He found his wallet and fumbled with it.

The pouch gaped open and her note was there—her handwriting.

The one he'd kept in his wallet as a reminder of her desperate need for milk. Something once funny now increasingly disturbing.

I can't do it anymore
Please pick up some God Damned MILK.

The cow doodle with the curly wig seemed to side-eye Brent with judgment now, disgust. He brushed his thumb over the indents of Marilyn's penmanship as her shoulder thumped distantly in the bathroom behind him.

He began to tear the note directly between the two sentences. The tear was gentle at first then all at once became panicked and frantic as he realized what exactly he was doing: framing her death as a suicide.

Purple Crayola noose.

He blinked against his dry eyes and prayed momentarily for more tears but they did not come. He then placed the doodled cow and second sentence back into his wallet before he jammed it into his back pocket. The leftover, torn note laid out in the palm of his hand like a curse.

I can't do it anymore

The strange suicide note was rolled anxiously between his fingers as he walked led steps back to the chilly, florescent bathroom. He kept his eyes low and his heartbeat steady as he entered below the buzzing light. Marilyn's hand hung in his peripheral of his dodging eyes and he reached out for it. He pulled it, careful not to lead her hung body with it, and placed it against the center of his chest for his heart to beat into. Her hands were icy and her nails had already begun to discolor into something grey. Brent suddenly felt as if he were mocking her. *See, my heart is still beating.*

A thick layer of vomit gurgled back up the inside of his throat and threatened to spew as he dropped the hand. It slapped into her side and her body turned again for her face to smear across the tile.

He placed the note on the bathroom counter. Whoever finds Marilyn, will find her note too. His mouth opened with a click then clamped shut as vomit spilled over his tongue. The wicked scented goo then dripped from the seal of his lips and his nose and he dropped his head forward to the ground.

Sweaty and feverish, Brent wiped his lips and took one more look at the kid. He memorized the curly kink in her hair for a long, still moment.

Then Brent turned his back on her and left.

To Be Continued.

EPILOGUE

It was silly, *savory*. The way her saliva dripped from a pointed tongue like greasy baby oil. Down her bottom lip, down her chest, against the stretched buttons of her shirt. Of course, there was always something quite *hilarious* about drooling at your office job.

Lillian sopped it up with the back of her hand bashfully and darted her eyes to the side of her, then to the back with a silent head whip. (*Of course, nobody saw you drool, you idiot. You sit window seat, back to the rest of the office–least suspecting if a coworker came in with a shotgun. Buckshot to the back! Boom. Boom. Boom.*)

She shook her head, away from the voice, away from the drool. Her eyes blinked hyper below the glare of brown framed glasses at the email on her screen. Her fingers danced like clicky little raindrops across her keyboard, careful and gentle not to actually press, *disturb,* any keys. Her thoughts twirled and the music in her headphones kept them in neatly tied *black, garbage bags.*

(Hey kid, pay attention. You're daydreaming.*)*

Lillian nodded agreeably.

Daydreaming.

A fucking olympian at–*daydreaming.* ADHD? Creativity? Nah, just fucking stuck in a warp of–*oh god, not this song.*

Her thumb bashed out at her phone that slept against her desk and opened the dark screen to her music. *What playlist? Exit Spotify. No wait, that's what you wanted to be in. Stare endlessly at your apps. Fuck. OH! Spotify. Yes, got it. What playlist? Stay in the playlist you're on. Dirty Rock.* Her head tipped back and her shoulders throbbed. *Headache! Great, this phone always gives me a headache. Pick a song, damn it.* Her head rocked back forward. *Maybe the way I sleep is why my head hurts. I do have a bad hip. God, I can feel it now, I should straighten my back. My posture. Oh, song. Exit Spotify. Get back in.*

Her back prickled in sweat.

"Fuck me," Lillian mumbled as she kept the song and threw the phone away from her, watching it slide carelessly into packets of paper and eraser debris.

(Hey.)

Lillian imagined looking to her side and seeing the soft, concerned stare of familiar man, leaning both elbows into her desk, face warm with new wrinkles and safe scent. *Hey,* she returned the thought.

(What are you listening to?)

Lillian's lip sunk deep into her mouth, shyly, as her imagination handed a headphone to the man.

He cupped it in his hand and held it to his ear, his eyes shifting up to look out at the light through her window as his finger tapped the beat. *(Nah, it's good, kid. Keep listening.)*

Lillian smiled.

(And kid,) his finger lifted from a tap and stood attentive to her double monitors, *(focus. That email isn't long.)*

The desk only held the young woman and the song again. She bobbed her head, she liked the song now. And the email wasn't long. Her fingers typed, and her phone stayed shoved away.

Thanks, Brent.

(Boom, boom, boom.)

If that's how I go, then that's how I go, Marylin.

ACKNOWLEDGMENT

Thanks God, I know you know what *Man, Mae, and the Moths* is really about. In a world full of moths, monsters, and man thank you for being the rock at the side of my boat.

Thank you to my Husband. Josiah, you never once doubted me, even when I was blanketed in thick, wooly self-doubt, you were there with your arm stretched six-feet-deep to pull me out. I will always be thankful for how strongly and openly you encourage me and for always being a listening ear when I need it. No matter what, when, where.

To my parents, Bill and Margi, for being the greatest supporters and also being so open-armed and willing to listen. In victories and failures I know I'll always have the both of you on my sideline, cheering. You two are my dream team, I wouldn't be where I'm at if it weren't for you. Thank you for that.

To my brothers, all three of you knuckleheads. Jaydon, thank you for reading my book! Even if this is the first book you've read since like, eight grade! I am SO proud of you, and I love you. Nolan and Harrison, thank you for being the little brother inspiration I needed to write about my sweet Davey. As much as I always wanted her to, Marilyn could never love Davey as much as I love you two.

To Derek, the greatest guitar instructor ever. Thank you for transitioning our guitar lessons into writing lessons so quickly and seamlessly once it'd been identified that I had a greater passion for the latter. Your curiosity and excitement for my writing are what pushed me to start writing this book, and two years after you sat down and helped me clunk through the first chapter, it is finished. Having Brique a Braq in Chapter 107 was my way of saying 'thank you so much!' I hope my reader listened as they read that chapter as I had intended. Your music inspires dreams.

To Mrs. Light, Thank you for your dedication to *Man, Mae, and the Moths*. Your willingness to spend your free time to read and correct my writing was a God-given blessing to me. Also, Thank you for your devotion to my characters, they loved the time that you spent with them. A lot. Your selflessness has blessed them and me beyond belief.

To David and Angie, my coworker/ book therapists. You two have been so supportive, interested, and electrified for me during this entire process and I truly appreciate it. I love you both!

Thank you to all of my other coworkers who have helped me, given their opinions, and encouraged me. Diana, Kevin, Keturah, Sam, Mike, Thomas, Heather. You all rock.

And Thank YOU, dear reader! I wouldn't have worked so hard on this book if it weren't for you.

Lastly, thank you to Brent, Marilyn, and Davey.

Your story isn't over.

A SPECIAL THANK YOU

To Tanya De, Angie Cochran, Emily Carlson, Grace Heisler, Kortney Sandlin, Margi Womack, David Rankin, Shannon Carlson, Shauna Peterson, Caitlin Clute, Lexie Brazil, Krista Henke, Matt Heisler, Heather Little, Mychal Sanders, Bill Womack, Ann Light, Reygan Carswell, Kaitlin Carlson, Sherry Graebe, Kevin Gray, and Josiah Timothy.

Thank you all! I am grateful for your help!

ABOUT THE AUTHOR

Lillian Rose was born and raised near Portland, Oregon where she now lives with her husband and their chunky cat, Chuck. Though always a late-night creator Lillian did not begin to take her insomniac writing seriously until the age of eighteen, when *Man, Mae, and the Moths* urged itself to be written. She is now held captive by the craft and eats, sleeps, and shits manuscripts.

Follow her on Twitter, Facebook, and Instagram!
@reallillianrose

LAST THING, SERIOUSLY!

THANK *YOU*! And DAMN! Look at you go, one hell of a reading machine. Marilyn, Brent, and Davey all appreciate your patience with them, as do I. Tulsa and Winnie probably appreciate it too, but like...they're super dead. So...

If you appreciated *us* then please let us know—leave a review! Brent could use a review right now, he's had a tough few weeks. You might just save his sad heart.

Or mine.

Let us know your thoughts!
And thank you again, you beautiful person, you!!!

Made in the USA
Lexington, KY
29 November 2019